CAST

The Palatinate of Carinthia

THE LEOPARD THRONE

Prince Gerhard V, the prince of Carinthia
Felix, his son and heir by his first wife, Emma
Caroline, his second wife
Ulf, her son
Trommler, his chamberlain

Allegretti, Felix's tutor

Schenk,
Ludl,
von Traunstein,
Hentschel, earls

Wolfgang Reinhardt, sergeant-at-arms of the White Fortress
Ehrlichmann, messenger

Peter Büber, huntmaster to Gerhard
Torsten Nadel, huntsman

THE ORDER OF THE WHITE ROBE

Eckhardt, a hexmaster

Nikoleta Agana,
Tuomanen, adepts

JUVAVUM, PRINCIPLE TOWN OF CARINTHIA

Messinger, mayor

Schussig, metalworker, guildmaster

Prauss, stonemason, guildmaster
Emser, cabinet maker, guildmaster

Seibt, journeyman carpenter

Aelinn, maid
Lodel, landlord

Taube,
Gertrude,
Heinrich, townspeople

Rabbi Cohen and Mrs Cohen
Aaron Morgenstern,
bookseller

Sophia Morgenstern, his
daughter
Rosenbaum,
Schicter,
Eidelberg, neighbour to the
Morgensterns
Avram Kuppenheim, doctor

THE LIBRARY

The Master Librarian

Frederik Thaler,
Thomm,
Grozer, under-librarians

Goss,
Fottner,
Otto,
Ernst Braun,

Erdlmann,
Ingo Wess, librarians

Glockner, head usher

Max Ullmann,
Reindl,
Manfred,
Horst,
Oswald, ushers

OTHER CARINTHIANS

Martin Kelner, woodsman
Oktav Groer, resident of
Hallein

Wulf Thorlander, from the
north
Ohlhauser, farmer

The Kingdom of Bavaria

Leopold, the king of Bavaria

SIMBACH, A TOWN IN BAVARIA

Fuchs, earl
Wiel,
Spitzel,
Metz,

Kehle,
Gerd and Juli Kehle,
townspeople
Bastian, smith

Mr and Mrs Flintsbach,   **Gretchen,** their daughter
farmers

Byzantium

Spyropoulus, ambassador
Agathos, slave

Schwyz

Tol Ironmaker, King of Farduzes
Thorson Heavyhammer

Franklands

Clovis, prince, son of King Clovis of the Franks

Vulfar, bargemaster

Teutons

Walter of Danzig, master of horse

PART I

Fimbulwinter

As Peter Büber climbed, he left spring behind him. The mountain peaks, stark and blinding, immense and razor-edged, made him feel the most insignificant creature that ever dragged itself across the land.

The valley behind him, narrow, deep and shadowed, was nevertheless showing the first flush of green. Ahead of him was nothing but white snow that stretched from summit to summit and covered everything between.

Büber stopped and planted his walking-stick in the ground. He pulled on a pair of fur-lined mittens, sat a furry hat hard over his shaved scalp, and took up his stick again. The wind was tearing loose snow from the exposed upper slopes and trailing it like cloud in the blue sky. The higher he went, the colder and more open the terrain became.

He aimed for the first cairn of rocks, a couple of stadia uphill – snow stuck to its top like a crown, but its flanks were dark and clear. His boots crunched through the crust of ice with every footstep, leaving a trail of holes through which poked the first moss and tough alpine grasses of the year.

He reached the cairn breathing hard. He needed to slow down; it had been months since he'd been up this high. His rough stubble was already coated in moisture, and it was threatening to freeze. So he wiped at his scarred face with his sleeve and leant back against the cairn, letting the weak sun do its best.

Recovered, he set off towards the second cairn, using a more measured pace. He planted the end of the stick, listened to the soft crush as it landed, then moved his feet, left and right. Repeat. There was a natural rhythm to his stride now, one that let him walk and breathe easily.

Past the second cairn, and on to the third – simple to find as only black rock against white snow can be, but he knew from bitter experience how hard it was trying to keep on course when the clouds descended and the precipices shrouded themselves in fog. Not today though. Today was glorious, bright and clean, and it was a pleasure to walk to the top of the pass and check the snow depth. It didn't even need to be clear, just shallow enough for the carts and wagons to wade through, and the short route to the Mittelmeer would be open again.

Büber, thinking contentedly of olive-skinned women, missed the first rumble of sound. He caught the echo, though. He stopped mid-stride, as frozen as the air.

Avalanches were common this time of year. He'd seen trees, buildings and people swept away and entombed in suddenly rock-hard snow that fell from mountaintops like a flood. They started with a crack and a whisper, then built like an oncoming storm to be the loudest thing he'd ever heard.

The last of it faded away, and he couldn't see the tell-tale sign of a plume of snowy air rising from the slopes. Everything was quiet again, the sound of even the wind muffled and distant.

It was said that there were foolish hunters and old hunters, but never foolish old hunters. Büber wasn't old, not yet, but he had every intention of living long enough to prove both his friends and his enemies wrong.

He stayed still for a while, scanning the east and west slopes with a practised, hand-shadowed gaze, but there was nothing he could spot. Perhaps it had been something in the next valley along, then, reverberating from peak to peak.

More cautiously, pausing at every cairn to listen, he walked higher and higher. The gradient wasn't that bad – the Romans who'd used it a thousand years earlier had picked out the route and built one of their wide roads south to north. Büber's ancestors had made the reverse journey, on their way to crack Rome's walls and set its temples ablaze. But up near the head of the pass, there were no smoothed stones or compacted gravel left. The via had worn away to soil and rock, just as it once was, and probably always would be.

He looked behind him. The line of cairns stretched away into the distance. Looking ahead, he could see three more before the slope took them out of sight. Almost there.

He trudged on. The snow rose over the turn-downs on his boots, and almost up to his knees. Not much, considering how high it would have been piled at Yuletide; warm air from the south helped clear the pass sooner. Difficult to walk in, all the same.

Difficult to run in, too.

The ground started to dip away to the south: he was there.

He plunged his walking-stick down, pulled out his knife and bent low to notch the wood. His breath condensed about him as he marked the snow level, not as proof – any idiot could stand at the bottom of the valley and guess – but for tradition. He'd been shown how to do it by a man now five years dead, and at some point he'd have to show some other rough kid from the mountains that this is what happens when you want to declare the pass open.

The flake of wood he'd cut fell to the snow. By the time he reported to the prince and the first ceremonial wagon was rolled up the via, even this covering would be little more than slush.

When he straightened up, he saw them.

They were in the far distance, coming down from the very top of the Aineck and almost invisible against the background: three large – and one of them was really very big – figures. They cast long black shadows that rippled against the contours of the snow, moving purposefully towards him.

There wasn't much meat on him, but giants weren't particularly picky about their choice of game. If they caught him, they'd eat him: quite how they'd spotted him at such a distance was a mystery left for later.

Time to go. If he turned around now, he'd just about beat them to the lower slopes, and at this time of year they wouldn't venture much below the snow line. While one man out on his own was prey, a crowd of them with spears was a predator. Giants were just smart enough to care about the difference.

Büber jerked out his walking-stick and took a last look around, just in case he'd missed something obvious. He was about to turn and follow his footsteps back when he saw a pack slowly sway into view. Then the ass it was strapped to. Then the man driving the ass on with a switch.

It wasn't him who'd attracted the giants' attention. It was this idiot.

And it wasn't just one idiot, because as Büber ran forward, his boots sinking deep into the snow, he could see a whole line of men and beasts snaking up the pass from the south.

He stopped again and stared. Maybe twenty donkeys, each with a pack tied high on their backs and roped together, and a dozen men at intervals down the chain, encouraging their charges to climb.

"Hey!" Büber waved his arms. "Hey, you!"

The lead driver raised his clean-shaven chin from his chest and looked uncertainly at Büber. He kept on coming though, switching the ass's hindquarters as it struggled upwards with its load.

"Giants," called the huntmaster. "Over there." He pointed.

The driver looked behind him and shouted something in a language that sounded like Italian. Büber didn't understand a word of it.

"Ah, fuck it." Büber squinted at the flanks of the mountain, but the snowy slopes were clear. "Fuck!"

He knew he should have kept the giants in sight. They could be anywhere now: together, split up, ahead, or coming over the ridge behind them.

"Giants," he said again. He mimed their size by lifting his hands as far over his head as he could and stamped the ground. What was the word? Stupid foreigners: why couldn't they speak German like civilised people? "Gigante. Si. Gigante."

Now he had their attention. The driver relayed the message down the line, and he definitely said "gigante" at some point. One man in particular took notice and slogged his way up the rise to Büber.

His clothes showed he was rich in a way Büber would never be. But then again, Büber wasn't about to see a substantial portion of his wealth eaten by giants, which was exactly what was going to happen if this man wasn't careful.

"Greetings in the name of the Doge, signore."

"Yes, that. Prince Gerhard, Carinthia, welcome. Giants, you Venetian cretin. Three of them, over to the east, though gods only know where they are now." Büber looked very carefully at all the places a creature twice his height might hide. "You have to get off this mountain now. And what are you doing here anyway? Didn't anyone tell you the pass is closed?"

"Pah. You Carinthians. You do not own this pass."

"Yes. Yes, we do. We open it and we close it and between times we make sure that people like you don't get butchered up here." Büber's head snapped around at something he thought he might have heard. "Save what you can and get ready to run."

"There are no giants," said the Venetian, warm beneath his furs. "Are you sure it was not dwarves you saw?"

"Oh, I'm sure." The donkeys plodded on. The first one was past him, the second one going by now. Their breath made little clouds and frost sparkled on their brown coats. They were making too much noise, and even he could smell them. Their scent must be driving the giants into a frenzy.

"You are a prince's man?"

"Yes." Büber's hand dropped to the pommel of his sword. It would be mostly useless against a foe whose reach was far longer – he carried a Norse-style blade, short and broad – but he felt better knowing it was there. "I'm the master of the hunt, and you need to listen to me."

"You wish for me to turn back because you think I should have waited for your permission."

"You should have waited until it was safe." Where were they? Giants usually just waded in, fists swinging. One blow was enough. What were they waiting for?

"Your ploy will not work. Besides, we have a little insurance of our own." The Venetian nodded at a man walking by. Dressed head to toe in a long red hooded cloak, it was only the tip of a nose and a sly, confident smile that Büber saw. "You Carinthians do not have a monopoly on magic."

"No. We just have the best." Büber had had enough. He'd seen the giants, he'd warned the merchant. He couldn't force them to turn back, or to abandon their cargo, or to sacrifice half the donkeys in order to try and save the other half, and themselves into the bargain. And besides, magicians gave him the fear in a way even a fully grown dragon didn't. "I've got my duty to do, and it's not to you. Good luck."

With all that donkey flesh available, the giants weren't going to bother with him, just as long as he got clear. When it was all over, when he'd got back down into the valley and made his report, he could come back with a squad of spear-armed soldiers and a hexmaster or two. And there might be something of the merchant's cargo worth salvaging.

The line of the train occupied the lowest point of the valley, so Büber turned perpendicular to it, and scaled the lower slopes of the mountain on the west side. He could keep them in sight, and put them between himself and the giants. Who were still nowhere to be seen. It concerned him that something that big could hide in plain sight. He had a commanding view over the whole of the upper pass.

He hadn't imagined them. He'd swear any number of oaths, to the gods, on his honour, on his parents' graves, that he'd seen those three long shadows shambling down towards him.

The lead driver tapped his jenny onwards towards the next cairn, and suddenly, from over the brow of the hill, came an immense rushing. When they wanted to, giants could move fast, using their long, tree-trunk-sized legs to devour the ground. Snow, knee-deep for a man, was simply kicked out of the way. They came in an arrowhead, the biggest one in the lead, the smaller two flanking.

The driver was rooted to the spot for far too long, and started running far too late. He was enveloped in a blizzard-like wall of white, along with his charge. He re-emerged, flying, limbs tangled, propelled like he'd been shot from a catapult. The donkey went straight up: giants did that, throwing their victims high in the air so that they would land, broken, behind them.

The animals were still tied together. The second one in line was jerked over and dragged before the rope snapped. The giants didn't stop. They thundered down the now-static formation, smashing their hands down like hammers and stamping on anything fallen.

And there was nothing Büber could do to help. The men at the back of the line ran more or less in the same direction, back to the south. The merchant, screaming uselessly at the wanton destruction of his property, and equally pointlessly for his guards to stand and fight, was knocked casually aside with enough force to shatter his ribcage, even with the cushioning effect of all his fine furs and padded coats.

The only one who looked like he was going to take the giants on was the Venetian sorcerer. He'd dodged to one side to avoid the initial onslaught: now he planted his feet and lifted his arms.

Three donkeys remained, still tied on to at least four or five of their dead or dying stablemates. They panicked and brayed and pulled, they rolled and twisted. The first giant slowed to a walk and reached down with its horny fingers splayed wide, catching a donkey's head and crushing it by making a fist.

With the animal still in its grasp, it turned to look at the magician.

The man had crossed to Büber's side of the valley, so the hunter had a good view, and despite both the urge to run and a clear path to take now the giants had gone past, he hesitated.

8

If this red-cloaked magician was any good, Büber might not have to run after all.

The giant dropped the donkey in a wet heap, and bared its long yellow peg teeth. It opened its mouth wide, wider than it had any reason to go, and roared out a geyser of white breath, spit and green mucus. The other giants – a female with pendulous dugs, and a juvenile already her height – stopped tearing chunks of bloody flesh and slippery entrails to view the scene.

The man in red rocked back on his heels and steadied himself. Büber had never seen such confidence, and he waited for the fireworks to begin.

The big giant was ugly even for its kind. Its face was more battered and scarred than even Büber's, and its hair was matted and growing in tufts. Old and angry, it glared down with its coal-black eyes at this weakling stick-thin figure that had the temerity to defy it.

The magician raised his hands, and the ink of his tattoos started to flow.

Nothing happened, and the giant charged.

It took a mere four steps to close the space between them and a perfectly timed duck-and-lift to scoop the man into the air. The cloak billowed as he flew: arms and legs flapped hopelessly against his useless scarlet wings.

He landed at the giant's feet, spread-eagled and on his back. He looked more surprised than hurt, but only because his surprise was very great.

The giant raised its foot, and a vast pale slab with curling toenails the colour of bone broke free of the snow. It brought it down hard on the magician, and then leant forward to apply extra pressure.

Büber heard the crack, and suddenly realised he was alone, up a mountain, miles from home, with only three pissed-off giants for company.

"Shit."

Now he started running.

There was a moment when he thought one of them would chase him: actually several moments, because every time he glanced fearfully over his shoulder, the baby of the group was looking at him even while it gathered up another handful of donkey – or man, he couldn't tell and didn't want to tell – and crammed it into its already red-stained maw.

When he thought he was far enough away, he slithered down the icy slope to the line of cairns, and kept his pace up until his lungs burnt, his vision swam and he could taste blood.

He leant his back against a cairn, hauling thin alpine air, and coughing like he had the plague. The sweat started to freeze on him, chilling his body and making him shiver. He knew what that would mean: he had to keep moving, but he still gave himself a few more moments to rest his hands on his knees as he tried to get his breathing under control.

There was a sound, stone on stone. Not right behind him, but too close all the same. He crouched down in the lee of the cairn and slowly, slowly, drew his sword. He stayed as still as he could, trying to trust his abilities to keep him hidden, but after a while, the waiting became unbearable.

He leant out ever so slightly. The giants' child was at the next cairn along, dragging some bloody morsel behind it, but searching for him. Büber ducked back, and prayed to the gods he hadn't been seen.

When he looked again, the giant had gone, and just a circle of red-spattered snow marked where it had been standing.

Büber hurried away, down the slope, to where spring was waiting for him.

2

Frederik Thaler was already sitting down in a quiet corner, his stoneware mug placed squarely on the table in front of him, when Büber arrived outside.

He only had to turn his head to see the light flicker at the windows, the image of boots and legs and torso warping as they moved behind the imperfect glass, a man in green and brown tripping down the steps from street level to the beer cellar's door. Then Thaler lost sight of him behind the heavy wood. The moment stretched out, beyond what could be expected of someone in need of a drink to turn the latch and push.

Thaler was almost resigned to getting up and seeing if the door was stuck when it finally opened. He sagged back down and waved.

"Peter, over here."

Not that there were many other drinkers in the cellar at that time in the morning; just a couple of old sots in opposite corners. Thaler knew them both, and their stories. They were harmless enough, and even at their drunken worst neither was fool enough to mess with one of the prince's men.

Büber didn't seem to agree with Thaler's judgement. He ducked his head under the black oak beams and looked hard at the cellar's patrons. It was a far from casual glance: he had a hunter's eye and he was looking for predators.

Thaler frowned and unnecessarily moved his drink a fraction to the left. Then back to the right.

With a grunt that might have signalled either grim satisfaction or unsettling compromise, Büber turned to Thaler's table and dragged a chair aside. As he sat down, he unhooked his satchel and placed it in front of him.

"Peter?"

"We're supposed to be alone." Büber twisted around and scowled at the host, idly wiping out washed mugs with a piece of stained linen. "Hey. Liquor. Now."

Thaler leant forward slightly and raised an eyebrow. "Are you trying to get me barred?"

"We have bigger problems than you finding a new drinking hole that meets your exacting standards." Büber scraped his stubbled chin with a hand that still had three fingers. He nodded at his satchel, and took another careful look around.

The host brought a platter with two short pewter cups, and a stone bottle of spirit. He was bandy-legged and rolled as he walked. But give credit to the man, he never spilt a drop, even when he was juggling half a dozen beers.

He put the cups down and unerringly filled them from the unstoppered bottle.

"Thank you, Mr Lodel," said Thaler, and he smiled weakly. His efforts were returned with blank-faced disdain. When the host had gone again, he thumbed the lid of his mug open and took a pull of the short beer inside.

"Look in the damn bag," said Büber. "But carefully."

Thaler put his mug back down in the exact position it had previously occupied, and put his hand out for the leather strap.

Büber's other hand – the one with only two fingers and a thumb,

11

which made it look like a claw – shot out and gripped his forearm hard enough to bruise. "Don't let anyone else see."

"Peter, you're hurting me." Thaler tried to shake free, but he was far too weak and the hunter far too strong.

Then, like he was breaking a hex, Büber shook his head violently and let go. "Sorry. I'm . . . just look in the bag."

Thaler started to undo the buckles, and noticed that whatever was inside was too long to be contained properly. Its cloth-wrapped end was poking out. He frowned again and continued pulling the straps through the metal rings.

The top of the bag flopped open, and he held the sides apart. The only thing inside was the wrapped object, just a little longer than his forearm.

"It's not going to bite me, is it?"

"Oh, it's dead. Very dead." Büber had taken hold of his liquor but hadn't raised it to his lips yet. He looked down at the trembling surface. "You'll be wanting something a sight stronger than beer once you've seen it."

Keeping most of it in the bag, Thaler teased aside the cloth with his fingers. They came into contact with fine, white ivory, still with a dusting of leaf-mould fragments. He stopped. He put both his hands down by his side to push his plump body more upright. His palms were moist. No, more than that: actually wet, and they weren't going to dry out in the smoky heat of last night's fire.

Unlike his mouth, which was suddenly parched, such that he had to force his tongue away from his palate.

He wiped his hands on his breeches and went back into the bag for a second go. He grasped one corner of the cloth and tugged it so that it unwound just a little.

The ivory was straight, conical, with a slight spiral at the point. The groove wound around the shaft, deepening with each turn.

He stared at the unicorn's horn for a while, then carefully rewrapped it and pushed the bag closed.

As soon as his hands were free, he snatched at his liquor and tossed it back in one throat-searing gulp. Nothing was quite in focus. Then everything slipped back into place, and he was able to speak again.

"What have you done?" he said.

12

Büber took a measured sip, the cup looking tiny in his fist. "Done? I've done nothing."

"If they catch you with that." Thaler looked down, and realised the bag was closer to him than it was to Büber. He pushed it pointedly back across the table. "If they catch you with that, they'll press you for sure."

The hunter checked he had enough digits for what he needed, and held up the two fingers of his two-fingered hand. "This isn't the first I've found."

"You're joking."

"Does this look like the face of a man who's joking?"

"Your face never looks like you're joking. Even though I know otherwise." Thaler remembered his beer and flipped the lid again. "Peter. It's a . . ."

Büber held a finger to his lips, then beckoned Thaler closer.

"With the first one, I did what anyone in my position would do. Mark where it was, tell the Order and lead them to it. I didn't even touch it."

"What did they do?"

"They turned out mob-handed and spirited it away. I got . . ." – he shrugged – ". . . not exactly a sack of cash, but enough for some decent whoring down Gentlemen's Alley."

Thaler chewed the tip of his tongue between his teeth, then said: "Is it real?"

"What? The money, the whores or the . . . that?"

Thaler scowled and nodded at the satchel. "That. Is that one real? I didn't feel anything when I touched it. Oh gods, I touched it." He hurriedly checked his hands for any spreading stain or erupting pustules.

They were already marked with ink, dark lines in the creases and folds of his flesh that only served to make the paleness that surrounded them stand out more. His nails were neat and whole, fingertips soft and sensitive. No creeping black rot or green decay. For now.

"You're a virgin, Frederik, and a good man. You're not going to die." Büber saw off the rest of his liquor. "And, despite not being either, neither will I."

"What happened to the . . . body?"

Büber shrugged again, like it was a thing of no consequence. "Wasn't there. No blood, or hair. No signs of butchery. Or even

13

a hunt. A bit of trampled undergrowth, a day old. And that, sitting in the middle. Like it was thrown away with the rubbish."

Thaler leant back and looked over his shoulder out of the window. Everything seemed normal out there. Townsfolk were walking past, both ways. A small cart, over-enthusiastically guided by a boy and his steering pole, propelled itself the other way. Voices were raised between him and the owner of a foot he'd run over.

No, the Old Town seemed much as he'd left it. It was only in the beer cellar that things had changed.

"Do you know how much that's worth?" asked Thaler.

"To the right sort of buyer? I've a fair idea." Büber took control of the satchel and fastened it tight. He placed it on the floor against the leg of the table closest to Thaler.

"It's worth more than either of our lives, that's for certain." Thaler knew that as contraband, a whole horn could empty a treasury. "Take it back to where you found it. Tell the Order and let them deal with it like before."

"There might be a problem there." Büber scraped his fingers at his cheeks, where the stubble was starting to show white. "Once. Yes, I can accept that. I've seen all sorts in the forest, some really strange shit that you only get to read about in your books. Twice? That's starting to be a pattern. I might not be able to write, and can barely read my own name, but I know signs. I know the sun and the wind. I know the rocks and I know the rivers. I know the peaks and the plains and, above all, I know the forest. And the hexmasters know that much about me. Though they look down on me and pity me, if I tell them about this second one they will come and kill me to keep me quiet."

Thaler had to concede that the huntmaster had a point, but still felt a duty to argue. "They wouldn't. You're a prince's man."

"The prince rules because it's beneath the Order to rule. Come on, Frederik. Don't pretend otherwise."

He was right, and Thaler gave in with a slump of his shoulders. "So what – or who – is taking them?"

"I don't know. I'll tell you what it looked like: as if the animal had curled up to go to sleep, and then simply melted away like snow."

"Leaving the most valuable part of it behind." A whole beast, blood and skin, valuable of course, but dwarfed by the riches the horn commanded. It didn't make sense.

"I'm scared, Frederik." Büber looked across the table at Thaler. His eyes were big and bright and blue. "I've been scared before. By bigger beasts than this. But this is the Order."

Thaler shivered, then steadied himself. "There has to be an explanation for this. Someone, somewhere will know. They'll have written about it."

"So you think the answer is in that vast pile of books you call work?"

"Yes." It was as close to a creed as Thaler would go. "It will be."

"What," said Büber, "if it's not? I've never heard of anything like this before. And neither have you, admit it."

"No, but that's the point of books, Peter. People write things down so they don't have to remember it all in their heads and it isn't lost when they die." Thaler realised he was banging the table with his fist, and he self-consciously wrapped his fingers around his mug to stop himself doing it again. "You should talk to a scribe: get him to write down everything you know. Or at least take an apprentice."

"I work better alone."

"And when you die, everything you know will have gone." Thaler opened the lid of his mug and swigged emphatically. "All that lore. All that craft. What a waste."

Büber chewed at the stump of one of his missing fingers and said nothing.

"Leave it with me," said Thaler. "I can hide it somewhere in the library – where no one will find it, obviously. As to what it means, I'll see what I can do. I'll be as discreet as I can."

"I never said I wanted your help," said Büber, raising his head.

"Of course you didn't. Proud man like you? Even your scars all face forwards." Thaler's beer had almost gone. He finished it off and flipped the lid closed. "Why would you need the help from some inky-fingered book-lover who's never done a real day's labour in his soft, comfortable life?"

"You want me to apologise?"

"No. I want to know why I had a messenger hammering on my door at an hour when a gentleman like myself was bound to be either in bed or at breakfast." Thaler waited. He was good at waiting. So was Büber, but it was the hunter who cracked first.

"Because . . ." he started, and pulled a face.

15

"Because?"

"There's no one else I can trust. That I know I can trust absolutely and won't sell me to the hexmasters for big bag of shiny coins. There? Better?"

"They could offer me books."

"Please don't make me beg, Frederik."

Thaler held up his hand. "I swear by all the gods—"

Büber interrupted. "Your word is enough. It's always been enough. No vows. How long have we known each other?"

"Twenty years. I can't even remember how we met."

"I do," said Büber, with a curious passion. "You were a wet-behind-the-ears junior librarian and my old huntmaster wanted my profession on the town's register. You put a line through the word 'apprentice' so that it just read 'huntsman'. We didn't even speak."

"But . . ." A memory flared bright in Thaler's mind.

"You reached out and shook my hand."

"So I did. And after that there was the faerie-lore."

"And I told you I couldn't read."

"So I read the whole damn book to you." Thaler sat back and stared out of the window again. "Was that really twenty years ago?"

"Twenty summers, twenty winters. I lost fingers, toes, my hair and my good looks." Büber ran his hand over his shaved scalp. "And you got fat."

Thaler poked his own belly with a rigid forefinger. It was true. It was the beer. And the pastries. And the books. His stomach had grown large and round, not exactly like a dumpling, but close.

"I'll find you some answers, Peter." He held out his hand, just like he had before. "You have my word."

Büber's claw came across to grasp it. There. Done.

3

Prince Gerhard stared down over the battlements at the procession coming up the road to the Chastity Gate. Two columns of spearmen barely seemed to contain the one shaggy-coated barbarian they

16

were escorting. The Teuton was big, with a long-handled axe strapped across his back, and his horse, led behind, was a massive, ill-tempered brute that needed two men just to keep its head down. The prince jutted his chin. The same damnable farce every year: a different face to be sure, but their sheer stiff-necked belligerence was a race trait.

"Felix. I want you to attend this audience."

The prince's son had to lean further over the bastion wall to get a good look at the Teuton commander, and Gerhard felt a moment of weakness, a cold wash in the blood that made him reach out to grip the back of the boy's tunic.

Oblivious to the drop and his father's reaction, Felix wriggled forward more, and lay on his stomach on the rough stone. "You think he'll fight you? That doesn't seem very wise."

"What have you learnt about the Teutons?" As the guard disappeared under the gatehouse, he increased his hold and pulled the boy backwards. He couldn't lift him like he used to, but the child was still small for his age.

"The Teutons are a barbarian people from the north where the land is poor and marshy. They lack all honour and hire themselves out as mercenaries to whoever has the coin to afford them. They fight mainly as heavy cavalry, and are brutal and ill-disciplined in battle. They call their hexmasters shamans, but their battle-magic is very limited."

"A little short on detail," grunted Gerhard, "but good enough for now. Do we give them leave of passage to join the armies of the south?"

"No, Father."

"Why not, boy?"

"Because," and Felix's voice became uncertain, "they are untrustworthy? And no one deserves having the Teutons set on them?"

"Maybe you should address this barbarian horseman: you've a decent enough appraisal of the situation." He placed his hand on the boy's head and buried his fingers in the dark hair. So like his mother. "We need to get ready. What do the Teutons fear most?"

Felix took his cue and glanced back down at the gatehouse. The man was back in sight, now without his horse and his axe. The way he leant forward, attacking the slope, showed his intent.

"They fear looking weak."

"So we must strip him of everything, while reminding him of

17

our strength. I'd rather not have that bunch of savages within a hundred miles of a Carinthian boundary stone, but that's not in my gift. I can keep them out of my lands though – that's something that the Protector of Wien can't take for granted."

Gerhard removed his hand from his son's head, and they walked along the battlements to the next tower. The town – his town – sat happy and warm in the spring sun, and outside the walls, so did the farms and the forests and the mines. All at peace, all prosperous, all content.

"Father?"

"Yes, Felix?"

"Do we fear looking weak, too?"

"Carinthia is never weak. This is the thing, boy: I could raise an army if the need arises, but that's not where our strength lies." Gerhard waited while the turret door was opened for him. The servant following him around was all but invisible until he was required. The pause was long enough for the prince to look across the river, to the steep wooded hill that squatted opposite both the crag the fortress sat on and the town that clung to its skirts.

On top of the hill was a tower, tall, black, glistening.

Felix followed his gaze. "Then why are we . . .?"

"Because our Teutonic friends need reminding. Every year, those that can head south for the fighting season, and none of them return. If they live, they invariably stay, given the choice between going home to a frozen swamp that'll be in perpetual twilight for the next six months, and warming their toes in the Mittelmeer while Italian girls peel them grapes. So every year I have to re-educate the sons-of-bitches that they should leave my palatinate free of their stench."

Even if Felix didn't yet understand the attractions of the girls, he could see the point. "So they don't love their home?"

"Gods, no. Why would they? It's a miserable shit-hole fit only for little bitey flies and eels." Gerhard waited again, and the door opened out into the courtyard. "And for some inexplicable reason, your stepmother doesn't like me swearing in front of you." He tapped the side of his nose.

A man, talking with men, needed to be free with his language. They needed to know their leader was someone who knew a good two dozen names for his manhood, and who wouldn't faint if he heard the gods being cursed.

Perhaps it was time to take more of an interest in the education of his heir. Not his only heir any more: thanks to his new wife, he had spares, but all the same . . . Felix was thirteen this year. It was about time he was weaned off the milk his tutors gave him. More riding, more hunting, more of the martial disciplines – that Genoese fop Allegretti could stay because of his ability to make an edge sing – and more of the civil arts too. Starting now.

"Dress plainly, boy. But put some steel on your belt. Something you know how to use. No point in turning up with some great pig-sticker you plainly can't lift."

"Signore Allegretti has been teaching me to use two swords at once. He says the style is very popular in the south," ventured Felix.

"Has he indeed?" Gerhard thought it sounded like a dangerous affectation. "Can you beat him yet?"

Felix scowled. "Not yet."

"And does the signore hit you with the flat of his blade when he wins?"

"Yes. Sometimes twice if I've been stupid."

"Good." It had been years since Gerhard had been thrashed by his old sword-master, but the lessons had stuck, both in his body and in his mind. Nothing fancy for him: just a longsword, light and strong, one-handed, two-handed, hews and blocks. If he had to, he could take that fat, greasy barbarian in single combat. Using a magical sword, naturally. "Go and get ready. Hurry."

Felix ran into the fortress ahead of his father, and Gerhard walked at a more measured pace through the doors and corridors and into the Great Hall at its centre. It was a big space, lit by both daylight and bright globes of enchanted crystal. Look up and, after the dimness of the entrance, a visitor would be blind.

At the far end of the hall was a raised platform. On feast days, the high table would be set out there: his lady on his right, his favoured men with him. Today, there was nothing but a single high-backed chair.

And Trommler. There was always Trommler.

"My lord."

"You know what we should do?" Gerhard stepped up onto the dais and slumped into the throne.

"What, my lord?"

"Send the hexmasters up to the Baltic coast and get them to

turn it into glass. That'd solve a few problems. And" – the prince wagged his finger – "half of Europe would thank me."

Trommler stroked his white beard with his fingers. "The Order wouldn't trouble themselves with a matter so trifling as the Teutons."

"Hah! Trifling or not, we've one at our gates, and another three hundred on our borders."

"They're camped near Simbach. The Bavarians have moved them quickly through."

"Who paid who this year? These calculations can be so difficult."

"Not that my lord would ever have to worry about that, but I understand not a single penny changed hands. The Teutons were granted forage, and a thousand spearmen ensured they went at such speed they could barely graze their horses." Trommler clearly agreed with the Bavarians' tactics, judging by his thin grin.

"I don't know whether to be impressed or just a little bit angry. Are those spears still poking at them?"

"The last I heard, they are, my lord."

"Send word to the captain of the Bavarian spears, and impress on them that the Teutons are to march through Austria and Styria. If he lets them cross the river before Passau, I'll have his bones mixed with those of the Teutons and dumped on the north bank. You might want to send that message to Mad Leopold too, just in case he feels led to countermand me."

"As you wish, my lord. I'll let the Order know."

There came the sound of running footsteps and the jingling of metal rings. Felix skidded to a halt in front of the dais and presented himself for inspection. As he'd promised, he wore two swords: a longer one on his left hip, a short one on his right. It would have looked better if the child had actually grown. Something he could always talk to the hexmasters about, for certain. A leader needed to be at least as tall as the men he commanded.

"Good enough, boy. Come up here and stand at my left. Listen to what I say, and watch the Teuton carefully. Don't speak, even if he tries to goad us. Remember that we're better than he is: stronger, richer, more educated and more civilised. We have every advantage that he doesn't."

"Yes, Father." Felix jumped up and took his place.

"We're doing this not because we enjoy it, but because we rule. Our subjects need to be protected from these creatures."

The doors at the far end of the hall clattered open. The light from outside darkened as the doorway was filled with figures. The Teuton strode in, and behind him, the guards, spears lowered for the threshold and then raised upright again.

The man was even more impressive close up. Tall, strong, pale, bear fur slung over his shoulder and mail on his chest. A man of note in his homeland, then.

Gerhard remained seated. He would have risen for an equal or a friend.

The Teuton's bow was poorly executed – nowhere near enough bend on that front leg – and his insolent eyes stared at Gerhard, not the ground. When he rose again, he crossed his arms in front of him and stood with his legs a shoulder-width apart.

Gerhard leant forward a little. The chair creaked behind him. "What's his name?"

Reinhardt, the captain of the guard, started to approach the dais, but the Teuton shouldered him aside and announced himself.

"Walter of Danzig," said the Teuton. If he'd hoped his fame had spread beyond the fly-bitten north, it hadn't made it quite as far as Juvavum. Unlike his stench, which was primal.

"So, Walter of Danzig. What do you think Prince Gerhard of the Palatinate of Carinthia can do for you?"

"I have a hundred horse to take over the mountains. I've come ahead to see there are no delays on the road."

Gerhard considered having the man executed on the spot and his body sent back to his companions in quarters. He looked to his right, where Trommler was as stony-faced as he always was at meetings like this, giving no sign of any emotion above bored detachment – perhaps having seen it all before, he was genuinely bored. To his left, Felix's tense fidgeting showed he knew the Teuton had shown total disregard for any form of civilised behaviour, but also that his father's warning was still uppermost in his mind.

There was no reason why Gerhard should let this Danzig off quite that lightly. A bit of play first, then.

"Let me consider this suggestion for a moment." He steepled his fingers and rested his chin on them, seemingly deep in thought. Then he straightened up. "No."

The Teuton stiffened. "What do you mean, no?"

"I would have thought the meaning to be self-evident, Walter of Danzig." Gerhard smiled warmly. "We appear to be able to talk to each other with some measure of understanding, so a simple 'no' ought to be easily comprehended by such an exalted person as yourself."

"I have a hundred—"

"Three hundred, my lord," said Trommler to Gerhard, his interruption perfectly timed.

Walter scowled and grimaced.

"And I believe both the road and the pass belong to you, my lord."

"And the land beyond the pass, Chamberlain?"

"Yours also, my lord."

"Ah." Gerhard stroked his lips and looked back to the Teuton. "You seem to want to give me reasons to refuse you: reasons I don't really need because my word is law in this land. You bring your brawling, thieving bunch of mercenaries halfway across Europe, and everywhere you go, you cause trouble. You arrive at my borders having been chased at spear-point through Bavaria, you lie about your numbers, you insult my ears with your accent, and then you have the gall to act surprised when I refuse you and your men passage."

The Teuton ground his jaw in silence, and eyed his guards. He was currently weaponless, but his snatching a spear was always possible. Then he grew very still. He'd noticed a figure all in white standing half obscured behind a pillar. All in white, even to the extent of having a veiled face.

Gerhard nodded in satisfaction. "Your act is poor, Master Walter. You came here expecting the answer you received, so you decided to be just plain rude instead. Perhaps you thought the Prince of Carinthia had grown weak, or stupid, since last year when a different ugly, sweaty brute stood in your place and mangled good, honest German with his stinking barbarian tongue."

"Wolfgang of Ludsen, my lord."

"And what did we do with him, Chamberlain?"

"Cursed his manhood, my lord."

"Pardon? I'm not sure I heard right."

"His cock rotted off, my lord, over the course of a few weeks."

"Yes. That was it." Gerhard rubbed his palms together, gratified

22

that, at last, Walter of Danzig had gone even paler under the veneer of dirt. "Clearly not deterrent enough. What shall we do this time?"

"I want to return to my men," said the Teuton, mustering as much of his dignity as remained. He glanced again at the white-shrouded hexmaster in the shadows, and Gerhard knew that although they'd brought their own shaman along with them, it was so much hedge-magic against the high arts of the Order.

"I have not finished with you," roared the prince. The spearmen flinched, and the order wasn't even directed at them. "This is my decision: I'm going to have you pressed, and when you're dead, I'm going to strap your shattered bones to your horse and send it back to your pox-ridden army."

The Teuton turned to find a score of broad-bladed spears pointing at his guts. He spun back, and reached up for his axe. His hand found nothing.

"This is what happens when you pick a fight with Carinthia," said the prince mildly. "You can't win. You just get to choose how you lose."

The Teuton straightened up. "You have done me wrong, prince, and you will pay for this."

Gerhard did no more than raise an eyebrow. Trommler hadn't moved, except to rest himself against the side of the throne, and Felix was stock-still.

"I see no reason to be provoked by you. A civilised man keeps his speech honest, and his temper checked. Take him away, and send word when the stones have been prepared. I'll want to watch."

Walter of Danzig spat on the floor and deliberately turned his back on the dais. He looked down at the spear-heads and, growling deep in his throat, knocked one aside with his hand.

The guards marched the Teuton away. Once the Great Hall's door banged shut again, the white-robed man – or woman, it was impossible to tell – drifted across the floor towards the dais.

"Father," said Felix, "won't the rest of them cause trouble for us?"

"Barbarians that they are, I don't think even they're quite as stupid as to ignore just how flat pressing makes a man." Gerhard rose from his throne and bowed. The white-swathed head dipped briefly. "Your presence honours us, as always."

Again, the slight movement of the head to acknowledge the

prince's will, then the figure walked off, stage right, back into the shadows. A door clicked and creaked, then shut with an echo.

Gerhard couldn't tell if there had been a real person underneath the concealment, or whether the clothes were merely animated. No concern of his really. He gave them the peace to pursue their studies, and half the palatinate's taxes. In return, their power shielded the land more certainly than any standing army. Like the tree and the mistletoe, they sheltered within his branches and made his rule sacred.

Or was it the other way around?

"Trommler?"

"Yes, my lord?"

"We could do with keeping an eye on the Teutons, just to make sure."

"Master Büber is in town. I'll have him fetched to the castle." Trommler trotted off, leaving the prince and his son alone.

"So," said the prince. "What did you think of that, boy?"

"You're really going to press him?" Felix looked at his hands.

"Yes. He deserves nothing less, and it'll keep his stinking brothers away from Carinthia at no extra effort to us. They can do what they like to Bavaria or Wien. My people are my concern."

"And you're going to watch?"

"Gods, have you really never been to a pressing before? That's a gap in your education, one which we can happily fill by the end of the day." Gerhard saw the boy grow white-lipped. "This is what princes do, Felix. They hold the power of life and death in their hands, and the sooner you realise that, the sooner you'll be ready to take my place, on this throne."

Felix glanced sharply around.

"Oh, I've a few years left in me yet. You won't be expected to assume these duties until you're ready. Now get down there" – Gerhard nodded at the space in front of the dais – "and show me your hews."

The boy reluctantly hopped down off the platform, and pulled out his longsword. The blade rang as he freed it from its scabbard, and as he moved into his roof guard position the edge of the steel glowed with a subtle blue light.

Felix held his stance, concentrated on his breathing, and, when he was ready, swung the point of the sword down and away, dancing lightly on his feet to execute a squinting hew, then again into a part hew. He pressed forward strongly, the tip always in motion as he slipped from one attack to the next, ending each move with the appropriate guard before bringing the blade around again.

When he reached the end of the dais, he retreated as if facing a stronger opponent, switching from guard to guard as the imaginary blows rained down on his slight form.

He was pink with effort by the time he reached his starting point.

"Not bad, boy. Not bad at all." Gerhard pushed his sleeves up. "Let me show you how to do that in battle."

4

Still completely covered by her Order's white robe, Nikoleta Agana left the fortress by the little-used Snake's Passage, and took the steep steps down to the riverside. Her soft shoes and billowing skirts made it look like she was floating. She could do that: her superiors hadn't even had to ink her and teach her levitation, as she'd arrived at the novices' house already able to fly. For her, it was as natural as breathing.

But she liked to walk. She enjoyed the feeling of stone under her heels, of grit against the soles of her feet, the meaningful stretch and ache of muscles as she moved. Some of her fellow adepts took it as a weakness, but after a bout of spell and counter-spell, it was they who were left dizzy and breathless, while she was alert and ready.

It was warm under the cloth. The days had turned from thrilling cold to showing a hint of summer. The townspeople, the merely mundane, had thrown off their winter clothes, but, whatever the weather, the Order wore the same white robes, and that was all anyone ever saw.

They saw it now as she approached the Witches' Bridge. Nikoleta didn't have to break stride, despite the road being busy. It was a centuries'-old concession, letting mundanes use the bridge, but the arrangement stood firm. Everyone had to get out of the way of a hexmaster or suffer the consequences.

They parted before her, and made Loki's horns at her behind

her back. Even though the bridge was narrow, the mundanes pressed themselves against the parapets and tried not to pitch either themselves or their loads into the swiftly flowing river below.

They weren't to know that she wasn't a hexmaster. They weren't to know that they never saw a hexmaster, and that it was anonymous novices and adepts that passed among them. The hexmasters stayed in their tower – plotting, researching, writing – unless there was dire need for them. And that was what she wanted for herself. A woman master: there wasn't even a word for what she wanted to become.

Her life – her adult life, at least – had been one of control and concentration. She could blank her mind of external stimulus, recall information instantly and perfectly, even slow her own heartbeat by an act of will. Freeing herself from the internal storm was more difficult: that was the difference between being adept at the secret arts and true mastery.

She used her learning song to calm herself; she sang it under her breath as she went, using the points of the simple, repetitive melody to inform her pace and fill her lungs. It was a song from Byzantium: that and her raw talent were the only two things she'd brought with her from the East.

"Hoson zês, phainou," she whispered, "mêden holôs su lupou."

It started to work. Not magic, exactly, but close.

The mundanes continued to move out of her way. Of course they did. Even a bare-faced novice would find their path clear. How much more would they scatter for one fully robed, muttering unintelligible words from under her hood?

"Pros oligon esti to zên, to telos ho chronos apaitei." Over and over again. She was so deep in a trance, she was almost blind and deaf. Her feet carried her like tiny automata into the town-beyond-the-wall, and up the shaded trail to the summit of the Goat Mountain.

Not a real mountain, more of a hill – steep, shrouded in trees – and no goats, either. The high peaks of the Alps that lay to the south dwarfed it, but it was more feared than any razor-sharp pinnacle. The slim tower balanced on its broad back was instantly recognisable by anyone who considered themselves wise.

She climbed under tall trees all the way to the top. She didn't know the route, had never before been permitted to approach the White Tower, let alone enter it. Yet it was easy: the slick black shine of the tower's walls peeked at her through the canopy during her ascent. It was only when she neared the summit, and the trees grew gnarled and wrong, that its size became apparent.

Her home city had inured her to architecture on a massive scale, but that was in the context of a city, the capital of an empire. The hexmasters had – not built, because that would imply the work of human hands – had raised themselves a spire that scratched at the heavens like a thorn.

Or so it looked from its base. Smooth black rock, half melted, windows like teardrops. One way in, a doorway, but no door.

An intruder would have to be completely insane to enter. There were things a sorcerer could do to a thief that were simply indescribable, and despite the fact she'd been summoned there and had express permission to go through the opening in the base of the tower, it was all she could do to prevent herself from turning around and fleeing as far and as fast as she could.

There were carved wards set into the stone either side of the doorway, faintly glowing in the shadow. She could see them for what they were because she wore the ink to do so, although their designs were arcane and their functions obscure. Those shallow engravings were responsible for part of her terror. The rest came from inside herself.

She took a step closer, and felt their full impact. If they'd gone for her, she'd have been a mewling, vomiting heap on the ground, unable to escape, utterly defenceless. Perhaps someone would have been along later to drag her away and trust she'd learnt her lesson. Or drag her inside, depending on their mood.

She'd seen it for herself, once, down at the novices' house. It had been instructive, but if she'd been asked to say what had actually happened, she'd have shrugged and said that the man had died, eventually.

It was still the effect of the wards. She swallowed hard and pushed through. As soon as she crossed the threshold, their influence faded, and she was left in the wide corridor that led to the main hall. Behind her, the outside had gone. There was nothing but a black wall. Ahead of her was a mess of hazy light, where blurred shadows walked.

She reached up and pulled her veil aside, folding it back over her head to expose her face. There was no point in hiding anything here, not from them. She served the hexmasters without question, obeying reflexively to avoid the pain of punishment. She went to find the master who had called her.

The space she was in was luminous, so bright that the hexmasters' white robes were grey in comparison. She couldn't tell how far the hall extended – even whether or not it was too large to fit inside the circumference of the tower.

There was no time to explore though, nor to wonder at the space. The moment she entered, she was surrounded. Figures coalesced out of the white mist, drawn towards her by the flame of her youth. Every one of them was old. All of them were shorter than her. They leant on their staffs and their hands were as white as parchment, as thin and brittle as twigs.

Mundanes could never attain that age. These men should all be dead. And yet . . . and yet, here they were, eking out their threadbare lives.

The air around her seemed to seethe with magic. She shuttered her usually impregnable defences down further to prevent her coming to inadvertent harm.

Her mouth was dry, though, and there was nothing she could do about that. "Master Eckhardt?" She didn't know which of them was Eckhardt. He had come down to the adepts' house, fully veiled.

"Adept Agana." A man taller and straighter than the others moved through the crowd. He was still old: the skin on his round head was heading towards his feet, and his owlish eyebrows were pure white. "What did the prince say?"

She closed her eyes to remember, and was suddenly aware of the pawing, the dry brushing of withered fingers against her robes, tracing the outline of her breasts, her belly, the hollow of her back.

Block it out, block it out. "Hoson zês, phainou, mêden holôs su lupou."

"The prince, Adept?" The mood of the master was plain. Eckhardt was quick to anger, slow to forgive.

"Gerhard is going to press the Teuton leader and send the body back to his men. He believes this will be sufficient warning to stop the Teutons crossing into Carinthia."

The touching didn't stop. If anything, it grew more intimate.

"Where are they now?"

"They are camped by the river at Simbach. If they cross, Gerhard means to call on you to kill them." Nikoleta shivered. The butterfly caresses fluttered away for a brief moment.

"This Teuton: what was he like?"

"Coarse. Rude. Tall. Strong. Smelt of horse." She wanted to leave, and knew she mustn't. "Brave. Unschooled. Cunning. Proud. Mortal."

Eckhardt grunted at her description. The light was blinding her, and it hurt to look at him. What little hair remained on his head shone like a halo.

"And Gerhard: what about him?"

He was their prince. Surely they'd know everything there was to know, even things that Gerhard himself had forgotten?

"I . . ." She found herself completely disorientated. It was the glowing, dream-like air, the inconstant, intrusive touching, the vibrations in her skull from being surrounded by so much magic.

"It matters not. All such men are the same, whether they rule few or many." Eckhardt reached out and took hold of her chin. He turned her head to the left, then to the right, not gently either. His fingers dug into her flesh. "Go. We might need you again. Wait at the adepts' house."

That was her dismissal; she knew better than to argue at her treatment or linger for an answer, and she didn't want to do either; she needed to obey. She turned, and the frail figures, hunched over their sticks, slowly, reluctantly, stood aside for her.

She took a step away from the masters, and another to get completely out of range of their hands. A smudge of darkness presented itself ahead and to her right. She walked towards it with the same steady gait that had brought her there.

The darkness expanded, swallowed her whole, and vomited her outside. She was shaking, retching, scrubbing her body through her clothes with her nails. She needed to lean against something to stop herself from falling. Not the glassy wall of the tower though, and not one of the nearby trees, which were tainted and untrustworthy. Nothing for it then but to stumble down the path towards the base of the hill, which led to the adepts' house and the novices' house beyond it.

The sun, clean and warm, filtered through the leaves. Its light was nothing like the syrupy, cloying incandescence of the White Tower. It was the same sun that had beaten down on her uncovered head as a child. She'd been barefooted then, her clothes nothing more than holes stitched together with remnants of weave; a wild, feral child, tormented and shunned.

She'd gone far enough from Byzantium to be safe then, and she'd gone far enough from the tower now. She slumped forward against the trunk of a chestnut and hugged its rough bark like it was her . . .

No, not that. Her mother feared her and hated her. If she was still alive.

The tree beat with rising sap, a slow, steady pulse. She could feel it if she concentrated on it, and it was so much easier to do that than consider her first, and only, meeting with the leaders of her Order.

After a while, when she thought she could stand again unaided, she let go and put her back to the tree, sliding down the trunk in a way that made her robes rise up and expose her legs, and the black ink under her olive skin. The palms of her hands were marked with ridges where she'd pressed them into the bark. But they soon faded. Her knuckles were smooth, her fingers straight. She was young.

In a hundred years' time, she would be like them, patting and stroking firm flesh when she could, because it was the one thing she'd never have again.

Or she might be dead. Broken, mad, immolated, disintegrated. Nothing was certain. And certainly not now.

"Is that what I really want?" she said out loud.

It always used to be. It wasn't just *her* goal, but every adept's, to be called to the White Tower and meet with the Master of the Order of the White Robe, to undergo whatever ritual was required of them, to be marked with the tattoos that would confer on them the power they craved.

In the three years since she'd been moved to the adepts' house, she'd known of two men who'd received that call. There had surely been others before then, and it was her turn next.

So where were the younger masters? They'd been conspicuously missing from the meeting she'd just had. Eckhardt had been the youngest one there, and no one would ever call him young again.

There was something else, too, undefinable and possibly unknowable: a niggling feeling that she was being built up, not for greatness, but for destruction. Eckhardt wasn't the Master of the Order, and yet he seemed to have assumed that position. The others, on paper just as powerful as him, appeared to take a subordinate role.

Nikoleta remembered their pawing hands, and swallowed bile. She picked up a shrivelled brown chestnut case from the ground by her side. The spines were brittle with age, sharp but easily broken. She shifted the ink on her exposed forearms, threw the seed pod lazily into the air and set it alight with a tiny fireball before it hit the ground.

It sizzled and crisped, a thread of black smoke lifted into the branches above her.

For the first time since she'd turned up at the novices' house – cold, all but naked, hammering on the door because, of all the places in the world, that place was the one where they understood people like her – she felt ambivalent.

The Order had recognised her abilities, taught her how to use them, scraped symbols on her skin and shown her power beyond reckoning. None of that came for free. She had paid, and paid dearly.

She dragged herself up and carried on down the path. Back in Byzantium, she knew she hadn't belonged. Here in Carinthia, she'd never felt that old unease until now.

5

Thaler sat at his desk in the library, the satchel burning a hole in the floor between his feet. He couldn't concentrate, couldn't even string one thought after the other. He fidgeted and moved scraps of paper around, and stared off into the distance across the cold, empty space between the balconies to the far side of the reading room.

He was surrounded on three sides by shelves, giving him a little alcove to work in, and a view of the rest of the library. Such were the privileges granted to an under-librarian. He had his own room in the dormitory, an allowance of a few shillings a week, and all the books he could want.

Lights – burnished globes of brass, glowing like suns – hung from the distant ceiling on great chains. He could read all day and all night under their perpetual light if he wanted, and he sometimes did. He was, he considered, the most fortunate of men.

To risk throwing such a life away was not a trifling matter. He hoped one day to contend for the position of master librarian, when the old master died. There would be fierce, but coolly polite, competition for that honour. And if he was caught abusing his position to secretly help a friend – against the hexmasters, no less – he could kiss that hope goodbye. Probably along with his flabby arse.

Even now they were preparing the pressing pit in the main square: not for him, nor Büber, but for some barbarian lord who'd stupidly threatened the prince. He'd rather avoid that fate.

He looked out to the opposite balcony, where one of the other under-librarians had their desk. Thomm wasn't there. In fact, Thomm was rarely there, and that merely added to the general malaise that had descended over the library of late. The last decade at least.

As far as he knew, the master librarian was in his eyrie, on the balcony one floor up that sat directly beneath the library's dome, while the apprentice master was one floor down with his half-dozen inky-fingered pupils. He'd counted seven other librarians moving listlessly between the shelves in the reading room. He pursed his lips, bent down to collect the satchel, and tucked it inside his black librarian's gown.

He listened. Nothing but the slight moan of a draught and the creak of a chain. He pushed his chair back, deliberately making its legs rasp against the dark oak planks. He listened again. No footsteps, no coughs, no squeak of a trolley.

Thaler moved into the next bay, and bent on aching knees to the very bottom shelf where the folio- and larger-sized books were kept. He dragged three of them out, piling them on the floor beside him, then eased a fourth a little way from the back of the shelf. He looked around again, making absolutely sure he couldn't be spotted by anyone, anyone except the master librarian, and he was always asleep until lunch.

He pressed the satchel into the gap, pinned it close with the book, then reshelved the heavy folios. He shuffled back to inspect his handiwork, and was satisfied. Those particular titles probably hadn't been moved for the better part of a century, and it was unlikely they'd be disturbed for another hundred years. All he had to do was remember where he'd put it.

He went back to his desk, but still clarity eluded him. He'd hidden the unicorn's horn. Now he had to discover why Büber had found two of them, without their attendant unicorns.

He needed fresh air. The library was windowless, and, with only the one main door that stayed mostly closed, was still and quiet and musty. Even the walls of the building were powdery with age: the Romans had worshipped their gods here, in their pantheon. That hadn't suited German ways; they instead raised great pillars of wood in forest clearings and on rock outcrops under the open sky. The statues of Jupiter and Mercury had been turned out and cast into the river, but the space had remained, unused and unloved until one of Gerhard's ancestors decided on a whim that he wanted a library.

Gods bless him for doing so.

Thaler got up from his desk again, and carried his outdoor shoes down the creaking staircase to the ground floor. From there, he made his way to the entrance hall, passing the huge desk that blocked the way to visitors – not that there were ever many, or even a few – and the dozing form of Glockner, the head usher, as crumpled and dusty as the books he supposedly guarded.

He kicked off his library slippers, nudging them back to a pair against the stonework of the hall, and eased on his shoes. As he fumbled his fat fingers into the heels, he looked up at the vast dome, the encircling galleries, the heavy lights on their solid chains, the stadia of shelves beneath. His lip trembled for a moment, before he stiffened it.

It could be brilliant, with a little more care, a few more librarians, a touch more of the prince's money. They could do only so much with the meagre resources they had, and that grieved him. When he was the Master, he'd go to Gerhard and tell him so.

The front doors were heavy, studded with iron, dark with pitch. It took genuine effort to lift the latch and pull the ring. The outside poured in through the crack, and Thaler had to keep the door moving until it was wide enough to get his bulk across the threshold. He turned, and strained again until the door banged shut.

There, that should wake Glockner.

He was under the colonnaded portico of the pantheon, in shadow and cold. Out in Library Square, a fountain played with the spring breezes, and over in the corner, a sausage seller was setting out his stall. In comparison to the inside, the square was teeming with activity. Carts, more or less steered by their drivers, rumbled across the cobbles, and busy people with baskets and sacks crossed from one street to another, disappearing up narrow alleys and emerging from doors.

Distraction and familiarity, that was what he needed.

He turned left, down the hill. The cobbles were still glistening with melting frost, and it was chilly enough in between the tall town houses to make him wrap himself tightly in his black librarian's gown.

Sunlight was striking the eaves of the east-facing roofs, so he chose to walk down to the quay. There was little heat in the spring sun, but it would be something, and the river didn't trap the air like the narrow alleyways of the Old Town.

He threaded his way by the most direct route, which is to say not direct at all, and suddenly popped out between two high walls onto the quayside. Two long barges were being loaded, bundles and crates passed up from carts and onto the flat-bottomed boats by a chain of shirt-sleeved men. A third was undergoing the reverse process, and when a cart was full, it was pushed off its chocks so that it wheeled itself across the wide quay, mostly in the direction of the waiting warehouses.

Across the river, beside the new town, were another two barges. One was casting off, orders shouted in the river-workers' cant ringing clear across the fast-flowing water. Its pointed bow aimed upstream, and for a moment the barge drifted backwards, its front threatening to turn across the current.

Then the heavily tattooed bargemaster put his hand to the tiller, his inked arms flashing darkly. The boat steadied and held its position. With seemingly no effort, and with the barge-hands busy with securing the ropes on deck, the vessel started to make headway. Little waves broke against its wooden sides as it pushed forward against the mountain meltwater.

Thaler walked upstream too, but the barge crept ahead of his pace. It threaded through the central arch of the bridge and he lost sight of it. His eyes were drawn instead to the forested flanks of the ridge that ran east to west across the valley, neatly bisected by the river.

On top of the western ridge was the White Fortress, bright and shining against the green of the wood and the blue of the sky. On the eastern side, the White Tower, as dark as the other was bright.

Everyone passing through – south to the mountain passes or north to the cities on the plains – was aware of those two authorities.

He looked from one monumental edifice to the other. It wasn't by chance or accident of geography that the town had grown up under the walls of the fortress, rather than huddling close to the flanks of Goat Mountain. As much as the prince's subjects feared their lord's temporal power, the laws that they were made to live by were at least comprehensible by mortals.

Magical things – like unicorns – were wild, quixotic, barely understood. That was the hexmasters' world, and poor Büber, who had always lived on the line between, had finally crossed over into it.

There were books about magic in the library, but no books of magic. Those were all carefully sequestered away and kept under lock, key, and far more arcane guards somewhere inside the ill-named White Tower.

An uninitiated man, even of Thaler's standing, would never get to see what was written in those books: it gave him an odd feeling in his stomach, to know that they were denied to him, even though the thought of opening even the most elementary primer in magic made him sweat.

There might be a way around that prohibition, though. It was risky, and he wouldn't take it yet. There were other avenues to be exhausted first.

This was better. He had started to plan, tentatively yes, but a solid course of action nevertheless. He breathed deeply, and caught the scent of pine on the wind. So: when he got back to the library, he would still have his duties to perform. His main work was overseeing the cataloguing and indexing of every book in the library, a task that had been barely started when he first entered the cool marble dome as a thin, pale youth, and that would still be incomplete when they carried him out feet first, however many years in the future that might be.

No one would be checking on him, though. He could, if he wanted, spend each and every day trawling the shelves for books of lore, the bestiaries and the philosophies, until he found his answer. He'd have to dig through the layers of manuscripts, and start with the very oldest. He would have to keep notes of his search – in code, perhaps. Yes, a code: a complex cipher, not one that could be solved with a moment's glance.

Thaler took one last deep breath of the morning riverside air, and turned to go back the way he'd come: the alleys of the Old Town were such that the shortest way to the library was to take the long way around.

Walking back along the quay, he paused to let a carter nudge the wheels of his barrow towards the waiting warehouse. As his gaze followed the man's broad back, he caught sight of a woman collecting an oilskin-wrapped bundle from a merchant.

He knew her, and guessed what she was now carrying, a heavy load caught up in both her arms and clutched to her chest. She was intending to go towards the Town Hall, away from where Thaler was, but she sensed she was being watched.

She turned quickly, curls of long dark hair escaping from her loose plait.

"Mr Thaler? Can you now *smell* books?"

She smiled and stopped. The weight she was carrying made it seem boorish to expect her to walk a single extra step towards him, so he went to her instead.

"Miss Morgenstern." There was something else he should be saying. "Happy . . ."

"Purim, Mr Thaler. It starts on Friday." She smiled at him. "Happy Purim indeed."

"And this Purim? You build tents, yes?"

"That's the Feast of Tabernacles, Mr Thaler. At Purim we get wildly, incoherently drunk and burn an effigy of the wicked Haman." She smiled again, and hugged the bundle of books a little tighter. "The men do, at least."

Thaler nodded with satisfaction. "Just like all *our* festivals, then. We'll make good Wotan-worshippers of you Jews yet."

"I think Father would have something to say about that." She hefted the books again. They were clearly heavy. She looked down at them, then up at Thaler. "I'm sure he'd welcome you to our house later, if you wanted to pay a visit. He's busy now organising the wood for the bonfire, and a hundred other things I'm sure."

"Do you know . . .?"

She looked up at the sky with a little flick and shake of her head. "A copy of the works of Josephus, which I'm sure you already have, a part of Maimonides – I'm not sure which part, and I don't think Father does either – and a Berber translation of a discourse on Greek geometry. Euclid? Or did he say of the school of Euclid? I'm sorry I can't be of more help, Mr Thaler."

That a Jewess knew of Euclid, let alone carried one of his books in her arms, was odd enough. "Tell your father I may well drop by. I'd like to check his Maimonides against ours."

"He'll be delighted as always, if a little distracted. I have to go, or I'll drop them on the way. Tell me, Mr Thaler, why do they have to make books so big?" She adjusted her load one last time and, before he had a chance to answer, started to stride up the quayside, her skirts flapping and snapping like a sail.

"The words, Miss Morgenstern," Thaler replied. "It's because of all the words."

She didn't wave to show that she'd heard, just carried on towards the bridge and the road that led off it, up the hill to the Old Market and Jews' Alley where most of her kind lived. There was even room for a man as unorthodox – that was their word, not his – as Aaron Morgenstern.

So: no more delay. To work – the first books to find would be whatever the library carried of the Rabbi Maimonides, and then he'd see about Büber's unicorn. The confusion he'd felt had gone like a mist burnt away by the rising sun. He set out, his footsteps over the cobbles almost energetic.

He hated winter, hated the cold and the dark and the damp. Even the library, bathed in perpetual light, seemed smaller and more joyless under a thick blanket of iron-hard snow. Everything was just more difficult.

And now it was spring. The Ostara festival had been earlier that week, an excuse for eating and drinking and being as merry as the Jews were planning to get for their Purim celebrations. Not that librarians were supposed to get drunk, though they sometimes did. Neither were they supposed to engage in the more earthy offerings of the goddess, though that, too, was sometimes honoured more in the breach. And they weren't supposed to marry: their books were to be their wives, their fellow librarians their family.

It was mostly enough for Thaler. Only sometimes – as with the mention of Büber's casual whoring – did it suddenly bite him hard. He kept himself insulated against the world for the most part, with an armour of leather binding, glued spines and black lettering.

Up Coin Street: windows were open, and the tap-tap of hammers and hiss of scalding steam drifted out from the workshops, bringing the smell of hot metal with it. Everyone seemed hard at work, except him. He felt ashamed, and started to hurry.

6

When it was done, and the guards had escorted Gerhard and a white-faced Felix back to the fortress, Büber stood in silent contemplation in front of the pressing pit, his teeth grazing at the scar-tissue of one of his finger stumps.

The crowd, which had gathered to hear Walter of Danzig's bones crack, started to leave, and Reinhardt, who'd been in charge of the execution, waited for Büber to give the nod and start the business of raising the massive stone slab.

The sacred grove of ash trees was in the main square of the town, surrounded by tall houses in the same way that the grove surrounded the bleached, smoothed pole of the irminsul. Büber looked up at the pale, ancient trunk, crowned with thick iron nails that bled rust.

The pit was at the base of the irminsul itself. Long ago, their priest-princes had sacrificed captives to Wotan One-Eye by hanging them from the trees. More civilised times had decided that the gods didn't need blood to keep the crops growing and the summer returning, and the pressing pit had been devised to execute criminals out of sight, if not out of hearing.

Quite how crushing a man's breath from his body until his ribs snapped and his skull shattered counted as civilised escaped Büber. There were quicker, cleaner deaths to be had.

"Come on then, Captain." He was weary of this already. "Let's get it done."

Reinhardt ordered his men to haul on the rope that passed through the block-and-tackle, and together they watched the stone winched, inch by inch, from the socket in the ground.

The Teuton had been spread-eagled and each limb tied to an inset iron ring. He'd been struggling and screaming and cursing, and it had taken strong men to hold him down. It would take only one to cut him free and remove him from the pit.

Büber pulled out the knife from his belt and went round each corner to saw through the cords, even as the stone carried on rising. As he stepped back, there was a sucking sound and a wet thud. That would be the Teuton's head.

There was a drain, but that didn't stop the flags that formed the floor of the pit from being stained almost black. It smelt of everything that had been in the man before the stone came down.

"It'll need sluicing out," said Büber, and when Reinhardt grimaced, he added plainly: "You want my job?"

"Thank you kindly, but no, Master Büber. The men'll see to it."

Büber unfolded the waxed canvas sheet next to the pit, and took hold of the Teuton's arms. He gave a tug, and decided that the rest would probably follow. He stepped backwards, easing the body onto the sheet. It was so disarticulated as to appear boneless.

The face was the worst. Danzig looked almost, but not quite, unrecognisable. The chest was a forest of white bone splinters, and his stomach had burst. In contrast, the hands and feet were pristine. Büber used the toe of his boot to arrange the body, then folded the edges of the heavy cloth together. He knelt down and started to sew the shroud up with a bodkin and thick thread.

Reinhardt and his crew chocked the pressing stone up on blocks of timber, and started pouring buckets of water collected from a fountain into the pit. They had stiff-bristled brooms to attack the gore.

Büber looked up from his task occasionally, catching Reinhardt's gaze. They wore the same expressions of grim-faced resignation. They had their orders, and they knew better than to disobey, even if some of the things they were told to do didn't make sense, or were foul.

At some point, someone from the stables brought a horse for him, and the Teuton's own. He wasn't much of a rider. He could do it, but preferred his own two feet.

The smell made his own horse shy away, but the shaggy Teuton mount seemed less affected: perhaps where it came from had inured it to the stink of blood and shit.

"Give me a hand here," said Büber, and he and Reinhardt lifted the sewn shroud across the Teuton's saddle. Some leakage was inevitable, as his needlework wasn't perfect. Reinhardt looked down at his surcoat. They both shrugged, and Büber tied the shroud on to the shuffling horse.

"Go carefully, huntmaster."

"I've no intention of getting within a mile of the Teutons," he said. "I'll leave that to the Bavarians."

"All the same, these things can come back and bite us little people on the arse." Reinhardt gave up and wiped his hands clean of sticky liquid, of the whole business. "The prince knows best, I suppose."

"Whether he does or doesn't is no concern of mine," said Büber. He fixed a lead to the Teuton horse's bridle and fastened it to his saddle, then mounted up. He had a way to go: he'd be lucky to make the thirty old Roman miles from Juvavum to Simbach before it grew dark. "He's the prince, and that's the end of it."

He rode down to the quayside and across the bridge, picking up the via that ran north. The river was on his left, the hill country to his right, and he hadn't gone far before he met two men.

The first was on one side of the road, the second on the other, walking almost in the ditches of the via, but both were shouting out the same name. Through cupped hands, they called for Georg.

Büber's horse drew level, passing between them. The man on the left turned to glance at Büber. Both of them were expecting just another traveller, and were surprised by the flare of mutual recognition.

"Peter?"

Büber looked again. It was Kelner. "Martin. What in the gods' names are you doing?"

Kelner put his hand to his forehead and tightened his fingers across his temples. "My brother's boy's gone missing." He looked around at the woods and the hills, and further away at the snow-covered mountaintops. "Can't find him anywhere."

The other man crossed the via and passed Kelner a water bottle. "The kid was looking after the pigs. The pigs were all there, but . . ." and he shrugged, "no Georg."

It wasn't his business, but Kelner was, if not a friend, certainly an acquaintance. Büber patted his horse's neck and swung himself out of the saddle and onto the stone road.

"No reason for the lad to run off, I suppose?" Life could be rough-and-ready in the wilds. Children had to be taught to attend to their duties, sometimes with the back of a hand. Even Felix was beaten by the signore.

"My brother's a good father," said Kelner, "and Georg has never

40

given him any real trouble. He's no paragon, but you know, he's a boy. It's not like him to just disappear."

"And the other kids?" Büber worried at one of his finger stumps.

"All accounted for. Peter, he's only nine. He hasn't run off with one of the other children, and he's not out chasing girls: his balls haven't dropped yet." Kelner turned slowly again, aware that he should still be searching for his nephew. His gaze took in the Teuton horse and its load. "What in Midgard have you got there?"

"I'm a prince's man, and I'm about my duties," he said.

"That's a body," said Kelner's kinsman. "Whose is it?"

"Some Teuton mercenary who pissed off Gerhard. He got pressed for his troubles."

"But why have you got it?"

"Martin, I don't have to explain myself to you, and I need to be on my way." Büber put his hand on his saddle pommel, ready to remount. Kelner snagged the reins in his fist.

"Has this got anything to do with Georg?"

"No." Perhaps he said that too quickly, or too slowly, because Kelner grew suspicious.

"Peter?"

"I don't know anything about where the boy is. Really I don't."

"And we're looking for my nine-year-old nephew." Kelner ground his heel in the dust. "Peter, remember when we had that bother up at the lake? The nixie?"

He did. The drowned man had come from Kelner's wife's family. But water spirits didn't make people – or unicorns – vanish.

"Nothing like that's going on, as far as I know."

"But you know something, right?"

"Look, Martin. I can't help you with the lad. I'm under orders, and it'll be my head if I screw up." His mouth had gone dry. "I want you to do something for me."

"We're out here until we find him. I'm not your errand boy."

"Martin. Calm down. This is the best I can do, okay?"

"What, then?"

"Keep looking. He could have wandered off. If . . . if you don't find him by evening, I want you to go to Juvavum and tell someone – one of the librarians."

Kelner was insulted. "A librarian? What the fuck for?"

"Because I want you to tell him about this, and him alone. A man called Frederik Thaler. It's really important you do. Don't

41

pass a message on, don't be put off by their black-gowned ways. Him and him alone. Got that?"

"And what's this Thaler going to do? Organise a search? He's a cocking librarian!"

Büber put his hand onto Kelner's shoulder. "Listen, Martin. I'm really sorry about your nephew."

His hand was thrown abruptly off.

"What aren't you telling me?" Kelner moved up close, so that Büber could smell wood smoke and sap. "This has happened before, hasn't it?"

"I don't know. It's . . ." Büber turned his head away. "It's complicated, all right?"

"I don't care how complicated it is, Peter." Kelner reached out and turned Büber back to face him. "This is about a kid. Nine years old."

Büber took a deep breath. Kelner was right. Of course he was right. But the boy had gone, and none of the others had come back.

Tell him enough, then. But not the whole truth.

He pushed Kelner's arm down, firmly but slowly. "There's something out there. I don't know what. I know that the masters know, but they haven't told me anything. I have to assume the prince knows too, but he hasn't told me either."

"And this something is taking children?"

"Maybe four over the last year. No one sees them go. Kids run away all the time, for all sorts of reasons. But probably four like this. Unexplained." Büber kicked at the stone road. "That's why you need to tell Thaler. Someone else other than the masters needs to know about this."

The urge to fight slipped away from Kelner, and he let go of the horse. "This Thaler? Can he help?"

"He's got all those books. That must mean something, right?"

"The masters, though. They can just cast a spell and find him, can't they?" Kelner didn't want to give up hope.

"That's been tried." Büber shook his head. As far as he knew, it had: the Order could have lied and there'd be no way of telling. Whichever it was, that particular child, a girl, was still missing.

"Crap. Peter, I can't go back to my brother and tell him some . . . *thing* has taken his boy. What's the prince doing about this?"

"I'm his servant. He tells me what to do, and I go and do it.

When I've done it, I come back and tell him I've done it. That's the way it works. And at the moment, I'm not doing what he told me to do." Büber reached up for the pommel again. "Tell Thaler. He'll take this seriously, and you won't get your arse kicked by one of the chamberlain's men. Which you will if you go directly to the prince."

He swung himself up, and his horse stepped right, forcing Kelner's kinsman away. Büber took the opportunity to jab his heels and get the animal moving.

"Good luck," he called, and Kelner half-heartedly raised his hand.

Büber felt wretched as he rode away north. Arguing over whether or not to look for missing children wasn't what he'd signed up to do – of course he should – but there'd be chaos if the Teutons chanced their arm and decided to head straight for the passes under the prince's control. There weren't just the horsemen to consider, either; it was their baggage train too. Carts of stuff, pots and pans and tents and blankets and weapons and armour and spare tack and clothes, piled onto low-bedded wains and pulled by cart horses. Packed in among the effects, almost as an afterthought, were women and children. Whether or not the women belonged to the men, and the children to the women, was a matter of conjecture. They were there, and they all needed feeding.

Three hundred horse. Pasture alone for that many would make sufficient fields bald to starve the local cows into stopping giving milk. That's if the Teutons didn't just eat the cows, kill the farmer and enslave his family for good measure.

What he was doing was important. He was saving many other Georgs, and their mothers, from going missing. Only if he did it right, though: he had to make sure the Teutons got the prince's message.

The Roman via was a broad road with a dressed stone surface that managed to stay usable in most weathers – but he could cut the corner off to get to where he needed to go more quickly.

So he headed up into the wooded hills and lake country where Kelner and his like lived, on tracks wide enough for a wagon and no more. This was Büber's country, too, more so than the high alpine pastures and the naked mountain slopes. He was never happier . . . no, not happier, for he was rarely happy, but content. He was at ease, at one with the landscape.

Except for today. When the trees closed overhead, he brooded over what had happened to Georg. He didn't know exactly, but something that could take a unicorn without a single sign of struggle could spirit a child away. Unicorns were tough bastards; he didn't let all the romantic talk about virgins and purity cloud his judgement, because he'd never forgotten the look in one stallion's eye as it levelled its horn at Büber's heart across the width of a forest clearing.

They were killers. And something had contemptuously left nothing but the most valuable part of it behind. Twice.

He hoped he'd done the right thing, sending Kelner to find Thaler. This knowledge was a dangerous commodity. He'd told the librarian about the unicorns, but not about the children, because, until now, he hadn't made the connection. Thaler would chew him out for that, since it was obvious.

What else had he missed?

He didn't know, because he wasn't used to thinking like that. His world was – it used to be – simple. Everything that happened had happened before. It was, if not explicable, predictable.

He kept on going, following the map in his head, through the villages that were no more than a strung-out ribbon of wooden houses by the track. Smoke and cooking smells reminded him he was hungry. He stopped occasionally, ostensibly to feed and water the horse, but really for his own sake. Wherever he dismounted, someone would come out and greet him, ask his business, and, satisfied that he was one of them, either go back in and leave him alone, or return with some bread, or cheese, or sausage, or beer.

Peter Büber, in the company of the dead, was craving the company of the living. He wasn't used to that feeling.

When he finally crested the last rise and saw the Enn in front of him, he was grateful to have something to do. His head hurt.

Simbach was across the wide river, a little Bavarian town with its own market and minor earl in charge. On the Carinthian side, nothing but five houses close to the bridge, and then widely spaced farm buildings dotted along the road.

The bridge, though. It wouldn't have looked out of place in a great city like Rome or Byzantium. A low, single span arched over the water, high enough at the midpoint for barges, but its slope sufficiently shallow for the rise to be barely perceptible. Wide, too:

traffic could cross north and south and still have room to stop along the way and admire the view.

It was, of course, physically impossible. No stone arch could support its weight shaped like that. But the bridge didn't depend on architecture for its existence, even if it was cast as a single block of black rock. There were engravings on each buttress bearing testament to that.

The bridge had been there a long time. The Romans had thrown a pontoon across on their way to conquer the known world, replacing it afterwards, during the time of peace they established, with a concrete and brick construction similar to their viaducts. That, despite the empire's engineering skills, had been swept away again and again. The hexmasters had come once and conjured a marvel, then left it for mortals to use.

Büber used his elevation to scout out the land. Simbach wasn't walled, and the compact centre gave way to farms and gardens. Everything seemed normal there: hazy air over the town, the sense of people moving in the streets, pack animals crossing the bridge.

Over to the west, however, was another, more concentrated source of smoke. That would be the Teutons, then, waiting for their leader to return.

The sun was setting, and had already started to slip behind the ragged mountain peaks to the south. Büber leant forward and patted his horse on the neck.

"Good boy," he said. The horse, sensing the day was almost over, looked around, sniffing at the saddlebags.

7

Thaler made his way through the town, his gown flapping around him. Nothing had happened in quite the right order that day, from Büber's early message to Kelner's late arrival.

The woodsman's story had left him confused and concerned. Missing unicorns, missing children, and Büber's almost child-like trust in the power of books which he himself couldn't read. Some force – an arcane force for sure – was at work, and it was becoming clear that the hexmasters couldn't or wouldn't confront it.

Which was deeply disturbing in itself. There was nothing that was collectively beyond them.

And now it was dark, and he was late.

He hurried up the side of the library to Franks' Alley, and then into the open space at the heart of the town, with its carefully kept ring of ash trees. They were in leaf again after a bare winter, their branches meshing with their neighbours' and providing a continuous circle of protection for the central pillar, whose top was lost at night in shadow and sky.

Tall, high-roofed houses, rich with money and servants, lined the square, and it was their uncovered lights that shone down and illuminated his way. Gold Alley on the far side was just as bright, even though the assayers and coiners had long since closed for the night.

Thaler trailed down the narrow passage, and came to another crossway in the labyrinth of streets. This alley was in shadow. No magical lights here: just a line of seven flickering candles in a window. It was a sign that a Jew lived there, and that he was at the entrance of Jews' Alley.

He found the right door and knocked on it. Old Aaron was getting a little deaf, so Thaler gave the small brass knocker some extra taps, loudly enough for faces to appear at other windows in the surrounding buildings. Maybe they recognised the shape of Thaler, or were just satisfied that there was only one man out in the street. Their faces receded, and eventually there was a shuffling behind the door.

"I'm coming, I'm coming," came the voice raised in complaint. "Who is it?"

"It's Under-librarian Thaler, Mr Morgenstern."

The door had bolts top and bottom, and they thwacked back like axe-blows. A chink of light appeared and, halfway up, a glistening-wet eye. "Sophia said you might call. I suppose this is about the Maimonides?"

"Partly," said Thaler.

"Partly?" Morgenstern shuffled aside and Thaler stepped into the hallway. "There's something else?"

Thaler dragged his fingers through his thinning hair. "It's been a strange day, Mr Morgenstern."

"You and me both, Mr Thaler." Morgenstern reclosed the bolts on the door. "I'll go and get the book," he said. "Go through to the kitchen."

Morgenstern headed up the narrow stairs on unsteady legs, and Thaler was left to creak along the corridor to the back room.

"Miss Morgenstern," said Thaler. He pulled back a chair from the long table and sat heavily.

"Mr Thaler," said Sophia, without turning around. She had her hair tied back and uncovered, with floury splashes down her apron. "Do sit down."

"I . . ." He'd done so already. "Thank you."

Wielding a long-handled wooden paddle, she delved deep into an alcove next to the fire. Then she pulled the paddle back out and deposited a round loaf on the table in front of Thaler.

"Eaten, Mr Thaler?" She knocked the oven door closed with her elbow and stowed the paddle.

"Actually, no. I haven't found the time." He hadn't, either. What with one thing and another.

Sophia tutted. "That's not like you, Mr Thaler. You have to look after yourself. So, some cheese with your bread?" She wiped her hands on her apron. She had a small smudge of flour on her nose.

Disarmed, Thaler acquiesced. "That will be . . ."

"Acceptable?" She laid three platters on the table and slipped a board under the cooling loaf. Its crust, previously smooth and brown, had just started to shrink and crack. "I'm sure Father will join us shortly."

The ceiling sounded with slow footsteps, and Sophia went into the larder to find the cheese and the butter.

Thaler looked at the low-burning fire, at the sparks rising up the chimney and out into the night.

Why did they do that? he wondered. Everything solid fell to the ground, but fire rose. Like the hexmasters and their levitation spells. Perhaps it was magic. Perhaps some types of wood were more magical than others.

Aaron Morgenstern shuffled into the room, and carefully laid the leather-bound book next to Thaler's place-setting. "The Maimonides."

The boards were rigid, unwarped and well cut, covered with a dark brown calfskin, tanned and stretched and nailed and tooled. He nodded with appreciation, then opened the book and ran a finger down the binding. Nice tight stitching. No loose leaves there. The frontispiece was clear and uncluttered, a Latin script with tightly controlled serifs.

"Good copy," said Thaler. "Berber Spain?"

"I believe so. It's no more than twenty years old, with very few corrections and marginalia."

Thaler turned the first page of stiff, fibrous paper. "Ah ha."

The text was interlinear Latin and Hebrew: he'd not seen that before. The Latin, Thaler could read, and his lips twitched as he muttered the opening syllables. Over the top, Morgenstern spoke the Hebrew, because he could understand both.

When they next looked up, Sophia was sitting opposite Thaler, a wedge of bread on her plate and a chunk of yellow cheese in her mouth. "What?"

"The blessing, child?" said Morgenstern. "Serving our guest first?"

"I swear I'd have starved to death before you two stopped." She wiped her mouth with the back of her hand and poured some watered wine from the pitcher into her cup. "Anyway, a reading from Rabbi Maimonides is blessing enough for a feast, let alone a simple supper."

To prove the point, she dipped her bread and chewed the end of it off.

"My daughter behaves more like a goy every day." Morgenstern threw his hands in the air. "Marriage. It's the only thing that'll be the saving of her."

Sophia smiled and dunked her bread in her wine again. "Can I get you anything, Mr Thaler?"

Thaler looked to her father for a lead, but he just shrugged and muttered in Yiddish as he took his seat at the head of the table, where he could warm his bones with the heat from the grate.

"Well, some of everything, I suppose."

Sophia dutifully cut a wedge of bread and leant across to place it on Thaler's plate, then returned with the jug of wine.

"So, will you be relieving me of the Maimonides?" Morgenstern held out his own platter for Sophia to load.

"We have translations, but not a Hebrew text next to the Latin one. Copying should only take a couple of months. It's not a huge book."

"And you have someone who can write Hebrew?"

"Even if they don't understand it, they can copy it."

"These words. Are words." Morgenstern trembled, and Sophia had to steady his hand. "Get one stroke wrong and you change the whole meaning. The text. Worthless."

Thaler's mouth sneaked a smile. "We have someone who can not only write Hebrew, they can read it."

The old man snorted. "You shouldn't joke about these things. It's important to us, and it should be important to you."

"I'm sorry." Perhaps he should be slightly abashed. Certainly Sophia was frowning at him.

"Sorry enough to return the sefer you have?"

Thaler raised his hands. "I can't do anything about that."

"But when you're the master librarian?" pressed Morgenstern.

"Not even then. They're part of the collection, and the collection is less without them. Let's not go round the square with this again."

Morgenstern shook his head and adjusted his little black skull cap. He was wearing the one with the gold-thread edging. "Each one a lifetime's work. Just sitting there. Not even being read," he muttered. Thaler's conscience was tweaked: he was sitting at the man's table, eating his food and drinking his wine, and insulting his religion all at the same time. "We don't have sacred texts," he said.

"Would it kill you to respect those who did?"

"Father," said Sophia, in a tone that brooked no argument.

"Yes, daughter mine." He bit into his cheese and chewed thoughtfully.

"You're our guest, Mr Thaler." She refilled his cup. "Guests are always welcome in this house."

"I . . ." said Thaler. "Look, I may never get to be master librarian. I'm not the oldest under-librarian. I'm not even the most senior, though that doesn't mean everything – the librarians usually choose their own master. And there are precedents."

"Don't worry yourself about it, Mr Thaler. What's done is done. More bread?"

"No, thank you. I'm fine." He drank the wine though, and stared at its glassy surface, stained slightly with the oils from the cheese transferred to the liquid via his upper lip. "If you would just come into the library . . ."

"Jews don't," said Morgenstern. "Even this Jew won't."

"Now who's being intransigent?"

"Gentlemen," said Sophia, "neither of you are behaving well. I insist on harmony at my table."

Old Morgenstern harrumphed. "*Your* table?"

"My bread, my cheese, my cooking, my going to market, my visiting the wine seller, my setting out, and undoubtedly, my cleaning up. So yes." She leant back and stared defiantly at her father. "My table as much as it is yours."

"Marriage."

"No one will have me." She looked quite pleased with herself.

"Is that any surprise? You make yourself unmarriable!"

"And who would look after you, you old fool? You'd spend all day wandering the house in your nightgown, wondering what time it was." She reached out and patted his hand, which Morgenstern rightly interpreted as being entirely patronising. "When you've gone, then I shall marry."

"If I thought you would marry, I'd go tomorrow."

"Perhaps I should leave," offered Thaler.

"He's just in a bad mood, Mr Thaler. Do stay." She smiled at him, but was looking at her father. "It's so rare I get intelligent conversation."

"And this from the mouth of my own flesh and blood? Oy."

"Tell Mr Thaler what's put you in a bad mood, Father."

"Apart from him taking my books and holding three perfectly good sefer captive?"

"He's only borrowing the Maimonides, and he's made certain that every other book the library has borrowed has come back, in the same condition, and quickly. He even had one of them rebound for you. Mr Thaler is your friend, Father, though I don't know why." She folded her arms. "You're an irascible old devil."

Sophia was right: Morgenstern was upset, and not at him. He'd tried hiding it, and with someone less familiar he might have succeeded. But, while Thaler wouldn't exactly describe the Jew as a friend, he was certainly an acquaintance of long standing.

"Come, Mr Morgenstern. If I'm not the object of your ire, what is? Is it something to do with your festival preparation?"

"What? Purim? No, no." Morgenstern pushed his plate away. "Sophia told you about the Euclid, yes?"

"Yes. You received three books. Josephus – we have both *War* and *Antiquities* already, the Maimonides, and the Euclid."

"I paid good money for the Euclid. *On the Balance*."

Thaler slowly sat more upright. "*Balance*? But that's . . ."

"Lost, yes." Morgenstern tugged at his thin white beard. "Which might give you some idea just how much I paid for it."

"Can I see it?" The librarian's palms were suddenly sweaty.

"I don't have it. They cheated me. Me, Aaron Morgenstern." He threw his hands up in disgust. "I've dealt with these people for thirty years and they've never let me down. I send them this king's ransom and I get some obscure Babylonian work no one's ever heard of."

"Who did you pay?" asked Thaler. Euclid. *On the Balance.* Gods, it was legendary! And no one had seen so much as a page from it for centuries. He wiped his hands on his gown and gripped the edge of the table.

"I can't tell you. It's a professional confidence." He sighed. "I can't even tell you if it was them who swindled me, or whether they genuinely sent it and it got switched in transit. All I know is I don't have *On the Balance.*"

"Have you questioned the bargemaster?"

"Gone. Quickly, too. Downstream. If I find it was them, I'll . . ." His anger slipped away, and Morgenstern seemed smaller and frailer than before. "I don't know what I can do. I can complain, but who's going to believe an old Jewish bookseller over a German bargemaster. I have receipts, a bill of sale, but no book."

"Do you even know who the bargemaster was?"

"I don't know his name," said Sophia, "but if you give me a moment, I'll remember the name of the boat."

"Wien is the obvious place to sell a stolen book," said Thaler. "I can get a message to the Protector's officials. You still might get your Euclid."

"And how will you get your message to them? Magic?"

"That's the way we normally do things. I know you don't like it, but . . ."

"Send a horse. Better still, send a man on a horse."

"All the way to Wien? Your bargemaster will have been, gone, and your book, if it ever existed, will have vanished into thin air." Thaler, having offered help, was irritated. And also: a previously lost Euclid? It was far too valuable to let it slip from his grasp – Morgenstern's grasp – without a fight. "You use the barges to move your goods. I mean, even if you think those tattoos are for show, how do you explain how the boats move upstream?"

"How other people send their books to me is their business. How they want me to send them is also their business." At least Morgenstern had the grace to look embarrassed.

"Then how I send a message to Wien is my business." Thaler knew he'd won that particular bout, and he swigged the last of his wine. "I'll go and do it now. An apprentice will call in the morning for the Maimonides, and I'll let you know if the Euclid is found. He pushed his chair back. "Good night to you, Miss Morgenstern, and you, Mr Morgenstern."

8

That Nikoleta could sense magic was a given: her first tattoo, since embellished and extended, allowed her to differentiate clearly between the enchanted and the mundane. That ability had nearly sent her mad. She was, after all, surrounded by sorcerers. She'd learnt painfully – there was no other way – to block out the roar in her head, so thoroughly that the only time in the last few years that it had proved inadequate was that very morning in the White Tower.

Now that she had cause to look at it again, in the quietness of her austere cell, it told her another story. She could still feel the magic around her, in her, and yet there was cause for real fear. She could now sense its absence elsewhere.

The knot in her chest tightened. The other adepts were confined to their cells by the master in charge, and she could tell from the auras around her where they were. But they were faint where they should have been vivid. They should have found her probing offensive and threatening. They should have retaliated.

That she was not under immediate assault from half a dozen furious adepts told her more than she wanted to know.

She waited. Waited for what, she didn't know, but it was all she could do. She had neither permission nor reason to leave the adepts' house: to do so without either would have been cause for severe punishment.

She heard footsteps. They were coming closer, and she shut down her magical senses completely. The adept master was stalking the cloisters. The pacing stopped outside her unlocked, unwarded door. Adepts were not permitted such luxuries as privacy and secrets.

She stood by the foot of her bed, as she'd been told to do countless times before. The door didn't open, but a parchment note slid under it with a crisp hiss. The footsteps receded. She didn't move for a few moments, making sure that the master wasn't going to return, then walked to the door and scooped up the letter.

It was novices who were used to pass messages on from mundanes, not masters. Which meant that the novices were confined to their quarters, too. She closed her fist on the stiff paper.

Then she opened her hand and smoothed the parchment flat. She looked at the letter. The wax seal was a library mark, with the Latin letters B and I prominent on opposite pages of an open book. That was how mundanes sealed their writing against tampering. It was little more than pathetic.

She almost destroyed the note. Instead, she opened it and read:

Felicitous greetings from Under-librarian Frederik Thaler in the name of Prince Gerhard V of Juvavum in the Palatinate of Carinthia, by the authority of the Master Librarian, to the Masters of Goat Mountain. By royal agreement and past custom, I require the following information to be transmitted with all due haste to the Protector of Wien. A Juvavum bookseller recently had the opportunity to acquire a previously unobtainable work, *On the Balance* by Euclid, but has been cheated. The library is determined to regain this invaluable book if at all possible – suspicion has fallen on the bargemaster and crew of the *Donau Bride*, which left Juvavum this morning, believed heading to Wien.

The Protector's men are requested to seize the barge and search it, before there is an opportunity to dispose of the book within Wien. I am authorised to offer a reward of one hundred shillings for information leading to the return of the book, and our prince's brother Protector Waldemar is assured of his goodwill and favour.

Written and signed this day, the fourteenth day of March in the fifteenth year of the reign of Gerhard V of Juvavum, Under-librarian Frederik Thaler.

It was perfectly reasonable. This Thaler was expecting nothing more than his due – invoking the name of the prince – to have a message sent to Wien. It would take no more effort than Thaler had taken to write his absurdly wordy letter for her to go to the projection room and transmit their contents near or far. It was a common transaction.

Except there now seemed to be a problem, and no one was telling her what it was. She would have to find out for herself.

Nikoleta took her courage and the letter in her hands, and stepped out into the cloister.

There was no rule requiring her to cover herself, but she felt the overwhelming need to do so, so she did. She felt safer, which was stupid because it was only a bit of cloth: she had a full repertoire of defensive and offensive spells, but she distrusted them to protect her from whatever was wrong.

She didn't run though, or walk quickly, to the projector. Decorum and order were nothing more than theatre, but she'd grown up in a city where the show of power was more impressive than the power itself. She understood such things and how effective they could be.

She walked along two sides of the cloister square. It was late, and the air spilling down from the mountains was cold. A fog was rising off the river and the lights of the adepts' house were haloed with mist. Because of the curfew, there was no one else about. It felt odd. There was always activity of some sort, even if it was just the sound of distant, rhythmic screaming.

Nikoleta stopped before she left the cloister and looked behind her. There, in the far corner, was the adept master. Almost, but not quite, impossible to detect, hidden in shadow and shrouded in white. He was watching her, to see what she'd do, to see whether she'd be obedient. Perhaps he hadn't thought she'd spot him, but he made no further effort to hide. Why should he?

She gripped Thaler's letter more tightly, and hurried down the vaulted corridor to the projector room.

When she'd first seen it, she'd been struck by its simplicity. For most novices, the discovery that spellcasting was a matter of will, disfigurement and rote learning that left little room for either aptitude or aesthetics was a surprise soon overcome. The same with the projector, which was nothing more than a glass sphere on a stand in the middle of an empty room. And even then, the stand was superfluous, and the sphere only there to be a focus. Masters, she was told, didn't even need that.

She was alone, which was good, because she wasn't used to

queuing, and she didn't need an audience, either, even though she'd projected dozens of times, never failing to connect after that first time, which had been humiliating and excruciating in equal measure. Not quite: the embarrassment had burnt long after the whip-marks had faded.

As she opened the door, she was struck by the smell, heavy and decaying, but on sight of the glass, she blotted it out. "Hoson zês, phainou. Mêden holôs su lupou."

Hesitation wasn't part of the spell. She walked straight up to the stand and rested the fingertips of her right hand on the top of the sphere, barely touching the cool, clear surface. The whole world was within, and Nikoleta had to search it all for a knot of existence that lay to the east of her. She closed her eyes and felt her concentration waver.

That shouldn't have happened. She stepped back, wiped her hand on her robe, then extended her hand again.

She stared through the convoluted refractions of the glass to its very centre, the place where she wanted to be, suspended in the middle of a ball of nothing. Then she closed her eyes again.

The glass was black, a black hole she could pass any object through, like a letter, to anywhere she imagined, such as the Protector of Wien's offices. Something was tapping at her hand. Slowly, rhythmically.

Nikoleta opened her eyes, and saw watery brown dribbles running down her wrist. She looked up.

She jerked back so fast she pushed the glass sphere away from her, the reflex too instinctive to overcome. She landed on her back, the stone floor jarring her all the way from her backside to her jaw. The sphere rolled up the indentation on top of the stand, and the whole thing rocked.

Her breath caught in her throat. The stand teetered for a moment, before the heavy glass ball rolled back, and the stand rocked again. This time towards her. The sphere launched itself into the air.

She unfroze and lunged for it, her hands spread wide like a net.

Nikoleta was entirely unprepared for just how heavy it was. It crushed her fingers against the worn flagstones and she gasped. The stand banged down next to her, narrowly missing both her and the projector.

Tears of relief welled up and trickled down the side of her nose.

If she'd failed to catch it, if it had been chipped or broken, she'd . . . she didn't know what they'd do to her. She was certain it wouldn't have been pleasant, and it would have lasted a long time. Bruised fingers were a good exchange.

Thaler's letter had flopped down on the floor by her side, lying like a wounded bird with half-open leaves for wings. She dragged it closer with her heel, and slid it so that she could roll the sphere onto it. The pressure left her hands, and her blood pulsed into them.

The pain was exquisite, and she tasted copper in her mouth. Her fingers were claws. It hurt to move them almost as much as it did not to move them. She gasped and gagged, but no one seemed to hear her.

She needed to right the stand, and somehow get the projector back on top. Instead, she lay back again, hooking a finger under her veil and drawing it back so she could breathe more easily. The cloth was stained with smears of whatever had landed on her hand.

With every beat of her heart, the ache in her fingers ebbed and flowed. It would pass. Her almost destroying the projector was far more serious. As was the pair of feet she could see, swinging slowly in the dark of the rafters.

It was that smell again, and the liquid was now pooling on the floor, splattering as it landed.

He – it looked like a he, it was difficult to tell, but there were few women adepts – couldn't have been up there long or there would have been more mess on the stones beneath. Long enough for his clothes to become saturated, though. Half an hour to an hour. Certainly dead, and no spell was going to change that. Not in a good way, anyway.

She glanced at the door. It remained closed. She stared up. The body would stay up there until someone fetched it down, or it rotted.

The projector's stand was still lying down, the sphere itself still on the sheet of paper. There was a man hanging from the ceiling, and foul discharge dripping off him. Her hands were starting to really hurt now, and one nail had begun to go purple. The message she should have already sent remained unreceived.

Yes, of course this could be worse, she thought. It could be a lot worse, and if I don't do something about it now, it will be.

She levitated up into the darkness above, until she was face to face with a fellow adept.

56

Even with his skin a dark purple, his staring eyes veined red with broken blood vessels, his fat, black tongue lolling out of the corner of his mouth, she recognised him. She lit a flame in her bruised hand so that she could make certain: Richart.

He'd joined as a novice a year after her, and had progressed further than she had. He'd had fewer floggings and more mentoring from the senior adepts, while she'd had to struggle for every spell that marked her skin. She knew him. She didn't like him, but there was so little fellow feeling among the adepts it was a wonder she didn't actively hate him.

He'd hanged himself. Slowly, quickly, it was difficult to say. The knot he'd tied around the roof beam probably wouldn't have withstood a long drop, so she imagined he'd slipped the noose over his neck and simply pulled himself up on the other end of the rope. Sorcerers didn't lack will-power, quite the opposite. It was a surfeit of self-importance that led them to the art. So strangling himself while retaining the ability to save himself wasn't surprising.

Neither was the fact of suicide. Novices tended to run away if they lacked sufficient steel to be degraded, beaten and humiliated day in, day out. Adepts either killed themselves or killed each other – duels were common, as were fatalities from the injuries sustained. There was no question of anyone else intervening. One less adept meant one less to compete for the prize of being received into the Order of the White Robe.

So she'd seen death, up close and intimate, for years, and for years before that, too.

It was that Richart had done it at all. She pulled back a little, and noticed the letter in his hand. It was similar to hers, but with a more impressive seal. Rigor mortis hadn't set in, so it was just a matter of coaxing her fingers into movement. Hard, but not impossible.

No letter from the library for Richart. His was from Trommler, Gerhard's chamberlain. There wasn't enough light to read by, and she didn't want to set the paper on fire, so she retreated to the ground and used the magical lights on the walls instead.

It was to Mad Leopold of Bavaria, warning him to keep the Teutons under close watch. Or else. Richart had plainly opened it and read it, tried to deliver it, and killed himself rather than explain why he couldn't do it. It seemed at first sight a weak, stupid, pathetic, impulsive response.

But he could no longer use the projector.

What if no one could? What if everyone was as weak as Richart? What if she, due to her natural and untaught abilities, was the only one left among the adepts who could still shift their ink and cast a spell? She'd felt plenty of magic at the White Tower. Or had that all been what she'd expected, and had she fooled herself into believing it so?

Nikoleta decided it was time to go. Richart could swing for a little longer; she didn't care. She briefly scanned again the contents of the second letter, and cast it to the floor. The projector could stay where it was, too. Both letters would remain unsent tonight, or any other night. She might need to fight the adept master as soon as she left the room, and she wanted to save her energy.

That was a decision quickly and easily made: if he confronted her, demanded to know why she'd failed in her task, then she'd duel with him. He must have known about Richart, because it must have been him who'd given Richart the letter. He'd wanted Nikoleta to join him.

She waited by the door to see if she could sense anyone outside. Nothing.

Using the latch was more difficult than it should have been, but it was only momentary pain. Closing the heavy door quietly behind her made her wince, but no more than that.

The corridor was crowded with shadows. Ghosts, real and imagined, swirled around her, but she pushed her way through. She covered her face again and strode out into the cloister. The adept master was not there.

Tomorrow, then. She would get her answers tomorrow.

9

Büber watched the sun rise in the east, over the broad Donau plain. He'd already made a fire, boiled some water for a mash, and let it cool out of reach of his tethered horse. It was his turn now, bits of sausage and day-old bread.

As he chewed, he kept one eye on the Teuton's camp. The fires that had burnt low during the night were restoked before dawn, and a great murmuring noise had risen from the site. They were packing up and getting ready to move on.

Büber had never seen a pitched battle between two armies before – skirmishes, yes, a few people on each side and none of them a hexmaster, but they weren't planned like a proper war with regiments and steel and horses . . .

The mere idea of three hundred horsemen arrayed with their banners and armour and lances fascinated him. Part of him wanted the Teutons to throw caution to the wind and come riding across the Simbach bridge just so he could see them. The destruction that would follow in their wake would be terrible, though. Not good for those caught up in it: not good for Carinthia at all.

Then there came the sound of another horse coming along the forest road. He reached for his saddle pack, pulled his sword out of its scabbard and hid it under his legs.

The rider came at a trot, his barrel-chested mount forcing his legs wide.

"Peter?"

Büber shielded his eyes. "Torsten. Just in time for breakfast."

Torsten Nadel slowed to a walk and gratefully sat back down into his saddle. "Fuck me, the things we have to do for His Majesty."

"Where were you?" Büber sliced some more sausage with his knife and poked it onto a green twig. "I thought you'd finished checking the passes?"

"I was on my way down. Up near Ennsbruck. Fucking giants chased me from pillar to post." Nadel slid out of the saddle and put his hands in the small of his back. His spine clicked.

"The same up at the Katschberg." Büber put the meat on to roast. "Some idiot Venetian tried to get a donkey-train over the top and got ripped to pieces for his pains. I've never known giants come down that low this soon. Did you tell the prince?"

"Wegener came through last night when he told me about Walter of Danzig's little show. Guessed that you could do with some help." Nadel crouched down next to the fire, warming his face and inhaling the smells of cooking. "But yes, I dropped by the White Fortress on the way."

Büber pointed to the far side of the bank. "That's the Teutons. Nearby should be some Bavarian spearmen, but I didn't see any last night. They're probably keeping the Teutons against the river in case they get the urge to wander further afield for forage."

Nadel watched for a moment, at the smoke and dust rising through the treetops. "How did they take it, getting the body of their leader back flatter than when they last saw him?"

"I didn't wait for a reply. Sneaked through the town in the dead of night, and just got close enough so that when I whacked the horse on its arse, one of their pickets spotted it. After that I was too busy running away to see what they did." Büber turned the sausages and reached for a chunk of bread. "They began striking camp from before first light, but they haven't started off yet, in whichever direction they decide. Maybe they stopped to burn him, if Teutons burn their dead."

"You've got your sword out, Peter."

"I didn't know it was you, did I?" He passed Nadel the bread and resheathed his blade. He chewed at a finger stump. "I'd rather have an honest-to-gods sword in my hand than make a mistake."

"We're prince's men, Peter. We're Carinthian. In Carinthia."

"I used to think that was enough. I mean, look at the pair of us. We've enough fingers between us for one normal man and scars enough for ten. We've been attacked by every bastard animal, real or magical, within the borders, and that's okay. It's part of the job."

"Sure, but . . ."

"You ever had to fight another man? When you hadn't been drinking?"

"I was going to say yes, but no. Not if you put it like that." Nadel reached out and snagged the stick holding the sausage slices. He ripped his bread open and slid the meat inside.

"Why's that then?"

"Because no one's fucking insane enough to try it? They don't want their mind burnt out or the ground beneath them turned into molten rock."

"I've done it. By accident. You come across some outlaws who've wandered too close to the boundary markers and forgotten whose land they're on." Büber stared into the fire. "Last time must have been ten years ago now."

"So why fill your sword-hand now?" Nadel was making short work of his food, and his horse was slowly advancing on the bucket of cooling mash.

"Another kid went missing yesterday."

"Fuck. Where?"

"Some village near the lakes. On the road you've just ridden down."

"Well," said Nadel, wiping his mouth with his sleeve, "*I* made it."

"You're not a kid. Whatever it is only takes kids. Kids and . . ."

"How many does that make? Five or six?"

"Torsten, this isn't some counting thing like a banker would do. I know this boy's uncle." Irritated, Büber ripped a handful of grass out of the ground and threw it at Nadel's horse. "Hey, you old nag. Wait your turn."

"Any ideas?"

"Not a clue." He wasn't going to tell Nadel about the unicorns any more than he was going to tell Kelner. "Just hope they all turn up alive one day."

Büber got to his feet and rescued the mash bucket, carrying it over to his own horse and setting it down in front of her.

Nadel looked off into the distance, and wisely changed the subject. "So these Teutons: how does His Majesty want it played?"

"They're expected to stay north. Where they cross the Alps is up to them, but if they come into Carinthia, they'll be slaughtered."

"Harsh but fair."

"Danzig was an arsehole. Remember what happened last year?"

Nadel cupped his balls. "I remember."

"I'll follow them on the Carinthian side until they've cleared our borders. If they turn south sooner, I'll get a message back to the White Fortress so that Gerhard can do whatever it is he wants to do to them." Büber wrestled the bucket away from his horse, and brought what was left over to Nadel's. "That's what I still plan to do, but what I could really do with is going to talk to the Bavarians and getting them to hurry the Teutons along. I've got better things to do than watch them crawl along for two weeks."

"I can watch them for you. Doesn't bother me how long they take." Nadel got up and stretched again. "You go and talk to Leopold's men."

Büber weighed up the suggestion. He got on well enough with Nadel, who could be crass and coarse but was otherwise a decent enough man. Trustworthy, up to a point – but the prince had said that he, his huntmaster, should do it.

"I don't know." Then he came to a decision. "I'll go and see the

Bavarians once the Teutons have started east. You keep an eye on them, and I'll catch you up. If they behave, good. If they don't, one of us can take the message while the other shadows them."

"Done. It's been a long, hard winter, and it's good to be outside." Nadel caught his horse, who was busy kicking the last of the mash out of the bucket. He began to strip the tack away.

Büber nodded and thought about doing the reverse. "This side of the river only. Doesn't bother me if they see you – it's probably better that they do, but the water's narrow in places. Easy enough to sling a quarrel into your chest."

"I'll stay out of bow-shot." Nadel looked down into the valley. "Fires are going out. White smoke, being doused."

"Better get going, then." Büber picked up the saddle and blanket, and advanced on his horse, dressing it quickly and efficiently. It stood there and took it, occasionally turning its head to see what its rider was doing. Büber patted its neck and quietened the beast at the appropriate moments. He liked horses well enough, and they suffered him being on their back, but he wasn't a natural. Not like the prince.

Horse ready, he packed his bags and hung them across the saddle. Sword, crossbow, seal of authority: the tools of his trade.

The steam from the quenched fires was dissipating, the thinning cloud stretched and fading over the town. Now that it was clearing, he looked beyond for the Bavarian army camp, and could see nothing.

"Maybe they struck earlier," he said to himself, but Nadel heard and answered.

"That's unlikely. Bavarians are lazy bastards at the best of times."

Büber checked the tack one last time, then put his foot in the stirrup, heaving himself up and on. The horse shuffled its feet and champed on its bit as he took up the reins.

"Stay alert," said Büber. "I'll see you in a day or so."

He nudged the horse into a walk and slowly made his way down the hill to the bridge. The first barges of the day were leaving the Simbach quays and heading east and west, and carts were heading to market.

The lower he got, the less he saw, and soon he was down among the houses on the Carinthian side. The bridge buttresses were ahead, their deep-set incantations shining faintly against the black rock.

Up in the mountains, where the border was less defined and held more in common than in law, he'd sometimes come across a group of soldiers or hunters from a neighbouring palatinate, and they'd share news and swap stories. Down here, in the lowlands where rivers and roads marked the beginning and end of territories, it was different. He was a prince's man on the prince's land. Outside it, he could only rely on Carinthia's reputation and his own right arm, and he'd never liked issuing threats.

"Don't be such a woman," he growled, and tapped the horse's flanks with his heel. "Get."

The crossing was as long as the river was wide, across the arch of stone that carried him over the water.

"Hey," said a voice, and Büber looked down to see four men, three of them holding spears, blocking his way.

"What?" He started paying attention. The unarmed man was better dressed than his companions, with a floppy hat perched on his head. The others were just townsmen, older, grey haired, but lean and competent enough. "What is this?"

"Toll."

"Fuck off." He said it more out of surprise than belligerence. "Since when did I have to pay to use a Carinthian bridge?"

"Everyone has to pay," said the man, ostentatiously adjusting his clothing to show the painted wooden plaque hung around his neck. "Earl's orders."

"Does Leopold know about this? More to the point, does the prince know you're taxing his subjects?" Not for the first time, Büber wished he could make a horse walk backwards. He was too close. Yes, of course he could afford a toll: he had money, but didn't see why he should part with a single red penny.

"Are you refusing to pay?"

Büber looked down at the men. "What're you going to do if I don't?"

From the look of confusion on the spear-carriers' faces, the question hadn't arisen before. They looked at each other, then to the man with the hat.

"We . . . will . . ." he started, and finally an idea came to him, ". . . take you before the earl."

"Good," said Büber. "Lead on."

"What?"

"Take me to this earl of yours." He leant back in his saddle and felt for his own royal seal. "I can find out why he's charging for something we provided for nothing."

He held up the token long enough for the man to inspect it, but not for so long that it was still there when a hand came up to take it from him.

The man wearing the plaque shrugged. "Show him the way."

"Why don't *you* show me the way?" asked Büber pointedly. "That way you won't tax anyone crossing our bridge."

"You're not in Carinthia, I'm not a Carinthian." He jerked his head in the vague direction of the town. "You arrogant bastards need to be taken down a peg or two. Now go and have it out with Fuchs."

One of the spearmen rolled his eyes and started walking up the street, and Büber followed slowly behind on the horse.

"I said it was a stupid idea," said the man over his shoulder, and Büber stopped his mount, swung himself off and took hold of the reins.

"What do you mean?"

"That. Charging a toll. Stupid. Gerhard was going to find out sooner or later."

"So why is your earl doing it? Did Leopold tell him to?"

The man spat on the ground and looked around for eavesdroppers. There were enough people around to suggest he shouldn't be so free with his words, but he decided he didn't care. "Leopold's an inbred, web-toed, six-fingered mouth-breather, and Fuchs is just cruel and spiteful. But they're both broke. Neither have a penny to their names."

Bavaria should be rich. It had farms and pastures and forests – all of it lowlands, not like Carinthia that was half mountains.

"Why not?" Büber had a flask somewhere in his saddlebags, a little metal one that contained something a bit stronger than water.

"Fuchs paid off the Teutons. Cleaned him out completely. That's why we're at the bridge."

"But you had a thousand spears at their back, hustling them through the land as fast as they could go." They were in the town square, where there was nothing as grand as Juvavum could offer: no fountains, no high houses, no rich merchants, no wide-skirted ladies. "What happened to the soldiers?"

"Leopold's cash ran out as well, didn't it? He's built too many stupid castles to be able to afford an army. So they all went home."

The man leant on his spear and pointed to a three-storey timber-framed house. "That's the Town Hall. You'll find Earl Fuchs inside. Doesn't bother me if you go in or not."

"Let's just get this straight," said Büber. "There's no one guarding the Teutons?"

The man shook his head. "Thank the gods they took the bribe instead of sacking the town. They're going away east now."

"I know where they're going. Or I thought I did." Büber chewed at his fingers. He looked at the Town Hall, and back down the road they'd just come along. The man with the spear pursed his lips and started to wander away.

"Where are *you* going?" asked Büber.

"All Fuchs told me to do was stand by the bridge and get some money." The man disappeared into the crowd of townsfolk, the top of his spear marking his progress towards a beer cellar at one of the corners of the square.

"Fuck," said Büber under his breath. Earl Fuchs and his explanation would have to wait.

He spent a little time and money – Carinthian coin being good in most places – on some bread and sausage and cheese, and some beer.

Then he turned and rode back to the river.

The man with the hat was still there with his guards, still extracting tolls.

"Hey, Carinthian. I thought you were going to see the earl?"

"I changed my mind," said Büber. He dug his heels in, and the horse trotted over the long span of the bridge. Once he had honest-to-gods Carinthian soil underfoot again, he turned east.

10

For anyone else, Nadel would have been hard to find. But Büber wasn't anyone, and a man on a horse left tracks that a man on his own would not. Neither was Nadel trying to hide, not from him at least.

Büber followed the riverside at a distance, stopping every so often to listen, and after a while he got down and led his mount on foot. The southern bank was steep and wooded before it flattened out into the farmed plain between the water course and the hills behind. He was shielded from sight and could still move more or less freely.

Shod hooves stopped leaving marks in the soft dark earth, and the ferns at the side of the path were trampled. He bent down and peered into the shifting greens and browns. After a few moments, the outline of a horse resolved against the shadows, and Büber carefully led his own horse into the gap.

He tied it to a branch, and crept down the bank to where Nadel sat, motionless, behind a screen of milk parsley.

"That was quick," murmured Nadel. He didn't take his eyes off the opposite bank.

Büber lowered himself to the ground and looked through the green stems and broad leaves. On the north bank, where the slope was more gentle, and the soil had partially collapsed into the river, a chain of women were filling buckets.

He looked further inland and could make out the carts and horses of the Teutons, scattered through the thin woodland. Carinthian carts didn't need draught animals, and it still surprised Büber that anyone else's did.

"We've got a problem," he said.

"What sort of problem?"

"Those Bavarian spearmen have gone home. No money to pay for them, so I'm told."

"That'll make things interesting. Have you seen some of these Teuton women? Faces like a robber's dog chewing a wasp."

"They'll be more used to fighting than you."

A Teuton mercenary rode slowly by the line of buckets and shouted something: encouragement or an insult, it sounded the same. The women took the opportunity to belittle his manhood, his bravery and his horse, in that order. That much Büber could make out from the gestures.

"And that," said Nadel, "is why they're barbarians, and we're civilised men. Our women just don't behave like that. Thank the gods they don't look like that either."

Büber gnawed at a finger. "They've got Simbach's money. The earl there paid them off."

"Really? Why would he do that?"

"Without the spearmen, maybe he thought he had to. The man

I spoke to said it was either empty the purses or they'd tear up the town." The horseman had ridden on, and the women resumed their bucket-chain. "I know they've got a shaman stashed somewhere, but I'm told just one of our hexmasters would be enough to take not only his skin off, but all the others too."

"Where are they heading?"

"South, somewhere. I know the Doge is spoiling for a fight with Milano. Plenty of coin to pay for three hundred heavy horse on either side. And if Bavaria has given them enough money, they could get there without having to take one of the alpine passes."

"All the way to the Adriatic," said Nadel. "Horses hate travel by boat, but I can't see that bothering this lot."

"This . . . this should have been simple, right?"

"Nothing's ever simple, Master Büber." Nadel leant forward slightly, tilting his head. "Barge?"

Büber listened for himself, and could make out the rhythmic wash of water against the upstream-pointed bow of a river barge.

"At least the Teutons seem to be back on the road." Nadel nodded at the direction of the women, who struggled up the bank with the last of their loads and disappeared back into the trees.

"We'd better get going ourselves." Büber stared across the river. "I'm wondering if one of us shouldn't go and tell the prince about the Bavarians being broke. I mean, apart from castles, what the Hel have they been spending it on?"

"Frankish wine? They've got this stuff called brandy. Very moreish."

The Teutons seemed to have vanished completely. The cart Büber had made out earlier wasn't there, but neither had he seen it move. Perhaps he'd been distracted.

The barge came into view, tracking the centre of the river. The painted prow and the decorated panels on the sides were a contrast to the natural browns and greens: eyes on the front, as tradition demanded, and a series of scenes of dwarves mining and forging metals down to the rudder, all flame and spark.

Büber was just wondering when he'd last seen a dwarf when the first arrow hit the bargemaster. It transfixed his tattooed arm, the broad head sticking out one side, the flights the other.

The man barely had time to look down and register the pain. He was struck half a dozen times in the torso, and one pierced his neck. More arrows had been loosed, and they looped across the water, their trajectories flat.

"Shit." Büber flattened himself against the damp earth and motioned for Nadel to do the same. The barge had almost drawn level with them, and with its master slumped on the deck, it was starting to slow and turn.

Feeling the change of pace, and hearing the odd banging noises on the hull, a bargee half-emerged through the little doors and stopped. He saw that his employer, colleague, friend even, was dead.

Another swarm of arrows flashed out of the undergrowth on the far bank. One hit the thin wooden door right by the bargee's head. The point scratched him and he fell backwards.

"Torsten, we have to do something." Büber raised his head enough to see that the barge was almost sideways across the river. Three men, dressed in Teuton-style chain shirts and half-helmets, stepped out into plain sight and judged the distance. Too far to jump, and the current was starting to carry the boat to the Carinthian side. They shouted instructions behind them.

"Hooks. They're calling for rope and hooks." Nadel knelt up. "If they get hold of it, they'll butcher what's left of the crew."

"It's coming our way first." Büber made up his mind. "Crossbow?"

"On my saddle."

Büber made a crouching run, only straightening up when he was almost at the horses. His heart was banging in his chest so hard it felt like it might knock its way through his ribs. Fear and anger both. He found Nadel's crossbow, and a bag of short bolts in the saddlebags, then he found his own.

Rattling, he ran back. Nadel held out his hands, and Büber threw him his weapon, then skidded to a halt beside him.

"Spread out. Two different angles," said Nadel. He heaved at the bow's steel lever, cocking it, and shook out a pile of bolts by his side.

"And keep moving. If they spot us . . ." said Büber, then he shut up. Nadel knew as well as he did. Keeping low, he moved a dozen paces downstream, slinging his bag of bolts over his shoulder. He put his back to a tree and looked for a target.

The Teutons had got their rope and hooks, and were fishing for barges. One threw too short. The iron hook at the end fell into the water, and he quickly reeled it in.

A stupid time to be having such thoughts, but perhaps Thaler was right: he should take an apprentice. If he lived through this, he'd consider it more carefully.

He worried a bolt out and laid it in the groove. He glanced to his left and saw Nadel watching him, impatiently waiting for him to be ready.

Of the three men on the opposite bank he could see, he had an uninterrupted view of just one, who was trotting down the river-bank to get ahead of the drifting barge. Büber raised the stock to his shoulder and sighted down it. The Teutons didn't know he was there, but they were about to find out – now was his last chance to change his mind and stay hidden.

His fingers curled around the trigger and squeezed. The bolt spiralled away, a flash of bright feathers making a rainbow blur. It buried itself in the man's chest, waving aside the metal links as if they were a matter of no consequence. The Teuton managed one last cry before his lungs filled up with blood.

Nadel caught one of the others in the leg. It broke against his bone, and he went down screaming.

Time for both of them to move. Büber ducked around a tree to reload, and the wood was suddenly alive with sharp black blurs. He felt a double concussion as two arrows smacked into the bark he'd put at his back. They were firing wild, though, with no idea where he was. And no Teuton hedge wizard would find him either; he was indistinguishable from the forest that hid him.

He ducked down again and scrabbled for the next tree-trunk. The leaves above him rattled and flicked. It was going to be blind chance whether they hit him or not, and he had to accept that or run away.

The stern of the barge was encroaching on the overhanging branches on his side of the bank, the bow drifting just beyond midstream. More of the Teutons had risked coming into view, with two of them scooping up the ropes of the fallen and another acting as spotter for the archers who stayed behind the tree line.

Büber needed to take him down. He uncoiled and straightened, aiming carefully.

His target shaded his eyes to see better. Perhaps he caught sight of a man-shaped figure, or a glimpse of coloured flights. He pointed, shouted and Büber fired all at the same time. Knowing he'd been seen, the hunter leapt away and found a fat sycamore to cringe behind as the ground around him sprouted a harvest of quarrels.

"Peter?"

"Keep away. They've got my range."

"They've also got the barge."

It was still too risky to even glance around. The barrage remained just as intense, and he was pinned down. Nothing for it, then.

"Hey, you on the barge. Now is the only chance you have. Tables, door, anything. You're on the Carinthian side but not for long."

He had no idea if they'd heard him, but he heard one of the Teutons get caught by Nadel's next bolt. The storm of arrows switched its focus: Nadel had deliberately shown himself to give Büber respite.

The stern of the barge hovered close to the bank. It was the only opportunity he was going to get before the Teutons reeled it in. He knew it would be impossible to move silently; there was almost nowhere to put his feet where there wasn't an arrow sticking out of the soft soil.

He turned and ran and jumped, landing next to the body of the bargemaster. The bulk of the barge protected him if he crouched down, which was a good thing as he'd attracted attention. All the arrows were coming in shallow, glancing off the hull, splashing in the water, but their noise made him cower.

"Wotan's one eye, this is stupid." He forced himself to bang on the hold doors. "If you're coming, this is it."

The door opened a crack and there was a faint reflection from a wide, white eye. Satisfied that Büber wasn't a Teuton, the occupant opened the door a little further.

The boat jerked backwards. The gap between the last board and dry land widened visibly.

"Now. Out."

There were two of them, one young, one old, both equally terrified. They'd heard the arrows striking the boat, now they saw the reality.

"We can't do that," the older man stuttered.

"Then you're going to die here." Büber recocked his crossbow, and slotted another bolt. "Torsten?" he called out. "Now would be good."

Nadel appeared upstream and killed one of the men pulling on the grappling hook. More willing hands took the dead man's place, and as before, the Teuton bowmen switched targets.

"Run," shouted Büber to the bargees. "Run and jump."

The boy crawled out onto the deck and crouched down, uncertain whether to go or stay.

"I'll leave you behind if you don't go now."

The boy nodded feverishly and managed to find his feet. It wasn't far, but he almost didn't make it. His first footing landed on the very edge of the undercut bank. It sank under his weight, but gave way completely only after he'd spilt face-first into the leaf litter and tree roots.

"You next." Büber grabbed the man's arm and hauled him into the open. The boy was just about starting to move, and was far too slow for the Carinthian's liking. "Don't just lie there, you arsehole!"

The rope connecting the boat to the far side of the river went taut with a crack, and the barge started to swing out into open water, away from the branches with their concealing leaves.

Büber stood up, put his hand to the bargee's back and pushed hard. Even as the man flew through the air, Büber braced his foot against the cargo hold and took the short run-up as fast as he could.

He landed awkwardly on the bank. The bolt he'd carefully laid on the stock of his crossbow bounced off, and he felt suddenly naked in a way he hadn't before. The bargee he'd pushed was struggling up the bank, and, almost without thinking, Büber reached down and grabbed a handful of the man's clothing between his shoulders.

Like a mother cat, he picked him up and ran a few steps before he overbalanced and crashed down again. An arrow whistled past his face, stroking his cheek before it puffed up the debris on the ground next to his wide-staring eye.

He rolled away, and put some trees between him and the Teutons.

"Torsten? Pull back. I've got them!"

The arrow fire dropped away, but only when Büber reached the edge of the trees and the track that followed it did he stop.

The boy emerged, his shoulder under the older bargee's arm, dragging him forward. The man cried out as the boy sank to his knees to drop his load to the ground. There was a thick black arrow in his buttocks. Then Nadel showed himself, face slick with sweat but pale as a ghost. His fingers were bleeding with the constant effort of cocking and recocking his bow.

"Peter? You crazy bastard."

Büber felt like he was on fire. Every nerve, every sinew was tight and ready. He was so alive, he hadn't noticed the blood dribbling in a fat stream down his face and neck.

He started to laugh with joy, with exhilaration and relief, and the others looked at him as if he were mad.

11

Gerhard was undecided. He customarily met his enemies in the throne room and his friends in his private chambers. He rarely met the men who worked for him anywhere, leaving the passing of orders to Trommler.

But here was Büber, master of the hunt, having ridden all night from Simbach. He had news of the Teutons, and the breathless messenger had said that half the man's face was obscured with blood.

The sergeants' quarters, then. Get him cleaned up and fed. Gerhard wrapped a cloak around himself and a servant opened the door for him. Trommler was already awake, up, and dressed.

"Good morning, my lord," he said, and gave a short bow.

"Am I allowed to suggest it's hardly morning?" Gerhard frowned at the greying sky outside.

"You are, my lord, but the gods decree that it is morning all the same."

The prince didn't often blaspheme against the Aesir, but he had to bite his tongue. Something told him that a day that started like this wasn't going to get better by nightfall.

In the sergeants' mess, Büber was cursing at a woman who was trying to mop his wound with diluted wine. He was sitting on a stool, his hands clamped on his thighs; she was standing next to him with a bowl and a bloodied cloth.

"Don't be such a baby," she scolded.

"Then stop scrubbing at it like it's a stewpot, you old witch." Büber turned and tried to grab the rag away from her. Then he saw the prince regarding him like a turd in the chamber pot. He batted the woman aside and stood unsteadily. "My lord."

Gerhard walked slowly over and reached out for Büber's chin. He moved it left, then right.

"Will you live?"

"Yes . . . yes, my lord."

"Then sit down and let the goodwife get on with her duties, while you tell me what's so important that my royal person is hauled from his bedchamber like a common labourer." Gerhard kicked one of the bench seats out and sat opposite him.

"Yes, my lord." Büber blushed under his dried blood crust. "The Bavarians have lost control of the Teuton horsemen. One of the Earl of Simbach's men told me that Leopold is broke, and since there was no coin to pay the soldiers, they went back to their homes. The Earl of Simbach has imposed a toll on the bridge to raise some cash locally, because everything he had went to paying the Teutons not to raze the town."

Gerhard's face grew increasingly immobile until he looked like one of the old Roman statues. After a while, he motioned with his finger to Büber's face.

"What happened there?"

"Me and Torsten Nadel were tracking the Teutons from the south bank of the Enn – they stopped to water the horses – when a barge came upstream. They attacked it, killed the bargemaster, and grappled the boat." He chewed at his lip. "We got the crew off."

"At some personal risk, I see." Gerhard was furious, but he'd show that later and in private.

"It was . . . they didn't care, my lord. Between us, me and Torsten put about six of them in the ground, and they just didn't care. Like they were animals."

"Perhaps, Master Chamberlain, we should have dealt with them all while we had the opportunity." Gerhard looked at his own pink-stained fingers. "And perhaps our brother Leopold has some questions to answer, too."

"Quite, my lord." Trommler made a rumbling noise in his throat. "Shall I request the hexmasters' pleasure?"

"Among other things, yes. But that's where we'll start. I want every one of those barbarian Teutons dead by dusk tomorrow." The prince's hand strayed unconsciously to where his sword-hilt

73

normally was, but not even princes wore swords in bed. "Now, huntmaster."

"My lord?"

"Two things. You did well saving the crew of the barge. I have no doubt they're grateful for their lives and that you were exceptionally brave. Well done."

"Thank you, my lord."

"And if you'd died, and Nadel also, I'd have absolutely none of the information you've just told me. Which makes you an exceptionally brave idiot. If you think I need to know something urgently enough to ride from one side of Carinthia to the other without stopping, you do that first. Then, and only then, do you risk your neck on some stupid and most likely suicidal rescue. Have I made myself quite clear, huntmaster?"

Büber swallowed. His Idun's apple bobbed conspicuously. "Yes, my lord."

"Good. Now get your face sewn up, eat something and get some sleep. I'll be needing you sooner than you'd like." Gerhard pulled a sour face and stood, with Büber struggling to follow suit.

The prince waved him down again. "Come, Trommler. We have work to do."

"My lord," said Trommler. "By your leave, huntmaster."

They left the sergeants' quarters and headed back to the prince's rooms.

"What appointments do I have today?" Gerhard was striding purposefully, and Trommler, with his much shorter steps, struggled to keep up.

"You were to meet with the council this morning to officially open the summer passes, and this afternoon you had promised my lady some hawking."

"Don't we have giants?"

"Yes, my lord. In both the Katschberg pass and the Enn valley."

"So doesn't that stop me from officially opening the passes?"

"No, my lord. Although it would be prudent to get rid of the giants before the first wagons attempt the journey."

"Events are running away from us, Trommler. I don't like that. It smacks of complacency. Bavaria treats us like we're a milk-cow, and the Teutons pretend they can act with impunity. Summon the hexmasters and have them meet me in the throne room in, say, two hours. Apprise them of the situation and have them make ready their battle-magic, however it is they do that. Tell the council, pressing affairs of state and so on, and I will see them another time. Apologise to my good lady wife, but the hawking will have to wait. Tell Reinhardt to assemble the guard, and send out messengers for the earls who live close enough to bring themselves and their squires. And baggage and attendants. And . . ." Gerhard tapped his lips and hesitated at his antechamber door, ". . . have my armour polished and sent to the throne room."

"The ceremonial armour, my lord?"

"No, the genuine article. If Leopold is incapable of keeping order in his lands, it's up to me to remind him how it's done." He leant against the door frame. "How long is it since a prince of Carinthia rode out to war?"

"One hundred and fifty-six years, my lord."

"Long enough for memories to grow short. It's time for a demonstration of power that should keep us at peace for the next century and a half. Even if we have to raze Simbach ourselves in the process." Gerhard punched the dark wood carefully with his fist. "That would be a legacy to leave Felix."

Trommler bowed low. "My lord has spoken."

"I'm going to enjoy this, Trommler. I think the boy should come along, too. The Fop as well. It's about time he saw how honest Germans fight."

"I shall inform them accordingly of my lord's wishes." The chamberlain spoke the same phrase that he'd used to Büber. "By your leave, my lord."

"Yes, yes, of course. A busy morning." Gerhard waved his hand, and Trommler bowed again before shuffling away.

The prince closed the door behind him and stalked around his room, poking at this and that, unable to keep still for a moment. By contrast, the servant beside the door stood motionless, all but invisible. Finally, the prince noticed both his own blood-stained fingers and the servant standing there.

"I need to wash. Then I need something to wear under armour."

The servant made ready with a bowl and water, a towel and a block of hard yellow soap. By the time Gerhard had finished scrubbing, suitable clothes had been laid out on the bed.

There was a knock at the door, and it was answered.

"My lady, the Princess Caroline."

Gerhard looked up, surprised. He was bare-chested, with only his breeks on. Not that he had anything to hide from his wife, but he had a softness about him that had come on like autumn. He'd once been as hard and supple as a mountain ash, so he regarded himself self-consciously. His wasn't a warrior's body any more.

"Show her in, then wait outside."

The servant was replaced by the princess.

"My lord?"

"My lady." She was very different from Emma.

"Gerhard, what's going on? Trommler's been stalking the halls like the Norns since dawn."

The prince picked up his quilted shirt and held it across his pale chest. He couldn't tell which was whiter. "The Teutons who were here the other day have attacked a barge downstream from Simbach." He struggled into the shirt and, eventually, his head popped through the neck opening.

"Can't the Bavarians deal with them?"

"Apparently not. They are, according to my man, so broke they can't afford to muster a single century of spears." He peered at the lacing of his collar, elbows and cuffs. This wasn't something he was supposed to manage on his own. "I don't know how that happened, or how I didn't get to hear about it sooner. I'll be having words with my brother Leopold – after I've cut every Teuton neck south of Bohemia."

Gerhard held out his arms, and the princess hurried to him, holding him tightly and pressing her head into the angle between his chin and neck. He'd only wanted her to help him with the ties, but this was unexpected: good, but unexpected nevertheless.

He'd needed another wife after Emma's death. A prince with a single heir was in a precarious position, as was his palatinate. So Caroline had been chosen from among the earls' families, and quickly too. Affection had not been a condition laid on either party.

He put his arms around her, and felt not a little confused.

"My place is at the head of the column. Carinthians don't start wars, but by the gods, they finish them." He raised his head slightly to avoid breathing in the stray blonde hairs that had escaped from her plaits.

Her fingers had found their way under his shirt. He shivered under her touch.

"I know, Gerhard. I understand. My place is here, with the children."

"Good. That's settled then. Hawking will resume when I return." Gerhard remembered what he'd told Trommler. "Felix is coming with me."

He felt her body stiffen, and her fingertips faltered. "He's still young, Gerhard."

"Twelve is old enough. And when he's sitting on my throne, the people will think back to today when he rode out with his father and claimed a famous victory. They'll respect him more than if he sat safe in a castle with his teachers. I'm taking Allegretti along too, so the boy'll come to no harm."

"I . . ." she said. "I've become fond of him. He's a good boy." She resumed her stroking.

"He is a prince's son," he said. Dark haired, dark eyed, like his Frankish mother, who was suspected of having something Hunnish in her ancestry. A marauding Hun, most likely.

"I didn't mean it like that, Gerhard."

"And neither did I. Caroline, I appreciate your concern, but I do have a battle to win."

"I know that. Just that this is all very sudden."

Gerhard moved his hand from the back of her housecoat to her shoulders and prised her off. "It is, but only because we ignored the signs. Do you know when there's a storm coming?"

"Of course."

"Because you look at the sky and see it darken. You feel the wind turn and strengthen. There hasn't been a storm for so long, we forgot to look up, that's all. Now" – he held up his wrists – "tie me into this thing. Not so tight it cuts off the blood, but the cloth mustn't bunch up under the plate."

She looked at the laces for a moment, then flattened the excess fabric against his forearm before looping the tie around and knotting it. "Like that?"

"Like a shield maiden of old," he said, and held up his other wrist.

As she worked, he realised that her heavy damask housecoat had begun to open, and she was naked underneath. Her breasts were fuller, her belly rounder, her waist thicker and her thighs heavier than when he'd married her – but she'd been a fresh-faced daughter of Carinthia then. Three children in six years had turned her figure more motherly than girlish. Then again, he was six years older too, and his tastes had changed.

Seemingly unaware, she lifted his arm and bent it slightly, gathering the loose material into a single flap before tying it off. "The other arm now, Gerhard."

Distracted by the increasing gap between the edges of her coat, he didn't respond. She brushed against him as she swapped sides, and his breath caught in his throat.

"Something the matter, my prince?"

"Weren't the Ostara celebrations enough for you, my lady?"

"Apparently not, my prince. Neither, it appears, were they enough for you." She gave up any form of pretence and shrugged her coat off her shoulders. The heavy material fell away, hanging only from her arms which she straightened behind her to leave the garment as a puddle of red and gold on the floor. "A man going to war should have some idea of the welcome he'll receive when he returns victorious."

Did Emma do this for him? Had she ever got over the fact she was simply a token in a political alliance between Carinthia and the Franks? Had she loved him before she died? Gerhard stared at the pale beauty standing in front of him, hands clasped at her back and slowly shifting her weight from the ball of one foot to the other.

Had he actually found the right woman second time around?

"I can't take long," he said.

"I won't take long," she said.

He nodded towards the bed, and she ran to it with indecent haste.

12

Almost everybody had assembled in the Great Hall by the time Gerhard arrived. Felix and his Italian teacher were at the foot of the dais, trading obscure Genoese insults along with each blow and block. Captain Reinhardt stood next to the armoury sergeant and watched the swordplay. The stable-master was deep in conversation with Trommler, and there were other servants: messengers, a herald, kitchen boys keeping the retinue supplied with bread and meat, enough men to carry the prince's armour, and another to bear the sword of state.

He ruled absolutely, and if he kept a room full of people waiting while he played hide the sausage with her highness, that was his prerogative. He jumped up onto the dais, and the conversation drained away before he reached the throne. He stood there for a moment, surveying the people below him, then sat down with a frown.

"Lord Chamberlain? There is a notable absence." He searched the room for a hint of a white robe: behind a pillar, perhaps, or skulking in the deep shadows. Or perhaps they were invisible, and only given away by a tremor in the air.

Trommler came to the dais. "My lord, a message has been sent. It was the first thing I did, knowing their somewhat erratic time-keeping and their concept of haste."

"So . . ." Gerhard paused, giving any hexmaster present time to reveal themselves with a theatrical flourish. There was no sudden appearance, and his good mood – no, his very good mood – started to evaporate. "Where are the Order of the White Robe?"

"They are not here yet, my lord." Trommler turned and scanned the hall himself. "Ehrlichmann? Where's Ehrlichmann?"

Near the back of the crowd, a man with dusty boots held up his hand. "My lord?"

"You went to the novices' house?"

"Straight away, my lord."

"And you delivered the message?"

"Yes, my lord." He scraped his boots on the stone floor. "Should I call again?"

Trommler pursed his thin lips. "Yes, Ehrlichmann. I think you should."

He had gone before Trommler had finished speaking, leaving the chamberlain to make his open-handed apologies to Gerhard.

"I'm displeased," said the prince. "They take half – half, mark my words – of every single penny we collect in taxes to spend on gods knows what, and I ask for nothing in return except that they come when I call." He unclenched his fist and gave a grunt of annoyance. "Perhaps our allies need reminding of their responsibilities as much as our enemies need reminding of Carinthian might.

79

Bring me my armour. It might be they'll grace me with their presence by the time I'm ready for war."

It was a show, but, without one of the principal players, it lacked meaning. Gerhard stood and posed his body as each piece of armour was strapped on. It was old, but it was functional. More to the point, it was enchanted. The metal itself was mostly for show, which made the whole suit light and easy to wear.

The sword of state was buckled to his waist and his helmet presented to him.

The Prince of Carinthia lowered himself slowly to his throne. Despite the armour's manufacture, it still weighed more than he was used to wearing. His mood soured further. "Where are the hexmasters, Lord Chamberlain?"

"They, they're not here, my lord." Trommler looked not just perplexed, but anxious. "My man hasn't returned yet." He glanced behind him in case Ehrlichmann had crept in without him seeing.

"Well . . ." said Gerhard, and momentarily couldn't think of anything else to say. "Well. In that case . . ."

Everyone was looking at him. Of course they were. He was the Prince of Carinthia in his battle armour. But it seemed he didn't command the total loyalty of all his subjects. Was this a deliberate snub? Why now? A thousand-year mutually beneficial alliance couldn't be unravelling because of a few hundred barbarian horsemen, could it?

What did this mean?

He saw the confusion on his face spread to the rest of the hall, and he got a grip on himself. He was man enough to leave his wife in gasping, sweat-sheened exhaustion; he was man enough to call the Order to heel.

"Perhaps it's raining," he said. "Or perhaps it's too cold for them. Or perhaps it's too early, and the messenger found them all in bed. True Carinthians don't care about the weather, or the hour. We're always ready for a fight." He laughed. "Well then, when we turn up at their tower ready for the battle that they're apparently unwilling to meet, perhaps we can shame them into joining us. Saddle the horses, form the men into files. I'm ready, and I'll wait for no one."

He lifted his helmet up and over his head. He held it there for a moment before he pressed it down. The padding inside gripped his skull, and Trommler's expression turned to one of pride.

Gerhard gripped the arms of the throne and levered himself upright. "Carinthia rides," he growled, a good deal more viciously than he had meant to. "Carinthia rides!"

The room cleared, every man hurrying to do his allotted job. Even Felix and the Italian: had he seen a flash of fear in the boy's eyes just now? Good. His heir needed to realise there was more to being a prince than being a good administrator.

He walked to the side of the dais and down the steps, to the soft whisper of chain against plate. The day outside beckoned him, and he hesitated again. Why hadn't they come? They'd come yesterday, unbidden.

Or had they? A figure in a white robe, face veiled, had walked in, taken no part in the audience, then left again. It could have been anybody.

There was only one way to find out, and that was to ask them himself.

He marched outside, and was handed the reins of his horse. Everything in the courtyard was now orderly, where moments before it had been in chaos. The castle guards were arranged in a neat column. The other riders were already mounted, horses clattering their shoes on the stones, raising sparks and rattling their tack.

Gerhard bent his knee and a servant quickly cupped his hands under it, pulling upwards and heaving the prince high enough for him to swing his other leg over. He settled himself in the saddle, and allowed his feet to be fitted into the stirrups.

"So, signore" – Gerhard found himself next to his son's tutor – "does your blood run hot at this sight? Are your sinews stiffened? Is your ardour stroked? Do you yearn for the ring of steel and the shock of impact in your arm?"

Allegretti, with whatever Italianate armour he possessed stowed on one of the wagons, looked as though he was out for a leisurely ride. His green mazzocchio was tilted back on his head at a rakish angle, and his expression of gentle bemusement looked singularly out of place amid the Germanic seriousness of his fellows.

"My prince, forgive me. My homeland is tormented by war, so I do not delight in these preparations." Yet he still looked puzzled.

"Then what?"

"Do you not need more men?"

Gerhard's jaw jutted out. They hardly needed what they had:

the men-at-arms and earls on horseback were only required to wheel the hexmasters into position. If he had to draw his sword in anger, he'd be surprised. He snorted at the sword-master.

"We've more than sufficient to deal with a handful of barbarians. The fewer the men, the greater the honour." He wheeled his horse around. "Have I entrusted my son to a coward?"

"No, my prince: to a cautious man."

"Often the same in my book," Gerhard sneered. He raised his voice: "Carinthia rides."

He nudged his heels into the flank of his horse, and it trotted towards the open gate. He was first through, and everyone followed in order, the cavalry, the infantry, and the spare horses, down the stone-edged road towards the outer wall. Of course they followed; he didn't need to look back and check.

Where were the hexmasters? Where were *his* hexmasters?

At the bottom of the hill, the wagons joined the back of the cavalcade, each one tended by a man with a long steering pole that he would occasionally slip under a wheel to keep the whole thing on course.

The column turned to mimic the flow of the river, clopping and marching down the quay, with merchants and stevedores stepping quickly out of their way. Children waved, woman curtsied, men bowed. He thought briefly about acknowledging their acts of obeisance with some small gesture of his own, but he would be riding past half of Juvavum and whatever he did would become rapidly tiresome.

So he stared straight ahead and concentrated on looking vengeful.

He approached the main bridge, and it cleared spontaneously: crowds gathered on both sides, either because they could or because they wanted to cross. Gerhard wasn't sure.

Damn them to Hel. There was no sign of a coterie of white-robed figures at the far end of the bridge. It would have to look planned; there could be no possible intimation that the Prince of Carinthia had to go begging to the sorcerers to protect him.

He was on the far side of the bridge now, and clearly the townsfolk were expecting him to head north, because they formed an arc across the road to the novices' house, the rooftops of which were just visible above the trees.

Just as he thought he was going to have to drive his horse into the people and force them to part, they parted by themselves. No, not quite: a single hooded hexmaster walked between the two straining rows of bodies to stand before him.

"My lord," she said.

Gerhard's heart hammered hard in his chest. How many masters were women? He didn't know of a single one, yet this gave him an opportunity to save face.

"Are you alone?"

The hood turned, left, right. "So it seems."

Gerhard raised his hand to halt the column, and the order was shouted in repetition behind him.

"So, hexmaster. Do you fly, or will you ride?"

"Give me a horse, and I'll ride for now." She stepped forward and lowered her voice, quiet enough that the prince had to lean from his saddle to hear her. "I have to speak with you. Alone."

He looked around and saw that one of the spare horses was being brought up. It was already saddled, but it wasn't suitable for a lady.

"Can you . . ." he started, then coughed, ". . . cope?"

The hood turned to look at the horse. "My lord will find I'll cope more than adequately."

"Good."

The squire steadied the horse's head, and the hexmaster – hexmistress? – raised her foot into the stirrup.

Her legs weren't that long, thought Gerhard, distracted. She'll need the straps shortening.

As her hands fastened around the pommel, her sleeves fell away. Both arms were covered with tattoos, dark and menacing. Then she swung herself up, and settled quite naturally on the horse's back, sitting straight and holding the reins loosely.

The prince tried to rub his chin with his mailed fist, but at first contact of metal on skin, he desisted.

"Where did you learn to ride, hexmaster?" He asked because tradition had it that all sorcerers rode like a sack of shit, assuming they didn't scare their horses half to death in the first place.

"Byzantium," she said, as if it answered everything. "My stirrups . . ."

The squire who'd brought the horse forward quickly adjusted them, then returned to his place.

"I'm ready, my lord."

"Damned if I am," he muttered, but he kicked his mount into

motion and deliberately let a gap grow between the two of them and the pair behind him, Felix and the Italian. The hexmaster matched his pace, drawing up on his right quarter.

"My lord?"

"This is not private," said Gerhard, continuing to look ahead. "Not yet." The street was still lined with people, spilling out from the new town and leaning out of windows to see them pass.

The houses finished, and the farms began.

"And now, my lord?"

He turned to her. She'd pulled her hood back, and she looked like a little Greek girl in white, riding a horse. Which she was. She encouraged her horse level with the prince.

"I'm not supposed to see your face. No one outside your Order's supposed to see your face." Gerhard wondered if his armour would save him. It was rumoured that it would, though testing it to destruction with him inside it was something he'd rather avoid.

"These are . . ." – and she pulled a face. Her skin was tight and unlined, showing just how young she was – "unusual times."

"So it seems. Are you really a hexmaster?"

"No, my lord. I'm an adept." She looked over her shoulder at the tower on Goat Mountain, then stared up the road. The via stretched straight and true ahead of them.

"Then where, in the gods' names, are the hexmasters?"

"I'm not going lie to you, my lord," she said.

"Good. Because that would be treason."

"There's a problem with the magic."

Gerhard's horse walked on, but he felt like he was floating above it.

"Say that again, Adept?"

She sighed and shifted. "I can't explain this well. The masters still have some residual power, and enchanted items still seem to work. But very little else does. I may be the only adept left capable of casting a spell. The message you wanted to send to Leopold?"

"Yes?"

"Was never sent. The man tasked with it killed himself when he failed. Your summons this morning?"

"Yes," whispered Gerhard.

"I was ordered – we were all ordered – to ignore it, and all other commands from the castle. Of course, you weren't to know of this, at all. Ever."

The prince's breathing was ragged, laboured, shallow.

"But you can, for now . . ."

"I was forbidden to leave the adepts' house by the master, but I calculated that if my masters couldn't answer your call themselves, they were incapable of stopping me. I remain, Prince Gerhard of Carinthia, your loyal servant."

"Your loyalty is commendable," he said automatically. Then he blinked at her, at the world behind her, as if it was new and terrifying. "Is this some sort of joke?"

She thought about it for quite a while before replying.

"If it is a joke, my lord, it's a joke on all of us."

13

Nikoleta was given her own tent, and she assumed that was because she was a magician and not because she was a woman. She'd been around long enough to know that German women didn't go to war, although they'd used to when the Romans looked down from the Alps and saw nothing but vast, rich, untamed forests. German women had been wild and proud, and, if the stories were to be believed, free.

A thousand years of civilisation later, and they gave her her own tent.

It was different in Byzantium, of course. Alaric had sacked only Rome, not her home city. She'd run away from there, eventually.

They'd given her a bed, too, a low wooden trestle with stitched mattress and thick blankets, and a brazier, filled with glowing charcoal. Used to the privations of the novices' house and the only marginally less austere adepts' house, she found the confines of the fabric walls too hot and airless.

They'd fed her. A board of bread, meat and cheese, and Frankish wine in a bottle.

The one thing they wouldn't do was talk to her. The mundanes were all scared of her – of course they were. Even though she'd got rid of her pointed hood at the beginning of the journey, her white robes were the only clothes she possessed. She was their hexmaster, so terrifyingly powerful she could defeat the Teutons single-handed.

She looked at those hands in the ruddy light, and lit a blue-white flame in her right palm. Could she do it? She thought she knew enough battle-magic, sufficient at least to scare a collection of barbarian marsh-dwellers into turning tail and running.

Then again, she'd seen their master of horse. He hadn't frightened easily, despite being alone in the midst of his enemies. His men would fight.

She didn't know what she was expected to face, or expected to do. She could guess, or she could go and ask someone. And there was only one man she could ask.

Picking up a blanket, she threw it over her shoulders and ducked through the unlaced part of the tent door. It was dark in the valley, and the soldiers the prince had brought with him were almost all crowded around the two large fires they'd made, their black shapes solid against the flickering flames and the ascending column of sparks.

Almost all, because there were guards set outside both her and his tents, and the boy's tent too. Presumably around the perimeter of the camp as well: it's what she would have done had she not been able to sense the beat of a heart at a hundred paces, along with the spirit that animated it.

"My lady?"

"Take me to the prince. We have things to discuss," she said, knowing that it didn't matter if the prince was alone, with others, asleep or simply didn't want to be disturbed. She wanted it, and she'd get it.

As the guard led her to another tent, its leopard pennant flapping in the breeze, she wondered at the truth: if she was right about the hexmasters' sudden impotence, she was the most powerful person in the whole of Carinthia.

Her guard spoke to Gerhard's, and though permission to enter was granted quickly enough, she knew he wouldn't be pleased to see her.

He wasn't alone, either. He had a boy with him, the child Felix – she'd seen him before and knew who he was – and another man, who she couldn't place. He dressed differently to the rest of the Carinthian court, and when he stood to greet her, his body betrayed a lean and natural grace.

"My lord prince," she said. She didn't have to bow, and if it had been just the two of them, she probably would have forgone the formality. As it was, she dipped her head for a moment.

The tall man with the strange floppy hat remained standing. He was staring at her, weighing her up and deciding whether she was a threat. No, not quite. He was trying to work out her weaknesses.

Adepts had very few of those: the gross ones had been beaten out of them, the subtle ones already exploited by their peers.

Gerhard sat in his travelling seat and growled. "You know my son. This long streak of piss is his tutor, Signore Allegretti."

She gave barely perceptible bows to both, noting that Allegretti carried two swords in the Italian fashion and that he could probably use both equally well. "My lord, we need to . . ." – and she shrugged – "talk."

Gerhard bared his teeth for a moment, then pulled back from whatever feral curse he was going to make. "The boy should sleep. We'll break camp at dawn and see what welcome brother Bavaria has to offer."

Allegretti's face was unreadable, but he turned to Felix. "Come, little man. A tired swordsman is one stroke closer to disaster than a well-rested one."

The boy was clearly revelling in his father's company, and the separation came as a grave disappointment. But he was obedient. He slid from his seat and hugged the suddenly surprised prince. "Goodnight, Father."

Gerhard's hands waved ineffectually in the air for a moment before coming to rest on the boy's back. "Goodnight, Felix."

Then it was just prince and adept. She didn't wait to be asked to sit; she just sat, taking Allegretti's seat and leaving Felix's empty between them.

"Do you have a name?" asked Gerhard.

"Yes," she said, "though revealing your true name when it can be used against you isn't wise. Or particularly survivable."

"And am I ever going to be in a position to exploit that?"

She lowered her head so that her hair covered her face. "Nikoleta Agana."

"Your German's good, but you weren't born here, were you? Byzantium, you said?"

"Yes," she answered. Her head came up. "I am loyal to you, my lord. More loyal than you could possibly imagine."

"Given that the rest of those snakes-in-white have chosen to abandon me in my hour of need, that's not saying much." Gerhard wiped his face with his hand. "One hundred and fifty years since we last asked you to turn out in force."

"Two, three months ago, your call would have been answered. The masters would have been elbowing each other out of the way to show what they could do." Nikoleta looked at her hands again, feeling the spark just under her skin. "I don't have an explanation for you."

"Are you sure?"

"No. All the signs are there, though. The novicemaster can't enchant the simplest tattoo on the most willing arm. That sort of thing should be child's play – for him, at least, as he's the one who inked me ten years ago."

She pulled up her sleeve and bared her forearm where, in among the black shapes and arcanum, was a simple circle centred on her wrist. Her pulse flexed the circumference – that was, in fact, the point. The needle had hurt like a bastard, but she hadn't cried once. When it was over, yes, but more out of relief that the tattooing had taken than from any physical release.

"It still works," she said, "for me, at least."

"What does it do?" Gerhard leant forward to inspect it.

"It allows me to see magic. Mundanes . . ."

"Mundanes? Is that how you think of us, of me?"

She let her sleeve fall. "Yes. I'm sorry if that offends you."

"Offends me?" Gerhard's voice rose for a moment, before he remembered that he was separated from his men by a single layer of cloth rather than a privacy-enforcing thickness of stone. "Carinthia gave you everything you wanted. Including money. Lots of money. And you dare to look down your nose at my royal person?"

"My lord, I'm trying to explain, and badly. You're the first mundane" – she screwed her face up as she said the word – "I've talked to for the best part of a decade. Within the Order, we're very direct. We don't talk around the subject, any subject, because that's just a waste of time. We all hate each other anyway, so why bother being polite?"

"You need to remember who it is you're talking to. I'm not one of your Order." He got up out of his chair and started pacing. The tent wasn't very big, so he spent most of his time turning. "Before my father died, he told me how to deal with you. He said, 'Don't bother them, Gerhard. Anything you can handle yourself, do so. But there'll be times when a little more is required. Then ask them for help. Nicely. When you see what they can do, you'll be glad you hadn't bothered them before.' So, Mistress Agana, what can you do?"

"That depends," she said, "on what you want me to do."

"I want you to kill every last murdering Teuton pig-fucker we find, then, on the way home, burn Simbach to the ground." Gerhard stopped his pacing and clasped his hands behind his back. "Can you do that?"

"I can't do the greater battle-magics. I can't do a moving pillar of fire, or summon lava, or curse them all dead." She saw that Gerhard was about to interrupt, and she held up her finger. "There is plenty I *can* do, though. If you use me right, we can still win."

The prince frowned as he digested the news. Then his jaw dropped. "Gods, woman, you expect us to have to fight!"

"Well, yes."

"The only fighting those men out there have ever done is to see who's first to the bar."

"Then you'd better hope they're well trained. Or you could always turn back." She looked up at Gerhard. "You're the prince. You decide."

He sat down next to her. "What *can* you do? Exactly?"

"All kinds of fire-magic. Elemental manipulations: if there's a fire, I can make it use all its fuel at once. Depending on the source, it can be quite a big explosion. Minor summonings which, if done properly, aren't really that minor at all. If they try to charge us I can guarantee I can drop the first couple of ranks."

"Before they reach us, you mean."

"Yes. I can throw a shield out – over some, though not all of us – that's impervious to all moving objects. Arrows, people, beasts. Centred around me. Some of the spells are quite close-quarters. There'll probably be casualties among your men, and I'm not a healer. Not even basic wounds."

Gerhard rested his elbows on his knees and his chin on his entwined hands. "I don't know. We're going to lose men just protecting you."

"Yes. How many Teutons are there?"

"Three hundred horsemen, excepting the ones killed in the fight over the barge. They're good with a bow, as well as a sword. They've got their women in a horse-drawn wagon train. Children too, for all I know. Against our hundred infantry and twenty horse. And you."

"If my lord wishes, I'll return to the adepts' house in the morning." She was certain he wouldn't accept.

He didn't. Instead he asked: "Why now?"

"I still have no explanation to give you," she repeated.

"What about the other sorcerers? The Teutons have one of their shamans with them."

"You didn't mention that before."

"I just have. What about them? What if only the Order are affected?"

"The barge. How many of your men were there?"

"Two. Hunters. No magic."

"And they rescued the bargees?"

"Yes."

"Then there's your answer. A half-competent shaman would have been able to rip their souls out and leave them shambling ruins, even over moving water. That they got away with it tells me that their shaman is either dead already or has run away."

Gerhard blew out his cheeks. "And what of enchantments? The barges, the lights, the millstones, the bridges. Our wagons. My armour. My sword. They're all working."

"For now," she said. "I can't guarantee they will in the future."

"You think everything will fail?" he said, then realised what that all meant. "Everything?"

His sword was around his waist, even though he'd taken the armour off for the night. He drew it and held it in front of his face, trying to detect if there was any change to the dark halo surrounding the blade.

"I don't know," said Nikoleta. "I'm just an adept. I've been able to enchant common items for a while, but I haven't tried recently. I've been busy doing other things."

"Busy? You've been busy? Well, that's all right then." He looked at her, and she noticed how his fingers tightened around the sword grip.

"Yes. Busy. You have to understand: what you do, what your people do, is of supreme indifference to a sorcerer. Your interests are not ours. Your father was right: don't bother us unless it's important."

"As long as the money keeps on coming in."

"Yes. We're expensive. Whether we're as expensive as having to recruit, feed, house and train a large standing army, I don't know. I've never paid attention to the cost of things."

"Carinthia is . . ." started Gerhard, but he stopped. His teeth ground together. "No. Not defenceless."

"My lord, the men out there, the ones drinking and eating and singing by the fire; are they all that you have?" They *were* singing, too: the "Climbers' Song".

"A single Carinthian is worth ten other men. We have an army of a thousand outside."

She chewed at her lips. "My lord, you don't have a single hexmaster with you. I'll do what I can, but whatever stories you've been told about how to fight a battle, even one as small as this, just don't apply any more. We cannot march up to the Teutons and simply kill them all before they even get into bow-shot."

"That's how it always used to happen," he said.

"You need more men."

"I need the hexmasters I have paid for."

"They're not coming, my lord. Perhaps they never will again."

Gerhard seemed caught between rage and terror. It left him looking impotent.

"Leave," he said, waving the point of his sword at the tent opening. "I need to think."

So she got up and slipped back outside. The night was cold, but the men were still singing.

14

They struck camp at dawn, and far from needing to be roused from an indolent lie-in, Nikoleta found herself ready long before soldiers came to dismantle her tent. She washed in water that wasn't even as cold as that used in the novices' house. Breakfast was the remains of supper she'd squirrelled away.

She found herself enjoying being outside the city's confines more than she'd thought she would. Before, sleeping rough and splashing meltwater on her face were signs of failure. Now, after years of having every aspect of her life regulated and every shortcoming picked apart, she felt liberated all over again.

And the thought that when she got back to Juvavum, she'd march right up to the White Tower and dare the inhabitants to do their worst had kept her warm all night.

She hung on to one of the blankets and stayed wrapped in it while she watched the men uproot the stakes they'd hammered into the ground, then slowly collapse the poles that held the canvas upright. All across the camp, the grey forms of men in the half-light busied themselves with storing everything away on the wagons, feeding and resaddling the horses, spending one last moment by the still-smoking fires.

Those were tasks she knew little about, and when her tent was folded and carried away, she followed to watch the men lean into the wooden cart and stow it neatly with the others. The wagon's wheels, propped up with a steersman's stick, rotated slowly, waiting for solid ground to bite against.

Afterwards, she wandered where her feet took her, soldiers and servants and wagon drivers falling silent and respectful as she stopped momentarily to watch them work, then murmuring softly to each other as she walked on. At one point, she found herself next to the two bonfires the men had lit the previous evening, and she frowned at the long iron rake being used to scatter the red embers across the scorched grass.

"What are you doing?" she asked.

"We always do this," said the man with the rake. "Grub the fire out."

"But why?"

The man, with more than a hint of grey at his temples, hooked a half-burnt log and rolled it to the side of the fire. As he did so, fresh little tongues of flame crept up its blackened sides. "Mistress, I suppose it's just down to good manners. If we were in a hurry, I dare say we wouldn't bother. But when are we ever in a hurry?"

She could feel the heat on her face from the exposed ground at the centre. Of course fire fascinated her. She'd spent her adult life learning how to control it, use it, create it – but never tame it. It was wild, like she was.

"Leave the other fire alone," she said.

"Mistress?"

"Just do it." She walked through the embers to the far side, kicking up sparks as she walked. She could have done it barefoot, but she'd already put her boots back on. From the other side of the fire, she looked over her shoulder. "Understand?"

"Mistress." The man looked down at the ground and wouldn't look up again.

She sat down a distance away while the rest of the camp was cleared. Yes, the soldier's captain questioned why both fires hadn't been raked flat, and the man in charge of the task pointed over to her and shrugged his shoulders. She didn't acknowledge the attention, only waited until everything was ready.

Doubt had no part in a sorcerer's mind. Doubt was for lesser creatures. It was for those who weren't supremely confident in their abilities and hadn't practised until their noses bled through the sheer effort of concentration.

Nikoleta's life had been forged in a hotter furnace than most: she knew that success and failure were sometimes out of her hands. What she had to do was to mould the world around her until it bent to her will.

She walked back through the line of ready wagons, files of spears and rows of mounted earls.

"My lord?" she said to Gerhard.

Back in his armour, the Prince of Carinthia looked down at her from his horse. "Mistress Agana, you've interfered with the orderly striking of camp."

She nodded, looking back at the thin column of smoke still rising from the remaining fire. "I wanted to make a deposit of sorts. Of trust."

Gerhard frowned under his helmet.

"Send the wagons on. We'll catch them up soon enough." She dismissed the servant holding the bridle of her horse, and put her foot in the stirrup.

Still frowning, Gerhard ordered the wagons down the via, and as the last one rolled away over the next rise, he rested his arms on his pommel.

The earls, the men, all were restless, concerned. Nervous. Nikoleta dropped her reins and nudged her horse around, using her knees alone. The fire was what? A stadia away?

Far enough for safety, and still close enough for effect. She could feel it, hot and energetic, like a wasps' nest ripe for kicking.

The heart of the fire flashed, and suddenly there were burning

missiles rising into the dawn sky. The highest rose almost verti-
cally, trailing sooty flame, while those on a lower trajectory buried
and bounced across the soft earth and the hard road. The sound
was like a thunderclap that rolled on.

Some of the burning wood started to land uncomfortably close,
and the soldiers began to shuffle backwards until Reinhardt growled
for them to hold. Some of the horses bucked and shied, whinnying
their fear, and their riders struggled to stay on.

When it was over, it seemed like half the hillside was covered
in smoking debris, and ash like snowflakes began to fall.

Satisfied, Nikoleta took up her reins again. Gerhard seemed
frozen. His son gaped. The Italian sword-master pushed his silly
hat back on his head and contrived to look both impressed and
unsurprised simultaneously.

"Father?" said Felix. "Did you see that?"

It was excusable for a twelve-year-old.

"Yes, I saw it," said Gerhard, brushing his epaulettes. "It was
very loud, too."

"How can we lose?" Felix grinned to himself.

Allegretti turned his horse in a slow circle. "Perhaps you should
concern yourself, young man, on detailing every possible way we
can lose, and determining a strategy for combating them, rather
than counting victory a certainty."

"Oh, signore," said Felix, but he was looking at the sorcerer.
As she rode past, she slipped him a sly wink while everyone else
was looking at the sky.

Eventually, Gerhard caught up with her. She glanced around
to see the soldiers marching along with considerably more spring
in their step than they'd formed up with first thing that
morning.

"Does that answer any of your questions, my lord?"

"You could, if you wanted, kill us all and take the palatinate."
He stared straight ahead. "If you're right, there's no one who could
stop you. Not now."

"Perhaps," she said, "but what would I do with it then? I've no
interest in it and even less idea of how things work off of Goat
Mountain. I'd have to resurrect you and all your advisers to show
me how it was done."

"You can do that?"

"No. It was a joke." The corner of her mouth creased into a

smile. "Even if I could bring you back, you'd be a mindless slave. Besides, I've no desire to turn you out of your throne."

Gerhard rode on in silence for a moment. "The boy . . ."

"The boy's a boy with wise masters. He'll become a man who's been taught well. At the moment, he's too young to be scared of war, or even of me. He'll learn that, too."

"The princes of Carinthia have been in alliance with the Order for nearly a thousand years. What happens next? Where will Felix's hexmasters come from?" The prince looked pensive. "I didn't sleep much last night. If at all. These things, going around in my head, all the time. Everything we do relies on the simple effect of magic. Without it? We descend to barbarism and worse. Tell me the Order's impotence is temporary."

"The Order's impotence is temporary," she said.

"But you don't believe that, do you?"

"I've no evidence one way or the other. Define temporary: is it a week, a month, or a year? Or a decade?"

"This brings me no comfort."

"I'm not here for that. I'm here because you called."

"Everyone must think that nothing's changed. The hexmasters are still in their tower, the prince is still in the fortress. All as it has always has been."

"But you can't keep them fooled forever. When the barges stop coming, the millstones stop grinding, the carts stop rolling – they're going to know."

The prince turned a strange shade of red. "They will not."

"My lord, the sun comes up every morning and sets every evening. If it didn't, just once, the whole world would know and there'd be nothing you could do about it. People talk. No law you pass can change that."

"They'll do as they're told." Gerhard was adamant. "No one, inside or outside Carinthia must know."

Nikoleta wondered how he was going to manage that. As far as the people of Juvavum were concerned, only one hexmaster had met the prince's summons. Wasn't that worth gossiping over? She'd heard a story once of a Danish king who'd given a simple but elegant demonstration of the limits of his authority by having his throne carried to the edge of a turning tide.

She wasn't in charge. She had no wish to be in charge and no idea what she would do if she was. Yet even she could tell that the prince's plan was unworkable. And not because he was stupid, but because accepting the truth was simply too much for him to bear. Gerhard was to be pitied, and she found that she did indeed pity him.

"As you wish, my lord." She eased off on the reins, and let him pull ahead. Several of his earls overtook her too, and she found herself at the back of the column of horse with Signore Allegretti.

"Good day, Mistress," said the tutor.

She raised her eyebrows, and he looked to the left and the right.

"My apologies. I had assumed that someone wishing to be on their own would not choose to ride next to me. Should I remove myself from your presence before you remove me more permanently?"

"Where's the boy?"

"With," he said, craning his neck, "his father. He can only learn so much from me: defending himself, mainly, not defending the palatinate."

She looked at him sharply, but he seemed not to notice.

"And, to be honest, he is already a good swordsman. I can still beat him, but my reach is longer and my fire burns brighter. Felix sees everything as a game. Even this. Even what you did. When he learns otherwise, he will outgrow my poor company."

"I'm sure you'll do whatever's best for the boy."

"Felix will have my best intentions, no matter what. However, this adventure seems singularly badly advised."

"And you say that for a reason, or because you have an ache in your left elbow?"

"Mistress, as impressive as your demonstration was, I would still like to know where your colleagues are."

"I . . ."

"One of the fundamental dicta of any fight, whether it is a brawl between two drunks or a clash of two empires, is to bring everything you have to bear on your opponent's weakest point. What we have is them . . ." – he pointed behind him and ahead of him – "and you."

"Your prince believes it to be sufficient." She looked again at Allegretti. Her experience of men, mundane or otherwise, hadn't been good.

"My employer," said the Italian, "believes a great many things, and believes that his subjects should believe a great many more. I am neither a prince nor one of his subjects."

"All the same . . ."

"I would be happier if there were two of you. Happier still if there were three. It is a shame my happiness is not the prince's concern."

Nikoleta wondered if she should lie, but she'd had little practice in deceit since childhood. Mind, she'd been really very good then, even though it got her into as much trouble as it saved her from. Lying to a hexmaster, however, wasn't such a smart thing to do.

"The prince is satisfied," she repeated.

"Are *you*, Mistress?" He angled his head in an attitude of contemplation. "I do not know the complexities of your craft – no one does – but I have seen a Sicilian conjurer brought down by sheer weight of numbers and literally torn limb from limb. *He* was on his own, too."

"I'm not on my own."

"I think you are always on your own, no matter how many of you there are. But I phrase myself badly. German is neither of our first languages, yes?" Allegretti made a deprecating gesture with one of his hands. "You are our most valuable asset. So the prince must concentrate on protecting you, while you win the battle. Not on winning the battle itself."

"The white robe." She looked down at herself, at the way she glowed in the morning light; she was clearly distinguishable from all the others, even the earls in their battle colours.

"Now," said Allegretti, "a group of figures in white robes, throwing elemental forces around as if they were a company of bandieratori, very impressive, very scary, very one-sided. One figure in a white robe, surrounded by nervous armed men? I may be the only man here who has ever experienced warfare in the flesh, so why not ask me where I would tell my archers to fire, where I would concentrate my strongest swordsmen?"

The sick feeling in her stomach didn't go away. Neither did the Italian.

"You would concentrate on me. Even as I was killing your men."

"No one expects you to sit passively while all these big, strong soldiers stand around you. They will hold their positions, even when they know that the further they stand from you, the less likely they will be to die. They are all brave, stout-hearted Carinthians, raised on the mountains and in the forests, and they have known nothing but peace for centuries. Who could possibly compare them with these blaggard Teutons, who are fed a continual diet of war and misery, and who have finally summoned enough sense to drag themselves out of the marshes of their birthlands and ride out to conquer more suitable lands?"

Allegretti finally shut up, and Nikoleta found herself mumbling, "I'll find something else to wear."

15

Büber came up behind the column as it approached the Simbach bridge. He'd snatched at some sleep, and managed to catch hold of it only fleetingly. When he'd been woken, everything that followed had felt rushed, including his ride back north.

At least there'd been no more distraught relatives looking for their lost children. He'd thought about that. A lot. He didn't like where his mind had taken him.

He was known enough not to be challenged – which was stupid, really, as he was known enough, equally, for it to be worth someone's while to pretend to be him – but he rode up the side of the via, past the marching soldiers to the first of the horsemen.

He looked again. The white-robed figure riding next to young Felix's tutor was a woman. Then he looked again. Since when did hexmasters ride? All the stories had them floating ethereally above the battlefield, wheeled there on great pantechnicons. Guessing that the other magicians would be ahead in the wagon train, he wondered why this woman was isolated.

"Ah, Signore Büber," said Allegretti. "A pleasant ride, I hope."

"No one tried to kill me, if that's what you mean," said Büber. He felt tired. More than that, his back burnt from too many days in the saddle. He could walk forever, but riding used different muscles.

He and the woman stared at each other. She frowned at him, and he at her. Her frown deepened, and he could see her concentrate hard.

"It won't work," said Büber. He held up his hands to show her his lack of fingers. She didn't appear to understand, so he explained. "No magic's touched me, ever."

She blinked. "You must have had some fall on you. Prayers? A naming?"

He shrugged. "If I had, it didn't take."

"Signore Büber is one of the prince's huntmasters?" suggested Allegretti, but she was now more confused than before.

"Does that make them special?" she asked.

"No, not really," said Büber. He spotted Gerhard at the head of the horsemen, and thought he really ought to tell someone he'd arrived. "Just . . . it's so that magical creatures can't use magic to find me and eat me. I get enough of that from the wolves, the boar and the bears."

"You," she said, "you were one of the men who rescued the barge."

"No. We lost the barge. We got the two bargees off, though, before the Teutons got to it."

"The other man. Was he a hunter too?"

"Nadel? Yes."

She went as white as the clothes she was wearing, and kicked her heels into the flanks of her horse. She rode up the line towards Gerhard.

"What did I say?" Büber hoped that Allegretti would supply some sort of explanation, but the Italian merely took off his hat, gave it a shake, and repositioned it on his head.

"The ways of wizards. And of women. Who knows, signore?"

"And since when did they let women into the Order?"

"From what I understand, at least ten years ago, because that is how long she has been on Goat Mountain." Allegretti watched her back recede. "They could all be women. When did you see one of their faces or hear them speak?"

Büber was about to answer, but closed his mouth on his words: it had been only a couple of months ago that he'd found the first unicorn horn, when they'd warned him not to tell anyone what he'd discovered. All the voices coming from under the white hoods had been male. He'd just assumed.

"The stories?"

"Stories have a way of filling the space that is required of them. They may start out true, but what do they end up as?" The Italian looked up at the sky. "Snow?"

Büber followed his gaze. The wind was at their backs, and the clouds were ragged and grey.

"It's not cold enough for snow, not now. Rain, later on." He was used to the elements, but he didn't know about the castle guard, who didn't really train if it was too hot, too cold, too snowy, too wet or too windy.

Allegretti's mouth twisted into a half-smile. "Rain. The gods do indeed piss on all our endeavours."

"Well, it's not like this won't be over quickly. We'll be home by tomorrow night."

"We have to catch the Teutons first, signore. They are a day ahead."

"They rise late and stop early. We can take them during the night and be roasting horse-flesh by sun-up." Büber's blood sang with the twang of his bowstring and the whistle of bolts and arrows. He wanted to experience the same intensity again, the closeness of death and the cheating of it in the same breath.

"Have you ever fought at night, signore?" Allegretti stroked the stubble on his chin with his thumb. "It is not to be recommended."

"And you have, I suppose?"

"I have seen and done a lot of things, signore. We foreigners within your borders all have our reasons for coming here and throwing ourselves on the mercy of Carinthia."

Büber noticed that Allegretti wore a ring on his right hand, which he played with as he spoke.

"We have the hexmasters fighting for us. Day, night, rain, shine. It hardly matters."

"You remind me of the boy," said Allegretti. The boy in question was now in the care of one of the earls, as Gerhard had drawn aside with the sorcerer. They were talking, heads close, but their arms were making numerous short, sharp, chopping actions, with repeated pointing to all directions.

"What are they doing?" asked Büber. "What did I miss?"

"That witch is our only hexmaster, signore. No one else answered our lord's summons. It adds an unwanted layer of complexity to our battle plans, most notably that we are both outnumbered and under-magicked." Allegretti sighed. "Yet we still march north."

Büber's horse plodded on. "*One?*" he eventually managed.

"Her ability is not in question – at least, I would not presume to question it – but yes. Just her."

"What happened to the others?"

"I am at a loss to know how to answer you, signore. Simply put, they did not come. It seems that everyone else is content that a quick victory over the Teutons is assured and that any Bavarians who might object to our marching through their lands will be swept away by our vast and powerful army." He leant in. "I do not share their confidence."

"So why did she suddenly ride off to talk to the prince? What did I say that made her do that?"

"You could always go and ask them. I am certain that they would be able to supply you with complete and satisfying answers, in a way that I am sadly unable to." Allegretti dragged the corners of his mouth down with his fingertips. "I am only Felix's tutor, not the Oracle herself. Apologies."

Büber felt that his world was suddenly and unnecessarily confusing, and that people were the cause of it. What he wanted to do was turn around and disappear into the forest for a month. What he actually did was slowly ride up the column until he'd reached the wheels of the rearmost wagon.

He waited for the prince to finish his business with the woman, and come back into the line. Which he did, eventually.

Gerhard looked distracted and sombre. Framed by his helmet, his face looked curiously rigid, far from the roistering man who led his own wild hunts and never seemed afraid of anything.

"My lord," said Büber quietly. He'd had little practice bowing in the saddle, but he made an attempt and didn't fall off.

"What? Oh, it's you. She" – and he flapped his hand in the direction of the only rider in white – "said you'd arrived."

Büber kept his eyes down.

"Everything still standing when you left?"

He looked up again. "Yes, my lord."

"At least something's going right." The prince grunted his annoyance. "Ride ahead. We'll be at Simbach in the hour, and I need to know what they have there. The earl . . ."

"Fuchs, my lord."

"Him. How many soldiers can he turn out, and will they stand against us? That sort of thing."

"The toll collector was guarded by just three men, my lord. I think they're as broke as I was told they were."

"Good. But I still want you to go to Simbach and see if anything's changed. Meet us on the Carinthian side."

Büber bowed again. "My lord." He encouraged his horse into a trot, and started to overtake the wagons. He looked in every one, but there were no more hexmasters.

So now he was a scout, a spy: weren't the hexmasters supposed to use their crystal balls, or whatever, to view the enemies' positions and report back? And since when had Bavaria been their enemy?

He rode on to the top of the next rise and looked ahead. The river curved around sharply, and the bridge was a black line across it. The town was hazy and brown beyond.

Then he looked behind, and saw things through Allegretti's eyes. There was something clearly lacking. There weren't enough troops to protect the wagons, let alone take the fight to the Teutons. Twenty horse against three hundred barbarian riders whose mothers were probably half-horse themselves. One hexmaster.

"Shit."

He had a job to do, though. He was already known in Simbach, had identified himself as a prince's man. There'd be no point in sneaking around, pretending. He wasn't used to telling lies, either: trees couldn't be fooled and the wild creatures he encountered appreciated only cunning and skill.

Büber passed through the farms on the Carinthian bank, and had got to the bridge when his horse refused.

There was nothing coming across the low arch at him, and nothing in the dark water beneath. Sometimes big birds circling overhead would spook a horse, but there were no shapes silhouetted against the low cloud.

He tried again, clicking his heels and making encouraging noises with his tongue, but the stupid animal wouldn't take another step.

Yesterday, it had been him who was reluctant to cross. Today, it was his mount. He slipped his foot from the stirrup and slid down to the ground, groaning at the burning in his back. He stretched and grimaced, then took the reins and tugged.

No.

He tried again, but nothing would induce the horse off the road and onto the stone bridge. He didn't hold with beating the thing, so he led it to the nearest house.

As he tied it to the fence that enclosed a well-tended garden, he was aware of being watched from the door. A child, blonde hair in coiled plaits, peeked through the gap at him.

"They won't cross," she called.

"Why not?"

"Don't know."

Büber tapped his purse, then opened it and pulled out a couple of copper pennies. "I need to go to Simbach all the same. Keep an eye on the nag for me?"

She nodded, opening the door a little wider, and he put the coins on the gate-post.

"Prince's business, mind," he said. "You'd better do a good job."

"I always do a good job," she objected.

"Then I'll expect to find my horse when I get back."

Büber took his sword from his saddlepack and strapped it on. He wondered about taking his crossbow, but that seemed unnecessarily provocative. He wasn't hunting anything except information.

He started walking, and he found himself hesitating at the threshold of the bridge. It hadn't changed. It was the same as it had been, as it had always been, since it was conjured out of thin air hundreds of years ago.

He consciously raised his right foot and pressed it against the black flagstone. Normal. Perfectly normal. He hurried across, slowing a little once he could see the far end of the bridge from the middle.

There were two horse-and-cart teams, driven by black-hatted Jews, and behind them, Bavarian carters with magical wagons. The Jews' horses were, like his, refusing to cross the bridge, and the jam was raising both voices and tempers. The Jews couldn't turn around with the Bavarians at their backs, and the Bavarians didn't seem inclined to allow them space, preferring to hem them in and shout at them, shaking their steering poles threateningly.

There were soldiers, too, spears waving above the mass in a futile attempt to separate them all.

Büber stopped and stared.

So it wasn't just *his* horse. It was every horse. Which meant there was a problem with this impossible, magical bridge that leapt across the river in a single span, against all common sense.

It was clear to him that the Carinthian forces wouldn't be going this way unless that woman could fix whatever was the matter with it. He didn't know how likely that was.

He hesitated there, on the highest point of the arch. Gerhard's orders had been quite clear: go to Simbach, find out how many troops the earl could raise and what their disposition was. But shouldn't he know about this first?

He turned and faced the other way. The prince would be along soon enough, coming down the same road he'd just used.

"Fuck," he said, and walked down the northern side of the bridge, towards Simbach.

The noise of horses and men grew louder as he got closer.

16

Gerhard leant forward onto his saddle's pommel, bringing his ear closer to Büber's mouth.

"Explain to me again, huntmaster. And this time, make it clearer than the insane babbling nonsense you gave me before."

Büber knew it sounded mad. But telling the truth was all that was left to him.

"My lord, animals won't cross the bridge. Horses, dogs, cats. I've tried all three." He had scratches on his face and a circular bruise on his leg where some mutt he'd borrowed had turned on him and bitten into his calf.

"That's not an explanation, man."

"I can't explain it! Something's wrong with the bridge and I don't know what. My lord." His cheeks stung with parallel cuts that beaded bright blood every time he changed expression. "I'm not a . . . I'm not like her."

"I'm surrounded by idiots." Gerhard straightened up. This expedition wasn't going the way he wanted. "Get back on your horse, huntmaster, and try and stay out of my sight for the rest of the day."

Büber slunk off to where his mount was being held by a tiny blonde girl, and the prince looked around for the next person to shout at. His gaze alighted on Allegretti, and his mouth tightened into a humourless smile.

"Allegretti. Ride to the middle of the bridge and then stop."

"My lord? Signore Büber says that it is impossible." The Italian made no sign that he would comply with the order. Instead, he lifted down his hat and inspected it for debris, brushing at the felt with his long fingers.

"Büber is an old woman."

"That is entirely possible, my lord, but he may also be correct regarding the bridge. I would advise we pay attention to his hard-won knowledge." He picked off some imagined speck of dirt and replaced the hat on his head. "The man who ignores it risks being made to look the fool."

"Which is why you're going to ride across the bridge. You, not me."

"As you wish, my lord, although trying every horse we have seems both imprudent and unnecessary. Either we all cross, or none of us cross, unless you wish to dilute your forces further."

"Signore Allegretti," started Gerhard, but to forestall any further conversation, Allegretti spurred his horse's flanks and set off at a canter. By the time he reached the bridge, he was at a gallop.

It was almost as if he'd ridden into a wall, the horse stopped that suddenly. Digging all four feet into the dirt, it slid to a halt, while Allegretti did not. He flew, having slipped his feet from the stirrups moments before. He almost had time to wave at Felix, before curling into a ball and bouncing on his shoulder and back.

He rolled to a stop. His horse backed away from the bridge, then turned and headed down the line of wagons, ears back and tail up.

Gerhard watched the Italian lie still on the ground for an exaggerated length of time, then finally unfold himself and bat the dust from his clothes. He retrieved his hat and started to walk back.

"Anything else, my lord?"

He ought to try for himself, but he wasn't going to. Allegretti's demonstration was proof enough. The damn fop could have killed himself, or his horse.

"Get me the, the . . . hexmaster." From what she'd told him, she knew nothing about stone forming. And that was how the bridge had been made, extruded from molten rock and shaped into a usable form, five hundred years earlier. Perhaps a proper hexmaster would know what was wrong, but this adept, this woman?

She was all he had, so he had to ask her.

"Tell me why, and whether, you can do something about this, this mummers' farce," he said.

She looked at him, her face neutral. "My lord."

At least she had the wit to dismount first, and hand her reins to one of the knights, before she approached the bridge.

She looked carefully at the runes on the bridge's parapet, walked cautiously up the first part of the rise, and even managed a little series of jumps, her feet stamping down as she landed. She walked back and stood in front of the prince's horse.

"I know what the problem is," she said.

"And?" sighed Gerhard. The Teutons were getting further away every moment they stood there, on the wrong side of the river. He needed to strike back at them, hard and fast, so that he could return to Juvavum and have a long, not entirely cordial chat with the Master of the White Order.

"The bridge has vanished. It's no longer there."

He looked at the bridge, at its black solidity, then at her. "Are you, are you all, out of your minds?"

"The bridge exists as an act of faith only. Animals do not have that capacity, so they think they are being led across a river on nothing but a ribbon of air. So, naturally, they refuse." She rested her hands on her hips and looked across to Simbach.

Gerhard dismounted and went to stand next to her. The bridge, the stone, the arch. It looked solid enough.

"It's like what you said last night, isn't it?"

"The magic that keeps it there is an echo. We remember what it was, so it still appears to us. When our faith in it to carry us across fails, so will the bridge. Poof. Gone."

"That's . . ."

"The way it works, I'm afraid. We never really understood where magic came from, only that it was there and we could manipulate the world using it."

"But you still can."

"Perhaps I just believe in magic more than everyone else." She stooped down and picked up a pebble, which she threw underarm high into the air. "The stone has no memory, no experience, no expectations."

They watched as the dirty yellow pebble fell onto the bridge and vanished. A moment later, a ring of ripples formed beneath the arch.

"It doesn't know that the bridge should be there. We give the lie meaning because of our belief." She dusted her hands clean.

Gerhard shook his head. "This . . . this whole thing. It's mad."

The adept twisted a strand of her hair between her fingertips. "I take it there are other ways across the river."

"Not here. Downstream. There's both a ford, and a bridge – a real bridge – at Obernberg. About fifteen miles away." Gerhard started to rub his face, and again encountered the cold chain-mail that protected his palm. "Farm tracks. It'll take the rest of the day to get there."

"The farmers use them. Why should it slow us down?"

"The last thing I expected of the Order: a practical sorcerer." He half drew his sword to see whether it still had the dark shine about the blade. "Is this it then? Is this how it begins?"

"So it appears, my lord."

Gerhard slammed his sword back and looked around pensively. "It's a strange sort of Ragnarok. I expected more, well, giant wolves and fire."

She was startled. "Why mention Ragnarok, my lord?"

"I don't know. Perhaps if the gods bring magic, their passing takes it away. Do you believe in the gods, Adept? We celebrate the festivals and offer the required sacrifices, because we're good Germans, but how many of us see Ostara as just an excuse for a massive piss-up and a chance to slip one to the neighbour's wife?"

He wondered what the Order's attitude to the gods was. Did they encourage worship, tolerate it, or try and beat it out of the novices? It wasn't anything that he'd ever been in a position to ask before.

"I have no opinion to offer," she said. "If there are gods, then I've never met one. I would suggest that we turn back, though. That's as much advice as I feel qualified to give."

"We're not running away." He wheeled his horse around, and caused her to skip back. "Carinthia does not run away."

"No one is suggesting that we run, my lord. But if this is happening here, what's happening back in Juvavum?"

He stared down at her, and growled. "I can only deal with one fucking thing at a time, Adept. Go and ride with Büber. Women together." Then he raised his voice: "East. We go east."

He kicked down hard with his spurs and his horse clattered its hooves on the stone via, before finding enough grip to head in the new direction. His earls followed, and then the infantry.

The wagons were laboriously turned and set on their trundling, one-speed way.

Gerhard glanced behind him once to check that all was in order, and didn't look back after that.

He had the river to his left, and it ran more or less directly east. The road was what he expected: beaten soil and stones. More than good enough for the wagons. He rode on in splendid isolation, and the column straggled out.

It started to rain: slowly at first, no more than mist in the wind as the clouds above churned and darkened, but it grew to become a steady drizzle, cold and uncomfortable. The road beneath him grew sticky, and puddles appeared in the potholes on the compacted surface.

"My lord," called a voice, and in turning to see who it was, Gerhard was forced to twist his head into the blustery rain.

"What is it, man?"

Reinhardt, swathed in a waxed cloak with only his head visible, ran up beside him. "The wagonmaster begs for a moment's rest. His men are finding the conditions difficult."

"Difficult?"

"Yes, my lord." Reinhardt, already apprehensive, lowered his head further. "The wagons . . ."

"May Sleipnir shit on the wagons." It had rained for barely an hour, and already they were whining, thinking of their beds and their beer. Meanwhile, the Teutons were ahead, pressing on with their rude horse-drawn carts. They could be crossing the Enn by now. So he came to a decision. "I've got new orders."

"My lord?"

"Those on horse will ride on to Obernberg, and scout the land ahead. Your spearmen will help the wagons get to us by afternoon. And when I say help, they'll put their shoulders to the wheels and push the fucking things all the way if they have to. Clear?"

The man knew better than to argue. "My lord."

Gerhard clicked his heels again, and his horse responded, breaking into a trot for a few lengths, before subsiding back into a walk.

He could hear what was going on behind him, though his helmet muffled some of the sounds. Barked orders, the rattle of tack, the stamping and splashing of horses' hooves against the ground.

They were doing what he'd told them to do. Anything else would be unthinkable: literally, because he couldn't genuinely think of a reason for anyone not to obey, and obey instantly.

The magic, though. He did think about the magic, and how the bridge at Simbach was real enough to take the weight of a man, but not a horse. He didn't understand that, and didn't accept it either. Perhaps it meant, at least, that the Teutons couldn't double back and cross the river there, but there were other considerations.

Everything he knew depended on the working of magic. His whole kingdom, down to the very last penny, relied on some sorcery somewhere along the process. The river flowed as the seasons dictated, but the barges that plied its broad reaches were driven by tattooed bargemasters who willed them upstream and controlled them down it. The whole network of trade on the inland rivers – the Donau, the Rhein, the Volga – would simply grind to a halt without magic.

And speaking of grinding: fields of golden grain didn't plant themselves in the soil in spring, or mill themselves into flour come harvest. The goods from the farms and the forests rattled their way to markets on wagons like those on the road behind him, ones that didn't need a horse and could travel tirelessly day and night forever.

Even the lights in the city's squares. Even the fountains.

Where were his hexmasters?

He almost stopped. He almost turned around and ordered everyone back to Juvavum, where he could take counsel and question his wizards and work out what to do next without having the smell of damp horse assaulting his royal nostrils and the uncaring rain running down his back in a small, cold trickle.

But Carinthia didn't retreat. Moreover, it didn't know how to retreat. It only knew how to advance, an irresistible, inexorable force that others either ran from or were consumed by. When Carinthia went to war, it rolled across the countryside like one of the magicked wagons. All it needed was to be steered this way and that, preferably directly at the enemy, and, as history had proved time and again, it was enough.

When they did turn for home, it was because they had been utterly victorious and their foes totally vanquished. Those who were not scattered after the battle had been annihilated during it.

109

How to lead a harried force safely away without loss wasn't in any of the stories he'd been told.

He had no wish to be the start of any such tale, so he summoned his nerve and remembered his ancestors. Three hundred horse: it was barely worthy of the name "army". He had his spears, his knights, and the adept. If he shied from a fight now, his name would be synonymous with cowardice. Not Gerhard Stoutheart, Gerhard Strongarm, Gerhard Widowmaker – yes, he liked the sound of that last one – but Gerhard Two-minds, Gerhard Pissblood, Gerhard Tiny-cock. Those, he liked not so much.

It was raining hard now, a constant, heavy blatter of water in fat drops that clattered against his plate. There was some ice in each, just for the extra discomfort.

His was royal blood, the same blood that had flowed in the veins of Alaric. What was rain? What was cold? His character was stronger than that.

Gerhard slowed his horse and turned it so that it walked diagonally across the road. His earls, heads bowed against the weather, looked a sorry sight, and he was ashamed for them. They were his nobles. One of them was his son. The only one of them who seemed to shrug the conditions aside was the witch.

"Straighten up in your saddles, you sacks of shit," he shouted, venting his frustration and uncertainty. "You are Carinthia, yet you ride like condemned men. Fuck the weather. Laugh at it. Scorn it. Mock it. The Teutons? Barbarians. Weak, ill-fed, ill-trained, ill-disciplined children. What do you fight for? The handful of gold florins you'll get for every one of their heads you lay at my feet? Or for your own honour? Because I'll tell you which is more precious to me."

He walked his horse in a tight circle. "Any of you lack the passion to defend Carinthia's virginity? Any of you who'd stand by and let its soil and its treasure be deflowered by Teutonic cocks? No? Good."

They looked back at him, those who dared. Others looked anywhere but.

"We've men to kill. Let's do it quickly."

Büber was still smarting from Gerhard's rebuke, and he rode at the back of the column of horse with the other disgraced: Allegretti, who didn't seem at all bothered, and the hexmaster, who did.

Gerhard may be a prince, but she was a sorcerer. If she'd been a man, she wouldn't have been spoken to like that. From the look on her face, she both knew and resented that fact.

What if she simply refused to perform when the time came? Büber had come to realise that the outcome of the whole expedition depended entirely on her, and the prospect of his lord and master screaming and begging for her to cast one simple spell to save them all while she smiled inscrutably and folded her arms gave him a vicarious thrill.

The prince could hardly have her killed for disobeying orders. In fact, and the mere thought twisted in his guts, all she had to do was to change sides. Here was Gerhard, here was Felix, here were most of his earls – those able to be mustered, at least.

The prince was right in one thing: Carinthia was here, and it suddenly looked vulnerable.

"Mistress?" he ventured.

"What?" She didn't even bother to look at him.

"Can I . . . can I ask you a question?"

"I suppose so. It passes the time."

"What will you do?"

Allegretti looked askance at Büber from under the dripping brim of his hat. Büber ignored him.

"I will discharge my duty to the prince. As always." She wiped water from her eyebrows, and used her long fingers to clear the rest of her face. She looked at him now, and something like a smile flickered across her face. "Why? Did you think that because he wouldn't listen to me, I'd get angry with him?"

Büber shrugged. "I suppose so."

"You'd be right. I am angry with him. But when has that ever made obeying his orders something I could choose to do? I'll do what's necessary when the time comes." She flicked a water droplet off the end of her nose. "He'll learn."

"The bridge, Mistress. What was wrong with the bridge?"

"Was it not obvious, Signore Büber?" said Allegretti.

"No. No it wasn't. Though it was to that bastard cat. What could it see that I couldn't?" Even now, the marks on his cheeks had set uncertainly, and the earlier wound from the arrow was looking puckered and white between the black stitches.

"That the bridge . . ." started the witch.

". . . was not there," finished Allegretti. He smiled to himself, and at the woman's consternation. "Oh, come. It is hardly a secret."

"No, that's exactly what it is," she said. "The prince said that no one must know."

"Hang on," said Büber. "Not there? I walked on it. So did you, Master Allegretti."

"I cannot deny it. But you asked what the cat could see – the answer is it saw precisely nothing. As did my horse, your horse, their horses."

"But . . ." said Büber, then quite deliberately he shut his mouth and looked away. They rode on for a while, and eventually the silence between them became unbearable.

"Something else you wish to say, signore?" prompted Allegretti.

All Büber could think about were the unicorns, how their horns were just sat in the hollows made by their missing bodies. He'd always assumed – he'd always been told – that the horns were the most magical part of them. What if that wasn't true? What if it were the exact opposite, and the horn was the only part of the beast that wasn't magical?

Nothing had stolen them away. They had, like the bridge, just ceased to be.

He stared at the woman, all in white. "Does the prince know?"

"He knows everything he needs to know to make the decisions he alone can make." She gave him another smile; thin-lipped, more desperation than mirth.

"But *you* can still . . ."

"Yes," she said, "and before you ask, I don't know why."

"But the . . ."

She sighed, the sound catching in the back of her throat, making it end in a growl. "Yes. I know."

"Apparently, signore, she knows. So do you. So do I, at least in part. As does the prince. Who else?"

Büber immediately thought of Thaler: had he worked it out? There were so many books in that library of his: what was the likelihood of finding the right one?

"I don't know. No one. I think," he answered.

"Not so," said Allegretti. "A great many people know. Except – they chose not to be here."

"The hexmasters?" Büber blinked. "How long has this been going on for?"

"Weeks, months even." The woman in white looked entirely resigned. "If magic started to fail, they would have been the very first to realise. They'd know the signs long before anybody else would even suspect anything was wrong."

Büber remembered the gold florins he'd been given for the first unicorn, and how very solicitous, very insistent, the masters had been. "I should have known, too."

"You?" There was scorn in her voice.

"Yes," he said, irritated. "Me. I don't suppose you know anything about any missing children, do you?"

It was her turn to get annoyed. "No."

"Nothing at all? Four kids, that I know about? About one a month? All under twelve."

"No."

"It's just that if you know how long this has been going on for, maybe you know about them?"

"The masters tell us nothing."

Allegretti narrowed his eyes and shook his head slightly, but Büber missed the expression and ploughed on regardless.

"What do you mean? You're one of them." Now he noticed. "Aren't you?"

"Signore Büber, may I introduce Signorina Agana, adept of the Order of the White Robe."

"An adept? You have got to be fucking joking."

There was a pause, and Allegretti eventually said: "Not the most tactful response. She can still immolate you where you sit."

She was staring at him. She hadn't raised her hands, or made any threatening gesture towards him. But her look was such that he suddenly realised that he needed to apologise, completely and at once.

"I'm sorry. I didn't mean that you couldn't, or weren't a . . ." He closed his eyes and wondered how death would take him. Magic terrified him, like it did most people.

"If I had a short temper, huntmaster, I would have died long ago."

He opened first one eye, then the other. Her gaze was steady, despite the cold wind and the rain blowing at her face. Then she laughed.

"It's what they do," she continued. "They goad you. Belittle you at every opportunity. Strip you and beat you, and you're too weak to resist. They call it training, but they actually enjoy every last humiliation they heap on you. If they manage to break you, they count it a success. If they don't, the next time you make a mistake, they are twice as vicious. I have survived all that. Your mis-spoke words? Hardly worth mentioning."

"I'm still sorry, Mistress." And he genuinely was. He'd had no idea.

"I think the man's suffered enough, signorina."

She turned her head with a flick. "He has no idea what suffering is."

"Signore Büber is well-enough acquainted with hardship, I think," said Allegretti mildly. "This is, however, a mere distraction, which we must turn away from and come to one mind over a different matter: what is to be done?"

"Us?" The adept seemed surprised that the conversation was to include her. "We follow, and the prince leads."

"A noble attitude, signorina. But our service would surely be rendered all the more valuable for being considered, timely, and, how shall we say . . ."

"Not stupid?" ventured Büber.

"I would have gone for wise. Your version lacks grace." Allegretti removed his hat, squeezed the excess water from it over to his side, then spent a while reshaping it. "Let me put it this way: we are twenty or so horse, travelling towards an enemy of considerably greater number. Our armour is back on the wagons, which may or may not reach us in time, and our spearmen – of considerable assistance when facing cavalry – are exhausting themselves else-where. We have our melee weapons, but little else. They have plentiful bows, as Signore Büber has discovered. Our esteemed sorcerer is with us, which is excellent, but whereas before we had infantry to protect her, now we do not. How can we three stop this turning into the disaster it threatens to become?"

His hat went back on his head, looking much sorrier than before.

"Why us?" asked Büber.

"Because we owe our lord as much? If he is Carinthia, and it is Carinthia we are sworn to protect, then it is us who are best placed to accomplish such a task."

"We are?"

Allegretti shrugged. "Who else? Signorina, can you protect the prince?"

"I don't know. I can try, but he'll be at the very front, won't he?" She frowned. "But I'll be busy. I don't see anyone else around here who can cast spells."

"There is always the Teuton shaman."

"I'm certain he won't be able to cast, and the prince has his earls to protect him, anyway."

"I have yet to see," said the Italian, "twenty horsemen win against three hundred. Especially when those twenty are on heavy horse but are essentially unarmoured. Signore Büber, do you know where the Teutons are?"

Büber scratched at his head. "I left Torsten Nadel to keep track of them. When we see him, they won't be far away." He chewed at his lip. "No, then. I don't know where the Teutons are. We could get no warning at all."

"All the more reason to make a plan now. Signorina, you cannot protect the prince. Neither can I."

"No?" she said.

"No. Felix is my first concern. Those are my orders from the prince himself. I will not save the man at the expense of the boy." Allegretti seemed content with his role, and looked across to Büber. "That leaves you, huntmaster."

"I can ride well enough," he said, "but I'm not a trained cavalryman. Are you honestly expecting me to charge the Teuton horse with the others?"

"No. Which leads us to one conclusion, does it not?" Allegretti waited for the others to mentally catch up.

"It means . . ." Büber screwed up his face with the effort.

"Gods, man," said the adept. "He means to let the prince die if he's so determined to carry on with this madness."

"We can't do that!"

115

"We can't prevent it, Büber. All we can do is plan for the inevitable disaster."

"But . . ." He was spluttering. He had no answer.

"The signorina is quite correct," said Allegretti. "If it comes to it, and we pray to the gods that it does not, if we are faced with defeat, what would you rather do? See Carinthia annihilated, or salvage something from the flames? Shall we fight to the last man – or woman – or shall we save the heir to the throne? The prince has not thought of this. We, his loyal subjects, must be ready."

Büber's throat was dry, despite the rain. He sucked at his sleeve to wet his mouth. "So what do you want me to do?"

"Your task is simple. The new prince will need a hexmaster. Since we only have one, you must protect her with your life. I will be Felix's shield. You will be hers."

"This is crazy. This is almost treason." Büber shook his head.

"It would be treasonous not to do this, signore. We serve the Prince of Carinthia to the very end."

"And from the very beginning," said the witch.

"We cannot tell anyone what we have agreed here. But we must be ready." Allegretti wiped the rain from his face, then dug under his clothes for a small silver flask. "Shall we drink to seal our fortunes?"

He unstoppered the container and swigged from its contents, before passing it across to the adept. She sniffed cautiously and took the smallest taste before leaning sideways to hand it to Büber.

"I don't drink spirits," she said. "It ruins my concentration."

Büber was more than happy to make up the difference. He tipped the flask skyward and drank deeply. The schnapps burnt on the way down, and put a fire in his belly, at least for the moment.

He didn't want this. He didn't want any part of it. Allegretti's plans felt wrong, yet were right enough to be convincing. What if they ran straight into the pack of howling Teutons? How long would they last? Long enough to grab the boy and run?

Someone needed to have the presence of mind to act in that moment. He gave the flask back to the witch, who passed it on without imbibing further. Allegretti had another nip before closing it up and hiding it away.

"I should be scouting ahead, not skulking behind," said Büber. "Obernberg is only a mile or two away."

"And yet the prince demands you stay at the rear." Allegretti bent his head, and a drop of water collected at the end of his nose. He curled his lip and blew it away. "He is a hard man to help."

"Well, I'm going to try. We're sleepwalking into this, and no one else seems to care." Büber nudged his sodden horse forward, and slowly made his way back up the line.

18

Büber was given grudging permission to ride ahead. His horse, cold and stiff, was equally reluctant to do anything but plod: it would trot for a short while, then subside into a heavy-footed walk. Büber was getting frustrated with the beast.

He tried to remember what Obernberg was like: a market square, maybe even as big as the one at Simbach, but the houses around it were pretty much all there was. The town was on top of the hill overlooking the river. There was a sacred grove, too, which he thought he'd have to pass on the way to the square. Then there was a big stone building, constructed from the remains of the old Roman fort. That was on the highest point, and it had commanding views of the bridge. In fact, there'd be very little about the place that a Roman wouldn't still have recognised if he'd stepped from his grave and looked around.

Farm tracks led left and right to squat collections of roofs. The light was piss-poor, and the rain was sheeting, coming across his vision in bands stretched from cloud to ground. The tops of the trees swayed hard.

Then he stopped. There were people ahead, sheltering next to a wall by the side of the road, and enough of them that they spilt out onto the road itself.

They had horses, he could see that much. He blinked away the rain and pressed his hand to his forehead to divert the water away from his eyes.

No, they *all* had horses. And they were all men, now moving from a close-packed knot where they'd huddled for warmth into a loose mass of arms and legs. It was as if he'd kicked an ants' nest.

The first man swung up on horseback and started towards him. Quickly.

"Shit. Shit shit shit."

Büber was facing the wrong way for a quick escape. In the time it would take him to turn, the Teuton would be on him, and moments later all his friends would be there, too.

To his left was a field, its boundary marked only by a ditch. That was the way he'd have to go. He hammered his heels down hard and shouted at the lazy nag to get going.

Stung, the horse reared. He hung on, barely, and was abruptly off, over the ditch and across the ploughed earth. He bounced around like a sack of cabbages until he'd got the rhythm; then, once he realised he wasn't going to fall off, he checked behind him.

He counted four Teutons. Two were heading down the road, two were following him directly. Soil was flying in clods behind him, and already his horse was showing signs of slowing down.

"No, no, no, you lazy-arsed animal." He kicked again. The ground sloped down to the grey-brown river, and lakes of standing water pocked the margins. He needed to avoid those, so he dug in with his left knee.

An arrow whistled by. At the speed they were going, the chances of them hitting him were low. But the mere fact they were firing at him, while riding, and getting anywhere near him was bad enough. If they hit the horse, the beast would throw him out here, in the middle of an open field with no cover whatsoever.

"Get a move on." He was out of the saddle, standing in the stirrups, crouching awkwardly over.

There was another field boundary coming up. Another ditch, but this time substantially wider.

"Ah, shit." He'd been surprised he'd cleared the first ditch. This one . . . "Jump, you stupid nag, jump."

He closed his eyes, and was airborne. His heart stopped, and only restarted with the impact of the saddle into his crotch.

"Fuck!" He could barely see. "Ah, my balls. Gods!"

And now, he heard one, then two horses landing behind him. Too close. He was being run down. If he turned to his right, he'd be in the marshy river bank. If he turned left, he'd be heading back to the road, and there were two Teutons waiting for him there.

Except, when he finally managed to blink away the tears and

black spots before his eyes, there were more than two horsemen on the road. For a moment, he despaired of ever seeing another sunrise clear the dew off an alp, or ever feeling the first snowflake of winter cold against his palm again, but then he realised that those other horses were Carinthian.

He veered towards them.

The other Teutons had ridden straight into the head of the Carinthian column. One was already down, his mount wheeling free, and the other was trapped between the armoured Gerhard and another earl.

Something glowed in the distance, and grew brighter. Quickly. It was growing, and it wasn't moving either to one side or the other.

"Shit."

He managed to get his feet clear and throw himself to the ground, just before the blinding, burning light roared past. He had a brief image of a churn of flame before his face dug a furrow in the sodden soil.

There were screams. By the time he had raised his head and spat the grit from his mouth, this . . . thing was on fire, staggering, then stumbling onto its knees. It was vaguely recognisable as a horse, and the shape on its back as a rider, but the heat and smoke and coils of orange and red obscured all the detail.

It fell towards him, and Büber scrambled back.

The second of Büber's pursuers checked his advance. He was close enough for Büber to see his snaggle-toothed sneer, the wash of stubble on his face, his bloodshot eyes. His horse whiffled and stamped at the ground, while the man continued to hesitate. His hand was on his bow, an arrow nocked, but he made no attempt to draw.

The smell of burnt hair and charred flesh was sharp and urgent. The rain hissed as it fell on the bodies: the flames flickered and began to die.

Büber's own horse was looking at him over its shoulder. It was exhausted, and even the stench of freshly roasted horse couldn't make it move. Büber himself realised that almost everything hurt, but he'd be damned if he was going to just lie there. He pressed his hands into the soil and clambered to his feet.

Some of the Carinthians started picking their way across the field towards him. They moved slowly and purposefully, spreading out in a line. They all had swords drawn.

The Teuton decided that Büber wasn't worth it. He wheeled away with a grunt of frustration and started to put some distance between them. Büber spat again and watched him go for a moment, before realising that he could do something about it.

He ran, splay-footed, to his horse, and dragged his crossbow free of the saddle. He worked the lever, his filthy fingers slipping against the smooth metal, but such was his determination that he took a second bite and the bowstring locked in place. He grabbed a handful of quarrels, threw all but one to the ground and slapped the last one on the stock.

The Teuton was galloping away, and the target he presented was getting smaller. Büber raised the bow and sighted. His heartbeat, his breathing, the tiredness in his arms, the cold, the rain, the pain: everything militated against his shot. The receding figure was impossible to keep in his sights.

Now or never. He took a deep breath, closed his eyes, then opened them again.

His finger twitched, and the bolt span away. It vanished into the distance, its bright flights lost in the heavy weather.

He thought he'd missed. No, he knew he'd missed. It was speculative at best, wasteful at worst. He might need that bolt and all the others he'd spilt.

The Teuton's horse mis-stepped and tried to kick back with its hind legs. Then it went down in a heap, and its rider barrelled over its head and into the mud. The Carinthian riders shouted and called, and gathered pace as the Teuton scrambled upright and started running.

The earls passed Büber, and the ground shook. Clods of earth spattered at him, and left him even more sorry-looking than when he'd first fallen.

They caught up with the Teuton and surrounded him. He'd drawn his sword and was spinning in a circle, trying to keep his tormentors at bay. Taunts and jeers were raised against the man's curses and the attempts of his horse to regain its feet.

Gerhard swung down from his saddle, his own sword in his mailed fist.

"Do you yield?" His voice was clear, and it carried all the way back to Büber.

The Teuton either didn't know what the word meant, or decided that taking the Prince of Carinthia with him was an exchange worthy of his own death. He swung his sword up and jumped forward.

Presumably, he'd intended to bring it down on Gerhard's shoulder, cutting his neck and torso, scoring a quick kill. Gerhard brought his own blade up and guided the inexpert blow aside.

The Teuton had overstretched himself, doubling over as his momentum carried the tip of his sword into the earth. He had one last chance to look up before the edge of the Sword of Carinthia buried itself in his woefully exposed flank. It didn't stop moving until it grated against his spine, and by then he was past caring.

Blood and offal spilt out, and Gerhard whipped the sword away, opening him up further. He was dead before he dropped.

"Someone put that horse out of its misery," he ordered, and threw his sword hilt-first to a knight for cleaning. He mounted up again and rode towards Büber, skirting the still-smouldering pyre.

"I'll be surprised if they didn't hear you back in Juvavum, huntmaster."

"My lord. Sorry." Büber bowed stiffly, because his balls still hurt.

There were flecks of blood mixed with those of soil on the prince's armour. "You have purged my memory of your earlier mistakes, huntmaster. A good shot. Heroic, almost."

"Just lucky, my lord."

"We make our own luck. Well done on not dying, too. Any more escapes like that and you'll be giving the rest of us a bad name." It was still raining, and it was running in ill-coloured rivers down Gerhard's breastplate. "The Teutons appear to have taken Obernberg."

"Yes, my lord." Büber was still cradling his crossbow. He'd very much have liked to stick his hand between his legs and massage some life back into his bruised plums, but that was definitely not something to do in front of royalty. He gripped the stock of his bow tighter to take his mind off the ache. "There were six Teutons on the road, just after the rise. But they only know I was there, not who else is coming."

"It's a piss-awful day, huntmaster, but we must strike sooner rather than later. We'll stop here. When the wagons catch us up, we'll arm ourselves and take back the town. When you have quite recovered," said Gerhard, snorting a short laugh, "I'll need you to scout ahead again."

"As my lord commands."

Gerhard went to ride on by, but he stopped again right next to Büber. "The other hunter: Nagel?"

"Nadel, my lord. No sign of him."

"The man better have a good excuse. I see no reason to be lenient with failure." The prince's smile soured to a frown. "We should have had more warning."

Gerhard flicked his heels, and the prince's horse extricated its hooves from the mud with a sucking noise.

Finally satisfied that he wasn't being watched closely, Büber slung the crossbow over his shoulder and gingerly cupped his balls. He gasped and groaned, but from what he could feel, he still had two.

He picked up the fallen crossbow bolts and retrieved his horse before heading back to the road. Both of them, he decided, would be better off walking. It took a while.

The woman in white was waiting for him.

"You could have killed me, you witch," said Büber.

She looked amused. "But I didn't," she said.

"I had to jump out of the way. It was coming straight for me!"

She sighed, and decided that, as they weren't going anywhere, she may as well dismount.

"Yes. That would be because the Teuton was right behind you, waving his big sword at your exposed back." She squared up to him. That was difficult, since he had a lot of height on her, but it didn't deter her for a moment. "Perhaps I should have left you to get sliced open. But then again, you're not the only one who's a decent shot. At least I hit what I aim at."

"I hit him," he objected.

"You hit his horse."

"Do you know how difficult that was?"

"No. Neither do I care, because what I did was much harder. I had to miss you as well."

"The fuck you did. I had to duck!"

"No, I had to count on you ducking at precisely the right moment. Which you did. Just." She folded her arms and smiled up at him. "Any later and I'd have ended up looking a complete idiot."

"But . . . but . . . That burnt thing out there could have been me."

"Good job you ducked then. Anything else you'd like to say?"

Büber's crossbow had started to slip off his shoulder, and he angrily pushed it back up. "Plenty. Do that again and I'll ⌄ . ."

"What? Not duck just to spite me?"

"Just to . . . yes. And gladly."

"And how is your precious manhood? Hopefully some sense has been knocked into it, because clearly it's the organ you use to think with best."

"This," said Büber, "this is exactly why men do the fighting, and the women stay at home."

"If this woman had stayed at home, your headless corpse would be lying in the mud over there." She nodded towards the field, then looked him up and down. "We're all worth more alive than dead, Master Büber. You can thank me later."

She led her horse away, and left him fuming.

19

Nikoleta watched the men with the wagons, saw how they laboured to keep their carts on the road, how they took every opportunity to rest on their steering polls, how hunched their backs were, how slow every necessary movement was. How tired they all were.

Even with the wagons parked – propped up with a frame under the ever-turning front axle to keep it clear of the ground – the men slopped and slipped about their duties.

The spearmen that accompanied them were in little better state. They had pushed and shoved and goaded for the miles between Simbach and Obernberg. It was nothing that a few hours' rest and a hot meal and chance to dry off wouldn't have cured, but they weren't going to get any of that.

Gerhard was determined to attack at once. A fool could see the lack of wisdom in such a decision. The Teutons were in a far better position than the Carinthians. In fact, they were in exactly the position the Carinthians should have been in. It should have been the Teutons cold and miserable on the road, shuffling nervously into their armour and fumbling with their weapons, dreading facing men who had turned out of a soft bed that morning and eaten a bellyful of meat.

For the first time, she found herself wondering if Gerhard was the best person to lead Carinthia in these new, interesting times.

"Signorina?"

"Signore Allegretti." He looked different now. Somehow, more business-like: the floppy hat and the rich clothes had gone, replaced with a plate-sewn coat and a half-helmet with nose-guard. Both looked well used.

He held out a rough linen tunic and a long canvas overcoat. "This was the best I could do, signorina. They have the benefit of being dry, but little else. Also this." He produced a brimmed leather hat and added it to the pile. It was wet, and clearly he'd taken it from someone else's head. "More important that you, rather than him, keep the rain from your eyes."

"Thank you," she said, and took them from him. There was nowhere private to change, just a few trees. For decency's sake, she ought to take herself away, but that would draw more, not less attention to herself. And it wasn't like any of the men here would so much as dare to comment on her nakedness, let alone try to take advantage of it.

Unlike the hexmasters, these mundanes were terrified of her. Good.

"Turn around, Master Allegretti." She put the clothes on the rail of a nearby wagon and shook the tunic out. It was a man's, but it would fall to past her knees. More importantly, it wasn't white.

She gripped the hem of her robes and peeled herself out of them, leaving them a soggy mass on the wagon. The cold rain on her tattooed skin made her shiver, and she dragged the tunic on over her head, quickly covering it with the coat. She wrung as much water as she could out of her hair, and topped it with the hat.

"Done."

Allegretti turned back to her. He said nothing.

"Well?"

"You look like a sorcerer in a long coat. But perhaps from a distance it will do."

"Is nothing ever good enough for you, Allegretti?"

"Nothing is ever perfect, signorina. No plan, no scheme, no deception is foolproof. The question is, will it serve its purpose?

In our case, probably. I would prefer it if you cut your hair: it makes you obviously different."

Unconsciously, she reached up and touched her hair, tugging on it. She'd worn her hair short, back in Byzantium. That she could grow it out was a mark of her control over her own life.

Other things: her height – she was shorter than most short men, but there were still some boys among the wagon train. Her shape – but she'd bound her breasts tightly that morning, and she wasn't so top-heavy that the coat didn't disguise them.

Allegretti was worrying over nothing. She could easily pass as a boy if she tucked her hair up under her hat.

"No," she said. "That stays."

"As you wish. Master Büber and two of the earls have ridden on ahead. Our attack will commence shortly."

"And this attack? Conducted to the old rules? March up to the enemy, cut them down and, when they run, hunt them like rabbits?"

Allegretti shrugged. His plate-laden coat was heavy with absorbed water. "More or less. The spears will advance, flanked by the horse. You and me and Gerhard and Felix will ride behind the spearmen. Very Roman."

"What will the Teutons be doing?"

"They will try not to engage with us, initially. They have bows and will use them. Their baggage train will be close by – Signore Büber is looking for it – and we need to close with that. They will make every effort to protect it, and they will melee with us at that point."

She closed her eyes and tried to imagine it. The Teutons travelling with the wagons would defend them, even it was just women and children. It would mean, when the Teuton horsemen charged them, the Carinthians would most likely be fighting both at the front and the rear at the same time.

"Is it a good plan, Master Allegretti?"

"It is not the worst I've heard. At least our lord realises that the town itself is unimportant. A lesser general would fight their way into the centre, only to find themselves surrounded. By seizing their baggage, he forces them to fight us. If he destroys it, they are destitute so they will continue to fight long after the moment when they should retreat."

"But? I can hear it in your voice."

"We run the risk of being overwhelmed. Every casualty we suffer is critical. Spearmen are only strong in numbers. If we have too few, they cannot support each other, and then it comes to their individual prowess as fighters." Allegretti looked over his shoulder at the nearest knot of spearmen, huddled together and talking in low voices. "These are not hardened warriors, practised in the shieldwall and the schiltrom, bloodied in battle and strong of heart. We must be ready to act, if it becomes necessary. These things can fall apart in moments."

A shout called the infantry to order, and they lined up in a field, three rows deep. They looked less fierce than they should have done. The horses split into two groups, which only served to show how few of them there were, and arranged themselves at either end of the line.

Gerhard and Felix came riding down the road towards them.

"See the flower of Carinthian manhood, Master Allegretti? The battle's as good as won."

"As you say, my lord."

Felix looked excited and nervous, and Nikoleta thought that he had absolutely no idea of what was going to happen. The boy held an oval shield on his left, his cavalry sword already unsheathed on his right, steering his horse with his legs only.

"You seem eager, young Master," she said.

He beamed back. "Who wouldn't be? This has to be the most exciting thing that's ever happened to me."

"Felix—" started Allegretti, but Gerhard interrupted.

"Gods, now's not the time for one of your lectures. The boy's got his blood up! Like his father, and his father's father before him." He banged his fist against his own shield. "Where's my huntmaster? We need our target."

Nikoleta untied her horse and slopped onto the back of it, while Allegretti resolutely remained on foot. At least the heat from the beast kept her warm.

Finally, Büber appeared over the hill, with only one of the earls behind him. They were riding at speed, then slowed to an energy-saving trot once they drew closer.

He was out of breath as he tried to explain to Gerhard.

"In the centre. Market square. They're all there."

"Where's Bruckner?"

"It wasn't easy, my lord. We had to get almost into the town. They've placed wagons across the roads to the square."

"Barricaded themselves in, eh?" The loss of an earl didn't seem to bother the prince unduly, so Nikoleta assumed he was a person of no great importance. "A static target."

"The wagons only. The Teutons are riding out to meet us."

"Good, good," he said, despite that not being part of his plan at all. They were now trying to take a defended position.

"How many roads into the square, Master Büber?"

"Two. One this side, the other to the north-east."

"And, like the town squares in Juvavum, tall houses on each side?"

"Yes," said Büber. He leant heavily on the horn of his saddle and wiped the sweat from his forehead. His exertions had opened the cuts on his face again, and even the arrow wound was weeping.

"Like a castle, then, and just as in the stories, the gates will be blasted inwards and we'll take the keep by force." Gerhard wheeled his horse around. "Mount up, Master Allegretti. Carinthia is at war and every man will do his duty."

He and Felix rode into the field to take up their positions, and Allegretti walked silently to his horse. He gave it a pat on the neck, and swung himself up.

"Every man?" she wondered out loud.

"Perhaps he has forgotten you are a woman, in the same way he has already forgotten how many drunken evenings he has enjoyed with the late Earl Bruckner."

The other earl went to join his assigned group, and Büber slowly straightened up, hauling in more air. "This. This whole thing . . ."

"Is madness?" offered Allegretti.

"There's too many of them. Even for you." He looked at Nikoleta as he spoke.

"That remains to be seen." Three of the four Teutons they'd already killed were laid out, headless, by the side of the road. The fourth, the one she had incinerated, had been left where he'd fallen. No one had wanted to touch him. "I've no particular wish to die, but neither will I counsel despair," she said. "The dice are cast; let them fall where they may."

"So said mighty Caesar, who had all the armies of Rome behind him." Allegretti reached across his body and drew his sword. "I would rather the gods' honest earth under my feet than this contrary animal, but my lord decrees I ride rather than walk."

He followed in the direction taken by Gerhard, and Büber shook his head violently. Spray from his hair and face flew off in all directions.

"I have to protect you," he said. "That sounds even less likely than when Allegretti first suggested it."

"Then there'll be little more for you to do today," said Nikoleta. "Be grateful that your work is done."

He snorted. "Of course it is. I'll believe that."

"The advance has been sounded. We're late."

"Oh, arse." Büber dragged his head up and indicated that Nikoleta should go first through the gap in the wall. She trotted off and slid into line next to Gerhard. On his other side rode Felix, and then Allegretti.

"Where are your robes, Mistress?" asked the prince.

"A simple subterfuge. I thought it wise." She left Allegretti's involvement out for the moment. Gerhard's continual sniping at his son's tutor was wearing, and she was much less likely to suffer his sarcasm. Teachers were replaceable. She, uniquely, was not.

Across the fields, in the distance near the town where the buildings ended and the farms began, there were horsemen. Enough of them to resemble a swarm of flies.

They were sufficiently closely packed for Gerhard to look at her again.

"Just over half a mile, my lord. Not a range I can make."

He tutted, but she knew the stories told by the mundanes didn't exactly match with what a hexmaster's abilities actually were. That thought sent her off on another wild chase through her memories: perhaps magic had been failing on a grand scale for centuries, and no one had noticed. Perhaps it had simply been used up, and they were now dining on the dregs.

When she looked again, the Teutons had spread out in a loose picket that extended far beyond their own line, and they were advancing.

Any moment now, and the arrows would start falling. At the rate the infantrymen were marching, they would be under fire for the whole ten minutes it would take them to reach the outskirts of Obernberg. They were struggling to stay in formation as it was, their boots picking up layers of cloying mud as they walked, and there was no hope of them speeding up, let alone running.

Nikoleta decided she'd have to start killing Teutons sooner, rather than later. Every one of them dead meant one less bow and a lot fewer arrows aimed at their own troops.

She fell back to ride with Büber.

"Can you keep up?" she asked.

He eyed her warily. "Does this mean you're about to do something stupid?"

"That depends," she said, "on how you define stupid. Can you keep up?"

"If I have to. I'll ask the nag too, shall I?"

"Is that a yes?"

"Gods, woman. Yes, just don't expect too much." Büber rolled his eyes. "You've seen me ride."

She had. She knew exactly what to expect. She pulled her horse around in a tight circle and started off towards the left flank. Büber trailed behind her, his horse already puffing. The ten Carinthian horse beyond the line of spearmen weren't looking particular purposeful. They had more the air of a bunch of nobles out for an afternoon's hunting, back before sunset for some feasting and other such entertainments that their lord had laid on for them.

She knew all about that. It was the poor bastards trudging along on foot she had sympathy for.

She and Büber were beyond the army now. She wasn't even sure if the prince had noticed her absence from the centre of the line. The nearest Teutons were more than dots at this range: fully realised men on horses, black and shaggy-maned, the rain shining off their armour, the light twisting on their helmets.

She reached out for them, and found them quite easily, their hot blood and beating hearts resounding in her mind like a chorus of drums.

"Are you ready, Master Büber?"

"Just how close are we going to have to get?" He reached down for his crossbow.

"Not that close, but don't you want to see the whites of their eyes?"

"Only if we have to." He pulled back on the lever, and the bowstring clicked into place. "You're nothing like I thought a sorcerer would be."

"Good, because I hate every last one of them." She clipped her heels into her horse's flanks and trotted out towards the enemy. The two at the end of the Teuton line started to take an interest in them. Unsure of what Nikoleta and Büber were doing, they pulled arrows from their quivers and took aim.

The air stiffened in front of her. She'd never done this on horseback before: on foot, the shield moved seamlessly with her. She had to assume it would work the same way now. The rain stopped falling on her, and instead ran in rivulets down the air.

The Teuton's arrows were arcing towards them, flights dark against an already dark sky. They would miss, but, unlike her opponents, she didn't need a ranging shot. She singled out the first man's heartbeat and concentrated on it until it was the only sound she could hear.

Her tattoos flashed and shifted on her skin, and her palm, empty moments before, held a tiny ball of white fire.

Concentrate on the sound of the double concussion, the opening and closing of flaps of skin, the squeezing of muscles. She had it completely, almost as if she could see it beneath his chest.

The fire flitted away. It swelled as it flew, growing from the brilliant pebble to a fist-sized storm of light. It didn't drop like an arrow would. It went perfectly straight, and it went faster than anything should have ever left a human hand.

The Teuton appeared transfixed by the oncoming storm. His comrade-in-arms shouted, but it was too late – had been too late from the very beginning. The man took the fire dead centre, and it consumed him in a wave.

Nikoleta heard the heart stop. The silence was abrupt, and she was suddenly aware of the world again.

She heard Büber say "fuck" under his breath. The second Teuton nocked another arrow and started for her.

Again, she felt for him, sorting through all the souls until she found his. The fire sprang to life, suspended by her will, cradled in her fingers. The Teuton stopped his ill-considered dash and loosed off his arrow. He was close enough that he would have hit her, or her horse, or Büber, but that didn't matter so much as that he was already dead when the arrow banged against the invisible wall in front of her and broke in two.

The flames and the greasy smoke had attracted attention, from both sides. The poor bloody infantry slogged on towards the town – quite why Gerhard hadn't used the road was lost to her – but the closest Teutons, and the Carinthian cavalry, started to converge on her.

"Are we going to pull back?" asked Büber. He felt for a crossbow bolt and fed it onto the shaft.

"No," she said. "We're going to take them on."

Her horse had seemed entirely unconcerned by the pretty lights above its head, but started to shudder and twitch as a dozen Teutons came at them from one side, and the Carinthians from the other.

The northmen fired their arrows at her as they rode. That not a single one reached her didn't lessen their accuracy, nor their rate of fire. Each crack and rattle made her horse more wide-eyed and rasp-breathed, and more difficult to control.

Her saddle wasn't a stable platform any more, and she realised why the Order were wheeled into combat on wagons. She tutted at her mistake and swung her leg out and over, ready to dismount.

"Where are you going?" asked Büber. He raised his crossbow and took aim.

"Forget about that. Hold my horse and don't let go." She dropped to the ground and felt it shake under the impact of so many hooves. It was more than just a little frightening; she felt her stomach tighten and grow cold.

But she had been taught to ignore fear. She had managed to cast spells under the most extreme conditions. Will and knowledge. They were the only things that mattered.

The Teutons were charging. They had swapped their bows for swords. They were waving them wildly, and she heard Büber struggling to keep both his and her horses under control.

She fixed the leader with a knowing smile and fire ripped him apart. She didn't stop there. The flames spread out like a curtain pulled from the ground, and the Teutons at the front were unable to turn. They plunged into it and through it.

Nikoleta knew how hot the air was, how it seared and cooked. She had never before tried it on targets that were so wet, though, so she was unprepared for the result.

On first contact, the water had exploded into steam, ripping into the Teutons' skin, bursting out between cloth and armour, scalding their lungs. She had boiled them, men and horses, inside and out, and the results were ruinous.

They fell, half-formed, slapping to the ground, momentarily obscured in a coppery-pink fog, but then revealed as the rain beat down and the flames licked their last.

The very rearmost of the Teutons had managed to pull up. He was abruptly alone on his portion of the battlefield, facing a Carinthian hexmaster and ten Carinthian earls. He turned and galloped away as quickly as he could.

She lost her concentration momentarily. Her shield flickered and fell, and the rain pattered against her hat once more.

Büber, the earls, they were all staring at her. She gazed at the gasping, twitching shapes in front of her. One by one, they shuddered and ceased.

What did she expect? For her targets just to disappear in a puff of smoke, clean and neat? These weren't mercenaries, hired by some lord. These were invaders, and they'd killed already.

She turned around, and took her horse's reins from an unresisting Büber, and mounted up.

"Sirs, if you don't have the stomach for the fight, Juvavum is back that way." She pointed south and east. "The enemy is over there. I suggest we attack them before we lose any more of our men."

She steered her horse around the line of still-steaming corpses, reintegrated her shield, and rode straight towards the next group of Teutons.

At least the earls knew they were no longer playing at war.

Her presence on the battlefield caused a change in tactics. Clearly, whoever was now in charge of the Teutons wasn't stupid. He'd been using his archers to keep the Carinthian horse at bay, while sniping at the infantry. Now his right flank was exposed, there was the threat that Nikoleta could simply roll up the line by herself.

He pulled back, melting away before her and leaving her nothing to aim at. Her horse was tiring. She was directly in front of the marching spearmen, a couple of stadia distant. The half a mile into town didn't seem so daunting now, although the Teutons were regrouping in the distance.

She stopped, and let her shield fall. She was tired too. And now she had to face Gerhard, who was riding towards her.

"You broke ranks," he said. She saw that he was both angry at her actions, and impressed at the damage she'd caused. Her advantage, then.

"Yes." She straightened herself and pushed her hat brim up to see him better.

"We conduct this battle according to my orders. Are we clear on that?"

If she killed him now, how many lives would she save? She batted away the thought as if it were a wasp, but it continued to buzz angrily around her as he blustered on.

"You have spent your life closeted away on Goat Mountain, while I have learnt the martial arts. You, Mistress Agana, are a weapon. Not a general. I will deploy you as I see fit. Understood?"

"My lord," she said.

"If you please, back in line. Just because it ended well this time, doesn't mean that the next you'll be so lucky." He turned away to give orders to his earls, and left Nikoleta purse-lipped next to Büber.

The infantry trudged past. There were slightly fewer of them than before, and Captain Reinhardt gave a grim-faced salute to her. He was grateful for the break in incoming fire, but had to march on nevertheless.

"They might thank you, but the prince won't," said Büber.

"I am becoming less concerned by that. Now, tell me what they're doing." She nodded in the direction of the Teutons.

Büber shielded his eyes and stood up in the saddle. "They're massing. It looks like they're leaving. That can't be right."

It was at the edge of how far she could reach out, but she tried it anyway. Points of existence, a couple of hundred humans and the same number of horses. Their blood surged and their hearts beat hot and fast.

"Unless they're planning to come around the back," she said. "We have to go towards the town, don't we? Or we'll end up trapped out here in the middle of a muddy field at nightfall."

Büber sat back down. "If they did that, they'd be driving us towards their wagons. That can't be right either. That is all their horse, isn't it?"

They were starting to get left behind again, so Nikoleta guided her horse towards the infantry line.

"Am I allowed to say that this is too easy? Gerhard's right: if we take their baggage train, we leave them with nowhere to go. All their women are there, and they won't just sacrifice them. Will they? Are they that barbarian?"

Büber scratched at his face, keeping his eyes on the Teuton horse that were riding around their right flank, well out of bow-shot. "What have we missed?"

"If we knew that . . ." She peered at the town, trying to sense her way around it, but it was just too far.

The Teutons carried on into the distance, but then started to come around, forming two packs. One stayed on the right, and the other started along the back of the Carinthian line.

Again, Gerhard seemed unconcerned, as long as they kept their distance.

"They are afraid," he said. "They have seen our might, and all they can do is watch us retake the town, destroy their meagre possessions and leave them paupers."

"My lord," said Nikoleta, "I don't think that's what they're doing."

He gave her a look, trying to silence her with thoughts alone. But he wasn't a hexmaster, and it didn't work.

"We're surrounded," she pointed out. "We have archers at our back, and gods-only-knows-what ahead."

Allegretti, riding close to Felix, leant towards the boy and muttered something in his ear. Probably getting him to work out how to kill every last Teuton with only a wooden peg.

"We are not surrounded," said Gerhard. He punctuated each word with a jab of his sword. "We will win this, and with few losses."

She tried one last time. "They still outnumber us."

"Good," said Gerhard emphatically. "More heads to display when we're through." He deliberately turned away from her and rode down the line, and then in front of it, holding the Sword of Carinthia up high.

All the houses were clustered around the market square on the top of the hill. The slope increased, and the last set of farm buildings — a house, a barn, a byre — marked where the road and the river were, off to their left. They were almost there.

"Master Büber," asked Nikoleta, "where is everyone?"

"Peter. You may as well call me Peter." He wiped at the stitches on his cheek. "It's shorter, if nothing else."

She looked out at him from under her hat. She'd told Gerhard her name; why not this man?

"Nikoleta. Though it's longer than 'witch'."

Büber coughed. It was an apology of sorts. She accepted it, and carried on.

"Where are the townspeople? Even if they've all fled, we should have found some of them on the road."

"Hiding, if they can." Büber frowned. "But if they couldn't? Prisoners?"

"In the town square."

"They're going to try and force us to surrender, which the prince will never do." He looked appalled. "I'm just a huntsman. I'm not supposed to have to worry about things like this. I rely on him to lead."

"We had the initiative. Then we handed it back to them. We have to pull out, now." She saw they were blocked in, front and rear, but at least it would be stalemate if they just stopped advancing.

"Are you going to tell him? He won't listen anyway. And how did Allegretti know it would turn out like this?"

"Because he's as good a scholar as he is a swordsman. Now, what do we do?"

Then the arrows started to fall again. But not from behind: from the front. Suddenly, the entrance to the town was blocked by men with bows who seemed to rise out of the ground. She should have noticed, but again she hadn't been concentrating. The first volley was already in the air, and the second was following. Fifty, maybe even a hundred black shafts reached the top of their trajectory and started downwards.

"Shields!" screamed Reinhardt, and yes, that was good advice. She locked hers in place, but some of the others weren't as quick.

The arrows clattered down. Some buried themselves in the sodden ground. Some bounced off hastily upturned shields or impaled themselves in the wood. Some hit the men behind them, and others still simply struck unprotected flesh, horse and man, and there was chaos. The second volley was already arcing down, and a third was on the way.

"Where did they come from?" yelled Büber. The arrows aimed at him and Nikoleta skittered harmlessly away, but that didn't stop them from being terrifying.

"Because half those horsemen aren't what they seem to be. They've swapped them with the women."

The Carinthian line staggered, and, over the grunts and screams, Gerhard's voice cut through. "Charge! Charge them!" He wheeled about and headed straight for the Teutons.

The attack was ragged. The earls were still trying to avoid the waves of falling arrows, and the infantry were broken. Time to recover was what they needed, and only Nikoleta could provide it.

She whipped her reins and charged with the Prince of Carinthia. It wasn't far. A stadia at most. She had to hit them hard, and try not to kill Gerhard at the same time. He was almost there, raising his sword out to his side and getting ready to strike.

No finesse, then. She raised a wall of fire across the Teuton line and let it burn for a moment. The flames scattered those who could still run, while others were ablaze.

Gerhard's horse went down in a heap, legs splayed, head to one side. It started to roll, and the prince leapt clear. She could save him if she could get close to him, but she had spells to cast and a succession to preserve.

She collapsed the curtain of fire, and turned her attention to the half-dozen Teutons burning like candlewicks. A moment later, it became apparent that the human body contained enough fat to fuel a good-sized explosion, and that someone wearing armour could become a source of lethal shards of red-hot metal, able to scythe down anyone close by.

The solid air in front of her was plastered with red splashes that stuck in splatter patterns like spiders. Her stomach heaved, and she gagged. The gore dropped to the ground as her shield collapsed, and she was suddenly in the middle of a pitched battle, with smoke and fire and the ringing of swords, the shouts and curses of men trying to kill and to avoid being killed.

Büber was at her side. He had his sword, and its edge was already dripping. "Forward. Can't go back."

She turned and looked. The Teuton horse had charged the rear of the Carinthian spears. The earls were fighting back, but their colours were few among the barbarian black.

A figure lunged at her, and instinctively her shield came back, tight around her. A sword-point scraped the air in front of her face. Büber kicked the man away and plunged his fist downwards. The steel went all the way through, and he had to drag it back out.

It would be stupid to die now, and to keep on being revolted by the results of her own magic was even more stupid. A deep breath, and concentration: if forward was the only way, then they'd have to cut through the last of the Teutons ahead and go through the town.

Her horse. She didn't even remember dismounting. It was nowhere to be seen, and neither was Büber's. Or rather, it seemed there were riderless horses everywhere, and it was futile to try and pick out her own.

Very well, then. The tall buildings around the market square had their backs to her. The gap between them lay up a short cobbled road with wooden houses either side. It was a walk of no distance at all, and at a run, would take mere moments to reach.

She stretched out her arms and fire poured from her palms. Not at anyone in particular, though a Teuton did get in the way and fell before the onslaught, reeling away, wrapped in flame. Despite the relentless rain, she set the side of a house alight. The logs hissed and spat, and the roof of shingles started to smoke.

"Get behind me," she said to Büber, and, without waiting, she tore the structure apart.

The blizzard of splinters cleared their path, and she set off up the street. Büber grunted with the effort of sprinting uphill.

"Where are we going?"

"Not back." She took a moment to look. "That would be bad."

There were two Carinthian infantrymen behind them. Whether they were running towards them, or running away from something, was moot. There was a Teuton rider coming up on them, his sword-arm poised. They could have kept him at bay with their spears, but it was difficult to tell whether they'd even noticed him.

She willed burning light into her palm and hurled it. Death was more or less instantaneous, and of the three men who fell to the cobbles, only two got up.

"Stay with us," she said, and the bloodied, battered soldiers fell in beside Büber, grateful they didn't have to think any more.

The town square: the opening to it was narrow, as Büber had seen, and blocked with laden wagons parked across it. Some of the barbarians' camp followers were at the barricades, women mostly, some boys not old enough to fight, some girls.

Behind them, the residents of Obernberg. Nailed to the timber-framed walls at a variety of angles, suspended by their necks from windows with their own bedsheets, impaled, butchered, every last one of them.

Nikoleta stopped, and Büber, and the two Carinthians, and simply stared.

What separated masters from adepts was a final surrender of

pity. If a sorcerer could not put to death that part of them which made them feel sorry for their victims, then they were forever condemned to inhabit the lower orders. Great feats of magic, yes: true mastery of the art, never.

Looking up at the walls of Obernberg and seeing its inhabitants strewn across them in a grotesque display of inhumanity was enough to kill off any remaining shred of sympathy within Nikoleta Agana.

She marked stepping across the divide by shrugging off her heavy leather coat onto the wetly shining stones and throwing her hat to one side. Standing their, the rain beating down on her head, soaking the simple shift that she wore, she had never felt so powerful, so at peace, so certain as to what she should do.

The ground trembled in anticipation.

The women on the wagons, beforehand all catcalls and ululations, were suddenly silent.

Nikoleta's tattoos shifted in new, unknown ways as she walked towards them and raised her hands.

20

In the end, Büber had to look away.

He'd passed from shock to rage, and then to calling for bloody vengeance for what they'd done to Nadel, nailed upside down and guts hanging out in a long, grey ribbon down the wall. Then it had gone beyond even that. There was an awful beauty about her and the way she went about the destruction of the Teutons. Inventive even, and he watched with a kind of horrid fascination as to quite how she would divide and slaughter.

When she had turned the square into a charnel house, and there were still the children to go; that was when he turned his back. His voice was ruined, his throat raw. Not from the smoke, but from the screaming.

The two infantrymen were huddled together, unselfconsciously crouching on the ground and holding each other. They were men, he and they, and yet they were all weeping like widows.

Büber bent down, dragged them both to their feet, and shoved them in the direction of the field of battle. They'd dropped their spears and shields in order to cover their heads better, and though he'd retrieved their weapons, he'd wondered if he should hand them back, or keep them well away.

He'd decided finally on the latter. They couldn't kill themselves with them, even though they could swear a pact and kill each other. After what they'd witnessed, it would have been a mercy.

The burning building at the corner of the town swept dismal smoke across his view of what was beyond. Only when he pushed through could he see that they had actually won.

What was left of the Carinthian horse had captured what was left of the Teutons. The spearmen he'd helped to rescue made their number fourteen in all. A drift of corpses lay across the road, twisted and soaked. The trampled soil oozed red. All across the muddy field, there were knots of bodies, dying where they'd fought.

There was no sign of Allegretti or the boy Felix. And no sign of Gerhard in that fancy enchanted armour of his.

He remembered that he'd last seen him charging the Teuton line, off to his right, and recalled roughly where the prince's horse had sunk to its knees. He threw the spears to the ground and went to search for the prince.

It was easy to find him, once he'd given it some thought. He just had to look for the largest pile of bodies, and in the centre there was the still-bright armour and the Sword of Carinthia.

They must have stuck him a dozen times through the joints where the plate gave way to broken-linked mail. He'd lost his helmet at some point, and still he'd gone down with his teeth clenched and his eyes open.

Büber waded into the circle, kicking away hacked limbs and ruined flesh until he could reach out and take the hilt of Gerhard's sword. The prince was still holding on to it, and the huntsman had to pull hard to free it.

His skin, his face. So pale, it shone. The flecks of blood only made it whiter. Büber edged closer and pressed his fingertips on first one eyelid, then the other, dragging them down, closing them to the world. He left pink smears behind.

"My lord," he said, and started to clamber back, up the bodies of the fallen Teutons and back down the other side. It was slippery.

He walked across to where the Carinthians had gathered.

"Master Büber," said Reinhardt. He looked exhausted. They all did. And Reinhardt had lost almost the entire castle guard.

"I . . ." He held out the sword. It was instantly recognisable, and the meaning of his holding it was instantly understood. "Has anyone seen Master Allegretti or Felix?"

They'd all known that Gerhard had died. Not wanting to believe it before, they had no way of denying the fact now.

"It was chaos, man. We barely rallied in time."

Büber understood. They'd been fighting for their lives, and a moment's distraction, like looking for a kid who had no right to be on the battlefield, would have been one dangerous distraction too many.

They'd done what had needed to be done. They'd persevered with the impossible task of hacking away at Teuton after Teuton until their sword-arms grew as tight as bowstrings and as heavy as lead, only realising there were no more enemies left when there was no one left to attack them.

Eight horsemen. Four infantry. Himself, and . . .

He turned and Nikoleta strode out through the smoke. It trailed after her like it loved her. Her hair, rain-slick and pushed back away from her face made her look even younger. Her face was radiant, serene.

Büber shivered uncontrollably. Her shift was plastered to her body, holding to every lean curve, her breasts, her waist, her hips, her thighs. She looked like a goddess, Freyja herself. Behind her, Obernberg blazed wildly, the flames leaping above the level of the rooftops, and sooty smoke hissed in the wind and the rain.

"The Teuton shaman," she asked. "Is he here?"

None of the Teutons would own up to being him, and none of the Carinthians knew enough to tell him from any other unkempt barbarian. Disarmed, unarmoured, kneeling in the mud, their hands on their heads, they looked wretched. Six of them, five men, one a woman disguised as a man: a deception that had so very nearly seen them overwhelmed and destroyed.

"I don't know. Some of them might have got away," replied Büber. The prisoners, if they hadn't lost control of their bowels already, did so now at the sight of her and the flowing ink on her arms.

"Then we will have to find out." She stopped next to Büber and inspected the prisoners one by one. "No. None of them. I hope he's not dead already. You, man," and she pointed, "stand up."

Even if he didn't understand her words, her gestures made it plain. He got to his feet, although his legs could barely support him. He barely breathed, and looked solidly at the ground, as if even catching her eye for a moment might lead to his death.

Not that they could expect a long life, not after what they'd done. Carinthia was civilised, but there was still the press if Nikoleta didn't turn him into a candle.

"Your shaman," she said slowly, emphasising every syllable.

The Teuton shook his head, all the time staring at his feet. He said something that could have been "no", or "not here", but it was difficult to tell.

She walked right up to the man and levered his chin up with her fingers. He resisted, briefly, but she was strong and he was terrified. He wouldn't meet her gaze.

"Where is he?"

He shook his head again – short, sharp movements, frantic and servile.

"Don't you know?" She tutted. "Then I've no use for you."

She let go of his chin only to press her palm against his forehead. Contact was only for a moment: it looked like she was gently pushing him away. It shouldn't have sent him crashing backwards into the churned mud, but it did.

Smoke was coming from his all-white eyes, and hot blood was bubbling from his ears. He didn't move again.

"Who's next?" she said simply.

Büber blurted out, "Stop", before he knew he was doing it.

Everyone, Carinthian and Teuton looked at him. Especially Nikoleta.

"Don't you want to find the enemy sorcerer?" she asked. "To see if he can do anything?"

"Yes, but not this way." It sounded feeble. What did it matter if the Teutons died like this, rather than some other, more painful and public way? He couldn't understand why he was protesting. Certainly not out of mercy.

Perhaps he'd just had enough for one day. Everything hurt, and he simply wanted it to be over.

"It's not for us to decide," he said. He held up the Sword of Carinthia in both hands by way of explanation.

It took her a moment, but eventually she realised. "Oh," she said. "He's dead, then. Where's the boy?"

"We don't know. He and Allegretti have vanished."

"He was supposed to keep Felix safe. It'd be a shame . . ." Her voice trailed away, and she closed her eyes for a moment. Then she span on her heel and pointed. "There."

At the furthest edge of the field, beyond which the boundary wall marked out the road, two figures appeared. They were both leading horses, and it was apparent that one pair was smaller than the other.

"Is that—"

"Yes," she interrupted. "How well do you know Felix?"

"Not very. Why?"

"I wonder how he's going to react to being told he's now the Prince of Carinthia." She furrowed her brow. "That is how it works, isn't it? Father to eldest son?"

Büber looked down at the sword in his hands. He noticed that it had lost its shine. It was supposed to glow, but the finely ground edges were as lifeless as its previous owner. He wondered if the armour had gone the same way, its enchantment fading as the battle wore on until it had turned from an impregnable fortress into little more than cheap, thin tin.

"It's gone. Look." He held it out to her to inspect, and she took it from him. She didn't hold it right, finding both its weight and its balance foreign.

"Is it still a good sword?" she asked.

"It's a fine sword." He took it back, glad of having distracted her from killing the prisoners by turning the contents of their skulls to fine ash.

"Then we should give it to Felix rather than throw it away."

"My lady," said Reinhardt, "that's the Sword of Carinthia. It's the symbol of our sovereign, of our land."

"Why don't we ask Gerhard how much that symbol was worth?" She smiled at him, and the captain visibly winced. "We can't, because he's dead. Gentlemen, if symbols are all we have, we're lost."

"Symbol or not, it belongs to the prince of the palatinate." Reinhardt turned away. "Let him decide."

So they waited. The rain continued to fall, and from the colour and height of the sky, it would carry on for the rest of the day, mourning for poor, lost Carinthia and her orphaned prince.

Allegretti's Italianate armour gave him the air of a Roman cavalry officer. His helmet lacked the plume, but that was all. He'd collected a few more dents that would need hammering out, and his right-hand sword had gained a notch halfway to the hilt that was going to be a bastard to grind out.

Felix was plastered in mud. His eyes were two white holes in a brown smear. He no longer carried a sword, and his right arm was tied across his body in a makeshift sling. Büber couldn't tell whether the boy behind the filth was Felix or not. It wasn't just his appearance that had changed, but his whole demeanour.

The enthusiasm had gone, literally beaten out of him. What was left was a sombre, serious child who might never find it easy to smile again.

They stopped, teacher and pupil, at the edge of the ring of Carinthians.

Felix scraped at his mouth with his left hand. "Huntmaster," he said, "give me my father's sword."

Büber staggered forward and lifted the hilt of the sword up to him. Felix took it, and held it in front of his face, tracing the patterns in the steel. Then he lowered it by his side. His gaze was unflinching as it tracked across the prisoners. "Why are they still alive when my father is dead?"

The earl who'd taken the prisoners pursed his lips. "My lord, I . . ."

"Kill them. Now."

No one moved. Not the five remaining Teutons, not the surrounding Carinthians.

Allegretti glanced at Felix, then at the earl. "The prince of the palatinate of Carinthia has commanded you. Kill the Teutons."

Still no one moved. A horse shook its mane and its tack jingled.

Nikoleta started towards the prisoners, and Büber couldn't let that happen to them.

"No. Wait." He looked for his own sword, but he'd lost it at some point. He still had his knife, though; a knife he always kept more than sharp enough to dispatch and skin his dinner. He pulled it from his belt, and muttered, "I'll do it."

They were all shorter and lighter than he was, but if they resisted, he had no idea what he'd do. Probably batter them senseless, then do what he was going to do anyway.

He went behind the first man, held him by his collar and put one foot on the backs of his legs. He pulled back the prisoner's head and pressed the knife-blade in like he'd done a thousand times before, into the sides of the neck, left and right, where the blood ran thick and fast in fat tubes. His hand came away coated in warmth.

He let him go, and moved onto the next one. Then the next. Then the next. The last man was crying, but that didn't stop Büber.

Quite why he'd left the woman until the end was a mystery. Maybe he thought Felix would change his mind and commute the sentence. Even let her go.

It became clear that wasn't going to happen. He reached out for her, but she turned and faced him. She spat full in his face, and deliberately stood in front of him, neck arched, eyes fixed on Büber.

He wasn't going to execute her like that. He started to step around her. She grabbed his wrist, and such was the speed and surprise of her move that she had plunged the knife into her own chest before Büber could jerk away and break her grip.

Her grip lessened. He pulled the knife free. She stared at him while she died, first one lung, then the other, filling with blood. A little welled from her mouth and she folded backwards on herself, her eyelids flickering and closing.

All done, and in silence.

Büber stepped back, dazed, his knife slipping from his fingers to stick in the mud of Obernberg.

"Huntmaster."

He looked up at Felix.

"My lord," he finally managed.

"Find the master and mistress horses," ordered Felix. Some grit had found its way into his startlingly pink mouth, and he spat it out. "Get my father, and we can go home." With adult irony, he raised his voice. "Carinthia rides."

PART 2

Ragnarok

21

When the lights failed, the library was plunged into a profound, almost sacred darkness. Thaler, sitting at his desk, surrounded by books and scrolls, had just dipped his pen and was scratching out some notes when he noticed the letters he was writing were becoming indistinguishable from the parchment.

He looked up to see the globes hanging from the ceiling fade like dying suns. Then it was night.

He didn't move.

The lights – the perpetual lights that had illuminated his work for the whole of his life – had just gone out. He felt a cold rush in his stomach and his pulse surge. He was still holding his pen, in a grip tighter than death. He forced his fingers apart and let it clatter.

It was perfectly black. He could see nothing.

But he could still hear. Frozen in his seat, Thaler heard the first desk overturn, the first chair being knocked aside, the first bookcase tip in a drawn-out tumble of books and the final punctuating crash of shelves. Fleet footsteps came towards him, then away, and with an unmistakable creak and cry, whoever it was pitched over the railings and into the void below. A thin, reedy scream was abruptly blotted out.

The lights have gone out, he thought. He couldn't even see himself blink. What do I do?

He could try and get out. There was more than one door, and if he kept a lid on his fear like he did a lid on his mug of beer, he could find his way to any of them by fingertip. They all could. Everyone who worked there knew the library as if it were a lover's skin. If they didn't panic, but it was already too late for that.

He stayed still. Someone made it to the front doors of the pantheon and eventually hauled them open. Weak light from the pig-awful day outside staggered in as far as the entrance hall, but no further. It wasn't enough to navigate by, but at least he could make out the space of the reading room and where the balcony ended.

He sat in his chair for what seemed like forever. When he finally shifted, it was mostly quiet; the occasional thump of a book, the creak of furniture. Someone was still moving down there, slowly picking their way towards the door.

He should really leave, collect outside with the others and . . . what? Stand in stunned silence, staring up at the stone walls of the library, and try and work out what to do next?

What to do next was straightforward enough: get a hexmaster with the appropriate spell, and relight the globes. It wasn't as if many had travelled north with Gerhard to see off the Teutons – only one had been deemed necessary, such was their power. He was sure that someone, one of the other under-librarians perhaps, had already dispatched a message to Goat Mountain to come quickly.

He frowned in the darkness, and carefully pushed his chair back. He felt the corners of his desk, and ran his fingers along one side, then another, until he'd shuffled himself to the other side of it and was facing the void.

What he was seeing was confusing him. Grey shapes and patterns imprinted themselves against the gloom, a visible glamour that would lead to him having a really stupid but entirely avoidable accident. So he closed his eyes and counted out the footsteps to the railings.

When he reached out, they were there, smooth and solid. But what if, he wondered, some of the hand-rails had been broken in the chaos he had so studiously avoided being part of.

Best go carefully then. Rather than turning left to start towards the stairs, he turned right, deeper into the maze of ladders and shelves. His progress was tentative, but he found his navigation more than sufficient. Here was the steep ladder up, here the rail that curved tightly around the short-circumferenced gallery.

He walked slowly, making sure of each footfall before taking it, and when he'd measured out enough steps to put him opposite and above his own desk, he stopped.

"Master librarian? Are you there?"

He listened, and was rewarded by the soft whisper of cloth. A divan creaked, and a throat coughed drily. "Who? Who's there?"

"Under-librarian Thaler, Master. I've come to help you outside."

"What's that?"

Thaler spoke louder and clearer. "Thaler, Master."

"I appear to have been struck blind, Under-librarian. Old age, eh? Bit of a bastard."

"You're not blind, Master. The lights have gone out."

"What? I'm not blind?"

"No, Master. You're not blind. Or I'm as blind as you are." Thaler took three paces towards the voice, and listened again.

"You're blind too? And you so young. A tragedy."

Thaler could hear the thin, reedy whistle of the librarian's breathing now, and he dropped to his knees and shuffled the remaining distance. "Hold out your hand, Master."

"Shouldn't we wait for someone who can see, Under-librarian?"

"It's the lights, Master. The library lights have failed. Once we get to the porch, you'll see what I mean." He moved his own hands through the air in front of him until he knocked against the sleeve of the master librarian's robe. He felt along it until he found cool, dry skin.

"Is that you, Under-librarian?"

"Yes, Master. I'll put your hand on my shoulder, and we can go."

He placed the master librarian's hand accordingly, and put his own on it. It was awkward, but it would have to do.

"Did you say the lights have gone out?"

"Yes, Master Librarian. Can you stand when I say?" Thaler got his feet under his body. "Now."

He ended up mostly dragging the man off his bed. He was shrunken and thin, whereas Thaler was big and more than just a little fat. The master was a weight that the under-librarian was used to, no more than a decent-sized folio.

"Did you say the lights have gone out?"

"Yes, Master. The lights have gone out all over the library. Not one is left."

"How extraordinary. That's never happened before, you know."

"Yes, Master. I know both that it's extraordinary, and that it's never happened before. There seems to be a lot of that about." He kept the bony hand pinned to his shoulder, and started to retrace his steps.

If reaching the master librarian's eyrie had taken time, getting back down again seemed to take several lifetimes. At least, Thaler felt he'd aged that much by the time they'd made it down to the ground floor.

They'd stopped for a rest so many times, he'd lost count, and the master librarian would ramble on so, often about exactly the same subject they'd just finished discussing and which, as far as Thaler was concerned, had been settled to the satisfaction of all.

"Where are the lights, Under-librarian?"

Inwardly, he groaned: his temper, already stretched to breaking point, was plucked taut. Outwardly, he barely did better.

"The lights," he said, "have gone. Out."

"Have they? How . . .?"

"Extraordinary? Yes. Very extraordinary."

"It's never . . ."

"Happened before. I know." Thaler decided that his humouring the old man had gone beyond what duty required. He could either leave him there, or tell him to shut up. "Master? Silence in the library."

"What? Oh. Of course, Under-librarian." And it was as if the gods themselves had intervened, for the endless flow of words simply dried up.

Why hadn't he thought of that three floors above?

He should, by now, be able to see the light spilling in from the porch. That he couldn't, worried him. Perhaps he had been struck blind after all. But that couldn't be right: the lights, as the master librarian had so perceptively and repeatedly noticed, had indeed gone out.

The doors had been closed again. Those outside had decided the building was empty and had attempted to secure the library against thieves. Yes, but anyone who had bothered looking would have realised that both he and the master librarian were missing. They'd closed the doors anyway.

Cowards.

There was nothing else to do but feel his way to the main entrance. "Master librarian? Hold tight. There'll be debris on the floor. Look, why don't I just carry you?"

It was the obvious solution, and again, if he could find his own arse in the dark, he'd kick it long and hard for being an idiot.

"Think, Thaler, think!"

"What was that, Under-librarian?"

"It doesn't matter. Now, put your other hand on my other shoulder. That's right. Keep still." He crouched down and backed up, reaching behind him and seizing the master librarian's spindly legs.

When was the last time he'd done this? He'd have been a child, playing with his friends in the streets and squares of Juvavum.

"Hold tight." Thaler straightened up and, in the event, hardly noticed the extra weight.

"Oh my," came the voice in his ear.

"Hush, Master Librarian. Silence in the library."

He set off, treading carefully, scuffing his feet to knock the fallen books, chairs and desks out of his way. The furniture could look after itself: the thought of kicking valuable manuscripts across the floor pained him almost to the point of paralysis. He got a grip on his wits, and continued the painstaking journey.

He knew that if he kept the wall to his left, he would eventually find the entrance. He found the main desk first: at least, that was what it felt like. Solid, immovable, and long. He crept along one side, then back down the other to the wall.

And there: light. Two thin rectangles that marked the library doors.

"Can you see now, Master Librarian?"

"My eyes! They're working again."

"Yes, Master Librarian. Yes, they are." Even that mean light hurt after the utter darkness, but he hurried towards it.

Thaler couldn't open the huge latch with his teeth: he'd be foolish to try, and he'd had enough of foolishness for one day. He lowered his burden gently to the floor, gripped the catch with both hands and heaved. The latch moved up against its stop with a bang and he heaved the heavy door back.

He was blind again, dazzled by the brightness, and he covered his face with his fingers.

"Mr Thaler!"

Wiping at his watering eyes, Thaler found himself surrounded by a semi-circle of ushers, and, at its midpoint, Glockner.

"Ah, Mr Glockner. Surprised to see me?"

Glockner lowered the switch he was wielding and glowered at Thaler.

"I thought . . ."

"Clearly your first mistake, Mr Glockner. I have rescued the master librarian, and would very much like some help carrying him outside." Thaler put his shoulder to the second door and pushed it back. Damp light poured inside, illuminating an area past where the main desk used to be and into the reading room proper.

The master librarian lay propped up against the wall, and the shaft of daylight showed two bodies stretched out against the opposite side of the entrance.

Thaler looked at Glockner with undisguised disdain. "The ushers are present, and are indeed paid, to keep order within the library. As head usher, you are responsible for their conduct and moreover, your own. Are those men dead?"

"I don't know, Mr Thaler."

"Then perhaps," roared Thaler, suddenly furious and seeking a target for his pent-up fear, "you had better all go and find out rather than cowering disgracefully behind each other. Order, Mr Glockner. Not chaos."

As Glockner and a couple of the other ushers recovered enough to dart forward, Thaler suddenly realised that he was momentarily in charge. Not just of the situation, but of the whole library.

He felt himself tremble. "Where are the other under-librarians? Where are Grozer and Thomm?"

None of the ushers responded, and Thaler looked beyond them and out into the square for the first time.

It was a melee, almost a mob. If it hadn't been for the rain dampening the impotent rage, there would have been a riot. Shouting, arguing, scuffling even: the good burghers of Juvavum were out on the streets and looking for someone to blame.

It wasn't just the library lights that had gone out. It was all the lights. And the fountain across the square. And the cart abandoned on its back near the entrance to Wien Alley.

The seriousness of it all hit Thaler like a hammer. He wanted to run out into the square and demand to know the meaning of this, just like everyone else. But in the absence of the other under-librarians, and given the incapacity of the master librarian, he was the senior officer. Not just for today, but for the next day too. And beyond.

He took a deep breath. He felt weak. He put his hand out and leant against one of the pillars that supported the portico. It was cold and slightly rough. More than that, though: it felt old. If the library was going to see tomorrow, then it was going to need some help.

Starting with some leadership from Thaler.

"You, what's your name?"

"Ullmann, Mr Thaler." The man was young and biddable, and less under Glockner's thumb for being so.

"Take two of your colleagues, and go to the Jews' Alley – you know where that is? – and knock on the second door on the left. An elderly Jew called Aaron Morgenstern will answer, and I want you to say this to him: 'Mr Thaler needs lanterns.'"

Ullmann frowned. "Is that it?"

"Yes, for now. When you have as many lanterns as you can carry – and make sure they are lanterns, not candlesticks – come straight back here. Go; hurry." Thaler shooed Ullmann away and turned to the next usher. "Who are you?"

"Reindl, Under-librarian."

"What I want you to do, Mr Reindl, is to find me a stretcher, or something we can use as a stretcher, to get the master librarian away safely and back to his rooms. Very important job, so take one other and go. Come back quickly."

He did a head-count of how many ushers he had left. Six. Not enough, but he needed to deplete their numbers further.

"You, you and you," he pointed. "Go back to the apprentices' dorm and the librarians' rooms. Get everyone you can and make them come here."

"Make them, Mr Thaler?" asked one.

"Yes, by the gods, make them. Beg them, cajole them, remind them of their duty, and, if all else fails, tell them that if they don't come, I'll have them thrown out on the street penniless and naked. We need every able-bodied man now."

They darted off in the direction of the library's dormitories, and Thaler gathered the remaining ushers about him. "Gentlemen? We have to defend the library at all costs. Reinforcements are coming, but for now, we're it. If anyone looks like they want to do the building harm, or to sneak in and grab a book or two for themselves, we repel them. Understand? Throw your switches away, and arm yourselves with broken furniture. Beat any transgressor as though they are barbarians. We're all that stands between the mob and sweet reason, so let's acquit ourselves well."

Thaler straightened up and stood squarely in the entrance.

"There will be order," he said, facing outwards and folding his arms, "in my library."

22

I am twelve years old, thought Felix. Twelve years old and an orphan. Twelve years old, an orphan and a prince.

He was a lot of other things besides, but at that moment, those three defined him. He was only just becoming aware of how little he knew: not just about the palatinate he was to rule, but about life as a whole. Today hadn't taught him much. He'd already known how to defend himself from the hairy, stinking barbarian horsemen who'd borne down on him, although he'd never quite grasped just how much it would hurt to parry their furious blows.

He did now, and he'd broken his collar-bone in the process. Signore Allegretti had laboured hard to save him, but even he could kill only one man at a time. So he knew something new about physical pain, and about how to act through it and despite it, when circumstances were desperate enough.

Then there was the other kind of pain, the sort that cut from the inside out. It had never seemed particularly important to him that his mother had died in childbirth, that his first breath had come as her last had gone in the same moment. It was a fact he'd grown used to, and there had been nurses and playmates and tutors for company; if his mother had lived, he'd have seen little of her and even less of his father. As it was, Gerhard had become more involved in his son's upbringing than would have otherwise been the case.

That part of his life was over. The body of Prince Gerhard V was laid across the horse behind him, wrapped and bound in several torn and blood-stained cloaks they'd found on the battlefield. He was now Prince Felix I of Carinthia, he was an orphan, and he was twelve years old.

He couldn't run a country. The idea was ludicrous. But he remembered one time he'd been shown into a jeweller's workshop over a baker's in the makers' market. He'd been younger by a few years – it was certainly before the signore arrived – and his tutor at the time had sat him down so that the nimble-fingered jeweller could explain how he crafted ingots of metal and rough-looking pebbles of crystal into engraved rings and filigree-thin necklaces set with stones that flashed in the light.

Of course, the object of the lesson, the one he'd missed entirely until now, was to teach him, not how to make jewellery, but that his father had craftsmen of high renown in his realm, and that this was how taxable wealth was created: it was a prince's duty to make it possible for such people to live and work and trade; do that, and they'd make him rich.

It was his duty now. He needed to fit his role, so that others could fit theirs. The clothes would be too big for a while, like the armour he wore, but he'd have to grow into them, and quickly.

"Signore?"

"My lord."

Already, their relationship had changed. Allegretti acted towards him in the same way he had towards his father, and the switch had been instantaneous on his realising that the game of succession had been played out. The Italian had even removed his helmet and knelt in the mud before him, something he'd never done before. Felix had moved from snot-nosed princeling bent over his tutor's knee one moment, to the master of all he surveyed with the power of life and death on the tip of his tongue the next.

"You will stay with me, won't you?"

"If you believe I can be of benefit to you, my lord, I will stay for a while."

They rode side by side down the potholed road, heading back towards the bridge at Simbach. The wagons, and most of their equipment, were back where Obernberg had been. The wheels had all stopped turning, and though the explanations offered by Allegretti and Mistress Agana as to why this had happened seemed inadequate and incomplete, it hadn't been possible to start them again.

If the magic had failed, why could the witch still cast her spells?

Apparently, she didn't know. She had pledged her allegiance to him, however, and promised to protect him. For some reason, her words brought tears pricking to his eyes in a way that seeing his father's corpse rudely laid out on scavenged cloth had not.

"A while? I want you to stay . . ."

"Forever, my lord? Forgive me, but I am good for teaching blows and blocks. You have already learnt those, and well, may I

155

add. A lesser man would have fallen." Allegretti nodded to himself. "But not you."

"You still have something to teach me, surely."

"A sword-master is for young earls, not for princes. You must learn other lessons now."

"But I trust you, signore." Felix changed his tack. "What if I commanded you to stay?"

The Italian shrugged. "Then I would be your prisoner for as long as you could hold me."

"And if I begged you to stay? For me?" He felt his lip tremble, which wasn't very princely. He looked away until he thought he had it under control.

"Then I will stay for as long as you need me, my lord."

Relief was like a warm bath. "Thank you."

"My lord, if I can lay one condition down?"

"Yes, of course. What is it?"

"That you use me," said Allegretti. "I would not want to be that old relic you keep around the castle, to be remembered once in a while, dusted off and aired, then put back in the cupboard where you found me. If you take me into your confidence, I will repay your trust."

"I don't know anything about what I'm supposed to do, signore. How do I get people to do what I want them to do? How do I make decisions? How do I even know what needs doing?" The task had come to him too soon, he knew that, and he felt frozen.

"All in good time, my lord," said Allegretti. "You will have me, and you will, in time, gather others around your royal person who will help you rule. A prince needs a court of loyal advisers who owe no man fealty but only to the throne."

"Like the mistress?" Felix twisted around in his saddle to look at her. She was on a Teuton horse. She looked different, sounded different when she spoke: less deferential, and more authoritative. She was back in her white robes, even if she had covered them with a waxed cape. She caught him looking, though she had been riding with her head down the moment before, deep in thought.

She was a hexmaster. Why shouldn't she know when someone was looking at her? She held his gaze for as long as he could take its intensity, then deliberately turned her head just before he did.

She was riding alone. The huntmaster, who up until the battle had seemed to be content with her company, was towards the back of the bedraggled line, guarding his father's body, which he could see bouncing with every laboured step of the horse that was bearing it. Felix didn't want to see that, so he turned back.

Allegretti pursed his lips. "My lord, if I may be so bold: you cannot trust Mistress Agana. Cannot."

"But she said . . ." and he wanted to turn around and look at her again, just to check she was still there.

"My lord, people lie. Even to themselves. But, eventually, the truth works its way towards the light, like a seed, where it will grow to full fruit." The Italian steered his horse closer to Felix's. "She will betray you, though she does not know that yet. She will seize your throne one day, and crown herself in your place."

Felix's instinctive reaction was to blurt: "That's just silly, signore. Girls can't become princes."

"Some barbarians have queens to rule them, my lord. It is not completely unknown." Allegretti sniffed. "Could you stop her? Could your army overcome her?"

"I don't have an army, signore. You know that."

"Then, until you do, she is a threat to you and to all Carinthia. You begged me to stay: I beg you to listen. If she is the only hexmaster left, there is no force in this or any other land that can oppose her. She could, if she wished, kill every last one of us and tell her own story to Juvavum. We are currently too weak to defend ourselves against her."

Felix felt his lip go again, and he used his good hand to clamp it tight against his face. He didn't trust himself to speak without his voice wavering.

Allegretti, on the other hand, spoke with the utmost conviction. "Your first priority, after your coronation, needs to be consolidating your power. She represents another flag around which the earls might rally. Civil war is . . . ugly, my lord."

"She said she would serve me," said Felix. His words squeaked out.

"But you cannot control her. She cannot control herself: one look at Master Büber's face tells you all you need to know."

And yes, his father's huntmaster now had eyes that had seen too much. That, and the complete destruction of Obernberg, gave credence to the sword-master's warning.

"At the very least, even if you will not dispose of her soon, you must devise a way by which you could dispose of her should the necessity arise. In the short term, she will be useful, I have no doubt, but the more you use her, the more powerful she will become."

Felix's stomach churned. After everything he'd witnessed, everything he'd done, he was now discussing killing someone in cold blood – at least, that was what he thought the signore was talking about. "I don't want to think about this now."

Allegretti immediately held up his hands. "Very well. Perhaps it is too soon to have such a conversation." He nudged his horse away from Felix's side, and they rode on in awkward silence for a while.

It kept raining, and Felix's shoulder ached in a way he'd never experienced before. Despite the strapping, despite his intention to keep the joint absolutely still, there was nothing he could do to immobilise it completely while still riding. Soon enough, it was all he could think about: it became the centre of his world and he began to sob.

Pain had always been a brief and transitory thing, sharp and hard to bear, but he'd always known that a healer, gruff and rough from the interruption to their studies, would be along soon and would simply take the pain away with a wave of their hands.

This? This was different: it was eternal and all-consuming.

Wordlessly, Allegretti passed Felix a small silver flask. Its top was already off and hanging from the neck of the flask by a short chain. Felix lifted the flask to his nose and took a cautious sniff.

He recoiled from the sharp, stinging fumes with a gasp of disgust. Allegretti looked heavenwards and shook his head in mock despair, and Felix decided that he would have to drink: this was schnapps, and it was what Carinthian men drank. He was, by any standard, a man. He might be only twelve years old and an orphan, but he was a prince. He was a prince first and foremost, whatever else he might be.

So he raised the open flask to his lips and dribbled some of the liquor into his mouth. It burnt so much; it tasted only of fire. His tongue felt flayed and his cheeks went so red that he thought they might burst into flame.

He swallowed. There wasn't much of the liquid left in his mouth by that time, but what there was scorched his throat and boiled in his stomach. His whole body shook involuntarily, but his collarbone didn't seem so important any more.

It took him a few moments to start breathing again. Did men really do this for pleasure? Apparently so. They even carried it around with them in specially made containers for occasions such as these. The sweet berry cordials he was used to belonged to another life: now, he supposed, it would be a diet of beer and wine and schnapps.

He handed the flask back, not trusting himself to be able to use his seared voice.

This time, Allegretti nodded approvingly. "My lord needs to give thought to where we will shelter for the night. The men are exhausted, the horses more so. While we need to return to Juvavum as soon as possible, arriving tired tomorrow afternoon will be better than arriving useless tomorrow morning."

"What . . ." Felix cleared his throat. "What do you think?"

"We are coming up on the Simbach bridge. It is your right to claim hospitality at the farms there, and they should be able to accommodate us easily. We are few: both horses and men."

"And the mistress," added Felix.

"As you say, and the mistress." Allegretti gave a weak smile. "Someone should ride ahead to prepare them for your arrival."

"Will you do it?"

"I could, but I have sworn to stay by your side and protect you for as long as you need me. One of the earls, perhaps, or Master Büber."

"Not the huntmaster," said Felix; "he's done enough." He'd butchered the Teuton prisoners on his orders, plunging his knife deep into their necks and bathing his hands in warm, slippery blood. It had been necessary – the signore had said so – to start his reign mercilessly. He wondered what it would take to make such a man as Büber angry, and wondered how unwise it would be to ever try. "Is Master Büber someone to trust? He seems a good man."

"A good man, perhaps. Huntsmen are simple and lack sophistication: they obey orders well, but thinking for themselves? I have not found it so."

"Oh." Felix was disappointed. So far, his court seemed to consist of just one man. "Then one of the earls, but I don't want to make a fuss, signore."

"Nonsense. You are the Prince of Carinthia. Whatever comfort a farmer enjoys will be yours whether or not he can spare it. It is yours by right and custom." Allegretti allowed a note of annoyance to seep into his words. "These are your people, my lord. It is your duty to rule them, and their duty to serve. It is as simple as that: whether or not you believe it to be true, you must act as if you do."

"I'll try," said Felix, chastened.

"You will make a good prince, my lord," said Allegretti. "Just listen to me, and everything will fall into place."

<h1 style="text-align:center">23</h1>

Their show of strength was enough. By mid-afternoon, the crowd in Library Square had mostly dispersed, the upsetting novelty of the day subsiding into grumbling complaint. That the rain had continued all day had clearly contributed to the muted reaction to the lights going out, but Thaler was still worried.

The militia were nowhere to be seen, and it was a matter of pride that the library staff were better organised than the mayor's men. The building was secured, the spilt books were stacked in piles ready for reshelving, and the bodies of those trampled in the most unseemly rush were removed.

The wounded – a few breaks and sprains, one crushed and breathless – had been taken to the refectory and were being tended as best a gaggle of inky-fingered apprentices could manage.

Repeated requests for some healers to come from Goat Mountain stayed unanswered, unlike Thaler's call for lanterns, which had been honoured to the full. Aaron Morgenstern might be an ungodly Jew, but he'd roused his neighbours and shamed them into handing over everything they could spare.

From his new desk just inside the main doors, Thaler wondered if Morgenstern's quick response was a ploy to extricate those religious texts he was so concerned about from the library's clutches. Perhaps. On the other hand, he hadn't needed to lift a finger to help. He could have chased the apprentices away and cursed their retreating feet.

Thaler looked at the ledger he had open in front of him and

read the entry: from the Jews of Jews' Alley, seventy-four lanterns and sixteen full boxes of candles, a score in each.

Put it like that, attributing some ulterior motive to old Morgenstern looked more than a little churlish. And hadn't they earned some credit?

He turned his head to look into the library. Tiny sparks of light moved in the profound darkness, and echoing voices checked the furthest reaches of the shelves for anyone left within. They'd found one of the other under-librarians under a bookcase, and it wasn't looking good for him. The other had completely disappeared. No one could say whether or not he'd been in the building.

With the master librarian incoherent or rambling, or both, Thaler was the one the whole staff looked to. He discovered he found the experience both terrifying and exhilarating. As orderly transitions of authority went, it was more de facto than he'd like: he was supposed to be appointed and ratified and handed his credentials by the prince. There ought to be speeches and toasts. Not this muddle.

He sat, chin on his chest, bemoaning the lack of ceremony, when a shadow fell across him. He looked up to see Glockner.

"Yes, Mr Glockner?"

"Mr Thaler. The library appears to be clear. Shall I . . .?"

"Appears?" Thaler sat more upright. "We have pairs of men searching – systematically, mind – each and every section. When they have all reported back here, to me, then and only then will the library be considered clear."

"As you wish, Under-librarian."

"I do wish it, Mr Glockner. I wish it very much." Did he have the authority to demote the head usher? Or even to remove him completely? There were books he could consult later. "I would also very much wish for you not to undermine or countermand my explicit instructions at every opportunity."

Glockner licked his lips nervously. "I meant only to assist you in your duties, Mr Thaler."

"Yes. Your zeal has been noted, Mr Glockner. Do we have any of your ushers spare to carry a message?"

"I do not believe so, Mr Thaler." Glockner looked momentarily self-satisfied, and Thaler narrowed his eyes.

"In which case, Mr Glockner, you will have to take the message yourself." There, he thought, that's wiped the smile off your face. He opened a pot of ink and dipped his steel-nibbed pen to write.

By the grace of His Majesty Prince Gerhard V of Carinthia and by the authority of the Master Librarian, to His Honour the Mayor of Juvavum. Under-librarian Frederik Thaler is delighted to inform you that the Great Library of Carinthia is secured, and requests an official guard to be posted overnight at its doors.

He folded the paper over, and conspicuously placed the seal of the library in front of him while he melted some wax over the join. When sufficient had collected, he pressed the seal down and held it while the wax hardened.

Thaler held up the note, and Glockner reluctantly reached forward to take it. His fingers closed around it, but when he tried to pull it away, Thaler held on.

"Mr Glockner, put this in the hands of the mayor himself."

"I know."

"None other. And . . . " – Thaler let go, and Glockner stumbled back a step – "I expect a reply. A sealed reply. Promptly. Whatever he's been doing these past few hours, I neither know nor care about. I want this building properly guarded overnight by someone with the prince's authority to be armed with more than a chair-leg."

Glockner tried not to let his lip curl into a sneer, and, sensing his failure, he walked away with Thaler's message in his fist. Thaler watched him stare up at the sky and adjust his gown over his head before stepping outside the portico.

It was very hard not to feel uncharitable. Men had died because Glockner hadn't been able to keep control. He had to go. Whoever succeeded the master librarian – either him or Thomm, wherever he was hiding himself – would have some hard choices to make.

But there was more: the lights had gone out. That in itself was a catastrophe for the windowless library, let alone everyone who had been plunged into darkness. Metal-workers, embroiderers, engravers, jewellers: almost every specialised trade in Juvavum relied on the ever-lit globes to conduct their business. The streets were kept clear of thieves and whores by light alone.

Then there were the fountains. The one in Library Square had stopped spraying playful streams of water into the rippling pool beneath by the time he'd got out of the building. Was there any good reason to assume that this fountain alone was affected?

If not, the entire town's plumbing had simply ceased to function. Fresh drinking water by pipe was a luxury: having their night soil flushed into the downstream Salzach was a necessity. It left them all, quite literally, in the shit.

The chances of the magic lights and magic pumps failing at exactly the same time were long odds, and Thaler – who was partial to a game of dice between friends – knew how to work those odds out. No coincidence could account for it. They had to be linked.

"Fuck."

"Sorry, Under-librarian?"

One of the returning pairs of searchers had materialised in front of him while he'd been thinking, and Thaler just stared at them like they were ghosts, or trolls, or the ghosts of trolls.

"Under-librarian? Are you feeling all right?"

Thaler seemed to have lost the power of coherent speech. All that would come out was a series of noises, ending in "fuck" again.

"We . . . we didn't find anyone," said the librarian, and he looked at his colleague.

Thaler blinked like an owl. His heart was racing, and he'd gone both hot and cold at the same time. He could think of only one thing.

"The unicorns are all dead."

"Under-librarian? What do you mean?"

"The unicorns. They're dead. Of course they are. I should have known." He smacked his hands hard against the tabletop and made the inkwell jump. He looked up at the two men, by now convinced he was having some sort of fit. "What a fool I've been."

He reached out, took another sheet of parchment, and then, gripping his pen, began to write. When the librarians started to edge away, he fixed them with fever-bright eyes.

"Stay. No. Different instructions. Can either of you ride a horse?"

One of them tentatively raised his hand, as if he were back in the apprentices' school. "Sort of. It's been a while."

"Good man." Thaler stopped writing mid-sentence and took a third note from the roughly cut pile. "Take this to the prince's stables; come back here with a horse. The fastest that the stable-master has left."

He scribbled out a requisition order without the certainty it would be honoured, sealed it, and handed it over.

"Under-librarian, what are you going to ask me to do?"

"Right now? Run."

Something about his mood was catching. The librarian left at a faster clip than Glockner would ever have managed. To the one left, Thaler gave another task.

"Find Under-librarian Thomm. If he's incapacitated in any way, give him all due aid. But bring him here as soon as you can. It's important."

"Where should I start?"

Thaler didn't know. "Start with the beer cellars, move on to Gentleman's Alley. After that, I don't know. Use your imagination."

"Yes, Under-librarian."

When the man had gone, Thaler continued to write his first letter, scribbling away and dipping the pen nib as necessary. It was necessary often, and he realised that he was rambling now. He thought he'd better finish.

"Can the Order still act?" he wrote.

Have they already solved this problem, and are they wilfully denying the prince the benefit of the solution, or are they now powerless? Be careful, my friend, whichever it might be.

    Your faithful servant,
    Frederik Thaler
    Under-librarian.

He folded it, dripped wax on the join and pressed the seal to it. Now, if only Büber could read – it was a gaping hole in his plan, transmitting written information to an illiterate. Instead, he was going to trust a man he'd barely been aware of before today to deliver the most important message he'd ever sent.

None of anything that had happened since that first sign of darkness was what he'd expected to be doing, so why not this? Why not entrust his life, and possibly the life of his friend, to someone who merely shared a vocation with him? Thaler didn't want Büber, nor himself, to get on the wrong side of the Order. By all the accounts he'd read in the last day or two, being well connected wouldn't save either of them. And, unlike Büber, he wasn't directly a prince's man.

The hollow ring of hooves on stone made him sit up. The first of the two librarians he'd sent out was leading a horse along the front of the portico, and Thaler hurried out from behind the desk to meet him.

It was still raining; perhaps not as heavy as before, but still a piss-awful day to be out in.

"I'm sorry. But there is no one else," he said, before realising just how young the librarian actually was. Just out of apprenticeship, probably by only a year or two. "Was there any trouble?"

"I gave the stable-master your note, and he told me to take whatever I wanted." He smiled uncertainly at Thaler from under the hood of the waxed cloth cloak he'd borrowed. "Where am I going?"

"First: what's your name?"

"Librarian Braun," he said, then hesitated before adding, "Ernst Braun."

"Right. This is a little complicated, so I want you to listen carefully." Thaler held the letter out to Braun, who turned it over in his hands and saw that it was blank apart from the seal. "I need you to take that letter to the huntmaster, Peter Büber, and him alone. If it looks like you can't do that, destroy it at once. Without reading it."

"Without reading it. Of course." Braun nodded, and put the letter in one of the leather saddlebags. "A secret, then."

"When . . . no, if . . . oh, you know what I mean. The huntmaster can't read. So you're going to have to read the letter to him. Then give him the letter and try to forget everything you've just heard."

"Under-librarian, isn't that going to be, well, difficult?"

"Yes. But it's a piece of fiction that we'll all try very hard to maintain. Büber will know what to do after that. Come back here, and as far as it's in my power, which is very little, you'll be well rewarded for your trouble."

"And where will I find the huntmaster, Under-librarian?"

"Good question. He's riding with the prince, so it shouldn't be too difficult. Between here and Simbach on the via, firstly, and east after that. I know I'm asking a great deal, but if Büber gets it in time, this could be of critical importance to the palatinate."

Thaler spread his hands wide. There was nothing more he could say. Braun more or less competently got his foot in the stirrup and lifted himself onto the back of the horse.

"Good luck, Mr Braun," said Thaler.

Braun beamed down from the saddle. "This is the most exciting thing anyone has ever asked me to do. I won't let you down, Mr Thaler."

24

"A librarian?" Büber bent back over the bowl of now-lukewarm water and scrubbed at his arm. Everything was bloody: the water, the container, the block of hard yellow soap, the towel, even the stubby brush he was using to scrape his skin raw. Most of the blood wasn't his, but he was continually finding new cuts buried under the grime.

The carter – the ex-carter now, since steering a magically propelled wagon seemed to be a profession wanting a practice – stood just inside the door of the barn and wrung his hands nervously. "A librarian, Master Büber."

"And he doesn't want to talk to anyone else?"

"No, Master Büber. Just you."

Büber looked down at his nails, those that he had left, and they were black crescents. He'd have to use something else other than the brush to get that out. A quill would do or, ironically, a pen nib.

"Then you'd better send him in."

There was very little hay left in the barn, and only some straw. Which was only to be expected after the passage of winter, but it left few places for the men to sleep. It was also cold, and it was damp cold at that. There was a fire, but it was in the house, and he didn't feel like company. Not unreasonably, he'd decided that all men were bastards, himself included. Mean, petty, vicious bastards. And the women: one woman in particular had shown savagery beyond mortal comprehension.

He had the urge to run, barely restrained by his bone-deep weariness.

"Master Büber?" The voice was different, younger.

166

Büber glanced around to see a mere slip of a boy, shoulders wet with rain. The crude lantern he carried made the droplets shine. But then, the librarian's lantern was no cruder than the one he was washing by.

"Yes."

"Under-librarian Thaler sent me. He said it was important."

"Did he now?"

"Yes, huntmaster. He wrote you this letter." He produced it with a flourish.

Büber tried to dry his hands on the towel, but it was already wet and dirty, so he stopped and just let them drip on the beaten-earth floor. "Let me see."

The messenger brought the sealed letter over to him, and held up the outside of the parchment for him. It was blank.

"You know I can't . . .?"

"Yes, Master Büber. Mr Thaler explained all that to me: I'm to read it to you, in private." He hesitated. "You are alone?"

"Yes," said Büber. "I'm very alone. I'll keep washing other men's blood off. Bring your lantern close so I can see better."

The librarian did so, and sat on an upturned manger before he cracked the wax seal and unfolded the creased letter. He tilted the words to the meagre light and cleared his throat.

"To Huntmaster Peter Büber, from Under-librarian Frederik Thaler, by the grace and authority of His Highness Prince Gerhard V of Carinthia: greetings." The librarian stopped. "Oh."

"There's no reason for him to know. In fact, it might be an idea for you to ride back as fast as you can with messages for the White Fortress and the mayor. Have you got pen and ink?"

"Yes, Master Büber, and paper, in case you wanted to send a reply to Mister Thaler."

Büber stopped scrubbing for a moment and rested his hands in the bottom of the bowl. "What's your name?"

"Braun, sir."

"Read the letter, Mr Braun." Büber picked up the brush once more, and listened to Thaler's words, relayed through the voice of the librarian.

"I have urgent news from Juvavum. The lights have gone out in the library, causing some small confusion, but that is not the worst of it. It appears that all magical lights have ceased working across the city, along with all wagons, fountains and consequently the fresh and foul water systems. Extrapolating further, it is most likely that the barges have stopped – this is true, Master Büber: when I crossed the river, the quayside was in chaos, and a barge was stuck sideways across the supports of the main bridge."

If Büber had given it much thought, he would have expected all that. If the hexmasters' magic had gone, if the bridge at Simbach had all but vanished, their own wagons left idle, then why not everywhere else?

"I know this. At least, none of this is new. What else does he say?"

Braun retraced the words. "Then it occurred to me that there was a pattern. Your discoveries in the forests of Carinthia were directly related to today's events. The sudden reluctance of the hexmasters to appear before the prince, or ride with him to war, and other seemingly trivial incidents suddenly all made sense. It has become clear to me that the source of magic, whatever that might be, has been dissipating for some time, and that the Order of the White Robe must have been, at the very least, aware of the possibility that this day's events would transpire, even if the timing was in question. That neither you nor I were informed does not exclude the prince having foreknowledge of the event, but consideration of his actions regarding the Teutons leads me to believe that he is acting without full command of the facts."

"Not quite," said Büber. "But no reason to make allowances for the boneheadedness of those who lead us. Like all warnings, they come too late. Go on."

"You must, as a matter of urgency, apprise His Majesty of the situation, so that he can best decide his future course. Juvavum is quiet but tense for the moment, but the militia are more conspicuous by their absence, as are the Order themselves. There is no reason for lawlessness, but when did lawlessness need a reason?" Braun looked up. "There is a little more."

"Give me all of it."

"Can the Order still act? Have they already solved this problem, and are they wilfully denying the prince the benefit of the solution, or are they now powerless? Be careful, my friend, whichever it might be. Your faithful servant, Frederik Thaler, Under-librarian." Braun folded the letter shut. "That's it, though I can read any part of it again, if you'd like."

"No, no. That's clear enough." Büber wiped his hands on his

undershirt and slumped into a pile of hay. It smelt of warm summer sun and tiny fleeting flowers. He could close his eyes and fall asleep, right there, and hope they never found him in the morning when the time came to move on.

"I'm supposed to forget the contents now, and never mention them again."

"It's probably better that you do," said Büber lazily. "No good can come from remembering such things."

"What are you going to do, Master Büber?"

"There's probably enough there to get me pressed for treason, though I'll be in good company. The whole Order of the White Robe will be under the same slab as me, though if they want to include Thaler, they'll need a bigger rock." The hay was pricking him through his clothes. It was ticklish, and he rolled this way and that to push himself deeper.

"Do you really think . . .?" Braun opened the letter again and re-read the offending paragraphs. "I don't see what you've done wrong."

"I relied on the Order to tell the prince about something I found. I shouldn't have: I'm a prince's man and that's where I owe fealty. I served two masters, and I was wrong. I was scared of the hexmasters. And now look where we are, without a prince and almost entirely without magic." Tiredness washed over Büber in waves. "If I'd have known. But then again, who knew? Not us mundanes, that's for sure."

"There are only three people who know what this says. You could burn it." said Braun, helpfully.

"Yes. I could." It was no use. Büber roused himself, dragging himself to his feet and brushing the hay from him. "But I could also do my duty one last time. Hand me the letter."

Braun held it back. "Or you could run."

Büber reached out and pulled the letter away. "I could do that too. But this is something that Felix needs to know. What he does after that is up to him: he is the Prince of Carinthia."

Braun tried one last time. "Mr Thaler speaks very highly of you."

Momentarily lost for words, Büber traced his finger along the pen strokes that made up his name. "I'm lucky to count him as a friend. My mind is made up, though. You should join the men in the stables, see to your horse, get something to eat. I imagine you'll be riding back hard in the morning. I'll go and do what I have to do."

He took his lantern by the end of its chain, where it was the coolest, and left the barn.

Braun was right. He could turn one way, and no one would see or hear from him again. Or he could turn the other, and let the dice fall where they may. That was what Nikoleta had said before Obernberg. That had worked out well.

Büber let the cold night wind chill his damp body and stir his clothes with its gustiness. He shrugged his tall, spare shoulders, and trudged to the farmhouse, entering through the kitchen to the room beyond. Both were banked with strongly burning fires: they should have been comforting, but all he could see in the flames were twisting bodies.

He was suddenly aware that the second room was full of people, and they were all staring at him gazing into the heart of the fire.

Allegretti cleared his throat noisily. "Master Büber. Heat escapes through an open door."

Büber took a deep breath. "My lord prince, I've received a letter from Juvavum."

The earls, Felix, Allegretti, all suddenly sat up. The farmer and his wife, who had been solicitously serving the prince and his entourage, looked uncomfortable, then relieved as Allegretti waved them away. They retreated to the kitchen and closed the door, quietly but firmly.

"A letter?" asked Felix. "What does it say?"

Allegretti stood between Büber and the fire. "More pertinent is why your huntmaster is receiving letters at all. Give it to me."

Used to obeying, Büber almost relinquished it without a word of complaint. Then, before Allegretti could snatch it from him, he put it behind his back. "It is addressed to me, Master Allegretti, and I'll give it to my lord."

For a big man, he could sidestep quickly. He knelt on one knee before Felix, who was perched on a milking stool in front of the hearth, nursing his shoulder. He held out the letter. His courtly language was lacking, not that Gerhard ever seemed to mind, but he tried his best.

"I think I may have done your father wrong, my lord. I have already shown you my desire to serve you, so whatever you decide, I will do it gladly." Büber bowed his head and felt the parchment

170

rasp against his fingertips as it was extracted by a curious twelve-year-old.

One of the earls started to speak, but before he had even got the first syllable out, Felix held up his hand and said simply, "Silence."

He shook the parchment out, and flattened it over his knee. He started to read. "Who is this Thaler?"

"Under-librarian, my lord."

"That's what it says here. What is he to you?"

"My friend of twenty years, my lord."

"Ah." Felix's eyes scanned the first paragraph with a frown. "Juvavum is in darkness. Everything has stopped working. The barges, too."

The earls muttered to themselves, and Felix's frown deepened. It looked strange on his face.

"Your discoveries, huntmaster?" he asked. "What did you discover?"

Büber swallowed hard. "I found a unicorn's horn, in the forest over near Mondsee. The . . . it was just lying there, it hadn't been cut or torn. No sign of the unicorn's body, or blood, or a fight, or anything. I told the Order, because by tradition and right it's theirs. They came and took it away, and told me not to say anything to anyone. Not even your father."

He looked up from his kneeling position to see Felix staring at him over the top of the page.

"And did you?" asked Felix.

"I didn't tell anyone." Büber lowered his gaze. "Not that time."

"Not that time?"

"It happened again. Or I found another one that happened at the same time, I don't know. I didn't even tell the Order this time. I thought that they'd kill me to keep me quiet."

"Why would they do that?"

"Unicorns are near-immortal, my lord: they don't just curl up and die, and when they're killed, they don't just disappear. They are the most magical of all creatures, so I'm told, more than dragons even, and if the hexmasters were scared of whatever was taking the unicorns, I was terrified. They bought my silence, my lord, with gold and fear. When I found the second horn, I knew the Order would make me disappear, too. So I went to Frederik Thaler, and asked him to look through all those books he has to see if anything like this has happened before. I told no one else, and neither did he."

"When was this?"

Büber counted up the days in his head. "Three? No, four days since I talked to Mr Thaler."

"Your Mr Thaler says the magic was already going long before now, and the Order knew." Felix put the letter down in his lap, and looked at the adults in the room, checking their reaction, before turning awkwardly back to Büber. "When did you find the first horn, huntmaster?"

"Last full moon, my lord. A whole month ago." Büber's legs were aching, locked in one position that he couldn't move from. At least he'd told the prince everything now. He felt lighter, though he knew a confession wouldn't save him.

"Where," said Felix, searching the shadows of the room, "is Mistress Agana?"

Allegretti looked at the ceiling. "Upstairs, my lord. She said her spellcasting had drained her completely, and she needed to rest."

The prince tutted and kicked his heels against the floor. "We can talk to her in the morning, I suppose."

"You are the Prince of Carinthia, my lord. You can talk to her now, if you wish." Allegretti made to stand.

"I do wish, signore. I wish it very much."

"Then it shall be done." But Allegretti didn't go himself. He waved at Earl Schenk to wake the witch.

Büber was still down on one knee, and Felix finally seemed to notice. "Get up, huntmaster."

"My lord." It came out more as a groan. He was stiff, and tired, and after everything he'd done that day, he just wanted it to be over.

"You should have told my father about this."

"Yes, my lord. I realise my mistake." Büber stared straight ahead: no one met his eye.

"This really mattered."

"I know, my lord." Here it comes. Will it be hanging, or pressing, or one of the old ways? The blood eagle, or the one where he'd have to walk around the irminsul, winding his guts on it as he went.

Nikoleta blundered into the room, breaking the tension. "My lord?"

172

She scrubbed at her face with tattooed hands, then lowered them to adjust her hastily thrown-on robes.

"Did you know?" said Felix.

She blinked, and rubbed her fingers through her loosely curling hair. "Know what, my lord?"

"That the magic was fading away."

She was still stuck by the door to the stairs, so she pushed her way through to the fire before answering.

"Yes," she said. She looked for a chair, then at Büber, sweating with his back to the hearth. "Peter? What's going on?"

"I've just told the prince that I found two unicorns' horns in the forests. I told the Order about the first, a librarian about the second, but his father about neither."

"Unicorn horns are the property of the Order throughout Carinthia," she said, curious. "Does that mean you kept one?"

"Yes. The unicorns didn't die, though: they vanished. The hexmasters were frightened by that, and they frightened me enough to keep me quiet."

Felix scowled. "Shut up, everyone. I'm the one asking the questions. Mistress, did you know the magic was disappearing?"

"Yes," and then to forestall any further argument she carried on, "and so did your father. I told him as soon as I could, and I'd only just found out myself. I told him to turn around, get more men, use a different strategy, but he wouldn't have it. You can't blame Master Büber, because he's a hunter and what do hunters know about magic? Nothing."

"I am the Prince of Carinthia," said Felix, jumping up and echoing Allegretti's words. "I'll blame who I like." The letter spilt onto the floor, abandoned for the moment.

"You could, my lord, but you would be wrong." She didn't shout it out, but spoke softly: admonishing a child, not defying a prince. "If you want to blame someone, blame me. If I hadn't answered your father's summons, he'd have been forced to turn back. I appeared and I gave him the confidence to carry on. My loyalty cost him his life and the life of every Carinthian who died today." Nikoleta clasped her fingers in front of her, a gesture designed to show she was not a threat, not now, not to the young prince or his earls. "I'm sorry. I'm sorry I couldn't persuade your father to take a different course of action. If Peter Büber failed you, so did I." She moved slightly, to stand next

173

to the huntmaster, shoulder to shoulder despite the height difference.

Felix didn't know what to do. His face was full of confusion, and he looked to Allegretti for support.

The Italian leant back in his chair. "Did the hexmasters know?"

"Of course they did. But I'm not a hexmaster. When I left Goat Mountain I was an adept, and the masters didn't tell us." She shrugged. "Go and ask them yourself: they're hardly in a position to turn you away. They can't do anything any more."

"And you are sure about that, signorina?" Allegretti pursed his lips and waited for an answer.

"Do you think she would be here," said Büber, "if they could?"

Nikoleta shushed him by laying her hand on his arm, and spoke first to the whole room: "They would have imprisoned me, or killed me. They would have done anything to prevent me from telling Prince Gerhard that the Order was powerless, and so was the palatinate. They needed the lie to continue: I wasn't prepared to let that happen." Then she crouched down in front of Felix, so that her face was close to his. His eyes were wide. "You have to understand that both me, and your father's huntmaster, did everything to expose the Order's secret before it was too late."

Allegretti reached forward and took up the letter again, scanning Thaler's precise handwriting. "It says here that the Order might be working on a solution. Is that true?"

"If the hexmasters were, then, once again, they never told me. I am not a hexmaster." Nikoleta narrowed her eyes at the Italian. "I repeat, why don't we go and find out rather than you asking me questions I cannot answer?"

It was Büber's turn to lay a hand of warning on her shoulder.

"I've confessed my part in this," he said. "She had nothing to do with that." Then he noticed the subtle shift of power. He was now answering to Allegretti, not the prince, who was speechless and swivel-headed, looking from one adult arguing to the next. "My lord, it's for you to judge."

Felix looked up at Büber, who towered over him as much as any giant would, and at Nikoleta, who slowly rose from her stoop. He backed onto his stool, held steady by the solicitous Allegretti, who leant over to whisper in the prince's ear.

"Can we all hear your advice, Master Allegretti?" Büber's words were sharper than he intended, but he suddenly saw the situation

174

for what it was: the horror of the day had been enough for a lifetime, and honestly, he'd be glad to lie down and die just to make it end sooner – but not so that someone who had pretended friendship would profit from it.

The silence in the room was as deep as anyone would find in the library. Even the fire was momentarily quiet, lazy orange flames flickering in a parody of the inferno from earlier.

Allegretti slowly turned his head. He had a different look on his face than when he'd suggested that Gerhard, seemingly bent on destroying himself, was a lost cause, and the only way to salvage anything was to do what he suggested. Protect the boy, he'd said.

Now Büber knew why.

"Master Büber, a prince may take advice from those he trusts, if he wishes, and no man has a right to interrupt."

"How about a woman, Master Allegretti? Do I have the right to talk?" There was an edge to Nikoleta's voice that she'd not used before. The earls seemed transfixed by the tableau, and especially with the position of her hands.

"Do not threaten the prince," said Allegretti, and that was all it took.

She hadn't. Of course she hadn't. But the earls Schenk and Ludl, von Traunstein and Hentschel, all reached for their swords. Which, in turn, made her raise her arms.

It now looked like they were defending themselves against her, and she was the powerful aggressor.

"Don't," said Büber. The fire was behind him, and he knew how much she loved playing with it.

"I didn't. I wasn't." She looked Allegretti square in the eye. "Nothos," she hissed.

"You are outlaws. Banished." Allegretti's two swords were abruptly in his fists. "Just say the word, my lord, and I will throw myself at the traitors."

Felix was lost, as surely as his father had been. Büber watched as a tight, bright light coalesced in Nikoleta's hand. He could carry on watching as she burnt the house down around them, or he could do something else.

"No more killing," he grunted. "Not today."

And he picked her up around the waist and carried her to the door to the parlour. He didn't stop, despite the door being closed, just charged it with his shoulder and kept on going, past the farmer and his wife, holding a witch in the moment of casting a spell, outside into the yard.

"Put me down," she said, struggling furiously. The light winked out, but he still didn't let go.

"Braun's horse is still saddled." He could see its wet coat shining in the dark, and hear it shake its mane as it waited.

Nikoleta's feet briefly touched the ground, and she dug her heels in against a crack in the slippery stone.

"We're going back," she said, but, as she wriggled free, he caught her wrist and held it tight enough to hurt.

"Who will you kill?" Büber demanded. "Allegretti?"

"Yes."

"Schenk?"

"If I have to."

"Von Traunstein?"

Her eyes burnt with the fire she so badly wanted to create. "All of them."

"Felix won't listen to you if you surround him with the dead."

Her voice became plaintive. "I have to try."

He picked her up and threw her onto the saddle. "The fuck you do."

She tried to levitate off, but even sorcerers could be disorientated by the rush of grappling. Büber grabbed at the reins and got one foot in the stirrup before she righted herself astride the horse's back.

Fire blossomed in her hand again and she held it at him.

Büber's body froze, but not his tongue.

"Allegretti was right about one thing only: I need to protect you."

"How dare you," she said. "I can protect myself."

"But not," said Büber, "from yourself."

He half expected that she would set him on fire and blow him apart, then go back for the Italian. He'd gambled everything – his life, the future of Carinthia – that she wouldn't. He grabbed the pommel and pulled himself up behind her, feeling her body stiffen in shock as their bodies pressed hard against each other.

She'd have to hold on as best she could. He was no horseman, and it took all his skill to wheel the beast around and set it out into the night.

He had no idea where he was going to go.

25

Thaler woke up and found that a sheet of parchment had stuck itself to his face. With his own drool. He looked at the world sideways for a moment, at the lightening sky and the pink-coloured clouds. It was peaceful, calm. Orderly. The rain that had persisted into the night had been blown away northwards and in its wake there was warm air and gentle breezes. Spring. He liked the season best of all.

His head was cheek-down on a table positioned in the library's entrance. He was there because yesterday something extraordinary had happened.

Thaler sat up with a start, gasping in air like he'd just run from the quayside up to the castle and back. The lights, the books, the . . . he peeled the rough parchment away and checked everything around him. He was whole – he patted his arms, his chest, his legs – and the ledger was still open in front of him. There was ink and spare paper, and a selection of pens. There was the heavy library seal and the stick of red sealing wax: the candle he'd used to melt it was no more than a white puddle.

He got to his feet, pushing the chair back against the wall. He seemed to be completely alone, and yet he knew he shouldn't be. He, Frederik Thaler, had set guards to keep the books safe from looters, and arranged them in shifts so that no man would have to watch for the whole night – except for him. He'd stayed on duty, and now it was dawn.

Where was everyone? Had they faded away too, along with the magic?

"Hello?" he called, and his voice sounded weak.

A vaguely familiar face peered around the library doors. "Mr Thaler? You're awake."

"I am?" He put his hand to his chin, and felt stubble. "I am. Yes. I'm awake."

Thaler tried to remember everything he'd done yesterday, but it still had the quality of a dream. Everything had been done with a purpose, and yet the situation was so extraordinary it hadn't felt real. And now, with the first sunlight striking the western side of Library Square, he had to pinch himself to be convinced that it had all happened, just as he'd entered it in the ledger.

"Are all the books still safe?" he asked the usher.

"Yes, Mr Thaler. There's been no trouble at all."

"Good, good." He pulled the ledger towards him and leant over it, examining each entry in turn.

Must thank Aaron Morgenstern, he thought, as he read about the lanterns. Do it this morning.

"Did the mayor ever send any militia?" he called out.

"No, Mr Thaler. Leastways, not so I noticed. Someone earlier in the night might have seen them."

Must see the mayor, urgently. This morning, too.

"Was Under-librarian Thomm ever found?"

"Not that I know of, sir."

Thaler looked up from his book. "It's Mr Ullmann, isn't it? I sent you to Jews' Alley yesterday."

"Yes sir. Max Ullmann. There's something you should probably know straight away, sir. The master librarian: he's not in a good way. Might be something you want to see to first thing, if you know what I mean."

"Yes, yes, of course." He'd have to do that this morning, too. So many things already. He emerged from behind the desk and stood with Ullmann and two black-robed librarians under the portico.

"Strange days, Mr Thaler," said Ullmann, leaning on his improvised weaponry, a turned and polished table-leg.

There was no one in the square, and the fountain was still.

"Yes. They are, aren't they?" Thaler rasped his stubble and noticed the emptiness in his stomach. There had been breakfast, and lunch too, yesterday, but he'd been too busy for supper and had eventually fallen asleep where he'd sat. He wasn't accustomed to missing meals, and he pressed his hand onto his ample belly to check whether it had shrunk.

"When do you think we'll get the lights back on, Mr Thaler?"

The question stopped any thought of food. It was a question that the whole of Juvavum would be asking. "Well, now. Here's the thing . . ." – but he was just talking to cover the fact that, if he was correct in his assumptions, the answer might well be never.

"Mr Thaler?" asked Ullmann.

"I don't know. The Order are strangely silent. Perhaps someone should go and ask them."

Ullmann's laughter sounded out of place. "I wouldn't like to be the man who tries that, sir. They're quick to anger and slow to forgive, so I'm told."

Thaler was inclined to agree, but then again: "I intend to see the mayor this morning, and I have a feeling this question'll come up." He scratched at his chin. Normally, he would have washed and shaved straight after rising. "I'm going to suggest that, in the absence of the prince, me and Master Mayor make a little trip up to the White Tower."

The two librarians, who were leaning against a supporting column, registered as much surprise as Ullmann.

"Yes, yes, I know," said Thaler, testily. "I expect it won't just be us – the guilds and such like will probably want representation. Though how many of them will actually want to come with us is another matter entirely." He patted at his pockets. "So much to do today, I don't know where to start. It would help if Underlibrarian Thomm would bother to show his face. Any word on Under-librarian Grozer?"

"Can't say, sir. None that's reached me." Ullmann hefted his table-leg above his head with both hands and stretched. "Are you going to open the library today?"

Thaler tutted and sucked air through his teeth. "No – not that I have the final say in the matter – but there's a lot of reshelving and tidying up to do. We should concentrate on that today, and try to reopen tomorrow."

"Very good, sir. I'll pass the message on."

Thaler was taken aback, and realised he needed to make sure there were no misconceptions. "I'm not in charge, Mr Ullmann," he said.

"Doesn't look that way from where I'm standing, Mr Thaler." Ullmann nodded emphatically. "Don't look so worried. The gods provide the right man for the right time."

"I'd be more believing in the wisdom of the Aesir if none of this had happened in the first place, Mr Ullmann." Again, Thaler experienced the nagging doubt that the gods, if they ever existed, weren't the slightest bit concerned with who he was or what he did. But perhaps in this case, Ullmann was right. Magic didn't just disappear; something must have caused it. "Still, this all very academic. If we don't get the water back on today, I doubt the doughty burghers of Juvavum will be as accepting of their situation as you."

"The water, sir?" Ullmann called after him as Thaler went back inside briefly for the ledger. And the seal. Can't go leaving that lying around. "Now that is serious."

"Yes, Mr Ullmann. It is, isn't it?" He hefted the book under his arm and pocketed the seal. "Now, I will be sending every available librarian back here as soon as I can. When they arrive, go and get something to eat, and get plenty of rest. I shall commend you for your diligence to Mr Glockner, and if I may say for myself, very well done, Mr Ullmann. Very well done indeed. If anyone needs me, I shall be in the refectory; after that, I will visit the master librarian and Mr Grozer, followed by the Town Hall. Disturb me if it is important; otherwise, carry on as you see fit."

He hurried away, the seal knocking against his leg as he walked. He passed the fountain, the surface of the water in the great stone bowl reflecting the sky in tremulous stasis.

The Romans had installed them, and they hadn't possessed the magic that up until yesterday the Germans had had at their command. So there was already a way of getting water through the city's pipework; he just had to find out how they'd done it, and copy that. How difficult could it be? The caesars had first taken the settlement fifteen hundred years ago, and Juvavum still had sections of the ramparts that dated back that far.

Thaler stopped in his tracks. He may not even have to copy the Romans. The original system might still be beneath his feet, lying dormant like some slumbering beast. What an extraordinary thought, having to rely on something so old.

He set off again, his quick steps devouring the distance between the library and the refectory. He began to smell the kitchens, steam wafting out of the high open windows. Some things, at least, were normal.

There were doors. Big doors with iron rings, and smaller ones closed with thumb latches, but he arrived in the refectory soon enough.

The room was long and thin: the ceiling went all the way to the painted roof, and high-set arched windows let slanting light stream in, illuminating the long table that stretched the entire length of the floor.

There were lights hanging from the roof beams, but, as in the library, they were extinguished, cold and grey.

Half a dozen librarians were already seated and eating, clustered at the far end nearest the kitchen. They seemed in good spirits, despite – or perhaps because of – their experiences. Normally, breakfast was taken in library-silence, with each man attempting to find an island of peace before the day's work. This morning was different in every way.

Thaler closed the door behind him, and walked down to join his fellows. Who rose as they saw him approach.

Embarrassed, he waved them back to their plates. "Quite enough of that, I think," he flustered. He placed the ledger next to him and helped himself to a mug of short beer from the jug.

"Is the library safe, Mr Thaler?" one of them asked.

"Yes, perfectly safe. I've left it in the very good care of Mr Ullmann for the moment." Thaler helped himself to a still-warm bread roll and dug his thumbs in to split it open. "Ah. Compliments to the bakers. I am in need, gentlemen, so no questions for the moment."

He dipped his bread in his beer, and savoured the yeasty, malty flavour. He cut some slices of sausage, and ate those one after another, then went back for more bread, and more beer.

The others were watching him. "Eat, eat!" he encouraged. "We must keep our strength up. There's work to be done."

So they kept going, even if they'd already finished, and after cramming enough in to fill the void in his stomach, Thaler slowed down enough to pass on his news.

"Well, my fellow librarians," he began. While he had been feeding, other librarians had drifted in, and now he was bordered on both sides by attentive faces. "What has been happening to the north is beyond our control, but what happens here is not: so, when my lord returns, he will find us in our library, working as we have always worked. Now, we are at a disadvantage in that our usual means of illumination is currently unavailable to us: we have what we have, thanks to the beneficence of Jews' Alley, but we must be very careful with our lights. We all know what happened to Alexandria, and that will not happen here.

"We have much to do. We have shelves to right and books to place on them. We have debris to clear and furniture to replace. When, gods willing, the master librarian returns to the library, he will find us as he has always found us: serving the prince as best we can, conserving and repairing our older manuscripts, copying and collecting and collating. It will be business as usual, and rightly so. Just because our fortunes change is no excuse. Our standards, already of the highest ethic, will not fall one iota."

He beamed around at them, hooking his greasy, crumb-covered thumbs around the edges of his robe. "I aim to have the library back to normal tomorrow morning, at the first watch, even if I have to work all night. Who else will stand now and say that he is an honest labourer, and that, while there is a job to be done, he will not rest? Who will join me in this great endeavour?"

They stood as one, and Thaler dabbed the corners of his eyes.

"Come then. To the library."

26

Outside, having started their day in darkness, the citizens of Juvavum were making up for their tardiness by turning out all at once. Despite the problems, they seemed determined – perhaps a little too determined – to carry on regardless.

Thaler found himself pressed to the walls of narrow Coin Alley on a number of occasions, all without so much as an excuse me or a beg your pardon. Relieved he'd made it as far as Wheat Alley without incident, he looked at the crowds there and decided to cut through to the open spaces of the quayside – with the barges tied up, there'd be room enough to walk sensibly.

It was almost true, and at least he found out where all the militia had got to. They were guarding all the barges and all the warehouses, from the city wall up to the very far end of Rudolf's Quay. And, conveniently, the Town Hall was directly opposite the main bridge, right on the waterfront.

He strode past the knots of spear-armed men, feeling increasingly indignant. Surely some of them could have been spared to guard other locations in the town? Like the library?

To cap it all, he was stopped as he was about to ease his way into the Town Hall itself. A spear-haft blocked his way, and a voice monotone with repetition said: "You can't go in."

Thaler bristled. "This is library business, man." He put up his free hand to push the spear aside, and checked himself just in time. Instead, he brandished his book, and the guard took a step back.

"The mayor said no one was to be allowed through . . ." said the guard, moustache twitching.

"Except on official matters," Thaler finished for the man. "It doesn't get much more official than this. I have the Great Seal of the Library in my pocket and I'm more than willing to stamp an imprint on your forehead to prove the point. Now, is Messinger in, or should I look elsewhere?"

The guard glanced up involuntarily, and Thaler spotted the open first-storey window he was looking at.

"He's in a meeting."

"Of course he's in a meeting. Anything else would be a complete dereliction of duty, given the shambles we currently have. Now, are you going to let me in, or am I going to have to shout my report up to him?" Thaler ostentatiously licked his index finger and opened the heavy ledger.

Defeated, the guard stood aside, and the librarian carried on up the stone steps and through the door.

The entrance hall was suitably impressive: tall, wide, with a double staircase at the far end, lined in oak and punctuated by the symbols of Juvavum's guilds. It would have been even more impressive if he'd found everyone hard at work rather than huddling together in twos and threes like frightened children.

These were the civic leaders of the town. Thaler found their behaviour shameful, and rather than look at them for a moment longer, he parted them to either side like the Jew Moses had parted the Red Sea and swept through the middle, all the way to the stairs, making sure that every step was purposeful and dignified.

Boots would have been better than library slippers. He seemed to be making a habit of that.

He turned the corner of the staircase, and caught a whiff of fear and foreboding. He recognised it for what it was: a contagion that could spread like the plague. Thaler's mouth formed a thin line, and he carried on up the stairs to do battle with the mayor.

Messinger was bent over a desk placed in front of the window, looking at a set of accounts with a gaggle of assistants and councillors. They argued to and fro, groaning and growling as appropriate, but never reaching a conclusion.

Thaler used his elbows to push his way to the front, and slammed his ledger down, narrowly missing the mayor's fingers.

"Mr Thaler, what is the meaning of this?"

"Well, Master Messinger, if you don't know, I can't imagine that you could possibly object to being interrupted." The mayor spluttered, and Thaler banged the Great Seal on top of the ledger. "The Norns appear to have decreed that authority rests with those who actually bother to turn up."

Messinger took a moment to recover. He looked at the seal, at the book, then at Thaler. "Mr Thaler, we are very busy."

"Busy doing nothing," said Thaler. "Now, what plans do you have for restoring the water supply?"

The librarian wasn't the tallest of men, but Messinger seemed to be related to dwarves. Perhaps he was. It wasn't unknown.

"We've already discussed the problems with the water. Really, Mr Thaler . . ."

"I didn't ask whether you had discussed them. I expect the whole town's discussed them. I asked what plans you have for getting things working again."

"Plans? Have you seen what's happening out there?" Messinger pointed a sharp finger out of the window, incidentally levelling his finger right at the ominous silhouette of the White Tower.

"I've certainly seen it, and I seriously doubt you've left the Town Hall since this emergency started." Thaler wouldn't let himself get distracted. "So, yes. Plans. I have two. How many do you have?"

One of Messinger's sycophants affected a laugh that died a natural death when the assembled men realised that Thaler was quite serious.

"Where is the master librarian, Mr Thaler?" asked Messinger.

"Incapacitated. Under-librarian Grozer is critically injured, and we are attempting to affect a cure ourselves in the absence of the Order. Under-librarian Thomm is missing, and has been since before the crisis. I and the other librarians have kept the library safe, no thanks to you, and now I come here to offer what appears to be some badly needed assistance. I am a servant of the library, and the library is the servant of the prince, Mayor. If you want him to return and find the council running and squawking like ready-for-the-pot chickens, so be it. He will not find the library like that. Do you have any proposals for dealing with this current situation, or should I seek both help and wisdom elsewhere?" Thaler straightened his back and folded his arms.

"Out," said the mayor. But when Thaler stuck his chin out and planted his feet anew, he explained his instruction. "Not you, Under-librarian. The rest of you, you useless, fawning, simpering, purblind idiots."

Consternation spread through the room, and Messinger span on his heel to confront his coterie.

"Out, you arseholes, you shitsacks, out!" He stamped and balled his fists and roared with a volume that belied his stature.

One by one, they left, shocked, wordless, until it was just the mayor and Thaler.

"Close. The. Door." A hand snaked back in and pulled the door tight shut. Messinger fell arse-first into a chair. "Gods, what a mess."

Thaler, surprised by the turn of events, looked around the mayor's chambers. They were richly furnished: the finest carpentry, the best tapestries, exquisite metalwork, and a cabinet of curios and gifts from across Europe. Very different from his own cell in the library complex. His gaze eventually alighted on a silver jug.

"Drink?"

"Gods, yes." The mayor put his head in his hands.

Thaler poured them both a generous measure of wine, and assumed he could sit down. He pushed the goblet in front of Messinger and sipped at his own. Very easy on the palate.

"Things are not as grim as they seem, Mayor."

"They're not? The lights our craftsmen use to work in the hours of darkness have gone out. We cannot produce goods. Ploughs will not cut the sod. We cannot grow food. The barges can travel downstream, but not back up. The wagons refuse to roll. Trade – trade we can tax – is ruined. Our drinking water has stopped flowing." The mayor snatched at his wine and sank half of it.

"I do appreciate that all these problems have landed on your desk, not mine, Master Messinger. We can still grow food, make things and send them to market: it might just be more difficult." Thaler's wine was too good to drink quickly, so he sipped at it again. "Has the Order offered any explanation for the hiatus in magical activity?"

Messinger shook his head. "No. No one's heard from them. And yes, I have asked around."

"Ah," said Thaler, raising his index finger, "but has anyone gone and asked the Order directly?"

"Are you mad? They'd as soon turn you inside out than bother talking with the likes of us." The mayor spluttered and swilled the remaining half of his wine before looking around for more. "No one needs to see your insides."

"I intend to go up Goat Mountain anyway, and I want you to come with me."

"Gods, man." The mayor leant forward into Thaler's face to make his point even more direct. "They'll kill you in ways you can't even begin to imagine. Possibly more than once."

"Rubbish. If they could resurrect people, they'd have done it to the prince's first wife. I don't think that's the only limit to their powers, either." Thaler leant back in his chair which was, like the wine, really very fine. "I don't think they can do anything any more."

The mayor blinked rapidly, and finally said: "What?"

Thaler raised his goblet and inspected the workmanship. "Nothing like this up at the library, Master Messinger. We're very much a beer-and-bread sort of crowd."

Messinger bit at his lip, his jaw trembling. "I will send a crate of my best wine to the library if you explain what in Midgard you are talking about."

"Excellent. A deal." The librarian sat upright and put his cup down, the better to wave his hands around. "Now, it strikes me that we mere mortals have been left in a quandary: do we sit around and wait for the Order to ride out of their tower and recast all the spells that have suddenly and mysteriously failed all at once, at the very same moment – which means we have to do nothing except appear suitably grateful and hand over even more of our hard-earned cash – or is this a permanent and irreversible occurrence which the hexmasters were powerless to prevent and are just as powerless to, er, reverse?"

"And you propose to go and ask them?"

"Yes," said Thaler.

"Despite the long-held convention that setting foot on Goat Mountain is punishable by death?"

"Yes."

The mayor considered matters for a moment, before getting up to collect the pitcher of wine himself and pour both of them another brimful each. "You are mad."

"At first sight, yes, my intention does appear a little foolish, but hear me out." Thaler slurped the top of his wine off without removing it from the table. "We don't know what to do without that information. If I have to reopen the library with no magical lights, I need to make other provisions – spending the next fifty years, or however long I live, blundering around in the dark and not being able to read a word indoors seems to me a fool's errand. You don't know what alternative arrangements you need to make regarding the passage of trade: if we have to revert to horse-drawn carts as the Romans did, or some of the barbarians do now, we're going to need many more horses. I'm not an expert in horse husbandry, but I'm led to believe that the process is not instantaneous."

"But what has that got to do . . .?"

Thaler held up his hand. "Please, Mr Messinger. What we do now, this day and the days following, will affect everything that happens hereafter. If we sit around on our ample backsides, waiting for the Order to come and rescue us, and they don't, we will have a situation far more serious than the one we face now. There is nothing for it. Someone will have to go up to the tower and find out. If they don't return, I suppose that is an answer of sorts."

Messinger guzzled at his wine again. "Yes, I understand that. Have you considered the third option?"

"A third?" Thaler looked pensive.

"That the Order have done this deliberately, and they want to watch us fail."

"It's possible. I've very good reasons for believing that I'm right, though."

"And . . ." – said Messinger. He looked at the dribble of red left in the bottom of his goblet, and decide it was better inside him than not – ". . . you're willing to risk your life on that?"

"Yes, Mayor Messinger. I am." Thaler needed a clear head. No more vintage for him. He picked up the seal and toyed with it a moment before putting it back down on the ledger. "If I don't come back, I'll be grateful if you could return these to the library."

Thaler stood up, straightened his robes, and walked to the door. He paused.

"Aren't you going to wish me luck?" he asked.

"Fuck it," said Messinger. He drank the rest of Thaler's wine, and got unsteadily to his feet. "Come on, then. Before I change my mind."

27

Sophia didn't cover her hair because she wasn't married, but she wasn't certain that she would have done so even if she were. Her hair was long and dark and only slightly curly, which meant that she could plait it into all kinds of interesting weaves such as the German girls wore, but that were forbidden to Jewish girls.

Well, not forbidden as such. It was frowned on, and Sophia had been frowned on a lot as a child. Her mother, when she was alive, had been desperate for her to fit in, because Sophia was such an odd daughter, more interested in her father's books than her mother's cooking.

She'd said – often, to anyone willing to listen – that husbands went to those girls who showed they kept a good house, not to those who could bisect a line or recite the opening stanzas of *The Iliad*. It turned out that Sophia's mother was right.

Being Aaron Morgenstern's daughter didn't help: he was a bad influence on her, indulging her when he should have been disciplining her. She was the bane of the local matchmakers, headstrong and contrary. She was, in short, a disgrace to her family.

She kept a good house all the same. Even though her father had given away, or lent, or something or other, all her oil lights and almost all of her candle lanterns to Mr Thaler's librarians, their windows had remained lit last night, and there had still been enough light to cook and sew and read.

Sophia called up the stairs. "Father, I'm going to see if the market has anything left."

"No, you're not. You're going out to be nosey and to get the latest gossip," came the faint reply. "No good will come of it."

"I'll tell you everything when I get back." She threw a shawl over her shoulders and unlatched the door. Her immediate neighbours, left, right and opposite, were gathered around the Rosenbaums' front step.

"Good morning, Mr Rosenbaum, Mr Schicter, Mr Eidelberg." She gave a little curtsey and remembered to reach back around her own door for the basket hanging there.

"Good morning, Sophia," said Rosenbaum. "Tell me again when I'm going to get my lamps back?"

"I don't know, Mr Rosenbaum. I'm sure the library will only need them for a short while." She pulled the door shut and looked down at the ground, then thought she didn't really need to do that, so she looked up and smiled. "I'll go and ask for you."

Rosenbaum wasn't used to any woman other than his wife smiling at him, and even that was rarely. "It wouldn't be proper for a Jewess," he said.

"You go and ask them, then." The rules about what she should do were more rules about what she couldn't do and, by the prophets, the list was already long enough without the Beth Din adding to them monthly. "If you think it's not proper for me to do so."

"A good Jew cannot set foot inside that place, Sophia. You know that."

"Perhaps you can stand outside and shout, then. Really." She stamped her foot. "I don't know why you bother talking to me, Mr Rosenbaum, if all you're going to do is find new ways to show me how much of a sinner I am."

She shouldn't rise to the bait, but she rarely resisted the temptation. Rosenbaum folded his arms across his chest and looked content, his thin beard wagging. Even though she was only just younger than he was – than all three of the men, in fact, and he'd been suggested as a possible match for her – she had to call him Mr Rosenbaum now he was married.

And she, unmarried, was still just Sophia.

She didn't have any answer to their sniping. It made her sad, and not a little bitter. So she left to the sound of their laughter and headed up Jews' Alley to the market in Scale Place. As she passed each door, she named the people who lived there – not all Jews dwelt in Jews' Alley, but everyone who lived in Jews' Alley was a Jew. She knew them all, and they knew her.

That used to be a blessing, but she'd started to see it differently. She didn't hate any of them. She didn't even find much to dislike about most of them. Everything, though, was all crammed in on this one narrow street with its high houses and thin walls, and it was very claustrophobic.

Books opened the world to her in a way life could never do.

The market was busy. It was busy with non-Jews, which was unusual, and some of them were poking at the kishke and the gelfilte fish with undisguised curiosity. Others were trying to buy hamantaschen without recognising their significance, and having to have the whole of Purim patiently explained to them. She didn't really need anything else, as she'd already done the shopping first thing; the disaster that had befallen the Germans had only partially affected them.

The water – that was the main thing. A Jewish household placed a bucket under the waterspout, and the women dipped from the bucket. As with her father's off-hand use of the barges to transport his books, they could claim they were getting their water from the bucket, not from the magically pumped spout.

Water for washing, for purification, for cooking. It was a concern. Perhaps it would come on again soon. Apart from this, though, Jewish boys pushed their handcarts through the streets, and sold vegetables brought to Juvavum from Jewish villages by donkey, just as they always had.

Sophia wandered around, trying to overhear what her German neighbours were saying, but in the end gave up and carried her empty basket down to the quayside.

She was surprised by the number of militiamen present, as she hadn't seen any in the upper part of the town, and even more surprised to find Mr Thaler in the company of the mayor, being marched towards the bridge by a company of spear-brandishing soldiers. They came towards her, the unmistakable shape of Thaler hurrying along the best he could, his black robe flapping behind him, and the mayor looking decidedly bilious, but more or less in step with the librarian.

She hurried too, apologising to those she bumped into as she trotted along towards the bridge approaches. "Mr Thaler," she called, "is everything all right?"

He didn't ignore her, but neither did he stop. "Good morning, Miss Morgenstern. Tell your father I will be along later to thank him for the lanterns."

"We'll be in the synagogue later, Mr Thaler. It's the . . ." – but she wasn't sure that Thaler would know what a Megillah reading was, let alone when it should be. "We won't be at home."

"No matter," he said. He drew level with her, and he smiled tightly in her direction. "Another time. Tomorrow." He seemed very determined, and she realised that he wasn't under arrest, but actually in charge.

Which, for an under-librarian, was a startlingly abrupt promotion.

"Mr Thaler, what's going on?"

Now Thaler had to look over his shoulder to talk to her. "That, Miss Morgenstern, is exactly what we're going to find out."

On they strode, though striding didn't quite describe either Thaler's rolling gait or the mayor's furious little steps. Those townsfolk who were on the bridge moved aside to let them pass, and, on nothing more than a whim, Sophia decided that she wanted to see where they were going.

That wasn't quite true: at some point, she'd have to atone for all those small lies that she knowingly told herself to justify her actions. She knew where they were going – to Goat Mountain and the novices' house, which was the only legitimate point of contact between the Order of the White Robe and everybody else. She knew why they were going – to ask about the fountains, the lights and the barges. She also knew that the Jews would be the last to be told the answers, as they were last to be told about anything that happened in Juvavum.

Perhaps, just this once, her community could be as well-informed as the Germans. Even take part in the conversation as to what happened next.

The soldiers swept past, rattling and chinking, and she waited for a moment to allow a reasonable distance to develop between them and her, before walking out into the middle of the roadway and over the bridge. Her empty basket banged against her side, but she tried to make everything look as natural as possible. Perhaps she was on her way to the makers' market on the far side. Or to collect some herbs, or just travelling to one of the farms on the outskirts of town.

She breezed across, worried that someone might turn around and order her away, but that never happened and, realistically, was never going to happen. Thaler and the mayor were intent on their task, and the soldiers grimly set to escort them, despite their better judgement. No one else cared what the unattached Jewish girl was doing, and it was just her guilty conscience that worried at her.

Thaler's group took the road to the novices' house and didn't stop anywhere on the tree-lined avenue. They carried on to the very end of the short, paved road and, having dodged from trunk to trunk, Sophia watched the mayor gesture sharply at the huge knocker on the tall recessed door.

Thaler wiped his brow and considered the architecture with his hands on his hips, taking in the short square tower, the high-pitched roofs, the grey stone walls. Then he stepped forward into the shadow of the doorway, and hammered out three sonorous knocks.

Sophia ducked back when Thaler turned around to talk to the mayor. When she re-emerged, they had already moved away from the novices' door. But not towards her; down the road to Juvavum.

They were taking the forbidden path to the next building up the hill.

It was as if she were watching her father tuck into a juicy pork chop and relish every mouthful. What they were doing was so incredibly transgressive that she couldn't quite believe it, even though she saw it with her own eyes. For a moment, she forgot how to breathe.

She clung to the tree-trunk until she could trust herself not to faint. The last of the soldiers disappeared from view – as far as she was concerned, forever – and she was alone.

Looking around, everything was perfectly still, and nothing out of the ordinary. Except that, when she really looked, she saw that the door at the entrance to the novices' house was half open.

She hadn't seen that: someone must have opened it, and told them to go up the forbidden path. So they might not die after all. But that they'd left the door ajar was very strange.

The compulsion she felt to go and pull it to was entirely of her own making, but it was strong nevertheless. She checked there was no one else around, then flitted from tree to tree until she was within striking distance of the porch.

Then she sprinted the rest of the way and stopped only when she was safely hidden within the stone arch. The knocker that Thaler had used was a huge iron hoop fed through the mouth of a dybbuk, so high up that it would have been as much a stretch for him as it was for her.

To say that she was the only Jew ever to see inside the novices' house would be a rare thing. No doubt someone like Rosenbaum would say it was forbidden, but he'd devour every last detail while frowning in disapproval.

Sophia dared to peek, not even touching the wood of the door, at what lay beyond. She couldn't see much, just part of a wide corridor. It was as dark inside as her own house was when she'd blown out the last candle, but the light leaked in through the gap.

It wasn't what she expected. She'd thought it would be much tidier. There were things – a book with its binding ripped, a few loose pages lying nearby like lost feathers, a drift of white cloth.

When she realised she couldn't make sense of the scene, she put down the basket that she'd been carrying all that time and pressed her fingertips against the door. It opened easily, swinging back and revealing that what she'd glimpsed was repeated everywhere she looked. Not just a mess, but as if the place had been ransacked.

Things she imagined would have immense value simply lay abandoned. Vandalised books, both paper and boards, had been systematically destroyed and cast into the air to fall where they might land. The piles of cloth she now recognised as the robes of the Order themselves; they, too, had been thrown off.

Other things she failed to recognise, but that looked arcane, were crushed and bent, or broken and shattered.

She took a single step inside, to see down the corridor better. She was standing in her own light now, and the shadows deepened and shifted, but she could see even more of the destruction wrought. The corridor that extended off to her right was filled with debris: some of it seemingly flung from the series of rooms to which it led.

Straight on was a set of stairs, and, judging from the pile of material that had built up on the staircase, things had been thrown from above and then trampled and kicked by the passage of feet heading down.

To her left was another corridor where detail vanished all too soon, consumed by the darkness. The story that had been told in the entrance hall was repeated. The whole place looked as if a mob had risen up inside and trashed everything on their way out.

She bent down and slid a single page across the floor until she could comfortably ruck it up against her shoe. Her fingers gripped the parchment, and she retreated back outside to inspect it.

The stiff paper shook in her hands, making a sound like distant thunder. To her surprise, it was written in Latin: she could read it, and she knew she shouldn't.

"Ecce iterum symbolum et a summo ac vincendo nomen Dei." Behold anew the symbol and the name of a sovereign and conquering god.

Enough. She threw the page back through the doorway and rubbed her hands together to remove any lingering taint. What was she even doing there? She peered around the porch to the road that led to the next set of buildings where Thaler and the mayor had gone.

They hadn't got permission from the novices' house at all. Thaler had glanced inside and come to the same conclusion she had. The novices, and their masters, had gone. And if Thaler was in the mood for demanding answers, even from sorcerers, the adepts' house would be their next stop.

It was either incredibly brave or incredibly stupid of them. Most likely, both.

Sophia couldn't see anything of the adepts' house but the high grey roofs, and she wasn't going to use the path to get closer, in case she was spotted. But if she walked up the slope behind the novices' house and through the trees, perhaps she could spy on Thaler's party from there.

She set off again, following the outer wall of the building as it climbed uphill and hid itself among the woods. It was hard going: the tree roots were forced to the surface by the rock of the mountain itself, and made a web of knots within which a foot could easily catch. The way steepened, and she found herself using her hands more and more to pull on branches and push her fingers into the thin soil. She straightened up every so often to get her bearings, and when she looked back across the valley to Juvavum, she saw it as so very few ever had. It looked different from that new perspective, although she could easily pick out the fortress, the river and its quayside, the library, and parts of the encircling town wall.

She was at the corner of the rear wall now. All she had to do was strike uphill, and keep down when she got to the top, and she could see without being seen. She glanced to her left along the length of the back wall, just to see if there was anyone there, but looked more closely when she realised that the midden heap centuries of novices had created had built the land up to almost the top of the crenellations.

The weedy, sherd-strewn rubbish had formed a bank that stretched along half of the back wall. It looked straightforward to climb, and if she picked her spot carefully, she'd be able to see over the top of the wall to the courtyard below. It would only take a short while, then she could get on with her illicit ascent of Goat Mountain.

The debris was dry and loose, crackling and shifting slightly under her, but the tough plants that eked out their existence on the older parts of the midden seemed to hold it together enough to stop her sliding back down. She lifted her skirts and took a short run at the slope, and found herself at the top.

She listened carefully, then looked over, her fingers gripping the stonework to pull her head to eye height.

The wall was thick enough to carry a walkway as well as the battlements. The courtyard itself was bare stone, with a drain in the middle covered by a round metal grating. Apart from that feature, and some sort of wooden frame that had been thrown down, there was nothing of interest.

Sophia craned her neck a little further, and her footing gave way with a sharp pop. Her foot only fell an inch or two before it reconnected with solid ground, but she caught her chin on the wall on the way down, and when she put her hand to it, she found that she'd grazed it enough to make it bleed.

She looked down to extricate her shoe from the hole it had made, and it slowly dawned on her that she'd broken someone's skull. Next to it was a disarticulated jaw, still with its teeth. And there, a finger, and the broken ends of ribs, and vertebrae: animal and human remains mixed in with the broken pottery and fragments of wood, all just thrown over the back wall to rot.

There had to be dozens of bodies. Everywhere she looked she could see an empty eye socket or weather-worn pelvis. And the mound on which she was standing was some fifteen feet tall.

Gehenna, the place of burning.

She scrambled down and stared back up at the wall. Her heart was banging against the inside of her chest and her breaths caught in her strangled throat. Who would do such a thing?

The Order would.

She thought hard about just running for home, where it was safe, where there was not, and never had been, any magic. Where the thickness of a wooden door could shut out the terror.

She might have even taken a few steps in that direction, down the hill. But she stopped. She needed to warn Thaler that the people he wanted honest answers from were not the kind of people who would willingly give them up. Sophia turned herself around and started back up the wooded slope.

28

Messinger stopped and looked back down the hill. "Do you have the feeling that we're being watched?"

"Only ever since I set foot on this accursed hill." Thaler mopped at his forehead and scanned the gaps between the trees for any signs of movement. "They can turn themselves invisible, can't they?"

"You said . . ." The mayor glared at the librarian.

"Apologies. They *used* to be able to turn themselves invisible." Thaler could pretend to be as confident as he liked, but up here, on Goat Mountain itself, with the White Tower looming over them, with the strange silence that seemed to infect the landscape? Confidence was a mere affectation: the place could be crawling with wizards and witches, and he'd never be able to tell.

The dozen guards the mayor had insisted they bring with them muttered darkly to each other, the rattle and chink of their armour the only other sound.

"We'd better get on," said Messinger. "Before I become convinced that this is a stupid idea."

"I thought you were convinced already." Thaler rested his hands in the small of his back and something went click. This was the most exercise he'd had in years.

"I am. I just can't think of anything else to do." Messinger kicked at the road, and set off again, Thaler in pursuit. "There's no doubt about what we saw, is there?"

"The novices' house? No. It's as if the novices had risen up, rioted, and run. The place was deserted."

"We didn't go in," said the mayor. "We could be being deceived, deliberately."

Thaler didn't think so. "When I was a young librarian, I sometimes ran the messages to the Order from the library. That front door was always locked, and with more than bolts. There was always someone on the door, too, no matter the hour of day or night. They made the library look slipshod and disorderly."

"So where in Midgard did they all go? I'm uncomfortable with the idea of gods-know how many apprentice sorcerers wandering the countryside." Messinger stopped again and looked around. "Are you sure we're not being followed?"

Thaler came to a halt, too, as did the militia. "Gentlemen, absolute silence if you please." He listened very carefully.

It was his name that came through the trees, faint but recognisable. He resisted the urge to snatch one of the soldiers' spears and brace it against attack. There had to be some rational explanation for this. Besides, no malevolent spirit would be hunting him down and calling him "Mr Thaler" at the same time. The last he'd heard, such beings didn't announce their intentions at all, let alone do so politely.

He went to the edge of the path and looked down to where he thought the sound was coming from. He squinted, and was rewarded with a flash of movement – a darker green against the browns of the tree-trunks and the leaf litter.

"There." He pointed the place out to the mayor. "A stadia or two away."

"I can't see anything." The mayor, being shorter, had a more restricted view, but he moved closer and was rewarded with a fleeting glimpse himself. Then a longer one. "It's a woman."

"Gods. I recognise her." Thaler tried to think of anywhere more unlikely to see her but halfway up Goat Mountain, but couldn't. "It's Aaron Morgenstern's daughter."

"I'll take your word for it." Now the threat had a name, and it was seemingly mortal, the mayor relaxed just a little. "What does she think she's doing?"

"I have absolutely no idea at all." The slope she needed to climb was steep, and he thought the best thing to do would be to go and help her. He hesitated for a moment before stepping off the path and slipping down to the next tree.

She chose that moment to look up, wild-eyed and dishevelled. "Mr Thaler!"

"Miss Morgenstern. A great number of pertinent questions spring irresistibly to mind, but they would be better served if we could communicate in something less than a full-throated bellow."

Sophia had no energy left to blush. She carried on using every handhold in her effort to climb, and eventually she and Thaler met at a mountain ash: he, hanging down from the slim trunk, extending his hand, and she, reaching up, her fingers encrusted with black soil and decaying plants.

He caught hold of her and pulled. He wasn't strong, but she was surprisingly light. And, fortunately, the tree they were both clutching took their combined weight.

"Mr Thaler," she gasped.

"Miss Morgenstern." Her face was bare inches from his, flushed and panting. "Does your father know where you are?"

She blinked, and growled at him, "Just get me to the top."

"Most people would use the perfectly serviceable road." Thaler looked up at the mayor and all the soldiers staring down at them. "*We* did."

"Never mind," she said. "I've come this far. I'll do it myself."

Sophia carried on scrambling up, until one of the soldiers lowered his spear-haft and she could hold on to it. Thaler followed after her, respectfully turning his head: she was, after all, wearing a skirt, and modesty made demands on him that his curiosity didn't quite overwhelm. Climbing was difficult, muddy work after all that rain, and the same soldier who'd helped the Jewess found Thaler a much weightier proposition.

"Gods," Thaler muttered. His hands were now just as filthy as hers, and the hem of his robe was snagged and littered with leaves. He batted himself down and tried to dislodge some of the grime with an expression of distaste. "Master Messinger, may I present to you Miss Sophia Morgenstern?"

The mayor made no attempt at pleasantries. The tension of being somewhere he knew he ought not to be exploded. "Wotan's one eye, girl, what do you think you're doing? Go back home this instant – it's death for you to be here."

Defiant, she said: "And for you, sir." She shook some twigs from her hair and stood her ground. "Yet here we all are."

Messinger's fists tightened. "Do you want me to beat you back to your father?"

"Beat me if you want," she said. "Now, do you want to hear what I have to say, or are you just going to ignore me?"

Thaler interposed his body between them. "This is all very irregular. We understand the risks we're taking, Miss Morgenstern. The mayor is representing the town, I am representing the library. Why are you here?"

"I followed you." She looked down at her exceptionally muddy shoes. "I suppose that wasn't very sensible."

"Indeed, young lady. I have no idea what I'm going to tell your father." Thaler glanced over his shoulder at the adepts' house. "This is no place for, well, anyone. As you say, here we all are, but some of us are not here by choice. You should really go home, Miss Morgenstern."

"I found bodies," she blurted.

Messinger shoved in front of Thaler. "Bodies?"

"At the back of the novices' house. There are . . ." she shivered, "skeletons. Hundreds of them, I think. Just thrown over the back wall. But the whole of the forest floor has bits of bone in it, just below the surface."

"Men?"

"Yes. And women, I suppose. Tossed out with the rubbish."

"Hundreds?"

"I didn't count them, but there were more than I could count in the time I had."

Messinger pressed his chins against his chest, digesting the news, so Sophia spoke over his head to Thaler.

"I had to tell you straight away. They must have been killing people for years."

"Not our people," said Messinger. "We'd know."

Thaler suddenly felt very ill indeed. "Gods. The children." He staggered, and was caught by one of the militia. Their arm-guards pressed uncomfortably into his flesh, but all he could think about was what Martin Kelner had told him.

"What is it, man?" asked the mayor. "What do you know that I don't?"

"That children have been disappearing over the last few months. But," and Thaler righted himself again, "that doesn't explain tens of bodies, let alone hundreds."

"If the woman's right, of course."

Thaler saw that Sophia was about to have her own explosion, and deflected it. "I'm certain that Miss Morgenstern saw what she says she saw. It may be that missing Carinthian children are the least of it." He turned his sights back to the adepts' house. "Perhaps we can find someone – anyone – at home prepared to give us an explanation for that as well as for why the magic has suddenly gone."

Messinger grunted with dissatisfaction. "I don't like it, Mr Thaler. This whole enterprise is looking madder by the moment."

"You may like the next turn of events even less, Master Messinger.

I propose that Miss Morgenstern stays with us until we return to town and I can repatriate her to her father's care. It would seem foolish in the extreme to abandon either our sworn task, or the young lady."

The mayor closed his eyes and shook his head. "Gods, man. Come on, then. Let's get this over with."

He tramped up the road, and Sophia mouthed a heartfelt "thank you" to Thaler, who raised a sceptical eyebrow and fell into step with her.

"I still fail to understand what possessed you to follow us. It's dangerous here – just how dangerous you appear to have discovered – and it's no place for anyone unaccompanied. I wouldn't have done it alone, which says something about either your courage or your foolishness, or both."

"I'm not brave, Mr Thaler. I'm quaking in my shoes."

"Well then," he said. "Let's call it what it is: foolishness. You've added an unnecessary complication to an already fraught situation. I would have expected better from someone who's read Euclid."

Sophia sighed. "I'm very sorry, Mr Thaler."

He kept looking straight forward, and despite his serious demeanour, he couldn't help give a grudging smile. Courage it was then. "And if you would at least pretend to mean it, I could pretend to believe you."

She had no answer to that, and neither was she supposed to. She had to realise that there was a line, and she'd crossed it. As had he, for that matter, but he felt his mission had more about it than simple curiosity.

The adepts' house slowly came into view. It looked both old and eternal: built in a late Roman style, added to and taken from until it looked more thrown together than designed. Perhaps the adepts had been expected to change the shape of a wall as a test of craft, create a new courtyard or tower to order. Or perhaps the masters had done so to frustrate and confuse their pupils.

Whichever, it looked wrong.

"Is there a door?" asked Messinger.

"There, look," pointed Sophia. Reminded of her presence, the mayor scowled, but she'd spotted a dark opening and the semblance of an arch.

"You did the last one," said Messinger. "I suppose I should do this one." He looked less than happy.

"Nonsense. We'll both go."

Except that when they set off for the door, there were three sets of footsteps on the path.

"Miss Morgenstern, what are you doing?"

"Keeping you company, Mr Thaler," she said.

The reason the doorway was dark was because the door itself was off its hinges, lying inside, and the corridor beyond was pitch black. The scene was similar to the one they'd found inside the novices' house, but with more violence. Some of the discarded robes were bloodied, and a few of them were still filled with the shrouded bodies of the dead.

None had died easily.

Messinger reached for a cloth to cover his nose and mouth against the sweet, rank smell.

"What d'you reckon, Mr Thaler?" he said, voice muffled. "This doesn't look like the reaction of a group of people who think they can get the magic going again."

"Not any time soon, at least, Master Messinger." Thaler stole a glance at Sophia, who was staring boldly at the corpses on display. "It seems the Order has deserted us, just as surely as the source of their power has deserted them."

"Aren't we going to go in and search, see if anyone's left?" Sophia had edged forward until she was at the threshold.

"No." Thaler reached out and pulled her back. "Firstly, we have no lights. Secondly, there are too few of us. And thirdly, it's the last thing anyone in their right mind would want to do. We want to question the Order: the Order is demonstrably not here."

The closest body seemed to have had its face smashed repeatedly against the floor: all sense would have suggested that the assailant might have stopped sooner, but clearly hadn't. There was a fourth good reason to leave, right there.

"What about the White Tower?" asked Messinger. It was lost among the trees, but they could all feel its presence.

"If we descend to the town now, we'll only have to return later. Better that we get this out of the way."

The path wound upwards.

"I can't imagine Carinthia without the Order," said the mayor. "Thaler, what are we going to do?"

"Hold firm, Master Messinger. What we do isn't our decision but the prince's." Thaler turned to his companions. "We must, however, give him the fullest account we can. That means we have one more place to visit before we can be satisfied the Order has completely abandoned us."

They started the ascent to the summit of Goat Mountain. The trees went from straight to crooked, and finally into shapes that were warped so far beyond true that it was a wonder they'd grown at all. The leaf buds that had dared to sprout were just as twisted as their parent branches.

In the broad circle around the base of the tower, nothing grew at all. The ground was bare, the soil gone. No mosses or lichens, none of the tiny alpine flowers that seemed to colonise the tightest of crevices. Nothing living.

"Well, this isn't promising," said Thaler, if only to hear his own voice. On every other peak surrounding them, wild green spring was breaking out. The top of Goat Mountain was like the desert he'd read about.

The tower loomed over them. The wind played against its glassy surface, causing it to hum at a pitch that made his stomach roil, and the sound seemed to emanate from the tower's entrance. Which was shaped like a mouth, an ancient, toothless sucking maw that wanted to consume them like slops.

The wind was also cold, but they would all have trembled no matter what the weather.

"It's as if—" started Sophia, but Thaler cut her off.

"Any allusion you may make will be no doubt apposite, but entirely unhelpful. We are all too aware of our predicament." He moved to set himself in front of the opening. "Why not wish me luck instead?"

"Good luck, Mr Thaler," she whispered.

Messinger had gone as pale as a ghost, but he wasn't going to be shown up by a mere librarian – as Thaler had intended all along. The darkness inside was thick and churning, or it was easy to imagine that it was, set between the melted uprights and half-formed lintel.

They walked together towards the tower, and were slowly aware of a lighter shape taking form in front of them. Then Thaler realised that it was no piece of architecture or artefact, but a man. He gripped Messinger's arm and brought him to a halt.

"Who's that?" He realised that he sounded like a terrified child. He forced himself not to bruise the mayor, and lowered his hands. "Who's there?"

The figure resolved itself: an almost-bald man, a roughly trimmed grey beard framing wine-red lips, wrinkled hands with hints of tattoos emerging from the ends of his sleeves. His robe would have been white once, but most of it was now stiff with splashes and smears of dark dried blood.

He carried a carved stick, but he appeared not to need it for walking.

It was blood on his face, too. It seemed to run down from the corners of his mouth to darken the hairs of his beard, as if he'd been drinking it.

Thaler wondered if he should have brought some sort of weapon. The mayor was carrying the ceremonial sword of office, but for all he knew, it might be just that: blunt, unweighted and for show only.

One look behind told him that only Sophia Morgenstern was holding her ground. The spearmen were edging back, towards the path down.

The man emerged into the light. He blinked as if unaccustomed to day, and looked first at Thaler, then at Messinger. Then finally at Sophia. His eyes narrowed.

"Good morning, Master," said Thaler. "May I present the mayor of Juvavum, Master Messinger? I am Under-librarian Thaler – the master librarian is currently indisposed, and I'm acting as his deputy."

The hexmaster finally turned his attention away from the Jewess to Thaler. Then he spoke, slowly and deliberately, without any semblance of emotion. "Why are you here?"

It was a very good question, and despite having had hours to think of an answer, Thaler was momentarily wrong-footed. "I . . . that is we . . . have come from Juvavum to enquire on the status of, er." He tried again. "Our magic has stopped working. What should we tell the prince?"

The hexmaster nodded very slowly, and planted his staff on the smooth rock in front of him. He closed both his hands over the grip and stared over the top at Thaler.

"Tell him . . . tell him the magic will flow again."

The mayor seemed to be pleased with the response, but Thaler was wary.

"Master, forgive my impertinence, but you appear to have lost all your novices, and all your adepts. Are there other masters within to help?"

"Other masters?"

And at that moment, Thaler realised precisely where all the blood had come from. He decided to stick to the original question. "The prince will ask when the magic will flow again. What do we say to him?"

"Tonight. As soon as tonight."

"That's good," croaked Messinger. He wanted to leave. In a hurry. "We won't trouble you any further, Master."

Thaler thought their departure just a little previous. He brushed away the mayor's hand tugging at his robe. "If I may be so bold, Master Sorcerer, isn't there something else you should be telling us to pass on to my lord prince? The magic will, as you say, flow, which is wonderful news, and perhaps that it might happen even tonight, which will certainly reassure the mind of the prince regarding the long relationship between the White Tower and the White Fortress." He scratched at his chin, painfully aware of the forensic gaze of the hexmaster and the consternation of the mayor. "How, exactly, do you propose to accomplish this miracle?"

"There will be some . . ." The sorcerer hesitated, not because he was dissembling, but because he was trying to translate his thoughts from the divine to the mundane. "Cost. Yes, cost."

"And good Master, if the prince enquires about this cost, shall we tell him to bring gold, or gems, or rare spices from the East, or else what?" Thaler feared that he already knew the answer, and his heart was beating hard in his chest as he waited for it to come.

The hexmaster had bloodshot eyes that made his blue irises all the more alarming.

"Is it children?" prompted Thaler. "Do you want more of our children?"

"It could be so," said the master. "I believe it might not matter."

Thaler reached out and slapped his fat hand over the mayor's mouth before he could utter a word in response. "For sacrifice?"

One bloodied eye twitched back to look at Sophia. "For fuel."

"My lord the prince will hear of your words, mighty Master. He might ask what the economy of this transaction is, though: before we leave, might he know how much fuel you require to restore the magic to a level of say, a week ago?"

Messinger had been rendered speechless, and Thaler let his hand drop.

"There will be a period of readjusting," said the hexmaster.

"Re-enchantment will be necessary. It is tiring. I cannot reanimate the common objects as one. Each must be ensorcelled, as it was before."

"But the fuel, Master. How much should we send?"

"One. Two a day. Sometimes more. I will tell you as I need them."

Thaler bowed. "Good day to you, Master. We shall leave you in peace and return only with the prince's word."

He started to retreat, and had to drag Messinger with him. He reversed into Sophia, who he shooed towards the path. She seemed almost drunk with horror, reeling, uncomprehending.

One last piece of information. The mayor may be neglecting his duty, but Thaler was damned if he would. He called out: "Who shall I say stands for Carinthia in its hour of need?"

"Eckhardt," said the man. "Tell him Eckhardt waits for him."

29

The bend in the road was familiar, and, slowly, the castle – his home, and now the seat of his throne – came into view. Yesterday's rain had washed winter away, and the fortress walls were whiter than ever, set against the black of the rock escarpment on which it sat and the grey of the sky behind. The alpine mountains that framed Juvavum were purple and green, and the river that churned heavy with sediment ran almost blue.

"My lord," said Allegretti. "Your kingdom."

"I'm not a king, Master Allegretti. I'm a prince, like my father was."

"And his father before him. But Alaric was king of the Goths. Perhaps it is something to be considered." The Italian gave an off-hand gesture. "Not now, of course, but in the future."

Felix wasn't sure. Everything had changed, and nothing could be taken for granted any more. Last night, he had fallen asleep where he sat, in front of the farmhouse fire and, as he dozed, he had heard the earls talking quietly among themselves: snatches of conversation as he drifted in and out of consciousness, barely more than a few disjointed words at a time.

Schenk had said: "We're lost. Carinthia with us."

And von Traunstein: "Bavarians. Wiennese. If they unite . . ."

Ludl: "We can save something, surely?"

Felix couldn't comprehend losing Juvavum. How did someone lose a town? How did they lose a palatinate? An invading army, yes, he knew that. He knew about siegecraft, and what that meant to a population trapped inside the city walls – but say the Bavarians turned up with five thousand soldiers, an unimaginable number not seen since the days of the Horde. There were three times that many people in the town, and what was the number of Carinthians within a day's ride? An army like that would be surrounded and overwhelmed in days.

It was simply impossible to invade Carinthia. Many of his earls had been lost, it was true, but he still had some, and the land would provide more. He was now their lord, and they needed to serve him.

He had these moments of clarity, times when he could concentrate on what he should be doing, now that he was supposed to be in charge, rather than on the past, his father's body, and the numbness that threatened to swallow him whole.

A boy ran out of a farmyard, still carrying a bucket. He stood at the wall, barely tall enough to see over it, gazing up at Felix. Perhaps he'd seen them ride past on the way north: the horses and the men and the wagons. What did he make of them now? So few, so bedraggled.

Felix tried to keep looking forward, ignoring the child, who had climbed up the wall and was now hanging over it, bucket and all, mouth open with incredulity. As he drew level, however, Felix couldn't help but turn his head, and stare at the boy, who was maybe only a year or two his junior, even as the boy stared back.

Eventually, his horse took him away, and he was forced to break the contact. The bucket fell. Feed – light-yellow barley grains – spilt out. The boy showed his heels as he ran pell-mell towards the house, shouting for his father, his mother.

Something that he, Felix, could not do.

"My lord?"

"Please, signore. Not now." He'd never wanted to become prince like this. Someone else should do it.

"You must think about your entry into Juvavum. We need to set the right tone. Seven days of mourning, and then the funeral."

That wasn't what he wanted either, but every time he tried to say so, the words caught in his throat. As far as he knew, the Carinthians didn't mourn their dead: they built a massive bonfire, burnt the body, and drank themselves unconscious. Allegretti was suggesting his customs as the only way things would be done properly.

"In Roman times," the Italian continued, "those of high rank would lie in state for a week, and the great would pay their respects. It will mean that your coronation will take place on the eighth day when all are assembled."

He didn't need some stupid ceremony. He was the Prince of Carinthia already. Everything that was his father's was his. Of course they'd expect him to sit on a throne and then everyone would bow to him, but that wouldn't make him anything that he wasn't.

"I don't care, signore. I really don't care." His shoulder hurt. His heart hurt. "Whatever you say."

And with that, he climbed stiffly off his horse, giving a small cry of pain as he landed heavily on flat feet.

"My lord, what are you doing? A prince must not walk like a commoner. Mount up." Allegretti started to dismount also, then checked himself. "We are expected to ride."

Felix took the reins of his horse and patted the animal's neck. The earls were behind him, and they stopped too, wondering what the matter was.

"Can we all just get off?"

"My lord," said Schenk, and heaved himself from the saddle. "What is it you want?"

"I want my father honoured," said Felix. He bit at his lip.

Schenk bent low, his moustache twitching. "And he will be, my lord. He will be."

"Bring him here."

The earl glanced up at his fellows. Von Traunstein shrugged and nodded. He too dismounted and went to the back of the column. In the distance, the farmer, his wife, their son, and another man stood at their gate, watching.

Ludl climbed off too, and soon all the horsemen but Allegretti were standing on the via.

Von Traunstein, head bowed and face set, led the horse bearing Gerhard's body forward. Felix took the reins from him, and gave him his own horse to lead.

"Signore," he said, "walk with us. We will walk, while my father rides. One last time."

Allegretti was caught out, and he quickly swung down. "Of course, my lord. This is a noble and gracious gesture you accord to him. The people will love you."

It wasn't why Felix was doing it, though. He just wanted the townsfolk to be able to see their prince. He took a deep breath, and started off.

The noise behind him told him the others were following: he compared the sound with that they'd made as they'd rode out. A bright clattering of hooves, a solid beat of marching, a sustained creak of wheels.

They had won the battle, but if there'd been another half-dozen Teutons, they would have lost, witch or no. And hadn't his hunt-master – his former huntmaster – killed that number when they'd fought over the barge? Felix wondered where Büber and the mistress were, and whether his own raw grief and obvious confusion had made something really very stupid happen without his intending it.

They were approaching the north quays, and there was already a line of people standing either side of the road. The houses that overlooked the river were slowly emptying: more came from the tied-up barges. Every word was whispered.

He led his father on, towards the bridge, which cleared ahead of him. He kept looking straight ahead, not seeing individual faces, just an unfocused blur. He reached the south side, and there were even more people, standing silently.

He continued along the whole length of the quay, the white walls of the castle growing closer and higher. Did his stepmother know? His half-brothers and sisters? It wasn't for anyone else to tell them but him: your husband, our father, is dead. Or were they on the Bell Tower, watching the sorry procession?

As he pulled the horse's head around to make the sharp turn up the road to the Wagon Gate, he happened to see what was going on behind him. There were his earls and the other horsemen, each walking their mounts. Following them, the surviving infantrymen, and then the camp followers: wagon drivers, cooks, armourers and squires.

And then a great mass of people, everyone he'd passed. They'd all fallen in step as the last man had passed, farmers and porters and tradesmen and bakers and makers, and not only that, women and children and old men and babies quietened at their mothers' breast. A great, silent mass was caught up in his wake, flooding the quay with bodies, overflowing into the surrounding streets and alleys, ready to break against the fortress.

He stumbled, either catching his toe against a tipping flagstone or simply because his legs were failing him. A sound like a sigh – a collective intake of breath – reverberated between the eaves and the gables. Allegretti was the first to reach him and hold him up.

"Courage, my lord. See how they loved your father." He pulled him to his feet again. "If you had ridden, you would not have fallen. No matter: what is done, is done."

Allegretti stood beside him, and the moment of Felix's weakness passed. He put one foot in front of the other, and the rest seem to follow naturally enough. The doors of the Wagon Gate creaked open to reveal the crow-black figure of Trommler. The chamberlain carried his silver-topped staff of office, rather than his appointments book.

The castle knew, then. There was no hiding place, no dark corner of the fortress in which Felix could pretend. Trommler came to meet him. At the sight of the body of the old prince he had served so faithfully, bound and wrapped in stained cloaks, his face trembled, and he looked all of his years, and then some more.

"My lord, Prince Felix of Carinthia." Trommler bowed as low as his back could manage. "Take the throne prepared for you, as you have been destined to do since you were born."

"Chamberlain. Mr Trommler. I . . . I'm sorry." It wasn't his fault, but he still felt the need to apologise. Perhaps he was apologising for coming back alive when so many had not. "There was nothing I could do."

"I will make the arrangements, my lord. It will be my duty and my joy."

Felix glanced nervously at Allegretti, who was watching the chamberlain with studied care. "Do you know how these things are done?"

"There is a book which details every funeral of every Prince of Carinthia since the time of Alaric. I have called for it from the library." Trommler straightened up and, despite the heavy lines on his face, looked for the briefest of moments like he was smiling.

"Valhalla will surely have opened its doors wide, my lord, and received your father to a high place at the table. What we do now is for our own comfort: right or wrong ceremony matters little when you are already feasting and drinking with the gods and your ancestors."

He reached out and patted Felix on his good shoulder.

"Thank you, Mr Trommler." The weight of expectation lifted ever so slightly from him. "I'm sure whatever is done, will be done well."

"Your stepmother's inside. She wants to see you." Trommler raised his head to view the crowd that was now spreading out along the lower flanks of the spur of rock that held the fortress. His thin lips drew back into a grimace. "Are you aware of our changed circumstances? The magic?"

"We've had . . ." said Felix, and he didn't know how to finish. "Our problems."

Allegretti intervened, "Mr Trommler, we cannot wait here while we discuss every last detail. Show us inside, and let us lock the doors. There are many things you need to tell us, and we have news of our own."

"If my lord wishes," said Trommler. He looked again at the crowd with narrowed eyes, and stood to one side as Felix finally walked his father back into the castle.

Reinhardt led the rest of the army – the victorious army, though it felt anything but – under the archway of the small gatehouse, and the tall wooden gates were closed firmly to the townspeople. A murmuring began. It became a cry, a howl, a wailing and a keening. A lamentation for a time past, its peace, its pleasures and its prince.

It broke the boy, in the privacy of his own castle, behind his own walls. He let the reins slip from his hands, and he knelt on the road. If he made himself small enough, he might be able to disappear.

Strong arms lifted him up and carried him. Barely aware of what was happening, he felt himself moved from downhill to uphill, from outside to in, from cool afternoon to dry heat.

Voices came and went, doors opened and closed. Something warm and soft enveloped him, and when he came back from wherever he was trying to hide, he was sitting in a chair and his stepmother was holding him to her.

"Felix."

He called her "mother", even though she wasn't. It was the least he could do.

"Do you want to know how it happened?"

She stiffened, then forced herself to relax. "Not now. We need to talk about other things, though. When you're ready."

His face was buried in her hair. It smelt of soap and smoke. "Like what?"

"Your succession. In other lands, things can get . . ." she hesitated ". . . complicated. Fighting. Killing. We've never done that in Carinthia. Not for a long time."

Felix disentangled himself.

"What?"

"Brothers fighting each other for the throne. Other royal houses might do that; I won't have it in this one. You are the Prince of Carinthia. The earls will pledge allegiance to you, as will your brothers."

"What?" repeated Felix.

"Oh, my boy. The stories you've heard of kings and princes all vying for a kingdom, of poison and daggers, traitors and turncoats. They're not just stories. That really happens." She wiped away the tear that was running down her cheek. "Your brothers and sisters are not your rivals. They are your family."

"They're just children." He'd finally worked out what she was saying. She was asking him not to kill them, and her. "I'd never do anything to hurt them."

"We'll leave just as soon as we can. My brother had land in Ischl, and I have a claim on it."

"You're leaving?" he said, pushing himself up with the arms of the chair. "Don't."

"Not straight away. But yes, we have to go. Ulf is only six, but he's now Earl von Ischl. And you are Prince Felix. It's better we do this now, and you can fill your court without my interference, intended or otherwise."

Felix gradually became aware of where he was: in his father's private rooms. The shutters were closed, heavy curtains blocked out the remaining light. A low red fire in the fireplace and half a dozen candles provided the only illumination, tiny haloes that did little to hold back the dark.

"Who made Ulf an earl?"

"My brother rode out with your father, his prince. He didn't return. And if we don't go back to Ischl soon, the freemen will demand that we do, or find another to take his place. I have obligations, and so do you." She said all this without rancour. She even stroked his cheek. "My children are too young to understand any of this: you, dear Felix, are not. I don't want Ulf to be used as a pawn in someone else's chess game. I want him gone from here so that he can grow up and become a man you can rely on, rather than a rival you're forced to do away with."

Princess Caroline got up from the floor and smoothed her dress out. Her gaze took in the room, and lingered on the bed.

"When will you go?"

"After the funeral. Perhaps even straight after." She put her hand on his head. It was warm. Almost so hot, it burnt. "You have so much to do, and I'm so sorry I can't help you with any of it."

"The signore wants my father to lie in state for a week in the Roman style."

"Signore Allegretti will have to contend with Trommler." Her hand trembled, and she removed it. "If I can offer one piece of advice, not just as a loyal Carinthian, but as someone who's tried to be some sort of mother to you?"

Felix nodded.

"Your duty is to the people of Carinthia. Let them be your first thought on waking and your last thought on sleeping. Those around you need to share that duty with you, until you can shoulder it yourself."

She kissed the crown of his head, and left the room.

Felix was alone, for the first time ever.

30

"Mr Thaler, where have you been?"

The sky was almost dark, and the streets looked as if they were going to be deserted for a second night.

"Yes, yes. I know, Mr Ullmann." Thaler put the Great Seal back on the desk in the foyer, and dropped the ledger next to it. "Gods."

Ullmann dragged his fingers through his greasy black hair. "I

sent to the mayor for you, because that's where you said you'd be."
He was almost hopping with nerves.

"And I was." Thaler leant on his knuckles, his whole body
sagging. "We went to see the Order of the White Robe."

Despite his agitation, Ullmann stepped closer and lowered his
voice. "You did? What did they say?"

"Gods," said Thaler again. "I can't tell you. I can't tell anyone."
Suddenly, he had Ullmann by the edges of his robe and was dragging him down, face to face. "It's madness. Utter madness."

Then he realised what he was doing, and released the usher with
an apology.

"Everyone's shaken by the news, sir," said Ullmann, adjusting
his clothing. "A terrible sight to see, the young prince leading the
old prince to the castle."

"Yes. It must have been." Not that he'd seen it himself, but
that's what everyone had said. Gerhard's death turned an already
near-impossible problem into one that was insurmountable. Felix
needed to know of Eckhardt's offer, but the boy had just lost his
father, and he was a boy! Almost everything that Thaler and
Messinger and Sophia had talked about on the way back down
from the White Tower – with Thaler insisting that Sophia put
forward her view – was now rendered entirely redundant.

"Mr Trommler sent a message for the Book of Carinthia to be
sent to the fortress."

Thaler screwed up his face. "Of course, yes. Was it found?"

Ullmann looked into the library beyond the doors, the dark
punctuated by the commas of moving lanterns. "Yes, sir. A librarian
has taken it already. And . . ."

"Thank the gods something's gone right." The under-librarian
started breathing again. "But go on: there was something else?"

"In order, sir." He listed the items breathlessly. "Under-librarian
Grozer is sadly no longer with us. Mr Braun has returned with
the young prince. Under-librarian Thomm has reappeared, and he
offers his resignation."

"This is getting a bit much, Mr Ullmann, for one man to deal
with." Thaler pinched the bridge of his nose. It didn't help. "So,
Under-librarian Thomm's resignation is refused. Did he give any
explanation as to where he's been?"

"He got married and had a family, sir." Ullmann edged back,
so that Thaler couldn't assault him again.

Thaler's jaw dropped. "What? In two days?"

"No, Mr Thaler. He was already married and had a child. The librarian you asked to find him finally tracked him down to a little house on Free Alley."

"Married? How could he support her? And a child, you say?"

Ullmann bit at his lip and said nothing, and Thaler choked back the outrage.

"He's been stealing books! Have him arrested, and have his rooms – and those of his so-called wife – searched. The greatest catastrophe Carinthia has suffered for a thousand years, the prince dead, the Order gone, and Thomm does this? I'll strangle him with my own hands. Gods, what next?"

"Mr Thaler, you've gone very red."

"As I have every right to be. Tell me that he at least kept a record of the books he pilfered."

"I don't know, sir." Ullmann took another step back.

"Does that mean there's more bad news?" growled Thaler through his teeth. "Out with it. Out with it all."

"I don't know how you're going to take this, sir. Mr Braun managed to deliver his message, but it sparked an argument between Master Büber and the young prince. Büber's accused of treason, and banished, as was the witch who travelled north with them. He even stole Mr Braun's horse."

Thaler went from red to white in an instant. He staggered back against the desk and clutched at it for support. "Peter. No."

"No one knows where they've gone. Some say that the witch even tried to kill the prince, but the boy's tutor forced her and Büber to flee." Ullmann risked coming closer again. "Can I get you a drink, sir?"

"Please: water."

"Water's still off, sir. I've some bottles of short beer hidden away." He disappeared into the library, and came back some moments later with two stone bottles. Thaler moved himself to the chair behind the table and slumped into it as Ullmann unstoppered both bottles and pressed one on the librarian.

The usher drank deep, and held his beer up to the dying light.

"Don't know how long these are going to last, Mr Thaler. Without water, the brew-houses are going to run out soon enough."

"Yes, they are, aren't they?" Thaler considered his own bottle. "There was nothing in that letter that could have led to a disagreement of such a magnitude. I accused the Order of hiding the problem, and perhaps of working on a fix in secret – we know the hideous truth of that now – nothing else. Where is Mr Braun? I'll have to question him myself."

"He's sleeping his journey off, so I'm given to understand." Ullmann nodded with satisfaction at the beer, and finished his, wiping his sleeve against his mouth at the end. "I don't expect you'll get any sense out of him until morning."

Thaler gripped his bottle tightly in both hands. "What Peter's been up to isn't the most immediate of my problems. Neither is what that scoundrel Thomm's been up to either. And neither is arranging a funeral for poor Mr Grozer. Nor trying to elect two successors. Gods, the jobs do stack up, don't they?"

"You've got yourself a pretty pile, and no mistaking, Mr Thaler."

"I have to go with the mayor and see the prince." Thaler looked up at the sky. "How long until sunset?"

"Give it half an hour, sir. It'll be proper dark by then."

"Not quite the Jews' new day." The under-librarian scrubbed at his stubble, and thought so hard it hurt. He took another pull of beer, and saw that he'd spilt some on the table, where it had formed a dark ring on the wood. He dabbed his finger on it, and drew a line away from the circumference. Beer flowed minutely into the damp mark he'd made. "Mr Ullmann, it appears to me that actions have consequences."

"Always have done, sir," agreed the usher.

"But if you do the right actions, in the right order, you can affect the outcome to your benefit, no matter that the situation began as a series of accidents."

"Looks like you've still got beer on the desk, sir." Ullmann leant forward and presented his sleeve for more wiping duties.

Thaler caught the man's arm. "No. The one thing we can't do is erase the past. But we can mould the present to change the future."

"What about the Norns, sir? Surely they'll spin a man's fate any way they wish."

"Things have changed, Mr Ullmann. If they have changed so dramatically here in Midgard, perhaps there's been an equally profound change in the other realms. Our only hope may lie in the idea that we are now masters of our own destinies." Thaler emptied the bottle, banged it back down on the desk, and stood, letting go of Ullmann. "If the mayor arrives before I come back, ask him to wait."

Leaving a bemused Ullmann in his wake, he shook out his robe and hurried down the steps of the portico, hurrying in the direction of Jews' Alley. The last remaining stragglers on the streets were heading for home. Juvavum had always been a lively place after dark, its lights extending the day's activities well into the night. This had always made the town appear rich, not just be rich. Now, it looked mean and cold, a provincial backwater full of nothing but faded glory.

He'd done a lot of walking that day, and there he was, walking some more. Under-librarian Thaler, pounding the alleys of the town, hot and bothered, rather than sitting neatly at his desk in the cool of the library: it was ridiculous, but there was too much to do, and only him to do it. It would have been churlish to blame Grozer for getting caught up in the frenzy that accompanied the lights going out, but Thomm? No excuses there at all.

Only the candles in the windows of Jews' Alley broke up the gloom. Despite the library having all the lanterns it needed, the Jews had still more. He worked his way down the street, excusing his way through the pre-Purim crowds until he got to the Morgensterns' door.

He was about to hammer his fist on it, when it opened and he was dragged unceremoniously inside. He was face to face with Aaron Morgenstern.

"What," he said, "did you do to my daughter?"

Thaler kicked the door closed with his heel. "What did I do? Why don't you ask her what she did to me? And the mayor?"

"You've led her astray. She's unclean. She needs to go to the mikveh rather than the Megillah, and it's all your fault." Morgenstern jabbed his bony finger into Thaler's chest for emphasis.

The librarian batted his hand away. "You old fool. She doesn't need me to get her into trouble."

"Oy, listen to the meshugener. Goat Mountain, what were you thinking?"

"I didn't invite her. Quite the opposite. And," said Thaler, "don't pretend you didn't know that Thomm was selling library books."

"Books? Why is this suddenly about Thomm? What about my daughter, my life, my joy, sullying herself with bones and magic?"

"Oh, do shut up, Father," said Sophia, coming down the stairs in a different dress to the one she'd muddied earlier. "I told you everything that happened and whose fault it was. Mine, I said. And what's this about you buying stolen books?"

Morgenstern squared up to Thaler. "You dare turn my own daughter against me?"

Sophia took hold of her father's shoulders and pulled him away. "I did what I did because I wanted to help us, the Jews. Mr Thaler is not to blame. You may as well go and find the mayor and shout at him, too."

"Who's to say I won't?" Morgenstern was genuinely angry, rather than his usual grumbling self. Even being accused of disposing of Thomm's contraband hadn't dampened his ardour. "You put her in danger."

"She put herself in danger," Thaler protested. "If anything, we rescued her."

"That's not actually true, Mr Thaler: I could have rescued myself, but I came to warn you instead." Sophia found herself between Thaler and her father, looking from one to the other.

"Despite our gratitude," said Thaler, "it was unnecessary."

"Enough," she said, and felt the need to repeat herself, and louder. "Enough! Father, shut up. You've had me explain what went on – twice. If you want to call me a liar, then go ahead, but you're not to take it out on Mr Thaler." Sophia turned her head. "Mr Thaler, why are you here?"

"I came to thank your father for the lanterns," said Thaler, weakly.

"You're welcome," said Morgenstern, flicking his fingers at the door. "Now get out."

"And to plead with you."

He had Morgenstern's attention, and his daughter's, too.

The bookseller edged closer. "If it's about those books of Thomm's, I had nothing to do with them."

Thaler brushed his excuses aside. "It's not about that. It's about your festival."

"What about it, Mr Thaler?" Sophia stood aside in the narrow hallway, to let her father by.

"Prince Gerhard is dead. How is it going to look if you're out on the square, celebrating and setting light to your bonfire?" It suddenly got very stuffy, and Thaler pulled at his collar.

"We have been commemorating the Feast of Lots for almost two thousand years—" started Morgenstern.

"Then miss one," interrupted Thaler. "You do not want to draw attention to yourselves tonight, to make yourselves look like anything but loyal Carinthians."

"But—"

"Your daughter's right, Mr Morgenstern. Shut up. Did she tell you what the hexmaster said?"

"Yes—"

"He wants sacrifices, you idiot Jew, to bring back the magic." Thaler really was too hot. He couldn't breathe and his heart was racing. "Do I have to spell it out to you, or can you work it out for yourself?"

Sophia whispered in her father's ear: "Eckhardt means us. Even we want the magic because of the water, and the trade and everything else we pretend we don't use, but most of all we want it because it keeps us safe and our neighbours happy. We are not safe and our neighbours are not happy."

Morgenstern glowered, but even as he rumbled in his throat, he said, "We are already loyal Carinthians, but go on."

"How long is it going to be for Eckhardt's offer to leak out into the town? How long after that before some hothead decides that it's worth the price? How long before you have a mob scouring the streets, looking for people to feed to that man's furnace?" Thaler had to lean against the wall. Short beer on an empty stomach; no wonder he felt unwell. "How long before they pick on you?"

"That's never happened here before."

"But it has happened. The Jews brought the plague to Wien. The Jews caused a drought in Gallia. The Jews conjured an earthquake in Attica. Who cares if it's true? You're different, with your one god and your frankly bizarre religious rules."

"They are not bizarre," objected Morgenstern, with enough vehemence to make Sophia interpose herself again. "We are a holy people, a chosen people."

"And every time something happens that the local sorcerers can't control, the mob chooses you to take out their anger on."

"Mr Thaler, are you all right?" Sophia looked at his sweating face and his luminous eyes. "I think you should sit down."

"No time for that. The reason it's never happened here is because our hexmasters are – were – so incredibly powerful that nothing untoward ever befell us. That's why there are so many Jews in Carinthia. Not that no one can hurt you, but that no one ever had reason to hurt you." Perhaps he should sit down. Ask for some water – except everyone was running out of water, running out of beer. He'd be no good talking to the prince like this.

"It's almost dusk, Mr Thaler," said Sophia. "I don't think we can change anything now."

"I don't think you can afford not to. But I have a compromise. I want you to tell your synagogue about it, and I want them to accept. It won't make you untouchable, but it will give us some time to come up with something else. And remember, I'm telling you this as a friend." All the turmoil of the day seemed finally to have caught up with him. He slid backwards until he was propped up by the angle of the wall and door. "Have the festival. Don't set the fire. Instead, give all the wood you've collected to Gerhard's funeral pyre. It's a generous gesture, and it'll be appreciated by those who can protect you."

Morgenstern seemed to be having a crisis of his own. He balled his fists and shook with impotent rage. "Why is it always us who have to change? Why not you pagans, just for once?"

"Because there are so many more of us than there are of you." Thaler levered himself upright for one final push. "Gods damn it, man. I'm not asking you to like it: I'm begging you to do it before we all find ourselves neck-deep in shit."

"Father. Stop arguing and go and do what Mr Thaler suggests." She shooed him towards the door, and had to drag Thaler aside to allow it to open. "Go and do it now, before it's too late."

"What about you?"

"Our bizarre religious rules have declared me unclean. I'll go to the mikveh later, you go to the synagogue now." She pushed him out into the street and closed his own front door on him. She gasped with relief and pressed her forehead to the cool wood. "Do you really think it'll work?"

"It's worth trying. Thank you, Miss Morgenstern." He closed his eyes for a moment, just a moment, in which she slipped her arm through his.

"I think you should come into the kitchen," she said. "And I think you should call me Sophia."

She led him unresisting to the table, and sat him down. Despite everything, there was water, and wine, and meat and little dumplings and three-cornered pastries, a feast, a Purim feast. She poured him water, which he gulped down, and bread, which he wolfed.

"I shouldn't be eating any of this, er, Sophia," he said, between mouthfuls. "I'm not Jewish, and have no intention of becoming a Jew."

"Are you poor?" she asked.

"Poor? I suppose, by any fair interpretation of the word, yes. But my needs are few, and the library supplies most of those. A few coins to buy beer and bread is all I ask."

"Purim is a time of sharing, especially with the poor. Although," and she looked at the inroads Thaler had already made into the dishes, "we normally wait until after the Megillah."

"I have sullied your board with my presence. And by now, the mayor must be waiting for me. I'll make sure that your report regarding the bodies behind the novices' house is given in full, to whoever we meet at the fortress." Thaler wiped his mouth to dislodge the crumbs. He felt not just better, but ready. "If it wasn't for your festival, you could come yourself. There will be detail in your first-hand account that I won't be able to do justice to."

"I'm not allowed to be a witness," she said. She started rearranging the food on the plates in order to make Thaler's ravages look less obvious.

"What? Yes, I suppose, but isn't that only in front of religious courts? What if the young prince commands you to appear before him?" Thaler glanced at the dark beyond the windows. He was late, and he pushed his chair back.

"All our courts are religious courts because all our lives are religious lives." She shrugged. "Though if the prince is prepared to take my testimony, despite my being a woman, then I would be prepared to give it."

"He'll hear you, I'm sure." Thaler frowned. "You can't go to this . . . reading, can you?"

"The Megillah, no." She looked at him, and he at her.

"All the Jews will be in the synagogue by now." Thaler glanced at the door. "Jews' Alley'll be empty."

"I'll bring a cloak," she said, and swept from the kitchen. Her footsteps sounded unconscionably loud on the stairs.

Thaler took one last pastry and popped it in his pocket, then went into the hallway to wait. Sophia appeared a moment later, wrapped in a woollen cloak that both skimmed the ground and covered her head.

"Are you quite sure you want to do this? Your father will have my head on a spike when he finds out."

"Quite sure." She looked pointedly at the front door. "I thought we were late already."

"Yes, I suppose we are." Thaler opened the door and peered outside. It was perfectly still and, but for the candles, perfectly dark. "Quickly and quietly, then."

31

It felt exciting, hurrying through the dark streets – the Germans hadn't yet worked out that putting candles in their windows would help their neighbours – and away from the synagogue, where almost everyone she knew would be crammed inside, hot and stuffy, with barely enough room to swing their graggers at the mention of Haman's name. Sophia doubted whether anyone would miss her in such a large crowd; everyone would assume she was in a different part of the building, and she thought it highly unlikely that her father would admit that she'd managed to exclude herself through being unclean.

If she was back home by the time the Megillah had finished, and the spiel was over, and the masquerade had processed . . . she might even get away without anyone knowing she'd never been there at all.

It was pitch black between the buildings, and only the slit of dark-blue sky indicated where they were heading. With her hood up, she was as invisible as Thaler in his black gown. So invisible, that she had to hang on to his arm, or else lose him, and him her.

She could hear his laboured breathing, and his tripping gait. She could hear her own panting and her boots on the cobblestones. And something else that might have been an echo between the high houses either side, or a dragging noise that kept pace behind them.

She looked, and could see nothing, and was almost jerked off her feet by Thaler pressing on up what she thought should be Sigmund's Alley.

"Mr Thaler. Stop a moment." She pulled back.

"What is it?"

"Hush." She lifted an entirely redundant finger to her lips, and listened. Nothing, nothing at all. "It doesn't matter. I thought . . ."

"We're late, Miss Morgenstern." Thaler tutted in the dark. "We've kept the mayor waiting quite long enough."

She trailed behind him the rest of the way, not entirely unable to convince herself that something nameless wasn't following them. But then there were lights ahead, and although the shadows twisted and flickered, there was no sign of anything behind.

The mayor's party carried lanterns on poles that they lifted above them to make little circles of illumination below, each with a dark centre that matched the solid base of the covered lights.

"The mayor is very fond of his guard, Mr Thaler," said Sophia. "He doesn't go anywhere without them."

"Until this morning, I would have agreed with you that it's a harmless affectation." Thaler lowered his voice. "Now it looks like prudence."

There were some eight men with Messinger, who looked as happy at being out at night as the squad who'd accompanied them up Goat Mountain had been. Half of them carried lanterns, the other half had spears at the ready.

Another lantern-carrier detached himself from the library portico, and Thaler seemed to know the man well.

"Ah, Mr Ullmann: well met, sir."

"'Evening, Mr Thaler. I told the mayor you'd be back in a minute. I think he almost believed me." The usher held up his lantern to see who Thaler was with. "A young lady, Mr Thaler? She's very welcome, of course. I'll just fetch another lantern."

Ullmann passed his lit lantern to Thaler and went back up the library steps. Messinger stamped over.

"Gods, man. What took you so long?" He eyed Sophia with patently mixed emotions. "Is she a permanent fixture now?"

"The opportunity presented itself that Miss Morgenstern could give her testimony in person. Having too much information is a rare luxury at the best of times, Master Messinger, and these are not the best of times." Thaler looked around the almost deserted square and scowled. He presented the chain of his lantern to Sophia. "Take this. Mr Ullmann will supply me with another."

"Where did you get so many lanterns from, and so quickly?" asked Messinger.

"The Jews gave them to the library, Master Messinger." Sophia took the proffered chain and inspected the lantern. The Hebrew letters scratched on the cage marked ownership. "Mr Thaler sent some librarians to my father, and he collected everything we had spare."

"Very impressive," said the mayor grudgingly. Ullmann brought another lantern, already lit, and gave it to Thaler.

"If that's all, Mr Thaler, I'll lock up," he said.

"Tell me," said Thaler, "does Mr Glockner have a deputy?"

"I don't think he's appointed anyone officially, sir," said Ullmann. There was a certain eagerness in his voice.

Thaler pursed his lips. "We'll have to see what we can do about that, Mr Ullmann. Carry on."

"Very good, Mr Thaler." He gave a separate bow to Thaler, the mayor, and, embarrassingly, Sophia, before attending to his duties. "Sir. Miss."

"Who's the boy, Thaler?" asked Messinger.

"Ullmann. Come out of the shadows in more ways than one." The sounds of long bolts being shut rang out. "Shall we go? The chamberlain's expecting us, I believe?"

"Quite what we're going to say to him – and the prince . . ."

"The truth, Master Messinger. What else but the truth?" Thaler looked up towards the fortress.

The mayor organised his men, front and back of the line, which he and Thaler were in the middle of. Sophia fell in behind them, and they worked their way up through the town to Fortress Alley and the Wagon Gate.

She didn't, despite the spears, feel any safer than she had earlier. She kept on looking at the slit of sky and the bright stars that glimmered there, as if something was going to descend on her from above and snatch her away. At least the noise the soldiers made drowned out any possibility of hearing odd sounds from elsewhere.

Thaler was deep in conversation with Messinger, discussing the water supply: nothing she could usefully contribute to, and they were still going strong when the Wagon Gate opened and they were within the castle walls.

Sophia had never been inside before, not even in the lower field where she was now. The white walls of the fortress glowed like ghosts above her in the reflected light, and she wondered if that had been the unseen presence she'd felt earlier.

Life behind the walls seemed little busier than in the town, whereas she'd always imagined intense activity: all the important people she knew lived lives of constant interruption. There were one or two sparks on the tower above her, and some of the windows glimmered, but otherwise they were unwatched, left to walk up to the next gate on their own cognisance.

"Mr Thaler, where is everyone?" she eventually asked while they waited for the Chastity Gate to creak aside.

Thaler blinked in the lantern-light. "My dear, they're all dead."

"Oh." The soldiers who'd marched out to cheering and waving were being plucked clean by the crows. No wonder the place appeared empty: it was.

From there, they walked between two high walls, across a bridge, along another narrow passage and through a tunnel. Only then did the sky open out and the keeps and towers that had seemed so far away throughout her life suddenly come within touching distance.

The guard dispersed, heading towards the main building, leaving her, Thaler and the mayor in the company of a boy who took them slowly across the inner courtyard towards one of the high towers – slowly, because he was shielding a guttering candle with only his hand.

The mayor had to open his own door and let the servant through, who then went ahead, leading them up stairs and along a corridor. Feeling totally lost, Sophia managed to resist the almost over-whelming urge to peer down side routes or behind curtains, in case she was momentarily forgotten and couldn't find her way back.

Then they finally arrived at what seemed to be their destination. The servant left, still carefully conserving his candle-flame, and it was just the three of them in some sort of anteroom. There were chairs and tapestries, and Sophia decided to sit and compose herself before her inevitable inquisition.

Thaler placed his lantern on a short round table that might have been a stool, and the mayor was content just to hold his.

"I don't like it, Thaler. The whole place has gone to the dogs."

"With respect, Master Messinger, it's a little soon to be recruiting a new castle guard, especially considering what happened to the old one." Thaler sat down briefly, before deciding that standing would be better. "And Prince Gerhard's funeral is still to come."

"I expected more, that's all." The mayor made a pretence at examining one of the wall hangings. "We've managed, haven't we?"

"Did you ever get around to answering my request for armed militia outside the library?" asked Thaler, with more than a little coolness in his voice. "Whose lantern are you using to examine that Rheinmaiden? Whose idea was it to question the hexmasters directly?"

"And look where that got us. Gods, what are we going to tell Trommler?"

Sophia sighed. "Gentlemen, please."

There was a slight movement to her left. She looked up and gasped. Thaler spun around faster than his size might normally allow, and the mayor actually jumped back.

"Apologies for keeping you waiting," said Trommler. As he turned to acknowledge each of them, he was revealed more clearly. "Master Messinger, a pleasure as always. You must be Under-librarian Thaler. And the lady? I'm afraid I don't know her, and I make it my business to know all who are in the castle walls."

"It's the Morgenstern girl," said the mayor. "The bookseller's daughter."

"Is it indeed?" Trommler stood squarely in front of her and looked down his sharp nose at her. "Rise, child."

When she stood, trembling, she was taller than him. "More than a girl, I think, Master Mayor," he said, and nodded slowly, seemingly coming to some sort of decision. "Wait here, Miss Morgenstern. I will call you shortly. Gentlemen, if you will accompany me."

The chamberlain went to the door at the end of the anteroom, and paused by Thaler's lantern. He regarded it in the same way he'd inspected Sophia.

"Interesting," was his only comment before picking it up by the chain. He opened the door, and the mayor strode through after him. There were lights, and voices, on the other side.

Thaler shrugged with an opened-handed gesture at Sophia, before slipping through the opening. The door was closed firmly behind him, muffling everything.

She had no idea how long she was supposed to wait. Trommler had scared her into obedience, at least for a while. She drew her knees up and laid her head on them, wrapping her legs with her arms. The voices next door started off calmly: Thaler's measured tones, the mayor's gruff barks, Trommler's indistinct bass rumble, and a fourth man whom she didn't know, whose voice was pitched higher than the others.

Even when she moved closer, she couldn't make out what they were saying: the odd word here and there, but infuriatingly not enough to sustain the flow of the conversation. But then, quite abruptly, Thaler was shouting. He was being answered in calm, flat terms, but he was agitated, and wouldn't stop.

Sophia moved away from the door: not only was her listening in vain, but she'd be unlikely to hear anyone approach, and she didn't want to guess at the penalties for overhearing affairs of state.

She sat back down in the same chair as before, and closed her cloak around her. Soon, it wasn't just the librarian raising his voice, but everyone. Uncomfortable and embarrassed, she bore it for as long as she could: eventually, she got up and stepped around the corner, taking her lantern with her. She could still hear them, though, so she moved even further away down the corridor.

Where she stopped, she found she was opposite a door ajar: not properly open, only a crack, but it was enough for her to hear the sounds of sobbing from inside. She looked up and down the corridor. Like the rest of the castle, it was woefully undermanned.

A choice, then. She could go back to the anteroom and suffer listening to the roar of full-throated argument happening behind the shut door. Or she could knock timidly on this open one and attempt to be of some use.

Sophia raised her knuckles to the frame, hesitated, then decided that nothing worse could happen than being told to go away. She was robust enough to take that, so she tapped at the wood and pushed slightly at the foot of the door with her toe.

The room beyond was almost dark. There were a couple of candles, and a low-burning fire. Her lantern added to the light, so that she could see a small figure slumped on the floor in front of the hearth. It was wracked with grief, shaking and moaning, curled in on itself in a tight little ball.

She lowered the lantern to the floor, knelt down next to it, and risked putting a hand out to rest gently but firmly on its shoulder.

The reaction wasn't what she expected at all. She was suddenly wrapped by the tight embrace of an arm, a wet face pressed hard into the angle of her neck, a body squashed shuddering against her own.

Her hands flapped for a moment, then came to rest on the thin linen shirt. She could feel the individual bones that made up – his? her? – spine. Her own hair was mixed with theirs, and she freed one hand to push her long strands aside, revealing collar-length, almost-black hair. No German girl would have hers cut so short, so it must be a boy, then.

She had no brothers or sisters. Her mother had been a long time in the grave. No one to learn from, and no one to practise on. She did the best she could with what little she knew. She made shushing sounds, she stroked the boy's hair, she rocked backwards and forwards, like she'd seen new mothers do to their babies.

It took a long time to quieten him, long enough that she started to get cramp in her folded legs and her back grew stiff. As he stilled and the quaking subsided, she took in the rest of the room over the boy's head. She couldn't see much without disturbing him, and most of the walls and furniture was in shadow.

But she could make out lots of decorative features: wood panelling, carved flourishes on the furniture, painted crests and shields on the plasterwork. Her eyes travelled up above the stone fireplace, and the yellow ornamental shield hanging there. The black panther emblazoned on it stared down at her, its red eyes alight and its red claws ready to strike at any unworthy touching the royal person.

Which, she realised with a gasp, meant her.

How had she got in unchallenged? How had she remained there for so long? Her heart raced like a downhill pebble, and she lost the ability to move, let alone talk.

He must have sensed the change in her, because he slowly and reluctantly slid his arms from around her back, though not letting go completely. He peeled his body away, and looked at her, gaunt and hollow-eyed.

"What? What is it?" There was a dirty loop of cloth hanging around his neck: a sling. And now she could see he held his right arm carefully. It wasn't the only thing about him that was dirty, either. His clothes were stiff with dried mud.

"My lord. I'm sorry." It was all she could manage. Felix I, Prince of Carinthia, all but sat in her lap.

He frowned, perhaps at her apology, perhaps because he didn't recognise her. "Who are you?"

"I'm . . ." She had an opportunity to just flee. He didn't know who she was. She could hide, and leave the castle, and he'd never find out. Except, except. It would never work. "Sophia Morgenstern, my lord, Aaron Morgenstern's daughter. I came with Mr Thaler and Master Messinger, but they're in with the chamberlain and having a huge argument over what the hexmaster wants us to do, I suppose, and they didn't need to speak to me yet, and I didn't like the way they were shouting so I walked down here to get away from them and then I heard you and your door was open and I didn't know who it was and please don't have me killed, my father has no one else to look after him since my mother died, just me . . ."

She had to take a breath, but then she'd have to stop talking and give him an opportunity to shout for help. Her voice petered out, and she hauled in so much air, she felt faint.

"Your mother's dead? My mother's dead too." Felix looked at his hands. "And now my father."

"Yes, my lord. I'm sorry."

That seemed to rile him, but only for a moment. She didn't know much about this boy-prince. Was he old enough for a Bar Mitzvah? That would make him a man, but even most of the Jewish boys were bigger than he was.

"Where are your servants?" she asked.

He looked blankly at her and attempted a shrug, which caused him pain enough to screw his face up, but not enough that he was going to let go of her.

"I don't know," he said. "They put me in here, and they left me. I think they're arguing over me, as well. Last night, I . . ."

"Have you had anything to eat, my lord, or to drink?" She looked around, and she couldn't see any empty plates, or even any full ones, picked at and ignored.

"No."

"No one's washed you, given you something clean to wear? Looked at your arm?"

"Shoulder," he said, and added with just a hint of steel: "I killed the man who did that to me."

"I should find someone who can help." She wondered why he was still clinging to her. He was a German prince, she wasn't anything but the shamefully unmarried Jewish bookseller's daughter.

"But you are helping," he said. "You're the only one who has."

"By accident, my lord." There was a smudge of dirt on his cheek, mud from his sleeve re-wetted by his tears. "I shouldn't have been able just to walk in here. I could have been anyone. A murderer, even."

His grip failed, and he slowly lowered his right arm by gripping his forearm with his other hand. "You don't look like a murderer."

She didn't move away, even though she was free. "Isn't that the point?"

"Probably. Signore Allegretti would have beaten me for this, before." He looked at her, and she at him. "How did your mother die?"

"She fell. She fell down some stairs because she was carrying too much, and she lost her footing. I wasn't quite two." It was something that had happened to someone else. She'd asked her father, and that was what he'd told her. She'd asked the same question every so often, hoping for more detail, but she always got the same bald explanation. She fell. She died. That was that.

She didn't ask Felix what had happened to his mother; she knew the bones of the story already. She'd died giving birth to him, even though the hexmasters had been called. She'd been ten, or eleven when the mixed news had been called out around the town: joy at a male heir for Carinthia, sadness at the loss of one so young and beautiful.

He didn't say anything, and she started to lose what frayed courage she had left. "This is wrong, my lord. I shouldn't be here."

"I command you to stay." His head came up, his chin set.

It was her turn to surprise him. She laughed at him, and instantly he was both angry and nonplussed, full of boyish rage and nowhere for it to go.

But she'd surprised herself, mistaking the little princes she knew from Jews' Alley with this real one. "I'm sorry. You are my earthly lord, and I am yours to command."

Now he blushed, and it was good to see some colour in the prince's cheeks. "I didn't mean it like that. I just want you to stay. You're . . ." and he looked away again without finishing.

The poor boy. "I can try and clean you up a little. If you want." She suspected that this was as awkward for him as it was for her.

She was used to waiting on her father, but not like this, and the prince was probably used to being waited on, but not like this either.

She got up from the floor and circumnavigated the room, seeing what was there, peering into chests and opening drawers. There were clean clothes, but made for someone much taller – the late prince, and surely she couldn't dress the son in the dead father's shirt and breeks? Did she have a choice? She didn't know where the prince's old rooms were, and she wasn't going to wander around the castle trying to find them. There was a jug half-full of water, and a bowl, which she set close to the grate to warm, and she decided that, as a prince, he could probably afford to sacrifice a shirt or two.

He watched her closely, and it made her more nervous. She barely had the strength to tear the shirts down the seams. She found that she barely had the strength to stand. She wavered between knowing what she was doing, and not having the slightest clue.

She knelt back on the floor next to Felix and decided that if she was going to do this, she was going to do it well. She laid out the pieces of shirt beside her, and splashed some of the water into the bowl.

"You need to look up, my lord."

"Felix," he mumbled as she took hold of his chin to turn his head.

"I know. But you're Prince Felix of Carinthia, and you need to be reminded of that." She dipped a sleeve in the water and wrung it out so that it was wet but not dripping.

"I could command you to call me Felix."

The water was cold on her fingers as she rubbed at his cheek. "You could, and I'd still add 'my lord' under my breath every single time. It wouldn't do to be over-familiar."

"Does that mean I have to call you Miss Morgenstern?" Rivulets of dirty water trickled down his neck. No matter: the shirt he was wearing would have to go. He ought to wash his hair, too, but she didn't have enough water for that, and anyway, a good brush would see off most of the filth.

"My lord can call me whatever he wishes. Isn't that the way it's supposed to be?" She lifted off the sling and, for want of anything better to do with it, tossed it into the heart of the fire. It smoked

230

and charred for a moment, before burning with a dirty flame. "This shoulder: is it broken?"

"There's a little bone that goes across here." He traced the line with his left hand. "The signore called it the clavicula."

"Collar-bone," she said. "It'll only set right if the arm is completely immobilised. Let me see."

He couldn't lift his arm up to get his shirt off, and she was going to cause him pain peeling it off him. So she sat behind him and ripped it off his back. She did warn him, but it was still shocking when the stitching tore, and they both covered their embarrassment by giggling.

Her laughter died in her throat. The boy's body was a bruise that varied only in colour. Red weals marked where the armour had turned blows away, and they were everywhere. His sword-arm was purple and black.

"How did you live through this?"

"I don't remember. It happened so fast."

Sophia eased the sleeve off the right arm, and moved around to the front to feel the break. It was clean, which was one thing, and there wasn't much swelling, but she could feel the ends move against each other when she pressed against them.

Felix winced, and said nothing.

"I know how to do this," she said. "It might take one or two tries before I'm happy with it." She needed to make bandages, and tie them together to make a long length. Somewhere in her travels, she'd come across a pair of good scissors, so she went to fetch those, and another couple of shirts which she proceeded to turn into strips.

"How do you know how to do this?" he asked.

"Because I learnt. We don't do it any other way."

"What do you mean?"

"By magic," she said. "It's not kosher."

He looked at her quizzically, and she sighed.

"Jewish law—" she started, but he interrupted.

"Jewish law? I thought—"

"Then you thought wrong. Anyway, these are extra laws, on top of the Carinthian ones, that say how we're to practise our religion. Food laws, mainly, and how to observe our festivals, but lots of other things too. We call it Halakha: things that are permitted are kosher, things that are not are treif. It can get complicated for

231

the . . . people who aren't Jews, but magic isn't kosher. It doesn't stop some, but we get by without, mostly."

She started knotting together the strips she'd made. Felix wasn't very big, so she wouldn't need as many as for a full-grown adult.

"You do without magic? How?"

"By doing things differently. We've done it for thousands of years. Three thousand at least. We're still here." She caught his unasked question, and suddenly she realised what she had to do. It suddenly wasn't about bandaging the prince's shoulder. "Carinthia can learn. It'll be hard at first, but it can be done. You can still rule a prosperous and peaceful country without the Order."

Felix chewed at his lip. "The Order's always been there. The stories, the battles: they've always been on our side."

"I know those stories too." Sophia took a chance, and hoped. "But do you know this one? I found something out today when I walked up Goat Mountain, all the way to the top, with Mr Thaler and the mayor."

She took the bandage and started to coil it up while he stared at her with wide-eyed amazement.

"You were on Goat Mountain?"

"At the top. At the White Tower." She nodded. "They've been killing people, in secret, for years, if not for centuries. They've killed their own, I think that's obvious, and Mr Thaler says they've been taking Carinthian children. To be honest, I don't think they cared who it was. But there are bodies. Maybe hundreds: skeletons, skulls, thrown out with the waste. There are bits of bone everywhere. Have you ever been told that?"

"No."

She slid her hands around his thin waist, wrapping it twice with the bandage to trap the loose end, then looping it up his back.

"Put your right hand on your left shoulder. Hold your elbow into your chest," she instructed, and he meekly complied. She drew the bandage diagonally across his front, down the length of his arm and under his elbow, before looping it around his bicep and tying it off.

She sat back and inspected her work. It was, if anything, a little tight, though it would relax with time. Felix didn't seem to notice any discomfort.

"There's more to this new story," she said. "We met a hexmaster at the White Tower – just the one, and I think he's the only one left. I think all the others have either been killed or run away. From the state of him, he must have killed a few himself. He says he can bring the magic back. That's what Mr Thaler, Master Messinger and the chamberlain are arguing about now."

"Won't bringing the magic back be a good thing, though? Everyone misses it, and we need it."

She leant forward to cut away the excess bandage, and let the scissors fall to the floor. "You can't do what the hexmaster wants, even if you believe him. Even if he can do what he claims."

"I don't understand," he said plaintively.

"He wants to use your subjects for fuel." She took the scraps of material and cast them at the fire. "That's what he said. Fuel. One or two a day. Every day. Sacrifices."

A noise in the corridor distracted her, and the door was flung open. A lean, angry man in fine clothes took one look and rushed at her. He moved extraordinarily quickly, taking hold of her hair in one fist, jerking her backwards to a half-standing position, and putting a dagger to her throat.

She barely had time to gasp, and when she did so, the point of the blade touched her neck.

"Let go of her," said Felix. He put his good hand on the floor and pushed himself up. He really wasn't very tall. He was half dressed and one arm was bandaged across his chest. But he was a prince. "Let go of her at once."

Despite the direct order, the man didn't relax his grip on her hair, or move the dagger aside. "Who is this woman? How did she get in here?"

Although both her hands were free, Sophia didn't dare move. She might get one hand between his knife and her, but he was very strong and she didn't want to die.

Having regained his colour previously, Felix was now shock-white again. He saw the scissors lying on the floor next to his feet, and he scooped them up, holding them in front of him in lieu of any other weapon. "Let. Her. Go."

The man still didn't obey. He clenched his fist tighter in her hair and pulled harder. It hurt. It hurt a lot. But she was transfixed by the boy-man in front of her, levelling a pair of closed scissors at the man's face.

Felix danced forward. His movements were almost as quick as

her assailant's: he had a leg either side of Sophia's in order to get close enough, but his footwork was assured. The point of the scissors trembled in front of the man's right eye.

"Signore. You're mistaken. She hasn't hurt me, and I insist you let her go, at once."

The man could have dropped her: sprung his hand and let her fall to the floor. Perhaps, with the threat of blindness an inch away and the prince clearly agitated, he decided that any sudden movements wouldn't be wise. He lifted his knife hand high, and lowered Sophia to the ground, disentangling his fingers with exaggerated care.

As soon as she was free, she scrambled away and put a heavy chair between herself and the man.

"Apologies, my lord," he was saying, "I am only ever concerned for your safety. That she has not mistreated you is both your luck and hers, not design." He looked at her like a cat would regard a mouse. "From the back I thought it might be the witch Agana."

There was a clump of her hair on the floor beside him, and when Sophia put her hand to her head, it came away wet. She almost picked up the chair and threw it at the man, this signore. Did she look like this witch from the front, too? He had had ample time to check. She pressed her fingers against her neck, and discovered a thin ribbon of blood running down to her collar.

The prince, though, seemed to accept the apology. He let his arm fall by his side, all the fight knocked out of him. "Why are you here, signore?"

"I came to find my lord and prince, to request his presence at a meeting of grave importance where the future of the palatinate may be decided."

Felix glanced at Sophia, then back at the signore. "I have to go," he said.

"My lord should at least consider putting on a shirt," she replied. What was she saying? She was bleeding from the head, the neck, and she was asking the half-naked Prince of Carinthia to put on some clothes. She wiped her hand on her skirt, and turned her back on them to look in the chests for something that might fit him without looking ludicrously huge.

She wondered as she searched whether she'd get that dagger between the shoulder-blades. She shuddered, and carried on regardless. Eventually, she found a suitable shirt that had ties which she could use to take in any excess.

Aware that the signore was staring at her all the while, she stepped behind Felix and asked him to raise his good arm. She dropped the shirt over his head, feeding his hand up the sleeve until it popped out the other end, then pulled the rest of it down over his bandages. She tied bows where she could, and even turned him around so she could lace his collar.

The signore's face was full of rage. He hated her. Yet after Felix had stammered his thanks and looked up at her looking down, when he turned back around, the man's snarl had vanished.

"We are in the solar, my lord. If you please." He gestured to the door, his hand still threaded with strands of her hair that glittered like web.

"I do have to go," said Felix.

"Of course, my lord." She dipped into a curtsey, and stayed with her head bowed until he left.

Then it was just her and the signore.

"I know who you are," he said.

"Then you lied to Felix." She moved to stand back behind the chair. "You lied to your prince."

The man shrugged off the accusation. "That idiot librarian thinks you have something useful to contribute to our discussions. You do not. You will not be heard."

Sophia was about to tell him that it was too late, that she'd already given her testimony about Eckhardt to the one person who genuinely mattered, when she decided that saying so wouldn't be a good idea. She was facing the sort of man who would kill her out of spite – not today, perhaps, but tomorrow, or the next day – and he'd make it look accidental so as not to arouse suspicion.

She had to rely on Felix not blurting it all out, of course. Her life was in the hands of a grief-stricken twelve-year-old boy.

"As you wish," she said, and he seemed satisfied that he had cowed her.

"Wait here. Someone will escort you to the Wagon Gate." The signore didn't even bother facing her as he carried on speaking on his way to the door. "Stay away from the prince, Miss Morgenstern."

It was just her, now. She didn't know how much time she had before a guard came to throw her out. She did know that she had to make the most of what she had.

235

Looking for likely bandage cloth had revealed a writing set. Ink, pen, cut squares of parchment. She raced to it, opened the box, and took it over to the fire, where there was most light.

She crouched down, and started to scratch out her words.

32

Thaler was too close to the fire, and he was sweating. He recognised that his seat had been offered to him quite deliberately to discomfort him. Messinger was in hardly a better position.

Things had started off well: Trommler had been in charge then, and Thaler realised that he'd met a kindred spirit, a man with a book under his arm. He'd listened gravely – there seemed to be no other demeanour that suited him – and nodded slowly as he gave them permission to proceed to the next part of their story.

The change had come with the entry of the Italian sword-master, Allegretti, from a door at the far end of the solar. He'd insisted they sit rather than stand. He'd insisted they drink, while surreptitiously abstaining himself. He'd made small talk, enquiring after their health, the state of the weather, the general disposition of the library and the town; anything but the most important matter of Eckhardt and his offer.

It had grown too much, and Messinger, already highly agitated, had blown like an over-heated kettle. Thaler, in his attempts to reason with both the mayor and the sword-master, had become roused himself, and it had taken all Trommler's skill to calm them down.

Thaler didn't even know why Allegretti was there. He appeared to have invited himself and excluded everyone else. He wasn't the prince, and it was the prince they needed to see. Yes, the boy had only twelve years under his belt, but it was obvious that Carinthia couldn't accept the demands of a deranged murderer, no matter what riches he proffered in return.

Yet Allegretti couldn't see that. He kept on accepting their points, only to completely overturn them with his next "But if . . ."

Messinger continued to explode. Who would have thought that such a short man could contain such boundless reserves of fury?

They'd even got to the stage of discussing whether or not to extend the number of capital crimes, so as to feed the boilers of Eckhardt's proposed magic-factory. Just a thought, a suggestion.

"Stop," said Thaler. "This is preposterous." He got up out of his chair and walked across the room to the windows, where it was cooler and he could think more clearly.

"Mr Thaler, I insist you rejoin us." Allegretti frowned at him.

"And I insist the prince hears what we have to say. We have rights of audience."

"The mayor has rights of audience, Mr Thaler. Under-librarians do not."

Thaler expected Trommler to intervene, but he didn't. He did, however, raise one eyebrow ever so slightly, and Thaler took heart.

"Master Allegretti, all free men of Carinthia have rights of audience to their prince, whether they're the lowest shit-shoveller or the highest . . . whatever." Thaler leant back into the wonderfully cool window alcove. "And I, through fate, represent the library."

"I accept your right, Mr Thaler, but we must have discussed the matter thoroughly first, in order to advise our lord wisely. He is tired, and distraught. Better we leave him to rest until we have something to say."

"Gods, man," growled Messinger. "You always have something to say. If your swordplay was as prodigious as your word-play, I'd be talking to Gerhard."

Allegretti's hand dropped to his right-hand hilt. "Where I come from, you would be on the end of this for such an insult."

"You're in Carinthia now, and we can tell blowhards like you to shut the fuck up as often as we like." Messinger leapt up and deliberately kicked his chair over on the way. "But if you like, I can see about learning some Italian ways."

Trommler rose like a shadow between them. "Gentlemen. We do no service to the prince by such actions. Neither does it appear we can usefully agree on a course of action to present to our lord."

"The mayor and Mr Thaler are intransigent, I agree," said Allegretti, and sighed dramatically.

"Who is this man anyway?" appealed Messinger. "Nothing but a glorified teacher."

"Perhaps I should teach you some manners." Allegretti half drew his sword, and Thaler decided that this meeting was already a disaster. He hurried over and interposed his bulk.

He took the mayor by the shoulders and pushed him back until they were outside the circle of chairs around the fire and in the orange darkness beyond.

"You're doing exactly what he wants, man. Don't rise to it."

Messinger shivered with frustration: "What *is* it that he wants? He can't honestly want to barter lives for magic, can he?"

"There will be many who will. Don't tell me you're not tempted." Thaler dropped his hands and clasped them in front of him. "Lights for the library. You think I want to spend the next however-many-years ruining my eyesight, reading by candlelight? All the other librarians, all that work, all that copying: how many lives do you suppose that's worth to me?"

"But you know as well as I do that once we've entered into this pact, there'll be no end to it. We'll run out of criminals sooner rather than later, then what? Who do we pick after that? Bavarians? Jews?" Messinger span away and paced the floor. "Yes, of course I'm tempted. It won't be like before, where everyone had magic, just not as good as ours. We had an edge then, enough of an edge to make us rich and allow us peace. We'll have magic and no one else will. Not so much an edge as an overwhelming advantage. Can we resist abusing that? If it means we don't have to feed our own to this Eckhardt's desire, but can take prisoners from the lands around us, who wouldn't?"

Thaler was struck by the differences in their ambitions. He just wanted a good light by which to read a book. Messinger was talking about invading their neighbours and taking sacrifices from the conquered lands.

"I'm a peaceable man, Master Messinger . . ."

"And so am I, Thaler. I know I bluster and strut, but that's what's expected of me. I can't countenance this . . . this, monstrous exchange, no matter how it might damage us otherwise. Because if the Wiennese, or the Bavarians, or even the Venetians get wind of what we're up to, we'll have three fuck-off-sized armies camped on our doorstep before autumn. And they'll know exactly what's at stake. It'll be either us or them." The mayor subsided momentarily as he gnawed at his fingernail. "I won't have it, Thaler, do you hear? Better we fade into obscurity than have our name remembered as a byword for this outrage."

Thaler hung his head. "We're of one mind. We must convince the prince."

"Will he believe us over his tutor?" worried Messinger.

"We need to gather the earls – the remaining earls, that is," Thaler corrected himself, "– and hold a grand council. If Felix hears many voices against and only one for, then we'll win the day. Surely."

"And if our lord already has his mind poisoned against reason? Gods, man: he's just a child." Messinger started to wind himself up again. "And now he's gone."

"Who?" Thaler turned.

"The Italian. Mr Trommler, where did he go?"

Trommler, with his back to the fire, answered. "Gone to fetch the prince."

"Time for our secret weapon, then," said Thaler, and went to collect Sophia from the anteroom.

She wasn't there. He went into the corridor beyond and looked up and down its length. She still wasn't there.

Had she wandered off? Gone home? Been chased away? Thaler clenched his jaw. It was one thing to hear two old men tell a story about a blood-stained hexmaster promising the world if they'd just give him people to kill. It was another to hear a young woman testify that the Order were killers, and that Goat Mountain was already a graveyard for countless victims.

She could help swing the decision in their direction.

He went back into the solar. "She's gone," he said.

Messinger groaned. "That's what you get when you rely on a woman. And a Jewish woman at that."

"I'm sure there's a perfectly reasonable explanation—"

"As to why she's left us in the lurch? Curse her." Messinger looked back at Allegretti's empty chair. "Do you think I could have him?"

"Who? Trommler?" Thaler was appalled.

"No, the Italian." The mayor rested his hand on his sword.

"Oh, you mean the prince's very own Genoese sword-master, the one who fights two-handed and has nothing to do but practise all day, every day, for what? Two decades?" Thaler considered the matter for a moment before concluding. "Don't be an idiot, man. He'd spit you like a partridge and pluck you to boot. Neither of which will help us find Sophia."

There was nothing for it but to admit her disappearance to the chamberlain.

Thaler cleared his throat. "Mr Trommler. Miss Morgenstern appears to have vanished."

Trommler stretched his calves by standing on tiptoe, and turned around to bake the other side. "Vanished, you say? Despite everything, I find that extraordinarily difficult to believe. You are normally so precise in your vocabulary, Mr Thaler: please try again."

"Well, she's not there." The librarian tutted. "Perhaps she's taken fright after all."

"Oh, I don't believe we're as frightening as all that. Civilised men can and do disagree passionately, something that Miss Morgenstern surely knows." Trommler rose again on his toes. "Even if she can't be found, I'm sure she has used her time wisely."

Messinger started to pace the floor. "We need to offer something in magic's place. Other than barbarism and defeat, that is. Can we do that?"

"The water," said Thaler. "The Romans did it. So can we."

"How? Deliver water to every house, every yard, every fountain in Juvavum?" Messinger snorted. "If you can do it, it'd be—"

"Magic, Master Mayor?" Thaler looked down at his boots. "Yet we know that the water used to flow without it." Somewhere beneath his feet, beneath the very fortress itself, was the answer. The Romans couldn't create water like the Germans: the spell for that, the associated rune, didn't exist then – yet they were still using Roman plumbing, and dabbling in Roman pools.

Then he looked up, so suddenly that the bones in his neck went crack.

"The mikveh," he shouted.

Messinger, startled, stopped his furious pacing. "What? What's that you say?"

"The ritual baths of the Jews. The mikveh, they call it. All this time, it's had water – it still has water – that doesn't come from magic." Thaler blinked in surprise. "So where does it come from?"

But there was no more time for questions. The prince, one sleeve of his white shirt trailing like a banner, slipped quietly into the room, and only Trommler seemed to notice.

"My lord Felix," he said. "The mayor of Juvavum and the library wish to exercise their ancient rights of audience."

Thaler expected Allegretti to be right behind the prince, but he hadn't appeared by the time the boy had nodded to both him and Messinger, and crossed to the fire. The night wasn't that cold, but he seemed to need the heat.

Trommler was also looking around for Allegretti. "My lord should be aware that a decision, or even an indication of his thoughts, is not required at this time."

"Thank you, Mr Trommler." Felix looked up at the chamberlain. "Mr Trommler, do you work for me now?"

"If it's your wish that I keep my position, then I'll serve you as faithfully as I served your father."

"I do wish," said the prince. "There's so much I don't know."

Trommler looked over to where the Book of Carinthia lay on a table. "My lord mustn't worry. Good advice is closer than you think. Gentlemen?"

Thaler and Messinger drew closer, and Trommler introduced them. The prince had met the mayor before, but he frowned at Thaler's name.

"The letter writer."

Ah. Thaler had wondered when this would come, and it was sooner than he thought. "Yes, my lord. Both mine and Peter Büber's loyalty to Carinthia are as solid as the foundations of this fortress. If he is at fault in fearing the Order, then I'm more to blame."

"He took the blame for himself." Felix blinked up at him. "Both he and the witch are banished. He admitted he should've told my father."

Thaler felt his heart sink. "Our fault was assuming he already knew. My deepest regret, my lord, is that we didn't discover the Order's perfidy in time. We failed Carinthia."

Instead of sending him away, or calling for the guard, what was left of it, Felix looked away. "I . . . mistakes get made, sometimes."

"My lord would not have a fiercer protector than Master Büber," said Thaler, knowing it was true.

It seemed that the librarian wasn't the only one with regrets. Felix turned to the chamberlain. "Is there any way I can change my mind?"

Trommler cleared his throat. "We can try and get a message to him, but he's the huntmaster and will be difficult to find. Such men are much more adept at disappearing than even Miss Morgenstern."

"She didn't disappear," Felix blurted. "She was with me."

Then Allegretti came back in, signalling his approach with the jingle of his scabbards. Thaler, open-mouthed, had his slack jaw closed by the back of Messinger's hand.

The Italian stalked to the centre of the room, looking at the faces of the others to gauge what had transpired while he'd been away. Thaler was examining Allegretti's features, with similar intent.

"My lord, gentlemen."

Messinger grunted impatiently, and seemed eager to state his case to the prince, but Thaler wanted something else first.

"Will Miss Morgenstern be joining us, Master Allegretti?" The Italian had returned some time after the prince had arrived. If Sophia had been with the boy, then so had Allegretti.

For a brief moment, the mask slipped and Thaler saw Allegretti's intent naked: only for a moment, because the urbane tutor reasserted himself quickly.

"She will not, Mister Thaler. As you well know, it is only free men who have rights of audience."

"If my lord Felix commanded it, however?" Thaler suggested, but the prince blushed and waved at the chairs.

"I don't need to," he said, and picked a chair for himself.

Allegretti looked satisfied. Self-satisfied, in fact. Thaler, however, thought he knew Sophia well enough to suspect she hadn't been entirely silent. The Italian took the chair next to Felix, positioning himself on the other side to Messinger and Thaler, creating the semblance of a faction and promoting himself to the prince's right.

Trommler hovered in the shadows while the other two took their seats.

"Mr Trommler, is there anything to drink?" asked Felix. "Or eat?"

"I'm sure there is, my lord. I shall return shortly." Trommler eased himself away, and Felix looked expectantly at the mayor.

Messinger scratched at his chin, and with a resigned shrug of his shoulders recounted the entirety of his and Thaler's trip up Goat Mountain. When he left something out, Thaler filled in the missing details, including the parts that should have been Sophia's to relate – and, judging from the prince's reaction, it didn't seem that he was hearing these things for the first time.

When the moment came to tell of the encounter with Eckhardt, the mayor reached forward and drank a good deal of the wine provided by Trommler. He could barely bring himself to speak of it to Felix.

So Thaler took over and explained what exactly the hexmaster had offered, and what he wanted in return.

"My lord, those are his terms, and he awaits your answer."

Felix stared into the fire. "How long do we have?"

"He didn't say." Thaler looked to his own wine. Despite everything, he was determined to sleep well that night. "Whatever you decide to do, you have to consider other factors as well."

Allegretti shifted in his chair. "We have heard your testimony, gentlemen. Thank you. Mr Trommler will show you out."

Felix looked from the Italian back to Thaler. His lips twitched. "What other factors, Mr Thaler?"

"We can discuss them when the gentlemen have left, my lord." Allegretti said firmly.

But the boy would not be swayed. "Mr Thaler?"

"Water," said Thaler quickly, before he could be interrupted. "Juvavum's water supply depends on magic to push the water through the pipes. Without it, we have no sanitation, no domestic or industrial supply."

"Be assured," said Allegretti, "that the prince has the welfare of all his people in his heart."

"Tell him, man," growled Messinger. "Tell him your plan."

Allegretti was about to cut the mayor off, when Felix held out his hand. He fixed Thaler with his fire-bright gaze. "A plan, Mr Thaler?"

The librarian went cold inside, and his mouth went abruptly dry. He took a mouthful of wine, and swallowed hard. "I do have an alternative, my lord." At least, he hoped he had.

Felix leant back in his chair. "Go on."

Thaler got out of his chair and started to pace the floor. "The Romans, my lord: their magic was poor, and their building excellent. When they founded Juvavum – or rather, razed the German town on this site to the ground and built on top of the ruins – they installed a water supply that worked without magic."

"Gods," muttered Allegretti, shaking his head.

"It is my belief that this underground system is still working."

"Ha."

Messinger gripped the arms of his chair. "If you don't shut up, you coxcomb, you gilded pig's . . ."

Thaler kicked the mayor's chair. Hard. And he was still in his library slippers.

"When did Rome fall, Mr Thaler?" asked the prince.

"A little over a thousand years ago, my lord. However, the Romans built to last. We have Roman buildings in Juvavum and throughout Carinthia. Parts of this fortress date back to Alaric's time, and as I'm sure my lord is aware, the library used to be a Roman temple."

"And what makes you think that the Roman water pipes are still there?"

"Because we still use part of the system. And because there is still water flowing into the Jews' ritual baths."

At mention of the Jews, Felix raised his head, and Thaler suddenly, dizzyingly, realised that he might actually pull this audacity off.

"If the ah, mikveh, still has water," he continued, "so could we. At least, I'd like your permission to investigate the possibility before my lord feels compelled to accept Master Eckhardt's bargain."

Allegretti looked disgusted, but the prince seemed intrigued. As for Trommler? He never gave anything away he didn't intend to.

"It's good to have choices, Mr Thaler. You taught me that yourself, signore."

"My lord, this hardly counts as a choice!"

Felix ignored the man. "What do you need, Mr Thaler?" he asked.

"I . . . I don't know." He looked to Messinger for support.

"He'll have everything he needs, my lord," said the mayor. "Men, materials, whatever."

"Thank you, Master Messinger." The prince nodded. "Mr Trommler said I didn't need to make a decision now, and Master Eckhardt seems to say he can wait a little while. Can you hurry, Mr Thaler?"

All hopes of sleep had gone in an instant. "My lord, I shall apply myself and my fellows to the task with all haste. Starting now. Mr Messinger, if you please?"

The mayor rose from his chair and looked sternly at Allegretti, before bowing to Felix. "We'll send news as we have it."

The boy shook his head. "Don't. That'll waste time. Just tell me when you've done it, or you know you can't."

"As you wish, my lord." Messinger swept from the room, pushing Thaler ahead of him. When they were alone, he hissed: "Do you really think you can do this?"

"I have absolutely no idea at all." Thaler cracked his knuckles. "But we're about to find out."

33

It was light when she woke. Sophia was vaguely aware of a hammering noise, and she wondered if it was her head. Purim drinking was both epic and legendary, and she'd taken some wine when she'd got back home, despite it only being the men who were obligated to get to the point where they couldn't tell the difference between cursing Haman and blessing Mordecai.

As she raised her head from her pillow, she realised that the banging was real, insistent, and coming from downstairs.

It was loud enough to wake the dead. More importantly, it was loud enough to wake her father, who, as well as being just a little deaf, had imbibed heroic amounts of syrupy sweet wine and danced the hora well into the night.

She threw back the covers, dragged her heavy housecoat over her night-clothes and tried to hurry. She fell against her bedroom door, hauled it open with difficulty and then crashed against the opposing walls of the staircase on her way down.

"All right already," she called. "Enough."

The knocking stopped, and she worked the latch, with no result. Seemingly, she'd had enough wits about her last night to close the bolts.

Last night. She pressed her fingers hard into her temples and leant against the wall. Then she put her hand to her neck, and felt the scab of dried blood, and touched the top of her head where it was sore.

"Who is it?"

"It's Mr Thaler, Miss Morgenstern," came the reply, bright and loud.

What was the idiot doing? She struggled the bolts free and heaved the door aside.

It was Thaler. It was also half a dozen librarians, two of the town's militia, and three high-ranking guildsmen.

She stared at the crowd, trying to understand what brought twelve men to her house before breakfast. They stared back at her, clearly expecting something to happen, Thaler the most expectant of all.

"What?" she asked. She moved the hair that was curtaining one eye. "What is it?"

Thaler looked behind him at the waiting men. "We need your help. What else would we need?"

"My . . . help?" Her hair fell over her face again, and she made more of a concerted effort to trap it this time. "I don't understand. Is this about the books?"

"Yes," said Thaler, "but not those books. I, we that is, have a plan."

He beckoned one of the librarians to him and plucked the roll of parchment from his pale hands. He unrolled it and held it up to her. It had lines and markings on it, with tiny annotations made in Gothic script.

"Yes. I see. You do have a plan." She leant back against the door frame. "What is it a plan of?"

Thaler let go of one end of the parchment and it rolled up again with a snap. "The water supply. Is your father up?"

"Up?" She looked back into the house. "You won't get any sense out of him before midday. And honestly, I'm not getting any sense out of you, either. What do you need my father for?"

"We need a scholarly Jew," said Thaler. "We have a book."

He waved at another librarian, who stepped forward and held up a black-bound book, the cover embossed with a menora.

"I can see you have a book. A book and a plan." Sophia shook her head to try and clear it. "Why do you need my father again?"

Thaler opened his mouth, but the man carrying the book got in first. "Begging your pardon, miss, but Mr Thaler's had no sleep at all, so if I might explain?"

"Someone needs to," she said.

"I think Mr Thaler's already told you that he thinks he can get the water running again. He has what we hope is a map of the underground cisterns, but we need someone who can read this Hebrew script. The library's got Hebrew readers, but they can't make head nor tail of this."

She focused on the man with his slicked-back hair and thin face. "Let me have a look."

She took the book from him and opened it at a random page near the middle. The spine creaked, and she had difficulty supporting its weight in one hand. She didn't want to drop it, so she only took a quick look.

"It's Yiddish, not Hebrew. Vernacular and old. No vowel marks."

Thaler looked pleased. "Your father can read it?"

"If I can, he can. But if I wake him up now, he'll still be drunk. As will every other male Jew in the street who might be able to make out what it says." Sophia handed the book back and stuck the heel of her hand into her eye socket. "Mr Thaler?"

"Miss Morgenstern?"

"At some point, we're going to have to stop doing this. Wait here." She stumbled back inside and pushed the door closed. This was insane. She had the fires to make, food to cook, dishes and clothes to wash, and today was Friday! The Sabbath wouldn't wait for anyone: two days' work to fit into one.

She couldn't afford to nursemaid goyim librarians through an obscure history book for the rest of the day. She needed to be here, in this house. Nursemaiding her father's sore head. Lighting the Shabbat candles.

But it was still very early, and her father wouldn't be conscious for hours. She ran a good household, so she could spare some time. Her neighbours would talk, but they hadn't seen the look on Eckhardt's face: the Jews needed the Germans like never before.

She growled at herself, and fled upstairs to get dressed, stamping back down again and flinging the door open on the still-surprised men.

"Where are we going?"

"The, ah, mikveh." Thaler pointed up the street in the direction of the synagogue.

"I know where it is, Mr Thaler." She closed the door behind her, and still they all stood and stared at her. "Oy. What are we waiting for?"

Sophia elbowed her way through and set off without them. Some of the window shutters were already open in the other houses, and as she strode past trailing a gaggle of black-robed men, spear-carriers and guildsmen, faces appeared at the openings, heads and shoulders leaning out to get a better view once she'd gone by.

The synagogue was at the corner of the street where it made a dog's leg into Scale Square. Stone-built, it was sturdy and squat, and underneath it, accessed by separate steps, was the mikveh.

She'd barely put one foot on the first step down when a window flew open.

"You men! Stop!"

They all looked up.

"You can't go down there. It's not allowed."

Thaler looked briefly confused. "But the prince has ordered it."

It was the turn of the woman stretched out of an upstairs window to be stunned. "The prince?"

"Yes, good lady. And the mayor."

Sophia retraced her path, and shielded her eyes so she could see. "Good morning, Mrs Cohen."

"Who's that?" She peered down. "Sophia Morgenstern? What are you doing?"

"I'm assisting these gentlemen in the execution of their lawful duty." She smiled. "I expect they'll arrest you if you try and stop us."

"Where's your father? Go and get him at once." The rabbi's wife's voice was sharp and demanding.

"My father is otherwise incapacitated, Mrs Cohen, as I expect your husband is. Now, if you'd like us to shout our business to the rooftops, I'll happily do so another time – but not now." Sophia cupped her hands around her mouth. "We're busy."

She'd pay for that later, especially if this plan of Thaler's didn't work. She turned back around and descended to the wooden door of the mikveh.

"Watch your heads." She ducked through the doorway, and collected the lantern from the alcove. The air was moist and cool, and the sounds of moving water percolated upwards. "Tell me you brought more lights."

"Ah."

"Don't worry, Mr Thaler. I've brought a few from the library."

"Excellent, Mr Ullmann." Thaler beamed. "Yes, Miss Morgenstern, we have lights."

The mikveh was at the bottom of a square shaft, wound around with steps. They all clattered down, as far as they could go. The stairs went on, under the water, and the lazy ripples in the pool twisted the candlelight back up at them.

"Oh." Thaler leant out over the water. "I expected something more . . ."

"Grand, Mr Thaler?" She'd stopped on the step above the water, and held on to the handrail. "Not this mikveh. I'm told the one in Spira is very much bigger."

"But look. The water's not still."

"Can we drain the pool?" asked a voice.

"There's a gate which slides over the inlet. It's not a perfect seal, but the water leaves the pool faster than it leaks in, through a grating at the bottom. That's the way we empty it. But Mr Thaler," she asked, "you've yet to explain why we're here."

"The answer, Miss Morgenstern, is very simple. We believe this is one of the access points to the Roman water system. That you still have water here is confirmation of that. Now, if you would care to translate a portion of text." Thaler took the book from Ullmann and sat down on the steps so that he could balance it on his knees.

He leafed through the pages, and Sophia held her lantern so that he could see what he was doing. Pages of closely written Hebrew characters passed under his fingers. Then he turned one final page, and there in the margin was a drawing that looked a lot like the mikveh.

"Here." He turned the book around and looked expectant.

"How did you find this? Out of all the books in the library?" She bent forward, tracing the lines of script.

"As Mr Ullmann said, none of the librarians have had any sleep. We must have checked several hundred books until we found mention of this one. Then we had to find it. And when we'd found it, I had to look through it, while other stout-hearted gentlemen went even further back into the past, to the very founding of the town."

"You worked all through the night. And you're still working this morning."

"There's much at stake, Miss Morgenstern. But we're in company, and I can't elaborate. So if you please?" Thaler pointed to the book.

"Yes, yes, of course." She read. "Once the site for the mikveh had been established, work began. Joshua ben Cohen gave his blessing and . . . how old is this book?"

"We believe it to be at least six hundred years old."

"This doesn't tell us why they chose this location, though." As

Thaler's face fell, she turned back one page. "A conduit passed in a line from Scale Square north-north-west to vomit . . . no, vent into the river west of the boatmaker's yard. Such living water as is passed through the conduit is by the Halakha suitable for a mikveh, and therefore determines its place."

"Which is exactly what we wanted, Miss Morgenstern." He turned around to address the men behind him. "Gentlemen? You may proceed."

The three guildsmen jumped down into the waist-deep water, one after another.

"Gods, this is cold!" one of them exclaimed, before reaching up for the chisel-tipped iron bar proffered by a librarian.

"What . . . what are you doing?" Sophia turned from the book to the men in the sacred pool, who were tapping at the stonework and looking up to orient themselves. "Mr Thaler, what's going on?"

"It should be self-evident, Miss Morgenstern. We need to break our way through."

"Break? You can't do that."

"Sorry, miss. Prince's orders," said the guildsman with the wrecking bar. He drove the point between two pieces of stone and heaved. The sound of rock grating on rock echoed up the shaft.

"I thought you were just going to look." Sophia stared wide-eyed at Thaler. "You can't do this."

"My dear, we'll make good any damage we do. But you have to understand, this is the only clue we have."

"You can't do this to me. Frederik, you have to get them to stop." It felt like she was in that ice-cold water too. Numbing. Bone-chilling.

The first lump of masonry fell into the pool, and Thaler quickly closed the book to keep it dry. "We have to get the water working again, Sophia. I'm trying to help your community."

"This is the heart of our community, Frederik, and you're ripping it out." A second, larger stone came free, and the guildsmen stepped back as it crashed down, sending a wave up the steps that engulfed Sophia's shoes. "You don't understand what this means."

Even as she watched, a guildsman gave a cry of discovery – "More light. More light!" – and started to hack hard at whatever lay beyond the gaping hole he'd already created.

Thaler passed the book back up the line for safe keeping. "Sophia, calm yourself."

"I will not calm myself, you stupid man; you've desecrated the mikveh. No one can get married. No one can be buried. No one can have children." A gush of water from the wall sluiced into the pool, and the level rose as far as her shins. "And no one will ever forgive me for bringing you here."

She looked down into the ruined structure, at the rubble lying on the bottom of it and the hole hacked in the wall. The gout had become a trickle, enough to allow the guildsman to crawl head-first into the gap. The light from the lantern he thrust ahead of him cast dancing shadows against the walls.

"Gods," he said. "It's huge."

And Thaler, distracted by the shout, was clearly more interested in what was beyond the mikveh than in her hurt, than the fact he'd betrayed her and destroyed her reputation so completely it could never recover.

"Get out of my way." She pushed past first Thaler, then the librarians, almost sending several of them spinning into the water below.

She raced outside. The rabbi's wife was there, her hand over her mouth. How much had she seen? How much had she heard?

Enough to condemn her, for certain.

She fled back down Jews' Alley, all the way home, and slammed the door shut behind her.

34

He watched her go – furious and lost at the same time – and he still wasn't sure exactly what he'd done. Yes, this was their ceremonial baths, but really: it was no more than a rough-and-ready stone-lined hole in the ground through which a river flowed. And hadn't he said he'd repair it? Whatever blessing their rabbi needed to perform to bring it back into use couldn't take that long.

All he wanted to do was borrow it so he could map out the underground passages, and hopefully they'd find a more convenient access point. The mikveh was at the bottom of a shaft with narrow stairs and, unsurprisingly, kept filling with water. Hardly what they wanted at all.

"Mr Thaler? Take a look for yourself." The stonemason's guildsman handed him the lantern, and there was nothing for it but to wade into the water after him. He found out for himself just how cold it was – a bitter, stinging cold like wet snow.

"Gods, that's . . ."

"Bit on the chilly side, Mr Thaler?" The man shivered. "That it is."

Thaler tiptoed to the hole in the wall and looked inside. He was startled: he hadn't known what to expect, but it wasn't an arched passage, white with lime, tall enough to stand in. It stretched away into the black distance both ways, with the water running in a trough along the floor.

The mikveh's water supply was achieved by doing nothing more complicated than placing an angled brick in the channel, so that some of the water diverted into a pipe while the rest of it carried on.

"The river is that way, yes?" He pointed downstream.

"It looks like it. What do you think of the construction, Mr Thaler? It's in a remarkable state of preservation."

"Nothing for it, Master Prauss, but to investigate further. If you'll so kindly assist me . . ."

The guildsmen, all three, heaved Thaler up into the gap. He barked his knees, grazed his hands and managed to bang his head on the curved roof, but he was in.

"The floor's very smooth," he said. His feet were wedged at the junctions of the wall so they wouldn't slip any further. "It's manageable, though. I suggest we head upstream and see what we can find."

Prauss scrambled up, followed by Emser and Schussig, who Messinger had assured him could fabricate anything made of wood or metal better than any man in Juvavum.

Then Ullmann poked his head through. "Room for one more, Mr Thaler?"

"I do believe there is, Mr Ullmann. Bring a lantern, and some spare candles. And a flint. I wouldn't want a sudden gust to plunge us into darkness and leave us with no hope of finding our way back." Thaler looked down the opalescent tunnel. "That'd be most foolish."

He slithered a little way onwards to make room and, with nothing to prevent him, kept on going. It was difficult, but not impossible. The air was cold, his wet clothes colder, but his curiosity warmed him. He inspected the walls and the roof as he went, moving his lantern from side to side.

"I don't see how this feeds the house plumbing," he said. His voice boomed in the enclosed space. "This is just a tunnel."

"We need to go further, then," said Prauss, behind him. "This is dwarvish work, I'd swear it."

"Begging your pardon, but dwarves? Mr Thaler said this was Roman." Ullmann braced his feet and shouldered the bag that was passed up to him.

"The Romans are supposed to have had a dwarvish legion, drawn from Schwyz." Thaler waved his lantern and started upstream again. "The Legio Ferus, they called it. If it's true, perhaps they had dwarvish masons."

The tunnel widened, and the channel cut in the floor branched into two. To the right, it seemed that the way was blocked with a single fallen block of stone. To the left, the tunnel stretched on. Thaler frowned. Perhaps things weren't as complete as he hoped.

Prauss came up behind him, and held his lantern high.

"Gods," he said. "Look at the size of that thing."

Thaler struggled to understand his meaning. "What?" But Prauss was already past him and slapping his hand on the curved wet stone.

"It's a wheel. A water wheel." He looked up the other tunnel. "There has to be a way to access the headworks."

The guildsman splashed off up the passage with Thaler and the others in pursuit.

"Careful, man," Thaler called. "We must be careful."

Then Prauss's lantern went out ahead. No clatter or crash, it just winked out. Thaler spread his arms wide, and everyone skidded to a halt.

"Master Prauss? Master Prauss! Are you all right?"

A reply, of sorts, hollow and distorted, rumbled back down towards them. It sounded like a man's voice, but Thaler couldn't make out any words.

"Slowly, then." They had no weapons, which was possibly a mistake. He thought he was right that there were no magical beasts left, but all the same, they could meet something down there that they hadn't planned for.

It was nothing more terrifying than a ladder of staples set into the wall, its rungs thick with the same white deposit that covered every surface. Thaler looked up, and Prauss looked down from the ledge above.

"It's even better than I thought," he said.

Thaler wasn't in the mood. "Really, Master Prauss. We must stay together: the party must not be split under any circumstances."

"Come up, Mr Thaler. You'll see why I'm so excited."

Thaler climbed up the first few rungs, then discovered he could slide his lantern onto the ledge. It was easier after that, and when he'd made it safely up, he shone his lantern around, adding its light to Prauss's.

It was the top of the wheel – what it was, now obvious – its hoppers white, its metalwork invisible. And it was huge, twice Thaler's height and easily twice his width.

"Very impressive, but what's its purpose?"

"Where are we?" asked Prauss, enigmatically.

"Master Prauss, I'm cold and wet, it's dark, and we have important business to attend to. No guessing games, please."

"We're under the fountain in the town square, just north of the irminsul." Prauss pointed at the ceiling. "This can't be a coincidence."

Thaler looked behind him. Emser, the carpenter, was climbing up to the higher level. Beyond him there was a ledge in the tunnel. Water would either run over the ledge, and fall down, or along the sluice and into the wheel.

"If this worked the fountain, then how?"

"There must be machinery . . ."

"Which has long since decayed away." Thaler finished for him.

Emser was looking thoughtfully at the wheel. "If that was made of stone, it would never turn."

"So we have an impossible stone waterwheel that powers a vanished device." The librarian's shoulders dropped. "Gentlemen, we're nine hundred years too late to save any of this."

"Not necessarily," said Prauss. He pulled out a small hammer from his belt, and got down on his knees in the mill race. He reached out for the wheel and gave it an exploratory tap with his hammer.

The sound was dull. If it had been solid rock, it would have rung.

"Aha," he said. He took a bigger swing, and shards of white flew off like tiny stinging insects. "Sorry."

He leant closer, and turned back to Thaler, grinning. "Wood. Preserved wood. Under this coating, the wheel's intact."

Thaler felt his spine straighten. "Then what about the fountain-maker?"

"We need to check the walls." Prauss set to with his little hammer, listening to the timbre of each impact. Emser and Thaler were left to rap their knuckles against the smooth surfaces, while Schussig and Ullmann made their way up to see for themselves, in lieu of any cogent explanation.

After a few minutes' fruitless searching, Thaler stood back and considered matters. If the turning wheel provided some sort of mechanical force, it would be transmitted through the axle. So the device used to push water through the fountain above – assuming Prauss was right – had to be attached to it.

The wheel itself was set into the channel so that the water would fill each section of the wheel in turn. The side of the channel which butted onto the parallel tunnel was too narrow to be anything but solid stone. But the other, where the dressed stone would have been laid next to the rough tunnel wall . . .

Thaler put down his lantern. "Master Prauss, your hammer a moment, if you please." He held out his hand for the tool, and gingerly stepped out onto the top of the wheel.

"Be careful, Mr Thaler," called Ullmann. "We don't want to be carrying you out of here on a stretcher."

It was slippery and damp, balanced on the circumference of the wheel. He felt across the wall, and on feeling a particularly lumpy part, took aim with the hammer.

Inevitably, he fell, though only as far as the hopper. The impact jarred his feet and ankles, and he cried out with a gasp.

The wheel trembled slightly, and it gave a high-pitched creak.

Thaler held his breath and steadied himself. When he looked up again, there was a small rectangular crack marking out a patch on the otherwise-featureless wall, and where he'd hit, the stone had peeled away to reveal the rusted end of a latch.

"You've found something there, Mr Thaler."

"Yes, my boy. Yes, I have." He was ankle deep in milky liquid, and he accepted the hands offered to him to extricate himself and get him back on the ledge. While he emptied his boots, Prauss hammered all the way around the crack, and watched satisfied as the veneer of white stone chipped away in large flakes.

The door was exposed. It was narrow – Thaler was going to find ingress difficult – and the hinges were corroded. He didn't really expect much to happen when Prauss lifted the latch and pulled, but after some initial resistance, the door juddered open, its hinges sounding like whips. It was dark beyond, and the guildsman called for his lantern.

"Gods," his muffled voice reported. "You need to see this."

Thaler was on his feet, and as Prauss eased into the gap, he started to squeeze through himself, holding on to the door frame and trying to make his stomach as small as possible. His size had never really been an issue before, but then again, he'd never been tramping around thousand-year-old tunnels before. Neither did he think he'd do it again in a hurry, but perhaps a little more walking and a little less sausage might help in more situations than this.

When he was certain he wasn't going to get stuck, he edged his feet through and released his death-grip on the stonework.

It was as if he'd stepped into a treasure room. All around him was the dull shine of metal: brass, copper, bronze and silver. Pipes and cylinders were plumbed in orderly rows against one long wall, and on the opposite side, a single set of wider tubes was connected to a fat brass vessel, itself at the centre of a wheel-and-cog arrangement.

"Well, Mr Prauss, I take it back. I take it all back." Thaler savoured the view for a moment, before asking: "Do you have any idea what all this does?"

Prauss was running his hands over the equipment, exploring and touching. "This is what we've been looking for. Extraordinary. This will move water, not just along, but uphill." He turned to the librarian, his eyes wide and bright. "If I could just take one of these apart . . ."

"Later, and at your leisure, Mr Prauss. If these pipes can indeed push water into our houses and restart our fountains, we must supply the wheel with a sufficient flow of water, which we clearly lack. Upstream, good sir, upstream!"

Back out in the main tunnel, they continued slithering their way deeper into the system. Another branch angled away to their left, down towards the river through a different part of town. Prauss wanted to investigate, but Thaler thought it more important to press on.

A short way further, there was a branch to their right that seemed to head towards the library. Thaler looked more wistfully at that one, thinking of the fountain in the square opposite the pantheon, but he steeled himself.

"That's right, Mr Thaler. We're making good progress," said Ullmann. "On to the end, wherever it takes us."

The young man was as cold and wet as he was, and yet he was undeniably enjoying himself. And Thaler had to concede it was all rather an adventure.

Even Ullmann couldn't prepare himself for the extraordinary sights they found under the fortress. Prauss was in the lead; he simply stopped dead, and everyone else, still concentrating on keeping their footing, clattered into each other's backs before looking up.

The roof was lost in darkness it was so high, and the water channels split into three separate sluices, each with their own mighty wheel. More delights waited for them when they climbed out and onto the ledge. Machinery, both installed and lying loose. Chains hanging from points out of sight that passed through pulleys and blocks. Pipes as fat as one of Thaler's legs heading down as-yet-uncharted corridors. Stairs, heading upwards.

"Gods," breathed Prauss. "The dwarves have been busy."

"Had been busy," said Thaler. "We must be the first people – the first men at least – to see this in centuries."

"And yet, Mr Thaler, this has been under our feet the whole time." Ullmann wandered by, almost in a daze. "Those steps lead to the fortress. Imagine opening a door and finding yourself in the Great Hall."

"More likely to find yourself behind some forgotten door in the prince's wine cellar." Thaler's breath condensed in clouds around him. He called Emser and Schussig back from their explorations: the cavern was bigger than the library, judging from the distant dwindling of their lanterns, and it took a while for them to return.

"What is it, Thaler?" Emser was impatient to get back to the wonders he'd found.

"As phenomenal as all this is, we still lack the basic ingredient:

257

water." Thaler rattled his lantern in the direction of the wheels. "Somewhere up ahead must be the source we seek. We cannot give a full report to the prince until we find it."

Schussig glanced behind him at the pipes and pumps. "The mayor never said, Mr Thaler, but I think it's time you told us why we're here." He raised his light so that it reflected off his damp, bald head.

"To see if we can restart the water supply," said Thaler, but he realised his explanation was lacking. These were intelligent men, and they'd already noted his single-minded urgency.

"Go on," prompted Emser.

Thaler sighed. He wasn't supposed to tell anyone, and yet . . . "There's only one hexmaster left. Eckhardt's his name. He's promised to bring the magic back – but at a cost."

"There are so many questions there," said Prauss, "I barely know where to begin."

Schussig moved his lantern closer to Thaler. Such a little light in the vast darkness, yet it burnt so bright. "Why not start with this one hexmaster business: what happened to all the others?"

"They're all dead. The novices' house was empty as far as we could tell, but we found bodies at the adepts' house. The White Tower?" Thaler shivered, not just from the cold. "I think Eckhardt killed them all himself. He's all that's left of the Order, but it's not like we can go to anyone else."

"You said there was a cost," said Emser, pulling at his beard. "Something more than half the palatinate's taxes?"

"Yes." Thaler's voice dropped to a whisper. "He wants sacrifices."

"You mean, like goats and cows?" asked Ullmann in all innocence.

"No. Like you, Mr Ullmann."

"No one would ever—" he started, but Prauss had got the measure of it.

"Yes they would. As long as it wasn't them, or their friends or family. Gods, that's . . ." Prauss shrugged. "Not a decision I'd want to make. We've lived for so long with magic, there are some – no, almost everyone – who can't imagine life without it."

"Precisely, Mr Prauss. Though the price is very high, there'll be plenty who'll be willing for other people to pay it." Thaler stamped his foot, and the sound echoed away. "I will not have it.

I stand to benefit as much as the next man, but I will not countenance the idea of feeding my neighbours to that monster – and Eckhardt's talking about one or two a day. If we have running water, like we did before, we make it easier for the prince to turn him down."

Ullmann spoke into the silence. "The young prince isn't thinking about agreeing to the master's demands, is he, Mr Thaler?"

"I don't think so. That he gave me permission to mount this investigation is a sign he's looking for alternatives. If you ask me again in a week, when there are hungry and thirsty mobs on the dark streets looking for people to send up Goat Mountain, I might have to give you a different answer."

Thaler straightened himself and regarded the small group, dominated by the space they were in, the machinery that filled it, and the enormity of their task.

"That, gentlemen, is why I'm in such a hurry." He paused and asked: "Who's with me?"

To a man, they answered yes.

"Good. To the source, then." Thaler lifted his lantern high. "Wherever that may be."

35

The banging on the door – did no one just knock these days? – had finally woken her father up. And to stop him from going out onto the street and learning for himself what she'd done, Sophia had had to tell him herself.

"Oy," was all he said. They were at the bottom of the stairs. He looked at the door, shaking with the impact of many fists, and turned aside towards the kitchen.

She followed him, at a loss to know what else to do.

"Close the door," he said, and the hammering became a faint but annoying rattle. "Sit down."

"Can't I get you something to eat?"

"Sit," he growled, and she took her usual seat at the side of the table, with the fire to her right.

Aaron Morgenstern rubbed his bloodshot eyes and scratched his fingers through his thinning hair. Then he drummed the tabletop and pushed on an empty bowl until it tipped. He let it go and watched it fall back.

"You need to eat," she said. "There's bread, and some of that soft cheese you like."

"Quiet, daughter. I'm thinking." He didn't look at her, just kept on poking the bowl and seeing how it rolled onto its base.

She sat there, suffering, listening to the rattle of pottery on wood. When she could stand it no longer, she snatched it away and forced him to turn her way. "What am I going to do?"

"Who's outside?" he asked.

"I don't know. The rabbi, probably, and the rest of the Beth Din."

"What do they want?"

"I don't know!" She considered throwing the bowl at the wall, but it was a good bowl and enough things had been broken already that morning. "My head on a spear, probably. How could I have been so stupid?"

"It's not how I brought you up," her father conceded. "You should know not to trust the Germans."

"But it was Frederik Thaler, father. He's sat, just where you are now, eating our food and drinking our wine. He's a good man." She leant across the table and placed the bowl as far away from her as she could. "He didn't tell me what he was planning to do."

"And you didn't ask." Morgenstern's face flushed with blood. "There's more you're not telling me, too. I looked for you at the Megillah, and I couldn't see you."

It wasn't getting any better for her.

"I was in the White Fortress, with the prince." Now it was her turn not to make eye contact. She studied the shelves on the wall, the dust on the panes in the window, the grain of the wood table.

Her father ran his thumb and forefinger down his beard, all the way to the end.

"You were in the White Fortress?"

"Yes."

"With the prince?"

"Yes."

"And who else?"

"The mayor and Mr Thaler. They were talking to the chamberlain, Mr Trommler, and the prince's man, Master Allegretti." She was now looking at her hands in her lap. "I was supposed to give my testimony to them."

"Testimony?" Her father's breaths were slow and deliberate. "Regarding what you saw on Goat Mountain?"

"Yes, Father. Exactly that."

"You could have been killed. You still might be, and there'll be nothing I can do about it."

"The prince won't let me die." Her head came up, and she chased away a tear. "He won't."

Aaron Morgenstern gripped the edge of the table and dragged in a huge lungful of air.

"Why would the prince care anything about a Jewish girl twice his age?"

Why indeed. But she knew he'd help her, just as she'd helped him.

"Because he's someone I can trust. I didn't get to give my testimony along with the mayor and Mr Thaler. I gave it to the prince."

"Wait: you were alone with the prince, who was also alone?"

"He's just a boy. A boy who's lost his mother, his father and everything he could ever count on." Her chin stiffened. "I know a little of what that's like."

Morgenstern smashed his fist onto the table. "He's the German Prince of Carinthia and don't you forget it. This is a catastrophe. Goat Mountain, the fortress, the mikveh: all of it." Then he echoed her own words to Thaler. "How could you do this to me?"

She should be weeping uncontrollably. All that came out was the occasional single tear. "There's more."

"I don't want to hear it." Morgenstern pushed himself away from the table, and was confronted by the closed door. "This would never have happened if your mother was still alive."

"But she's not, is she? You brought me up: I am exactly how you wanted me to be."

"So you're blaming *me* now?" He addressed the door.

"I'm blaming you for making me educated, headstrong and unmarried at twenty-four. Who else is responsible for that?"

"Mensch, such an ungrateful girl."

She was on her feet, and yelling. "Would you rather I was some stupid milch-cow? Who'd take care of you? Who'd do all the Sabbath preparations? Who'd cook kosher for you? Who'd run all your errands? It's not like the widows have been lining up at the doorstep to take you on."

"No, we have Rabbi Cohen and the elders instead, but they're not here to marry either of us." Morgenstern listened to the continued hammering on the front door, and sat back down at the kitchen table with a grunt. "This isn't solving anything."

She moved around and sat next to him. She took his hands in hers and squeezed. "I'm sorry."

"The mikveh's ruined, you say." Morgenstern slid one hand out and rested it on hers.

"They went in through the wall with iron bars. Mr Thaler said they'd repair it, but it'll need blessing, and whatever else. They had the prince's authority: I couldn't have stopped them, even if I wanted to."

"Peace, little one. They used you unthinkingly, which is what I'll say to that bunch of ravens on our doorstep. You, however, need to fly like a dove, at least until everything is as it was." He drummed on the table again. "You've an aunt in Halstadt."

"Halstadt? It's no more than a shtetl." The thought of village life, with all its crudities, didn't exactly fill her with joy.

"Like you can afford to be so picky. I'm not the one who led the Germans to the mikveh." Morgenstern glared at his daughter. "I'm trying to help."

"That doesn't get me out of the house." Even if she appeared at the door, bags packed, ready to leave and prepared never to return, it wasn't going to save her. She had to be gone without anyone knowing.

"Don't worry about that. You go and get some things together: I'll see to the other." He shooed her out, and she had to pass the front door again. They were still banging, but at least their noise masked whatever sounds she might make.

All the same, even while she was concentrating on collecting together enough clothes to last her, but not so many that she couldn't carry, she could hear strange thuds and scrapes coming from the back room. It was where her father kept his books: on a series of heavy wooden shelves around the walls, only because it was unlikely that the middle of the floor could have taken the weight of so much paper.

Sophia took what she'd placed on the bed and halved it. She sincerely hoped he wasn't going to expect her to carry books, too.

In fact, she'd refuse. She wrapped up in the bed blanket what she'd decided to take and tied it tight with two belts. When she stepped back to examine it, it was both depressingly small and alarmingly heavy.

It would have to do. She heaved it from the bed, and walked lopsided to the back room. She barged the door and found several piles of books, an empty bookcase shoved to one side and a hole in the plaster wall. But no father.

She crossed the floor and, crouching down, put her head through the hole. "Father?"

The reply was distant and indistinct. "Come down."

She crawled in on her hands and knees, dragging her bundle behind her, and found herself in a narrow passage that went the whole length of the wall. There were books here, too: wrapped in soft skins and lined up like a hidden army. A lantern hung from a nail above a hole in the floor: the top of a ladder poked through.

Shouldering her load, she started down. There was an intermediate landing, and another ladder. At the bottom was her father, tapping at the stiff bolts of a door she never knew existed. She looked up at where she'd just come from.

"Are we behind the kitchen?"

"Mostly." Morgenstern used more vigour on the bolt, hitting it with a fist-sized piece of stone.

"So where does this lead?"

"Rowlock Alley." He glanced around at her. "Why do you think we live in this house, rather than any other house?"

"Father! Those books upstairs . . ."

"Hush. A man's got to make a living, and times can be hard, especially with the library's interference." The first bolt gave, and he started on the second.

She put her luggage down and took the rock from him. "You obviously haven't used this way for ages."

"No, but it's always been here, just in case. I never thought I'd be smuggling my own daughter out through it." He drew his sleeve across his forehead. "Needs must."

It was quicker for her. She soon shot the other two bolts, and all that remained was to heave off the thick wooden bar that fitted snugly behind the door in two iron hangers.

"As soon as you're outside, down to the quay and across the bridge: take the road to Wolfgangsee, past Ischl."

"I know the way, and I can always ask if I'm not sure." She gave him the rock, and picked up the blanket by the straps. "I don't want to run away. I want to stay and explain what's going on. I haven't even told you everything yet, and you need to know."

"There's no time, Sophia." Morgenstern lifted the latch with difficulty and pulled hard. The door opened a crack and caught jarringly on the step. He went to push his fingers into the opening, but she put her hand against the door.

"No. You have to hear this. You have to tell the Beth Din, because I know them: they won't listen to me. We met a hexmaster," she said, "probably the last hexmaster because he seems to have killed all the others. He offered the mayor and Mr Thaler the chance to bring the magic back."

Her father eyed her cautiously. "Go on."

"Necromancy. Human sacrifice. And when he said it, he looked straight at me." She pulled the door open herself, and dim light from the narrow alley filtered in. "If the Germans want their magic badly enough, then that's what's going to happen."

"What did Messinger say?"

"He didn't say anything to the master then. But we all went together to tell the prince what the offer was, and since the prince has given permission to Mr Thaler to try and get the water flowing again, then I imagine they don't want to accept. But," she continued, as she bent down to take hold of the blanket, "that doesn't mean they won't. And it won't be Germans they're sending up to the White Tower."

"No," said her father sourly, "I don't suppose it will."

"Get rid of those books. Especially if they're from the library. Give them back to Mr Thaler, or just throw them in the river."

"Sophia!" He clutched at his chest as if he'd been run through the heart.

"I don't care. Just do it. I'll send word when I'm safe. Now get this door shut." She leant forward and kissed her father on the top of his head, then stepped out into the alley. There was no one around, and she spun away, hefting her bundle on her back. The door slammed shut behind her, and the bolts began to grind into position. She walked to the end of the alleyway, where it faced out onto the river, and looked for a moment at all the tied-up barges, their crews idling away their time on deck.

They were staying, she was running away. She couldn't remain in Juvavum: certainly not in her house, that much was obvious, and no one else would take her in. Going to some distant relative's house deep in an alpine valley where no one would hear of her transgressions was – for a time – a good solution.

Yet it still felt wrong. Yes, she'd followed Thaler up Goat Mountain, but good had come of that. Yes, she'd gone to the fortress and ended up with a dagger at her throat, but she'd talked to the prince, and more. Yes, she'd taken Thaler to the mikveh, but she hadn't known what they were going to do.

What, exactly, was she running from?

Other people. Other people who didn't respect her or think her worthwhile anyway, something they made abundantly clear every time they addressed her.

Where was she running to?

A community that was even more conservative than the one she was leaving, and that would look on her educated, book-reading ways and unmarried status even more severely than her neighbours already did: they were a whole new group of people she'd inevitably disappoint.

As choices went, neither was particularly palatable.

Then, as she stared into the distance at blue-white mountains, she heard a shout which was unremarkable on a busy quayside, except that it contained her name.

She looked around so fast, her neck clicked.

Coming down the quayside from the direction of the Witches' Bridge, was the rabbi and the rest of the Beth Din, their black hats and coats instantly recognisable. They weren't outside her house any more: they were here.

She started walking away from them, and the four men quickened their pace. After a few steps, she started to run, and after a moment's hesitation, so did they.

None of them were dressed for a prolonged chase. She was carrying a heavy, lopsided bundle that banged against her legs; they were hampered by their long coat-tails and the broad-brimmed hats they had to hold in place.

If she dropped her load, she'd get so far ahead of them they'd give up. But then what? She'd have nothing save what she stood in.

It was inevitable that the only movement amid the enforced stillness of the quayside would attract attention. A bargee called after her, and another from a different boat took up the cry. In a sudden eruption of noise, the whole river bank was alive with jeers and hoots.

Then there was the militia, who were at first amused by the spectacle, but grew concerned at the same rate as the bored bargees grew raucous. She passed them, standing in pairs, curious, half-smiling, uncertain. The first bottle from a barge arced through the air, thrown from in front of her, aimed at those behind her.

It shattered on the stone pavement, sending shards spinning and spiralling across the quay. Sophia realised that the bargees had found a new sport and, in the time it took them to arm themselves, the sky was thick with missiles. She ran with her head on back-wards, dreading to think what would happen if Cohen or one of the others was hit.

Her escape came to an abrupt halt against the mail-shirted chest of a militiaman. She struck him full on, and fell back on her bottom before she realised what had happened.

He looked down at her, and she up at him.

"Miss Morgenstern?"

It was one of the guards that the mayor had taken up the mountain yesterday. She raised her arm, and he helped her up.

"Sorry, sorry," she apologised, and batted at his armour as if she'd damaged it with her face.

"Never mind that. Better get you inside while we sort this out."

She was outside the Town Hall, and Messinger was staring out of the wide upstairs windows. He frowned at her, shook his head and disappeared back inside. The guard ushered her through the line of soldiers that was forming up, and closed ranks with his fellows.

There was nothing for it but to retreat up the steps and into the wood-panelled calm of the foyer, pulling her bundle after her. But if she thought that shelter would be momentary, and that she could continue her journey after order had been restored, she was wrong.

"Sophia Morgenstern." It was the mayor, leaning over the gallery balustrade, and she climbed the first few stairs to see him better.

"Master Messinger." It lacked something as a greeting, so she added. "Good morning."

"Are you responsible for the riot outside?" He wasn't smiling.

"Responsible? No." Which also lacked something, namely the truth. "I am the cause of it, however."

"Gods, woman. It's not like I haven't got enough to do." Messinger rolled his eyes towards the painted ceiling bosses. "Come up. Leave your washing downstairs; I doubt anyone will steal it."

"My . . . oh." She supposed it did look like washing. She put it the other side of the banister and, to the distant accompaniment of cracking bottles and cracking heads, she slowly walked up the stairs.

36

"We need more castle guards, my lord." Trommler looked in his book and frowned at the numbers. "I've instructed Captain Reinhardt to go and recruit an initial century of men, with another to be gathered in a month's time."

"Do I have to do anything about that?" asked Felix. He rested his head on his good arm as he slumped onto the solar's long table.

"Only pay for them, my lord, something which we can currently manage quite comfortably. Our treasury is large, and the strong-rooms are well stacked with coin."

"I can feel a but, Mr Trommler." He turned his head so as to speak directly into the table.

"Carinthia has never needed a standing army. The princes of this land could always rely on the earls to supply sufficient spear-carriers, and the real fighting was done by the Order." Trommler ran his finger down a list of names. "We have lost a great many of our earls, and all but one of the Order."

"Two," said Felix. He told Trommler about Nikoleta Agana, and the chamberlain received the news with one eyebrow raised.

"And she left with the huntmaster?"

"Well, sort of. More dragged away by the huntmaster." Felix raised his head briefly. "Have I done another bad thing?"

Trommler stroked his hooked nose. "Not one that cannot be redeemed, my lord. I've prepared a proclamation declaring a pardon for Master Büber; it will be a small matter to append the name of Mistress Agana. I'll take care not to identify her as a hexmaster, however."

"She said she was loyal to me, and then . . . I don't know what happened. After I read the librarian's letter, something went wrong." The prince put his head back on the table. "I can't remember."

"I'll see they come back, my lord. Now, our army."

"Do we have to do this now, Mr Trommler?"

"Yes, my lord. We do. A palatinate that cannot defend itself is not a palatinate at all. There will be . . ." and Trommler dried up for a moment.

"What is it?" asked Felix.

"Can I be blunt, my lord?" Trommler looked at his figures, sighed, and closed his book with a thump.

Felix groaned. "If you have to."

"My lord's full attention would be appreciated. What I must tell you is of the utmost importance." Trommler licked his thin lips.

"Shouldn't we wait for the signore to return from . . . from wherever he's gone?" Felix glanced around at the closed door, the empty chairs and the smouldering fire.

"The utmost importance," repeated Trommler, and without pause he delved inside the folds of his gown to retrieve a surprisingly large scroll of paper. He dropped it on the table; it bounced and stayed closed.

Intrigued, Felix parted the curls with his thumbs and unrolled the sheet. Trommler placed a heavy object – his book, a jug, a small box, a plate – on each corner.

It was a map, not just of Carinthia, but of the surrounding countries. There was the top of the Adriatic, and at the other end of the page, part of the Baltic coast.

"We are here." Trommler pointed with a faintly trembling finger at the little castle that marked Juvavum, at the very centre of the map. "We control the lands to the north as far as the Enn, east almost up to the gates of Wien, south to Over-Carinthia and the mountain passes, and west where we butt against the dwarven kingdom of the Schwyz."

"It's not that much land," said Felix. Even though he'd seen maps of the region before, this was the first time he'd looked at one in earnest while being responsible for the palatinate. Also, it was the first time he'd appreciated that being at the centre of everything made the little bit he owned – highlighted with a faint yellow wash – look fragile.

"It might not be very big, but it's strategically placed. The same rivers and roads we use to conduct our trade can transport invaders into the heart of Carinthia just as easily. I said I would be blunt, and so I will." Trommler pointed to the north. "The Bavarians. They have no money, their mad king having frittered it away on ludicrous buildings of no purpose. They had their own inferior sorcerers, useful only for mass actions against other, less magically inclined lands – and for protecting the royal person. I cannot imagine that the Bavarian earls won't rise up against Leopold, if they haven't already done so."

His finger moved east. "The Austrians. They can cut off our direct trade from much of the south; easier to move goods by boat than over the Alps, but what becomes of that route is anyone's guess at the moment. The Protector of Wien is an ordinary, decent pagan who owes Carinthia a continuing debt for saving Europe from the Horde. But even then, I'd offer concessions before he forces them from you."

Across the peaks of the mountains. "Oh, how the Italians love fighting! They squander their lives and their money in pursuit of the slightest advantage over their rivals. The Doge of Venezia and Duke of Milano have been locked in a duel to the death before the current incumbents were even born, but if they ever made peace, they'd march north and try to empty our coffers together."

"What about the dwarves?" asked Felix. "What will the dwarves do?"

"Honestly? I have no idea. I haven't seen a dwarf for the better part of a decade. Perhaps they've gone the way of the unicorns. What I do know is that every treasure-seeker and brigand will be heading their way to find out. As for any aid we might have got from them? They might be asking *us* to help them."

"And this is why we need an army?"

"Even if it is just the appearance of an army at the start, my lord. Look at where we are." Trommler stabbed his finger down on the parchment. "We are at one of the world's crossroads. Know this for certain: sooner or later, someone will come across the border in force. How we meet them is of the utmost importance: do we field a rabble, which is a sure sign to our enemies that we're ripe for picking, or do we dispatch them with typical Carinthian efficiency?"

Felix frowned at the map as if it were alive with threats already.

"But haven't we just done that? Only just about won a battle where we should have blasted them off the . . ." and he looked down at the space where Obernberg would have been marked had it not been so insignificant, "off the map?"

"My lord sees the situation with wisdom beyond his age." Trommler bowed.

"How long do we have?" Felix glanced out of the long line of windows. The white tops of the mountains peeked over the bailey walls.

"It's spring. The short summer months will follow. If we can get through those, then winter will close down the passes again. All the countries surrounding us will have their own particular problems." Trommler tapped his chin. "We can expect skirmishes along our borders – if we decide to protect them – from now on. A major attack? Not until next year. It takes time to organise a large army, especially if most of the troops are from the levy. The soil's warming up: seeds need to be planted now if starvation is to be avoided later. Then there's harvest time. There's precious little space for a proper campaign. However, my lord should consider sending spies to the other lands, and an emissary to the dwarves to gauge their intentions both plain and covert."

"I thought it was impossible for anyone to invade Carinthia. Surely, Mr Trommler, there are just too many of us?" Felix bent over the map, tracing the lines of rivers and mountains with his fingernail.

Trommler pulled in his chair again and settled into it. "It depends on how many of us will fight."

"And if I tell them to fight? If I lead them into battle?"

"My lord," said Trommler, "you've seen what happens. The enemy might simply be stronger. The Romans regularly fought, routed and annihilated much larger forces because they were better trained."

"We beat them," said Felix.

"Even then, we had wild magic on our side." Trommler started to remove the weights from the corners of the map. "We haven't now. Obernberg may be remembered as the last battle fought with a sorcerer."

The released map rolled itself up with a snap, and Trommler hesitated.

"What's wrong, Mr Trommler?"

Trommler picked up the map and stowed it away in whichever pocket it had come from. "I need direction from you as to what to do about Master Eckhardt."

"What . . ." said Felix, ". . . what do you want me to say?" His advisers had presented him with two contrasting responses; he couldn't decide between them on his own.

"You've directed Mr Thaler to investigate the water supply, which gives me reason to believe that simply accepting the hexmaster's offer is something that you don't want to do. What if Thaler comes back and says it's impossible, or that it will take years of work?"

"Then we'll have to do something else, I suppose." Felix reached out for the box. There was something inside.

"Are there any circumstances under which you'd be willing to pay his price?"

"One or two people – a day?" The prince shuddered. "I'd have to be desperate."

"How desperate?" asked Trommler gravely. "The ending-of-your-rule desperate? The sacking-of-Juvavum desperate? The-end-of-Carinthia desperate?"

"I don't know. Perhaps I never will know until I see it."

"You need to think very carefully about that, my lord." Trommler looked away. "There will be some, perhaps even many, who'll reach the point of desperation long before you do, over much less. There might be irresistible pressure to accept Eckhardt's plan, simply to make people's lives more comfortable."

"Wait, Mr Trommler, are you saying that the people, my subjects, would have their neighbour killed by a . . . a necromancer, just to provide them with running water?"

Trommler hung his head. "Oh, my lord, water is worth rioting over. As are healing spells for your sick child or wife. And how about wheels that turn by themselves, rather than having to be turned? Or lights that don't need lighting and never go out? Or all the other everyday tasks we used magic for just three days ago? I appreciate that you're lighting your father's pyre tonight . . ."

"I know," said Felix through gritted teeth. "I know."

"It would be very much easier for you if you could mourn your father's death properly and decently, and not have to worry about affairs of state for a few months. It's a luxury you don't have, because these are not normal times." Trommler walked to the window, and leant heavily on the sill. He suddenly looked very old indeed, his whole body sagging under the weight of worries. "If you're to survive to your thirteenth birthday, you need to act quickly."

Felix rubbed his sore shoulder through the cloth and bandages. "You said we might have until next year."

"And so we will. My lord, your neighbouring princes are not the immediate threat." The chamberlain turned around slowly, almost shuffling. "It's your own people. And while I'm being completely candid, if there was no hope of going back to the old ways, they would find the transition very much more palatable."

Felix screwed his face up and thought through the consequences. "Are you suggesting it would be better if there were no hexmasters at all?"

"Yes. That's exactly what I'm saying. And I would go up Goat Mountain myself and do it, but I'm afraid my lord finds me at a time of life when words are significantly easier than actions." Trommler held up his trembling hands. "You should find someone who'll do it for you, quietly and quickly."

"But what if we need him, as horrible as that might be?" Felix dragged his fist across the table. "Not today, but some other time?"

"Accepting his offer will tear the palatinate apart: initially neighbour would turn against neighbour, and eventually the demand for foreigners to be given to Eckhardt will become overwhelming. Perhaps my lord needs to consider where we would get such a steady supply of sacrifices, especially if we weren't going to scour our brother princes' lands for captives."

"I understand," mumbled Felix, and his face coloured up.

Trommler continued. "Rejecting Eckhardt and letting him live would be just as bad, because he would become a standard about which dissenters will gather. No prince can survive having a murderous band of brigands on their doorstep, getting stronger with every victim they take. As unpleasant as this choice is, I advise you to have it done now, before word of Eckhardt's proposal ever reaches the populace. Master Messinger and Mr Thaler's testimony indicates that it is more than likely he killed the other hexmasters."

"Can't we press him?"

"A hexmaster? If we can't get a blade between his ribs without him knowing, we're all in a great deal of trouble." The corner of

Trommler's mouth twitched. "Huntmaster Büber would have been an ideal choice: magic tends to look the other way where he's concerned. Nadel died at Obernberg. There are other hunters; they're all away from Juvavum at the moment, but I expect them at tonight's ceremonies."

Felix had a thought. "What about the signore? He's the best swordsman in Carinthia. He'd do it if I asked."

"My impression," said Trommler, "is that he believes you should consider Eckhardt's offer seriously."

"But I agree with you, Mr Trommler. I can do that, can't I?"

"You can, my lord. All that your advisers should do is point out the consequences of each of your choices before you decide. The decision will always be yours alone to make."

"Good. I'll talk to the signore this morning, and I'll order him to . . ." Felix thought about the word he should use. He was an honest German, though, and had been brought up to call something what it was. "To kill Master Eckhardt."

37

The tunnel was more or less featureless, and more or less straight. Having left the huge mill-wheels under the fortress behind, the only thing they'd discovered was the depth of their willingness to suffer in the cold and the wet and the dark for mile after mile. They lost all sense of time, and only had Prauss's word as to how far they'd travelled.

It had long since stopped being wonderful, and was now just a slog. Thaler felt as though he'd lost inches of fat around his middle: perhaps that was why he'd become so very cold. He'd lost feeling in both his fingers and toes, and the end of his nose had grown pale and waxy.

Their direction of travel was difficult to ascertain, though it appeared to be mostly southerly. They were certainly somewhere well outside the city walls and deep in the Carinthian countryside, in a region known for its lakes. They'd had to discuss the possibility that the tunnel might end under one.

If a rock fall had blocked the inlet, and only the steady but small river that passed over their feet could get through, what if they dislodged something critical? They'd die, drowned or smashed against the machinery further down the tunnel, assuming they lived that long.

Not an appealing prospect, thought Thaler. And if their way was blocked at the far end, would they have enough light to make it back down at least to the fortress?

But if his resolution wavered at all, it was bolstered by remembering the look on Eckhardt's face as he'd talked about people as merely fuel.

So they splashed on in weary silence; sometimes slipping, sometimes falling on their knees, and sometimes ending up face-first in clear alpine water barely above freezing. They helped each other up, and after a nod to show they were still capable of continuing – what else could they do? – they carried on.

Finally, they came to a jumble of rocks that barred their way, an ancient fall coated with the same white crust that covered the rest of the underground system. At its base, water flowed through the cracks to form the river.

"Well," said Thaler. "That appears to be that."

Prauss looked sour in defeat. "All that way, and to fail. Arse."

They stared at the bubbling water and readied themselves for the trip back, but Ullmann held his lantern up high, almost to the apex of the arched ceiling.

"Now, I don't know much about mining and digging, and I beg Master Prauss's patience, but if the tunnel was flooded on the other side, wouldn't the rocks at the top be running with water, too. But look." He slapped his thin, long-fingered hand on the white-rimed boulder nearest the roof and showed his palm to the others.

It was damp, but not dripping.

"He's right," said Thaler, and Schussig moved in for a closer look. He spotted something in among the jumble of stone, and fished it out with the tip of his knife.

"What is it?" asked Emser. The guildsman made to pass it across but, his fingers numb, he dropped it.

Thaler stamped on the object as it floated past, with a speed that surprised everyone, not just himself. He smiled sheepishly. "Got it."

He bent down and scooped it up, then held it to a lantern to inspect it: pale, thin, bendy, with a slight furriness about it.

"It's a root, Mr Thaler," said Ullmann.

"Yes. Yes, it is, isn't it? Which means," said Thaler, looking up, "that we can't be far from the surface."

"What do we reckon?" Prauss reached for his hammer. "Do we risk it?"

"As you said, Master Prauss: we've come all this way." Thaler looked at Emser, then at Schussig, gauging their mood. Ullmann was invariably so enthusiastic about everything that what he wanted wasn't in doubt.

"Well, you're the leader of this expedition," said Prauss.

"Leader? Gods, no. Gentlemen, we must agree together. Master Schussig?"

"As much as I'd welcome death at this moment, I'd rather see the sun again. If you believe going through the fall is the quickest way of doing that, I'll dig with the rest of you." He tried to massage life back into his cheeks by slapping them, but they stayed as white as the root.

Emser grunted. "We have little to lose and everything to gain. And Ullmann's right. If the tunnel was flooded, there'd be jets of water squirting out, not that damn trickle."

"Master Prauss, we are guided by you." Thaler stepped back.

"Start at the top. See if we can shift some of those little stones first, then the big stuff might free itself." He stepped up to the rocks. "Careful, now. If I say stop, stop at once. Got that, Mr Ullmann?"

"Loud and clear, Master Prauss." The usher reached up and started to wriggle a river-worn pebble free. It came out after a struggle, and he dropped it behind him. "It's a start."

They did what they could, which for Thaler meant the reduced role of removing debris and offering general encouragement, shifting the rocks that came free away from the base of the fall further on down the tunnel. At least the work helped to warm him a little, but they seemed to be getting nowhere. They removed some of the larger stones, only to find more behind.

Thaler considered the volume they'd already moved. They were, at least, that much closer to freeing the tunnel, but what if the fall just went on and on? At some point, they'd have to admit defeat and turn back. Preferably, before they ran out of candles.

Ullmann, balanced at the very top of the heap, wrestled with a large block, but the one he was perched on suddenly gave way.

He toppled over backwards, still clutching his load, and Schussig, to his right, tried to catch him. Simultaneously, the clatter and grind of shifting rock grew from a whisper to a wild growl.

Dust billowed and covered everyone and everything. Thaler, at a remove from the rock face, turned his back and covered his eyes from the stinging, choking cloud. The tunnel was full of noise and chaos: coughing, shouting, booming, skittering.

And when the worst was over, and Thaler's dropped lantern had been extinguished along with everyone else's, he realised he could see light from between his fingers.

He cautiously took one hand away, then the other. No, not the Valkyries come to take him to whatever Valhalla had to offer portly librarians; he was still underground in the cold and the wet. Except for a shaft of daylight, unbearably bright, spearing through the settling dust and down the tunnel.

"Everybody all right?" he asked. Two figures emerged from the dark, filthy and bruised: Prauss and Emser, only their eyes and teeth showing white.

"Master Schussig? Mr Ullmann?"

"At your feet, Mister Thaler." Ullmann spat out a mouthful of grit and heaved a rock of his chest. "I think Master Schussig has been struck a blow to the head. I can hear him breathing, though."

The brilliance of the shaft was contrasted by the deep shadow it cast, but overall there was enough light to work by. Schussig was bleeding from a cut near his crown, but seemed otherwise intact. Ullmann declared himself entirely unharmed.

"We seem to be somewhere," he proclaimed, and started to climb up the loose debris to put his eye to the gap that had opened up.

"Careful, man," said Prauss, but the usher wouldn't be put off.

"It's daylight all right, powerful bright. There's green, too. Let me see if I can push my way through."

"No," said Prauss and Thaler together, and Thaler gave way to the mason.

"I'll check we're not likely to bring the whole damn thing down on our heads first, if you don't mind," said Prauss, summoning Ullmann down with a tug on his tunic.

He exercised much more caution than the younger man had done, inspecting both the roof and the walls, making his pronouncement only when he was sure.

"This is the end of the tunnel – it's been deliberately blocked off – and the tunnel entrance itself appears perfectly intact. We just need to take stones from the top. Here," he said, and he passed the first one down. "Let's do this quickly, and get Master Schussig outside."

They formed a chain, passing rocks down to be piled up by Thaler, who could barely lift some of them. The gap gradually grew bigger as they removed the infill, until there was just one large boulder in the way.

Prauss squinted around it. "If we all push, we can move it. Mr Ullmann, Master Emser?"

They arranged themselves around the base of the rock and heaved. It shifted, but then settled deeper.

"Again."

They strained. It rocked forward, but then became stuck against something, and they had to let it roll back. The smell and sight of outside was tantalisingly close, and Thaler couldn't wait any longer.

"You're doing it wrong," he said. He picked up two fist-sized stones from the pile at his feet and positioned himself carefully beside Emser. "Now push again."

They did, and when the boulder rocked forward again, Thaler jammed one of the stones in the gap at its base, hammering it home with the other. He bent down a second time and came up with a bigger rock.

"Again."

It was harder work pushing this time, and Thaler had to smash the wedge into position with all his frustrated strength. He looked up, and saw a slit of sky.

"It's working, Mr Thaler," said Ullmann.

"Of course it's working. Archimedes. Basic stuff." Thaler hunted on the floor for a tapered stone, and knocked it in under the boulder. "Push again."

With grunts and groans, they took the strain. The boulder moved, and Thaler mashed the face of the stone like a berserker.

"Get in there, you fucker. Get in."

The boulder was at an angle now, and the gap between the roof and the rock almost wide enough for the smallest of them to squeeze through. Thaler tossed his makeshift hammer to one side and pressed his own palms against the gritty surface.

"One last push," he said. "Don't let it fall back."

He took a deep breath and dropped his shoulder against it. It was going, it was definitely going. He gasped and grunted, and started to straighten his legs. Then he was falling forward with the weight, still pressing hard against it. Spread-eagled on it, almost.

Thaler looked up, and saw sky and clouds and trees. It was cool and sunny, and insects buzzed about him, tasting his salt sweat.

Ullmann pulled himself up the incline and out, standing on the very rock that had blocked their way.

"It's a lovely day up here. Though I'm not sure where here is, exactly."

Prauss and Emser dragged Schussig to the entrance and Ullmann helped pull him out.

"You feeling up to coming out, too, Mr Thaler?" Ullmann extended his hand. "That was a mighty effort from you at the end."

Thaler mentally checked himself to see if anything had gone pop. He couldn't remember the last time he'd been called on to exert himself so strenuously. If this was what life would be like without magic . . . He clenched his jaw at the thought. The cost of his ease had been shown to be great, too great.

He lifted his hand and let Ullmann haul him upright, giving his dark-adapted eyes time to adjust to the bright colours of aboveground. They were in a valley, with a particularly tall mountain towering almost directly over them – they'd emerged from an opening at the base its flank, right down by the valley floor where a river flowed between the trees.

Thaler frowned, and looked back. The tunnel opening was, as Prauss had said, intact: the top of the tooled stone arch was visible now they'd climbed up and out. He looked along the line of the tunnel from the entrance to the river.

At first sight, and even on closer inspection, it looked as if the tunnel was just cut into the mountainside. Yet water was somehow flowing from the river, through the ground and into it, all the way to the mikveh and beyond to the quayside in Juvavum.

"How is Master Schussig?" he asked.

"Beginning to come round. Lump on his head the size of a hen's egg." Prauss scraped grime from his chin and inspected his ragged fingernails. "Any sign of people?"

"No, no," said Thaler, distracted. He slowly climbed down the rock pile and onto the soft shade-dappled ground. The tree roots were knotty under his feet, and he knelt down, tearing at the soil with his hands. He found a jumble of rock fragments a little way down. He stopped and moved on towards the river, stopping again to scrape away the leaf litter and loam.

"What is it, Mr Thaler?" called Ullmann.

"Come here," he said. "Put your ear to the ground and tell me what you hear."

Ullmann thought it a strange request, but he complied anyway. After a few moments, he looked up at Thaler. "Water. There's running water under there."

"There is indeed, my lad. Now," he said, looking at the river, "that can only mean one thing."

"It can?"

"One thing," repeated Thaler, and he trotted to the river bank. He crashed around in the undergrowth, kicking and stamping until he'd found something that didn't sound like waterlogged soil. He pointed downwards. "Here."

He dropped to his knees and started to dig, joined shortly by a bemused Ullmann. The top of a piece of dressed stone, chisel-marks clear for both of them to see, appeared: the pointed capstone of a pillar.

"If that's here, there should be another . . ." – Thaler scrambled up, shook the dirt from his fingers, and judged the distance – "over there."

He walked a little way away from the river, but at right-angles to the line of the tunnel. The second stone pillar was even easier to find than the first, the top of it lying just below the surface.

"Can you see it now?" Thaler spread his hands to take in the whole of the valley. "The Romans diverted the river to run under the mountain. Right here. The tunnel was blocked off later, when our ancestors used magic instead; the aqueduct was filled in; and the gate that must have been here was lost or buried. But it's all right under our feet."

"And has been all the time." Ullmann nodded, satisfied. "Well done, Mr Thaler."

The librarian blushed and slapped Ullmann on the back. "Well done to you too, Mr Ullmann. With a team of men to dig this out, we could have it working in a crude fashion in, say, a week?"

"There's a lot to do inside the tunnels, too, Mr Thaler."

"Then we'd better make a start. First things first: find out where in Midgard we are." He looked down at his belly. "And perhaps get something to eat. I don't know about you, but I appear to have regained my appetite."

38

The prince sat by the window, watching the sun hovering low and orange over the mountains. Trommler slipped in like a shadow and stood behind him, waiting to be noticed. Felix, chin on the window shelf, was as far away as the sharp snow-covered peaks he could see through the glass.

The chamberlain coughed politely, and then a little less politely.

"My lord, it's time."

"I know," said Felix. "I know that someone else can't do it, that I have to, but it doesn't stop me from wanting to be . . . Oh, I don't know . . . what's the furthest place you know of?"

"They say there's a great emperor in the utmost East, who commands flights of dragons and wears cloth woven from spider silk. They call him the Son of Heaven, the Lord of Ten Thousand Years." Trommler held out the Sword of Carinthia on the flats of his hands. "I imagine that would be far enough, even for you."

Felix took the sword just above the guard, but there was no way he could strap it on one-handed. Then he realised that the ceremony had started, and there was no escaping its inevitable conclusion.

"Prince of Carinthia is the best I can hope for." He handed the sword back. "However long I last."

"Be assured of your subjects' support, my lord." Trommler fed the belt around Felix's waist and fastened it in front.

"That's not what you said this morning," said Felix. "You said they'd turn on me if they realised there was magic still around."

"They will support you tonight, at least. Everything is ready, and you needn't even speak. It's certainly not required, nor even expected."

Felix looked down at the sword. "Can you hang this on my

right? There doesn't seem any point to having it where I can't even draw it."

Trommler looked to see if he could change it, but the fittings were on one side only. He solved the problem by turning the whole belt around, so that the buckle was at the back. "My lord hasn't eaten anything today."

"I had something for breakfast."

"Which is contrary to what the servant I sent to you told me." Trommler gave a mirthless smile. "I shall have him beaten."

"Maybe I didn't. Don't beat him." Felix looked across at the table, with its untouched plate of cold meats and bread and beer. "I'm just not hungry."

"It is, I'm afraid, your royal duty to eat, and drink. Especially drink, and I'd rather you had some ballast inside when you take the horn tonight. I've made sure that the Gothi waters the mead down for you: it wouldn't do for you to either collapse or spew." He guided the boy over to the chair and pulled it back for him. "Anything would be better than nothing, even though it might taste like wood."

"Has the signore returned, Mr Trommler?"

"Not that I know of," said Trommler. "But you cannot wait for his return."

"He can't have failed." Felix poked at a small wheat-flour roll with his finger. "Perhaps he's just waiting for the right moment."

"I'm sure that's the case."

"He couldn't have left me, could he?"

Trommler pursed his lips. "No. I very much doubt that he has. The signore will return when he is done."

Felix sighed and dug his fingers into the roll, splitting it apart and revealing its close-textured middle. "I've got another question, one that I don't want to know the answer to."

"Oh?"

The prince reached behind his bandaged arm and retrieved a small square of folded paper. "I . . . no, just read it. You don't need to know where it came from."

Trommler reached out and opened up the paper. The writing was tiny, almost illegible, and he had to hold it well away from his face in order to see anything of it.

"Trouble seeing, Mr Trommler?"

"The enchantment on my eyes has failed, my lord. I'm reduced to this now." He looked over the top of the note. "And no, I don't wish for it back, even though I'll miss easily being able to read even the smallest handwriting."

He finally deciphered the note. In silence, he folded it back up and slid it across the table to Felix.

"It's a very good question," he finally said. Felix waited, and waited some more. Trommler grew increasingly uncomfortable, and eventually went to stand by the fire.

"But is there an answer?"

Trommler's hunched back tightened. "There is, my lord. But, as you wisely said, you don't want to know what it is."

"What if I did?" Felix pushed his chair back and adjusted the sword of state at his hip. He walked slowly across to Trommler. "What if I felt that, as the Prince of Carinthia, I needed to know."

"And not just because she was your mother?" Picking up a poker, the chamberlain riddled the half-burnt logs with something approaching anger.

"Why did she die?"

"She died in childbirth. She died having you."

"That's *how* she died," said Felix. "Not the why. The note that . . . the note asks why she died. I always assumed that the how explained everything. My father never said any more than you just have. There is more, though, isn't there?"

"It's getting perilously close to late, my lord." Trommler replaced the poker and wiped his hands. "Your escort's waiting for you in the courtyard."

"I am the Prince of Carinthia. Let them wait."

Trommler raised an eyebrow. "Just what your father would have said. Perhaps now is not the best time to answer this. Later."

"If I'm to remember my father properly, then now is the only time I can ask. Later will be too late." Felix stood between Trommler and the fire, the heat uncomfortable at his back, but at least it forced the man to look at him. "Why did my mother die? Why was she allowed to die? The Order? They performed miracles: in the old days, it's said they could resurrect someone. A princess of Carinthia died giving birth: I want to know why."

Trommler stroked his scraggy little beard. "Because your grandfather, the king of the Franks, had managed to anger the Order sufficiently for them to want to take revenge. Your mother was the price of that."

Felix stared up at the chamberlain for a moment, then walked away.

"Your father didn't know of the feud," Trommler called after him, and the prince came back.

"What do you mean?"

"It happened when your father was just a boy, far younger than you are now. King Goderic had just ascended the Frankish throne and he tried to detain a hexmaster travelling through his lands: first by bribes, then by force. There could have been a war, but treaties were made instead. One condition was that Goderic's daughter would be given to Gerhard when the time came – the bride-price nearly beggared them, which served them right – but that wasn't enough for the Order."

Trying to add up dates in his head, Felix murmured, "That's . . ."

"Fifteen years later. Oh, they made all the right noises, apologised that their magic was insufficient, that she was too far gone to save. She died, and those few of us who'd served long enough to remember vowed never to tell your father."

"Carinthia needed the Order to survive."

"You see? What would Prince Gerhard of Carinthia have done in his grief if he'd found out that the Order of the White Robe had let his wife die?"

"He would have fought them."

"And he would have lost everything. Now I'm the only one left of those old servants and, by fate, I've lived to see the day that Prince Felix of Carinthia finally took steps to break free of the Order." Trommler glanced over at the table where they'd been sitting. "Who gave you the note?"

"A . . . friend," said Felix.

"Sophia Morgenstern, then." The chamberlain clicked his tongue. "She is quite perspicacious, for a woman. There's no possible way she could have known."

"Unless she'd read it in a book."

"Ah, yes. She's the bookseller's daughter." Trommler looked down at Felix. "Allowing her here into the fortress, leaving her outside in the corridor, expecting her to sit and wait until she was called. What *was* I thinking?"

He turned away quickly and walked stiffly to the door. He held it open for Felix.

"My lord. Your final duty to your father is ahead of you. Have courage, and don't be afraid."

"Mr Trommler, are you . . .?" Felix didn't have the words.

"I am your servant, my lord." Trommler bowed. "We really must go."

Felix left the solar and walked down the nearest set of stairs to the ground floor. He thought of his growing up as the only royal child in a castle. His half-brothers and sisters were significantly younger than him, and he hadn't had much in common with them.

He would give them titles and see them make marriages – he knew that much was expected of him – and in return, they would owe him fealty. What did that even mean? They were just children, and so was he. But he had the Sword of Carinthia on his belt, carefully cleaned of the muck and gore it had collected in his father's hand at Obernberg.

It was no longer a magical blade, one that would cut through wood, leather, chain and plate with little more effort than it would cleave flesh. It was, however, still potent. As long as he held it, he could claim the palatinate as his. There might be some point at which friend, or even foe, would pry it from his cold, dead hand. By then, he'd be past caring.

Unlike his father, though, he'd go to meet the gods in full knowledge that his mother had been left to die because of something that someone else had done when she was still a baby. Having ordered Allegretti to go and kill Eckhardt, he wished now that he'd gone to kill him himself.

The honour guard, sitting around the courtyard, were called to order by Reinhardt. Felix hadn't thought he had that many soldiers left, and from the way that the captain growled and kicked at them as they formed up, he suspected that some of them weren't part of the garrison at all, but were cooks and porters and stable-hands pressed into ill-fitting armour and handed unfamiliar weapons.

They mostly looked the part, though, and it was dark. The first stars showed in the northern sky, and a crescent moon was low to the south-east. When the torches were lit, the effect would be complete, as long as no one dropped anything or tripped up over a spear-haft.

Trommler fussed about, making sure everything was ready as tradition demanded. Felix's stepmother appeared from another part of the keep: her children huddled around her, their expressions ranging from pensive to uncomprehending. They had lost not only their father, but their home too. Perhaps, thought Felix, they blamed him for that. He hoped their mother would explain.

"My lord," she said formally.

How was he to reply? Trommler leant in and whispered in his ear.

"My lady," said Felix, adding, for want of anything better to say, "Are you well?"

"We're going to Ischl in the morning. They're expecting us there." She wore a dress so dark in its redness it appeared almost black.

"Hello, Ulf," he said to the boy by her side, almost lost in the folds of her skirt.

"Mother says I'm to call you my lord now," he said.

Felix crouched down, sword scabbard scraping against the flagstones. "I don't mind if you still call me Felix. Otherwise I'll have to call you Earl von Ischl."

"Are we going to say goodbye to father?"

"Yes. That's what we're going to do. Did Mr Trommler tell you what's going to happen?"

Ulf nodded. "He said there would be a boat, and a big fire, and the boat would sail away with father and take him to Valhalla."

"Then we come back here." Felix felt the first pricking of tears. "Can I come and visit you in your new house? Not straight away, but soon?"

"Of course you can. We can go riding and hawking and fishing, though I don't know the best places yet. There's a big lake, and Mother says sometimes the spirits come up and talk to you."

Not any more. "That would be lovely." Felix patted the boy's mop of golden hair and straightened up. "I think we're ready, Mr Trommler."

The chamberlain called for Gerhard's body to be brought out of the Great Hall: the doors were flung open, and the bier was carried out by the few remaining earls. The black, red and gold cloth, covering both the shrouded body and the wooden frame, rippled with movement, but nothing came untucked. Trommler had seen to everything, even making sure that the colours of Carinthia had been tacked at the corners.

At his signal, the torches were lit, and fire bloomed from dozens

285

of sources, the flame being passed from one to another until the courtyard was alive with leaping shadows and twisting flames.

He recalled watching as Obernberg burnt, flames consuming the whole town like a handful of dry twigs. He'd had the signore with him then to steady him, and the Italian's absence gnawed at his guts. Where was the man? Why hadn't he returned?

His ashen-faced stepmother stepped up beside him. It was a well-meant gesture, but he shook his head. "Stay with the children. I'll walk with Mr Trommler."

She nodded, patted him on his good shoulder, and shepherded the boys and girls together at a respectful distance. Trommler came and stood next to Felix, his hands clasped around a walking-stick.

"My lords," he said, "if you please."

It began. The earls carried Gerhard at shoulder height towards the Hel Gate, with everyone following according to their rank, and the soldiers taking up the rear. Servants carried the torches along beside the procession, the hiss and crackle of their tar-soaked wood just as loud as the murmuring of their feet.

At least they could still make the torches, thought Felix. We haven't forgotten everything.

"Has there been anything from Mr Thaler?" he whispered to Trommler.

"No, my lord. Neither is now the time to worry about that."

"Oh."

They walked through the echoing gatehouse and down between the high crenellated walls, across the bridge and along the path to the Chastity Gate. The fortress was a huge presence above them, and there was still further to go – down to the outer wall and through the Wagon Gate.

Then into the maze of deserted alleys and houses, dark and silent except for them, their boots and their burning.

Felix had never heard the collective hush of thousands of people, just waiting. They were lined up on both sides of the river, downstream from the bridge, a black mass that strained and shifted like a living thing.

The prince hesitated, and Trommler's hand came out to steady him.

"Remember who you are, my lord."

I am twelve years old and an orphan. And the Prince of Carinthia.

I faced down a charging Teuton horseman and killed him, even though he broke my shoulder. I killed another, even though my shoulder was already broken. The battle was won, in part, because of me.

He took a deep breath and carried on.

The bier was carried onto the bridge. He followed, and everyone followed him. A small barge, loaded with firewood, was anchored under the bridge between the piers. The ropes holding it in the midstream flow creaked with the effort.

Trommler halted the bier, and stevedores attached ropes to it as the sweating earls stood back. Then, slowly, carefully, Gerhard was lowered over the side. The bier swung, was steadied, and arrived on its final resting place with little more than a bob of the boat.

Felix looked around once more, to see if Allegretti would emerge from the crowd, or perhaps Thaler, or even, possibly, Sophia. All he got was the Gothi, in white and green, ceremonial hammer at his belt. The old man held up a ram's horn, and gave it to the prince.

The mead was sticky, sweet and potent. Whether or not it had been diluted was of little matter: he would have had to drink it even if it had been liquefied goose fat.

The first few mouthfuls weren't too bad. It was harder after that, but he forced himself to swallow all but the last few drops. Those he poured over the parapet, onto the banner and his father's body.

A servant passed Trommler a torch, which was so heavy he struggled to hold it. Felix had to take it from him quickly. His head buzzed, and his own fingers felt fat and unresponsive.

This was it. He held the fire up, feeling its dirty heat on his hand and face. The river was ahead of him, Trommler behind. He reached out, and let the torch fall.

It burnt brightly as it fell, then almost disappeared as it dropped between the gaps of the stacked logs. A distant, obscured flicker shone through the pyre for a moment.

Then the fuel caught. Flames leapt out, and the flag glowed at its edges. Felix stepped back as the first sparks rose into the air. The ropes holding the barge were paid out, and it started to drift downstream. The earls took torches and hurled them towards the flames. His stepmother cast hers with a strong and practised right arm. After that, he lost sight of quite who did what: everything became a teary blur of flames and reflections.

But he could hear. The solemn stillness suddenly broke with an incoherent shout, and the murmur that ensued rose and rose until it became a howl. The people of Juvavum were mourning their lost prince, giving voice to their grief.

Trommler gripped his sleeve. "My lord, look."

Felix wiped his eyes.

"Look," urged Trommler. "The White Tower."

A cold spark, blue-white and intense, was descending from the peak of the mountain. It was so bright that it shone through the trees and picked out the new green leaves, as if the moon itself had descended to Midgard and was coming to meet them.

He checked in the sky, an involuntary movement: the horns of the crescent moon were still wheeling towards the western horizon. He watched the light, neglecting to follow the course of his father's pyre that was still aflame mid-river.

"Eckhardt," he whispered; then, to Trommler: "What are we going to do?"

"It depends what he wants . . ." started the chamberlain, but Felix shook his head firmly.

"No. We know what he wants. He's just fed up with waiting." He found his hand dropping to his belt. "Wherever the signore is, we need to stop Eckhardt now."

"You have to get to safety, my lord." Trommler spread his arms wide and started to usher him back. "Guards! To arms!"

"Mr Trommler, I am the Prince of Carinthia. If I have to do this myself, alone, then that's what I'll do." He hauled his sword out and held it aloft. "To me, Carinthians. To me!"

Trommler tried one last time. "My lord, now is not the time for bravery."

Felix disagreed. "Now is always the time for bravery. Get my stepmother and her children back to the fortress. Go, Mr Trommler, go."

The first by his side was Earl Hentschel. "A hexmaster?"

"The last," said Felix.

"But I thought the magic had gone."

"Almost gone."

"Isn't that wonderful news?"

"Wond . . .? No. You don't understand. This isn't good."

"But the Order has always been for us, my lord." Hentschel was jostled by one of the castle guard, whom he pushed roughly away. "Watch where you're going, man."

"My lord Hentschel, I've learnt today that the Order has always been for itself. As for Master Eckhardt, he's become a necromancer. Do you know what that means?"

The funeral barge kept moving with the current: it was past the city wall, beyond the houses on the north bank. Its light was dwindling, the flames settling to a deep red glow, while the sharp, uncomfortable light coming from Eckhardt was growing.

People began to move.

The crowd on the quay on the far side started to thin as they chose to meet Eckhardt coming down. Those on the southern wharf had to cross the bridge to join them. They numbered thousands, and no militia would be likely to hold them back.

"We have to hurry," said Felix. "We have to get to him first."

The press of bodies was like a rising flood, slow, strong and irresistible. Those who'd formed the funeral procession were forced across the bridge, and those servants that Trommler had dressed up as guards didn't know what to do.

Felix couldn't control them. He'd lost contact with the earls, and Reinhardt was somewhere else, somewhere he couldn't see. Some of the guards broke and ran. Others lowered their spear-points and tried to hold their ground.

A trained man would have known what was going to happen, but Felix only realised too late. The order to pull back died in his mouth, just as the first of the crowd, frantically trying to evade the lowered spears, was shoved forward.

They screamed, and the guard let go of the haft, scrambling backwards, but there wasn't enough room for the impaled man to fall. The spear-haft waggled onwards.

In that moment, the guards became frantic, and the crowd became a mob.

Felix found his voice. "Off the bridge. Off the bridge." He lifted his sword again, and led the running, stumbling retreat to the relative safety of the far quay. The fight midstream was over by the time he looked, and the people of Juvavum were pouring noisily over the stone bridge and up towards the blue star that appeared to have settled on the road to the novices' house.

His father's pyre was now invisible – either sent to the bottom of the river and extinguished or around the bend and out of sight. The only light was the cold glow created by Eckhardt, and Felix realised he simply couldn't compete.

He could hear what they were saying. "He can bring the magic back."

What was left of his retinue gathered around him, no more than a dozen men. He couldn't tell in the dark who was there, and who had been swept away, or consumed by madness, or caught up in the mob. But despite them being mostly pot-carriers and door-openers, they closed around him and did their best to shelter him.

It had taken three days for his rule to be overthrown. Three days for rioters to chase him off the streets. Three days of dark nights, no water, no transport, no ploughs or mills or grindstones or lathes to turn calm, law-abiding Carinthians into a disorderly rabble who'd follow the merest hint of an enchantment. Even as his father's body burnt, they'd lost their reason.

"My lord." It was a familiar voice in his ear: Reinhardt. "We have to retreat to the fortress. We have to go now."

The bridge was almost clear.

Felix pushed out between adult shoulders to see better. "Where's my stepmother? Where're the earls? Where's Ulf?"

"They've gone, my lord." Reinhardt had lost his helmet, and his grey hair was black in the night. "Please, I beg you. The fortress, while we still can."

"Gone? Gone where?"

Reinhardt shrugged helplessly. "They're just gone."

What was he going to do? He was responsible for everyone and everything within his lands, and yet he'd spent those three days curled up into a ball feeling sorry for himself.

Maybe he deserved to lose the palatinate. But perhaps there was something he could still do. Being a twelve-year-old orphan simply wasn't an excuse any more.

"We can't stay here. We'll go to the . . . the Town Hall." It was at the other end of the bridge, and perhaps some of Messinger's militia had made it back there. "If anyone tries to stop you, get them out of the way, hit them, kill them if you have to. We have to go together: follow me."

He strode from the shadows by the bridge and started back across the river.

39

Sophia watched it all happen from Messinger's office: everything, from solemn procession to final chaos, as the lights on the bridge winked out one by one until there were none left. After that, there was only roaring noise.

The light from the White Tower shone out, steady and bewitching, illuminating the flanks of Goat Mountain. It reflected on the faces of the people drawn towards it, faint scratches of blue against the dark.

Downstairs from the office, all was silent. The front doors had opened once or twice, and footsteps had tapped against the tiles, but if anyone was still there, they were staying determinedly quiet, presumably to avoid attracting attention.

Below, out on the quay, the last of the crowd hurried over the bridge. Sophia, suddenly realising how conspicuous she must be – a candlestick with three burning candles sat on the table behind her, framing her silhouette in the rectangle of the open windows – stepped to one side.

The prince, and his whole party, seemed to have been swallowed up. Messinger was nowhere, the militia had melted away. She'd read enough histories to know what was coming next.

Her people were at prayer. She was not. They had lit their Sabbath candles; she had not. They had recited kiddush; she had not. They were at the synagogue, and she was not. It was a sin for her not to be there, and yet HaShem had chosen her to be a prophet, and had conspired for her to be here instead.

She took another look out of the window, and she could see nothing that might stop her leaving. All the same, it was better, she decided, to be prepared. There were two spathae mounted across each other on the wall, their hilts and points protruding from behind the leather-covered auxilia shield they were displayed with. She drew up a chair, stepped up, and lifted the shield free.

Sophia had never held a sword before. She didn't know what it would feel like, or how to wield it without slicing her own leg off. She'd just have to learn as she went.

Both swords were polished bright. Even though they appeared merely ceremonial, and were far removed from what she imagined battle-ready blades should look like, she hoped that they were the genuine article. She wrapped her hand around the grip of the leftmost sword and pulled it free of the bracket.

She had imagined it heavier, that the point would drag down towards the floor. Instead, it fitted her neatly and sat up keenly. It might have been a presentation piece, but it was no toy.

She climbed down off the chair and levelled the spatha at the door, sighting down it. It was perfectly straight, and the candlelight dripped off it like butter. HaShem had provided again. She felt like Deborah.

She glanced up at the other one, and regretted having to leave it, as well as the many other weapons on the walls. She opened the door a crack and listened. It was still quiet, so she wedged the chair in the gap and scooped up the candlestick to light her way.

There was the upper gallery, the staircase and the hall to negotiate. The wood creaked as she walked across it – there was no way it would not – so she speeded up, flitting down the first flight and turning the corner for the second, holding the sword down by her side, but ready.

She paused. The candlelight barely reached the bottom of the stairs, let alone the deeper recesses of the entrance. She didn't even know if the bundle of clothes she'd stashed were still there. Not that it was important any more. There were, she knew, other people in the building, but she hoped they wouldn't try to prevent her from leaving.

Sophia was halfway to the double front doors when their wood shuddered. A moment later, the latch rose, snicking loudly against its stay. She blew out the candles and spun away, just before a door was flung open, and a gaggle of people burst in. Crouching down in an alcove, she waited, not daring to breathe. The door banged shut again.

Someone coughed. Others wheezed and gasped. Then a voice.

"Is there no one else here? Mr Trommler? Mother? Master Messinger?"

She knew who that was. She uncoiled in the dark. "I don't know where they are, my lord."

He knew her voice, too, despite the gasps. "Sophia?"

She stepped closer to him. "Someone came in a little while ago, but I don't know where they've gone. No one came upstairs."

"Eckhardt's out there."

"I know."

"I have to try and kill him."

"My lord, it's too late—" objected one of his men.

"No. I refuse to accept that."

Her hands were full, candlestick and sword. She knelt down and put the candlestick on the floor, then reached out. She found his bound-up shoulder, and moved up to rest her palm on his cheek.

"Felix, whatever you do now, it's too late for the Jews. We have to run, and quickly. When your German subjects cross the bridge again, it'll be for one thing and one thing only."

"It won't happen," he said fiercely. "I won't let it happen."

"You know it will. Without us being here, you might have a chance to restore some sort of order come the morning." She put her hand behind his head and pulled him to her. "With us here, we're all dead."

She held him for a moment, then pushed him away.

"I can protect you," insisted the prince.

"You might be able to protect me. But you can't protect us all."

Felix didn't answer for a moment. He sheathed his sword with a long metallic slide, and let out a series of grunts and grimaces. Then he found her hand and pressed something into it.

"What are you doing?" she asked. "I have to go."

"That's my father's ring. It's my ring now. Get everyone you can and go to the fortress. You'll be safe there."

"The . . ." The thought simply hadn't occurred to her. Princes simply didn't make that kind of gesture.

"If I have to, I'll hold them at the bridge. Ring the bell in the Bell Tower, and I'll know you're safe. Reinhardt: take the rest of the men back to the Chastity Gate and make sure the Jews are let in."

"My . . . lord?"

"Just do it, man! That's an order."

"Thank you," Sophia said. She was already breathless, ahead of all the running she'd have to do.

"Open the door," said Felix, and it inched back open. "Good luck."

She crept outside, and the first thing she did was to check on the light coming from across the river. It seemed steady enough, except that there was a glow around it, as if a fog was rising.

Whether it was just the collective breath of thousands, or something more sinister, she couldn't tell. But there was no baying mob yet.

Felix's ring was too big for any of her fingers. She jammed it on her right thumb, working it painfully over the joint. It felt cold and heavy, and since she never wore jewellery, odd and obvious.

She ran back along the quayside and up into the town, taking the narrow cut that led to the Old Market. The moonlight illuminated only half the square and, as she darted into the shadows towards the start of Jews' Alley, she ran headlong into someone, something.

They fell and she fell. Sophia was on her back, trying to tell which way was up, when the sky darkened and metal glittered. Without thinking, she brought the sword up, expecting to do no more than bat her assailant away. Such was the force of her swing and the length of the blade that the point sliced through something significantly more substantial.

She heard a single bellow of pain, and the shape above her fell all over again. This time, it didn't get up.

The man – it sounded like a man, and smelt like a man – groaned deep in his throat. He'd landed partially across Sophia's legs: she dragged one free and kicked him away. He groaned again, more quietly.

She couldn't see what she'd done, who it was, or tell anything about him. She didn't know what to think, even. Had he been going to attack her, or had she just wounded, or killed, an innocent man?

She scrambled to her feet, and the sword dragged along the ground for a moment before she remembered to lift it. It seemed welded to her arm, something to cling to. "Sorry," she stammered, "I'll send help." She ran the length of Jews' Alley: the candles in the windows lit her way, and she could see that there was no one else around.

She'd grown up in streets that were never dark, thanks to the same magic she'd been taught to reject. Now she knew the truth of the cost of it, she was glad, but she still missed the light.

The synagogue doors were still closed: she'd arrived in time. She crashed through the first set, into the porch where the stairs went up to the women's balcony, and instinctively turned to climb them.

No. Not today. She could hear the words of the Aleinu through the doors ahead of her, and that's where she needed to go. She put her hand on the handle, and realised she was more scared of going in than of what would happen if she didn't. She trembled and her knees started to buckle.

By the lantern-light, she spotted that her sword was smeared with blood. Flecks were on her hand and bodice. And her skirts were heavy with it. There were even splashes of it drying on her face.

If she didn't act, they were all going to die a far worse death than the man she'd cut at.

She pulled the door aside and marched down the aisle to the bimah, where the Torah scroll lay, unrolled. Rabbi Cohen, yad still in hand, stared at her: at first, open-mouthed, then with increasing fury.

"Get out," he roared, "get out, get out, get out!"

"No," said Sophia. "They're coming to kill us, and everyone needs to listen to me."

She turned her back on him, the bimah and the open ark. She looked up to where she would normally sit, up on the balcony at the back. There were a handful of women present, whereas downstairs it was full, and every man was dressed in his Shabbat best.

They were as shocked as Cohen was, but their anger was giving way to uncertainty.

"She is not permitted to speak. Throw her out," thundered the rabbi, but instantly her father was on his feet, shouting over the top of him.

"Shut up yourself, Cohen. Sophia, what happened to you?"

"I don't have time to explain. The last hexmaster's coming for us, and he's got the whole town behind him. We have to leave now. Everyone." It wasn't getting better, it was getting worse. She was dripping on the floor. How was that even possible? How much blood can one man contain? And they were still sitting there – except for her father – looking at each other to see who would say something first.

"You're all idiots," said Aaron Morgenstern, and he climbed over three men to get to the aisle. "The girl turns up covered with blood and carrying a sword, and you think, 'what could this possibly mean?' Mensch, what do you think it means? I'm going home to pack."

"No. There's no time," said Sophia. "They're coming. We have to run."

"But to where?" someone called, and she held up her sword-hand.

"See this ring?"

"You've gone mad," said the rabbi behind her. "Possessed!"

She turned and levelled the sword at him. It weighed deceptively little, despite being almost as long as her legs: he was easily within reach. "Look at the ring. Recognise it?"

He was forced to examine it, the edge of the bloodied blade at his neck. "No."

"It's the ring of Prince Gerhard. His son gave it to me to get us – all of us – into the fortress. Assuming you choose life over death, of course." She lowered the sword and tried to be slightly less threatening. "I know it's the Sabbath. I know I shouldn't interrupt the service, I know I shouldn't be down here in this state. I wouldn't do this if I wasn't telling you the truth and I wasn't terrified of losing everyone here to Eckhardt."

"But what about the prince? The mayor?"

"Felix said he'd try and hold the bridge for as long as he could, but we have to give him a signal when we're safe. He's going to die too if we don't move." She looked up at the balcony, and it was empty. The women had gone, not that the men could see. "If you're coming, get your wives and children and be in Scale Square as soon as you can. Go. Go!"

She hoped she'd done enough. She headed for the doors, pushed them aside and stepped out into the cool night. She leant back against the wall of the synagogue and closed her eyes. The doors banged open again, and again, and again: up and down Jews' Alley, people were running in and out of houses, collecting everyone with a hurried tale about the Morgenstern girl and the prince.

"Sophia?"

"Father." She opened one eye.

"Are you all right? Your mother would never forgive me if anything happened to you."

She laughed. It was a little late for that. "I'm fine, Father. None of this . . . this mess is mine: someone attacked me – I think he was going to attack me – in the Old Market. I think I killed him. With this."

"You were supposed to be in Halstadt." Morgenstern's whole body ached for an explanation. "What happened?"

"Oh, the rabbis saw me and chased me down the quayside, then the bargees threw bottles at them, then the mayor called out the militia, and I've been hiding in the Town Hall all day. By the time everything was quiet, there was no way I could get to aunties' before Sabbath. The mayor's a good man, Father: no love lost there for the Order. I just hope he's still alive. Felix's stepmother and the children are missing, too. It was . . ." she shuddered, "terrible."

Her neighbours started to stream by, and despite the urgency of the situation, almost everyone was clutching a bundle of something or other; treasures that they didn't want looted.

"Sophia, since when did you start calling the Prince of Carinthia by his first name?"

"Since last night." She stopped, scandalised. "Nothing happened. He's just a boy. We're . . . friends."

"Never trust the Germans," Morgenstern said.

"Some Germans, yes." She shook her hand in his face.

"And now you have the prince's ring on your finger."

"It's on my thumb, Father." No one had passed them for a little while, and she grabbed his arm and propelled him towards the square. "It won't fit anywhere else."

And from what seemed not so very far away came the sound of thousands of voices raised in a shout.

40

Büber slipped out of the doorway and crossed the wide quay quietly, not that he needed any of his skill to remain unseen: there was simply no one looking, least of all the diminutive figure of a boy with a sword in his off-hand.

He couldn't be heard, either, over the tumult that was beginning to wind back down the lower flanks of Goat Mountain. Gods, they made a lot of noise; he never missed this city with all its attendant human and mechanical chattering.

The boy stood on the approaches to the bridge, resolute but alone. In front of him was the curve of the stone arch reaching towards the other bank, and dotted on it, in ones and twos, were bodies.

If it made him contemplate his mortality more keenly, so be it.

"Has everyone deserted you, my lord?"

For someone not yet adult, and injured too, he brought his blade up far too quickly.

"Hold."

Though Büber had a sword at his belt, and a bow on his back, he had nothing in his hands. "You're as stubborn and graceless as your father. It got him killed, and you seem to be determined to go the same way."

He pushed his hood back and let the prince take a good look.

"You came back." The sword-point didn't waver.

"I thought I owed some measure of respect to Gerhard. I've paid my dues, and I should really go, since I'm banished." Büber glanced across the river. "There are good reasons to stay, though. If you come with me, I'll show you."

"You're not banished," said Felix. He lowered his sword. "I made a mistake."

"Well, that's refreshing: a prince saying he was wrong. There's hope for you yet, my lord." Büber rubbed at his stubble. "Why are you standing here?"

"Because there's no one else left to do so."

"It's a good answer," said Büber, "but it was the wrong question. What difference do you think you'll make? "

"I promised . . ." The prince tapped the sword against the ground. "The Jews are going to the fortress. They're supposed to give me a signal when they arrive: the bell, from the Bell Tower."

Büber turned around and looked up. He could just about see the top of the tower above the roofs of the warehouses. "And you think that staying here is going to slow down a mob like that? You'd have a better chance of holding back an avalanche. Your Jews are going to either make it or not: anything you do here won't count."

People were starting to filter onto the far bank, dark shapes rimed with moonlight. There was an awful lot of them.

"But I promised," said Felix.

"Then you were a fucking idiot, my lord. You are very young, though, and it'd be a shame if you never grew up to learn either wisdom or humility."

"You . . . you shouldn't speak to me like that." The Sword of Carinthia started to rise again.

"Maybe I shouldn't. But if you don't get your arse off this bridge, you're going to be the prince of a mass grave. So it doesn't really matter how coarse my words get, does it?"

They saw him. Someone shouted, and a group of them speeded up, trotting and full of nervous energy.

"Really," said Büber. "No one is going to remember this as a heroic gesture, because I'll be too embarrassed to tell anyone about it, and they'll be too ashamed."

The first of the mob had reached the crest of the arch, half a dozen of them, then joined by half a dozen more.

Felix coughed into his sleeve and raised his voice.

"You men. Do you recognise your prince?"

Perhaps they did. Or perhaps they recognised the dark outline of Büber better than that of a dark-haired twelve-year-old. They slowed, but didn't stop.

"You need to get out of our way," one of them called. "We've work to do tonight."

None of them seemed to be armed, but numbers were very much against Felix and Büber.

"You mean you're to do butchers' work, thieves' work, rapists' work," answered the prince. "You're no true Carinthian if that's your business."

Gods, his voice is still a child's, thought Büber. "You're going to die here, and there'll be nothing I can do to prevent it." he said in Felix's ear. But even as he spoke, his hand dropped to the grip of his sword. He could smell the blood already.

"Carinthia's always had magic, little prince. We can't be doing without it now." There was a score of them, edging down to the southern side of the bridge. "My advice is that you stand aside, or—"

"Or what?" Felix held up the Sword of Carinthia again. "Treason?"

"Out of the way, boy. The master will get what he wants."

Felix charged them, his war cry sounding exactly as any twelve-year-old's would.

After a moment of surprise, Büber drew his sword and raced after him, for no other reason than that he was there, and that there was nothing else he could do.

The group on the bridge stopped. One or two started to step back. Then Felix was on the first one, felling him with a single blow. He didn't slow down. He swung and lunged, and each time the sword darted out – high blow, low blow, stab and slice – a man went down. He cut his way through enough of them to make the rest run.

When Büber caught him up, the boy was barely out of breath.

"You see, Master Büber, a prince of Carinthia keeps his promises. Even if they are idiotic." He wiped his blade on the back of one of the dead.

The huntmaster bowed. The prince had his good arm tied up tight, and could still wield a sword better than him.

The main mass of people had arrived, colliding with those fleeing from the bridge. Their mutterings and movement seemed unnaturally loud.

"I was wrong before," conceded Büber, "but I'm right now: the two of us will never hold this bridge. Anyway . . ." – he twisted around – "there's your signal."

A bell tolled repeatedly, slow and sonorous, echoing across the town.

Felix stared up at the huntmaster. "I hadn't given any thought as to what to do next, Master Büber."

"How about run? Running would be good."

"But where?"

"Follow me."

Büber took off with a long, loping stride that he knew he could maintain for hours if he had to. Felix had shorter legs, and had to chase the huntmaster along the quay before he caught up with him at the left turn into Wheat Alley.

They cut through the line of houses there where a narrow arch pierced the brickwork and led into a courtyard. Büber took a moment to close the iron gate behind him and bolt it.

"They'll go looking for easier doorways than this," he said, and moved to the far side of the small cobbled square where an even narrower exit led into a passageway.

"I need to get back to the fortress," said Felix, hopping with agitation.

The clatter of boots grew, as did the shouts and cries of the townsfolk.

"We're not going to the fortress, and for gods' sake keep your voice down," warned Büber. "This isn't going to be pretty, whatever happens."

"My place is there."

"This lot aren't going to damage so much as a stone in its wall. Now, if Eckhardt makes an appearance, that's a different matter, but the fortress, and everyone in it, is safe for now, as long as they don't do anything stupid." Büber had to turn sideways to get down the passage: the stonework pressed against both his chest and the crossbow across his shoulders.

"So where are you taking me?"

The huntmaster felt for the latch on the gate at the passage end, and opened it slowly. He didn't push out into the next alley immediately, but waited and listened.

"This way."

"Master Büber, I demand to know where we're going."

Büber smiled grimly down at the boy. "When a prince has to kill his subjects with his own sword and sneak around his own capital by the back alleys, it means he's not in charge any more."

Felix bristled, but Büber slipped away and down the street. He counted alleyways as he went, until, coming to a particular one, he thrust the gate aside. The prince passed under his arm and Büber pulled it shut just as shouting started close by.

"They'll be in Jews' Alley by now, breaking windows and kicking down doors." Büber pushed Felix along the passage between the two buildings. High up, there were windows. Down at the bottom, there was no need for them. The bricks were rough, the mortar damp. Black doorways faced on the walkway, and they held different imaginary terrors than those conjured in a moonlit forest.

The gate at the other end of the passage was stiff, and the hinges squealed as Büber reached over to shove it open. The sound was louder than he liked, and he gritted his teeth.

"Out, out." He put his hand against Felix's back and propelled him into the next street.

"The library?"

The ancient pantheon glowered down at them across the square.

"Yes, the library." Büber looked to his right, and sensed more than saw that they'd been seen. "Main doors, go."

He covered the open ground as fast as he could, and took the steps three at a time. His shoulder struck the door, and he hammered on it with his fist.

"It's me, open up."

The shadows around them seemed to swarm with figures. Büber drew his sword, and they shrank back. Noises from inside the library boomed and echoed, but slowly; gods, too slowly. He was back to back with Felix.

"It's the prince," said someone. He sounded surprised.

"What will the master do for us if we bring him?"

"You won't live long enough to find out, you pig." It was dark under the portico, but that didn't mean Felix was blind. The boy lashed out first, fast and low, impossible to duck or dodge, and

301

then Büber roared and went hand over head, carving an arc from shoulder to toe.

The library doors cranked open, and lantern light spilt out.

Three, four, five bodies lay on the library steps. One of the mob blinked and instinctively put his hand up to shade his eyes: he lost both his hand and his head.

Both sides retreated, the townsmen to the line of pillars, and Büber and the prince to the doorway.

"We can take them," said Felix.

"Until they rush us, pull us to the ground and disarm us, then carry us off screaming to our fate." Büber edged back further. "Don't be like your father."

Felix had no choice: a hand reached out and dragged him inside by his collar, and Büber stepped smartly through the closing gap. Librarians were ready with the bar of seasoned wood and dropped it into place.

The doors shuddered and bowed inwards, straining against the barricade as the mob thrust against them. They creaked in complaint, but did little more than that.

"It'll hold," said one of the librarians. He dusted the palms of his hands against his library robe, turned to Felix and bowed. "My lord, Master Büber."

The prince rested the Sword of Carinthia point-down on the stone flags. "Master Büber, why am I here?"

"Because we've all been living in the mistaken belief that this place is unimportant," said Büber. "Just something to show how rich you are; you and your father and your forefathers before him."

The doors rattled again. They held perfectly firm, so he continued.

"But it's not. Right now it's the most important place in the palatinate, and if we lose it tonight, we may as well just go and live in the forest and eat berries and wear skins."

"The . . . library?" Felix frowned. "You're talking about the library?"

"Come with me," said Büber. "I'll show you what I mean."

He led Felix to where the front desk usually sat. Lantern-light made a soft orange glow in the rotunda, and the shelves of books shone with promise.

"Frederik Thaler would be able to explain this better than I can. But I don't think he's realised himself yet." Büber dragged over a chair. "And he's fooling around underground somewhere, so I'm told, so sit yourself down, my lord, and I'll give it a go."

The doors boomed, and they all – prince, huntmaster, librarians – looked up with annoyance.

"Maybe we should block that a bit better," Büber suggested, and some of the librarians flitted away to move furniture.

Felix sat slowly down and laid the still-bloodied sword across the arms of the chair. "Go on, then. Tell me why."

"It's like this. Carinthia has always had two powers, right, staring at each other across the river: the White Tower and the White Fortress. There was a sort of balance between them, except there wasn't really. The only reason the Order weren't in charge was because they couldn't be bothered with all the problems that running everything would mean. And for you, for the princes of Carinthia, it was like playing with loaded dice. Not cheating exactly, but no one would gamble with you any more, because you'd always win."

"What's this got to do with the library?" asked Felix, and Büber, realising that he had an audience of librarians creeping closer, got flustered.

"Nothing," he stammered, "nothing at all. But that's the point."

"Well, I'm missing it," said the prince.

Büber appealed for help: "Mr Braun, you understand this. You're better at it than I am."

"Nonsense, Master Büber. Keep going."

"Ah, fuck it," growled Büber, and he tried to compose himself. "You see, we were all half-right. There *were* two powers, but, begging your pardon, the White Fortress was never one of them. The prince collected the taxes for the Order, and spent the half they didn't take on whatever took his fancy."

"I think," said Felix, "my father did a little more than that."

"We can argue about that later. The Order needed someone to run Carinthia for them: the princes were a safe choice. Father would tell son about the great battles the hexmasters had fought, and, in turn, the son would tell his son. They had us just where they wanted us, and, let's be honest about it, we were all happy with the arrangement."

Felix worried the scabs on his hand against the wood of the chair. His eyes had narrowed to thin, angry slits.

"Oh, you can press me for this later," said Büber, "if you can catch me, that is. But one of your ancestors had a really smart idea. Perhaps he realised, just as I did, but a lot sooner. There really are two powers in Carinthia, and we're standing . . . well, you're not, you're sitting . . . anyway, this is one of them. The library. So many words, carefully collected over the years, by men like these." Büber swung his arm out and encompassed the whole meagre staff. "I can't read a single one of these books, but I'll tell you this: they've saved my life on more than one occasion, and if they can save me, rough and illiterate as I am, what else can they do?

"Their way – the magic way – it's over. Whatever Eckhardt comes up with, he can't keep it going. Not even if he kills every man, woman and child in Carinthia and beyond. One day, he'll run out of time or sacrifices, and that'll be that. But there'll be nothing left after he's done. No way back for anyone who has the misfortune to survive. If we save the library, we can start again, and on the right path this time, not the one that the hexmasters led us down."

The prince had let his head drop, deep in thought. Now he raised it. "It would take an army to defend this place."

"My lord, you haven't got an army." Büber laughed out loud. "You've got two."

Felix picked up the Sword of Carinthia and got up. He circled the huntmaster. "Two armies?"

"Librarians and Jews. I thought we were going to have to rely on just these pasty-faced scribblers, but you've created another force of fighting men simply by not throwing the Jews to that wolf across the river."

"There are thousands out there, Master Büber. We've got no more than two score here!"

"Does that matter?" Büber asked.

Felix was in front of him, shaking his bloodied sword. "Are you stupid, or something?"

Büber bit his lip for a moment, and resisted the temptation to knock Felix's blade aside with his own. "No. You think we're fighting the townsfolk? You need those people: when we've won, you'll need them to bake their bread and weave their clothes."

"They're rebelling against my rule, huntmaster. Or haven't you noticed? Where's my stepmother? Where are my half-brothers and sisters? Where's my chamberlain and my mayor? Where are my

304

earls? For all I know, they're dead, killed by those bastards outside. If I can kill every one of them, I will."

"What sort of man do you want to be when you grow up, my lord? Do you want to be loved, or feared?"

"Both. Is that too much to ask?"

In the silence that followed, the doors boomed again. Then again. A regular, dull crash that meant only one thing.

Büber tried to hide his smile. "If there was time, I'd tell you how I saw Signore Allegretti in a beer cellar this morning, whispering loudly to anyone who'd hear that the magic would come back if only they could find a way of giving the last hexmaster what he wanted."

"He did . . . what?"

"He didn't see me. For a big man, I can hide in the smallest shadow. I was more than close enough, though. I take it you didn't send him out with that message?"

Felix's sword-point clattered against the floor, and he barely held the grip.

"But I ordered him to kill Eckhardt. Are you saying he betrayed me?"

"Yes." There was no way to soften the blow, and little reason to do so. "We'll kill Eckhardt all right. It's the only way to stop this madness. Right now, though? This is where we need to make our stand. Right here among the books. We can let the library burn. We can let all the librarians get dragged away. Or we can fight. What do you reckon, my lord? Can we save this place?"

Felix looked around him at all the pale, nervous, candle-lit faces, and beyond them to the rows and rows of spines, each with their lettering and decorations.

"We can try," he said.

Büber nodded. "Then raise your sword, Prince Felix of Carinthia. There's a lot of work to do."

41

Sophia didn't know what to do. Actually, she did know what to do, just that she had no idea how to accomplish it.

305

Felix was out there, somewhere, and he hadn't come back.

The streets she could see – she was surprised by how many she could look straight along from one of the fortress's many walls – seemed alive with shadows and light. The townspeople had found the fallen torches from the funeral party, or hastily made their own, and tall smoky flames flickered against the window glass and painted shop signs.

There was, inevitably, a concentration of people around the Old Market and Scale Place at either end of Jews' Alley, but they seemed to drift back and forth without direction.

The quayside still shone brightly, and beyond that ghastly blue light glistened over by the novices' house. There was, however, a lot of commotion in front of the library. Which seemed odd, until she considered that there might be librarians inside.

She listened, and over the general noise of tumult, she could hear a rhythmic bass banging: the gaps between each concussion were long, drawn-out, like the beating of a giant heart, the sound echoing out over the town and up to her.

Taking her lantern, she wound her way down to the main courtyard, where many of the Jews still were. The women and children had mostly found shelter inside the workshops, unwilling to go anywhere near the kitchens or storerooms where the preponderance of pork-based foodstuffs was simply too much.

They outnumbered the servants vastly, who had retreated to the places where the Jews wouldn't go. No one seemed in control any more. Reinhardt was doing his best, but he had no guarantee that the two elderly guards he'd left at the Wagon Gate wouldn't let Eckhardt's mob in, just because they'd been asked nicely.

There was certainly no thought of going back into the town and searching for the prince.

She found her father in the crowd of Sabbath-best men.

"We've got to do something. Lots of somethings."

"Calm yourself, daughter, and do you really have to drag that pig-sticker around with you?"

She was maintaining a death-grip on the sword she'd taken from Messinger's office. "Yes, apparently. We're not safe here. Not yet."

"Some of these walls are twenty feet thick, child." They were, too. Passing through them was more like entering and leaving a tunnel.

"And some of the gatekeepers are just as dense, Father. We can't rely on them."

"What do you suggest we do? Seize the castle ourselves?" He looked at her determined expression. "Oy. You're serious."

"In the prince's name, Father. If that mob gets in here, it's not just us who are lost. The whole of Carinthia will go up in flames." She wanted to sit down all of a sudden, to hand over the whole business to the men who, surely, had more experience in dealing with matters like this. Tired, that was it. She was tired and wanted it to stop.

"I'll talk to them," said Morgenstern.

"That's not enough," she complained. "I know what you're like. Talking, talking, never deciding. We don't have time for talk."

Her father was affronted at first, then had the grace to look abashed. "It's how we decide things. Yes, it can take a while, but at least we can all agree."

"Can you all agree right now that you'd rather not be hanged from the fortress walls or fed to Eckhardt?" she asked, loudly enough to begin to attract attention.

Morgenstern, his back to the rest of the men, equivocated. "Most likely, but Sophia, we've nothing to worry about. We're here under the prince's protection."

"And how long will that last without a prince? Where is he? Where're his earls? They're dead and he's lost. There's nothing to stop Eckhardt coming up here and doing whatever he wants. Unless you think a couple of old men with spears are going to stand in his way?" She had an audience again. When all this was over, she determined that she would do nothing else in her life but read. "Yet we have over two centuries of able-bodied men cowering behind these walls, shaking their heads and pulling at their beards, thanking HaShem for their deliverance."

"We have been delivered," said Rabbi Cohen, and he added, somewhat reluctantly, "thanks to you. Let the Germans do what they want outside: it's no concern of ours."

"No concern? No concern?" She spluttered and her blood-stiff skirt scratched as it swung. "We've just left our homes, run for our lives, and all we have to show for it is a better class of prison in which to die. How can you say we're not concerned with what happens outside?"

"Sophia, you've done what you can. Go and wash. Put the sword down. Give thanks to Elohei Sara, Elohei Rivka, Elohei Leah v'Elohei Rakhel."

She closed her eyes. It was useless, and, worst of all, Cohen was right. They hadn't started this, and they certainly weren't going to finish it either. But still the insistent bang of heavy wood on heavy wood filtered up over the high walls and down to her ears.

Into the midst of them ran a man in a black robe. He was gasping for air, and he couldn't speak. He couldn't stand, either. He crouched down on his haunches, coughing and spitting. He was a librarian.

"Which . . ." he said, "which of you . . .?"

"Someone find him a drink," said Cohen. "Tell the women that someone out here needs a drink of water."

The man pushed himself half-upright, resting his hands on his bent knees. "Gods, which one of you is Sophia Morgenstern?"

The Jewish men all looked at the librarian, then at Sophia.

"I am," she said. "That's me."

The librarian peered up at her from his half-bent state. "Prince Felix sends his greetings and requests every loyal Carinthian to arm themselves and come to the library at once."

A woman crossed the courtyard and pressed a cup of water into the man's hand. He rasped his thanks and gulped until the cup was dry. Straightening himself, he took in the curious stand-off between Sophia and the rabbi: she on one side, and every male Jew on the other.

"Miss Morgenstern?" He turned to her, and lowered his voice. "They can understand German, can't they?"

"Oh, they understand perfectly. Mr . . .?"

"Braun. Ernst Braun, at your service." He bowed to her. Sophia wore the prince's ring: why wouldn't he?

"Perhaps hearing themselves described as loyal Carinthians is so much of a novelty, it's shocked them into silence." She frowned at the rabbi, and at her neighbour, Mr Rosenbaum, who stood just behind the cantor. She knew all of them, and in turn each of them looked down and away.

Except her father.

"I told all of you that if we were loyal Carinthians, we'd give up the lion's share of our bonfire wood for Gerhard's pyre," he said. "We did. That must mean we're all loyal Carinthians." He momentarily took his hat off and wiped his forehead. "Where do they keep the weapons?"

Braun blinked. "Grandfather, the prince didn't mean you."

"Less of the grandfather, boy. I can still break skulls if I have to."

Sophia intervened. "Stay and guard the castle, Father. Better still, stay and be in charge of the castle until Felix gets back. Go and find Reinhardt. Get him to open the armoury." When he hesitated, she didn't. "Father, go."

The sound of him shuffling as fast as he could across the stone flags merely served as a reminder that he was the only volunteer so far.

"Please," said Braun, addressing the men, "the library is surrounded. The mob is outside. Only the prince and Master Büber have swords. All the librarians are with them, but we can't hold out alone."

"Young man," said Cohen. "Why the library? Why not here? Surely the fortress is the safest place to be."

"But," said Braun, "the library isn't in the fortress. It's down there. If it burns, it's gone forever, and Master Büber has convinced the prince it's the most important building in the whole of Carinthia. Without it, nothing will be worth saving."

His reply silenced the rabbi. So Sophia asked instead.

"Mr Braun. Why would he believe that?"

"Because we have to learn to do without magic, Miss Morgenstern. We have no one to teach us except those books."

She smiled. "How long have we waited to hear that? Listen to him, please. The Germans want to live without magic, and we can help them." She deliberately stood next to Braun and planted her sword between her feet.

"Miss Morgenstern, I don't think the prince meant you, either," whispered the librarian.

"Shut up, you fool," she said. "Don't you know how shame works?"

"Honestly? No." He forced himself to look away. "I'll take your word for it."

They stood shoulder to shoulder, and Sophia fixed her neighbours with her dark eyes. "Prince Felix is against Eckhardt. If we stand with him now, we'll be honoured throughout the land. We'll live and prosper in Carinthia as long as the story is told of how the brave Jews of Juvavum took the prince's side and defeated his enemies. And don't think that Eckhardt isn't our enemy: he'll take every one of us, your wives and your children, until there are none of us left to remember. If the prince falls, so do we. If he wins, so do we." She kicked her foot at the sword-blade so that is grated against the stone. "HaShem has given us this opportunity. Do we spend our lives or do we squander them?"

It took a while, but, eventually, one of them broke.

And it was Rabbi Cohen. He ruefully turned around and raised his arms high as if in blessing. "So what are we waiting for? Pesach? Our families will stay, and we'll go. David, go and find out what's keeping Aaron. If you think you're too old, too young or too infirm – and yes, I do mean you, Enosh – you be gatekeepers. Being too scared isn't reason enough: if you want courage, ask El ha-Gibbor to provide."

Cohen took over organising the men into groups, and Sophia moved away. They weren't going to take orders from her directly anyway, even if they agreed with what she wanted them to do. She twisted Felix's ring around and around her thumb as she waited.

Spears and swords and shields emerged, along with more advanced armour: helmets and chest pieces, mail and lorica. They were distributed with a good deal of nervous laughter, as they tried to fit chain coats over their clothes. In the end, most of them settled for the basics – something to fight with, something to hide behind and something to stop their brains being dashed out on the unforgiving pavements.

They weren't fighting an army – neither were they an army, which became painfully apparent when they tried to line up in the semblance of a century.

All of this was done to the rhythmic battering of the library doors. When it stopped, the silence was chilling.

Braun tried to shout over the rabbi, "We have to hurry. They've broken in," but it didn't seem to do any good.

Sophia picked up a round shield with a metal rim, and struck at it with the flat of her sword. When the din had quietened everyone down, she shouted, "We go now, or not at all."

Throwing the shield down, she started for the Hel Gate, Braun hurrying after her, trying not to trip over his spear-haft.

"Miss Morgenstern, you really aren't supposed to be part of this."

"Mr Braun, did the prince tell you explicitly that I wasn't included in the call for all loyal Carinthians to rally to him?"

"No, but I'm sure he meant . . ."

She handed him her sword for as long as it took her to gather up her hair and tie it in a knot at her neck. "I'm sure he meant that too. However, in the absence of a direct order from him, to me?" She shook her head and took the sword back.

The start of the Sabbath was ruined already: they had worked, carried, and lit fires. Now they faced the prospect of fighting, killing, and perhaps dying, on the holy day. Atonement would have to be sought, and they would pray and fast and listen to the Torah until their sins were blotted out.

It wasn't just Sophia who was considering the enormity of her actions: the mood spread from man to man. The novelty and playful heroism leaked away to be replaced by a quiet anger that their worship, their celebrations, their whole pattern of life had been broken.

By the time they reached the Chastity Gate, they no longer walked like they were out for a Saturday night: they almost marched in time.

Even Braun sensed the change, his eyes round with mounting dread.

"How do we do this, Mr Braun?" asked Sophia.

"I . . . don't know." He looked at the spear in his hands with a reaction close to surprise. "I'm a librarian. Books are almost all I know."

"Books are almost all I know too. Has anything you've read got any relevance at all to what we're about to do? Any Homer? Any of the Gallic War?"

"Not that I can remember. Bestiaries, mainly." He drew in his lips. "And maps. I like maps."

They marched on to the Wagon Gate. The guards weren't quite sure what to make of them, but when they saw that Sophia was at the head of this suddenly large column of armed men, they automatically started to unlock the gate.

"Look at them. They don't even question what we're doing." She called over her shoulder: "Father? Take charge here."

"As you have?" asked Braun.

"Tomorrow I'll go back to being plain Sophia Morgenstern. For now, I am HaShem's chosen, just as Deborah was in her day. The hand of a woman delivered her people from the Caananites; so will it be tonight. Onwards."

42

The left-hand door was off its hinges completely, and was leaning back against the pile of furniture that had been stacked behind it. The right-hand door was splintered at its furthest edge, but still grimly hung on to the wall, as it had done for the last thousand years.

Hands slipped around the side of the fallen door, trying to pull it away. It was too heavy for an uncoordinated mob to shift, which bought the library a few more seconds.

Felix, his back to the entrance, inspected his troops. They didn't amount to much: pale men, the young too thin, the old too fat, more used to wielding a pen than parts of a banister. The only advantage he had was that they appeared more than willing to defend their library with their blood.

"Won't be long now," he said to Büber.

"No." The huntmaster rested his sword against the upturned table he stood behind and cocked his crossbow. He held it out to the nearest black-robed man. "You. Come here."

"Yes, Master?"

"What's your name?"

"Erdlmann, sir." The librarian stepped forward hesitantly.

"Can you point your finger, Mr Erdlmann?" asked Büber, laying a bolt on the bow.

"Yes. I think so."

"Then you can aim and fire this." Büber took a few moments to instruct the man in the rudimentary operation of the weapon. "First man past that door, kill him. Got that?"

"Kill, Master Büber?"

"Gods, man, yes." Büber looked roofwards. "You'll get something worse if they take you."

Felix slapped the librarian on the back. He'd intended to say something about his being the first of his profession in Valhalla, but the instant he touched the man, Erdlmann's nervous finger twitched against the hair trigger.

The bowstring snapped taut and the bolt became a blur in the lantern-light. The unaimed shot ricochetted off the wall and into the back of the door with a thud. That it also managed to fix some-one's hand to the wood was an entirely unintended consequence.

The screams came to them, high-pitched and urgent, rising in volume when the owner of the hand tried to pull free and found himself trapped.

Büber took the bow from Erdlmann's sweat-soaked grip and recocked it.

"A silver florin if you can do that again," said Felix, "in fact, a silver florin for every man here. Mr Trommler says Carinthia's rich, so I might as well spend it on those who deserve it."

The door – impaled hand and all – was pulled out of the way. The screaming kept on, and there was something about its tone that made Felix want to climb the barricade, find a path through the deliberately strewn furniture, and end that gods-awful noise once and for all.

He resisted, and urged everyone to do the same. "Hold. Remember the plan. Think as one, act as one."

At the far end of the entrance, still under the portico, the shadows moved. The light from inside the library reflected off their eyes and little else. There were hints of steel, but mostly the dark bulk of clubs and swags of sacking and rope. They were there to take, not to kill. Eckhardt wasn't going to reward them for a life-bled corpse.

"My lord?" said Büber.

"Yes, huntmaster, I know." Felix stepped up on a chair to the flat of a table and cleared his throat. "Carinthians. You have rioted, murdered, and rebelled against me, your rightful prince. The traitor Eckhardt is under sentence of death for treason. If you don't want to share his fate, then go home, lock your doors and stay inside. The library is under my special protection. Anyone entering here will pay the price for their disobedience, and no mercy will be shown." He climbed back down.

If some in the mob had thought they'd only be facing librarians – terrified, disorganised, weak – they now realised they'd face the Prince of Carinthia too, and whoever he might have in there with him. Those with clearer heads, who preferred easier prey, slipped away. Many hung back, waiting for others to be first. But those who immediately needed what Eckhardt offered, or thought they did – a healing, a boon, an advantage over others – they were the ones who pressed forward slowly and cautiously, hoping that the prince's threats were nothing but bluster and bluff.

And a few were fanatics who would follow Eckhardt unquestioningly.

A man, bare-chested and holding a hatchet over his head burst through the advancing mass and tried quickly to close on the defenders. As he ran through the strewn furniture, he hit a chair with his shins, causing him to stumble into another which had its legs sticking in the air. He fell, and when he rose again, it was without his axe.

That he blinked and was possibly regretting his folly was moot, because a moment later he took Erdlmann's bolt square in the chest. Flecks of foam from his mouth spun away in the lantern-light as his head snapped back. He dropped, but the others pushed on, stepping over and on him, as if he were now no more than another discarded piece of furniture.

Felix drew his sword and placed himself front and centre. Büber stood to his right. Erdlmann ducked down and cranked the crossbow lever like he'd been shown. He came back up again just as the front of the mob reached them.

He fired at point-blank range into them, threw the bow behind him, and picked up his baluster.

Felix had organised the defences into a deep and narrowing horseshoe shape. Tables turned on their sides and wedged against more furniture stopped any easy access over the top, and allowed the librarians to batter anyone attempting to clamber across. The prince and Büber had positioned themselves at the narrowest point of the arc, where the pressure of the crowd would naturally propel people.

The arrangement was the best they could do with the limited forces they had. As long as everyone stuck to the plan, it might work. If any section was left undefended for so much as a moment? They'd be overwhelmed.

The time for hoping he'd done enough was over. Büber lunged with a simple thrust against a man pinned against the barricade. The sword-point smashed the bridge of the man's nose and kept going until it hit the back of his skull. Jerking it free, Büber found another easy target and thrust again.

The librarians used their weapons to poke and bash. They set upon an attacker who was trying to haul himself across a table, the rise and fall of square-ended pieces of wood slowly reducing him to a bloody wreck of twisted limbs and unrecognisable features.

He made it into the library proper, but only when he was dead, tossed aside by the red-handed staff.

The noise: Felix had thought it would be a howling, screaming, roaring cacophony. Instead, it was strangely subdued. The great dome echoed to grunts, strains and gasps of effort and concentration. To the crack and crunch of bones. The meaty hiss of a metal blade passing through skin and muscle. The hollow hammering of fists and feet. The scrape of wood on stone.

There was no room for the bodies to fall. The weight of those entering held them up. The length of the entrance became a funnel that led to inevitable death, and once caught up in it, there was no way back. Not that it stopped those in the second and third rank from trying to claw their way out of the range of Felix's and Büber's swords.

The prince's arm was tiring. He glanced at Büber, who was sweating and gritting his teeth with every strike. His own blows were becoming less and less effective at reaching the living through the dead.

The barricade moved towards them. A foot nearer across the slick floor. A gap opened up between the tabletops. Corpses rolled and slid, filling the opening.

"Master Büber," he called.

"Keep going. Break them."

"They need to know they're broken first."

"The plan, my lord. Stick to the plan." Büber plunged his sword into the guts of the man in front of him, twisted it, and heaved it out again.

The bodies were so thick on the ground that the attackers were rising above them. But it was an uncertain footing, and they were hopelessly exposed to thrusts and cuts at their abdomens, groins and legs. They fell even quicker than before, brought down and either run through or beaten mercilessly.

The relentless onslaught didn't allow for a moment's rest. Every time a target died, or was clubbed insensible, there was someone else to replace them. And there were casualties starting to appear in the ranks of the librarians. A cut here, a concussion there; it made a difference to the effectiveness of their defence. The tables kept being pushed back. Their previously compact perimeter was expanding. Weaknesses were appearing. They didn't have enough reserves to plug the holes. Where defenders flagged through exhaustion or injury, there was no one left to take their place.

Felix found that he was taking a step backwards more often. And he couldn't feel his left arm any more. Most of him was numb, except his shoulder, which was on fire. He had to force himself to fight on.

This is how it ends, he thought.

The line finally broke, not with a shout but with a sigh. They had no plan for this part. He raised his sword-hand high and brought it down on top of a man's head. The blade stuck for a moment too long, and he couldn't use it to chop at the next target.

Büber threw himself between them, his big hand closing around a throat and punching.

Chaos.

Knots of men were struggling at close-quarters. In some, the black robes outnumbered the townsfolk, and they forced the attackers down. In others, hard boots and fists beat a bloodied librarian into submission and started to drag him away.

Without his sword, Felix found he was useless. He was a twelve-year-old, taking on grown men, some of them strengthened by years of manual work, and while they were fresh, he was so tired he could cry.

Büber hacked and cut and swung. He put his head back and bellowed his defiance. "Carinthia! Carinthia!"

Even as Felix clattered into a bookcase, the huntmaster raged and foamed and finally disappeared under a melee of bodies pulling at him, trapping his arms, holding his legs.

Then he was up again, his tormentors hanging from him like burrs. Unarmed, he simply tore at them with his nails, gouging and rending, throwing them off one by one, scattering them like leaves. Ignoring his fallen sword, he ploughed into the next band, barely sparing the crumpled librarian he was supposed to be saving.

Felix darted forward, scooped up Büber's sword, and swung at the bent shoulders of a man trying to rise.

"Carinthia, to me!" he called. He stabbed down, impaling a thigh, then cutting up as the body twisted away. Blood arced black in the orange light. "To me!"

But then Felix went down. He'd slipped. They were on him. He struggled, but their full weight was on his chest, crushing the breath out of him as though he were being pressed. He couldn't move. No, he could move, but it had no effect. He couldn't free himself. They were kneeling on his broken shoulder. The pain was incandescent, beyond feeling and sense.

A hood descended over his head, and it was dark. There seemed little point in resisting, but he did his best, which was to say very little. Someone took hold of his ankles and started to pull him, a step at a time, across the floor. Felix's good arm flailed ineffectively at them.

He was released. He stopped moving and his heels hit the ground. He lay there, waiting to be picked up again, but nothing happened. He realised that no one was going to stop him from taking off his hood, so he did so in one movement, casting it aside and propping himself up on his elbow.

The only figures left standing were librarians, and one of them spotted him with a cry of relief.

"My lord, you're safe."

"Where . . . where did they all go?" He used the man as a prop to regain his feet as he tried to make sense of everything.

There was barely space for the dead to lie. It was as if an autumn gale had blown a pile of dried brown leaves through the doors and into the reading room. Tables and chairs and the weapons both sides had used protruded like trees and twigs. He raised his eyes towards the main entrance. The doorway was uncannily clear.

"I don't know," said the librarian, looking around, more stunned by the possibility of victory than the inevitability of defeat. "I think we won."

"Where's Master Büber?" Felix couldn't see him. "Master Büber?"

"I'll find him." But the librarian first groped on the floor and hauled out the Sword of Carinthia from under the still form of a well-dressed man who had fallen across it, obscuring all but the pommel. "Yours, my lord," he said, as he pressed it into the prince's hand.

He reeled away, asking his fellows if they'd seen the huntmaster, and eventually one of them pointed towards the outside. The librarian retrieved a baluster and picked his way warily towards the gaping darkness where the doors used to be.

Felix found an unbroken chair, righted it and fell into it. If they were to be attacked again, be bound and hooded and dragged across the bridge, there'd be nothing he nor the librarians could do about it. They were spent. Better to gather his allies and tell them to escape, if they could, than let Eckhardt have his way with them. Fuel, he remembered, and shivered.

The signore had switched sides. His stepmother was missing. His half-brothers and sisters were missing. Chamberlain, missing. Earls, missing. Order, scattered or slaughtered. Library, lost. He still had the fortress, but he wasn't in it, was he? No army, no magic, no way of holding back the night.

The librarian who'd volunteered to find the huntmaster was returning, not with one person, but with two.

The first was Büber, looking more animal than man. His clothes were ragged, his arms bloody, his teeth bared. His eyes were reduced to thin slits and his whole body appeared almost lupine, touched by a madness that was yet to leave him.

By contrast, the other was cool, self-possessed and controlled. It was Sophia Morgenstern, just as gore-covered as Büber, but regal where he was feral, magnificent instead of maleficent. She seemed to have acquired a dwarvish-made spatha from somewhere, carrying it drawn by her side, the blade stained red and black. She wore the ring Felix had given her on the thumb of her right hand.

"My lord," she said, "we have Library Square." She seemed not at all perturbed by the strewn dead lying between them.

Felix looked up at her. "You came."

Her face cracked into a half-smile. "We all came. All the Jews of Juvavum, except those who've made the White Fortress secure."

"But you could have been killed." Felix was out of his seat.

"Then I would have died in the service of my earthly lord, the Prince of Carinthia. When you sent Mr Braun to us, you knew I'd come, even if I had to come alone."

Felix nodded dumbly.

"What do you want us to do now? The mob has fled, and we're guarding Vienna Alley and Corn Alley."

"What do I want to do?" The prince's shoulders slumped. "I want to kill them all for what they've done. I want to kill them all and replace them with subjects who won't turn on me and each other because some magician promises them the world."

She looked at him with her dark eyes, sad and sombre. "You *could* do that."

"Do we have any prisoners?" He raised his voice. "Librarians. Any prisoners?"

"Yes," answered Erdlmann. He'd found Büber's crossbow, and he offered it to its owner. "Some. Not lots, but a few."

"Bring one to me."

Büber took his crossbow, slowly and reluctantly. Civilised men used weapons like that, and he seemed unsure of his right to carry one.

A man, his head matted with stiff blood and both eyes blackened, was thrust in front of Felix. He knelt, knowing that he would have been forced to anyway.

"I warned you," said Felix. "No mercy if you entered the library."

"I . . . didn't hear you, my lord."

"I should just kill you." He examined the sword in his hand. Not magical any more, but it didn't need to be. "But I'm going to use you instead."

He put the sword on the chair behind him and pulled his knife from his belt. He turned to Erdlmann: "Hold him."

The man was held, and Felix knelt down on the floor beside him. He held up the knife. "Just to be clear: the man with his arm around your neck will kill you if I tell him to. I'm willing to do so, too, with my own sword or this, and I may well decide later that that's what I'll do. This, however, will do for now."

He carved a diagonal line down from left hairline to right cheek across the man's face, then, as the blood beaded and dripped, he went back for the reverse stroke so that the two cuts crossed on the bridge of the nose.

"Listen to me, because your life depends on this. I want you to go through the streets of Juvavum and declare a curfew. No one is allowed on the streets until the Bell Tower rings. If the curfew is observed, you live. If it doesn't, I'll hunt you down and kill you tonight. It's not like you can hide any more."

The man snivelled and gasped, but nodded.

"Hold his right hand out," Felix told Erdlmann, and when the prisoner's hand was thrust out palm-down towards the prince, he stuck his knife into it so that the point came out the other side.

The man screamed once, then shut up.

"Never take up arms against me again. I might be only twelve, but I know what to do with traitors." Felix pulled the blade out, and straightened up. "Take him outside and he can start."

Sophia was looking at Felix, unblinking.

"What else am I supposed to do?" he said to her, and he called out again to the librarians. "Bring me the next one."

43

Dawn broke across the south-eastern sky as lines of blossom-pink cloud. Büber glanced up from his task – stacking the bodies in ranks in the town square – and reached over to open up his lantern. He blew the candle out and closed its hatch.

"It's morning, Master Büber," said Braun, working alongside him. He'd brought a fresh handcart piled with corpses, and had stayed to unload. "Last night . . ."

"We all thought that," said Büber. He took the arms of the topmost body and pulled it clear. "Yet here we are, and here they are. When we tell the story of what happened, it'll be because we were more worthy, more loyal, more true. But really? It was because they needed to take us alive, and we didn't need to do the same."

He dragged the stiffening corpse into place and dropped it down. He'd never been that good with numbers, tending to group things into ones, pairs, a few, a handful, lots, and fuck-loads. By that count, they'd killed lots of people, and every one of them a Carinthian. He wondered if the same scene was being played out all across Europe as monarchs fell and cities burnt.

It could still happen. Eckhardt was across the river, his power most likely waxing. Until he was dealt with, Felix's throne was vulnerable. The longer it went on, the worse it would get.

"I need to see the prince," said Büber. "Where is he?"

"Still in the library, Master, with that Jewish woman."

Büber wiped his hands on the back of his breeks. "Careful, Mr Braun. Not only did the Jews haul our arses out of the fire last night, for which we should be properly grateful, but we'll have a Jewish princess as regent before long. I'd keep your mouth shut if you value your neck, whatever your mind might say."

"No one's saying they didn't do a good thing." Braun checked around him before he spoke further. "They only have one god, Master Büber. How can that be right?"

"And how many gods do you think we have now, Mr Braun?" Büber looked up and down the rows and rows of still forms set out in the square, and at the gyre of crows circling above. A kite wheeled with them, its outline dark against the lightening sky, reminding him of one time he'd happened to glance upwards and see the outstretched wings of a dragon pass overhead. "Do you think this lot are feasting with Wotan in Valhalla? Or are they just going to stay rotting here until they're either claimed or tipped into a hole? Seems to me that the gods have gone the way of the unicorns, so what does it matter any more that the Morgenstern woman believes in one god or many?"

Braun wore a sour expression for a moment, before he shrugged. "It just doesn't feel right, that's all."

"Well, get used to it, man. A group of people used to living without day-to-day magic? Until we learn how to do that for ourselves, we're beholden to them." Büber started off across the square, along the files until he reached a gap and cut through. When he was at the entrance to the alley, he turned. The bodies were grouped in lines of ten, and Braun was crouched over a cart parked halfway along the seventh line.

Büber shook his head in disgust and despair, and went to find Prince Felix.

The librarians were scrubbing the flagstone floor: on their knees, with buckets of steaming water and stout-haired brushes, sleeves rolled back and hands red with effort.

Now *that*, he had to concede, was dedication. The left-hand door was propped up against the wall outside, with the fortress's carpenter fussing over it. Another mob could swarm across the bridge again that night and walk right in, yet there the library staff were, scraping the blood and shit off the ground in case it contaminated their books.

He had no choice but to step in his boots right where they'd cleaned. He assumed they wouldn't mind.

"Mr Erdlmann?"

The man was intent on his task, and Büber moved to stand right in front of him. Weary, bleary eyes gazed upwards.

"Master Büber?"

"You have to sleep sometime."

"My turn soon," he said, and sat back on his heels. "The prince is on the first landing on the right."

The handrail had gone: of course it had, denied support when the banister had been de-constructed for weapons. Büber stuck to the wall side and climbed up to the gallery, letting his eyes adjust to the gloom. A single lantern flickered on the floor, illuminating two blanket-shrouded shapes.

One lay curled up like a cat, and, separately, the other was propped against the curving wall.

"Master Büber," said Sophia Morgenstern. Her hand moved away from her sword, lying within reach on the boards beside her.

"My lady," he said.

"I'm not my lady of anything, Master Büber." She sat up further, moving slowly, almost painfully.

"I won't have been the first to call you that. Pretty sure I won't be the last."

"No," she admitted, "there is that." She pulled the edge of the blanket in, indicating that Büber should sit next to her.

He lowered himself down and found himself staring at the prince's sleeping form. "Poor kid," he said. "Must be knackered."

"He wouldn't stop until I made him." She snorted softly. "He listens to me. Don't know why."

"I'm not well-versed in the ways of kings and princes," said Büber. "But even I know that the normal rules don't apply to the likes of him."

"Whatever could you mean, Master Büber?"

He missed the irony in her voice, and attempted an explanation. "Just that who they marry, and when they marry, aren't matters that concern ordinary folk. Some are betrothed before they're born."

"Felix was telling me that just that happened to his father. His mother was a Frankish princess, taken as the price for offending the Order." Sophia made her lips go thin. "And many years later they let her die in childbirth, simply out of spite."

Büber raised his eyebrows. "When did he find that out?"

"Yesterday. Mr Trommler told him, presumably to stiffen his resolve and act against what his tutor was saying." Her hand went back to her throat where Allegretti had pricked her. "I don't suppose there's any word on either of them?"

"They haven't turned up among the dead, if that's what you mean. You know that Felix sent Allegretti to kill Eckhardt?"

She nodded. "And that you overheard him yesterday, singing Eckhardt's praises."

"He's a dangerous man."

"Oh," she chuckled, "I know all about that, Master Büber. It seems the only person who didn't was the one that mattered."

"There is a way we could end this, but it's not without its risks." Büber straightened his legs in front of him to stretch them. Yes, he was tired, but he was used to being tired. Not like these townsfolk. The woman, mind, she was still awake and alert.

"Go on," she prompted.

He looked at her sharply. Anyone else, he would have told them that he was a prince's man, and, as such, had the ear of the prince directly. Even a future princess of Carinthia. She had saved him, though, from being carted away across the river.

She pre-empted him. "If it's none of my business, you only have to say. I've no authority over you."

Büber grunted. "Not yet."

"Not even then, Master Büber." Sophia made to get up, and he stilled her with his hand.

"Eckhardt isn't the only sorcerer left. The one who rode out with Gerhard: she can still do magic, and she doesn't need what he calls 'fuel', either." Büber worked some dirt from underneath his fingernails. "She might be prepared to, well, kill him – and Allegretti – for us."

"Is she more powerful than the hexmaster?"

"Yes. Probably. Maybe." He shrugged. "I don't know. This is the Order we're talking about. She isn't even a proper hexmaster herself; she's an adept, though I think after what she did to Obernberg, no one's going to worry about that."

Sophia shifted against the wall. "What did she do?"

"She burnt it to the ground. Along with everyone still in it." He grimaced. "There wasn't the time to call for her last night. Probably a good job, too. Juvavum would be a pile of ash by now."

"No half measures?"

"No," said Büber. "She's elemental. In more ways than one. The prince knows her, knows what she's capable of."

"And so do you." Sophia toyed with the pommel of her spatha. "This woman . . ."

"Nikoleta. Nikoleta Agana."

She looked up and caught Büber's gaze. She raised an eyebrow, and Büber gave a little shrug. Somehow, she'd guessed at more than he'd been willing to say.

Scratching at a cut on his face, he said: "Felix banished her, though that was more Allegretti's doing than the prince's. He might yet decide that he doesn't want anything to do with magic any more, and she's still not welcome."

"If he does that, would you leave with her?"

He thought about it. "I don't know how he's going to deal with Eckhardt without her help. He can't overwhelm him with numbers, and as for sneaking up on him? I could do it, but I'd be lucky if I got half a chance at him. Then there's the fucking sword-master to worry about, too."

"I'll talk to Felix," she said.

"You? A Jew? Prepared to use magic?"

"Don't mock, Master Büber." She shifted her shoulders again, uncomfortable against the cold stone. "You're right. We don't have enough soldiers. We don't have any soldiers, just untrained boys and men trying to look the part, and they're most of the people I know. If Eckhardt kills them, that'd be the end of the Jews of Juvavum, and that can't happen."

"And what will your god have to say about this?"

"Honestly? That I should have faith and trust in Him, rather than rely on witchcraft to save us. That HaShem will send His angels against His enemies." She rolled onto her hands and knees, and Büber could see she'd changed her clothes at some point. The blood-soaked skirts of the night before had gone, and she was in something else, clean and bright.

"If he did, that'd solve a lot of our problems. Do you really think it could happen? I've never had dealings with any god, let alone yours."

"There are stories . . ." she started, and he finished for her.

"All from a long time ago." He rubbed at his face. "They always are."

"Go and talk to your witch," said Sophia. "I'll tell the prince when he wakes. How soon, assuming she's willing, could she be here?"

"Midday?" He got to his feet, and she to hers. They faced each other in the gloom. "Last night you saved the prince and the palatinate. That was well done."

"I didn't do it on my own, Master Büber."

"We both know differently." He kicked at the floor. "If you are going to be our queen, then you'd be a worthy one."

"Carinthia needs its friends, huntmaster. We serve where we

can." She reached forward and lifted his chin. "How long have you known you're a berserker?"

"Last week, probably." He wouldn't meet her gaze again, and pushed her hand away. "I don't plan to make a habit of it." He barely remembered meeting her outside the library. He'd been tearing and snapping at the mob, using one of the librarians' makeshift clubs to lay indiscriminately about him, when the Jews appeared, seemingly from nowhere, bristling with weapons and armour to drive the insurrection from the square.

He'd almost fought them as well, but the sight of Sophia Morgenstern, bloody-handed and in command, had stilled him just enough that when she levelled her sword at him, he had the presence of mind to recognise friend from foe. The Jews had charged on, roaring their battle-cries in their foreign tongue, everyone taking fright at their ferocity. Sophia and Büber were left circling each other until he sprang his hand and dropped his club, letting it clatter to the ground. The madness had left him, and he was just the huntmaster once more.

"Like I said, we serve where we can. Some duties are more painful than others, that's all." She rested her hand on his shoulder. "Godspeed, Master Büber."

He nodded, and left her, making his way back down the stairs to the ground floor, deep in thought.

Getting back to where Nikoleta was waiting – waiting for him? – wasn't going to be as straightforward as infiltrating the town in the first place. The Gaisberg was across the other side of the river: the next, much larger peak in the chain that included both Goat Mountain and the fortress crag.

He'd crossed the bridge yesterday, hidden among the crowds. Today, any large group of people was to be avoided, even the Jews guarding the crossing: trying to explain to them that bringing in another magic-wielder of uncertain temper would solve their problems wasn't a conversation he wanted to have.

A boat, then, and away from the town to where awkward questions would be scarce.

The East Gate through the walls on Well Street was open. Perhaps it should have been closed and guarded, but the curfew seemed solid. He had his hand on his sword, and he made sure he walked down the middle of the road. Yes, there were faces at some of the windows, but he was a recognisable figure, and a prince's man.

Outside the walls, the houses grew more sparse and widely set. Rich men's manors – merchants and guildsmen – lined the waterfront. Many of them would have a boathouse. He chose the last building on his left and self-consciously scaled the locked iron gate set in the tall brick wall.

The gardens in front of the house were immaculate, all squares of hedging and neat borders. The gravel path crunched underfoot: it was the only sound, and served to heighten his nerves. He had no idea who lived there but, on reflection, didn't really care. It was just another faux-Roman villa, complete with a statue-lined approach, and couldn't compare to the dark splendour of the forests.

Büber went on unchallenged: around the back and towards the river bank. More gardens, taking in the vista towards the lake country of the east, the Gaisberg now visible, rising from behind Goat Mountain, grey and indistinct in the morning mist.

The boathouse was new. It smelt of fresh-cut pine and still oozed resin, more so inside where the air was still and the river lapped at the base of the piling that supported the walkways either side of the tongue of water. The boards creaked as he walked to the far end to peer out through the opening at the far bank. He stayed still for a while, letting everything settle, watching and waiting.

There was no one over there. He climbed down the ladder to the smaller of the two boats and carefully sat on the bench seat as it wobbled under him. Two oars lay in the bottom, and after casting off, he used one of them to push himself out into the open water.

The current slowly took him, turning him in the direction of town again. Quickly, he fitted the oars to the rowlocks and began to pull himself around, aiming the prow of the boat upstream and towards his destination.

He stretched his legs, brought his arms into his body. The oars dipped and caught. The boat surged on.

44

Before, his appearance – his mere presence – had always been a surprise: that she could see him and not sense him. When he'd left her the previous day, he'd stepped out of the clearing and was suddenly absent, where moments before, he was there and they were together.

Now, there was a subtle change. If Büber hadn't previously been invisible, she'd never have noticed.

"Is it done, then?" she asked benignly. "I saw the fire."

Büber said nothing, walked up to the rock she sat on and squeezed on next to her. She never noticed the temperature, but sitting there, like that? She felt hot inside.

"Is it done?" he said. "Oh, it's done, and more besides."

He carried injuries. Superficial cuts, spotty bruising. He'd been in a fight. But that wasn't what concerned her.

"You've been . . . prayed over." That was the taint that hung over him: prayer.

Büber worked his jaw. "Sophia Morgenstern. I didn't even notice."

"So what has Peter Büber been up to, to warrant a blessing from a Jew?" She took his chin and turned his face left and right.

"Saving Carinthia. Apparently." He shook himself free. "I learnt a new word yesterday, though I don't think it'll be new to you."

"Go on."

He stared down at the White Tower. From their vantage point, they had a perfect view of both it and the White Fortress, with the town crouched in the gap between them.

"Necromancer."

"Who?"

"Eckhardt." Büber spat on the ground beside him. "The rest of your Order have either fled or been killed. By each other, or by Eckhardt himself."

She digested the news slowly and fully. "Just two of us left, then," she said. "What's he doing?"

"In the middle of Gerhard's funeral, he came down from the tower, as bright as the full moon. And that idiot Allegretti had been putting it about that Eckhardt could bring the magic back. All the townsfolk were lining the quays, and there was a fucking stampede." He hunched his shoulders. "Gerhard's widow, her kids, the remaining earls, Trommler – all gone. No one knows where: either they've been taken to Eckhardt or they ended up in the Salzach."

"And little Felix?"

"He – gods, he fought like a man, like a giant. Eckhardt has promised them magic if they bring him sacrifices. Some – more than enough to matter – came back from Goat Mountain to do just that. They went for the Jews first."

"They always do," said Nikoleta.

"They didn't succeed this time. The Jews were all up in the fortress, thanks to Felix. Thanks to Sophia Morgenstern." He looked down at his hands. He really ought to scrub them clean. "So they turned on the library, and I managed to convince Felix that losing that building would cost him the country. We had a pitched battle, right there, in the middle of the library, and we so nearly lost. Then the Jews came back down into town with two centuries of men."

She raised an eyebrow. "The library, Peter?"

"I'm not stupid. I know what that place means." He shrugged. "Besides, Frederik would have killed me himself if I'd let anything happen to it. Those librarians are furies when they're roused. Gods, it was close. Closer than Obernberg."

She leant more firmly against Büber's side. "Are we still going away together? Your banishment, and mine, remember?"

"We're not banished any more. We weren't, even before I reappeared. Felix apologised, and admitted his mistake."

"Not very princely," she said, even though she knew the banishment was Allegretti's doing in the first place. She waited for the catch.

"If they come across the bridge again, they're lost. He's lost. They could hold out in the fortress for months, but if Eckhardt gets enough power together, he'll shatter the walls and it'll fall in half a day." Büber growled in his throat. "The boy deserves better than that."

"Even if his own subjects would rather follow some mad sorcerer?"

"They've caught the madness from Eckhardt. If he was out of the way—"

"You mean dead."

"Yes, all right. Dead. The magic's gone. It's not coming back, is it?" He looked at her accusingly. "Is it? Those poor bastards have to learn to live without it, like I do, like the Jews do. Eckhardt's just a mountain path that ends in a sheer drop, and he's going to take everyone with him."

"Why do you care, Peter?" She shifted away from him. "Let

328

them eat themselves. We'll be hundreds of miles away and you'll never even hear of them again."

Büber looked down into the valley, at all the little houses that were normally coughing up wood smoke, but that were instead cold and silent. "It's not just the town, is it? So they kill all the Jews and all the librarians and burn all the books to keep themselves warm. What are they going to do next? Who else are they going to give to Eckhardt? I've got friends who live in the forests: they've got wives and children, and gods only know they've lost some already. Then there are the villages, and the farms, and travellers and, fuck it, Nikoleta, I don't want to come from a place that mothers use to scare their kids with."

"If you don't behave, the Carinthians will come and get you?" She laughed, but he was serious.

"I love this place. It's all I know. I've spent my life trying to make sure that the enchanted and the normal – the mundane, if you want to call it that – can live side by side without killing each other. But Eckhardt's like a dragon: a big scary fucker with an unending appetite who can't be talked to or reasoned with." Büber drew his knees up and worried at his knuckles.

"And what do you do with dragons?" she asked.

"You can't chase them off – doesn't work. You can't buy them off – they always want more than you can offer. In better days, we'd have called for the Order, and got half a dozen hexmasters out to bury it under a mountain."

She scoffed. "Exactly how many dragons have you seen, to give you such a wide experience?"

"Two. But," and he jabbed one of his half-fingers at her, "and this is the whole point, Frederik Thaler read a book to me about dragons. So although I've only ever seen two, I know how to deal with them all. And without magic, all we could do is march up to it in the company of the maddest bastards in the land and hope one of us can take it down before it torches the entire party."

"You don't have enough mad bastards left to do that, do you? For a dragon or for Eckhardt."

"Torsten would have been up for it. So would some of the other hunters: he's gone, and I've no way of finding the rest quickly, and this needs to be done now."

"You can still let Felix deal with this. If he can't, he'll have to . . . I don't know . . . come to some arrangement with Eckhardt.

Perhaps the Jews' god will intervene now ours have gone. Or not: I don't know him. Maybe he's gone, too."

It wasn't as if she didn't know what Büber wanted, or even that she would refuse him. Fate had always been one of her least favourite aspects of the gods. Capricious whim and venial self-service she could deal with, and even understand, but not the idea of a long drawn-out inevitability, so that no matter what she did, her actions brought her, like the curve of a bow, back to one unavoidable point.

"Say for a moment that I agree," she said with a sigh. "What about afterwards? What do I do then?"

"Then you come away with me. I can leave knowing that Carinthia is safe, and we can go and find somewhere where having a skin full of tattoos doesn't mean you're a witch. I'll teach you what I know."

"Because what *I* know is useless? I've spent my whole life learning not to be vulnerable again. What if we leave now? I'll have my power. We can do whatever we want."

"At some point, it'll come down to you against Eckhardt. When he finds out about you, he'll try to destroy you, and the longer you leave it, the more powerful he'll become. Whatever life you've built for yourself elsewhere will count for nothing, because he'll come and take it away from you. You can't pretend he's not there, Nikoleta."

"I don't want to believe that I've been left behind, by the gods, as a weapon against Eckhardt."

"Then it's up to me. I can't let the boy face him alone. Or Sophia Morgenstern and her band of Jews." He slid off the rock and made a show of checking his sword and his crossbow. "If I can get Allegretti at the same time, I'll be even happier."

"You're determined to do this, aren't you?"

"This isn't someone else's job. It used to be your job – to protect Carinthia from its enemies – but everything's changed. So now it's up to me."

"Why you?" she demanded.

"Who else then?" he countered.

She had answers, but none of them satisfying. "So, in the absence of other heroes, Master Büber steps forward."

"You haven't been listening to me. I'm no one's hero." He looked away, out over the valley again. "I'm a workman."

They lapsed into an angry silence, staring at each other. Büber

330

was big: tall, strong, comfortable with his scars and his missing digits. His was a body that had been lived in, and every one of his years showed in the lines on his face. She wasn't any of those things. She was a tattooed Greek runaway slave who'd got where she was by being as cruel to those under her as those above her had been cruel to her.

Without her magic, she was worse off than when she started. Her magic: wasn't that the problem? She'd always looked on it as something she'd earned, paid a price for, rather than as something she was only borrowing.

"I don't want to face Eckhardt," she said.

"Then don't. No one can make you."

"That's not true." She dropped her gaze.

"What? Me? What can I do to you?"

"Be kind to me, expecting nothing in return. Ask my opinion rather than force me. Make love to me rather than rape me." The ends of her fingers burnt, and she needed release. Ink shifted and the carpet of pine needles around her started to smoke in little puffs: individual pieces of foliage glowed cherry red and consumed themselves in fire. "I don't want to face Eckhardt, because it means staying here for longer. I just want to go far away from where I sold myself, body, spirit and soul to the Order. I could have done anything with my life. But I wanted revenge on each and every person who ever hit me, spat at me, whipped me or fucked me, so I came here and learnt how it felt to be feared."

"You were just a child," said Büber.

"And now I know better. I'm not a child, and I'm not even that child any more." The undergrowth threatened to spontaneously combust, so she stopped. "I'm not used to being good, Peter."

"And I'm not used to leaving a wolf in the sheep-pen." He seemed unperturbed by the smoke drifting past. "Ragnarok is supposed to destroy all nine worlds, and maybe it still will. Doesn't mean I can't go down fighting." ·

"I don't want you to die. I want you to live." She sounded needy. She didn't mean to, but after years of suppressing any emotion, she couldn't express herself normally.

"I don't want to die, either." Büber kicked his way across the smouldering ground towards her. "I have responsibilities. I'm still a prince's man. When it's done, I'll walk away, whatever riches Felix offers me."

"What if he offers you everything and anything?"

"What can he offer me that I haven't already got? Gold? Titles? Fancy clothes? Land?" He spread his arms out wide. "I have all this."

She bowed her head. Fate had caught her in its wide net. Even this stupid, sudden passion she'd found for this rough beast only served to entangle her more firmly and drag her more quickly to her own, very personal doom.

"If Felix wants me to, I'll fight Eckhardt." She thought about it for a moment, and changed her mind, but only slightly. "No. You're right. Eckhardt needs to be killed, no matter what. Even if Felix tells me not to, I'm going to do it anyway. Why should the word of a prince trump the will of the gods? The magic ends with me."

45

"It's damn quiet," said Prauss, looking around nervously. "Where is everyone?"

Thaler, trudging along, looked up to see the town wall, and where the alpine road pierced it. The gates were open and idle. No traffic, no guards, no tolls. He stopped, and after a few more weary steps, so did the rest of them.

There was a house on the right with a high brick wall and tall ironwork, just the sort of house a rich merchant would build for his new wife: all classic Roman architecture and perfumed gardens. The house was still, and the whiff of wood smoke was absent.

"What time is it?"

Ullmann looked up at the sky. "Must be nearly midday, Mr Thaler. Something fearsome strange must have happened."

"The boy's right," said Emser. "I don't like the look of this at all." The guildsman took in their situation, and started moving towards the edge of the road.

Thaler thought that wise, and belatedly ushered everyone to the cover of a line of blackthorns planted on the verge.

"What do you suppose happened, Mr Thaler?" Ullmann managed a stage whisper.

"The unavoidable conclusion is that Eckhardt's made his move." Thaler leant out and studied the top of the town's wall carefully.

"He is, however, just one man, and one man, no matter how powerful, can be in only one place at a time."

The White Tower was across the river, the White Fortress up and to his left. There were thin ribbons of white-grey smoke rising from the buildings inside the whitewashed battlements, something he'd seen a thousand times before.

"The castle?" asked Schussig. He worried at the grimy bandage that was wrapped around his head and half obscured his vision. His bright blue eye peeked out from the shadow.

"Seems, by any reasonable measure, our best bet. If that's fallen, then we've worse problems than being cold and tired." What Thaler really wanted was a hot bath, a hot meal, and a warm bed. What he was going to have to put up with was some more ridiculous sneaking around. He felt affronted. "Curse him to the deepest part of Hel."

"The way's clear," said Prauss. "One at a time or together?"

"We've nothing to lose by going together. Any trouble we might run into is better handled by five stout Carinthians." Thaler stepped away from the hedge, and started an awkward, crouching shamble towards the next piece of cover.

The others followed, all equally visible to anyone who cared to be looking, but they made it to the gate unmolested.

Pressing their backs against the solid stone of the wall, they rested for a moment.

"What's the plan?" asked Prauss.

Bemused, and slightly annoyed that everyone kept deferring to him, Thaler huffed. "The Wagon Gate is the closest, but we have to go through town to get to it. We can circle the castle to the south, and try and gain entrance through the sally at the base of the Arrow Tower. That way we'd be mostly hidden. What d'you say?"

"Sounds reasonable." Prauss patted Thaler's back in a way that indicated the librarian should take the lead.

Thaler rolled his eyes, and deliberately broke cover in the most nonchalant way he could managed. It was more of a stroll through the gate than a mad dash, and he even put his hands on his hips and stared about him when he was under the shadow of the arch.

The others were more careful, keeping to the wall, and trying, in an exaggerated manner, to avoid letting their feet clatter against the cobbles.

Then there was a shout, and Thaler found himself looking at a group of twenty armed men coming up from the quayside. At first glance, they looked irregular, each of them wearing and carrying something different from the next. At the second, he realised that, despite their appearance, they were more organised than some rioting mob.

"Gentlemen?" he said to his colleagues. "Run."

With the wall to their left, and the fortress crag on their right, there was only one way to go. The guildsmen and library staff were unencumbered, but exhausted: their pursuers seemed fresher but rattled in their unfamiliar kit.

Thaler, inevitably, ended up at the back, with Ullmann sprinting for his life like a deer in front. Schussig though, after an initial burst of speed, was slowing down. As they ran, Thaler couldn't shake the thought that some of those chasing him were familiar, but incongruously so.

He risked a look behind him. In among the men with spears and swords, some struggling with shields and holding their helmets on, was one face he definitely recognised. A man who had every reason to be extremely angry with Thaler in particular, but not one who would necessarily kill him.

They were never going to make it to the Arrow Tower. The road wound uphill, and steeply. Schussig was starting to stagger, his legs bending and bowing as they gave out. Only Ullmann looked capable of escape. Thaler caught Schussig just as he buckled completely, which brought them both to a grinding halt.

Prauss looked back, hesitating.

The armed men were close enough now for Thaler's suspicions to be confirmed.

"Call those curfew breakers back," shouted the group's leader. "In the name of the prince."

Thaler let Schussig down gently, crouching behind him to support him, and stared up at the wild-eyed and bearded warriors bearing down on them with iron spear-points. "Rabbi Cohen. What in Midgard are you doing?"

"Thaler." Cohen had a spear and he jabbed it uncomfortably close to Schussig's blind-sided face. "I should run you through for what you've done."

"We said we'd repair it," said Prauss, dragging his feet. Ullmann hovered in the distance, uncertain whether to stay or go, but Emser was waving at him to come back.

"So if I was to chop down the irminsul, but promised to put another one up, that'd be fine?" The rabbi shook his spear with genuine fury, and the rest of his men – Jews all – started to surround them.

"That's . . . different." Prauss finished lamely.

"You Germans. What did we ever do to you?" Cohen pulled his spear back a fraction and pointed at Schussig. "Can he walk?"

"If we're allowed to help him," said Thaler. When no one said he couldn't, he put his hands under Schussig's armpits. "I appreciate we haven't always seen eye to eye," and he winced at the rabbi's barking laugh, "but since when were Jews allowed in the militia, enforcing a curfew we've never had, in the name of the prince, on the Sabbath day?"

"Since," said Cohen, reversing his spear and poking Thaler in the ribs, "we saved your precious library."

"The library?" Thaler almost dropped Schussig, and if Prauss hadn't caught him, the guildsman would have ended up in the road again.

"Enough talk from you, Mr Thaler." The rabbi pulled at his beard and pointed his finger. "You're breaking the curfew."

"The curfew we didn't know existed," muttered Emser, scowling.

"Ignorance is no defence," said Cohen. "Bring them."

Thaler was relieved from his Schussig-holding duties by Ullmann. "Where are we going, Mr Thaler? They seem awful cross."

"Cross they are, Mr Ullmann, but I'm more concerned with what's happened to the library." Thaler stared around at the motley collection of arms and armour. "And to the militia, and the mayor, and normal, decent order. Rabbi Cohen seems in no mood to explain. We appear to be at his mercy."

"He did say, 'in the name of the prince', though," said Schussig, lucid for a moment. "He'll see us right."

"I hope so, Mr Schussig."

They were marched, quicker than was strictly necessary, through the streets. There were signs of damage, mostly broken windows and broken doors, but nothing too serious.

Until they passed the top corner of the main square, where the bodies were laid out in rows and rows, and the crows flapped and feasted.

Their guard seemed used to the sight, but Thaler faltered in his hurried march and clutched at Ullmann, who followed Thaler's horrified gaze with his own. Their open mouths formed circles of shocked surprise.

"Gods!" said Prauss. "What happened here?" Schussig pushed his bandage out of the way, the better to see, and Emser started to walk mechanically towards the square.

Cohen growled at them to keep moving, and they were pushed away protesting and down the next alley.

"My family. I have to check on them." Prauss reached out for the rabbi's shoulder, and was fetched a crack across his knuckles.

"The prince first," said one of the men. "No exceptions."

"But my wife . . ." started Prauss. He still had his knife – their guards were inexperienced enough to have left him with it – and Thaler had to intervene when he saw the guildsman reach for it.

"Hold, Master Prauss, hold. Something terrible has happened, but getting yourself killed won't reveal the truth any faster. The good pagan qualities of courage and fortitude will have to sustain us until we see the prince; he knows we're not rebels."

He hadn't marked Prauss out as a hothead: perhaps the stone-mason had simply had enough of strangeness.

They were driven down the side of the pantheon, with Thaler trying to inspect the stonework for fire damage, and into Library Square. The ground outside was stained black with blood, a torrent of which had apparently cascaded from the entrance down the steps of the portico.

One of the doors was off its hinges, and a line of tired-looking librarians were on their knees, sleeves rolled up, scrubbing at the stone with hard-bristled brushes.

"Gods," breathed Thaler. Splashes of blood had reached head height on the pillars, and some of the men toiling away were bandaged. "Gentlemen. What terrors have you faced here?"

One of them looked up, then sat up on his heels. "It's Mr Thaler."

He was an apprentice – Thaler couldn't be expected to remember his name – but the boy greeted him like a son, until he was forced away by a Jewish spear.

"He's our prisoner," said Cohen.

"He's our librarian," objected the apprentice. "You let go of him at once." The situation, with tired, angry men on both sides, momentarily threatened to get out of hand.

Thaler stepped between them, an outstretched palm directed at each man. "I believe we're all on the same side here, gentlemen, and it's painfully clear that we should not succumb to fissiparous urges, no matter the provocation. Librarians, you continue with your duties, and I'll address you all in good time. Rabbi Cohen, our safety is your responsibility: you're charged with bringing curfew breakers before the prince, so that's what you must do, without delay."

When he thought that tempers had cooled sufficiently, Thaler slowly dropped his arms back to his side. The apprentice lowered his brush and stood aside, gathering with his fellows in a sullen, mutinous crew.

Rather than have Cohen force him onwards, Thaler took the initiative and marched into the library on his own cognisance. This was his home, so why should he do anything else?

The prince was sitting at the long table, placed in its traditional position at the front of the circular space. On his left was Sophia Morgenstern, leaning her head towards him and listening intently. She had parchment and ink and pens in front of her. To either side were more librarians, patiently writing away by lantern-light.

Although the table had been restored to its rightful place, much had changed: the banisters had gone, and, apart from the shelves, there was no other furniture on the ground floor. All the reading desks and chairs had vanished. Thaler looked down at the freshly cleaned floor and decided that answers might have to wait.

His approach was noted, and the prince broke off his conversation and rose to greet him.

"Mr Thaler!"

"My lord," said Thaler, and bowed low. "I am the bringer of good – no, excellent – news."

The boy's shoulders, broken and unbroken, seemed to straighten at his words. "I like good news, Mr Thaler. You and your men need to tell me about it straight away."

"My men?" Thaler took the opportunity to prise the guildsmen and Ullmann from Cohen's clutches and bring them forward. "May I present Master Prauss, Master Emser, Master Schussig, who met with a slight accident, and Mr Ullmann, an usher here at the library who has rendered assistance above and beyond his duties."

"We need chairs for these men," said Felix. "We need food and

337

drink." He looked through the group in front of him to the rabbi behind. "Thank you for bringing them to me, Rabbi Cohen. Your service has been noted."

Chairs were found – from the first gallery – and Ullmann found himself persuaded to sit in the prince's presence despite his reservations.

"We've had some problems," said Felix, "and they aren't over yet. Telling me we can get the water back on will go a little way to solving some of them."

Thaler looked down the line, and found that everyone was looking at him. He lifted his hands in a gesture of exasperation, and said, "Yes. It'll take a little while for everything to work perfectly. There may be unforeseen difficulties, but essentially, yes." He rubbed at his chin. "Does my lord know of the huge cavern underneath the fortress filled with dwarven machinery?"

Felix blinked, looked down at Sophia, then back at Thaler, who pursed his lips.

"That'll be no, then," said Thaler.

"Under the fortress?"

"Master Prauss believes that's where the cave is, my lord. There are staircases going up which we didn't have time to explore, so we don't know where they come out, but we presume it's somewhere in the fortress."

"A cave, under the castle, which no one knows anything about?" Felix sat down warily. "What do the machines do?"

"We don't know exactly. Big wheels. Chains." Thaler shrugged. "Master Schussig may have more to say on the matter, but our conclusion at the time was that we might need to go and ask the dwarves themselves."

"Someone make a note of that," said Felix. "How quickly can you get something working to show the people?"

They looked at each other again. Prauss judged their expressions. "A week, perhaps. We need a crew to dig, craftsmen to make good. The tunnel comes out beside the river near Grodig, under the Marktschellenberg. My lord, what's happened to our families? We saw the bodies in the main square. We were arrested for curfew-breaking by Jews."

Felix glared at Prauss from under his browline, and suddenly looked a lot older than twelve. Prauss subsided, and the silence grew longer.

"Master Eckhardt happened," said Sophia. "We can issue you with a pass to travel through the town, but the north side of the river remains out of bounds, certainly if you value your life. If your family is home, then they're safe. If they're across the river, they're outlaws, and you're not to go looking for them. If they're in the main square, then . . . you can claim the bodies."

One of the scribes scraped his seat back and presented Prauss with a still-drying pass written in both German and Hebrew.

"Master Prauss," said Felix, "all of you. Some of your friends, your family, your work colleagues will have gone over to Eckhardt. If you aid them, you defy me. If they want to come back, they have to come and look me in the eye first. Understand?"

There was a clear chorus of "my lord".

"There's food and drink waiting for you over there. You've served Carinthia well, and Carinthia forgets neither its friends nor its enemies."

They stood, bowed, and started to walk away.

"Mr Thaler?" said Sophia.

Thaler stopped and, taking a moment to usher Ullmann on with the others, approached the desk.

"Miss Morgenstern." She was sitting to Felix's left, the position usually occupied by a royal consort. It seemed too deliberate to be accidental. Calling her Sophia in such a situation? There were shifts in power that Thaler would do well to track.

She reached behind her and laid the heavy library seal on the table in front of her. "This is yours."

"It's . . . sorry?"

"The master librarian cannot perform his duties. You're the only remaining under-librarian." She smiled hopefully up at him. "And it's not like we have a surfeit of good men willing to risk everything for an idea."

The seal's engraved surface winked at him in the lantern-light.

"This would be most irregular," said Thaler.

"Take the godsdamn seal," growled Felix. "We spilt our blood here last night defending your books when we could have been behind the fortress ramparts. You know how this place works – now it has to do something. It has to teach us how to live."

Thaler bowed his head. "I'm not worthy of—"

Felix grabbed the seal and thrust it at him. "I am the Prince of Carinthia and I demand you take this, even if I have to bury it in your belly."

"That won't be necessary, my lord." Thaler held out his cupped hands, and Felix dropped the seal into them.

"Swear your loyalty to me."

"By everything I hold sacred."

It was good enough. Felix leant back, making the wood of his chair creak. "Go and eat, Master Thaler. Then assume your duties."

46

Felix's life was completely different, not just from what it had been before, but from what he'd expected it to become. He'd been transformed from someone who did nothing but play all day, into someone who did nothing but work all day.

Playing was the best way of describing what he'd done: training with the signore had had a purpose, but the purpose hadn't been serious. No one had expected him to have to defend himself against anyone who might genuinely want to kill him. The fighting manuals he'd pored over were fictions. The two-handed swordplay was just that: play.

The riding, the hawking, the hunting of boar and bear and more exotic beasts, the music and the storytelling: everything he knew how to do well was little more than a game. And for what purpose had he been taught those things? So he wouldn't get bored when he was prince, and wouldn't engage in some stupid, reckless foreign expedition and risk the palatinate simply because he couldn't bear the tedium a moment longer.

Other people were supposed to do the work. The chamberlain ran his household. The mayor ran Juvavum. The earls ran their fiefdoms. He needn't lift a finger: his sole duty was to make sure the Order was given everything they wanted, and summon them at times of crisis. That was it: that was all he'd been expected to do, and had been trained for accordingly.

Trommler and Messinger were missing, probably dead. His earls, most definitely dead. The Order was – with two notable exceptions – gone. He couldn't even tell who was on his side any more.

So there was all the work of fifty men falling on his broken shoulders, and very few he could trust to hand it on to. That would have to change. Right after he'd dealt with Eckhardt.

And if Peter Büber couldn't persuade Mistress Agana to intervene, that was exactly what he'd have to do. Deal with Eckhardt. Something else his training hadn't adequately covered.

In all the stories, the magicians – the good ones – had always won. Always. There were fragments of knowledge to be gleaned from the ways the heroes had battled with the villains, but more often than not it had come down to the gods being on their side. That, and raw power. He had neither the gods nor the brute strength required.

He narrowed his lips and looked over his shoulder at the rows and rows of books behind him. He remembered what Büber had said about them saving his life.

The librarians on either side of him were busy writing out orders and making lists. Sophia had gone back to the fortress to enlist some more Hebrew scribes. He was using the language like a code: his side could find someone to read it, Eckhardt's side couldn't. Felix was left sitting in the middle, scowling at everyone who asked him questions and already knew the answer. They were just requesting permission, really, but that they felt they had to do so didn't make sense.

If he wasn't there, would everything simply grind to a halt?

"You, man. What's your name?"

"Wess, my lord."

"Go and find Master Thaler, and bring him here."

"My lord."

As the man put down his pen and wiped his hands on his gown, Felix looked at him again. He had a cut on his head, barely hidden by his close-cut hair, and a dark line of blood had run down from it to behind his ear. He hadn't manage to wash since last night, yet here he was, faithfully copying words and acting on instructions.

How could his father have missed this, this deep well of competence? Büber was even more right than he'd first thought. It wasn't just the library that mattered.

A short while later – in that time, he'd taken three verbal reports and ordered the town wall gates to be closed and guarded rather than left wide open – Thaler appeared, looking groggy and damp. He, at least, had changed his lime-slicked, sweat-stained clothes and attempted a wash.

"My lord."

Felix kicked his chair back and turned to face the library. "How is the old master librarian?"

"He's best described as being in a state of pleasant delirium." Thaler shook his head. "He may continue like that for years, but we'll care for him."

"Yes. Master Thaler, walk with me." Felix stepped into the space where the reading desks had been, and looked up at the galleries and the dead globes that hung from the domed ceiling. When Thaler had joined him, he said in a low voice, "We have to get rid of Eckhardt."

Thaler held up his hand, and motioned for the prince to follow him to a point away from the centre of the room. "If you stand there, my lord, the whole of the library can hear you. I don't pretend to know how that happens, but it's so, just as there are places on the upper galleries where a whisper will carry from one side to the other without seeming to travel through the intervening space."

"Is that magic?"

"My lord, the library is – was – one of the least magical places in your palatinate. We were able to bring devices inside, like the lights and the magnifying lenses, but the walls were opaque to any form of magical interference. The Greeks had their amphitheatres for their plays, and the actors' speech carried from the stage to the seats at the very back. A similar principle may apply here." Thaler glanced over his shoulder, checking for eavesdroppers. "If we didn't insist on silence in the library, no one would be able to work."

"Getting rid of Eckhardt?" said Felix.

"Quite. An endeavour I can wholeheartedly support."

"Is there anything in any of these books that will help us? Histories, legends? A group of brave men tackling an evil sorcerer?" Felix reached out and dragged randomly at the spine of a book in a way that made the new master librarian wince. "Anything in this one?"

Thaler gently took the book from his hands and tapped on the cover. "This is a treatise on geography by Pomponius Mela. It won't help us at all." He reshelved it and stood with his hands on his hips. "I'll have to consult with the other librarians."

"But haven't you got a list of your books, and what they contain?"

"You mean the Great Catalogue, my lord. One day, gods willing, we'll finish it."

"You don't know what you have?" The notion astounded Felix. "How can that be possible?"

"Previous generations simply collected, conserved and copied manuscripts, and no systematic attempt had been made in years to collate a library catalogue until, I think it was ten years ago. We have a made a start—"

"Not good enough!" shouted Felix. His voice echoed, and the murmur of voices elsewhere drained to nothing.

Thaler's face clouded. "There are at least a hundred thousand individual books, scrolls, monographs and pamphlets housed here. Perhaps twice that number: only Alexandria in Egypt can boast as many, and they keep on catching fire, so gods only know how they catalogue theirs. My lord, simply caring for these works takes a good deal of time, as does copying those which appear to be beyond saving. Then there is the collecting of new works, copying those, and training in a dozen or more languages . . . if we had more librarians, we could have done better."

Felix went from petulance to comprehension. "You never had enough money."

"No, my lord. It went across the river."

"That will change, Master Thaler." Felix kicked a bookcase with the toe of his boot. "What can you do that'll help us now?"

The man's face went through a series of contortions. "I don't know," he finally admitted. "Texts concerning battles between sorcerers and the non-magical that might yield useful information? The Order would have cleared all the obvious ones from our shelves years ago. Something might have slipped through, though. My lord, I'm going to have to talk to the other librarians. One man can't know everything, but someone may know where to look."

"We have to kill Eckhardt soon. Tonight, tomorrow. This can't go on. I won't have it."

There was another long silence, then Thaler finally said: "My lord, it might not be possible to kill Eckhardt. He might be too powerful, or too well protected."

"Or it might be as easy as sticking a dagger in his back." Felix made the motion. "We don't really know, do we?"

"You could send someone to spy on him," said Thaler. "Do you have anyone suitable?"

"I don't know. We've always relied on the Order for scrying." Felix thought of all the people he might use, but those he really trusted – Thaler, Büber, Sophia – were already known to Eckhardt, either by sight or reputation. He needed someone anonymous. "Do you know of anyone?"

Thaler stared at the floor. "Mr Ullmann? He might do it, if you asked him. It'll be incredibly dangerous, of course, but he's a lively boy and quick-witted with it."

"Go and get him," Felix said. "Do you know what time of day it is, Master Thaler?"

"Past noon, I believe, my lord." Thaler bowed and left, crossing the library and disappearing through a side door into the librarian's quarters.

Felix tapped his foot. Büber was late, and even though the huntmaster had promised to come back, there had to be a plan in case he didn't. Yet sending someone over the river to spy on Eckhardt, then come back with information that could be used to help kill a hexmaster, was incredibly risky. He might as well have this Ullmann pressed and save Eckhardt the bother.

Kill a hexmaster. How could that be done, when all the stories he'd read, what he'd seen Mistress Agana do, told him that even an army of mundanes would be slaughtered before they'd laid hands on him?

But hadn't the signore told him a story of seeing an Italian magician being brought down by weight of numbers? If Allegretti had been there now, Felix could have asked him. But he wasn't. Not only had the signore manifestly failed to carry out Felix's orders, the prince had Büber's words regarding the sword-master rattling around inside his skull, looking for a home.

He was short of men. He had a couple of centuries of Jews, perhaps half a century of librarians, a berserker huntmaster, and an adept he'd previously banished. The only thing he had in excess was books. He wandered the shelves, running his fingers along the mismatched spines in the hope that one might literally jump out at him and flop open at the right page.

Too many of the wrong sort of stories: nothing fantastical like that was going to happen. He had what he had, and he had to fashion a victory out of that.

He was so lost in his thoughts, he failed to see Büber draw alongside him. The huntmaster had to clear his throat, and Felix reached for his sword as he turned.

"My lord'll need to be sharper than that," said Büber. He was somehow looking even taller and more scarred than before.

"Will she come?" he asked.

"She's here," Büber replied, then smirked at Felix's sudden head-turning. "Not here here. She's waiting outside the walls."

"Will she, you know . . .?"

Büber said nothing, and just nodded.

Felix felt his whole body flood with the gentle heat of relief. "Can I see her?"

"Perhaps afterwards. She accepted your apology, barely, and her moods are mercurial." Büber smile hardened. "If we don't take Eckhardt by surprise, none of us are going to get a second chance."

"Master Thaler is going to ask one of his men to act as a spy," said Felix, and the smile flickered back.

"*Master* Thaler now, is it? But a spy's a good idea, if we can get away with it. Who's he chosen?"

"That man there. Mr Ullmann."

Thaler and Ullmann stood momentarily at the front desk before being directed further towards the prince, Thaler steering the young usher like a barge, with a hand on his shoulder all the way. Perhaps he thought Ullmann would bolt.

"Peter," said Thaler. "I thought you'd . . ."

"And good afternoon to you, Master Librarian."

Thaler stepped forward, and before Büber could skip away, he was encircled by stout arms and thick-fingered hands. "Thank you for saving my library."

Büber, flailing, eventually patted Thaler's round back. "It wouldn't have been right to let it burn. It's an important place, Frederik. It's all we have now."

"Yes it is, and it shames me that I wasn't here to help." He showed no sign of letting go.

"We did what we did, and that's the end of it." Büber peeled the librarian off. "Introduce me to your colleague."

"This is Mr Ullmann." Ullmann found himself propelled forward. "Huntmaster Büber."

"Max Ullmann, at your service, sir. My lord," he added for Felix's benefit.

"Do you understand what we want you to do?" asked Felix.

Ullmann screwed his face up, trying to remember. "You want me to cross the river, make my way to where Master Eckhardt is, find out who else is there and how he's protected, then come back and report to you."

Büber leant on a bookshelf. "You missed the part where you don't get caught."

Ullmann cleared his throat and looked at his boots. "And don't get caught."

"I'd go," said Büber. "But most people know my face." He rubbed ruefully at the latest scar on his cheek.

"I'd go myself," said Thaler. "I am, however, sadly aware of my limitations."

"While any one of us would go," said Felix, "Fate seems to have cast you in this role, Mr Ullmann. Are you up to the task?"

"Yes, my lord. I'll do my very best for you." He reached up and tugged at his hair. "I'll come back with what you need to know."

"Talk to Master Büber about the best way to get close, and the best way to get back." Felix saw the boy in the man. Ullmann was only a few years older than him. Gods only knew if he'd make it to the end of the day, let alone to his next birthday. He pulled out his dagger and presented it, grip-first, to the usher.

Ullmann slowly took the grip, and stared at the mirrored surface of the blade. "My lord, I'm . . . honoured."

"Not as honoured as I am, Mr Ullmann. Take it, and use it as you need."

47

Büber took Ullmann to meet Nikoleta in the boathouse. And why not? The main house seemed deserted, and perhaps it was: the family who lived there would have been at Gerhard's funeral, and probably their servants too. Anyone left behind would be eating their way through the larder and drinking the master's wine cellar rather than daring to find out why no one had come home.

It was as safe as anywhere, and out of sight. Sophia's warning about the Jews' reaction to Nikoleta's existence held true, and they had enough problems to cope with already without adding the prospect of driving the only militia they had into revolt.

Ullmann reminded him of a baby deer, all arms, legs and curiosity, and magnificently innocent.

Nikoleta sat cross-legged on the edge of the walkway, having positioned herself so that she could see the base of Goat Mountain through the boathouse's river entrance. Only when he sat down next to her did he realise she could also see up as far as the White Tower.

"Who's the boy?" she asked, glancing up.

"This is Max Ullmann, one of the library ushers."

Ullmann abruptly grasped that he wasn't being introduced to just anyone. She might not be wearing a long white robe, but the tattoos on her arms, neck and legs gave her away.

"Master Büber? I thought . . ."

"Yes. Not a word to anyone else. This is Mistress Nikoleta Agana, the last surviving hexmaster who can still do magic."

Nikoleta got her feet underneath her and stood, holding on to Büber for support. Her hand stayed on his shoulder as she examined the usher.

"And what role do you have to play, Ullmann?"

"I'm . . . I'm a spy. I think. Master Büber, does the prince know about this?"

Büber looked up. "He wants the mistress to kill Eckhardt, having judged that we mundanes aren't up to the task. He's probably right. There aren't enough of us, and one hexmaster's plenty."

"I have to get close to him first, Ullmann. Do you understand why?"

Ullmann met Nikoleta's gaze. "Because you might only get one chance, and you need to make it count."

"He's not stupid, Peter. We could do a lot worse." Nikoleta nodded. "You're not invisible to magic like a hunter is, yet your aura doesn't radiate like a Jew. An ordinary, decent pagan, am I right?"

"Very ordinary, Mistress."

"It's not an insult, Ullmann. Ordinary means you won't stand out. Ordinary means you might make it back. I need specific information regarding Eckhardt – not just how he's guarded, or who's guarding him, especially if there's an Italian sword-master hanging around him – but what he does and how he acts. That means you have to get yourself into a position where you can observe these things without anyone suspecting you." She pushed her hand back through her curls. "Do you know what'll happen to you if anyone guesses what you're there for?"

"They'll kill me?"

"Only if you're lucky. I don't know much about necromancy and precisely how Eckhardt takes a life and turns it into raw magic, but the little I do know tells me that it's very likely to hurt. A lot." She flashed him a smile. "Are you sure you still want to do this?"

Ullmann swallowed hard. "Yes, Mistress."

"Right. Now listen. He doesn't know I'm coming for him. He doesn't even know I exist. When I do come for him, what he'll feel is a big knot of untamed fire getting closer. I need him alone, if possible, not because my power is weak, or that I have scruples about killing any number of mundanes, but because . . . why don't you finish that thought, Mr Ullmann?"

"Because while you're dealing with others apart from Master Eckhardt, what will he be doing?"

"I'm genuinely impressed. All my concentration needs to be on Eckhardt: he's been a hexmaster for longer than I've been alive, and he'll know all kinds of nuances that I don't. The first contact between us is the most important. If I'm still alive after that, I can grind him down: his magic will eventually fail, whereas mine won't." She walked around Ullmann. "Get me my chance, and I'll do the rest."

"I'll row you across the river and come with you as far as I can." Büber stood up to untie the waiting boat. "I'll bring you back, too."

Ullmann nodded. His mouth had gone dry and rendered him speechless.

Büber scratched at his chin.

"No one is forcing you to do this, and no one's going to think any less of you if you decide that it isn't for you. Even after I've rowed you over and you've got out, you can still run in the opposite direction."

Despite being drained of colour, Ullmann clambered unsteadily into the rowing boat, and waited.

"You're a brave man, Max." Büber turned to Nikoleta. "I don't know when we'll be back. Go up to the house and see if there's any food left, but try not to be seen."

She grabbed him by the collar and dragged his head down to meet hers. "I'm not an idiot, Peter."

"There are too many things that can go wrong. I should see if I can pick Eckhardt off with my bow, or slip a knife between his ribs."

"No you don't." Her breath was hot in his face.

"He won't hear or see me coming."

"Peter, no. He can do things you can't imagine possible. I won't take that risk."

He tried to take a step back, but she had him off-balance. "You can't tell me what to do," he said.

"But I can beg you not to do it, and know that you'll listen to me." She finished with a hard kiss, savage and tearing.

He came away with blood on his lips and pressed what were left of his fingertips against them to ease the soreness and sourness away. She walked out of the boathouse, and Büber climbed down into the boat opposite Ullmann.

He reached forward and closed the usher's mouth for him. "It's her way of telling me not to get involved in a magicians' duel." He slipped the rope off its iron ring and pushed at one of the jetty's piles.

The boat drifted out and into the river. Ullmann was still staring at Büber.

"Look, lad. She's . . . she's not from round here." He tried to think of the best way of explaining it to Ullmann. Her foreignness would excuse much. "They do things differently in the empire. And then she was closeted away with the Order for years. They did things differently there, too."

He turned the boat and pointed the prow upstream, where he could keep an eye on the town. Ullmann twisted in his seat so that he could see as well.

"Where do you think Master Eckhardt will be?" he asked, finally recovering his voice.

"Difficult to say. He could be up at the White Tower. That's what he's used to, and Nikoleta tells me that hexmasters stick to their routines. On the other hand, that's not where he showed himself last night: he came all the way down to the novices' house, so he may be there. That would make more sense than having folk traipse up and down the mountain."

"So I should start at the novices' house?"

"If you think like that, you're going to get yourself killed. You start as soon as we land." Büber pulled hard on the oars. The boat was midstream, and exposed to anyone who might look their way. "Remember that. One slip-up and it might be over."

Ullmann was suddenly apologetic, which annoyed Büber.

"I'm serious. I can't say I've had much experience with sneaking around people, but I've had plenty crawling on my belly like a worm as I come up the windward side of some beast or other. I'll get you as close as I can without us having to break cover, and we'll decide what's best then. Unnecessary risks – in any job – are stupid. And you're not stupid, are you Mr Ullmann?"

The usher pursed his lips, then agreed. "No, Master Büber. I know I'm not."

A few feet later, they were covered by the overhanging branches of some riverside willows. "So tell me, Mr Ullmann: why didn't you become a librarian?"

"Because I ran away from my father's farm and my earl, Master."

The boat bumped against the soft earth, and Büber reached out to hold the bank. "I see. I don't think that'll be a problem now, though."

Ullmann grabbed at a thick root, and held it tight while Büber levered himself up onto the bank using the painter. In turn, he held the boat still while Ullmann pushed himself on his elbows into the long grass. When he was out of the way, Büber continued to heave, and manhandled the boat in between two trees, where he rolled it over.

"You think serfs should be free to leave their land?" said Ullmann.

"I think people should be free to go wherever they want." He kicked the bottom of the boat, which gave a hollow boom. "Life, Mr Ullmann, is short, and I can't honestly say whether anything we do here makes a difference one way or another."

"Saving the library like you did, though. That has to count."

"And tomorrow, some mad fucker could break in and burn it down. And now that the only lights in the library are lanterns, it could happen by accident. Then, all those men I killed, all the skulls the librarians cracked: what would it have been for? So yes, roam where you want and take opportunity where you can." Büber reached over his back for his crossbow. "There'll always be plenty of other things to worry about."

He led the way towards the road that ran along the north bank, and crouched in the undergrowth at its side. It seemed strange to have someone with him: uncomfortable, even. He was so used to working alone, but that was going to have to change, considering the promises he'd made to Nikoleta.

"From now on, don't talk unless I say so. Don't move unless I say so." He glanced around. "And lose the robe. Just bundle it up and throw it behind you. Should have thought of that before."

Ullmann shrugged off his loose-fitting usher's robe and disposed of it as Büber had said.

"Ready?" asked the huntmaster.

"Yes."

"Did I say you could talk?" Büber gave a sly smile. "Did I?"

"No, Master."

"Then don't." He checked the road again, and darted across its rutted stone surface to the far side. He ducked down once more and listened carefully. All he could hear to start with was Ullmann's over-excited breathing, but, after a moment, he managed to blank it out and pick out sounds from beyond.

He could hear the river. He could hear the wind in the trees. He could hear something else, too: a murmur, soft and distant. He frowned. He didn't like it because he didn't know what it meant.

Between them and the novices' house was the flank of Goat Mountain. He knew that, halfway up, was the adepts' house, and knew also, from Thaler's report, that it was full of bodies and detritus. Perhaps the best way to proceed would be to climb up, and then descend on the novices' house from above. People naturally avoided heights if there was an easier option, and he'd expect most of those who'd gone over to Eckhardt to be down on the lower slopes.

They moved off, uphill. To Büber's trained senses, it felt like Ullmann was deliberately trying to attract attention by snagging his clothing on every briar, stamping on every dry twig and clattering against every low-hanging branch. It was almost exactly like torture. No matter how fast or how slow he went, the usher banged from trunk to trunk like a drunkard.

But then, gradually, the noises diminished. By the time they'd found the path up to the White Tower, there was a noticeable difference, and as they descended, the effect wasn't perfect, but it was certainly passable. He raised his hand and crouched down. There was barely a whisper as Ullmann squatted beside him, looking impossibly young and smooth-skinned.

Büber listened again. The murmuring was still audible, louder but remaining indistinct. Then, as he was about to indicate they should move on, the tone of the sound changed. It grew angrier, more urgent. There were distinct shouts and cries, before it settled down again.

The men looked at each other, and Büber shrugged theatrically. They'd have to get closer.

They crept on, with Büber stopping them every few steps to check his bearings and his quarry. He'd never tried to sneak up on a crowd before. A herd, yes, but there was a big difference between the two, and he wasn't willing to take any risks. Most creatures — plant-eaters, at least — would merely turn tail and run if they scented him, but these people? It'd be him doing the running.

He slowly manoeuvred the two of them into position among the trees above and to the left of the back of the novices' house. A path ran in front of them, and they had a reasonable view of the space in front of the building and along the avenue leading to it.

He sat down, his back straight against a trunk so as to not offer a silhouette, the muted browns and greens of his clothing helping him to blend in almost instantly. He tucked his legs in front of him, controlled his breathing, and kept his head still.

Ullmann, watching him closely, did the same, choosing a tree a little way behind him.

They sat, and they watched.

With the emptying of the town, first onto the quayside, then towards Goat Mountain, he'd expected to find most, if not all, of Juvavum's missing inhabitants here. But it became clear that the crowd wasn't as large as Büber had feared.

Those who were left had divided themselves into groups — huddles was a better description — and seemed intent on watching each other, which helped to render them oblivious to the two men looking down on them from between the trees.

Though he would have to contend with Eckhardt's supernatural abilities, Büber was certain that he, of all people, could get closer without being spotted.

He pointed at Ullmann, made a sign that was unambiguously "stay", then eased himself further downhill. He could, if he chose, use the wall of the building to hide behind, but he couldn't see through that any more than the next man. He stuck to the trees, swinging around in an arc to give the closest group a wide berth.

This was better. Now he had a good view of both the novices' house and what was happening in the space in front of it. He sat down again, back straight, knees bent, willing himself to appear as gnarled, flaking bark.

The group nearest to him were all facing the other way, looking at the two groups closest to them. In turn those groups eyed each other, and those behind them. In the middle, surrounded by them all, was Eckhardt, sitting in a high-backed wooden chair. He had a glowing staff resting across the arms, its brightness paling in the daylight.

Littering the ground in front of him was a pile of wan, bloodless bodies, naked and thin like worms after a rainstorm.

Büber narrowed his eyes and looked closer. There was another figure beside the chair, chained to it by his neck, limbs tied, mouth gagged and eyes blindfolded by an expert in knotwork. Some high-status prisoner, obviously, but it took him a while to realise who it was kneeling in the dirt, blind and dumb, hobbled by a rope around his ankles.

Allegretti: Eckhardt had apparently found the Italian as trustworthy as Felix had.

Büber shifted his gaze and concentrated on the group directly below him. Individuals seemed to have different roles within the mass. Some, those closest to the edge, were armed with whatever they could lay their hands on, the sort of weapons that the mob had brought to the library last night. At the centre of the group was a curious hollow, until he worked out that the prone and sitting figures were bound captives. Between the "soldiers" on the outside and the prisoners in the middle, were the "guards", preventing escape.

He could smell the tension. Eckhardt, though, didn't just appear content, but seemed to be actively enjoying the madness that had taken hold of them. He turned his head this way and that, like a bird eyeing a crumb, then eventually gave a tiny gesture, so small Büber almost missed it. His wrist tilted up, not even moving from the chair arm, and a finger waved in the air. The sort of signal a great lord would make to his attentive servants to clean a spill, or pour more wine.

Pandemonium broke out. Each group exploded into frantic activity, trying to be first to deliver a wretched prisoner to Eckhardt's feet, while attempting to prevent the others from achieving the same goal.

They fought with each other. They rucked and mauled and seethed and pushed. The participants ebbed and flowed across the open space, groaning and grinding until, finally, one of the filthy captives, frozen in fear, was grounded near the chair. Again,

Eckhardt did his little finger gesture, and the winners held their ground while the losers slunk back into their positions.

Eckhardt ordered the prisoner to be untied and stripped. The man lay there in the dirt, unresisting, as his clothes were torn off. He seemed dead already, and didn't move as the hexmaster started his ritual.

The hexmaster rose from his seat, placing the glowing staff behind him, resting it in the angle between Allegretti's bent legs and stooped neck. He was using the sword-master as a stand for his symbol of office, and Büber felt a twinge of sympathy. A traitor for sure, but to end up like that?

Eckhardt drew a circle and signs around both himself and the sacrifice, then straddled the man, kneeling across him in a disturbing mirror of the position he and Nikoleta had been in last night. Blood-encrusted robes covered most of the victim's naked body, and Eckhardt reached down. Büber couldn't see what happened next – the hexmaster's back obscured his view – but there was an audible sigh.

He expected to see a pool of blood form, but there was nothing. And when Eckhardt staggered to his feet, the ink on his arms running like clouds before a storm, there wasn't a mark on the man.

Now came the boon. Someone presented Eckhardt with a some-thing or other – a trinket, or necklace maybe – even while others were stacking the limp body with the others. The magician took it back to his chair and held the chain in his hands so that the pendant hung free in front of his face.

There was a flash, and Eckhardt simply tossed the necklace back. That was how it the enchantment was done. The ink stopped boiling and settled into its predictable patterns, and the master leant back, retrieved his staff from Allegretti, and closed his eyes.

Büber thought he could take him there and then. It was a distance, but his target wasn't moving. He'd have all the time he needed, and it'd be an easier shot than the one he'd made in bringing down the Teuton horseman back at Obernberg. If he missed, of course, he'd have a pissed-off hexmaster and a clearly insane mob howling at his heels. He thought of what Nikoleta would say, and reluctantly pulled his empty hand back out of his quiver.

He could see Ullmann. The usher had gone an unhealthy shade of grey, and he judged it was time he went back to him. He crept from tree to tree until he was within reach, then gently took

Ullmann's arm. He led him away, unresisting, until they were far enough away to be no longer concerned about being spotted.

There was no way anyone could go down into that sea of madness alone. They'd have to think of something else.

48

Nikoleta was furious. Furious enough to let small flashes of fire escape from her fingertips that threatened to burn the boathouse down.

Büber tried to calm her in his oblique and reasonable way, but she was having none of it. Ullmann was poised by the door, one foot in, one foot out, and ready to run for it if her fury overtook her common sense.

She had gone from dangerously over-controlled to dangerously unpredictable in the space of a few days. The battle at Obernberg had been the start of it, but not the whole reason. If the Order had still been intact, perhaps she'd have found another hexmaster to take her under his – naturally a his – wing and show her how to rule her seemingly unlimited powers rather than allowing them to rule her. That was impossible now, and it simply served to stoke her rage.

"I'll do it now."

"No," said Büber, "it's not for you to decide."

"You put too much store in the prince. He's a twelve-year-old boy, for Zeus's sake. What does he know about anything? He wants Eckhardt dead? Good. So do I. But I'm not going to have him tell me how I should do it."

"Nikoleta . . ."

"Don't. Just don't. I've had enough of being pissed about by mundanes. Tell me of somewhere where there are no people, and I'll go there in a moment. I've had enough of princes and masters and free men and earls. To Hades with the lot of them." She pressed her palms together, and when she pulled them apart, there was a ribbon of flame connecting them.

Büber sat on the walkway beside the boat, swinging his legs, apparently unconcerned by her petulant pyrotechnics. "You can't do this on your own. The mob still needs distracting."

"No, they don't. All that Felix's army of Jews and librarians are going to do is get in the way. Either Eckhardt will dominate their minds and turn them against each other, or he'll make them drop their weapons and allow the mob to take them prisoner. Eckhardt will get stronger and Felix will be left too weak to defend anything."

"Then we need to think of something better. Perhaps Frederik has found something in a book we could use." Büber stared into the distance.

"No one is going to get to Eckhardt except me. I can resist his domination attack, I can avoid the mob, and he's wasting his power on making little magical gew-gaws for his followers. He'll have a couple of spells in hand at most: I have everything. I don't even know why I'm waiting."

"Can you handle a rowing boat?" asked Büber, mildly.

"I can fly, you idiot."

"Over running water?" He had this knack of saying just enough to remind her that she was, after all, mortal.

"Yes. I can row a boat." Of course she could. It didn't look that difficult.

"You've made the point that I can't stop you. And I doubt if Max over there is up to the task either." He shrugged in Ullmann's direction. "Don't take it badly, Mr Ullmann."

"No offence taken at all, Master Büber," said Ullmann.

"I'm still not going to let you go alone, though. If this is what you want, I'm coming with you." He looked up at her.

She wanted to stay furious. She felt that passion and fire were better for her than the cool analysis she'd been taught for all those years.

Then she realised, and stamped her foot on the wooden boards. "The bastards."

"What now?"

"They . . . they lied to us." She was astounded. The whole method of learning magic, by stoic endurance, by pain, by effort of will, was a fabrication. It had served her masters well over the centuries, for certain. If novices were the slaves and victims of their system, the adepts were both their playthings and their enforcers. It was only when an adept broke through their conditioning and embraced their fear and loathing would they ever achieve mastery of their craft. By then they would be so bitter as to be ideal material for joining the highest rank.

No wonder they had hated each other.

"That doesn't come as a surprise. Now, are we going to do this or not?" Büber put his feet onto the walkway and levered himself up.

If she had been burning before, now she was the queen of winter. Her anger had crystallised into a block of ice, cold and hard and heavy in her heart.

"Yes. Let's do it. Let's do it right now."

Büber clapped Ullmann on the shoulder, and the usher winced. "This is not for you, lad."

"But I can guard the boat and wait for you to return, Master Büber."

"If Eckhardt dies, we'll be able to walk across the bridge. If he doesn't, there'll be little point, and probably very little left of us, to return." Büber purposefully reached past the man to close the boathouse door, with both of them inside. "Your job is to wait until dusk, then go back to Felix and tell him what we tried to do. If we've succeeded, we'll be there already. If we haven't, well. Not quite all hope is lost, but my lord may well wish to sue for peace."

"Not before the sun goes down," warned Nikoleta. "Otherwise I'll be very disappointed in you. I have every intention of coming back, and I will find out."

"I wouldn't, Mistress," said Ullmann. "But I could bring the boat back, rather than leave it on the far side for anyone to use."

"He has a point," said Büber. "Get in the boat, then."

They all climbed aboard, and arranged themselves for balance: Büber in the rowing position, Ullmann facing him from the stern, and Nikoleta squeezing past them both to sit on the prow. She looked down at her warped reflection, and found the water closer than she'd like. She'd never learnt to swim, and wondered how difficult it might be and how long it would take.

Büber slipped the rope and pushed out. When he'd rowed her across the first time, it hadn't seemed far. The buildings of Juvavum had been something to aim for, to concentrate on. And there had always been the possibility that she could still avoid her fate.

Now that she was crossing again, towards what the gods had planned for her from the very start, all she could see was a wide, fast-flowing stretch of muddy brown water and, looming above her, the White Tower.

It took an age. Perhaps Büber was tired. With three of them in the boat now, it was bound to be harder work, and he'd been across four times already. They should have rested, made more of their time together.

She wasn't going to lose a duel with Eckhardt. There was no conceivable way she could lose. She was going to set him on fire and watch him burn for a while, then explode burning chunks of him over his so-called followers. He was mad and weak, and she was fresh and strong. She'd go in hard, disrupt his concentration, put him on the back foot from the very start. By brushing aside his domination spells, he'd have nothing left to hit her with.

Quick, if not clean.

Büber pulled on the oars, dragging them closer.

The mob? She had a plan for them, too. Not to kill them, but to humiliate them. She could do that. Part of it would be through killing Eckhardt as if he were no more than a beetle beneath her heel. The rest would come in good time.

And Allegretti. Eckhardt was her priority, but she knew they wouldn't be dragging the tutor back across the river in his chains. She wasn't going to give the man the opportunity to talk his way out of his treason.

She was almost within touching distance of the river bank. She couldn't feel Eckhardt. Presumably he couldn't feel her yet, either. What would he do when he first sensed her and her raw, naked power?

The bow of the boat bumped against the earthen bank, and she skipped up and off onto dry land, painter in hand. Büber scrambled up with far less grace, and Ullmann carefully shifted around to take the oarsman's position.

"Straight back, mind," said Büber. "Don't let yourself drift downstream."

Nikoleta let go of the rope once the usher was confident of his grip, and she watched his first few strokes, assured and deep. The boat surged back into the flowing water, and she found she didn't have the inclination to watch it leave.

"Shall we go?" she asked.

Büber unslung his crossbow and held it loosely by the stock. "We only need to be as careful as you think necessary. They're over by the novices' house. There's no one else in between us and them."

"He'll know I'm here before long. Why don't you go on ahead? Get in a position where you can see his reaction. Then come back and tell me what he did." She stood with one hand on her hip, weight on one leg, relaxed, calm. "I'll give it a little while, then follow you."

"Makes sense. If he's going to prepare any sort of defence, then you need to know about it." Büber looked at the limb of the mountain where it swept down to the river. "I'll take the same route I did last time."

As he made to leave, she pulled him back and kissed him. Almost tenderly this time.

He wiped his mouth and frowned, but set off all the same. It was impressive to watch as he merged seamlessly with the wood.

Of course Büber didn't suspect anything. There was no reason why he should. And there was no reason why he would ever think of looking up.

She gathered herself, remembering all the indignities that had been heaped on her, both as a child and as an adult. The times when she'd been freezing, starving, terrified and worse. The times she couldn't remember at all, the blank holes in her memory where she knew something had happened, something ghastly enough for her mind to reject it completely.

All the pain she'd endured to become an adept. All the lies she'd been told. All the services she'd been made to perform.

Eckhardt was her enemy and he was going to die.

Nikoleta rose into the air, avoiding the branches, fending the twigs aside and brushing through the crowns of the trees. As she flew into clear air, she started forward, heading straight for the novices' house. Poor Peter Büber below, thinking he was ahead, taking his circuitous, careful path. He'd forgive her. Of course he would.

Now she knew where Eckhardt was, she reached out, focusing her efforts in that one direction. There, at the limit of her senses, was a twisted, writhing knot of energy, dirty and seething with corruption. It was going to take him a little more time to find her, and she spent that time wisely.

She would need a shield, not against physical weapons but against Eckhardt's will. If such a spell existed, she didn't have it drawn on her skin — but she'd overcome such limitations before. Now she could read them right, her tattoos told her not of rigid defin- itions, but of potentials. She already had a shield against physical attacks; she would change it to make it proof against Eckhardt's magic too.

The air in front of her shimmered and set, and the wind that was blowing her hair out behind her dropped to almost nothing. Then she poured her loathing of personal invasion into the shield, and the ink on her arm shifted, configuring itself to a subtly different pattern.

She felt it change, and Eckhardt's presence on her mental map, along with the aura of every other creature nearby, ended.

That was an unexpected consequence, but at least it told her she'd succeeded in reconfiguring her abilities at the first attempt. What else was she capable of?

Though she could no longer sense Eckhardt, she knew where he'd been a moment ago, so she flew on at tree-top height over the shoulder of the mountain and down the other side. As she crested the rise, she could see the roofs of both the adepts' and novices' houses, and the avenue of trees that marked where the road was. There, right there.

Spreading her arms wide in the imitation of an eagle, she swooped down. The first pass was the most important. Was he oblivious to her, or had the sudden hole in his perception alerted him? No matter. What he did next was immaterial, because he'd have no answer.

Her outstretched hands filled with bright fire, and she caught a first glimpse of those with Eckhardt, still divided into their mutually warring tribes. Faster, lower: that roaring sound was the wind battering against her shield. She could make out the seat, Eckhardt's throne. She could see the pale figure seated on it and his shining staff, together with the crouching, tied man next to him.

A river of flame poured out from her. Not just from her hands, but her mouth, her nose, her eyes. She breathed fire, vomited fire, threw fire. It fell like a column, reducing the wooden chair to burning matchwood on impact and splashing out in a flood, engulfing whoever was in its radius. Allegretti died in that instant, his flesh blasted from his bones. His death was incidental, along with a dozen others who were too close, and the candle-bright twists of fire that danced and spun away shrieking weren't even distractions, because she knew, instantly, that Eckhardt wasn't one of them.

She snapped around as she overshot the target and she spotted a figure rising clear of the ground. He'd lost his staff, but how significant that was, how much of his power he'd stored in it, she didn't know. Then her shield shuddered as if she'd just run into a cliff.

The skull-jarring shock bruised her all over and left her screaming in pain. But the shield held. Eckhardt, like her, had held nothing back for his first spell. Now it was down to who had enough left to bring the other to their knees long enough to deliver the mercy-stroke.

She doubled back and gave him everything she could. Face to

face, over the distance of a stadia: fire boiled out of her again and flowed towards Eckhardt's hovering form. As it seethed and roiled, it dripped flame on the ground below. She was dimly aware of shouts and cries, but they were just mundanes, stupid, gullible and weak mundanes who weren't worth saving. She used their fear to feed her fury.

Her destroying fire reached Eckhardt's shield, and it flowed around it, enveloping it. She willed the mass on, to become more intense: thicker, hotter, brighter.

At some point, she had to stop. Blood was coming from her nose and ears, and her vision was obscured by a red mist that she had to blink away. The fire flickered and faded.

Eckhardt wasn't dead yet, but she'd succeeded in wiping his maniacal grin off his contorted features, and his filthy-dirty robes smoked with residual heat. She'd cooked him red-raw, his skin cracked and baked and oozing.

She was going to hit him again. She'd almost got him last time, and now she was looking for a kill.

Something invisible held her and started to crush her. She pulled in her arms and legs, ducked her head down to her chest to bring her to the centre of her shield. Vast and incalculable pressure weighed down on her, a mountain's worth of rock that made shrieking sounds as the structure of her defence deformed and buckled under the relentless, impersonal force.

She held on. It was a storm and she would endure. When it passed, she would remain. It grew dark outside, and she concentrated on the core of her being. Eckhardt was trying to snuff her out, but she was determined not to be extinguished.

Then, with a creak, the attack faltered. It became light again. She could see him on the bare ground in front of the novices' house, on all fours, exhausted amid the ruin of charred, smoking corpses and tongues of bright fire. .

Now.

Her very fingertips seemed to burst with ribbons of flame.

And suddenly, he was gone. The space he'd occupied filled with a thunderclap.

Fire growled down and out, spilling up the stone steps and into the open door of the novices' house, licking around the walls and scorching the roof shingles. Eckhardt had escaped, and she howled in frustration.

He couldn't have gone far. He was weak. It was his final throw. Where would he go?

Her gaze travelled up to the White Tower. Where else? She lowered her shield for an instant, just to make sure, and looking at Eckhardt's aura was like staring into a furnace. She slammed the shield back into place and set off again, up the mountain, over the trees, until nascent green gave way to gnarled and warped brown.

The entrance to the tower was clear, and she flew down, almost into it and then through to the space beyond. But there was a note of caution sounding in her head. When the dragon was in its den, it was the most dangerous of all.

The sygils drawn into the doorway had no effect on her; whether or not they still worked, she didn't know or care. She brushed by them and entered the hall.

There was a single blue-white light in the centre of the vast room; such a contrast from its previous overwhelming brightness. Now it was shadows that obscured the exits.

But not the dead. They were obvious, little mounds of decay lit on one side only. If Eckhardt had had more imagination, or power, or both, he'd have reanimated them. Corpse armies were hard to deal with, since their constituent parts were dead already. But however good undead were at terrorising mundanes, a decent magician could always either sever the tenuous link that controlled them or more prosaically, destroy their bodies.

It would have cost her more power. It would have slowed her down. But the dead stayed dead, and she flew over them, looking for a passageway. There were several – she needed the right one.

She dropped her shield momentarily. Gods, Eckhardt was starting to cast again. She could feel it, a dark star below her. He was too busy to deal with her, frantically carrying out the ritual that would suck the life from one person and give it to another, a ritual that could neither be abbreviated nor hastened.

Necromancy was a stupid and dull dead-end, relying on rote and cant. She could take him now, almost at her ease. She wouldn't even need magic to do it.

She started into the tunnels beneath the tower, and made her own light for the journey in the palms of her hands. Finding Eckhardt wasn't going to take long. She was getting closer with every step. How hurried he seemed. How futile it all was.

She came, finally, to his door. She could have opened it in the normal fashion, but chose instead to blast it. Pausing only to notice the lifeless wards etched into the wood, she brought up her shield again to protect herself from splinters.

The door frame came away with the door itself, slamming into the opposite wall and taking several pieces of furniture with it. Burning fragments spiralled away like missiles, sooty trails following.

She walked through. There he was, captive in the circle along with his victim, and behind him, all the previous victims, children, grey skinned and still but for their wetly gleaming eyes.

Eckhardt was astride the barely breathing chest, his hands around a man's throat. He looked up at her, and she down at him.

This deranged murdering vagrant who smelt of death was a hexmaster. The second-to-last hexmaster. His rooms were already ablaze; tinder-dry books, powders and volatile liquids popped and flashed and crackled.

It was, in the end, easy. She held out her hand, and a ball of fire closed the distance between them in less than a heartbeat. It clung to Eckhardt's face like a burr, then consumed him.

He twisted and turned as he burnt, staying upright for a long time, longer than any mundane could have stood. Eventually, he put one hand to the floor, and tried to rise, but there wasn't enough of him left to hold him up.

The individual fires were coalescing into one all-encompassing inferno. She started to back out of the room, her strength spent. It was over. Her spells dropped away and she felt the full force of the heat for the first time.

She turned, saw a man, felt something cold and hard piercing her heart.

Nikoleta looked down and recognised the hilt of Felix's dagger. She looked up and saw Ullmann, his eyes narrow, his jaw set.

"I'm sorry, Mistress. But it's for the best."

She reached for him, her hands fluttering, but there was no force in her efforts. Instead, he pushed her back through Eckhardt's doorway, back into the fire she'd started.

As the blade left her, her blood poured out. She knew why he'd done it. She knew exactly why.

She just hadn't expected it to be him.

49

Thaler climbed to the very top of the library, to the master librarian's gallery. The sparks of candlelight that fluttered below seemed so very far away, as if he was watching spirits at the bottom of a lake; something he assumed had come to an end along with everything else. Also, the walkways, the banisters, the balconies: they seemed less substantial than they had before.

It was just the effect of the dark. In full light – and that would happen, he was determined of that – the library was warmer and more friendly. That was partly why he was up here, poking about. The Romans, when they'd built their pantheon, hadn't filled it with magical light. He vaguely remembered seeing an illustration once, not of this pantheon but of a similar one in Rome. There'd been a feature in that picture that was absent from the library building, and now he was going to see if the sketch was true, or just a fiction.

He couldn't reach the ceiling. He'd need a ladder, and someone to hold it, or better still, someone to hold it and a different someone to climb up while he directed activities from the safety of the master librarian's platform.

All the same, he dragged the heavy desk to dead centre and climbed up. It gave him another three feet of reach, and he was almost there. He happened to glance down, and his guts churned. It was an awfully long way down, and he'd have quite a while falling to contemplate his folly, or to give a drawn-out scream: that was far more likely.

He crawled off the desk and gave himself a few moments to calm himself. He wished he was brave, brave like Büber, like Felix, like Ullmann, even like Sophia Morgenstern whose courage was equal to any man's. He couldn't even stand on a desk without breaking out into a cold sweat.

Banging his hands on the thick wooden top, he summoned up his resolve.

"Come on, Master Thaler. Greater things are expected of you than this, so why do you quail like a frightened child?" His own voice chided him.

"Quite right, quite right. It is all very silly," he replied. He took hold of a heavy chair and heaved it up onto the desk. "As the master librarian – acting master librarian? No, master librarian – I have responsibilities."

He climbed up onto the desk again, and sat in the chair. That wasn't so bad. He reached down for the lantern, and slowly turned around. He put one foot on the chair seat, then the other, and straightened up.

He was standing on a chair. Hardly a feat worthy of Hercules, yet he felt like he'd slain the Lernaean hydra all by himself. He held the lantern in one trembling hand and pressed his other against the ceiling to steady himself.

The domed roof had always been smooth inside at the very top, repainted white every decade or so at great expense and no little disruption to the work of the library below.

Yet he held in his mind two things: firstly, the image of breaking away a layer of rock to reveal a door underneath it, and secondly, the book illustration that showed the pantheon with a circular hole in its roof, the edge of which began almost exactly where he was looking.

The paintwork was old, and the plaster beneath even older. It was nothing but a patchwork of cracks as fine as any mosaic. But he thought he could make out the beginning of a wider line that extended away from his probing fingertips. Outside, the concrete dome was completely covered in greened copper sheets, with no hint of what they might hide underneath. But if he was right, if there was a hole at the top of the dome, which could let in natural light, they would only have to peel back the copper to reveal it. Of course, the hole would then have to be covered by something to keep the weather out. But no one made glass in sheets that big, and the weight of a leaded window that size would be enormous. How would they get it up there, let alone place it without it collapsing?

Life was complicated where it used to be simple. All those questions to answer.

The sound of commotion came from beneath him, and he wobbled. Cold sweat drenched his skin as he braced himself between the ceiling and the chair. He held his breath and closed his eyes, and convinced himself that he wasn't going to fall.

Someone was shouting, and not in a good way. Büber: it sounded like Peter Büber.

He opened his eyes again, one at a time, and carefully climbed down until he was kneeling on the chair, then standing on the table, then back onto the platform. It was inviolable tradition for the master librarian to be stationed here at the top of the library, but he really didn't fancy it all.

Time to find out what was going on. He peeked over the edge of the gallery to see. Yes, there was Büber, and the prince, and Sophia, and the librarians, and he couldn't make out a single word any of them were saying.

He hurried down the staircases and along the walkways. The noise had subsided by the time he arrived, red-faced and panting, on the ground floor. Büber was crouched on the stone flags, his knees under him, his long back arched like a boulder, his hands pressing his head down as far as it would go.

Around him was a circle of concerned-looking people, each apparently unable to do or say anything to help.

Thaler pushed his way through, and instead of asking them what the matter was, he went straight over to his friend and put his arm across his shoulder. He bent his own head low.

"Peter? Peter, it's Frederik." Büber smelt of smoke, bad smoke, the sort of smoke that was acrid and dangerous. "Talk to me, Peter. Tell me what's wrong?" He looked up to see if Ullmann was also present, but there was no sign of the usher. Instead, everyone was staring at him. If they weren't going to help, why didn't they just go away?

"She's gone," Büber said.

"She's . . . gone?" Thaler glanced up again, and noted that both the prince and Sophia looked neither at him, nor at each other. "Who's gone?"

"Nikoleta."

The magician with whom Büber had been banished. The one who still had power.

"What happened?" He was beginning to sound as bewildered as Büber. "Did she and Eckhardt . . .?"

Büber's head came up off the floor. "They're both dead. They're both dead, Frederik."

And Büber clung to Thaler and wept.

The knowledge that Eckhardt was gone made Thaler's heart flutter, but there was clearly something more. Büber, the man who had never cried before, who suffered disfiguring pain with little more than a shrug, was in torment.

"Ah. I understand." Thaler looked over Büber's shaking shoulder and pursed his lips. "My lord, if you could afford the huntmaster a moment's privacy, we would both be so very grateful."

The onlookers had been looking for an excuse to go: now, Thaler had given it to them. One by one, they stepped back and pulled away, their pace increasing. Sophia took Felix's arm and eased him in the direction of the portico. He left reluctantly, repeatedly turning his head as he went.

He was young. He'd learn.

When they were alone, Thaler urged Büber to his feet. "Come on. Let's find somewhere sensible." And, unresisting, Büber allowed himself to be pushed ahead, towards a side door and down a narrow corridor pierced through the wall of the pantheon.

There were stairs, and doors, and windows through which Thaler was able to catch fleeting glimpses of outside: he saw that there was smoke rising from the far side of the river. Something seemed well ablaze and there was little sign of it diminishing: the black cloud he could see over the rooftops of Juvavum seemed dense and consistent, no matter which part of the sky he searched.

He just about managed not to comment aloud on the fire, though he was itching to know its cause.

Guiding Büber to the last door, he reached past him to open it. It led into the library's refectory, and they were alone. There were still the remains of a fire in the hefty grate, and Thaler moved them to the end of the table closest to it.

He pressed Büber onto the bench seat, and went in search of something to drink. It was what his friend needed right now, even if Thaler himself would have preferred a plate of bread and a thickly sliced sausage.

The kitchens were deserted. It was likely, he concluded, that some of the library staff, cooks and the like, had gone over to Eckhardt. The thought grieved him, even as he banged around, opening cupboards and peering at shelves.

He finally found a crate of beer under one of the benches, and rather than carry just two bottles back, he unloaded half onto the floor and heaved the rest of them to waist height.

When he got back to the refectory, Büber was in exactly the same position that he'd left him in.

Thaler sat opposite, opened the stoppers on two bottles and slid one across the table. He took a swig from his own and waited.

Eventually, Büber snagged the stone bottle without looking up, and clutched at it without drinking.

"You loved her," said Thaler.

Büber nodded miserably.

"Bloody disaster all round." Thaler put his beer back on the table. "I'm really very sorry, Peter."

Büber nodded again, and showed no sign of talking.

"What was she like?"

That got a reaction. Büber looked up sharply, and his whole body tensed as if he was going to fight. There was only Thaler, though, nudging a bottle of beer around the table with his thumbs.

"She's . . ." he began, and choked up. He loosened his throat with several gulps from his own bottle. "It was crazy, Frederik. Like a madness. We just circled around each other until we couldn't stand it any longer. Then we just tore at each other like we were rutting animals."

Thaler's eyebrows crawled up his forehead, and he had to make a conscious effort to drag them down again.

"I don't even know why. She didn't either. After that first time, we should have left each other. She to go one way, me another; the world's a big place, so I'm told. Look at me, Frederik: I'm not the sort of man a woman goes with willingly."

"You have other qualities," ventured Thaler.

"I look like a fucking troll. I swear that the whores on Gentleman's Alley take it in turns with me so that I don't subject any one poor girl to the horror of bedding me twice in a year."

"I was talking about loyalty, honesty, friendship. But never mind."

"And now I expect all the trolls are dead, too, so I'm the ugliest bastard left walking Midgard." Büber sank the rest of his beer, tossed the bottle to one side and reached for another.

Thaler watched the bottle roll along the table, getting closer and closer to the edge. It teetered and fell, bouncing against the bench seat on its way to cracking apart on the floor.

"There was a deposit on that," he murmured. "Although in the grand scheme of things, that's not really important. Peter, what happened?"

Büber sighed, drank beer, and rested his elbows on the tabletop. "Ullmann couldn't get anywhere near Eckhardt. The mob had descended into a . . . I don't know what you'd call it . . . a pack of wolves, except wolves work together. They'd have ripped him to shreds and thrown what was left to Eckhardt. But we'd seen enough to understand that attacking with a militia would just have given him more fuel for his spells."

The huntmaster stopped, and didn't start again for a long time. "Allegretti was there. Eckhardt had made him his . . . I don't know . . . his pet?"

"Did he . . .?"

"He died. Lots of them died." His face turned sour. "I should have taken out Eckhardt when I had the chance. I was close enough to take a pot at him with my bow, and he was . . . busy."

"Busy."

"They're still alive, afterwards, his victims. Just. What he does to them: it turns them into little old men, starving-thin, no strength to move, speak, breathe. They lie there and blink. Gods only know what's happened to them." His shoulders slumped. "I should have had a go. Nikoleta didn't want me to, so I didn't. I should have ignored her."

"I imagine she thought she was protecting you." Thaler finished his own beer. He set the bottle carefully back in the crate, and collected another.

"She ignored me instead. We were supposed to go together: Eckhardt couldn't sense me, and I was to get close enough to be able to tell her when to strike. She left me like a fucking idiot and just went at him with everything she had. And it worked. She had him beaten. He used a spell to get back to the White Tower, and she chased after him as fast as she could. She was on fire, and I don't think she even noticed. I'd run all the way to the novices' house in time to see Eckhardt vanish, and then I had to run all the way up the fucking mountain, before working out which of the tunnels she'd gone down, and by the time I'd got there it was over." He took a shuddering breath. "One of the caves. It was like an oven. I saw her, Peter. I saw her burning."

"I'm sorry."

"That fucker Eckhardt crawled out of the fire. The flesh had boiled from his bones, and he looked up at me from the floor, with his grinning skull and his eyes all melted away, and he reached out for my leg."

Thaler hung on to the table for support, and Büber looked him in the eye for the first time since they'd sat down.

"Don't worry. He's not coming back after what I did to him."

It was Thaler's turn to nod and be silent.

"What happens now?" asked Büber, reaching for his third beer.

"Whatever it is, it's out of my hands. We have a boy-prince and no earls, and I don't know how that's supposed to work." Thaler contemplated his bottle, and looked up at the high windows that were now the refectory's only illumination. "I do know what I'm going to do, though. That's about the only thing I can control at the moment."

"What's that?"

Thaler couldn't tell if Büber was just making polite noises to humour him, but he carried on regardless. "I'm going to finish cataloguing the books. In fact, I'm going to start again. We're going to go through every book, every scrap of paper, and we're going to work out exactly what each one contains. And then, we're going to shelve each and every one of them so we know where to find them again. We're going to organise them not by how big the book is but by subject; all the maps in one place, all the bestiaries in another, the histories and the geometry and astrology next to each other."

"Is that all?"

"No. No, it's not. We're going to learn from them. We're going to find out how this world works, and we're going to bend it to our will. That is our destination. If we want water that flows, wheels that turn, barges that run, lights in our homes, then we're going to have to do all of that for ourselves."

Büber shook his head. "Frederik, there's no more magic. The days of miracles are over."

Something stirred inside Thaler's chest. It might have been been no more than hubris, but to him it felt like the first sight of land after a long, storm-chased voyage.

"Those days, Peter, have only just begun."

PART 3

Ember

50

It only occurred to her later that she'd been the first woman in the library, not just in living memory, but perhaps forever. That night, when she'd led the men down from the fortress to the town, forced the mob back with swords and spears and clubs, then crossed the threshold to greet her prince.

Neither Jews nor women entered the library. The spell had been as broken as the door by the time she'd entered, if it had ever been anything more substantial than habit and history in the first place; the magic might have gone, but those two forces stayed just as strong.

Sophia walked up the scrubbed steps to the portico, and into its whispering shadows. The rehung door was open, the coat of paint on it fresh and bright, and a newly constituted group of ushers guarded it.

If the library was the most important building in the entire palatinate, possibly the entire continent, then using a bunch of boys to look after it wasn't necessarily the best decision Thaler could have made; habit and history again.

But they knew her, and stood aside for her. She collected a lantern from the rack, had it lit by the librarian on duty, and asked for Master Thaler's whereabouts.

The librarian shrugged good-naturedly. Thaler was never in one place. Thaler was everywhere, all at once, his actual presence only detectable by the trail of harassed note-takers frantically scribbling in his wake.

"I'll find him," she said, "even if I have to stand in one place and wait for him to pass."

"A sound strategy, my lady."

"It's Wess, isn't it?" She had a decent memory for faces. "Now under-librarian?"

"And he has me handing out lanterns." Wess smiled ruefully. "There are still so very few of us, and, as Master Thaler points out, making sure a faulty lantern doesn't burn the library down is a vital task."

"All the same, Mr Wess. I'll have a word with him." Her brows crinkled as she frowned. "No, I'll have more than a word."

She carried on into the library proper. Carpenters were replacing the missing balustrades on the stairs, and in the centre of the dome, a huge scaffold was taking shape. In the dark, high up, there were lights and figures, hammering and augering.

It was hardly silent, yet all around the base of the structure, librarians were hard at work, pulling books off the shelves and placing them on tiered trolleys. In another part was a long table where senior staff were attempting to categorise each book as it came along.

It reminded her of an ant's nest. No one was still.

She took a deep breath, and, despite her given title of Princess Consort, bellowed in a most unladylike way, "Master Thaler?"

A momentary pause in the activity, then everyone who wasn't Thaler got back to work. The one who was peered over the edge of a second-tier balcony. "Mistress Morgenstern?"

She cupped her hands around her mouth. "Stay there. Exactly there, Master Thaler. Do not move. I'll be right up."

She had to negotiate passage with the carpenters, but after that, things became easier. Despite her haste, Thaler was itching to move on by the time she reached him, although the cloud of scribes surrounding him seemed relieved at the prospect of a rest.

"Mistress Morgenstern, surely this can wait. I am a very busy man."

"Yes you are, Master Thaler." She looked left and right. "I'd like to talk to the master librarian alone, please."

His assistants were more than pleased to comply, and Thaler found himself frustrated.

"Really, this is . . ."

"A moment between friends, where I tell you in all honesty that you cannot carry on this way."

"I don't know what you mean," he blustered, but even by lamplight, she could see him blush.

"You're exhausting everyone. You have poor Wess handing out lanterns. How many languages does he know?"

"I believe it's about the half-dozen mark."

Sophia put her lantern down on a table, and pushed a chair towards Thaler. "Then you are wasting his talent, and yours. Sit down, Frederik."

"But I . . ."

"Sit. Down." She dusted off a chair for herself and sat upright on it, hands folded in her lap.

Thaler sighed and sat down. The chair creaked with his weight, though less than it would have done previously.

"You've been eating, of course?" She gazed absently upwards at the growing scaffolding. It had almost reached the top of the dome and the master librarian's eyrie.

"Sometimes. There is a great deal to do, Sophia."

"I know. But it doesn't have to be done by you, does it?"

Thaler was silent for the first time in days, and eventually said: "I suppose not. But I feel responsible for everything. It's all so important."

"You'll have no argument from me about that. Felix asked me to find out how everything is, whether you have what you need."

"If I had twice as many people it'd be too few." Thaler rested his hands on his knees, and visibly sagged. "We don't have enough of anything. We don't have enough craftsmen to make the internal alterations, make trolleys, and knock up new shelves. What will happen when we start to take the roof off is anyone's guess. We don't have enough librarians to read and catalogue the books, classify them, move them to their temporary positions. We don't have enough candles, even. We're working from before dawn to long after sunset, and we don't have enough cooks, nor enough to cook with or cook on. It's all a bit of a mess really."

"It's early days, yet," said Sophia.

"It's getting worse, not better. You're right. We can't — I can't keep going like this, yet what alternative do we have?"

"We have lots of alternatives," she said, "which is why I'm here. To talk to you about them. Make you see sense."

"Very well," said Thaler, leaning back. "Convince me."

"Mr Trommler, of blessed memory, kept very detailed accounts. They show we've many thousands, many tens of thousands of florins at our disposal. And that's not all. Teams are being sent into the White Tower each day, and are coming out with more silver and gold than they can carry. We can bathe in the stuff."

"That's beside the point. We can't eat it. Neither can we use it to read a line of Greek or Latin, or make a plank, or hammer in a nail, or render a candle, or anything else good." Thaler saw her expression. "You've got an idea."

"I have lots of ideas," she said, "but specifically one. The food and the lanterns and the carpentry, someone else can see to. Your problem is that you don't have enough librarians."

"Well, yes . . ."

"So buy them."

Thaler stopped mid-objection. "Buy them. Where from?"

"Everywhere. Wien. Bavaria. The Franks. Venezia. Genova. Byzantium. Alexandria." She waited.

"It'll take too long. And they won't be suitable, anyway. Some of them will be married, they'll have families. We take boys, and we train them in the ways of this library." Thaler wrung his hands together. "It simply won't work."

"Frederik, you're going to have to change the way you do things. Half the Jews in Juvavum can read German, Greek, Latin and Hebrew, yet they're clanking around in armour and lording it over the townspeople. Would you rather they did that, or that they were in here, helping you? It's not like you're going to catch Jewishness from them, are you? Or just take my father." Her even smile slipped. "Please. He's driving me mad."

"But Jews won't work in the library."

"I'm here, aren't I? And by the way, how about returning those sefer you've got?"

"They're library property."

"Give them all back, and one will be returned on loan. You don't need three." She leant forward. "You *can't* go on with the old ways. So, while everything is up in the air, establish a new way of doing things. Let the librarians get married. Start paying them. Hire the best people from all over Europe. Don't insist they live as though they're members of the Order: you don't have to slavishly imitate what they did, not any more."

Thaler looked out at the scaffold, and the men working on it.

"How much money do I have?" he finally asked.

"All of it, if you want. It has to last though, so I'd like to think you wouldn't spend it all at once. Am I right in thinking the other under-librarians you served with are gone?"

"Grozer died. As for Thomm? Has your father returned those stolen books he bought yet?"

"I'll see to it. I know where he hid them. This is getting off the point, Frederik. Change the way the library is run. Just do it. You don't have to ask anyone's permission, and you don't have an old guard to humour."

"You're right, of course. But there's so much else to do." He looked again at the scaffolding, and went to stand at the edge of the gallery from where he could survey his domain. "I haven't so much as looked at a book in a week."

"Then can I suggest you're doing it wrong?" Sophia came to stand next to him. "The library building is less important than the work going on down there, yet what impression do I get from up here? That the catalogue is running second-best to everything else."

"But . . ."

"Frederik. You've got Mr Wess handing out lanterns. So this is what we're going to do: I'm going to take charge of the alterations and all of the non-library tasks. You are going to do what Felix has made you master to do."

"But you're a woman!" Thaler blurted.

"Yes," she said. "I had noticed. I can also read and write several languages, add, subtract, and solve geometry problems, run a household, talk to guildsmen and suppliers and haggle for the best price on anything from a book to a broom. I can also, if you'd forgotten, lead an army into battle and be the prince's chosen consort. Anything else you'd like to say?"

Thaler considered his options. "No, Mistress Morgenstern. Nothing at all."

"Good." She patted his arm. "It's better this way, Frederik. If you don't think the men will listen to me and take my instruction, you're wrong. I have the prince's authority and the prince's purse. If they want his coin, they'll have to deal with me."

"Are you . . ." asked Thaler, his sudden nervousness making him grip the handrail tightly, "are you all right with this?"

"With overseeing the building, dealing with Germans, or with being Felix's consort?" She looked at him sideways. "Ah."

"I don't mean to speak out of turn, Sophia."

"If I was eight, no one would even blink in surprise." She rested her forearms on the same handrail. "I'm not, of course. I'm twice his age. And I'm Jewish. And not a princess. Completely unsuitable, really, and he'll probably end up marrying someone else. But until then, I intend to use whatever position I have to help him."

"And," mused Thaler, "helping the library will help him."

"Just so there's no misunderstanding: the fate of Carinthia is in the hands of people like us. That's why having you choose what wood to use for the new shelves is a waste of everybody's time."

Thaler nodded, then frowned. "Can I show you something?"

Without waiting for an answer, he disappeared up the stairs to the third gallery and came back shortly with two leather lunch-pails.

"It won't be kosher," she said automatically.

"There's no food in them, more's the pity. Look."

He showed her the contents. One was empty. The other had part of a roll of soft lead sheeting in it, making it almost too heavy to hold in one hand. Thaler got down on his knees and balanced both pails on the very edge of the gallery, between the upright balusters.

"Which one do you think will reach the ground first?" he asked, looking up.

"The one with the lead in it, of course." She leant over the handrail. "Assuming it doesn't land on someone's head first."

"And yet yesterday, when a workman dropped both his hammer and the wedge he was trying to fix, this happened." He jumped up, shouted "Clear down below!" and then ducked back to push both pails off.

There was a pause, and a single loud bang.

Sophia was watching very closely, and to her it looked as though the containers hit the stone floor at the same time.

"How is that possible?" She squinted down at them, trying to judge whether she'd seen what she thought she saw.

"I don't know. I've tried them both empty, both full, one full and one empty. They fall at the same rate, every single time, in direct contradiction of Aristotle. I've tried it from the very top, too. I suppose it might not be far enough for the difference to show, but this building is one hundred and fifty feet, floor to ceiling. Some of the fortress's towers are taller . . ."

"Yes, I'm sure you'll get permission. Perhaps." She stopped, and frowned. "Perhaps Aristotle was wrong. Or the world has changed, and Aristotle is no longer right."

Thaler sat back on his haunches. "Have you noticed how we simply don't have explanations for almost anything that happens? Things fall, yes? Then why do sparks rise? The sun at midday in winter is lower than in summer: is that because the sun is hotter in summer, or what? A barge floats, yet put a hole in it and it sinks. Has the barge lost its boatiness simply because of that hole?"

Sophia laughed. "Boatiness?"

378

"I don't know what else to call it. Plato would have it that the more a boat diverges from the ideal, the less of a boat it becomes." Thaler heaved himself up. "My head is so full of questions, I don't know where to start."

"Start down there, Frederik. Start with the books. I'll find someone to look after the lanterns and let poor Mr Wess do some proper work. And my father, too. Just make sure you search him at the end of the day."

5 1

Felix couldn't help thinking how small Carinthia looked on the map, and how it wouldn't take much movement of the lines that marked the border to erase it completely. The parts that lay over the mountains, the Drau and Danz valleys, could be swallowed up by Venezia without him even noticing. The land between the Enn and the Salzach was vulnerable to the Bavarians, and in the east, Wien could march around the top of the Alps along the broad Donau plain.

Being left with the area immediately around Juvavum, and the lower reaches of the Salzach and the Enn, was all but unsustainable. All the good land would have gone, with the trade routes that he currently controlled falling into other hands, and the mines at Durrnberg, too.

The palatinate would collapse, and someone else would be installed in the White Fortress, to rule on behalf of a distant king who didn't care about the land or its people.

And the stupid thing was, he *did* care. He cared more than his father had, whose one excursion to protect Carinthia from invaders had ended with him dead and his orphaned son on the throne. But Büber was right. It was the Order who'd held all the power, and they were gone, all of them, for certain this time. His father, and his father before him, had been figureheads. Not puppets, exactly, but the faces of men put before other men so that no one would see the monster that hid behind them.

For the first time in a thousand years, a Carinthian prince was solely responsible for the safety of his people, and it happened to be him. The gods weren't noted for their sense of humour, but he imagined a mocking laugh echoing from the mountaintops and down the steep wooded valleys.

There was a knock at the door, and he absently called his assent, but not so absently that he didn't momentarily rest his hand on his sword and look around to see who it was.

"Mr Ullmann. Thank you for coming."

"My lord." Ullmann walked to the table and waited to be addressed, but inevitably his gaze wandered down to peruse the map.

Felix wondered what he made of it, so he asked him plainly. "What do you see, Mr Ullmann?" He waved his left hand across the map. His shoulder was sore. It was always sore, and he wondered if he was going to spend the rest of his life favouring it.

"Carinthia is here, my lord, and . . ."

"No. I've been schooled in geography. I want to know what *you* see when you look at this. What does it mean to *you*?" He adjusted one of the boxes that kept the map flat.

Ullmann scrubbed at the bridge of his nose while he thought. "That we're surrounded by both enemies and friends, but the ink on the parchment doesn't tell us who's who."

It wasn't an answer designed to please. But it was honest. Felix leant his elbows on the table. "Nor does it tell us that the Bavarians are broke and have no money to pay for their soldiers. It doesn't tell us whether the Doge or the Duke have the upper hand in northern Italy. It doesn't tell us what's happening in München or Wien or the Eastern empire, or in the Franklands." He pointed to each place in turn. "We're blind. We always have been. It never mattered before, but suddenly we need to know whether they're in as much trouble as we are, or whether they're plotting to carve us up like a roast boar." He stared at the hand-drawn lines, trying to make sense of it all. "If you'd arrived in Juvavum just two weeks ago, we'd have appeared as strong as we ever were. Now look at us. If the Teutons come at us again, in the same numbers as they did before? A tiny army, a few hundred horse. They could walk in and take over, and there's very little I could do – that anyone could do – to stop them."

Ullmann shifted from one foot to the other. "My lord . . ."

Felix drummed his fingers on the tabletop. "I don't know what I'm supposed to be doing, Mr Ullmann. Really, I have no idea.

Everyone else, they seem to be busy at what they do best, and I'm left gazing at the stupid map, wondering if I should be trying to raise a huge army to defend us, or writing letters to my fellow princes. I'm twelve. The people I used to trust to tell me what to do have gone, Mr Ullmann. I need new advisers, a whole new court, and that takes time we might not have."

"Then it strikes me, my lord, that you need to call a grand council, to hear the views all the people. I'm sure Master Thaler can tell us from his books how to run one." Ullmann tapped Juvavum with his forefinger. "Hold it here, in the fortress."

"I don't see how that's going to help. The few earls I have are even younger than I am, Mr Ullmann, or their families are still arguing about succession." Little Ulf had been eventually fished out of the river, along with a dozen or so other bodies, none of which was his stepmother. She hadn't been found among the other bodies either. She was lost, more surely than he was. Felix stared out of the window at the mountains, and wondered if that was another pain that would never cease.

Ullmann cleared his throat and spoke softly. "My lord, you can't wait on these things. The town needs a new mayor, even though we don't know what happened to Master Messinger yet. You gave Master Thaler the library seal, remember, even though the old master librarian is still with us."

"So I should just make new earls? Perhaps," said Felix absently.

"Not quite what I meant, my lord. You could rule that all the earldoms have reverted to you, and that you'll portion out the land in a way that suits the new ways."

Felix sat back so quickly he jarred his whole body. "Take the earls' lands? I don't think so."

"My lord, there are so few earls to take them from. Some families have been completely wiped out. Rather than having distant cousins squabbling – and fighting – over who's the heir, which'll go on for years and become impossible to make right, just cut them out now, while everyone is still willing to accept that we have to do things differently." Ullmann took the chair next to Felix without invitation, but the prince decided he didn't mind.

"Are you after an earldom, Mr Ullmann?"

Ullmann reacted as if he'd just been offered a freshly squeezed cup of aconite. "No thank you, my lord. Not at all. Shall I tell you what I'm thinking?"

Can I stop you? wondered Felix. He welcomed the distraction, though, and waited as Ullmann pulled the map closer.

"When the Romans went on the march, they promised every legionary their own piece of land in return for twenty-five years of service. They were well paid, and they knew what they were fighting for."

"A professional army, yes: I know this."

"What better way to get an army than to promise this for our people? Most of them spend their entire lives working land that their earl owns. Give them their own land, and they'll fight for you."

Felix looked at the map again. "So I take away land from the earls, and distribute it to the peasants?" Even as he said it, he couldn't quite believe that someone was seriously suggesting it.

"Forget that they're peasants. Some of them have worked the same land for generations, and it's a hard life that just got harder. If you make them give you their sons for a few coppers a day, then," Ullmann shrugged, "all your fears will come true. If you ask them for their sons and tell them that, in return, the soil they've sweated and bled on is their own? They'll love you, my lord."

Felix scratched at his nose and eyed the usher – no, not usher any more – he was wasted in that post. "I'll have to think about this. Your parents . . ."

"Serfs, my lord. I'm not apologising for that." Ullmann sat taller and straighter. "Please don't think that I'm just saying this to give my mum and dad an easier time; that's not what this is about."

"So how did you get off the land? What did your earl say?"

Ullmann looked away for a moment. "Should I lie, my lord?"

"Not to me, Mr Ullmann."

"My dad could see how much I might do, if I could only get my chance. So he pretended I'd run away to seek my fortune in Italy."

"And yet you're here, in Juvavum." This Ullmann lad was definitely lively, as Thaler had noted. Ambitious, but in a good way. Felix was warming to him.

"I needed to learn to read, I knew that. So I found work in the library, cleaning and washing and carrying for the librarians, and after my day's work, I used to sneak a book off the shelves and find a quiet corner – if a round building can be said to have corners, that is – and see if I could make out what it said. When I was found out I thought I was for the road again, but the librarian – no names, my lord, don't want him in any trouble – asked me if I could read, and I had to say I couldn't, so every night afterwards, he'd spend a while schooling me in my letters, and now I can read honest German as good as any man alive, and some Latin and Greek, too."

Felix tapped his finger against his lips. "And a year and a day later, you were free of your obligations to the land."

"That's when I asked to be an usher, my lord. I knew I couldn't be a librarian because I was too old to be apprenticed, but being an usher was the next best thing. Then I got to help Master Thaler on his adventure, and that made me feel like I could be useful, not just to the library, but to the palatinate."

The prince looked askance at him. "Useful? Oh, you've been more than useful, Mr Ullmann. Which is why I asked to see you. To thank you."

Ullmann was very still for a while, except that his eyes darted about in their orbits, his gaze lighting on the map, the door, the fireplace, just for a moment, before darting like a fly to another place.

"Thank me? For what, my lord?"

"For giving Master Thaler the help he needed in securing the library, and later underground." Felix scraped his chair back and found a jug with wine, and another with water, and two cups. He poured Ullmann half a cup, and watched as the man added the same amount of water. Sober, then. Self-reliant and self-restrained. If he was putting on an act, it was a good act. "Without you, the expedition would have failed, and for that, you have Carinthia's thanks."

Felix realised, sitting there in the solar with Ullmann opposite him, that both of them were playing the grown-up and that it wasn't just that he had to take risks, but that any decision he made was a risk. The map on the table between them was instructive, but it told him what things used to be like, not how things were now. The borders of Carinthia, a pale yellow wash on the paper, meant nothing if he couldn't defend them. That was the threat. The opportunity was that borders went both ways.

If he was going to count holding on to the lands his father had left him as success, he could guarantee the similar calculations were being made in throne rooms the length and breadth of Europe.

"Land for service," said Felix, returning to Ullmann's earlier suggestion. "What you're suggesting overturns a thousand years of history. We Germans have never done anything like this before."

"We know it worked for the Romans."

"Up to the point we destroyed them," said Felix.

Ullmann pressed his hands together. "We had magic then, my lord. Now all we have is muscle, like the Romans had. In a straight fight, it served them well enough."

"An empire." The Romans had carried their eagle standards to some unlikely places, and it had only been the dark woods, deep rivers and raw magic that had prevented his barbarian ancestors from being overrun. "I don't think I want the Carinthian leopard to travel at the head of an army and conquer my neighbours."

"But my lord would like them to leave your lands alone."

"Yes." Felix looked again at the map, the smallness of Carinthia. "Professional armies are expensive, and from what I've read of the Romans, they had to conquer to keep the money coming in."

"It doesn't have to be a big army, my lord. It might even be better if it was small. Elite soldiers, trained to the hilt. A cohort or two. And you'd have your own Praetorians to guard you. The cohorts would support local militias; that way, you'd be able to field a large number of men quickly, anywhere."

"You've thought about this a lot, and you've clearly read your Roman histories. I'll have to see."

"There's something else my lord needs to consider, too."

"Which is?"

"Spies, my lord." Ullmann circled the border with his finger. "We need eyes that will see for us, and tell us about those plotting against us in secret."

Felix made some sort of decision. Again, it was a risk, but doing nothing would be worse. "I want you to find me another dozen people, just like you, and bring them here. Don't tell them what I want them for, just ask them if they're willing to give their lives in the service of the prince. Because, if they say yes, that's exactly what they might end up doing." Felix nodded towards the door. "Time is short, Master Ullmann."

"Mas . . .?" Ullmann jumped to his feet, almost knocking the chair over in his haste. "My lord."

He almost ran to the door and out. Felix realised he'd found a fanatic, more deadly in his way than the berserker tendencies of Büber. What could he do with loyalty like that?

384

He wondered just how many more Ullmanns there were out there, wasting their time and talents ploughing the fields and tending chickens. How could he find them, and use them?

52

Even Büber couldn't help but look up. The peaks either side were enormous white-wrapped spires that pierced the clouds and tore swags of fog free so they could roil down the high Alps and into the valley below.

The river rumbled and fluttered, fed by fast-flowing tributaries that tumbled as waterfalls from the rock walls. The spring melt-waters had only just started to form this far up in the mountains, nowhere near full spate, but it looked full and cold.

He'd been this way before, and knew how far he had to go, but then again, the route would have been obvious to even the most inexperienced lowlander. There were the mountains soaring either side of the flat-bottomed valley. There was the river at the bottom. There was a path that went along next to it. Trees covered everything that wasn't rock or river or road. That was it.

The air was clean and sharp. No taint of smoke on the wind, no greasy, meaty smell of cooking flesh, no cloying reminder of alchemy and death. It was, for a while, easier to forget than it was to remember.

Sometimes he rode the horse. Mostly, he led it. There'd been a Roman road here once, but that had all but gone in the annual cycle of flooding and freezing. And these were debatable lands, nominally on the edges of Carinthia, of no use to the Bavarians, and outside the Franks' influence, which ended where the mountains started.

Then there were the dwarves to consider.

He stopped by the bank of the river, ostensibly to refill his water skin, but also to watch the half-sunken remains of a small boat bob past, surrounded by grey wavelets.

His horse tore at the scrubby grass behind him as the broken bow dipped down, then re-emerged, lower in the water than before. There was no obvious cause for the damage: it seemed just to have been knocked about as if it had gone uncontrolled through one too many rapids. He kept his eye on it until it was well downstream, heading towards the warmer plains to the north.

There weren't any rapids on the Enn until well beyond the bridge, and he couldn't account for the wreck. Filling the skin, he splashed some of the freezing water on his face and neck, wiping it across his stubbly head.

His horse, a stubby cob still with its shaggy winter coat, shook its head and made its bridle rattle. It raised its head at the same time Büber did, to look around and check that nothing was coming to eat it.

There used to be giants here; still might be for that matter. He didn't know if they were magical or mundane, but he'd bet a bag of silver shillings on some kind of enchantment.

Büber slung the waterskin on the saddle and patted the horse's neck.

"Steady now."

The horse whiffled at him, and he took hold of the reins inside his misshapen fist.

Apart from his horse and a couple of eagles soaring spread-feathered above him, he could see no sign of any other creature. His gaze bored into the forest, but nothing stared back.

There might be wolves out there somewhere, though it was early in the year for them to have crossed the pass. And wolves couldn't sink a boat, of course.

No; as Büber had found to his cost, men made the worst monsters. He unhooked his crossbow from its place near the pommel, and hung a quiver of bolts from his belt.

He walked on, passing a well-weathered mile marker a little further along. If he'd been numerate, he could have counted them all the way from Juvavum and known how far he had left to go. As it was, the corroded stone was mute. All it told him was that it was a mile since the last one, and a mile until the next.

A noise up ahead broke through the rushing of the river and hushing of the trees. He could hide himself, but concealing his horse wouldn't be so easy. He tugged on its bridle and pointed its head to the valley-side, where the forest was thicker and a silhouette less likely to show against the shining water.

Crossing what was left of the roadside drainage ditch, he cajoled his horse in among the trees and tied it to a low-hanging branch.

Then – because despite everything, he still valued his life – he moved half a stadia away where he could keep one eye on it and the other on the road.

Büber wasn't an expert with horses. It might not stay quiet even with his best efforts. He cranked the wire on his bow and slid a bolt into place. At least he could be still, even if his mount couldn't.

Then he waited patiently. A handcart rolled into view, piled with parcels. It was being pushed by a man, and every time the wheel went around, it groaned. Just when Büber thought to relax, he saw another figure, a woman. Then trailing behind her, one, two, three children. Following her, another man – no cart this time, just his back to carry his load. Then still more. The few ponies and donkeys were heavily laden.

He quickly lost count of the procession. From the set of their shoulders, their subdued voices, their whole demeanour, the people weren't enjoying their journey, and since all of them, from the youngest to the oldest, seemed to be carrying something, it looked like they'd packed up their possessions and walked out of their homes.

Which they probably had, but he was never going to find out why by skulking around in the woods. He broke cover, moving back towards the road, but no one seemed to spot him until he stepped out of the trees.

The stragglers of the column eyed him cautiously, and his loaded crossbow even more so. He'd be damned if he was going to unstring it any time soon, though, so he just held it loosely, his hand nowhere near the trigger.

"Where are you from?" he asked. No one seemed to want to stop, so he was forced to walk along with them, back the way he'd come.

"Who's asking?" said an old man. His load was tiny, but his back was bent with the effort and he was using two sticks to help him along. If, as Büber suspected, they hadn't long left their town, this man was soon going to find himself struggling on alone.

"Master Büber, huntmaster of Carinthia."

"Is that so?" The man turned his good eye on Büber and totted up the number of scars. "There's nothing for you up there."

"You're from Ennsbruck, aren't you?" Büber looked down the line. "You're abandoning it.

"Nothing for *us* there any more, either, Master Büber." He said Büber's name with no little sarcasm. "So we're going down the valley, to start somewhere else."

"Why?"

"The magic's gone, if you hadn't noticed."

Büber bit his tongue. Actually put the tip of it between his teeth and closed his jaws around it until it hurt and he knew he wasn't going to spear the old man through the heart.

"Yes," he finally managed. "I had noticed."

"Go and ask the dwarves why we're leaving. You'll get your answer from them."

Büber stopped and the man walked on. The last few people drifted by, stepping around and ignoring him, and soon enough they were swallowed up by the bend in the road.

"What the fuck is going on?" he said out loud. He turned again and went to collect his horse, but this time he kept his crossbow in his hand. He led the animal back onto the path, and continued up the valley.

He kept hearing things: a keening noise, almost a lament, that carried on the wind. It could have been the sound of a high col catching an updraft, or he could have imagined it.

Eventually, the trees thinned out into grazing land. Ennsbruck sat in the fold of the river in the distance, seemingly secure behind its ramparts. There should have been a pall of woodsmoke above it, but there was nothing.

As he approached the city, he passed goats and long-haired cattle eking out a rough existence between drystone walls, waiting for the brief, rich months of summer. Their herdsmen appeared to have left them. They'd abandoned their wealth, and no one did that lightly.

The bridge that gave Ennsbruck its name was stone and solid, flat and supported by two piers. It ran right up to the gatehouse, and the gates were open, entirely unguarded. And the boats tied up by the river bank appeared to have all been deliberately holed; they sat wallowing on the gravel bar, their ropes wet and slack.

Büber looked at the gates, at the town inside, at the lateness of the hour, and decided that he wasn't going to get a better offer of a decent bed, perhaps some left-overs, and maybe even a forgotten bottle of schnapps.

He led his horse through the gates, its hooves sounding hollow as they passed under the arch, and then he stood for a moment, wondering which way to turn. A cat, black and sleek, trotted across the cobbles on the way from one alley to another. It stopped dead in the middle of the street as it spotted the man and his horse, green eyes wide. Then it was off again, and vanished from view.

It had been years since he'd been there, yet he vaguely recalled a marketplace beneath the wall, set in an open space at the end of the right-turn.

When he got there, he found the stalls tucked way against the corner turret, the market empty, and a crude picture of a lidded beer mug swinging in the wind from one of the buildings. He needed to see to the horse's feed, but there was no reason why he couldn't do it on a full stomach.

He tried the door, and it opened. Light showed through the dusty window glass: a crude bar, barrels behind it, rough tables and chairs, and a cold fireplace. The ceiling was low enough that he had to duck, though this was no cellar. He laid his crossbow on the end of the bar as he went around the edge of it, and tapped the barrels with a knuckle. One was half-full, and he poured himself a beer.

Why would the owner just up and go? Ask the dwarves, the man had said, but the dwarves lay at the other end of the valley, almost a hundred miles away.

Büber raised his mug, tasted the beer, then drank. He came up for air with a frothy moustache, which he wiped away with his hand. He'd ask the dwarves when he got to Farduzes.

A movement beyond the window caught his eye, something that was more than his horse striking one of its hooves against the cobbles. He ducked down behind the bar, then half-rose to collect his bow.

As he did so, he caught sight of the vague shape of a man patting down his saddlebags. He guessed that when Ennsbruck emptied, not everyone had gone. What was left was likely to be the dregs.

He raised himself up again, sighting over the bar. The man was still there, working his way through each and every pocket, delving down to the bottom of the deepest bags. Not that he was going to find anything of particular value, or anything that couldn't be found in one of the abandoned houses, but it was Büber's horse and Büber's meagre belongings.

He didn't like thieves, no matter what. He'd paid his way in the world, and saw no reason why everyone else shouldn't. Moving quickly and quietly, he leant around the door, bow first.

"Stop there," he said, but the man ducked under the horse and started off at a rare turn of speed across the market square.

So he wanted to make it interesting? In two steps, Büber had a clear view of the man's back and the bob of his blond hair. The idiot didn't seem to realise that he should dodge from side to side to make hitting him more of a challenge. The huntmaster raised the bow-stock to his shoulder and squeezed off a shot.

The bolt blurred and spun across the distance between them. The whirring noise it made preceded it, but only just.

The edge of the broadhead sliced a line of flesh on the outside of the man's thigh, and he stumbled as he ran. Büber cranked the bow again and lined up another quarrel.

"Next one's through your heart," he said, and this time his target skittered to a halt, still feet away from any useful cover.

Büber walked over, and when he was close enough to guarantee his next shot would be an easy hit, he told the man to strip.

The man had his back to Büber, and there was blood staining his breeks, the cloth gaping around the wound. "Strip?"

"You've stolen from me. I'd like back whatever you've taken."

The man finally turned, and it wasn't a man after all, but a boy of somewhere around Ullmann's age, thin faced, thin limbed, thin fingered.

"I've taken nothing."

Büber was reasonably certain it was a lie, and he didn't have to worry about niceties, either. "I can take whatever you've got from your corpse."

"You're not from around here," observed the boy. The gash he'd been given had to hurt, but he played it as if it was of little consequence.

Never one for small talk, Büber raised the bow and tickled the trigger with his finger. "If you wanted to parley like a Frank, you should have announced yourself. Now, strip or find yourself with an extra hole in your head. I'm not in the mood."

"It's cold."

"Find someone who gives a fuck."

"You shot me."

Büber sighed. "I could count to five, but I'm likely to lose my way. So I'll just kill you now."

The boy put up his hands. "I'll do it, I'll do it."

He did. Neither Büber's crossbow nor his forensic gaze wavered. Yes, it was humiliating, and now there was blood dripping down the kid's skinny leg as far as his knee, but the huntmaster was unmoved.

"Step away. Over to the wall. Put your nose on the stonework."

Barefoot, bare everything, he complied, and the huntmaster shook out the boy's clothes. There was Büber's purse with his silver and copper, and there was also a thin leather thong with a seashell tied to it.

The money, he'd expected that: the rat-faced kid was a thief and a chancer, after all. The bracelet? That was a different level of injury. Sticking him to the wall would have been surprisingly easy, and momentarily satisfying. He considered it, but eventually decided against it.

Picking the bolt from the stock, he slid it back inside the quiver, before easing the bowstring off the catch. He looked up and saw the boy watching him.

"Did I say you could turn around?"

"You're not going to murder me?"

Büber's eye twitched. Murder was a strong word. Justice was another. "There's no law here except my own scruples, and I'd be within my rights." He held up his recovered loot. "Keep away from me, boy. I'm in a dangerous mood, and you've used up what little mercy I keep about me."

"Can I put my clothes back on?"

"You can prance naked from now until midsummer's day for all I care." Büber turned his back on him and stalked back across the empty market square to the beer cellar.

He patted his horse as he passed, then poured himself another mug. This time he sat at a window seat where he could keep an eye on things. The thief, all pale goose-flesh, picked up his pile of clothes and hurried away with them, out of the square and out of sight.

Büber held up the shell on its strap, and watched it twirl in the muddy, fading light. He didn't want to lose the token, but he didn't want to wear it either — too easily damaged. He silently toasted the woman who'd given it to him, and drank deep.

Time to move: find somewhere to stable the horse, and probably bed down next to it, the prospects of a soft mattress stolen from him by the mere presence of the boy. No wonder the rest of the town didn't want him along with them. He was an irritant, incompetent and petulant, not worth the energy to deal with once and for all, but like a biting fly, draining.

He led the horse around the square and down side streets, eventually spotting something that resembled livery doors. He had to shoulder them open, but they gave, and inside was everything he needed. Unbuckling the tack, he set to brushing the animal's brown flanks down.

As he worked, he was aware of being watched.

"I could have killed you, and you wouldn't have known," said the boy.

Büber shook his head and carried on his broad arm sweeps.

"Come on then, little assassin. Come closer with your sharp blade and I'll leave it in your chest."

The boy stayed by the doors. "I could have had a bow."

"If you had both a bow and the wit to use it, I'd have strangled you with the cord by now. What do you want?"

"You're not scared of me, are you? You should be."

Büber peeled the mat of horse-hair from the brush and let it fall to the floor. "Scared of you? If it'll make you go away, yes, I'm terrified. Now fuck off."

"I know all the houses, been in most of them. Know all the routes across the roofs and alleys. They always suspected it was me, but they could never pin anything on me."

"Of course they couldn't. That's why they tied you up and left you here."

"They didn't."

"Then what are the rope-marks on your wrists and ankles? They're fresh, made this morning, and you've a few bruises where they had to hold you down to do it. It's a mark of their basic decency that they didn't execute you because, for certain, that day was coming. Now . . ." – Büber turned and put his hand out for his bow, resting on a loose-tied bale of hay – "last chance. Leave me alone. I can break all of your fingers, hamstring you, break your knees in a way that'll mean you'll never walk straight again, or just cut out your tongue. Pick one."

"I can tell you why they left."

"You could have told me that at the very beginning, and I'm likely to have believed you. You could have shown me where the stable was, but instead you decided to rob me. You could have joined me for a drink. You had the chance to make a good impression on me, even if just to make me trust you. You didn't. Instead you just carried on like you always have done. No wonder they hate you."

The boy scowled hard. "They don't hate me. They're afraid of me. It's different."

Büber was weary, weary of everything, but right now so very weary of this. Most likely Ennsbruck didn't even have a lock-up, or the boy would have still been shut in it. "Remember when I said 'last chance'?"

He walked towards the doors, and the boy scuttled backwards to the house on the far side of the narrow street. Büber swung the first door shut, then the other, and dropped a pitchfork through the hangers to serve as a bar.

"Don't you want to know why they left?" came the plaintive cry. "I can tell you. I was listening."

Büber didn't bother answering, just went back to his horse and threw a blanket over its back.

"Mister? Don't you want to know?" The door rattled, then rattled again.

"Mister?"

53

No one else was in the library, and it was perfectly still. The great scaffolding had risen up from the floor and attached itself to the galleries, spreading out like the branches of an oak, reaching the apex of the dome. Ropes and buckets hung suspended from the framework, ready for the day's work of chipping away plaster and opening out the oculus.

They'd started the previous evening, and in concert with their brethren outside, had made a small hole in the very top of the dome. Thaler could look up, and where no natural light had penetrated for a thousand years, a thin beam of pale blue shone through and washed against the inside.

Mirrors, thought Thaler. We can't control the sun, but we can predict its movements. We can intercept the light and reflect it to where we want it most.

The beam brightened as the sun came out. Motes of dust danced in the shaft of light, and something attracted the librarian's attention: a picture painted onto the pale plasterwork, of clouds and sky and distant mountains.

Upside down.

Despite everything, he started to climb. The scaffolding was substantial, perfectly secure. There were even ladders between the platforms, tied on with stout cord to stop them moving. The first level wasn't so bad. The foot of the ladder was on the floor, its top against the planking. He could crawl onto that, on his hands and knees. The next one was more difficult, in that the ladder started in the centre of the frame, and ended dangling over the abyss. He'd have to turn around at the top to get to the next safe space.

He hung on to one of the uprights. The clouds in the picture were moving. Moving, as if they were real clouds. He cursed himself for his timidity, and climbed the ladder to the third level. He was sweating and breathing fast by the time he made it. The labourers made it look so easy, hanging off the edge with only a single foot to support their weight and a casual hand to steady themselves, throwing tools to each other and catching them without worry.

He was only as far as the first gallery, and there were plenty more to go. The tower seemed to be narrowing, so as well as having to manoeuvre backwards onto each platform, he had to swing himself out to even start the next climb.

Above him, always above him, the clouds blew by.

Finally, he was level with the image. It wasn't just a picture of the sky. It *was* the sky, projected all around him – most obvious where it was best illuminated, but in fact running in a band – faint in places – around the whole circumference of the dome. He ignored his sweat-slick palms and his drum-beat heart for a moment, and realised he could spot the towers of the fortress on one wall, and the spine of the White Tower on another.

The sun went in, and the picture faded, though it was still just visible. When the sun came out again, the brightness flashed and the images grew in clarity. He could see outside, inside.

It wasn't a painting. It wasn't even a magical painting. Somehow, the opening of the roof had made this phenomenon possible. A bird flew past, and he could track its flight around the dome, and away. Things were distorted: angles weren't true and straight lines appeared curved. That wasn't the point though.

"How is this possible?" he asked the deserted building. Not quite deserted, as it turned out.

"Who's up there?" called a voice.

"Master Thaler. Who's down there?"

"Mr Wess, sir. I came to open up."

Thaler risked leaning over the edge of the platform, and called down. "That can wait a little while longer. How are you with heights?"

Wess was much better with them than Thaler. He climbed like a squirrel, and his vigorous action made the whole structure shake. Thaler was dry-mouthed all over again by the time the under-librarian reached him. It was really a very long way up, and Wess seemed unconcerned about hanging off inconsequential handholds on his way.

In the end, Thaler had to close his eyes and hold on tightly until the scaffolding stopped rattling. There was one last solid thump as the man joined him, and then Thaler risked opening his eyes again.

"Look at the wall and tell me what you see."

Wess leant forward – and out – to get a better look. When he started to tilt his head sideways, Thaler knew that he wasn't just imagining things.

"That's astonishing." Wess stretched over and waved his hand in front of the wall, watching as his shadow blocked out some of the scene. Another cloud drifted over the face of the sun, and the image dimmed. "Oh."

"Wait just a moment," said Thaler, "and please be careful."

The ribbon of cloud passed by, and the panorama was restored.

"How . . .?"

"I don't know."

"But . . ."

"I know. It must have something to do with the light coming in through the small hole, and then . . ." Thaler was mystified. "It's not magic."

"It looks like magic, Master Thaler."

"That's the one thing it can't be, Mr Wess. Do we have any works in the library on the property of light and the nature of the eye?"

"We have Euclid and Ptolemy, among others. But, Master Thaler, doesn't light come from the eye? At least, that's what Empedocles said, and Plato agreed." Wess tried again to make shadows on the wall.

"I'm becoming increasingly disenchanted with the Greeks' theories," said Thaler: "they appear to be so very often wrong. For one thing, if our eyes did indeed emit light, then where does darkness come from? It seems self-evident that light comes from objects that make light, and rays springing forth from our own eyes are an unnecessary complication. In fact," he continued, "we seem to have been wallowing in ignorance for far too long."

Wess stopped making shapes and turned towards Thaler. In doing so, he now had his back to the unguarded edge, and appeared oblivious to the danger. "We're educated men, Master Thaler. Ignorant is the one thing we're not."

"I – and please do hold onto something, Mr Wess – am as guilty as the next man. I read Aristotle, Euclid and Plato, and clearly I take note of what they say. But some of their conjectures are contradictory, in that they describe the nature of things in different ways, and they cannot all be true. We haven't actually thought about these things for ourselves."

Wess was troubled by the whole idea, and Thaler hardly less so.

"What do you suggest we do then?"

"I'm at a loss. I mean, who am I to challenge the greatest geometers of any age? How would I do it? And yet, what they say about light coming from the back of the eye and illuminating the objects so that we can see them? Over here we can see the Bell Tower of the White Fortress, yet our eyes aren't even looking at it – just an image of it on the wall of the library."

Wess rubbed his hand over his chin. "Master Thaler, there has to be an explanation."

"Of course. But how to arrive at one? That, my good man, is the question." Thaler momentarily looked down, and wished that he hadn't. "Open up the library. We have work to do today."

"Are you going to be all right?" asked Wess, his gaze straying to Thaler's death-grip on one of the uprights.

"Oh, I'm fine. No help needed. None. Not at all." He nodded emphatically. "Off you go. I'll just stay here and study the phenomena a little while longer. Yes."

"As long as you're sure, Master Thaler." Wess sat on the edge of the platform above the ladder and lowered his feet until they made contact. "See you at the bottom."

He was as vigorous climbing down as he'd been climbing up, and the structure vibrated with his footsteps. Thaler felt a curious weightless sensation in both his legs and the pit of his stomach, as if he were already falling, but he wasn't really going anywhere. And that was the problem. The workmen would be wanting their scaffolding back shortly, and an overweight librarian perched at the top like an eagle's chick who refused to leave the nest was an impediment that they'd probably rather do without.

"Master Thaler?" called Wess. "Mistress Morgenstern is here. She has books."

"Good morning, Master Thaler." Sophia paused. "What in heaven's name are you doing up there?"

"I'm investigating a . . . a thing," he called back.

"Well, stop it at once and come down. I've got the books Father bought from Thomm and they need to go back into the catalogue."

There was nothing for it. He could be lowered from the roof like a sack of flour at a mill, and suffer endless ridicule and shame, or he could climb down by himself. It was perfectly safe: Wess had proved that. As long as he kept a hold of something at all times, it would be absolutely no trouble at all. Child's play, even.

He started, and quickly found there really was no substitute for looking down and seeing where he was going. Closing his eyes was no good at all. The only thing that got him through the whole stuttering, terrifying descent, was the thought that he was now the master librarian, and that he needed to show some backbone.

If he'd sweated on the way up, he was saturated by the time he reached solid ground again. His whole body was trembling, and he had to resist the overwhelming urge to sink to his knees and kiss the stone flags.

He looked between his feet, and saw shapes and whorls embedded there. Some of them looked like snails, some like creatures he'd never seen except frozen in the smoothed, sawn rock. How did that happen? How did living animals end up trapped in something so permanent?

"Master Thaler?" Sophia's hand was on his shoulder. "Have some water, please. You look terrible."

He grimaced and tried to straighten up. "I assure you, Mistress, I am in rude health."

"You can assure me all you like." She motioned to Wess for a chair. "I'm inclined to believe the evidence of my eyes."

"Which, it appears, do not radiate light as the Greeks suggested."

"Didn't Euclid disagree with Plato?" Sophia forced him down into the chair. "Though it was all forms with him."

"Oh, I think they were probably both wrong." He took the cup of water from her and drained it. Beer would have been nicer; the water tasted a little odd. "Almost everything we know is wrong."

"Almost?"

"Trying to work out which parts are true is going to be a lifetime's work." Thaler handed the cup back, smacking his lips. He tested the ground under his feet. It neither shook nor rattled. Perhaps he should only undertake climbing again as a last resort. "You said something about books?"

"First, Master Thaler, the sefer?"

He had enough energy left to raise an eyebrow. "You're not still going on about those, are you?"

She pointed to the long table where she'd placed a pile of folios. "I'll even write the letter of authorisation for you. Frederik, this is important. If you want Jewish men to help you in here, you're going to have to give them up."

Thaler sighed. "Very well." He dragged himself upright and walked the few feet to the table, where he sat down again. Sophia gathered ink, pen and parchment, and started to scratch out German words.

He watched her for a while – she had a good penstroke and wrote more evenly and cleanly than many a librarian – and then turned his attention to the returned books.

Speaking of Plato, there was a copy of *The Republic* among them: he heaved it down in front of him and checked it for damage. He turned the pages carefully, then looked down the spine. There was a fine copy, also, of the *Commentaries on the Gallic War*. Both books together would have been the start of a good private library, Greek and Latin. Of course, his library had several copies of both, and Thaler began to see a pattern: Thomm had only taken books that were duplicated. The master librarian's attitude to his former colleague softened just a little.

"Ah, Mr Thomm. If only you could have kept it in your breeks."

"Sorry, Master Thaler?" murmured Sophia, not looking up.

"Nothing. Nothing at all." He reached for the third book, a much smaller volume, almost duodecimo in size. Looking first at the cover, he then opened it to peer at the title page.

She must have felt him stiffen. "What?"

"This book. Where did it come from?"

She glanced over. "That's the one my father received instead of *On the Balance*. He clearly doesn't want anything to do with it, so I brought it to you."

Thaler slid it across to her. "Can you read it?"

She put down her pen and held the page closer to the lantern. "It's in Persian. It says, ah, *Balance of Wisdom*. Yes, that's right. Not *On the Balance* at all. There, it might have even been an honest mistake." She ran her finger right to left across the curved lines and uprights. "Abu Ali al-Hasan ibn al-Hasan ibn al-Haytham. That's the author. You seem very interested in a book you can't read."

"The frontispiece," said Thaler, "look at the picture. There is a man, presumably this al-Haytham, at the top of a tower. Can you see what he's doing?"

She leant in very close. "He's dropping things. Spheres. You can see some of them on the ground at the bottom."

Thaler pointed to dotted lines proceeding from the man's hands. "And these objects here are those same spheres in flight. They get progressively further apart. Is that what happens?"

Sophia looked up at the gallery from which Thaler had thrown the lunch-pails off the edge. "It might be."

He took the book back and turned several pages until there was a diagram. It seemed to be of a large ball of fire surrounded by concentric circles, to which single smaller circles were attached.

"And what's this?"

"I can't tell without reading it."

"Or this?" The same ball of fire was juxtaposed with stars, but, without being able to read the text, he didn't know what it meant.

"Frederik, calm down. I'm not that good at Persian, but my father is an expert. When he gets here, he can read some to you. But remember, this isn't what you're supposed to be doing: you should be cataloguing, working out what we have, separating them into subjects." She pried the book out of his hand. "Where would you put this?"

"I don't know." He was angry, with her, with this long-dead al-Haytham, with himself for having spent his entire life believing the explanations of Greek philosophers. "Astronomy?"

"Then put it in the catalogue. Shelve it with the other astronomy books. That's where it'll be when you need it." Sophia picked up her pen again, but only after moving the Persian book to her far side, out of Thaler's reach.

While they'd been talking – arguing – the library had filled up with people. Workmen were laying siege to the lowest ladder on the tower, and librarians were carrying piles of books in their arms, both away from and towards the table, loading and unloading barrows with quiet efficiency. Around the table itself, the more senior librarians had taken their seats, and the cataloguing had already begun.

Up above, out on the roof and out of sight, skilled hands assaulted the cover of the oculus. All of a sudden, what had been a tiny hole became a fist-sized space, which in turn widened out rapidly.

Light, natural light, poured in like a flood.

Everyone stopped and looked up, including Thaler. The effect was startling, eye-watering. A bright oval struck the side of the dome, and partially illuminated everything. The lanterns they were using looked dimmer, and the library larger and more solid.

Sophia smiled. "Vayomer elohim yehi or."

Thaler didn't ask for a translation, because he was already thinking again about the mirrors they'd need to put up.

Big mirrors.

54

The first thing Büber saw when he opened the door in the morning was the boy's face wearing an expression of pugnacious desperation. He almost closed the door again in the hope that it would go away, but no, fuck it. Why should he?

He was hungry, and needed something to eat. The horse was catered for; there was probably only so much bulky animal feed that the townspeople could carry with them, and they'd rightly surmised there'd be grass lower down the valley. Human food? Not so much.

He went back into the stable for his crossbow, and the quiver of bolts, and strapped on his sword, making sure his knife was on his belt too. All that effort for one kid. He dragged the door mostly shut behind him and stalked down the narrow street, all too aware that he had a shadow.

Büber went back to the same tavern on the corner of the market square. He poured himself a beer and let it settle while he went through to the back room. There wasn't much: pickled eggs, pickled vegetables, a jar of what looked like boiled fruit. The shelves were unsurprisingly empty. Certainly no sausage, or sauerkraut. Nor, apparently, plates.

He sat in the morning sunshine, behind the dusty windows, with his open jars and ate his fill. He'd not had to hunt or forage for it, so that even though it was mostly disagreeable stuff that was still hanging around after a long, hard winter, he didn't mind. The beer helped, too.

All the while, he was watched.

Perhaps this was a tactic the boy used often, standing there and staring but not crossing that thin line between being a pain in the arse and an outright criminal. Even this far up into the mountains, outside of any palatinate's control, people had a code of law and they stuck to it. No barbarians here.

It was meant to be intimidating, but it didn't stir Büber to either fear or anger. A little while longer, and he'd be gone. He finished up, wiped his hands on his breeks and fixed the stoppers back on the jars.

The boy followed him all the way back to the livery. Büber left the doors wide open while he fitted the saddle and fastened the bridle. He unhooked his weapons and tied them on, then put the saddlebags over the patient beast's back.

He was ready, and he'd not had to exchange a single word. One last look around, to make sure he hadn't left anything, one last pat of his pocket to make sure his purse and shell bracelet were still there.

They were, and there was no reason to stay a moment longer. He led the horse out and they walked side by side up the alley to the space behind the gatehouse.

The boy, from following him, darted in front and stood between him and the open gate, the bridge visible beyond.

"You can't just leave."

Büber considered his options. "Out of the way."

"You have to take me with you."

"No, I don't. Now, get out of the fucking way, before I make you."

The boy hopped from foot to foot, the cut on his leg now hidden behind a clean pair of breeks. "Take me with you, or . . ."

"Or what? You're no use to me, boy. You're too stupid to learn that what you want isn't what you need." He mounted up, putting his foot in the stirrup and heaving himself onto the saddle. "This isn't some sort of fairytale that mothers tell their children, complete with happy ending. Do you know why that is?"

"N . . . no," the boy stammered.

"Because all the fairies are fucking dead, and you're a complete shit. You want to be king of Ennsbruck, the big man in town? Well, you are, until a bigger, uglier shit wants to take it from you. Good luck."

He dug his heels in, and the horse trotted forward. The boy had to dodge aside or get trampled. A moment of shadow as he passed under the gatehouse, and then he was on the bridge. The mountains were ahead of him, behind him, and to his left.

People. That was the problem. Maybe he'd have better luck with the dwarves.

Across the bridge, left towards the pass. Ennsbruck's black walls slowly receded, and he began to relax, just a little. He looked around once, to make sure. The road behind him was empty.

Then it was lost in the trees, and his path went onwards. After a while, he dismounted and walked, his long legs eating up mile marker after mile marker. He wasn't concentrating on anything but each foot fall, but he still heard the racket ahead while he was far off, the sound of many voices all shouting at once.

He stopped, listened, and decided they were stationary. Leading his horse off the path again, he tied it to a tree, and stalked off, weapons ready to see who it was.

They were trying to light a fire, and arguing over the best way of doing so. Getting a flame didn't seem to be a problem – from his hiding place, Büber could see sparks and puffs of white smoke – but nothing to show that they'd caught so much as a pile of kindling alight.

The men themselves looked odd. Not just because of what they wore, which seemed ill-fitting, but because they all had a way of moving that made them look drunk. They stumbled, dropped things, and were all talking at the tops of their voices, growling and barking orders at each other that none paid the slightest attention to.

There was an awful lot of beard going on, too. Germans didn't do beards: neither did the Franks, and the effete Italians shaved all the time.

Then the penny dropped, and Büber eased himself from cover.

His sudden appearance made the men scurry for their discarded packs: every one of them had an axe or a hammer. Büber slowed down and held his hands out wide. No, he wasn't going to put down his sword or his bow, but he wasn't going to use them unless he had to.

He approached them slowly. They were all short, some well below his shoulder, but he expected that. They were now silent, as was he. He wasn't at all sure they'd understand him if he spoke. His actions would have to speak for him.

They parted and stood around him as he crouched down next to their lamentable attempt at a fire. He tutted, and sorted through the wood, discarding the green timber and the stuff that was thoroughly rotten, until only the dry wood remained. Breaking it into smaller lengths, he piled it up, leaving a hole in its centre.

That, he filled with crumbling bark and dry leaves from under the canopy.

Caught up in the ritual of fire-making, he pulled out his knife. Hands stiffened around axe-hafts, until he picked up one of the sticks and started to cut it into curls with strong, steady strokes of the knife-blade.

He was done. His own flint was back in his saddlebags, so he mimed to his audience the sharp, short motions of raising a spark. One of them reached into a pocket and handed him a small tin and a rough metal rod.

Büber wasn't quite sure what to do with them. He popped the lid of the tin off with a thumb and sniffed the dark grey powder inside. It smelt of stone. The rod was hard, and he scraped his knife across it. Fat orange stars, brighter than the day, crackled and smoked thin trails through the air.

He didn't want to look stupid any more than his hosts did, so he did what he thought was best: put a generous pinch of powder on the kindling and tried to light it with sparks from the rod.

The result was slightly more enthusiastic than he'd anticipated, and the hairs on the backs of his hands crisped with the wash of heat as a puff of acrid, sulphurous smoke billowed out.

He coughed, and kept on coughing, even while he remembered to feed the nascent fire with sticks and more bark. Then it caught properly, a tentative tongue of fire licking out and tasting the broken branches above.

A little longer, and he was able to sit back on his haunches and let the flames do the rest. Büber took a moment to study the onlookers: there were as many of them as he used to have fingers – shaggy haired, bearded men, alternately staring at the fire and scowling at each other.

He hadn't made a mistake: their dress, their weapons, the way they looked. Another foot off their height, and they'd be dwarves. Which is what they were, or at least had been once.

"Peter Büber," he said. "The Prince of Carinthia sends his regards."

They looked as one to the man-dwarf-thing who'd handed him the tinder box.

"You speak German?" asked Büber.

"Yes."

They looked miserable. Not just unhappy, but defeated. There was something of himself in their slumped, sullen expressions.

"You were trying to light a fire. Now you have one." He hadn't heard of dwarves ever having problems making a fire before, but he conceded that dwarvish hearths burnt black rock, not green wood. "If I could share it with you, I'd be grateful."

The spokesman – spokesdwarf – grunted his assent. "You know who we are?"

"I think I've worked it out. If it makes you feel better, I could pretend I haven't."

"What's the point, human?" He kicked the ground, perhaps wishing it was honest stone.

"I need to get my horse. We've lots to tell each other, so don't go away."

He almost sprinted down the road and into the forest. He found his bemused horse, and led it back out.

"They've grown," he told it, patting its neck. "They've grown and they don't know why."

404

He wracked his memory for the other preternatural characteristics of dwarves: fierce, untrusting, greedy almost to the point of evil, expert miners and smiths, cunning makers of machines. By gaining height, what had they lost?

The pillar of white smoke was starting to fail by the time he returned, and he fed the fire with more wood, placing green timber around it to dry it out. They'd have done better collecting the resin-rich branches of the local pines, which burnt hard and fast. He'd point that out to them later.

As he squatted by the fire, he held his hands out to its heat. An instinctive gesture. He wasn't cold.

The German-speaking dwarf looked and frowned. "Your fingers. You lack many of them."

"Most of them ended up in the belly of some beast or other. A couple I lost to a sword-blow. That was . . ." He put his hands in his pockets. Again, instinctive.

"Hard?"

"Yes. Yes, it was."

"And your magicians?"

Büber looked at the iron pot supported by an iron tripod placed over the fire he'd made, and at the wisps of steam rising from its black lip.

"That's not what hunters do. Did. They could have healed me, but then enchanted creatures would've been able to feel me, and either run from me or attack me." He shrugged. "It wasn't what was wanted. Not then."

"Why are we like this?" the dwarf asked suddenly. "Why are we . . .?" It was his turn to struggle with his words.

"Tall."

"Yes. Tall. Big. Long-limbed, ungainly, tottering, fumble-fingered, poor-sighted. Why are we becoming like you?"

"I can't tell you why." Büber breathed out. "Well, maybe I can. Ragnarok. The twilight of the gods. They've gone, and they've taken the magic with them. No more spells, no more unicorns, no more wood and water spirits, no trolls or dragons or anything else with a spark of magic in them. And no more you, so it seems."

"Who told you this?"

"The last sorcerer. Sorceress."

The dwarf snorted.

"I know, I know," said Büber. "If it had been one-eyed Wotan it would have been better. More believable. It happened anyway, just like she said."

"What of the unicorns?"

"They just melted away. Too much magic, I suppose. I don't know about the dragons. Big, flightless lizards? I don't know. We've had problems of our own."

One of the other dwarves put dried meat and mushrooms in the now-boiling pot. He glared at Büber, then stalked away.

"Problems, human? Compared to ours, they're nothing."

The huntmaster thought about getting angry. "Not nothing, no."

The dwarf looked sideways at Büber. "The extinction of your entire race?"

"No. But still not nothing. Let's not get into a pissing contest: I doubt you want my sympathy any more than I want yours."

"True."

They contemplated the fire together.

"What brings you out of Farduzes?" asked Büber.

"Do you know what it's like," said the dwarf – and he growled at the indignity – "to live underground for your whole life, and then to become scared of the weight of rock above you? Of feeling afraid of being buried? Of even having to duck through doorways you once strode through? We are not dwarves any more. We are short, ugly men."

"You're all leaving?"

"In groups. Like this one. When it becomes too much to bear."

"So what do you plan to do?"

The dwarf stared into the heart of the fire. "Survive, I suppose. The best we can. It will be difficult." He leant closer. "Our women are losing their beards."

"Losing their beards." Büber nodded. It was clearly significant. "The people – the humans – at Ennsbruck, have gone as well. Left what they couldn't carry and gone down the valley. They told me to ask the dwarves why."

The dwarf pulled at his beard. "There might have been something said. About closing the pass. Forever."

"They didn't look pleased." Büber picked up a branch from the wood pile and poked the fire. "They scrabbled a sort of existence through farming. Take away the trade they relied on for the extras, and they had no reason to stay."

"They have somewhere to go, human. More than we do."

"You have Ennsbruck now. It's empty, and it's just down the road. You may as well take it." Büber thought of the boy-thief, and of how he would react to the arrival of these short, dark, angry men-things. "You'll have shelter and stone walls to protect you while you get used to living above ground."

The dwarf pulled at his beard again. "That has merit. I can suggest it to the others. It is a small place, though."

"There aren't that many of you."

"It's not us I'm thinking about."

"How many?"

"You don't get our secrets from us that easily, human."

"The Prince of Carinthia," said Büber, "wants to hire you. Whoever will come. There are tunnels under Juvavum, dug by dwarves in Roman times and filled with dwarvish machinery that puts water into every house. The prince wants them working again, and we don't know what we're doing."

"Dwarves don't work for humans."

"You did for the Romans. You fought for the Romans."

"That was a long time ago, and our honour is still tainted."

"I usually find that putting food in your children's bellies commands a higher price than honour." Büber shifted uneasily. He didn't want to have to either run or fight, but there was room enough for only one person to wallow in righteous self-pity, and he'd got there first. "I said I'd put the offer to the Lord of Farduzes."

"The pass is closed, human."

"I'll take my chances."

"Do you value your life so little?"

Büber smiled. "Yes. Death would be some sort of release. What keeps me alive is the thought that I might change my mind at some point, and I'll regret giving up now." He threw a pine-cone into the fire and listened to it hiss and spit.

"Your prince," said the dwarf, "does he have gold?"

"The prince will share it with those who choose to help. They can live with us, or they can build themselves somewhere." Büber relaxed again, and watched the other dwarves bumble around the makeshift camp.

"If you have gold, do you also have silver?"

"We have mountains and forests and lakes and rivers and pasture. We have gold and silver and iron and copper and salt. We have meat and milk and bread. We'll share it all." He scratched at his nose and waited for the obvious question.

"You need us for now." The dwarf had gone from suspicion through hostility and threats to arrive at a rare glimmer of hope. "What if, when the work is complete, your prince changes his mind?"

"Carinthia will share its land and wealth with any of the dwarves of Farduzes who will come. When the prince made his offer, he didn't know how your . . . situation had changed. But he'll honour it, in full, or I'll be a liar and an enemy of Carinthia forever." Felix would keep his word, one way or another; Büber was determined about that.

"And you wish to speak to the Lord of Farduzes?"

"No, I *will* speak to the Lord of Farduzes." Büber emphasised his intention clearly.

"Then I will be your guide." The dwarf nodded just as emphatically. The matter was settled, and there appeared to be no way to argue against it.

Büber scratched at his chin. So much for being alone in the mountains again.

55

The solar was full of men, and not the sort of men that the solar usually saw. It used to be a place where the rich, the powerful, the influential gathered to make small talk and become richer, more powerful and better connected. Not today.

Then the long, sunlit room became slightly fuller, and slightly less manly. The door opened, and the babble of voices, some of them barely broken, cut off as quickly as beer from a barrel when the tap is closed. Felix walked in with Sophia behind him, and navigated his way to the far end of the room through the gap that opened for them between the worn boots, dusty breeks and patched jackets.

Ullmann was waiting for them there.

"Is this enough, my lord? I could have taken more, and I could have taken less, but I used my judgement and presumed two dozen, plus myself, would be a good number to start with. All true Carinthians, with Carinthia's best interests at heart."

Felix looked up at the front row of men. To a soul, they looked honest and poor, hard-working and keen. To them, this was an adventure. To him, they were simply tools to be exploited and used as weapons. Perhaps not simply – it was needful and expedient – but Ullmann had called them and they'd come. He needed those who were loyal not just to him, but to the idea of Carinthia.

"You've done very well, Master Ullmann." The numbers were more than he'd asked for, and it was possible that some of those gathered might have previously gone over to Eckhardt. There was no way of telling; Ullmann's judgement was the only measure he had for now. "Now find me a chair."

Ullmann took one from next to the table, set it in the middle of the room, and steadied Felix as he climbed onto it. Sophia passed him a folded piece of parchment from the stack she was carrying.

The room, already silent, was now still.

Felix looked down at every man there, then at Sophia. If there was a weakness here, it was the lack of women. He already knew there were things a man would tell a woman that he wouldn't tell a man. Ullmann would have to go out onto the streets again and see what he could do.

"Gentlemen," he started, wishing that he would grow and that his voice would deepen so it didn't sound like a mouse's squeak. "Master Ullmann has picked you because you want to protect Carinthia from its enemies. Your duties will be varied. Sometimes it may be taking a message securely from my hand to another's. Sometimes it may be going to another town beyond our borders and sending back information. Sometimes it may be dangerous. Some of you will die. If any of you don't wish to be involved, leave now, with my blessing. If you stay, you are sworn to oaths of loyalty and secrecy."

He waited, and the men in front of him waited too. Not one moved so much as a foot. They did glance at each other though, perhaps seeing if any would bow out. None did.

"Very well. I have letters of authorisation – not enough to go around yet, more will be written – letters that permit you to take anything and do anything in my name. Misuse that freedom of action, and I will have you pressed in the main square, along with your collaborators. Use it properly, and you will be properly rewarded.

For now, you answer to Master Ullmann, and he answers to me. After twenty-five years' service, you will have land and titles for you and your families, because Carinthia rewards its loyal sons."

That was the end of his prepared speech, the one he'd been practising all morning and had only partly written himself. He knew he shouldn't go on, that he should let Ullmann take over, but as he searched the men's faces for a sign that he'd said enough, he caught the opposite mood. He needed to leave his script and say what he felt.

"When the magic failed, we found we were all living in a different world. It's not the world we were born to, any of us, but it's where we have to make our homes now. If we want to keep those homes safe, we have to do things differently. You're our scouts, the ones ahead of the troops. Before we think about raising an army or what weapons to use, you'll be telling us what we have to defend ourselves against. If you fail, Carinthia falls. It's as simple as that."

Perhaps they weren't so used to someone in authority being so candid, and the mood of the room grew uncomfortable. Sophia frowned at him, and pointed subtly towards the floor.

He didn't want to stop. He wanted to explain.

"I'm trying to make you understand how important your role is. It's not more important than what others are trying to do now, but I've told them the same thing. If you're going to build something, you need stone and wood and tools and someone to wield them. If you're missing one of those things, nothing happens. We're at that point. We need to get everything together first. Then we need to build, tall and strong. When the storm comes, which it will, we need to be ready."

Now he was done. He jumped off the chair, and stood next to Sophia as Ullmann took his place.

"This is your first job: to announce a grand council that is to take place here in Juvavum two weeks from today. You'll be divided into pairs. Each pair will go to the furthest part of the land, and call all those with something to say to arrive no later than the full moon. Start with the most distant places, work back towards here.

"Now listen: this isn't just for the earls and merchants and freemen. Anyone who wants to come can come. They can leave their land like a freeman can, and don't you suffer any nonsense: earls' lands won't be earls' lands for much longer, no matter if there's an heir or not to claim them. When the prince calls a grand council, he means what he says. All Carinthians are welcome, and no one's to be left out.

"We'll divide the map up, find horses for those who can ride. Get your warrant from Mistress Sophia, your purse and your assignment from me. Let's form an orderly line."

Felix watched carefully how Ullmann handled the proceedings. His easy manner with the men made them feel like part of a street gang, but beneath that was a hard core of determination. The mostly rough-and-ready apprentices, carters, vendors, stevedores and messengers – they knew who was in charge, this bright and articulate chancer from the countryside.

Sophia, too. She was confident and aloof. She rarely smiled, and when she did, it was at their eagerness and their mistakes, not at them personally. They were much closer in age to her than Felix was: they could be forgiven a little banter, but she did nothing to encourage it. She rewarded politeness and frowned on familiarity, making it abundantly clear that she was untouchable, unassailable, like the fortress walls themselves.

Felix himself was the source of their authority, but he didn't know how to use it. That troubled him. He'd made mistakes already, been betrayed by people he'd trusted, and he had little idea of how to avoid making those same blunders in the future when the stakes were just as great. So much to learn.

Ullmann dissected the map of Carinthia, detailing different pairs to visit the towns and villages, from the Venezia border down to the Bavarian lowlands, from the high valleys to the gates of Wien. If there weren't enough horses in the stables to carry them, they could take them from elsewhere and compensate their owners. If there wasn't enough food in the kitchens to keep them going, they could take it from wherever they wanted. They were to claim swords from the armoury, even if they had no idea how to use them: they could learn another time. Making it up as they went along, much like he was having to.

It felt all very hasty. Perhaps that was a good thing. Making quick decisions meant that at least they were doing something, even if it was wrong.

Suddenly, it was all over. Lists of names had been taken, the amount of money given to each man recorded, their routes through Carinthia noted. They probably wouldn't reach everyone, but they'd catch enough that almost all would feel included.

Ullmann took the lists with him as he went, bowing at the door. "My lord, it'll be done, and done well."

The door closed, the latch clicked, and they were alone.

"Sophia?"

"Yes, Felix?"

"We should be glad he's on our side."

"Who? Max Ullmann?" Sophia crossed in front of him to sit next to the fire. "He's an interesting find, for sure."

"He has the common touch. He inspires people."

"Felix, come over here." She reached out and pulled a chair close to hers, and he reluctantly joined her, fearing a lecture.

"Having a common touch and inspiring people," she said, "makes him sound like he's walked straight out of the pages of Cicero. And I very much doubt he'd enjoy wearing a toga."

"He has ideas. Radical, dangerous ideas."

"All of which you told me about last night, and I told you that the only thing that makes his ideas radical is that they haven't been tried before. Or that they have, but not for a very long time. There's nothing wrong with ordinary people owning their own land: in the Torah, that's one of HaShem's promises, with everyone sitting in the shade of their own vines and fig trees."

"It's not the way we've done things."

"And you know that we can't carry on with that old way. You know that, Felix." She reached out and took his hand. She had strong fingers, and his hand in hers looked small and fragile. "Have courage. I know that your mother died, your father died, your stepmother died, your chamberlain and your earls died, your tutors left you, and your sword-master betrayed you. And died. But I have no intention of going anywhere. Neither does Master Ullmann, or Frederik Thaler, or Peter Büber. Well, perhaps Master Büber isn't the best example to use here."

Felix tried to pull away, but she held him firm. "We can't change our fate," he said. "Everybody dies."

"This is why nothing's changed in a thousand years. Did your Alaric dream for a moment that he could challenge the might of Rome and shatter its walls?"

"It was foretold," said Felix. "It was his destiny."

"If that's what it takes, then I will prophesy over you and tell you that you're destined for even greater feats." She pulled his hand closer, and he had no choice but to move with it. "Did Alaric bring the Roman Empire down on his own?"

"No, but . . ."

"You won't save Carinthia on your own, either. No king, no prince, ever rules alone. Your authority is not diminished when you share it; it grows. Every time you trust someone enough to make them a prince's man, then your power and your reach increases." She leant forward and pressed her forehead against his. "You're not a tyrant, although that temptation will always be with you. Remember that tyrants get overthrown, but a well-loved prince is respected by his people."

"Sophia," he said, "I'm scared."

"We all are. Part of me wishes that you'd stop telling everyone how close we are to disaster, but they have the right to hear it, I suppose."

"Lying to them isn't honest," he mumbled. Her breath was hot on his cheeks, and it made him feel more than a little strange.

"Sometimes you have to lie to them to make them think they're going to win. It only becomes a lie when they lose." She disengaged one of her hands and rested it at the back of his neck. It was both cool and hot at the same time.

"You mean, like when you say I'm destined for greater feats than even Alaric the Goth?"

She laughed, and he laughed too.

"Yes, just like that. There's no one to tell me I'm wrong, though. Felix, you've been left by everyone you knew when you were a child, and you can't be the prince they expected you to be because that's just not possible."

"I'm still a child," he said.

"No. By any measure, German or Jewish, you're a man. You've had blood on your face and blood on your sword. You've fought in battle and you've won. I don't see many children doing that."

He sighed, and let her stroke his neck for a while. He didn't feel like he was in charge – that was the problem. No, *his* problem: despite the moment of madness that had overtaken some of his subjects when Eckhardt had appeared, promising them a return to the old ways, they all seemed content now to maintain the fiction that he was still the Prince of Carinthia.

His princeliness was the only aspect of the past to survive.

"Can you get a pen, and some parchment?" he suddenly asked.

"Yes, yes of course." She fetched them and sat at the table, poised ready to write. The sun broke through for a moment, temporarily dazzling the two of them with its brightness.

He could see more clearly in that brief, blinding interval between one cloud and the next than he had ever seen before. Perhaps Sophia was right: he could become greater than Alaric. But she could just as easily be wrong, and he'd die along with his palatinate.

He'd aim high.

"Write this: a decree against magic. Magic in all its forms and practices is from this time forbidden throughout every part of Carinthia. All magical books and items are forfeit. Various fines and penalties will be levied against those who keep forbidden items and practise forbidden arts. For the crime of necromancy, the punishment will be death by pressing."

Sophia wrote clearly in a neat Gothic script, and added, "By order of Felix I, Prince of Carinthia" at the bottom.

"Would you get another piece of parchment?" he asked, and she fetched one from the drawer while he composed the words in his mind. He stared out of the window for so long that he was only reminded of her presence by her polite cough.

If the first decree of his reign was going to cause trouble, the second was likely to cause worse.

"A proclamation of general freedoms. All those who call themselves Carinthians will be subject to the same laws, the same taxes and the same freedoms granted by Carinthia, without favour. Given the great service shown by the Jews of Juvavum to the palatinate, all Jews within Carinthia are considered true Carinthians, and no man is to say otherwise."

The scratching of her pen stopped. Her chair rasped against the boards, and her footsteps came up behind him. He found himself enveloped in her arms, with her tears running onto his head.

Being a prince meant something, he decided.

56

She went back to the library, to order the scribes to copy more of the spies' letters of authority. She was also clutching Felix's new laws. The one against magic? She was surprised that it had taken him so long, and had been going to suggest it herself in time for the grand council.

The one forbidding discrimination against Jews? It burnt in her hand. She'd never even thought of that. A few concessions, here and there. Wresting the sefer from the grip of the library was as far as she'd hoped, and Thaler, distracted as he always was these days, had already signed the transfer without so much as a murmur.

There, echoing down the alleyways of Juvavum, was the sound of the shofar. How long had it been since that had been heard, proud and joyful outside the walls of the synagogue? She turned the corner into Library Square, and Rabbi Cohen was at the head of a procession – an armed procession, Jews with spears and swords and helmets over their kippah – in which two huge scrolls, ornate with gold and silver, were lifted shoulder-high.

Cohen sounded the great coil of ram's horn and the cantor raised his voice in one of David's psalms. The people – her people – sang to celebrate the liberation of the sefer: the men-at-arms were surrounded by a cloud of women calling out praises at the tops of their voices, and children ran among them all, their Purim rattles finding a new use.

They marched by, heading for Jews' Alley, a noise, an event, that distracted the Germans from their journeys and their labour, and made them stare and wonder. Some of her neighbours spotted her, and their reactions were curiously mixed. She was, in turn, acknowledged, ignored, frowned at and smiled on.

She looked down at herself. Her own clothes, the ones she'd fought in, were . . . somewhere. She hadn't given it much thought. She was dressed now like a German princess for the want of anything else to wear – there were chests of women's clothes in the fortress, unused and unlikely to ever be worn again. Practical and thrifty, she'd taken them over.

And her neighbours were no longer that: she and her father lived in the fortress now, and their house was empty and cold and still.

Sophia watched the backs of the processors, a curious longing to be in among them mixing with the creeping realisation that she was now irrevocably separate; that was the price she personally had to pay.

They were waiting for her in the library. She'd lingered long enough.

Library Square resembled a builder's yard. There were stacks of timber and piles of stone, and the sound of sawing and chiselling rattled off the walls of the surrounding buildings. Inside was barely quieter. The cap on the oculus was almost completely removed, with buckets of material going both up and down the tower of scaffolding in the centre.

At last, though, there was natural light. Not enough that it didn't need supplementing, but it was a start. Glazers and leaders were already attempting to construct something like a window to fill the gap, but the sheer weight and size of it was defeating them.

Every problem they tried to fix simply provided them with another. And they were mounting up.

Everyone wanted to speak to her and claim a moment of her time. Of course they did; she had the palatinate's purse. She listened carefully and then, surrounded by clamouring tradesmen, simply held up her hand.

Eventually, they fell silent. Taking one, two, three steps up the stairs to the first gallery, she turned to face them. They had followed her, waving bills and receipts in the air.

"Gentlemen. This simply cannot continue. There is business and there is chaos, and this is chaos."

"Our suppliers need paying. Our men need paying," called a builder.

"They do." Rather than accuse them outright of trying to gouge the royal treasury, she tried another way. "I am aware that your costs are greater than they would once have been because everything has to be done by hand. Food costs more, materials cost more, labour itself costs more. However – they are only worth what someone is willing to pay for them. There's a natural, and understandable urge to add a little to each account in this time of emergency. However, for the moment, only the palatinate is hiring."

She suddenly wondered if she should consider directly employing craftsmen at standard guild rates – as set before the crisis. It would be substantially cheaper, but she also thought of the nightmare that would ensue if she directly challenged the guilds.

"I need to talk to the guildmasters. We all need to eat, and prices that keep on rising are going to hurt the widows and the orphans harder than a master or a journeyman. Especially those whose husbands and fathers have died most recently."

There, that was magnanimous. The bodies laid out in the main

416

square hadn't all been men, but the lion's share of them had. They were all burnt now, ashes on a pyre, but some of them would certainly have been guild members, whose guilds now had a responsibility to look after their destitute families. Higher charges from the guilds meant higher costs for the guilds.

From the look of some of them, the lesson had hit home. They didn't want to see their own wealth destroyed.

"But what about the money we've already laid out?" called someone.

"I'll pay guild rates," she said, and left the rest unspoken. If they'd been foolish enough to get caught holding an excessive bill, then they were twice as foolish thinking they could simply pass it on. Neither would she countenance any surreptitious redrafting of their promissory notes. "Hand everything to me. Tomorrow, I'll pay what they're worth."

She called on the library ushers to help her, easy enough as they were already looking her way, and they made sure that the merchants and craftsmen handed their papers over. The bills made a tidy pile, and she wasn't going to be able to both sleep and enter all the items in her ledger. Perhaps it was time to co-opt a librarian or two, ones that were numerate as well as literate.

She shooed everyone away. They had work to be getting on with. Now, of course, so did she. Clutching her bundle of notes and laws, she walked around the scaffolding and the wheeling barrows to the long table, where books were being catalogued at a furious rate.

Thaler was in position at the head of the long line of readers, muttering comments to a scribbling librarian as he inspected the manuscript in front of him. A square of paper had been pinned to each book, each piece of parchment or vellum beforehand. By the end of the cataloguing process, Latin numbers written on the square told the shelvers where the book needed to go.

She didn't disturb the master librarian. He was so absorbed in his task that he hadn't even noticed her presence, so she turned instead to Mr Wess, who was receiving a book and opening it to inspect the frontispiece.

"Good morning, Mr Wess."

"Ah, Mistress Morgenstern." He leant back in his chair. "Thank you. This is much better than handing out lanterns."

"I'd save your thanks, Mr Wess," she said, and his smile slipped a fraction. "I suddenly find myself overwhelmed not just with paperwork that needs to be copied and distributed, but with adding and subtracting too."

Wess frowned. "A clerk?"

"No. Yes. A dozen clerks, and someone to oversee them."

"A dozen?" Wess closed the book cover with weary resignation. "My lady, we are running out of men who can read and write sufficiently competently to carry out even the most basic tasks."

"Then we need a school in every town." Yeshivas. Her people had done it for centuries, and there was no reason for the Germans not to. "And school teachers in every town."

"And until then?"

"Mr Wess, I'm aware that if the Jews run everything, it would cause some comment, and not a little disquiet. Please save me from that."

Wess sighed. "Mistress." He pushed himself away from the table, and made his excuses. "Gentlemen, my apologies. It seems my duties lie elsewhere."

The others at the table barely looked up. Perhaps they thought he'd be back in a little while. Sophia knew that if he returned it would be as a master in his own right, and that it would take years, if not decades, for him to get back to the library.

"I'm sorry, Mr Wess. We're all having to think on our feet, and having agreed to oversee the library alterations, I failed to notice that I was also agreeing to restructure the entire economy of the palatinate."

"You're what?"

"Nothing costs the same as it did before. And the craftsmen are all adjusting their prices in one direction only." She pressed the stack of receipts onto Wess. "We need to control prices or we'll run out of coin and the people will starve. I've already asked for a meeting with the guildmasters, but until then, we pay what we would have done previously."

Wess looked at the first bill in his hand. "Mr Gluckner, master mason, for removal of stone and disposal of same. Work for a master and two journeymen . . . how much? Gods!"

"Quite, Mr Wess. Your first job is to find out how much I should be paying, then to rewrite all those notes we have in hand. Prompt payment will allow these good gentlemen to eat: I will not, however, be taken advantage of. After that, I have plenty to keep you busy."

"Where are we to work?" Wess continued to scan the bills, peering at the amounts requested and wincing. "Is there anywhere in the fortress that's suitable?"

It was something she hadn't planned for, but inspiration came: "The Town Hall. We don't have a mayor, and Master Messinger's old room is large and bright. If a dozen men are too many for now, pick half a dozen. Tell me by the end of the day how much treasure we've spent so far, and I'll have it delivered to you in the morning."

Just as Wess left to scour the library for personnel, her father walked in.

He didn't see her at first. He looked up at the light streaming down from the oculus, at the men working high above, then at the industry going on around the long table; the barrows of books and the bowed heads of the librarians.

He even looked at her, his own daughter, who he'd shared a house with for twenty-four years and who had looked after him for all her adult life. The slow turn of his head took her in, and passed on.

Even though a moment later he snapped back, finally registering who it was in that heavy, ornate dress, she felt more lost than she'd ever done. While he – of course – held that instance lightly, joking at her clothing, how he hadn't recognised her, it was nothing but noise and confusion to her.

When she came to again, she was standing to one side of the reading room, with two folded pieces of parchment in her hands, with her father standing in front of her with a quizzical expression on his lined face.

"Sophia?"

She shook herself out like a dog emerging from a cold lake. "I'm all right. You can take Mr Wess's place at the table. And you have to follow instructions, Father; if you make a mistake, a book might be lost forever in the wrong place."

"Yes, yes." He glanced up at her. "Have you been back to the house?"

"I . . . might have," she ventured.

"Did you go into the room. The one upstairs?"

It was about his secret library. She steeled herself. "Yes."

"Did you . . .?"

"For heaven's sake, Father, yes. They weren't yours. They were stolen and you had to give them back."

"I paid good money for those books," he said, making a poor attempt to speak quietly,

"Then go and get your money back off Mr Thomm." She scowled hard and raised her voice. "And while you're at it, get him back in here and put him to work. Tell him that, if he does, Master Thaler will consider not having him pressed. It's not like we're deluged with Latin and Greek readers. We'll even pay him."

Morgenstern took a step back. "Calm, daughter, calm."

"No," she said. "I will not. I'm fed up already. I've done everything I've been asked to do, and none of it is good enough. The last thing I need is my crook of a father arrested for fencing. Which reminds me. That book you got instead of *On the Balance*?"

"Yes?"

"I took that, too. To apologise."

"Sophia!"

"Well, you didn't want it, and it turns out it might be very important. So when Master Thaler—"

"Oh, it's Master Thaler now, is it?"

"Yes, and you'd do well to remember that – when Master Thaler gives you a break from your catalogue work, you can start translating it from the Persian."

Her father pressed his lips together and tugged at his beard. "Did I raise you to be this ungrateful?"

"Clearly." She gave him Felix's new laws. "Read them."

He took the papers from her and scanned the first. "That'll be difficult to enforce," he said. He opened the second, and his eyebrows threatened to crawl completely off his forehead they were raised so high.

"Well?" she said. "Any other comments about how you raised me?"

"Perhaps, I didn't do such a bad job after all," he conceded.

He presented his cheek, and she kissed his whiskery face. He gave a grunt of contentment, and took his seat at the table. It took him a while to get comfortable, then a little longer to open the book in front of him. He crouched forward, running his finger along the text, then looked up to consult the large painted board on which Thaler's classification scheme had been chalked.

She smiled to herself. At least one of them was happy again. She went to inspect how work on the glass covering for the oculus was progressing. A solution would present itself, eventually.

57

Ullmann strode through the town, aware of his newly elevated status but even more conscious of the effect it had on other people. He had been quietly invisible before, hiding under his black usher's robe. Now that same robe marked him out as being associated with both the prince and the library.

Moreover, the town's rumour-mongers were hard at work, associating Ullmann's name with something dark and secret: that he'd been collecting together some very rough characters and sending them up to the fortress, that Ullmann was in charge of something important, that he was now a prince's man.

He needed neither to confirm nor deny a single thing. He only had to smile and leave the rest to their imagination.

The latest letter he carried would, no doubt, surprise and shock even the most dedicated fantasist. Yet the ruthless logic of its contents couldn't be denied. Thaler, of course, only saw one side of it, but he could see the other: you kept your friends close, and your enemies closer. Felix had taken some convincing, mainly because my lady had set her face against the matter from the outset.

She trusted Thaler though, and he'd talked her around while Ullmann looked thoughtful and waited to the very end to tip her over the edge. It was well done, and he hadn't had to show his hand at all. Even Thaler thought the idea was his own.

All that was left to do was for Wess to copy the proclamation and for his spies to carry it across Carinthia and beyond. He stood for a moment on the quayside, looking at the tied-up barges and considering both the necessity of getting them moving again and the problems arising from having the bargees idle and increasingly destitute within Juvavum's walls.

Then he looked up, up at Goat Mountain and the White Tower. His heart beat a little faster, and he was glad Büber had not only gone to see the dwarves, but seemed determined never to return.

He turned towards the Town Hall, walked up the steps, and climbed the stairs to the mayor's old office. As he entered, he saw Wess as just another of the clerks seated at a half-circle of desks, writing steadily. Paper was piled at each man's left, and again on his right. Wess himself was scratching out numbers from a bill and writing in new figures underneath, his calculations – marked on a piece of broken roof slate – propped up in front of him.

Ullmann cleared his throat, and Wess put his pen down deliberately, almost violently. His sigh of exasperation was clear.

"Disturbed, Master Wess?"

"Continually, Master Ullmann. There's too much work for us as it is, and" – he eyed the contents of Ullmann's hands – "it looks like you've brought us even more."

"Oh, this?" He stepped forward and slid the parchment square onto Wess's desk. "I need these today, as many copies as you can manage."

"There has to be an easier way than doing it all by hand." Wess ground his teeth, noted the seal, unfolded the sheet, and read the words. Then he read them again, just to make sure he'd completely understood what was being asked of him.

"This . . . this is the prince's will?"

"It is, Master Wess. You've read it to the end?"

"Yes. Gods. This won't go down well." Wess saw that the other clerks had all stopped working and weren't even pretending not to listen in. "Your duties, gentlemen."

The sound of nib on parchment resumed, and Wess looked again at Ullmann's note, written in Sophia Morgenstern's neat hand. He appeared to be all but speechless, so Ullmann chose to explain.

"Former members of the Order can all read and write, some of them languages that the librarians can't even pronounce, let alone translate," said Ullmann. "My lord has asked Master Thaler to keep an eye on them, and he said he would with my help: to be honest, it's probably the best they can hope for. Their tattoos are permanent. They're marked for life, Master Wess, and they'll never be able to pass as ordinary folk. It's a kindness, of sorts."

Wess threw the letter down in front of him. "It'll cause all sorts of disquiet, but my lord commands," he said. "We live in a world where magic still works, but the only way to raise it is so demonstrably evil that we have to ban it. We've just spent our blood ridding ourselves of the Order, and now we're asking for them back." He shook his head.

"Where would you rather have them?" asked Ullmann. "In a

torture chamber belonging to one of our enemies, or in the library of one of our friends?"

The clerk picked up the paper again and studied its words.

"What with you, the impending paper crisis and the Bavarians, it's a wonder I'll get anything done today. These accounts . . ."

"Bavarians?" Ullmann's eyes narrowed. "What have Bavarians to do with this?"

"A Mr Wiel and his companion came from Simbach to enquire about the possibility of a new bridge. I sent them on their way. In your direction, in fact. Have they seen you yet?"

Wess tried to turn his attention back to the pile of bills, but Ullmann moved right up to the desk: no Bavarians had been to see him, and he'd rather no Bavarians knew of his existence at all.

"What did you tell this Wiel?" asked Ullmann. "Exactly."

"I . . ." Wess's mouth had gone inexplicably dry, and his throat had started to close. "The truth?"

"The truth?" Ullmann didn't like the sound of that. "What sort of truth? Not the actual truth that the Order couldn't put the bridge back because we have no Order?"

Wess nodded.

"Anything else?"

Wess nodded again.

"Everything that's happened in the last two weeks?" Ullmann's demeanour changed from affable to coldly furious in a moment. "Where did this Wiel and his friend go?"

"I don't know."

"What did he look like?"

"He looked like . . ." – and Ullmann realised Wess was actually scared of him – ". . . he looked like a man who'd been travelling for a couple of days. Dusty. Battered. A hat – he had a wide-brimmed hat."

"Tall or short? Dark haired or blond or bald? Old or young? Thin or broad?"

"I can't remember."

Ullmann leant over the desk. "Try, Master Wess. Try very hard."

One of the other clerks came to his rescue. "Taller than you, Master, shorter than Master Wess, short blond hair starting to go at the temples, a few lines around his eyes and mouth, thin under his long riding coat. Definitely a Bavarian accent."

"Thank you. At least someone pays attention." He straightened up. "In case I need to spell it out, don't tell our business to everyone who asks: they're going to find out eventually for certain, but let's not make it easy for them."

He fixed Wess with a stare that made the older man shrink down into his seat. Then he was gone, door banging firmly behind him. He left the Town Hall fuming. His face felt hot and dry, and his heart beat hard and fast in his chest. Stupid, naïve Wess, giving away all their secrets at once.

And stupid, naïve Ullmann, for thinking that Bavaria – slow, backward land of farmers and mad kings – wouldn't get into the spying game before Carinthia. He'd shown himself to less competent than Felix believed, and he wasn't about to compound the error. He was a quick learner – everybody said so – and he didn't need a teacher to tell him what he'd done wrong.

First things first. He ran to the bridge, and to the Jewish guards on duty.

"Master Ullmann," said the man with the sergeant's coat.

"Two Bavarian spies have entered town. Don't let anyone pass until we've caught them."

"No one?" The sergeant leant on his spear. "People aren't going to like that."

"When the Bavarians overrun us, they'll like it a lot less. And don't say why you're stopping them. The less warning these bastards get, the better."

"As you wish, Master Ullmann. We'll wait for your orders." He touched his hand to his helmet. "Orders coming only from you, of course."

"Right then." He turned on his heel, and spotted two children walking by, a younger boy and an older girl. "You two. Here."

They looked at each other, and stopped. Were they biddable? Ullmann wondered. Could they take a message? He could have done so at their age, he decided, so he trotted across to them, crouched down and tipped out the contents of his purse into the palm of his hand. Flipping two shilling pieces between his fingers, he held them out. The boy went to take them, but Ullmann held them higher and gave them to the girl.

"Can you run? Both of you?"

They nodded.

"I need one of you to run to the East Gate and the other to the

West Gate. Tell the guards this: 'Master Ullmann says close the gates in the prince's name.' Master Ullmann, got that?"

They both nodded again.

"It's important you do this right. Your prince is depending on you." He started to pour the rest of his coins back into his purse. "Go! Run!"

The boy started towards the East Gate. The girl caught him and whirled him around. "No. West Gate's closer. Meet you back here." She hitched up her skirts and started down towards the quay. The boy hesitated for a moment, then hared off in the opposite direction.

With a bit of luck, thought Ullmann, the Bavarians were now trapped. All he had to do was find them before the already disgruntled and idle townsfolk decided they didn't want to be trapped along with them. He needed more help, and quickly.

There weren't so many militia that he could take them from their posts. And his spies would be still up at the fortress, getting ready.

The library ushers. He ran again, through the narrow streets, making himself thin as he hurtled through gaps that were only briefly present, and all the time looking out for a man with a broad-brimmed hat who looked like he'd been on the road for a while.

Library Square, in comparison with the rest of town, was stupidly busy, crammed with craftsmen and piles of sand and stone and wood. There were the ushers, though, under the portico: a group of six of them, and more importantly, he knew them, and they knew him.

"Lads," he called when he was close enough. "To me."

"Well, look here," one of them replied, "if it isn't Master Ullmann. Want your old job back, Max?"

He skidded to a halt on the gritty stone steps. "Leave it, Manfred. Less banter, more doing. There are two Bavarian spies in town, and they mustn't get away."

"Bavarian what? You're pulling our legs, right?" The usher nudged one of his colleagues with his elbow.

"I think he's serious," said his friend with wonder. "Where do we start?"

"Gods, I don't know. I've never done this before." Ullmann thought furiously. "Start up by the castle and work our way down to the bridge. They can't leave, I've made certain of that."

"Are they armed?"

"I don't know. I don't know anything about them except that one of them is a bit taller than me, has short blond hair, is older, and is wearing a big hat." He puffed out his breath. "Goes by the name of Wiel. It's not much to go on, but we have to try."

The ushers shrugged and muttered until Manfred rolled his eyes. "Come on, then. It's not like we're even busy here. You owe us all a jar – two jars – of beer. Each."

"Done," said Ullmann. "If we find them, I'll buy you enough drink to drown in."

They descended the library steps and headed up Wien Alley. "Did they come on horses?" asked Manfred.

"Possibly."

"Horst? Check Stable Street, will you?"

The seven of them filled the alley: they looked like they were out mob-handed, and their robes resembled a uniform of sorts. Ullmann couldn't tell whether that counted in his favour or against it. They turned left into Gothis' Alley, while Horst took the wide right-turn and started to peer in each livery yard and shout questions at the stable boys.

No one, but no one, was wearing a hat like the Bavarian. The main square was thinly populated, with just a few hungry people sitting around waiting for something to happen that might have some coin in it for them. Ullmann scanned each face in turn, while the ushers spread out.

He heard a faint shout behind him, then a sudden clatter of hooves. Without turning around, he threw himself to one side, pressing his face to the wall of a tall town house.

A horse burst into the square, a mountain of brown flanks and flashing white feathers. The rider on its back looked around wildly, his head twisting and turning as he sought an escape route.

His gaze took in Ullmann. They knew each other's purpose in that instant; a professional understanding, no more, no less. It wasn't the man with the hat, but most likely his companion. Why else would he be running?

"Stop that man," bellowed Ullmann, and he reached down for his sword. The ushers, frozen for an instant, came alive and converged on the Bavarian.

The rider didn't seem to have a weapon, but he had a horse, which was more than sufficient. It was going to take a brave man to stand in the way.

The horse darted forward, and the ushers scattered out of the way, Manfred making a darting lunge for the bridle. His fingers caught the leather strap, and his feet left the ground.

The horse's head came down, and it stumbled. Manfred was bowled over and lost his grip, ending up on the cobbles right in front of the sparking hooves.

Ullmann leapt, sword forgotten. He managed to connect with the rider's boot, and pulled hard. It was enough to slow the rider for a moment, and Manfred rolled out of the way just in time.

The horse started to pick up speed again, and Ullmann's feet were dragged out from underneath him. The Bavarian leant down to beat him away, but started to slide from the saddle himself. He desisted and crouched low, assuming that he'd shake the Carinthian free shortly.

Ullmann was caught in a dilemma. If he let go, he'd crack his skull on the ground. If he didn't, his legs would sooner or later tangle with the horse's, and he'd be trampled.

He had to do something different, something unexpected. They were halfway around the rapidly emptying square. The ushers were chasing, but didn't look likely to catch up.

It was up to him, then. He started to reach for his knife, but the jolting was too great. Pulling himself close, he sank his teeth through the man's breeks into the flesh below.

There was satisfying shriek of pain and a less welcome clubbing blow to the side of his face. The rider was losing control, and the horse was slowing. Ullmann bit harder, shaking his head like a fighting dog. He was hit again, and again, but then he managed to find his feet and jump clear.

He staggered back, the taste of the man's blood on his tongue. He reached for his sword, determined to draw it, just as the rider, now furious, wheeled the foaming horse around directly at Ullmann.

A broom-handle struck the Bavarian, square in the kidneys. He arched his back, and the horse reared. Ullmann caught sight of a woman through the milling hooves, brush end in hand, stepping clear and readying herself for another strike. His sword cleared his scabbard, and the ushers were right behind him, yelling and roaring.

The terrified horse rose higher on its hind legs, and the rider pitched off backwards with a wail.

"Get the horse," said Ullmann, and he darted around it to the stunned man lying spread-eagled on the square. The woman was red-faced with exertion as she set about the Bavarian with her broom, hitting him over and over.

"Enough, Mistress, enough." He pointed his sword at the man's chest. "Do you surrender to a prince's man?"

He was in no position to answer one way or another, which was for the best, because neither of them were in any shape for a fight. Ullmann held his sword point-down and crouched over, blowing like bellows. He felt a hand on his back.

"Max?" said Horst. "You mad bastard."

"I thought I could see the Valkyries for a moment there." Ullmann blinked away the pain and the sweat, and looked up. "Thank you, Mistress."

When she gave him a crooked smile, his spine straightened just a little. "You're a bit young to be a prince's man."

"Older than the prince," he said. "Manfred, get some cord and tie this fucker up before he comes around."

Ullmann tried to stand up. Everything felt uncertain and insubstantial. When he came down he'd be in so much pain.

"Horst? What did you say to him?"

Horst held onto the horse's reins and attempted to settle it down. "I didn't get chance to say anything. He damn near ran me down from the off."

"We need to find the other one, and quickly." Ullmann got to his feet, and saw the state of his boots. The soles had separated from the uppers, and were flapping every time he moved. "But not wearing these, it seems."

He turned again to the woman with the broom-handle.

"Mistress, that was timely. Saved my neck and no mistake."

She leant on her broom the same way he leant on his sword. "So what is he? And who are you?"

"He's a Bavarian spy, suspected anyway, and I'm Master Max Ullmann, at your service."

"So, not a horse thief: either of you." She twirled the broom around in her hands. "That's good. Since when did Bavaria see the need to spy on us?"

Shortly before we decided to spy on Bavaria, he thought, but didn't say. "I'd be neglecting my duties if I told you more, Mistress."

She came back with that ready smile. "A shame, Master Ullmann, because I'd like to be told more."

Manfred returned with some braided cord, and the ushers

gathered around the stirring man. They turned him over and, despite his weak attempts at resistance, they bound his hands and tied a loose loop around his neck so that one jerk would have him throttled.

"What do we do with him? Take him to the fortress?"

Ullmann frowned. "I don't even know if it has a prison. It's a castle, so I suppose it must. Yes, two of you take him. Oswald, you're a big lad: go with Manfred. The rest of us will dig his friend out from the rock he's hiding under."

He handed Manfred his sword, and nodded at their prisoner. "Check him for knives in all the obvious places, and when you've done that, check him again. Come on, lads. We've got more to do."

"As have I, Master Ullmann." The woman put her broom over her shoulder. "At the Odenwald house. That one just there on the corner of Gold Alley. You will remember that, won't you?"

He made certain she was talking to him. "So when would the mistress like to be remembered?"

"You're obviously a busy man with lots of important duties. I can wait."

"And who will I call on, when I have time?"

"Aelinn, Master Ullmann." She walked back across the square, and he watched her go while he absent-mindedly rubbed the blood from his lips.

"Max. Max?" Horst's elbow dug deep into his ribs. "Haven't we got something else to do? There'll be time to chase women later."

"Horst, a little bit of respect, please." He wiped his hand on his breeks. "If Wiel heard any of that scrum, he'd have gone to ground. We'll look in the beer cellars around the Old Market, and then down Sigmund's. We need to keep him moving, and flush him out."

Looking down, Horst said: "You need new boots, Max, before we go anywhere."

"You're not wrong. Manfred? Hold up. Get his boots off. He ruined a perfectly decent pair: let's see if his fit me."

They did, more or less. He'd need a thicker pair of socks, but he could find some later.

"Right then, lads. Let's look lively."

They ran on towards the Old Market, passing the house on the corner of Gold Alley as they went.

No sign of Aelinn outside. Ullmann's gaze wandered from the door to the windows to see if she was looking back at him, but they went by too quickly, and the house receded behind them.

58

It was difficult enough to find someone to guard the door, aside from the problem of finding an appropriate room to shut them in. It had been a very long time since the fortress had housed prisoners.

In his father's day, justice had been swift, and there'd been little call for prison cells, except the lock-up for drunks.

"What are my options, Master Ullmann?"

"Pressing, my lord."

Felix glanced around from the solar window. "Only one path is not options."

"They're foreign spies, my lord. They expect it. As do we."

"Yes, I know that. But we're not ready to have a war with Bavaria." He looked back out at the Alps. "Are they ready to have a war with us?"

"No one goes to war because their spies have been caught, my lord." Ullmann sat at the table with the unrolled map. "It's just expected that when you find them, you kill them."

"And everybody knows that." Felix paced the floor. "I've made bad decisions before. Killed prisoners because I was angry. I don't want to do that again."

"You don't sound angry now."

"I'm not. Master Ullmann, I know what a prince is supposed to do. What I want to know is what I should do."

"You are a prince, my lord." Ullmann raised his head.

"Advise me, Master Ullmann. Tell me not just what's expected of me, but what's possible." Felix took the chair opposite and leant his elbows on the table. It felt good to get his arm out of the sling, which he'd draped around his neck, ready to put on again should Sophia come near.

Ullmann pursed his lips and started to count out the options on his fingers. "You could have them pressed. You could hold them

430

for as long as you like: they might be valuable to the Bavarians, and useful if any of our spies get caught. You could torture them for what they know."

"We know what they know, because Master Wess told them more or less everything."

"I meant about Bavaria, but there'd be no way of knowing whether the information they give is accurate or not. They'll tell us whatever they think we want to hear." Ullmann held up another finger. "You could try and recruit them."

"Oh?"

"Turncoats: traitors to their lord."

"I know what it means. I just hadn't thought of it. Carry on."

"You could tell the Bavarians we have their spies, and ransom them. Or, of course, you could release them."

"Or any number of those things together." Felix studied the map in front of him and wondered just how accurate it was. The distance to München didn't look that far at all. "Can I talk to them?"

"I . . . suppose so." Ullmann frowned. "It's not usual, my lord, for a prince to dirty himself with such things."

"We left what was usual a while ago, Master Ullmann. Everything we do is different, so why not this?"

Ullmann shrugged. "They're in the Hare Tower."

"Tied?"

"Shackled to the wall, but their hands are free. We're not animals, my lord."

Felix's eyes narrowed. "You don't want them pressed either, do you? Despite you almost dying trying to catch them."

"I never mentioned that, my lord."

"No. More accurate reports in future, Master Ullmann."

Ullmann smiled ruefully.

"It's not that they don't deserve it, nor that, if any of my lads got caught in their lands, they wouldn't get the same, but we need to know who sent them and why. What's Leopold up to, and does he have designs on Carinthia? He could be as scared of us as we are worried about him."

"We don't have to be enemies," said Felix, "though they might think otherwise. Which is why I want to talk to these spies. They don't seem to be . . . I don't know . . . very good spies. Perhaps they're like ours, just people they've picked out of a line and told to do their best."

Ullmann pushed his chair back. "Shall we try to find out, my lord?"

They left the solar and went down the stairs to the courtyard.

"One question, Master Ullmann. Do you know how to use your sword?"

Ullmann hesitated for a moment. "Enough to point the sharp end at my enemies."

"I'll train you myself. I'll start a sword school right here, in the main courtyard. What I teach you, you can then teach to others. Every leader should be able to hold his own with a sword."

"Like Mistress Morgenstern, you mean?"

Felix wasn't quite sure how to take that. Sophia's exploits had become increasingly unlikely the more times the tale was retold, whereas, first-hand, she made it sound as though men had simply thrown themselves onto her blade. That was more probable, he supposed, than her HaShem guiding her arm.

"If she wants to learn, then I'll teach her too."

The thought of her, bloodied spatha in her upraised fist, calling curses down on her foes and blessings on her friends . . . He shivered.

"My lord?"

"Doesn't matter. Has there been anything from Master Büber?"

"No." It was Ullmann's turn to look uncomfortable. "Do you think he's going to come back? I mean, really?"

"I don't know. I think he'll go and see the dwarves, but what happens after that? There's nothing to stop him just keeping on going until he reaches the ocean." Felix thought it would be a loss, but was well aware it was up to Peter Büber whether he turned around or not. The mountains and forests might call him home, or he might be so consumed with grief that he'd lose himself in some forgotten valley and never return. "I'm not sure I can order anyone to do anything; only hope that they choose to do what I say."

"You have authority as Prince of Carinthia."

"Yes, I know that." Felix gazed up at Ullmann. "But if I don't find it a good enough reason, I can't expect others to. I'm only twelve, and I haven't done anything yet: no one needs to fear me, and no one thinks me wise. The people don't love me, either. They're simply used to doing what the arse on the throne says, and we know what happens when they forget that."

They were at the tower, and Ullmann put his hand on the door latch. "My lord, you shouldn't dwell on such things."

"What right have I to run not just your life, but those of people I've never even met and am never likely to? I could do what my father did: give power to the earls, and have them rule their little bit of Carinthia for me. But where are the earls at the moment? Mostly dead." Felix kicked at the wall. "Outside of Juvavum, there's been little trouble. The palatinate seems happy to run itself."

"The people crave order, my lord. They know that if there's no law, there's no security. They won't make plans for a harvest if they think someone else is going to steal it from them at spear-point."

Felix stopped kicking and frowned. "That's a good point, Master Ullmann. Open the door: let's see these Bavarians."

They made their way up the steps inside.

"We don't have a name for the second man yet," said Ullmann. "He's not volunteering it, though I dare say we could beat it out of him, or Wiel."

"We can call him whatever we like. It's not like Wiel will have given us his real name," said Felix. "How about Mr Spitzel?"

"That's a good one, my lord. Spitzel it is, then."

The jailer was perched on a stool outside the locked room. He wasn't asleep, and even stood up when he heard them approach.

"Open up, man. The prince wants to interrogate the prisoners," said Ullmann.

It wasn't exactly what Felix had said. If anything, he wanted to see the faces of people who might be his enemy, even though he'd done nothing to them.

The guard took the key from around his neck and wrestled it into the lock, heaving it around until there was a satisfyingly heavy clunk. He peered through the bars in the door to check everything was still in order.

"The chains go halfway across the room, my lords. Stick close to this side, and the bastards won't be able to get at you." He heaved the door aside. "Up, up, you fuckers, the Prince of Carinthia is here."

It was quite clear that neither man had come quietly. Black eyes, cut cheeks and chipped teeth were the order of the day. The man who Ullmann had bitten had a crude bandage on his leg. They looked up as the prince and Ullmann entered, but did not stand, a slight that enraged the jailer.

"Wait outside, good sir," said Felix. "My chains around their ankles are enough of a sign of their submission."

"The boy Carinthia," snorted one.

"That's Wiel," whispered Ullmann.

"Good afternoon, Mr Wiel. Mr Spitzel." It got a reaction from the other man, who pushed himself up to a more upright sitting position. "Are you being treated well?"

"Treated well?" Wiel leant closer, and the links tightened behind him. "Why are we here? You chase us, beat us and throw us in here, all for asking about the Simbach bridge."

"So you deny you're Bavarian spies then?" said Ullmann. "I suppose you didn't try to run my lads down, Spitzel, or to knife one of us, Wiel? We didn't find a sack of coin on you, worth far more than an honest messenger should be carrying?"

"It would be useful if you stopped denying it," added Felix. "We know what you are. I want to talk to you so that I can better decide what to do with you."

"You haven't opened the pressing pit for us, then?" said Wiel, sitting back down. "I'm surprised."

"I'm not my father." Felix sat too, cross-legged on the floor, the Sword of Carinthia scraping across the stone. "Forget whatever he used to do. I'm my own man, and I make my own decisions."

"Man? Man? You're just a child. Does this long streak of piss with you have to hold your hand while you're straining out the royal shit?"

One of the reasons why he'd sat down was so that it would be more of an effort to get up again. Felix managed to ignore him.

"Mr Spitzel. Yes, you. What do you say?"

"I think you're going to be screwed like a tuppeny whore."

"And why do you think that?"

"Because you have nothing." Spitzel stretched his leg uncomfortably, but still gave a little smile.

Felix steepled his fingers and rested his elbows on his knees. "Tell me, Mr Spitzel: are all Bavarian spies as good as you two?"

Ullmann snorted at the man's sour expression. "There you go, my lord. If we have nothing, they have even less. Old Leopold ran his kingdom into the ground long before the magic disappeared."

"That's true," said Felix. "Not even enough coin to pay for a few spearmen. Ended up scrabbling around for coppers, taxing Carinthian bridges."

"Leopold was a fucking idiot," growled Wiel.

"Was? So he's gone, has he?" Felix could see the point of this now, this testing of an opponent and seeing how much they'd give away. "Who's in his place?"

"Shut up!" spat Spitzel at Wiel. "Shut up now!"

"One of the earls, then? Or has Bavaria fallen apart, and every fiefdom is for itself? The Earl of Simbach sent you, is that right?"

Wiel stayed white and tight-lipped.

"Answer the prince, you Bavarian cock-sucker," said Ullmann. Felix looked up at him, eyebrow raised. "If you don't mind, that is, my lord."

Swearing like a stevedore hadn't been in the prince's lessons, although he'd picked up a few choice phrases from his father. Being around Ullmann was an education in itself.

Felix tapped his sword. "We'll find out soon enough for ourselves, Mr Wiel. One thing that Carinthia hasn't done is set earl against earl."

"They're all dead. That's hardly a triumph," said Spitzel. He reached down to scratch at his injured leg. "You'll be joining them soon enough, princeling."

Wiel wasn't the senior partner. It was Spitzel. Interesting.

"So Simbach thinks it can take what it wants of Carinthian land and treasure? The last time we paid you a visit, you couldn't even make a toll booth."

Spitzel considered the insult. "You're right, of course. No point in worrying about us. You may as well just let us go. A gesture of goodwill between neighbours."

Ullmann stiffened. "Is that the same gesture you gave me with your fists, you pig-fucker?"

"You gave as good as you got."

"You won't be saying that when we burn Simbach to the ground and send all the prisoners as slaves to work in the salt mines."

Felix rested his hand on Ullmann's shin. "Steady, Master Ullmann. We don't have to force them. Perhaps the people of Simbach would jump at the chance to earn a share of Carinthia's good fortune."

Wiel jerked on his chains. "We're better than you. We're just better than you. We've had to watch for centuries while you throw your weight around like a bloated boar with its head in our troughs, rooting up our crops and shitting on our floors, and all the time it's been 'the Order will come and get you' if we stand up for ourselves. The Order has gone. No more hexmasters: you're weak now, and we're going to gut you like a fish."

Felix made sure that Ullmann wasn't going to jump in and try to silence Wiel, then asked: "When was the last time a Carinthian army invaded anyone? I know the answer to that, because I was made to learn it. Do you know?"

"You've always been there, right in our faces," shouted Wiel. 'Do what we say,' you tell us, 'or we'll burn your houses and salt your land.' You threaten us just by breathing."

"A hundred and fifty years ago, and it was Wien, not Bavaria, and that was after they blocked trade on the Donau, which hurt Bavaria as much as it did us. We didn't even sack Wien, just made it plain that we could." Felix played a complicated rhythm with his fingertips. "I've every reason to hate the Order. Certainly more reason than you. But if you say we charge around like a bull in a field . . ."

"Boar, my lord."

"Whichever. You're wrong. If anything, the history I've learnt tells me we ignored everything that happened outside our borders because it didn't make any difference to us. So why do you hate us? Bavaria has been better off for having Carinthia as a neighbour."

Wiel breathed heavily, still straining against his iron chain. Spitzel roused himself and ordered the other man to sit back down.

"We hate you," he said, "because you've never had to struggle, never had to try. Everything's come easy to you Carinthians. Peace and the wealth to enjoy it are the only two things worth worrying about in life. When our harvests failed, or we were at war, or the Death came calling, you passed us like a beggar in the street. Now that you're on the street with us, we're not going to forget."

Ullmann shook his head and walked out, and Felix unfolded his legs. "One of you hates us for interfering. The other hates us for leaving you alone. And you call *me* a child."

He got up and dusted himself down. His shoulder was still sore, but it wasn't too bad. He thought he might leave the sling off even if Sophia told him otherwise.

"Prince Felix?"

"Yes, Mr Spitzel?"

"Have you decided our fates yet?"

Felix rubbed his face and pinched at his nose. "No. It'd be easy enough just to have you pressed. That's what I'm expected to do, and don't think that my being twelve will save you from the stones. What could save you is that I'm not my father, or my grandfather, or his father either. Good day, gentlemen."

59

His name was Thorsun Heavyhammer, in the usual dwarvish style that sounded more than slightly ridiculous to human ears. From Büber's limited experience, Heavyhammer was a dwarves' dwarf: dour when he wasn't being grim, full of fate and doom.

Despite the thinness of the air, Heavyhammer kept up an almost continuous monologue. About how they'd make Farduzes by night-fall, unless something ate them first. About how the sky terrified him and the rocks oppressed him. About how, ultimately, his people would be forgotten in a cruel and uncaring surface world. After two days in his company, Büber was left contemplating murder to make at least that part of the dwarf's wyrd come true.

They were in the high passes, far beyond any human habitation, in a land locked in snow and haunted by wind. The path – only the most optimistic would have called it a road – gripped the valley bottom as if it were a lifeline, disappearing occasionally under a drift or a landslide for a hundred feet or more before carrying doggedly on westwards.

The trees had given out. The landscape was cold and dry and bare. Rock and snow, grey and white. Their breath – that of man, horse and dwarf – condensed in clouds ahead of them and beaded skin and hair with dewdrops that initially sparkled, then soaked in.

It was almost a relief to be interrupted by the howl of a giant. If there'd been any sign of it before, it had been lost in the low drone of the dwarf's voice. Büber reeled in the leading rein and held the horse's bridle close. The beast's ears swivelled and its eyes grew large.

Büber listened carefully, tracking the echoes from peak to peak to see if he could work out from where the sound originated. Poor dead Nadel had had problems with giants up here; perhaps it was one of the same group. A family, he'd said, like the one Büber had encountered to the east.

Heavyhammer opened his mouth to speak and Büber raised one of his remaining fingers in warning. Do not speak, it commanded. Make no sound. Don't even move.

The only reason a giant called like that was to communicate with other giants across the vast open spaces of the mountain landscape. It had probably been left to watch from some vantage point – the eyesight of giants was as legendary as their temper – while the rest remained hidden beneath a drift or in a gorge.

He looked for a tell-tale sign: a flurry of snow, a rattle of rock. Nothing. He reached for his sword, nonetheless.

"They're not going to attack yet. Later, probably, and we won't get much warning." He wiped the moisture from around his nose and mouth with the back of his sword-filled hand. "I thought the giants were closer to Ennsbruck."

"Then you thought wrong, human."

"They must have wandered up here over the last month." Büber looked down at the dwarf. "You have less love for the bastard spawn of the Jötun than we do. At least draw your axe. You won't get a second chance."

"Death in the ravening maw of a giant would be welcome compared to the living twilight of this misshapen body," answered the dwarf. But he put his pack down and freed the axe from its bindings.

"Gods, I should have travelled alone."

The giant's single ululation had apparently served its purpose, whatever that was, for now the only sounds were the wind and those they made themselves: flapping cloth, scraping boots, crunching hooves.

"We'd better get going. I take it there's just one way we can go."

"Yes. Up here. To our certain slaughter."

Büber pulled his horse on, barging past Heavyhammer on the narrow path. He understood that the end of a whole way of life was a terrible thing to face, but they needed to get to Farduzes before nightfall. If they went too quickly, they might miss any ambush the giants had set, but conversely they'd be so much fresh meat in the dark. Best, then, to press on and hope.

He kept a watch out for hiding places, for trampled snow, for a sudden shift in the shadows on north-facing slopes. Nothing. Staying alert for such a length of time was immensely wearing; his head hurt with the strain of it.

He needed a drink of something, a bite to eat, a moment to rest his eyes, so he pulled up and turned to speak to Heavyhammer.

Two giants, a stadia distant, were padding up the path side by side, arms swinging loosely by their side. He looked the other way, only to see two more on the path ahead.

"Shit."

They'd appeared out of nowhere, just like giants always did. They'd probably passed the two who were now behind them by no more than a few sword lengths.

Bow or sword? Sword. Giants would cover the distance quickly. Forward or back? Four giants at once was suicide. Two at once was scarcely better odds, with another pair roaring up behind him.

Forward then.

Heavyhammer dropped his pack, while Büber smacked the horse on its rump with the flat of his sword to scare it away. Then he started to run up the track.

He was closing fast. The giants were lumbering towards him. They'd meet sooner than he'd anticipated. He'd thought they were further away, but they were right there, almost on top of him.

His reckless charge faltered as he suddenly realised they were tiny. Well, not tiny exactly. They were still taller than Büber, but for giants – and they were indisputably those, with their peg teeth, filthy claws and shock-white skin hanging off in great flaps – they were small. The first of them charged Büber, milling its fists as if they were still great clubs of flesh and bone.

Gods, it was slow, thought Büber. Ponderous, even. He'd never thought of himself as agile, but even he danced easily between the flailing arms and drove his sword-point hard through the creature's stomach. When the blade grated against bone, he'd knew he'd gone in far enough, and he dragged it out at an angle.

His face was almost level with the giant's. Its mouth formed a circle and its yellow eyes bulged. Büber had seen only two expressions on a giant's face before: rage and hunger. Now, he'd found a third. Regret.

He turned to avoid the inevitable spew of guts, shoving the giant behind him as he spun. He'd pushed a giant, and the giant had fallen.

Watching the overgrown dwarf and the second shrunken giant batting at each other with ineffectual blows was like seeing two children scrapping in the street. Their contest should have been epic and fierce, not embarrassing, and Büber felt compelled to end it with a single swing that severed the giant's spine. It lost the use of its legs, and folded to the cold ground, bleeding to death.

These creatures were shadows of what they'd once been. This was what the world had lost, writ plain to see. He could feel himself well up inside. He'd killed two of them, and wasn't even breathing hard.

"Turn around, Master Dwarf," he called. "Here come the others."

The dwarf raised his axe, and Büber his sword. The chasing giants slowed, and came to a halt just out of reach.

"What are they waiting for?" asked Heavyhammer.

"For Death to take them. Look at them. They have no idea what's happening to them. They only know their old habits, and they have to obey them."

"Then why aren't they tearing at us?"

"Because somewhere deep inside there's a voice that tells them it's all for nothing." Büber looped his sword in front of him. "They'll attack though. It's all they know."

They stared at each other, and eventually one of the giants threw its head back and howled.

It was answered, plaintively, at a distance. The call echoed between the valley sides, and Büber wondered if that was the last time anyone would hear such a sound again.

Then the creatures started forward again, driven by their animal-istic desires.

Heavyhammer lacked his former martial skills, but his courage was never in doubt. Though the giant was still twice his height, he swung his axe at the giant's thigh. It bit deep, even as the giant battered at the dwarf's head with its fists.

Büber faced his own opponent. Stepping out the way of its first swipe, he cut up against the giant's forearm, then slashed at the giant's pale neck. Air frothed out of the wound; there would be no getting up again after that.

The other giant was down on one knee, still trying to reach the dwarf, clawing at the air with its horn-coloured nails. It over-reached, and toppled forward with a groan. Heavyhammer's axe sliced its skull in two.

Büber lowered his guard. There was nothing else coming for them. The only movement was his horse picking its way across the scree further up the slope.

"Well, that was pointless," he said. "Stupid fucking idiots. They could have left us alone and lived."

The dwarf put his foot on the giant's head and worked his axe-blade out. If he'd looked grim before, now he was sepulchral. He rested on the haft as bits of brain and bone slid off the steel, and his mouth set into a thin line.

For a brief moment, Büber thought that Heavyhammer had finally run out of words. Then he started quoting poetry.

> "Hrafn flýgr sunnan,
> af hám meiði,
> ok er eptir þar
> örn í sinni.
> Þeim gef ek erni
> efstum bráðir.
> Sá mun á blóði
> bergja mínu."

Büber raised his eyes skywards, and unbidden, the dwarf offered a translation.

"The famished raven flies from the south, the fallow eagle flies with him, I shall feed them no more on the flesh of the fallen: on my body both will feast now."

"Gods, please."

"They were once noble foes, and they are reduced to this pathetic state. The mighty fall, the kings of this world are humbled, the proud are laid low. This world is dull and lifeless and without joy." Heavyhammer snorted and drooped his head in dismay.

Büber inexplicably thought of Thaler. "You're wrong," he said. "And I doubt you've ever felt joy. I'm going to catch my horse now."

He clattered after it, whistling, and it not only acknowledged his presence, it came plodding back towards him. They met, and he patted its muzzle awkwardly, confessing that it managed better conversation than the dwarf.

He led it back to the path, retrieved his sword and, wanting for any vegetation, he found a rag in his saddlebags to wipe the gore away from the blade. When he was done, he tossed it to the ground next to Heavyhammer.

"Don't tell me it's a dwarfish custom to allow your weapons to remain caked in the brains of your enemies."

"Those creatures were not worthy enough to be considered enemies, Master Büber. They were like cattle to the slaughter, lowing even as their lifeblood drained into the rock below their still-shuddering carcasses."

"Wipe your fucking axe, you miserable old sod, and let's get going. I'm not going to get caught out here at night with no fire or food." He sheathed his sword and led his horse past Heavyhammer, the path still heading inexorably upwards.

Büber wondered if he ought to strike out alone and find Farduzes himself. It couldn't be that hard, and it had been the original plan, as had blundering around and hoping to find the entrance to the underground city. But he'd been offered a personal introduction to the dwarvish king. He should take the crumbs that fate threw his way.

"Come on," he called back, a little more conciliatory. "We've miles to go. You swore an oath to me, Thorsun Heavyhammer. I thought that sort of thing was important to you."

"What is the point, human? We are doomed, you and me. We will pass from Midgard and no one will remember us. My oath?" He picked up the cloth Büber had thrown down and gave his axe a few desultory wipes before casting it onto the body of the nearest giant. "You would do better trusting Loki himself."

"That always works out well," said Büber. "But all I have is you."

Heavyhammer hauled his pack back on, staggered under its weight – something a dwarf would never have done – and carried his axe to where Büber was standing.

He strode past with a quick gait, and didn't look back.

60

If Thaler had had his own way, the work of the library would have carried on, in shifts, throughout the night. How dare people get tired, hungry, irritable and bored? And even while he cursed the frailties of others, there was his own corruptible body that itself would succumb to his base instincts despite his best efforts.

Perhaps it was better to work from cock-crow to nightjar's croak, but possible? No. Eyes that were sharp in the morning became blurred by mid-afternoon.

"Dismissed," he murmured from his position at the head of the long table.

"Master Thaler?" asked one of the librarians busy filling a barrow with catalogued books.

"Dismissed. Done. Finish for the day. Back to the dormitory, or wherever it is you intend to lay your head tonight. Eat, drink, rest, for tomorrow we do the same thing again. A Sisyphean task, gentlemen, but ours nevertheless."

He rubbed his slack, grey face, and pressed his knuckles against his closed eyelids. When he'd finished reaming, the seats around the table were empty except for his and Aaron Morgenstern's.

Thaler rested his elbows on the tabletop. "Thank you for your help today, Mr Morgenstern."

Morgenstern leant back in his seat and twisted his neck, first to the left and then to the right. Two cracks like falling slates rang out. "You've an impressive library. I didn't know just how many books you had."

"Neither did we, and indeed, we still don't. Quite what possessed my illustrious forebears in putting off the cataloguing is anyone's guess. Extraordinary business. I suppose, if I was being generous, that at some point in the past the sheer volume of titles became simply too daunting and someone decided that it had reached the level of an impossibility."

Morgenstern cracked his knuckles next. "Did Sophia remind you she'd brought back the books Thomm stole?"

"You are, without doubt, a most generous and law-abiding Jew, and a credit to your people." Thaler endowed him with a beatific smile. "She also made reference to the pseudo-Euclid book you received by mistake."

"The one she gave to you."

"Again, generous to a fault. My thanks. I trust the scrolls of your religious writings have found their rightful place in your synagogue."

"Each one needs an ark building for it, but yes." Morgenstern softened a touch, and Thaler thought that perhaps returning the

443

sefers would mark a change in the relation between the library and the literate Jews.

"We're very short-staffed," he ventured. "Especially when your daughter keeps finding new jobs for my librarians. If you could possibly . . ."

"I'll see what I can do. The young men are busy earning their shekels, but the old men? They sit around and do nothing but kvetch." Morgenstern got up, but instead of taking his leave and walking out, he picked a chair next to Thaler's. "May I?"

"Of course, please do."

Morgenstern sat again, and readjusted his kippah. He seemed nervous, but the only sounds were the last few librarians wheeling trolleys and shelving books in the deep recesses of the library.

"Sophia."

"Yes?"

"How are the Germans taking it? I mean, it must be strange for them."

Thaler countered. "And the Jews? Your religion is exclusive. One God as opposed to a pantheon, strict laws and formal obser-vance as opposed to occasional propitiation, a written tradition as well as an oral one. From your point of view, I suppose she's taking a bigger step than Felix."

"If they were married, then perhaps things would be more settled." Morgenstern pinched at his nose. "Do you know the word concubine?"

"I know that it means less than a wife," said Thaler.

"Your handfasting is less than what we'd like."

"And I've observed your marriage processions before."

The two men ruminated on their differences.

"Honestly," asked Morgenstern, "will the Germans accept Felix taking a Jewish wife?"

"Eventually? I expect so." Thaler had heard the usual grumbles. Though, since Morgenstern had requested honesty, he ought to be honest. "They're confused. Your people have lived more or less separate lives in our midst. Like those parallel lines Euclid is so fond of. To suddenly find a Jew in the royal family, and one older than Felix, and more importantly, Felix being only a boy and Sophia a woman? It's a hard thing for them to take. A prince of Carinthia is supposed to marry someone close in rank, and for duty, for the country, for peace, not for . . ."

"Not for love, you mean." Morgenstern rumbled into his beard. "I'm worried about her."

"As is right and proper. You're her father." He paused. "Would she withdraw if you objected?"

"Objected? She's with the prince. Objecting would have me locked in a tower like those Bavarians." Morgenstern sniffed. "Not really. She'd just ignore me. Oh, for certain, she'll consider what I have to say, but I can't order her around now, if I ever could. She's her own woman. Takes after her mother. "

"If there was a marriage, how would your people treat her?"

"My . . . Yes, I understand that you Germans are more lax about taking a wife, but for us, it's important. It's a father's duty to see his daughter married well."

"In which case," said Thaler, "you should be delighted."

"You mistake me. A Jewish woman's duty is to provide Jewish children for her Jewish husband. Marrying out is a particular fear we have. There aren't many of us, Master Thaler."

"In the circumstances, calling me Frederik wouldn't be out of place."

Morgenstern smoothed the hair between his nose and his lip. "Frederik, then. We have to marry within the faith, or we're lost. It'd take only a generation."

"But think of the protection she could give, Aaron."

"Is already giving. There are . . ." and Morgenstern waved his hands, "precedents. And any . . . ah . . . issue would be considered Jewish."

"Matrilineal? Interesting. A son would be . . ."

"A Jew. Yes. By our measure. How would the Germans take that?"

Thaler bent his head, deep in thought. It was a conversation that Morgenstern simply couldn't have had with anyone else. He felt strangely honoured by the level of trust imparted between two men who had, up to that point, had a mutually competitive interest in books: rivals, even, and Thaler had always had the upper hand.

He still did, of course, on paper. He was a prince's man, and the holder of arguably the most important position in the whole of the palatinate. Except he was sitting across the table from the prince's de facto father-in-law.

"I don't know. It's never happened before. Gerhard's mother was an Italian, and his first wife a Frank. If you were to be strict about these things, Felix is less than a quarter German already." Thaler thought he'd seen a book earlier with lists of kings and queens in it, and he looked around to see if he could immediately spot it. "We were never strict about inheritance, though. In the earliest days of the palatinate, the earls elected the prince from among themselves. The succession could, and did, swap families."

Morgenstern was discomforted. "And if the earls take it on themselves to do that again?"

"Most of the earls are dead, Aaron."

"But not the earldoms. There's always someone who'll claim to be the heir."

Thaler patted the table. "They take their authority from the prince."

"Who is only twelve."

"We're not going to solve all the problems of Carinthia tonight. The great council's coming: that should settle matters." Thaler reached into his pocket and pulled out the work of ibn al-Haytham. He slid it across the table. "It might not be by Euclid, but I'm still interested."

"If the great council is going to be anything like our synagogue meetings, all we'll get is a bunch of old men shouting at each other. And I speak as one of those old men." Morgenstern took the book and idly flipped open the front cover. "If this had been Euclid, I could have commanded a price that would have kept me in luxury for the rest of my days."

"*On the Balance* would have been a dramatic find, Aaron: a lost work, rediscovered. This one, though, has some promise."

Morgenstern leafed through the pages, looking at some of the illustrations and frowning at their novelty. "I thought at one point that *you* might have been interested in Sophia."

Thaler kept his face guardedly neutral. "I'm a librarian. We don't marry."

"You're still a man." Morgenstern affected studying the text in front of him closely. "Look at the state Mr Thomm got himself into."

"Sophia is an intelligent and learned woman. I enjoy her company in the same way I enjoy speaking to anyone of a similar disposition." Thaler pursed his lips, as if to indicate his disapproval. What if he had, briefly, ludicrously, entertained thoughts of Sophia

Morgenstern? He couldn't have had both her and the library, and now, whether or not it was possible, he'd made his choice and she hers. No point in wondering what might have been.

Aaron Morgenstern grunted. "You realise that this isn't just one book, rather several sewn together?"

"No, I didn't," said Thaler, glad of the change of subject. "What else do we have?"

Turning back a few pages, Morgenstern consulted the title. "*Risala der Mehel: a Treatise on Place*, which discusses moving bodies, I think, and another risala, this time on optics."

"Optics?"

"The behaviour of mirrors, curved glass, and such. Here, listen to this: 'Suppose then that the enquirer views a phenomenon they cannot explain. They must observe similar occurrences, which in itself is not enough. They must propose a solution that encompasses all those occurrences, which is not enough either. To truly seek answers, the enquirer must also carry out such experiments as are necessary. This is in order to prove the solution correct in all circumstances that are applicable.'"

"Experiments?" Thaler glanced up at the scaffolding tower. "So if I were to propose that all objects fall at the same rate, no matter how heavy they are . . ."

"I imagine you'd be the laughing stock of the town."

"No, hear me out. I could carry a variety of weights up to the top of a tower, release them at the same time, and if they strike the ground at different times, I'd be proved wrong."

"Yes. That's what'll happen. Everyone knows that."

"Everyone? Well then." Thaler pushed his chair back and stood. "Shall we prove *them* wrong?"

"What? Now?"

"We still have daylight, and it's not something I can do by myself." The master librarian reached forward and took the book from Morgenstern's hands.

"One old man and . . ." – Morgenstern regarded Thaler's physical form with scepticism – "another out of his prime, climbing towers and throwing weights off them, and to what end? It's foolishness."

"But I've already done it once." Thaler looked lost. "I went up to the gallery and I pushed two of the workmen's lunch-pails off, one empty and one full, and they hit the ground at the same time."

447

"You only think they did, Frederik. That gallery up there isn't high enough to prove anything." Morgenstern snorted. "Everyone knows that the heavier something is, the quicker it falls to the ground. If you take a feather and a stone—"

"Yes, yes." Now he was getting cross. "But a feather is supposed to push back against the air."

To illustrate his point, he grabbed one of the prepared quills on the table, and waved it back and forth. He could feel the pressure of it against his fingers. It wanted to fly, just like the goose it had come from.

"Well, there you go," said Morgenstern. "You have to consider the nature of the thing as well. A pound of feathers will fall more slowly than a pound of lead."

"Ah! Ah hah!" Thaler pounced. If an empty container fell at the same speed as one with a pound of lead, then he was absolutely confident one stuffed with feathers would. "A hundred florins says it won't."

"A hundred florins? Merciful God in Heaven, where is a poor bookseller supposed to find a hundred florins?" Morgenstern mopped theatrically at his brow. "You may as well make it a whole talent of silver and have done with it. A hundred florins would break me."

Thaler didn't have five florins to his name, let alone a hundred. He had no idea why he'd said that amount, unless it was to embarrass Morgenstern, and that wasn't his intention at all.

"A translation of this book, then, if I'm right. To be done at your earliest convenience."

That wasn't asking much. Sophia expected her father to do it anyway. Morgenstern considered the penalty.

"And what do I get when you inevitably fail? A book from the library? Any book I choose?"

"These books are not mine, Aaron, any more than they were Thomm's." Thaler even stamped his foot. "I'm missing an under-librarian now that Wess has left me to push paper on behalf of your daughter. How about Under-librarian Morgenstern?"

"Oy. I'd have to work for you? And this is supposed to be a good thing?"

"The book trade will take years to recover, even if we avoid war with every single one of our neighbours. Yes, you could spend every day in the fortress, sitting on your thumbs, or you could be down here, in among the books." Thaler held out the al-Haytham. "Smell it, Aaron. Smell the age on it. The knowledge in it. Where else are you going to get such an offer?"

Morgenstern pressed his hands together and held them against his chin, his lips and his nose. "Hmm. Put like that, I might even want you to be right."

61

"This," said her prince, "is a sword."

Sophia felt the announcement was more than a little redundant, since the Prince of Carinthia was holding the Sword of Carinthia above his head to the assembled trainees. Sitting on a barrel to the side of the courtyard, she sunned herself in the slanting sunlight that squeezed over the battlements and watched the motley crowd of faces, both familiar and strange.

Rabbi Cohen was there, and her neighbour Mr Rosenbaum, and Master Ullmann, and Master Emser, one of the guildmasters who'd gone exploring underground with Frederik Thaler.

Felix had unbound his right arm – against her wishes, but he was young and he'd learn – but still held the sword in his left. The sunlight caught the blade and it glittered marvellously. The men looked to their own swords, a mixture of old Roman-pattern cavalry swords and Goth-style longswords. Not one of them was as fine, and they didn't look at all convinced that they'd be able to learn anything.

She frowned. Did he realise? Should she tell him?

She'd help set up the wicker dummy behind him, as well as the deer carcass hung on chains from a wooden drying frame. That was as far as her involvement seemed to extend.

"Rabbi," said Felix, "come here."

Nervous, fingers flexing on his hilt, Cohen took a pace forward and stopped.

"No, over here." Felix beckoned.

With a glance over his shoulder, the rabbi walked towards Felix.

"Prince Felix?" Ah, getting a "my lord" out of that man was harder than milking a stone.

Felix gave him the sword he held, and exchanged it for the notched, dull, hammer-beaten one Cohen had chosen from the armoury.

"This," he said, "is also a sword."

The men laughed, and Sophia's heart inexplicably soared.

Left-handed, he rotated on his heel and landed a blow across the neck of the dummy that left the blade embedded where the Idun's apple would be. Felix let go, and the hilt hung suspended in the air. He brushed off fragments of willow from his tunic.

"Respect your weapons, gentlemen. I'm not going to promise to turn you into master swordsmen, but today you will go away with a better idea of how not to get yourselves killed. If you come back tomorrow, we'll practise the other part. Spread out so that you're two lengths apart but can still see me."

They complied, and in good humour. Felix started slowly, almost ponderously. His slight frame didn't seem made to make such exaggerated shapes. It was almost like dancing: raising the blade point-down in front of the body on the step back, holding it horizontally at waist-level on the step forward.

Repetition seemed to be the key, training the body to adopt the most rudimentary of guards. He moved, they copied. Ragged at first, uncertain, timid even. Then more confident, as if they could see the point of it.

She got up from her seat and walked slowly around the rear of the group, where she stood watching the strain and heft of their backs as they blocked, lowered, and blocked again.

She picked up a spare sword from the trestle where they'd been displayed. It was similar to the one she'd borrowed from the Town Hall, long with a slight widening before the tip. It fitted neatly in her hand, and balanced well.

The next time the men slid and held, she did too, just the foot movements. It *was* a dance: she was poised and steady, she was already good at this.

Felix was speeding up. Each form he made was less discrete and more fluid, seamlessly folding from one to another and back. She tried following, and found it easy, even when Felix decided to go faster still.

He stopped, and stood in front of Rabbi Cohen, who was still using the Sword of Carinthia. He held out his sword, drew it back, and aimed a lazy swing at the rabbi's guts.

Metal clanged against metal, eliciting a grunt of effort from the man. Then Felix whipped around and went for the reverse blow. Cohen instinctively raised his blade and another clang echoed around the courtyard.

"Good," said Felix. He moved on to the next man and did the same thing.

Each man got his turn, until there was only one left, and she wasn't a man.

"My lord," she said.

"Are you sure about this?" he asked. "It's not usual . . ."

"I know." She nodded. "All the same, I'd rather do this properly than not."

He gave her no warning, and didn't pull his blow. She parried at once; her hand buzzed with the impact and she grunted with surprise, but there was no time to rest or consider how it felt. He stepped back, she stepped forward, and he brought the sword across her again.

Step back, raise blade, bang.

"My lady," he said, "always with the flat. Always. And with the half of the blade below the hilt if you can." He walked back to the front. "Ride the blow. Don't be rigid. The best way to avoid being hit is not to be in the way. Failing that, deflect the blow, move with it, make it safe."

He turned and faced them again. "Blows from above. Raise your sword over your heads, blade horizontal. Brace it halfway with your other hand on the flat. I can't do that bit, but you can."

He put his back to them. "Like this." He bent his knee and braced his other foot against the ground, lowering his head and bringing the sword over it. "One movement."

Felix straightened again, and then bent. The others mimicked him, and so did Sophia. The seams on her sleeves were tight, and resisted her raising her arms. Courtly dresses weren't made for sword fighting; not really a surprise. But she wasn't going to hold back if it meant not completing her guard. If the stitching went, so be it.

They went through the same procedure, starting slowly and gradually building up speed until it became second nature.

He attacked them all. His pupils, eager and attentive, all blocked Felix's overhead swing. He came to Sophia again, and she readied herself.

"My lord."

He swung at her. But not at her head. At her side. She leapt back, hand raised high, sword-point dipping down. Felix's edge scraped up as far as her hilt. She stepped forward, levelling her blade and forcing his down. Her opponent back-handed a blow up and over, towards her neck. She brought her hands high, just as she'd been taught, and her arms shuddered with the effort.

Felix let his sword rest on hers. "Too stiff, my lady. Your elbows should be bent, not locked."

She pushed his arm away and snapped, "Are you actually trying to kill me?"

Felix looked shocked, then mortified. "No, Sophia, no. I wouldn't. I'm trying to show you what it's like."

"Then why is it that you're tapping at their swords but hammering away at mine?" She was acutely aware of her sudden anger, of the way her fingers flexed against the corded sword grip. That she could reach out and smack this child with either her open palm or her filled fist. "My lord."

"Because you're already better than they are, Sophia." He lowered his sword, resting it point-down on the ground. He was disappointed, not just in her, but in himself. "I should find someone else to teach you."

There *was* no one else, and she was being as petulant as he was. No one had made her do this. She could choose to put her weapon down and never pick it up again, or stay and see this out.

Everyone was watching her, to see what she did. And, no doubt, what she did would be gossiped about in those beer cellars that still had some beer left.

"Elbows bent," she said, raising her blade. "Then we'll do it again until I get it right."

His next blow was soft. It didn't trouble her, and she narrowed her eyes.

"Harder. How else am I going to learn?"

"But—"

"Harder."

He complied, leaning away from his swinging arm. His sword bounced off as she timed her parry to actively block, not just passively receive.

"Better," she said.

He smiled uncertainly at her, and she brushed his sword-arm

452

away with hers. She looked down, and saw that with a little extra effort she could pin the tip of Felix's blade against the ground with her boot.

Felix was watching the direction of her gaze. He danced back. "My lady."

The men looked uncomfortable. Good. Let them realise that Sophia Morgenstern wasn't content to sit in the solar practising her needlework. Let them see their prince's consort with a sword in her hand and her hair plastered to her forehead with sweat. She was no blonde Valkyrie, but if they remembered her like this rather than as an outsider first, a Jew, then a little suffering was nothing.

Sophia straightened up. She made certain that she didn't smile, didn't give anything away. "Your students are waiting, my lord."

She could tell that he didn't know how to take that. As he walked back to his place again, he kept on looking behind him. He took his stance at the front, taking the first position, holding it until everyone had copied him.

Sophia put her arm up, angled the blade down.

Felix moved into the overhead block, then back. Two fluid movements faster than ever before, each with their own step.

It was simple. Her muscles followed her instructions perfectly. No need to get over-confident, either. Not every blow was going to come from the side or above: there were lunges to think about, and low blows. And using a shield, and a spear, and possibly doing all those things on horseback.

He didn't come around again to see if they'd mastered their twin parries. The sun slipped below both the fortress ramparts and the surrounding mountains, and the courtyard grew gloomy.

It was enough for one day. Her sword-arm ached dully by the time she placed it back on the table, and she squeezed her muscles to try and get them working again. Felix remembered to relieve Cohen of his sword before he made off with it, and the men trooped out, with good-natured banter and bragging.

Now Felix was in pain. He gingerly sheathed his sword at his belt and dragged his feet over to Sophia. His left hand was feeling under his shirt at his clavicle, trying to tell if the bones had become unravelled by his exertions.

"Am I allowed to say I told you so?" she said.

"Who else would get away with it?" His discomfort made him irritable. Or perhaps he was grumpy because of her treatment of him.

"You could have left it for another week. We might have been able to have some practice-swords made."

"We can't afford to waste a week. So we train now, with real swords." He allowed her to push his hand away and manipulate his shoulder for herself. "Did I really hurt you?"

"You surprised me. I don't know why." His young bones had set straight, with only a small knot to show for it. "If I'm going to learn how to defend myself properly, I shouldn't have gone into it thinking I was just playing."

He looked up at her. "And were you? Playing?"

"To start with. I was wrong, and you were right." She pulled his shirt closed. "You need to put your sling back on for the rest of the evening. I can understand why you didn't want to wear it in front of everyone, but they're not watching now."

Felix nodded meekly.

"Come, my lord. Let's see if the kitchens have managed to scratch something together." She placed her hand in the small of his back and guided him over to the keep.

"Sophia? Are people going hungry?"

"Not yet. Food is getting more expensive the more scarce it gets. The supplies aren't coming into town. It's more difficult to bring them to market now, but that doesn't mean it's impossible."

"So where's all the food?"

"It's still at the farms. They're keeping hold of it because they don't have the confidence to send it here." She reached ahead of him and hauled open the wooden door. "They're still waiting for the sky to fall."

"And the water?" he asked.

"They've been digging for over a week now under the instruction of Master Prauss. It has to come soon." That one problem had become the symbol of all their problems. It made life difficult for everyone, so difficult that some had considered packing up and leaving for elsewhere. "Is it true that there are caves full of machines below the fortress?"

"That's what Master Thaler says. He also says there are stairs up, but I've never found the top of them." He leant against the doorway. "I should have. There wasn't much to do but poke around in dark corners, when I wasn't being schooled by the signore."

If her shibboleth was the loss of the mikveh, his was the betrayal

454

by his sword-master. He couldn't deny Peter Büber's gloss on events and pretend that Eckhardt had somehow tricked Allegretti.

"Someone's going to have to go down the tunnel and up through whichever blocked door it goes to." She shrugged. "It's not so important as the other things."

"Someone we can trust. These walls don't need a back door." Felix closed his eyes and rested his head against the stonework. "My father never had days like this. He never trained troops, made laws, hired spies or locked up Bavarians."

"He didn't know, Felix. If he had, he would have done something."

"You think? You didn't see him at the end: he didn't believe it was happening, so he just did what we'd always done."

"I know you miss him," said Sophia.

"I don't, though. I don't miss him at all. If he was here now, all I'd be doing is shouting at him for getting everything so wrong and then leaving me with all this mess. He spent his life riding and hawking and hunting. Sometimes he had to dress up and play at princes, but he wasn't serious about it." Felix sighed. "I've done more in a month that he did his whole reign."

"I'm sorry." What did she really feel for this boy, this man, this prince? They needed each other for the political advantage it gave them: he'd saved her and she'd saved him, and they went on saving each other every day. He needed someone to mother him, even though she had no experience of that. She needed someone to rescue her from being an outsider in her own community.

If they both found meaning in that, expedient as it was, was that so bad? Only good had come out of it so far.

"And tomorrow," she said, "we do it all again. Except by tomorrow, the workmen at the library will have been paid, and they'll want to buy food, and the market traders will send out to the farms, and the carts will start arriving again, even if they are pushed by hand."

"Horses. We need horses. And the tack that goes with them. And carts designed to be pulled by them."

"Donkeys do just as well. And you can use cows. Bullocks. We use them to pull our carts and ploughs. We'll teach you how." She stood bolt upright. "The Jews need to show the German farmers how to live a non-magical life."

"Your market in Scale Place—"

"Is as well-stocked as it usually is. Lots of Germans buying there, too. Most of us have relatives who live on the land. They can lend their plough teams out. Work out a breeding programme for livestock. Make patterns for yokes." Ah, the irony. They were all going to be Jews from now on. "Threshing and grinding. Everything."

Felix rubbed at his face, his exhaustion showing. "Can we do this? Can we really make things work?"

"No reason why not. We've been living like this for thousands of years. We're still here, and not just surviving, but thriving. Especially here in Carinthia." She reached out and brushed at his hair, which had become as unruly as hers. Next time, she'd tie hers up, or cover it like a respectable Jewish wife should. "The shtetls and dorfs have grown, both from children being born and Jews coming from other palatinates. I'll take you Halstadt. I've an aunt there."

"That's good," he said, and caught her finger in his own, dragging it down. He added with a mumble: "That wasn't what I meant, though."

"Oh," she said. "You can always change your mind. Now, or later. You're the prince: you can do more or less what you want."

"People will say I'm just using you to keep the Jews loyal."

"Then the people would be very wrong, Felix. My being here isn't popular with anyone. It might become acceptable, when they take the time to think it through, but for the moment, no. They won't be saying that at all." She hooked her finger to keep contact. "If you were older, then . . ."

"Would that make a difference?"

"Probably not." She shrugged. "Your . . . years make things more complicated, but it's not the cause."

He grew quiet, and she jiggled his hand.

"Why don't we find our supper, and see what tomorrow brings?"

Felix nodded, and allowed himself to be led away.

62

It was fated that they arrived at their destination just after the sun's last red line shimmered on the far distant horizon. Moments before, the wall of rock that was Farduzes had been lit like a beacon fire. Now it was shrouded and silent, and the path they were following slid away into uncertainty.

"Fuck," said Büber. It was Heavyhammer's fault. The miserable bastard had been dragging his still-stumpy legs for the last five miles, while retaining enough breath to spout dreary kennings about rocks more or less at will. Now they had to pick their way down to the entrance in the twilight, a descent that would have been bad enough when they could have seen what they were doing.

"It isn't far, human." Heavyhammer walked a little way down what appeared to be an entirely contextless ledge and stopped.

"You can't see in the dark like you used to," muttered Büber. "You don't know the way any more than I do, and when the stars start to come out, you're going to curl into a ball and start rocking backwards and forwards." He looked around. The only safe way down the mountain was to back up and wait until morning. There wasn't enough room for his horse to turn around, but he could reverse it up with careful coaxing.

The drop in front of them wasn't sheer, but it was loose scree almost all the way down to the valley floor. Above them loomed sharp, blocky outcrops; whether their shapes were natural or deliberately carved, it was impossible to tell. "If you'd just admitted we were lost, then we could have made camp somewhere other than halfway up a cliff." Büber patted his horse on the muzzle and shortened the reins to a stub. "Now we have to do something dangerous and stupid because of you."

And better do it now than wait any longer. He stood in front of the horse and, holding its head, started to nudge it backwards up the path. It resisted, quite understandably, trying to gain purchase on the joints in the rock. Büber was insistent, however, and eventually it had little choice but to move. It took a few steps, decided that was enough, and tried to dig its hooves in again.

"Come on. A little more." He eased the beast back. "I'm not carrying you."

He reached a place where there was enough room – just – to lead the horse around in a circle. Then he realised that Heavyhammer had gone, and there was no way the dwarf could have got past him.

"Ah, *fuck*."

He completed the manoeuvre anyway and climbed up to where he knew the path cut across a broad, flat shoulder of rock. So, some or all of the dwarf's laggardness had been an act, designed to strand Büber out here, on top of the mountain, in the dark and the cold, while he went on, into the city to do whatever it was that lying, cheating dwarves did.

The stories told about them were clear enough, and the moral obvious. And Büber was perhaps one of the few people who could throw a dwarf further than he wanted to trust one.

He got some food out of his saddlebags, but there was nothing for the horse, and he felt like a bastard for having dragged it all that way without even the sniff of a bale of hay while he gnawed on the end of a spear of dried meat.

There was nothing to tie the horse to. He had to use the only material to hand – stone – and devised a wedge that would hold a tether. When he'd managed to convince himself that it wasn't going to slip, he dragged the saddle from the horse's back and threw a blanket over it.

They were both going to get cold, no matter what. There was nothing to burn. Dwarves might have their black rock, but Büber had none, nor any wood. He wrapped his cloak around himself and tried to find somewhere out of the wind, finally making camp in the angle of an overhanging outcrop, surrounded on two sides by hard grey walls.

He made sure he had his sword, bow and bolts to hand. Giants weren't going to be the problem they might have been, but there could be other monsters abroad. There was always Heavyhammer's possible return, too.

Büber wondered what he was up to. An oath was an oath, but if it was made to a human, did it still count? If the dwarves wanted to talk among themselves for a while, he wouldn't have minded waiting inside somewhere, instead of halfway up an exposed rockface.

He pulled his knees in and rested his chin on them, trying to make himself small. It was almost completely dark, with clouds skittering in from the east and racing away across the valley. The flashes of stars in the breaks were the only light, until, just as Büber's eyelids were sinking closed, a flickering orange flame caught his attention.

Another fire appeared behind it, and another, until a line of wind-torn torches stretched out across the high ground. They wound towards him, and Büber assumed that the dwarves must know where he was: he could hear them as they came closer, muttering and clattering.

"Come out, human." It was Heavyhammer's voice, or at least it carried the right note of regret and weariness.

"You could have just told me you needed to go on ahead," said Büber, scooping up his sword and holding it in its scabbard.

"It was necessary. No human sees the way into Farduzes unbidden."

"Even though you're going to abandon it soon? That makes sense."

One of the torches closed on Büber's resting place, and the shadows that fell down Heavyhammer's face made it look like he was melting. "These are our laws. You will not mock us."

The wind tugged at Büber's cloak and the flames from the torches stretched and roared. It wasn't a good night to be out, so he curbed his tongue.

"So what's your decision?"

"The king of Farduzes will hear your petition."

"Good." Büber got to his feet. "Now, or in the morning?"

"The halls of Farduzes are timeless, and the king is waiting." Heavyhammer turned his back, and the torches started to move away.

Büber called after them. "I need to get my saddle and my horse – unless dwarvish hospitality doesn't extend to bed and board for both me and the animal?"

It might not have been something they'd considered, but Büber was going to make them consider it now.

The dwarves seemed to be dithering. The question was straightforward, as was the answer: he was a messenger from a neighbouring prince. It was common custom to treat them well.

Büber decided for them. He picked up the saddle and heaved the tack on loosely. He tied on his sword and bow, and slipped the tether from the rock.

"I'll see the king now," he said.

Rather than argue or fight, they acquiesced. The line of lights moved off again, with Büber and the horse trailing after them.

There didn't seem to be a path, just a wasteland of jumbled rock from giant-sized boulders down to pea-sized grit. They were following a trail he couldn't see that wound around a pinnacle so tall it blotted out even the night.

Then a door appeared, its shape – tall and broad, like the opening of the fortress gatehouse – shown by the light coming from inside. The lead torch swung from side to side and the line of warm light split and grew. The doors were levered apart soundlessly to reveal a high-ceilinged space beyond.

The torches were extinguished, one by one, and the dark shapes that carried them resolved into the same odd-shaped, ill-clothed man-things that he'd seen the like of beside the river.

He crossed the threshold, and the huge doors closed behind him with an inappropriately soft shush. He steadied the horse and peered around at the smooth, carved stonework. Even high up on the vaulted ceiling, the work was immaculate, the joints all but invisible.

"Leave the beast here. Only your presence is required." Heavyhammer pointed way down the hall to another equally impressive doorway. Oil lamps flickered in niches along both walls. Their wavering light made the dragons carved up the pillars appear to shift in an unnerving way, especially to someone who'd seen them in the flesh.

Büber once again dragged the saddle from the horse's back and, wanting for anything else to tie the reins to, fixed them to the pommel. One more thing: inside his saddlebags was a small leather satchel, in which was Felix's letter. He fetched it out and slung it over his shoulder.

"I'm ready."

At first, it was possible to convince himself that he was in some kind of building. But after the second set of doors opened to reveal a pit of impossible depth, around which ran a wide road spiralling downwards, the illusion was lost.

There was, at least, a high stone banister to guard against accidents, but he stuck to the wall side, avoided looking down after that first glance, and certainly didn't think about how far underground he was going. The bottom of the staircase was lost below him, and the central well deep enough to have its own weather.

If they meant to impress him, it was working.

And if the dwarves were growing wary of the weight of rock above them, he understood. It worried him, too.

"How . . . far?" he asked.

"The secrets of Farduzes are just that: secrets. You are the first man to have walked this way in a thousand years." Heavyhammer had dispensed with the poetry, but was still as doom-haunted as ever. "You will not be the last. There is a time coming when every thief and robber in Midgard will tread this way, looking for plunder, and there will be nothing to stop them. Our memories, our achievements, our history, despoiled and stolen by those who will ill-use them in their own bitter service."

"Don't you have a way of sealing the doors, or closing off passages?"

"Farduzes was not designed to be our tomb, but a living monument to our glory. Why would we build in mechanisms to destroy it, that could be triggered by some madman?" Heavyhammer pulled at his beard, and muttered: "There were enchantments we could have used – they are useless now and we are defenceless."

They were in the heart of the mountain: galleries led off the main staircase, wide enough to suggest whole towns complete with smelters and forges, farms and gardens. All now were plunged, if not into darkness, into the twilight gloom of smoky orange flame. No wonder they were dying.

Büber looked up at the way they'd come. There were pin-pricks of light from the entrance hall, then long curves of lamps like beads on a necklace. If this place had been lit by magical light, he'd have been able to see all of it, all at once. It would have been terrifying.

They were nowhere near the bottom. Büber finally moved from the wall to a position where he could glance into the abyss again, and their were faint lights at the limit of his vision – or was he simply imagining things? There was no opportunity to check. The lead dwarf headed along one of the galleries, and the procession followed. Runes were carved in letters a foot high above the arch, as they had been above every arch, but it wasn't just German that the huntmaster couldn't read.

"The king is old and irascible," said Heavyhammer. "I doubt if there is anything you can say that will persuade him from his chosen path."

"I'm here to deliver the prince's letter. I'm not here to persuade anyone to do anything." How far below the mountain was he now? Did the world have a beating heart, and how close was he to it?

"You will try, human. It's in your nature. You live like birds, all movement and noise, building your nests and always fearful of the next storm. Even when your labour has been dashed on the

461

ground, your eggs broken, what do you do?" The dwarf glowered at the uselessness of it all. "You build it all again, in the hope that it'll be different next time. It's not hope that propels you, but vanity. And foolishness. Nothing ever changes."

"Everything has changed, Heavyhammer. None of us can escape that."

"It's brought the moment of our destruction closer, that's all." He looked up at Büber. "If you cannot keep a civil tongue in your head, then things will go badly for you."

"I don't intend to say anything at all." Büber patted the satchel. "I'm the delivery boy, and there's no reason for kings to listen to the likes of me."

The dwarf bristled indignantly. It might have worked had he been in his pomp, but his appearance now reminded Büber too much of the petulant child from Ennsbruck.

"If the king questions you, you will answer."

"I'm not an idiot, Master Dwarf. I know how to conduct myself."

"Good," said Heavyhammer, "because we're here."

If the mere corridor had been impressive, the space beyond was vast. Pillars sprang from the floor with such energy that they lost themselves in the space above, and Büber's footsteps, far from echoing, simply fled in fear and never returned.

In the distance was a dais, and on that dais was a throne.

Büber thought of the time when Gerhard had sought him out in the fortress's mess room. There had been something — no, a lot — to be said for his ability to speak to other men on an equal footing, while maintaining the gulf in authority that existed between them. For all his faults, the late prince had been approachable, and not only from one end of a stupidly long hall.

"This king of yours: if I'm to greet him properly, I'll need to know his name."

Heavyhammer grunted. "His name is Lord Tol Ironmaker, Master of Farduzes, King of all the Dwarves, Mountain Hewer, Spark Quencher, Doom Monger."

"My Lord Ironmaker has an impressive set of titles."

"You mean for one so short?" Heavyhammer's voice rose from a whisper to a shout.

"Not at all," said Büber mildly. Perhaps, he decided, it would be better if he did say nothing after all, given how touchy they all were. "Just that human lords tend to style themselves more simply."

462

Tol Ironmaker had a sizeable ceremonial guard, but their numbers simply proved to Büber the hopelessness of the dwarf king's situation. All their armour was too small, their pikes strangely foreshortened, their demeanour less than splendid.

Büber's own escort halted well before the throne, leaving him to make the trip to the foot of the dais with only Heavyhammer by his side.

Ironmaker glowered down from his throne. It was high-backed, high-sided, and the grey-bearded king looked squashed in. His legs were too long to rest easily, and he moved his arms from his lap to his thighs, then folded them in front of him. His sceptre was still impressive, containing the largest gemstone Büber had ever seen, set within a golden cage: never normally one to look for symbolism, the huntmaster thought it quite apt.

Something of a staring contest ensued, until Heavyhammer glanced up from his almost-supine position. "Bend your knee to the King of the Dwarves, human."

Büber knew how to bow, so he did that instead. Honour seemed to be satisfied, and while Heavyhammer told his lord of the messenger's credentials, Büber opened the satchel and retrieved the letter.

He proffered it to Ironmaker, and the king gestured for Heavyhammer to take it.

"What language is this written in, human?" Heavyhammer asked him.

"German, I assume. Unless Felix managed to find a dwarvish speaker in the library. Which he might have done, I don't know."

"What sort of messenger—"

"One that can't read, Master Dwarf." Büber pursed his lips. "I never had the reason to learn, though you'll find me skilled in other ways. Like lighting fires."

Heavyhammer approached the king with the letter, and Ironmaker took it from him with about as much joy as he would have received a dead stoat a week after its passing.

The king gave his sceptre to a waiting servant, and cracked the seal on the letter. Still scowling, he opened it and scanned the first few lines. He raised one of his bushy brows and looked over the top of the piece of parchment at its deliverer.

Büber wondered if he should be afraid. The thought of the mountain hanging over him certainly concerned him. The thought of never seeing the sky again likewise. But afraid of these tragic figures? It was difficult to think of them as anything but lost children, abandoned in a world where nothing made sense any more: much like the hexmasters, although at least the dwarves had managed not to turn on each other in bloody revenge.

He gazed evenly back, trying not to show what he was thinking.

King Ironmaker turned his attention back to the letter. It was presumably written in Dwarvish, thought Büber; either that or German-speaking was more common than he'd realised.

It took a while for the king to look up again.

When he did, he let the parchment hang from his hand, allowing Büber to catch sight of a forest of little runes as spiky as pine needles. Ironmaker leant forward to examine the human, then said something to Heavyhammer.

"The king wants to know why you are so scarred. He thought all humans were smooth-skinned."

"Tell the king I'm huntmaster of Carinthia. Tell him I've never been healed because spells would have left a taint on me and left me unable to carry out my duties."

Heavyhammer translated, and the king listened. He spoke again.

"The king wants to know if your Felix can be trusted to keep his word."

Büber looked askance. "I'm not the Oracle," he snorted, "and it ill fits the Master of Farduzes to expect me to judge my own lord's honesty."

Rather than passing Büber's words back, Heavyhammer explained further. "Carinthia's offer is to the dwarves. Will he honour his offer now we are changed? Will he reject us or enslave us instead?"

"Ah," said Büber, and he froze. The king had sent him to ask for help in operating the machines below Juvavum, expecting no more than a few dozen dwarves to make the journey. King Ironmaker now seemed to be suggesting the entire dwarvish kingdom decamp for Carinthia. How many of them were there? He'd seen, in all, no more than . . . well, less than half a century for sure.

But he'd passed numerous galleries on the way down. There could be legions more dwarves, more of them even than Carinthians. He had no way of telling.

What he ought to do was go back to Felix and explain. He was the prince. It was up to him to decide. That was why they had princes, after all, so that people like Büber didn't have to make decisions of this magnitude.

All the dwarves were looking at him, waiting for him. He didn't know whether a wrong word now might mean death. He'd no idea, even, what the wrong word might be.

He'd always believed himself a capable enough man – he knew his areas of expertise, and understood also when he was out of his depth, as with the unicorn horns – but here was a decision that might decide the fate of whole peoples and nations.

He remembered how Felix had ordered him to kill the Teuton prisoners, and his later mumbled regret. He remembered his banishment with Nikoleta, and the apology that had followed. He remembered standing on the bridge, and defending the library, and how the boy had matched him blow for blow, afterwards marking every man who'd taken up arms against him. He remembered his insistence that Eckhardt had to die. The boy had steel in him, for sure. And he was man enough to recognise his mistakes.

What would Felix have done if he was standing in front of King Ironmaker? Büber knew what he'd have said: that he was a twelve-year-old prince whose fledgling sense of honour had just been questioned by a once-mighty dwarf-lord.

Büber cleared his throat: "The Prince of Carinthia's word is always trustworthy," he said. More than that, he found himself believing it.

Heavyhammer translated, and the king's expression didn't change a jot. Perhaps something was lost in the interplay of words, from German to Dwarvish and back. Büber felt he'd played his part as best he could: let them do what they will.

Ironmaker swapped Felix's letter for his sceptre. He spoke briefly.

"The king says Carinthia will have his answer soon."

They weren't going to kill him yet, then. One corner of Büber's mouth curled up.

"It is time to go, human."

Büber turned to see that his escort had already reformed behind him.

"Thank the king for his time," he said, and he walked away, not knowing whether protocol demanded that he should reverse out, bowing all the time.

Behind him, Heavyhammer, approached the throne on his own, and spoke with his lord.

The climb was long, and without rest. It seemed that one thing the dwarves hadn't lost was their ability to simply keep on going. Büber had descended perhaps half the height of the peak in one go, and it was a struggle to keep breathing on the journey back. By the time they led him back into the hallway, he was exhausted.

And now what? Were they simply going to push him back out into the night?

Apparently not. The horse had already been fed, and there was food and drink and blankets set out for him.

The stone was hard and cold, even with the odd-smelling rugs, and the food tasted, not poisonous, but off – mushroomy. The drink was beer with dwarvish character, bitter and heavy and dark. It sent his head reeling, and if he hadn't been tired before, he was now unable to stay awake a moment longer.

He all but fell down the wall he'd propped himself against, and he barely had time to rearrange the blankets around himself before he was gone.

63

Ullmann turned over, and realised there was an arm across his chest. Not *his* arm, either. Light fractured the curtain, and gave him enough to see the back of a crown of golden hair.

It was a narrow bed. They were jammed in together like piglets, naked and pink, and their clothes lay strewn with indecent haste across the rest of the mean lodgings – a room at the top and back of her master's house.

"Aelinn? Aelinn, wake up. It's morning."

She stirred, felt behind her to touch the outside of his thigh, and sat up suddenly. "I need to lay the fires and boil the water."

"Wasn't there enough laying and boiling last night?"

She hit him lightly across his bare chest. Her breasts bounced, and Ullmann was distracted.

"Work is hard enough to come by these days, and there'll be a dozen like me wanting to take my place if I don't get on."

"Aelinn . . ."

"Up, dressed, and out, before the rest of the household wakes."

She pushed his questing hand away. "We can talk about last night later."

"Aelinn—"

"Max, please. This is important to me. I have a job to do, even if prince's men can order their own hours." She slid from the bed and went hunting around the room, gathering up her clothes and throwing Ullmann's at him. He was hit in the face by his own breeks, and he laughed inappropriately.

She gave him a look – no, *the* look – that made him realise that he really ought to do what she said, but she was still as blonde and slim and pretty as she had been before, and they hadn't been drunk except on each other.

He'd sought her out. They'd walked and talked and eaten and flirted. He had, up to the point they'd kissed on the doorstep, been the perfect gentleman. It became a little blurred after that point, but they'd ended up in her room doing all manner of things to each other, for quite a long time, before falling sated onto the mattress.

She was dressing, and reluctantly he started to do the same. Ready long before he was, she found his boots for him. He didn't recognise them, then remembered they were the Bavarian's.

"Thank you," he said, and she waited, arms folded, while he pulled them on, unfamiliar and ill-fitting.

"Max, you're going to have to go. Now."

He dragged his shirt on over his head, and struggled into the sleeves. "You seemed more than happy last night to have me stay."

"That was last night. There may well be other nights."

"May?"

She half smiled. "Yes, may. But it's morning now, and I've a day's work to do." She reached out and snagged his arm. She was surprisingly strong, and he didn't have the will to resist her anyway. He found himself propelled towards the door.

"Can I call on you again?"

"Yes." Her hand was on his back, pushing him down the narrow stairs.

"Tonight?"

"I thought prince's men had important duties: ones that might keep them from calling."

He stopped at the turn of the stairs, and looked up at her shadowed face. Above her was a defunct light. "Aelinn, have I done something wrong?"

"No," she said. "This is a bit quick, that's all. I didn't mean to . . ." – and she gave a small squeak of frustration. "Give me a little while, yes?"

Ullmann worked his jaw. "Whatever you want."

"Don't be like that."

He started down the stairs again, thought about deliberately making some noise, but resisted the urge. He didn't know what was going on here. It should have been simple, but apparently it wasn't. "Like what?"

"Huffy," she said. "All I'm doing is trying to get you out of the house before I get into trouble. Any more trouble."

"I'm going. I don't mean to be a nuisance."

"You're not, it's just everything else. Now, quiet as you can." She squeezed past him, front to front, stifling a giggle at his startled expression, then tripped through the remaining rooms on her tiptoes.

The front door was substantial, and bolted. He helped her draw the bolts back and ease the latch up. Outside, the sky didn't look promising, and it was colder than it had been the day before.

He raised his eyebrows at her and started to slip through the gap between door and frame. She caught his chin and kissed him hard on the lips before sending him across the threshold with a shove.

The door clicked shut again, and Ullmann found himself looking out over the main square. The fortress was a grey slab above the rooftops and greening branches of the sacred grove, and wood smoke flavoured the air. Breakfast, then. No man could tell him he hadn't worked up an appetite.

He could find a beer cellar or street vendor: he had a purse of florins and shillings now, but was unused to wealth. What he should do was send some of it back to his parents to help them pay for the things they'd need for the farm that would soon be theirs by right, no longer beholden to any master or earl.

His only immediate desire was another pair of boots. And another night with Aelinn. Not just because it had been the first uninterrupted sleep he'd had after stabbing Nikoleta Agana, but because he liked her more than he thought possible in such a short time.

His daydreaming had brought him to Library Square. A trickle of workmen were beginning to arrive – apprentices and journeymen

– making ready to begin their labour, even though the doors to the library itself were still shut. The library refectory would be open, though, he remembered, so – ignoring the few enterprising bratwurst sellers who had turned up in their carts to make the most of the prince's coin – he slipped in the side door.

It was early, even for librarians. The hall was almost empty: a sprinkling of people at the kitchen end of the table. He thought about turning around, but was called over.

"Master Ullmann!"

It was Master Thaler, waving across at him. Ullmann took his place next to the man.

"Good morning, Master Ullmann. Up with a larks and ready to seize the day?"

"Carpe diem indeed, Master Thaler." He reached forward to claim a wedge of bread and chunk of cheese. "The world is full of possibilities, and it's up to us to make the most of them."

"Indeed it is. As I was just explaining to our newest librarian, our circumstances may have changed but our skills are still valued by the learned." Thaler affably raised his mug to his colleagues.

Ullmann raised his own and glanced around the table. His skin prickled.

On the far side of the master librarian was a man not much older than Ullmann, who he recognised as Fottner. Opposite the junior man was Braun, and next to him . . . The man . . . no, woman – though with her rough, short-cropped hair and pale northern features, she could have passed for a boy – reached out for her mug to return the toast. Her black robe pulled back from her wrist to reveal a maze of tattoos.

"She's . . ." His first bite of bread remained unswallowed.

"As you yourself argued before the prince, it is what she is and can become that now directs all our behaviour. What she was is immaterial. The past is indeed a foreign country. We know it not." Thaler swigged his watered-down wine. "To the future, where we will journey together, as one."

The woman fixed Ullmann with her pale eyes. She lifted her mug, but her salute was mocking, and her gaze never left him as she drank.

He was instantly suspicious. She'd swapped her white robes for black, but she couldn't be mistaken for anyone else. He'd taken the instructions regarding the Order to Wess only yesterday afternoon. He wet his mouth with his wine. "You move quickly, Mistress."

That was an understatement: it was almost as if she'd been waiting for such a letter to be written, possibly even predicting its appearance. Had he made a mistake?

"I've learnt through bitter experience to do so, Master."

All Ullmann could see was Nikoleta. Her tattooed hands trying to cover the wound in her chest. Her fever-bright eyes wide and round as she recognised her murderer. The flames as they caught the clothes she was wearing, her hair, her skin.

His hand brushed the place on his chest where she'd touched him, marked now by five silvery oval scars, and composed himself. The woman opposite wasn't Nikoleta, and didn't resemble her in any way. She had a thin, sculpted face. Almost elfin. Ullmann couldn't see the tops of her ears. They were hidden in her hair, but it was entirely possible that they ended in points.

"Apologies," he mumbled. "I was just surprised at the speed of your arrival. I should have been told if and when hexmasters enter the town."

"There's scarcely been time," said Thaler, "and now you know. We must also remember that the mistress is not a hexmaster, and never was. But whether a novice or adept, she is literate, and gods know I need as many of her as I can get. She is both welcome and wanted."

"If I could still do magic," said the woman quietly, "do you think I'd be here?"

Thaler beamed at his newest recruit. "If you thought the transition to our new world is painful for us, Master Ullmann, can you begin to imagine what it is like for those who are now adrift in it like shipwrecked sailors? The library is their Pharos, showing the way home."

The tension that had built up started to spill away. With conscious effort, Ullmann reached out for the jug and offered to refresh his dining partner's drink. After a brief moment in which he thought she might refuse, she held up her pottery mug, still resting her elbow on the table.

He poured the wine-pink stream until her cup was half full. "Mistress."

"Master." She drank slowly, lowered her mug slowly, and returned to her meal slowly, all the while enjoying Ullmann's discomfort.

"Excellent," said Thaler. "Now where was I? Yes. You are free to come and go as you please: a salary will be paid, with a small deduction for board and lodging while you remain in library accommodation. Working hours are, perforce, during daylight alone now, until we can invent something better than a lantern. If you find something you'd rather be doing, then let me know – you've sworn no oaths and made no promises regarding the length of your stay, but of course if you feel the work and the life suits you, you are welcome to join our small band of brothers."

"And now sisters," said Ullmann.

"What? I . . ." and Thaler sat suddenly upright. "Gods yes. I hadn't even thought of that. I hadn't thought of that at all. Well then: if the Order took women, then so do we. Another tradition on the bonfire."

He charged his mug and gulped down its contents to cover his confusion.

Ullmann noticed that the woman opposite now seemed to be regarding him with less hostility. He joined in the small talk and, because he was a good talker and knowledgeable about the town, the others listened to him. He observed how she ate and drank; freely, taking what she wanted, when she wanted.

He'd visited the novices' house. He'd picked over the jumbled pile of bodies behind it, and wandered its empty corridors, confronted again and again with devices that could only have been used to inflict various grades of pain. Everyone who'd been through that school would be a formidable opponent. He suspected that the former witch was never going to be content to be a mundane like everyone else.

Finally, he thanked them all for their company and left the refectory, intending to head to the fortress. He was halfway to the outside door when he heard his name called.

It was her.

"Mistress?"

The corridor was almost completely dark. She came towards him, only stopping when she was uncomfortably close. "We need to talk privately, Master Ullmann."

"We do?" Ullmann judged his exits.

"Yes," she said. "Master Thaler is a good man, and well suited to oversee the library. Do you agree?"

"There's none finer in the land, Mistress. Master Thaler lives

471

and breathes books, and he has a rare passion for knowledge." He wondered where she was taking the conversation.

"Do you also agree that he's ill-equipped for any measure of intrigue and politicking?"

"I can't say whether he is or isn't, Mistress." All Ullmann could see of her was her silhouette. "I dare suppose Master Thaler could turn his hand to anything if he chose."

"Come now. He's a naif, an innocent. He projects his own good intentions on others, and expects them to treat him honourably. You, however, realise that the Order trains people differently."

Ullmann's hand strayed to his belt almost unconsciously. "Mistress, I only know a little of the Order's methods—"

"All your suspicions about me are true, and you cannot begin to comprehend the depths of depravity which the masters imposed on me." She tilted her head to one side, and her voice sounded almost wistful. "Master Thaler is wholly different. His nature is light to their darkness, and, astute as you are, you surely realise that I have nowhere else to go. He is ignorant of what I really am in a way that you are not. If you turn him against me, I'm finished."

He had his fingers on his knife. "I'm content to let Master Thaler oversee your conduct, and as long as it pleases him, it'll please the prince."

"Are you still afraid of me, Master Ullmann?" she asked. "Are you afraid I'll somehow regain my power and try to take everything back?"

It would be easy to drive his dagger into her guts. Easier now that he'd done it to someone else. After the act, though, he'd have Thaler to answer to, and the prince after that. "I'm quite convinced that your witchery is in the past, Mistress, and if necromancy ever tempted you, we've already dealt with Eckhardt."

She leant forward on tiptoe. "I need you to be convinced, Master Ullmann, as much as I need Master Thaler to be convinced. I recognise a potential enemy when I see one, and, right now, one is one too many. I might be the first adept to come over to the library, but I won't be the last. If others start to plot and plan, I'll come and tell you. Ask me questions and I'll hide nothing from you."

Ullmann consciously moved his right hand to behind his back. "That's a fine offer, Mistress . . ."

"Tuomanen," she said, filling in the gap.

"But what do you expect in return?"

"What do I want? I want to live. Master Thaler thinks the townsfolk will simply accept us in their midst: we both know he's wrong." And with that, she turned and walked away, a slight and small grey shape in the gloom.

Ullmann stared at the space where she'd been, and thought that, just as Thaler had under-librarians, and masters had their journeymen, he needed his own people around him: nothing less than a private army to protect him and do his bidding.

All in the name of the prince, of course.

He had coin, and access to more if he made the case for it. It was time to make some appointments.

64

Felix joined Sophia at the window as she peered down into the courtyard. She pointed at the man in the rich cream-coloured cloak.

"Is that him?" she asked.

Felix nodded. "His excellency Spyropoulos, ambassador of the Eastern Roman Empire."

The ambassador had gold thread embroidered into the hem of his cloak. It glittered as he walked towards his entourage.

"I'm sorry I missed him," she said. "Something came up."

"I can't be trusted to deal with ambassadors now?" Felix watched as the ambassador, a tall man with tightly wound oiled black hair, snatched his reins from the child slave acting as his retainer. "He has a temper."

"What did you say to him?"

"That I couldn't lend him half a dozen hexmasters to put down a slave revolt."

The Byzantine slapped at his slave with the back of his hand, and followed it up with a kick for good measure. The boy fell to the ground, cringing, and Felix felt his hand slide to his belt.

"How did he take it?"

"Badly. It must be a very big slave revolt to need the services of six hexmasters." Felix glanced at Sophia's face, and at the serious expression she wore. "Do you think I should ask him to stop that?"

"It's hardly the boy's fault," she said, tapping her lips with her finger. "Perhaps I should go down."

Felix looked at the ambassador's fine white horse and the five other riders with him, dressed in Roman-pattern cavalry armour. They all had young men or boys as retainers, and none were exactly dressed for the climate. Their short tunics and sandals seemed wholly out of place. "We're not supposed to threaten the ambassador or his retinue. It's not done."

"Even if he beats a child to death in front of your eyes, in your own courtyard?"

Felix struggled with the catch on the casement, and finally managed to open the window.

"Ambassador? Ambassador Spyropoulos?"

The ambassador was so intent on stamping on the boy's huddled legs that he didn't hear at first. One of the other riders gained his attention and pointed up to the solar.

"Yes, most illustrious prince?"

Felix murmured to Sophia. "How come *you* never call me 'most illustrious'." Then he raised his voice. "You shame yourself and me with your conduct."

Spyropoulos looked momentarily perplexed. "The slave? You concern yourself about a slave?"

"Yes, ambassador, I do. Stop kicking him. Now."

Glowing with his exertion, the man stepped back.

"How much?" asked Felix.

"My esteemed prince?"

"The boy. He's a slave. I'm buying him from you. Name your price." He felt Sophia's hand on his arm. He smiled.

"Keep him. One less slave to rebel against the emperor." Spyropoulos spat at the boy and took up his reins again. "Is our business done, my noble prince?"

Sophia leant in to Felix. "He doesn't mean it, you know: 'most illustrious'."

"Yes, I know." Felix smiled, then called down again. "It's done, ambassador."

He watched the Byzantines ride away towards the Hel Gate, the horses' iron-shod hooves clattering and sparking on the flags.

"We could have done with those horses," he said. "Instead, I have a slave."

"Trust you to think about horses."

"You're not sore, are you?" he asked her. Below, the boy started to uncurl like a bruised flower, eyes blinking at the twin thoughts that he'd been both saved and abandoned.

Sophia moved awkwardly. "My, you know. Tusch."

"Arse?" suggested Felix.

"Yes, that. I won't be sitting down all day."

Felix smirked. "You had the fattest, most docile nag left in the stables and it barely broke into a walk."

They returned their attention to the courtyard. The slave-boy had finally found his feet, and was looking around at the high walls, sniffing the the cool damp air. He limped first in one direction, then another, not knowing what to do.

"Someone needs to go and take care of him," said Sophia.

"Wait. I want to see what he does."

"Isn't that . . ." she frowned, ". . . cruel?"

"He's free," said Felix. "Is freedom cruelty?"

"The boy's hurt."

Despite his evident discomfort, the boy circled the courtyard. A servant came out of the kitchen, on the way to the well for water. She broke step when she saw this under-dressed child, and kept a wary eye on him as she hauled on the rope.

Felix studied the woman thoughtfully. "That well," he said, "might come up from the caves below the fortress that Master Thaler discovered." He glanced around at Sophia. "Do you think that's possible?"

"Who are you going to send down to find out?"

"I'll ask for volunteers."

The woman at the well was now speaking to the boy, who clearly didn't understand a word. She didn't give up, though, her mouth-movements becoming more and more exaggerated as she attempted to make herself understood.

"The lad can work in the library. Master Thaler speaks Greek, doesn't he?"

"Among a dozen other languages." Sophia stretched her back, but continued to look out of the window at the courtyard. "I do too."

The boy was standing close to the kitchen woman. He was pointing to the rope, and she was laughing, shaking her head. The bucket emerged, and her strong arms lifted it clear. She poured the contents into the pail she'd brought, and left the other on the ground, surrounded by coils of rope.

She was halfway back to the kitchen when she turned and beckoned the boy to follow her. He tried to hurry, despite his thin legs being stiff with injury. She waited for him all the same, and he trailed beside her skirts as she was lost from view.

"You were late back from the library. Something's happened, hasn't it?" Felix rubbed at his shoulder.

"You'd better sit down." Sophia declined to do the same, but instead poured them both a cup of watered wine. "Master Wess had to intervene at the bridge this morning. A farmer had found some Bavarians hiding in his barn."

"Not more Bavarians." Felix pressed his forehead against the table. "We're going to run out of towers to hold them all at this rate."

"It's not like last time, Felix. It was two families. They were fleeing Simbach."

His head came up. "Fleeing? Are things that bad there?"

"So Master Wess says. Their earl has decided that as well as sending spies against us, he's going to rob his own people." Sophia walked back and forth beside the length of the table. There was something distracting about the swish of her skirt as she turned.

"Can't we leave the Bavarians to deal with him?" Felix asked her. "Who's on the throne instead of Leopold?"

She stopped briefly. "No one knows. This Fuchs seems free to do whatever he wants."

Felix pulled a face. "We don't have enough soldiers to patrol the river bank."

"We have to do something, though. If all of Simbach decides they've had enough, we're the first obvious place for them to go. And then Fuchs will follow them."

"My father would be choosing what he was going to have for lunch about now," murmured Felix, looking at the surface of the wine in his cup, and at how it shivered with each of her footsteps. "Then perhaps thinking about an afternoon's hawking. Ask me again if I want things to go back to the way they were?"

"They can't, Felix, and we're left having to do something about this." She stood behind him, and rested her hands on his shoulders. Gently, as if she might damage him otherwise. "Fuchs has already sent spies here to find out what we could do to him. He's testing us."

Felix leant back into her touch. "We can't do anything to him.

I'm sorry for the people of Simbach, but what do they expect us to do?"

"They expect us to help them."

"With what? We don't have an army, Sophia. We don't have hexmasters and we don't have men-at-arms and we don't have horsemen and we don't have crossbowmen. And even if we had, I wouldn't want to waste their lives like my father did at Obernberg." He twisted around in his seat, despite the pain this caused him. "We have to choose which battles to fight. We don't have to fight this one. Not yet, anyway. We're not ready."

She stepped back, let her fingers slide off him. "We can't ignore it."

"We're not. We're arguing about whether we can invade Simbach when we haven't even repaired the water system." He slumped back onto the table. "If Fuchs crosses the river, then yes, we'll have to force him back, somehow."

"Wouldn't it be better to think about that now?"

"Yes," he groaned. "But I can't magic up an army I don't have. And I'm not hiring mercenaries – I know what'll happen if I do that. We'll be able to protect ourselves by next spring. We'll have militias by then, and enough arms and training for them to make anyone worry. We'll have troops we can move quickly through the palatinate when we have to. It'll just take time, that's all."

"Simbach doesn't have a year, Felix. Neither do we." Hands that moments ago had been gently touching him were now slapped on the tabletop with force. "We've been given this information. We haven't had to work for it, and it's cost us nothing. Surely we have to do better now than just sitting around waiting for something horrible to happen."

Exasperated, Felix got up and kicked his chair away. "What do you suggest then? Are you going to lead your neighbours up to Simbach and rout the earl?"

"Felix, I don't have to. How many men does this Fuchs have? A score? Two? How many men – and women – in Simbach are fed up with his pillaging? They don't need an army. They need hope and a leader. That's it. That's all." She bent down and righted his chair, pushing it back under the table.

Felix felt she was missing the point. "Simbach is in Bavaria—"

"There is no Bavaria, Felix! It's gone. Even Byzantium is coming to you for help: if they can't kill enough slaves, they'll go the same way as Rome did. You spend hours staring at that map when you know it's meaningless." She reached across and snatched it up, shaking it at him. "Carinthia is only real because the people who live in these inky scratches are happy to call themselves Carinthians."

"And not because I'm their prince?"

She lowered her arms, put the map back down on the table and smoothed out some of the creases she'd caused. "What made us – most of us – turn to you rather than Eckhardt?"

Felix was prince because his father had been prince, and his father before him, all the way back to Alaric. Yet Sophia was asking why people followed him.

"I . . . don't know." His high dudgeon was burst like a pig's bladder. "Do you?"

"Yes," she said, "which is why you're going to do something about Simbach. You can offer them something better than they have now. If they want to get rid of Fuchs, you'll help them. It's your nature."

"What can I offer them? Honestly?"

She put her back to him for a moment and reached into her bodice. When she turned again, she was holding out a piece of parchment. "I kept the original," she said. "This. This is enough. You could raise an army in a valley bottom or on a mountaintop with this."

He took it from her – it was warm from the heat of her body – and opened it. The words he'd written almost casually, carelessly, stared out of the page at him. All those who call themselves Carinthians will be subject to the same laws, the same taxes and the same freedoms granted by Carinthia, without favour. At the stroke of his pen, he'd upended a thousand years of the privilege of wealth and land and status. His own included. It hadn't seemed like that at the time, but it was still the right thing to have done.

"You really think so?" he asked.

"Yes. That and a bargeload of weapons. We can take Simbach in a single night, and not lose a man – if you're prepared to extend that guarantee across the river. Tell them you'll divide the earl's lands among them. Appoint a mayor. No more Fuchs, and no more homeless townspeople drifting into Carinthia." She took the paper back, and turned away once more to stow it inside her clothing.

"Just tell me it'll work." He had no idea. But she was convinced, and that counted for a lot: for everything, in fact.

"If it doesn't, we can try something different. Perhaps a more . . ." Sophia considered her words, "usual response."

"Well, I suppose we should call for Master Ullmann," said Felix. "As for those Bavarian families: let's see if they have the stomach for a fight."

65

What would have happened if she hadn't followed Frederik Thaler up Goat Mountain? Would they all be dead by now? Would Eckhardt still be feeding his appetite with Jews, or would he have run out of them and moved on to other game? Had her decision been a whim or had she been guided as part of a greater plan? Was her meeting with the prince, and the fine dresses and unaccustomed authority that had followed, an accident, or had the God of Abraham, Isaac and Jacob had used her to save His people?

Sophia thought that some sort of sign might have been appropriate: a burning bush; a pillar of smoke; an angel; a still, small voice. A talking ass, even. It wasn't much to ask. Instead, all she had was the indisputable fact that, when she spoke, people listened, including all the men who'd previously only ever frowned at her for being too intelligent, too well-read, too opinionated, to make a good wife: exactly those qualities that made her useful – necessary even – to Felix.

She had plenty of time to entertain such thoughts on her walks between the fortress and the town, but at least she no longer had to worry about her father: since falling in with Thaler, and losing some obscure bet with him, he was mostly out of trouble and more or less content.

She was at the quayside, to talk to the bargemasters, who were taking their sudden unemployment badly. It was still early, but if she could find one of them sober, she'd count herself lucky.

Most of them were rumoured to be found in the beer cellars at the bottom end of Wheat Alley, and beer cellars weren't somewhere that Jewish men ever went, let alone good Jewish women.

And yet, and yet.

She steeled herself at the top of the cellar's steps and gathered her coat around her. The windows were brown and streaked. Above the door was a complicated rope knot, bent and spliced and intertwined. She had no idea what she would find inside. Drunk Jews celebrating Purim was one thing: drunk Germans despairing for their livelihoods was another.

If she was scared, she shouldn't show it. Like most things in her life at that moment, if she could act the role, she was the role.

She walked down below street level, and opened the door. The smell was – distinct and unpleasant. Everybody in Carinthia smelt more than they used to – the lack of running water had seen to that – but this was a different level of odour.

Those men still conscious turned to see who it was who dared disturb their maudlin reflections.

Most just turned away again. A handful kept on staring, and two stood up – not out of deference, but in a belligerent, resentful manner. The cellar's host put down the mug he was cleaning and flicked a damp cloth over his shoulder.

"Mistress Morgenstern? You're welcome, of course, but this isn't a place for the ladies."

"I'm looking . . ." she said, surprised at how small her voice sounded, "I'm looking to hire a boat and its crew."

"Fuck off back to Jew-land," said one bargemaster, and he put his back to her, his tattooed face twisted in a sneer.

Sophia hadn't come unprepared. To the consternation of the drinkers, she parted her coat up to her waist and drew her sword. The sound was unmistakable, the soft slither of iron against the leather and brass of the scabbard, and the man who'd insulted her stiffened.

She rested the tip of the blade on his broad shoulder so he could feel the weight of it. "That's 'Fuck off back to Jew-land, my lady' to you."

She had their attention.

The bargemaster reached slowly for his mug and took a long pull. "Do you expect me to apologise?"

"An apology would go a long way to helping me forget your face and not bother to find out your name. What's it to be, bargemaster? A day in the lock-up or a grudging admission that I have a point?"

"Do you have balls under that skirt as well as a sword?"

"Not yet, but I can always cut yours off and wear them as a trophy."

Someone laughed. It gave permission to others to guffaw and snigger, but it wasn't her they were mocking. This was no harmless sport, though: reputations were being made and lost.

She held her nerve. The bargemaster finished his drink and brushed the sword-point from his shoulder. She held the weapon level. He got up, slowly, and showed her just how tall and wide he was, how bloodshot his eyes were and how yellow his teeth.

If he laid so much as a finger on her, Felix would have him pressed. He knew it. She knew it. The sword was superfluous, the law an extravagance. Had she judged the situation wrongly after all?

No. Apparently not.

"My lady," he said, dragging the words out of somewhere deep inside and refusing to look at her. His line to the door was far from straight, but it sufficed. The door closed. He'd gone. There were still two dozen or so bargemasters and bargees, and she rather hoped she wouldn't have to face down every single one of them.

She lowered her sword, and looked around the room. Several of them were still smirking, but none gave any indication they might want to talk to her. That was, in her opinion, stupid. She had coin, and it wasn't like any of them were going anywhere soon. Quite where they found the money for drink escaped her.

A few grins started to slip. She wasn't going anywhere either, they realised. They started to glance sideways at each other, to see who would break first.

Finally, a grey-haired man with a cross-shaped tattoo on one cheek and a spiral on the other ousted the clean-skinned bargee off his seat at the end of a table. He raised his eyebrow at Sophia and nodded towards the empty chair.

She could poise and swagger as well as the next man, but something told her that this bargemaster wouldn't be impressed by that. She laid her sword lengthways along the beer-soaked tabletop and, gathering up her skirts, sat down.

"Thank you," she said, "I'm—"

"I know who you are, my lady." The man had the look of a Frank about him, right down to his thin but long moustache. "Vulfar."

"And you own a barge, Master Vulfar?"

"Used to ply it from Ulm all the way to the Black Sea, and, gods willing, I will again. The thing is . . . you'll know by these marks" – Vulfar turned his cheeks and pushed up his sleeves – "what I can't do any more."

Sophia felt herself colour up. "I wouldn't be hiring you if you could."

"Very pragmatic of you, Mistress Morgenstern." He sat back and tweaked the end of his moustache. "I think we might have had dealings with your father in the past. Indirectly, of course."

She looked at the rest of his crew, and wondered if these men didn't feel the loss of magic most keenly of all. One day, the open river and a thousand miles to navigate; the next, tied up on the quayside of a single town.

"The trip will be downstream only, Master Vulfar. We'll try and get your boat back here afterwards, or we'll buy it outright if that's what you want. And there'll be pay for you and your men. I don't believe in chiselling every last red penny, so I hope we can come to a fair price."

"A fair price for what work, exactly?" Vulfar examined the bottom of his empty mug.

"Something we should discuss in private, perhaps," said Sophia. She didn't know how much cellar beer cost, so she guessed, counting three shillings from her purse and placing them on the table in front of her. "I'm sure your crew can drink to the prince's health while we're talking."

She closed her purse and pulled her sword back along the table. Vulfar's men watched its steel simplicity withdraw and then pounced on the coins.

Vulfar led the way back outside and, with a wary look around at the street, waited for Sophia to join him.

"You don't think I should have crossed that other bargemaster, do you?"

"He was your enemy before you entered the cellar, my lady. Why should it be any different now?" He had a club at his belt, far more effective in a bar brawl than her own weapon. "I do think you shouldn't be walking the streets of Juvavum without a guard, no matter how proficient you are with that pig-sticker."

"Pig-sticker?"

"You know what I mean, my lady. I might not share either your religion or your country, but the prince's mother shared mine and I've more than a passing interest in his well-being." The barge-master smoothed his moustache again with a pinch of yellow wax produced from a silver container. "The boy leans on you, and you need to be more careful."

She pulled her coat aside to sheath her sword. "I've lived here all my life, Master Vulfar. I know the risks."

"Do you?" He stopped for a moment. "Do you really? I was on the quayside the day your priests chased you into the Town Hall. They took a pounding from our bottles then, and ever since, whenever I've seen them, they've been in armour, and always in company. Far be it for me to point out who learnt what that day."

He carried on and made for one of the barges tied up, nose pointing upstream towards the bridge.

Sophia folded her arms and regarded the length and width of the vessel. "You're probably right. You're not the first person to mention it either."

"Oh, they're not going to take on Felix. The boy's got a good arm on him and fights like a Jötun. And he's a son of Carinthia, no matter that he's a Frankish prince too. You? The magic might have gone – if just for a season – but there're many that accuse you of witchery." He jumped aboard with practised nonchalance. "You've got away with it so far by being proud and fierce. It won't always be enough."

"Thank you for your concern, Master Vulfar." She held out her hand, and he steadied her as she stepped up. The boat wallowed under her. "You've a cargo already?"

"Salt. That can go back on the quay if you need the space. What's the job?" Vulfar sat astride the covers of the cargo deck and stretched his legs ahead of him.

"I need you to go to Simbach, arriving at night somewhere upstream of the town, and unloading men and cargo there. Can you navigate that far without your river-magic?"

Vulfar's eyes narrowed. "I've heard the gossip. Are you planning to kill the rogue earl?"

"No," she answered mostly truthfully. "Although if he ends up dead, then so be it. We want to give the people of Simbach some-thing to fight with, and something to fight for. What happens after that is up to them. We're not going to mass an army and march it across the river, but neither can we ignore what Fuchs is doing."

The bargemaster drummed his heels. "If it goes wrong, I'm stuck on the Bavarian side of the river in the dark, with angry earl's men wanting to separate my head from my neck."

"If it goes wrong, you can swim the half a stadia to the other bank," countered Sophia. "I'd recompense you for the loss of your boat."

"Still a risk. I'll be straight with you, my lady; while trade isn't what it used to be, and being laid up for such a long time is hurting my purse as much as the next man's, that's no reason to throw caution to the wind and take on a job that might end up with us drowned or hacked to pieces."

"Master Vulfar, stop building your part up and name your price. We can take it from there." She looked away to the north, down the river and the steep-sided valley that contained it.

"A hundred florins."

She turned slowly back. "If I returned to that stinking pit of depravity you call a beer cellar and slapped a hundred florins on the counter, I could find half a dozen bargemasters that would follow me to Sheol and back. Why don't you try again?"

"If you went with any of those chancers, you'd still be trying to land as you passed through the Iron Gates. I'll get your men and your weapons – and you, if you want to come along – to the right place at the right time. A hundred florins to stop a war before it starts is cheap, my lady." Vulfar swung his feet over the far side of the hold and slid down to the deck. "Besides, it's not likely that this earl could afford to buy us out at that price."

"And, to your credit, you decided to talk to me when no one else would." She smiled at him. "Such generosity of spirit shouldn't go unrewarded."

Vulfar patted his thinning hair. "I've an eye to the few years I might have left, my lady. If I'm not to die with my hand at the tiller, I need to invest in a different business."

Sophia stamped her foot against the wooden boards. The barge was solid and heavy, and it was difficult to imagine such a vessel moving without magic. "A smaller, slimmer boat? One you could sail or row, or even pull upstream?"

"That sounds like a young man's game to me. Now, if you

wanted someone to build such boats and sell them to idiots seeking their fortune . . ." His voice trailed off and he faced away from Sophia, staring out at the river and the woods beyond.

"A hundred florins would go a long way to setting up a boatyard and buying timber." She relented. "A hundred it is then. To be settled in full on completion."

Vulfar looked over his shoulder at her, eyebrow already raised. "My lady—"

"You and your crew won't see so much as a red penny until we're done. I'm not having drunken bargees broadcasting our business in the brothels and beer cellars of Juvavum. Tell them as little as you can get away with, promise them money, and leave it at that. You wouldn't want Fuchs hearing about this any more than I would." She jumped across to the quay unaided. "Afterwards, they can do what they like, and probably will."

The bargemaster stroked his beloved moustache again. "A deal, then. I won't insult you with written contracts or a spit and a shake. Your word is good, Mistress Morgenstern."

"I'm still unconvinced I had the better of this bargain," she said. "Start unloading your salt, Master Vulfar. We'll need the space."

66

The armoury wasn't empty, and there seemed to be still more rooms further and deeper that were piled with weaponry. Quantity wasn't a problem. Neither was the quality of spears being carried out in bundles of ten and twenty. The spearheads were discoloured with age, and on occasions blunt, but they could be cleaned and sharpened. The shafts were old, but of seasoned timber that could still take an impact. They'd do the job, even if they just looked the part.

Ullmann's worry was that they were handing over perfectly good pole arms to the Bavarians without any guarantee that Carinthia wasn't going to see the wrong end of them at some point.

He watched while Reinhardt closed and locked the door behind him, rehanging the key around his neck. Then they walked out into the courtyard together, where a handcart was already laden with spears. The servants fitted the extras on top and tied them on.

"This had better work," he said to himself, but Reinhardt heard him and scrubbed at the back of his neck while he formulated a response.

"I agree, Master Ullmann, but we do as we're ordered."

"That goes without saying. But I'd be happier with Carinthian weapons in Carinthian hands. The Bavarians owe us nothing." He looked up at the Hare Tower. "There's two up there who can't agree on anything except their hatred for all things Carinthian. One of them thinks we interfere too much, the other that we intervene too little. Whichever it is, it's all our fault."

"Press them, I say. We're wasting good food on them."

"My lord Felix says they stay for now." Ullmann was worried about them. Incompetent spies though they were, they could still do damage if they got away. Perhaps it'd be better for everyone if he could engineer both their escape and their immediate recapture, followed by their inevitable visit to the main square.

Later. He'd think about that later. The cart was loaded and ready to be rolled away, a man at the front and a man behind.

"If everything goes to plan," said Reinhardt, "it won't matter one way or the other. Without Fuchs, they've no reason to cause us trouble."

"You think they need a reason?" Ullmann let it pass and called to the servants. "Come on, then. Let's get going."

The cart rattled away, and once it was out of the fortress precincts, it attracted attention: there was no hiding what they were moving. A glare from Ullmann seemed to send people on their way, but he was aware that doing all this in daylight where they could be seen by anyone was a risk.

Mistress Morgenstern wanted them to leave now so that this Frankish bargemaster Vulfar could get in position by nightfall, but to his mind it seemed rushed. They weren't ready to extend their rule over other towns. They didn't even know if they could keep hold of the ones they had: what had happened in Simbach could just as easily have happened in Villach or Hallstadt or Linz with their own earls, and they'd only just be learning about it now.

They passed through the main square again, and his gaze was drawn to the house on the corner with Gold Alley. He wasn't going to be there tonight, or the night after that, or even . . . and he had to admit that the thought of Aelinn was distracting him from his duties, just as she'd warned him it shouldn't.

He told the carters to take the wide road to the right of the square that led to the quays, rather than try and steer through the narrow alleys, a path that would lead right past her front door.

Vulfar was standing next to a pile of barrels, each of them as tall as his waist, and stacked two-up so that the pile looked like a wall of wood. The previous cart-load of spears was almost stowed away, the last of the bundles being threaded between the supporting struts of the hold, and overseeing everything was Mistress Morgenstern, sitting on a single barrel of salt.

She waved him over, and he inspected the barge sourly.

"Not partial to the water, Master Ullmann?"

"Far from it, my lady. The quality of the boat and the crew are more my concern."

Vulfar curled his moustache around his finger and scowled, while Sophia laughed. "Master Vulfar has assured me on both those matters. At the price we're paying, that's the least he could have done."

She stood up as the second load of spears was unloaded onto the quay and the laborious task of carrying them into the barge began.

"Gentlemen? We need to conduct a few introductions in the Town Hall." Sophia pointed the way, and the two men fell in behind her. Ullmann was a little taller and considerably younger than the Frank, but it didn't help him to feel safe in his company. A hundred florins was a huge price, five years' wages in his old job as an usher − and all for two or three days' work. While it had been a wise decision to keep every last penny away from the bargees until the deed was done, the amount itself was just another worry.

He wondered if they couldn't have found a Carinthian barge-master instead.

For his part, Vulfar seemed happy with the deal he'd struck, and why wouldn't he be? The risk was all Carinthia's.

In the Town Hall, there were men waiting for them. Master Wess, of course, as this was his lair, and three men he'd never seen before. One reminded Ullmann of his father: broad and barrel-like, with rough hands and a weather-beaten face. The other two were smaller, shorter, less used to a life of hard physical work.

Sophia gathered them together. "This is Mr Ohlhauser, a farmer on our side of the river, and these are Mr Metz and Mr Kehle: they'll all be travelling with you. Master Vulfar will let Mr Ohlhauser off on the east bank before the turn to Simbach. You know what to do when it gets dark?"

Everyone nodded, Metz and Kehle more nervously than the others.

Wess held out a sheet of parchment to Ullmann, a map of sorts, with lines and shapes. "This is roughly" – and he rolled his eyes – "what Simbach looks like. Spend your time on the boat wisely, Master Ullmann."

Ullmann took the map, turned it this way and that, then folded it into quarters. "Very useful, I'm sure, Master Wess. Thank you."

"Are you ready, Master Vulfar?" asked Sophia.

"More or less, my lady. We have our barge polls and our cargo, Master Ullmann and his gang. All that remains is to gather my crew and we can cast off."

"Then gather away, bargemaster." She thanked Ohlhauser for his assistance in taking care of the families who'd ended up in his barn, slipping him a purse when she thought no one else was looking, and told the Bavarians that it was up to them from now on. They looked as convinced as Ullmann felt.

He lingered, when everyone else had been released.

"Mistress Morgenstern," he started.

She cut him off. "I'm aware of your concerns, Master Ullmann, but both you and Felix are still obsessed with the lines on the map, and with who lives on which side of them. Do you really think a river or a mountain makes that much difference? Do you think that Mr Ohlhauser is any different from Mr Metz, except for who he pays his taxes to? Do you think that ideas and people see a bridge and refuse to cross over?"

All he could manage was an "I—" before her lips formed a thin line, and a little growl escaped from her throat.

"If you were a Jew, Master Ullmann, you'd realise just how ridiculous that is. We Jews have washed like a tide across this map for millennia: sometimes we stay, sometimes we go. If we've learnt anything in the last two thousand years it's this: the lines mean nothing."

Ullmann gazed at his feet, which only served to enrage Sophia more.

"This is the first time since the magic failed that we can turn a whole situation to our advantage. We don't have to burn Simbach down, and we don't have to occupy it. All we have to do is offer them what we have here. The Bavarians want the same things for themselves and their children as we do." She huffed. "To the boat, Master Ullmann."

They walked side by side across the wide quay, and she softened her voice.

"We can't afford not to share everything we are and own, because if we try to hang on to it with our clenched fists, it'll leak out and we'll be left with nothing. So we're sharing you and the others, our weapons and our money, and, in return, Simbach will become a good place to live and work in again."

She stopped and pinned him in place with her gaze until he had no choice but to back down. He'd had his way concerning the hexmasters, but not here, not now. She was becoming increasingly confident and assertive. It was something he needed to watch carefully.

"I understand, my lady. We'll see Fuchs gone and everything as it should be." He drew back and stalked to the riverside.

The barge was loaded, and the two Bavarians, together with the Carinthian farmer, were waiting on the quayside in one knot of people, Horst and Manfred – two of Ullmann's fellow ushers – waiting in another. The carts and the servants had gone – everyone was waiting for Vulfar.

The bargemaster arrived back with his four crew, each of whom looked so disreputable they could have been dredged from the bottom of the Salzach. If appearances were what counted, the trip down river was going to be both short and eventful.

In all, there were eleven men and a barge full of spears, and Ullmann was responsible for all of it. It wasn't so long ago that he'd been a plain usher, yet it felt like a lifetime away. He glanced at the Jewish woman, who was smiling at Vulfar and even joking with his bargees.

Control, he decided. It was all about control.

"Are we ready now, Master Vulfar?" he called.

"We certainly are, Master Ullmann. Everyone on board, and try not to break anything."

Ullmann looked askance, and Vulfar laughed at him. The other passengers clambered into the hold through the open doors, and Vulfar's crew started to untie the ropes that held the barge fast to the quay, downstream first and working their way up until just one lead wrapped around a cleat held it in place.

"Master Ullmann, please. We've reached the point of no return."

Apart from the biggest bargee, braced with the rope in his huge hands, he was the only one left to board. He stepped across the widening gap, glancing down at the rippling water, and onto the barge-board.

Sophia Morgenstern raised her hand in farewell.

"Carinthia will win this, my lady," said Ullmann.

"If only it were that simple, Master Ullmann. It'll suffice, though, until the next problem needs fixing; all we can do is fix the ones we can see. Go, with HaShem's blessing."

He would rather go with the expectation of this being only the first of many great victories for Carinthia, but a small one would do for now. The bargee unhooked the rope and jumped with it alongside Vulfar, and the other crew set about the barge poles, pressing them against the stone quay and stern of the next boat, steering the bow out into the faster-flowing mid-river.

"It's probably too late to ask," said Ullmann, as he watched the scene unfold, "but have you ever done it like this before?"

"Such little trust, Master Ullmann." Vulfar gauged their progress and adjusted the tiller accordingly. "But since you ask, no. I am, however, certain of two things. First, of my knowledge of the river, and second, of the competence of my crew. Fortunately, your Mistress Morgenstern is paying handsomely for both."

The bow started to slew to the left, and the stern to the right, threatening to turn the barge sideways-on to the river banks. Vulfar dragged the tiller back, and shouted down the length of the barge in a language only the bargees knew. They climbed on top of the hold and lowered their poles over the side.

They pushed, with their faces red and knuckles white, and slowly – much slower than Ullmann would have liked – the bow came about. They were already downstream of the quay, passing the edge of the town wall.

"You see?" said Vulfar, moustache bristling. "Nothing to it."

Horst leant out of the hold to tug at Ullmann's breeks. "Max?

Are you going to tell us now what we're doing on this tub? Or does that stay a secret forever?"

Reluctantly, Ullmann ducked back down and left their erratic progress down the river to Vulfar: there was nothing he could do except scowl, and he'd rather the bargemaster's full attention was on keeping the boat pointing roughly in the right direction.

He reached into his jacket and retrieved the map that Wess had drawn. Unfolding and smoothing it out, he beckoned the Bavarians over to try and explain it.

"This is where we're going, lads. This is Simbach."

67

"Who's the boy?" Morgenstern murmured without looking up.

Thaler, who was passing, stopped and leant over to inspect the work. He had proven to Morgenstern that objects fall at the same speed, no matter how heavy they are. Consequently, the Jew was deep in his al-Haytham, translating the Persian into Latin. They had discussed whether German would be better, but Latin was widely read and understood among the educated of their part of Europe.

"Oh, some Greek slave my lord Felix rescued. Apparently the Byzantine ambassador called this morning, and didn't receive the answer he wanted."

"So he left a slave behind as a warning?"

"No. He was busy killing the boy in the inner courtyard when Felix and Sophia decided such a spectacle was unseemly." Thaler scanned the library and waved the boy over. He rattled towards them, carrying a tray stacked with bottles and plates.

"Are you letting people eat and drink around the books?" Morgenstern raised his face from the page. "That's a little dangerous."

"It's the workmen," sighed Thaler "I can't stop them leaving their debris all around. At least now I have someone to tidy up behind them."

Morgenstern put down his pen and flexed his fingers. "So he's *your* slave now?"

"Agathos's status is a little ambiguous, mainly because I can't convince him he's now free. The boy'll get exactly the same treatment as an apprentice would, so the point is moot."

The Greek boy slid his tray onto the table and looked up at Thaler, who frowned back.

"I'm certainly not used to such obedience."

"I'm sure once he realises you won't thrash him to death, he'll become as uncooperative as the rest of the youth of this town." Morgenstern beckoned the child closer and peered at him. "He's a bit bruised. Perhaps you should give him a day or so to recover."

"Light duties, Aaron. We all have to pull our weight, no matter how fast it falls." Thaler smirked and dismissed the boy.

"Yes, very good." Morgenstern retrieved his pen and dipped it. "So what precisely are your duties this morning?"

"Trying to persuade the existing librarians to work with Mistress Tuomanen is one." Thaler sat on the edge of the table and scraped his fingernails across his scalp. "I mean, you don't have any problem with that. She was what she was, and now she is what she is: literate and with nowhere else to go."

"Do you want this book finished any time soon?" Morgenstern put the pen down again. "Very well. No, I don't have a problem with former sorcerers as long as they remember they're as mortal as I am. I can't imagine that they won't have problems with me, but as long as they leave me alone I don't really care. Any tensions they cause are, as you suggest, for you to deal with."

Thaler swung his legs. "You don't like her."

"She works for you, Frederik. My opinion is of little matter." He tutted. "You might set her to sorting out all the arcana that came out of the White Tower. No one else really wants to touch it anyway."

"I'm not so sure about that." The master librarian pulled a face. "We know necromancy works, and I have a feeling it would be a grave mistake to allow her, or anyone trained in the magical arts, to go poring through their order's greatest secrets. At best, she'll become so dispirited she'll leave. At worst, she might rediscover her appetite for ruling us. Homer and Virgil are a better diet for the moment, no? Until things settle down."

"I hadn't thought of that." Morgenstern returned to his book. "This won't translate itself."

"Of course it won't. Can I get you anything? More light? Paper?" Thaler slipped his feet to the floor again, ready to be off.

"Actually, yes." Morgenstern picked up the al-Haytham and flicked back a few pages. "Can you find me some of these? He calls them lenses."

"Lenses?" Thaler took the book from him. "What are they?"

"Sections of a glass sphere. Like a chord of a circle. They keep on coming up again and again, and they seem to have . . . properties that might be useful." Morgenstern tightened his lips.

"We've glass spheres from the Order in relative abundance, from small to very large. I'll ask the glassmakers if there's anything they can do with them." Thaler examined the book, trying to interpret the densely packed lines. "If all this is true, al-Haytham was a clever bastard, wasn't he?"

"From what I understand, his king locked him up in a tower for years over some misunderstanding about the Nile." Morgenstern retrieved the book from Thaler's fevered hands. "He had nothing to do but think and write."

"That sounds – much as I'm enjoying the challenge of the present days – like a librarian's idea of Valhalla." Thaler looked up. "I do wish they'd get on with glazing the oculus. Nothing but hair-brained schemes that'll come crashing down on our heads so far."

"Perhaps when you see that daughter of mine, you could tell her to crack the whip a little harder." Morgenstern set the book open on the desk and found his place again. "Is that offer of an under-librarianship still open?"

Thaler started. "Yes, Aaron. Yes it is."

"It strikes me," said Morgenstern, wiping the dried ink off the nib with his sleeve, "that Sophia is going to become more, not less, involved in the affairs of state. I have no one to look after me. Oh, I'm sure she'd pay someone to keep house, but my work there is done: for better or worse, she's off my hands."

"I'm sure we can come to some sort of arrangement," said Thaler.

"Can some of the cooks learn the kashrut? It'll need to be done in a separate kitchen. Or I can just get one of the Jewish families to send me meals." He shrugged. "It's not difficult."

"You'd be a welcome addition, Aaron." Thaler patted the man on the shoulder, and left him to his translating. He needed some fresh air.

Stepping out under the portico, he found the square full of piles of building materials, together with the builders who'd brought them. Some of the guildsmen were arguing over scale models of what they wanted to place on top of the library dome. When they spotted him, they hurried towards him, each seeking to have their design judged better than their rivals'. The contract was lucrative, and worth fighting over.

Thaler retreated quickly to the safety of the entrance hall, where, to his relief, Sophia came to his rescue. She shooed the craftsmen away.

"They're right, of course. We have to come to a decision soon," she said.

Thaler allowed himself to be guided back inside.

"But none of their designs are suitable. They're either too heavy or too flimsy: better to have the wind and the rain get in, than for the ceiling to fall in and crush us, or the construction to fail at the first whiff of a storm."

She held up her hand. "There is one design among them that's caught my eye. Why don't we go and have a look?"

"But they're like ravening beasts out there."

"Frederik, I'll be with you, and you need to see this." She turned him around, tucked her ledger under her arm like a shield and, with Thaler sheltering under her wing, she marched him across the square to a group of men sitting next to a small wood-and-glass building. He couldn't remember having seen the building – which resembled a giant lantern, tall enough to hold a full-grown man – the day before.

As they approached through the bustle, the men stood and dusted themselves down.

Thaler looked at them, they at him.

"Where is it, then?" asked Thaler. He peered through the windows.

"That's it." She pointed at the octagonal building. "The whole thing. Who's in charge here?"

"Me, my lady. Seibt."

He appeared to be no older than the journeymen around him, who all appeared to be barely out of apprenticeship. As he spoke, he tugged at his black hair.

"Master Seibt," said Sophia, "please show your construction to Master Thaler."

"Us? Yes, of course." He was momentarily transfixed, but, on recovering, pushed his colleagues into action. "And it's Mr Seibt, my lady."

Thaler watched as they removed the glass: it came out in frames held in place with toggles. It took them moments to take down a whole side, stacking the individual panels together on a blanket. They worked their way around each of the eight sides in turn, and when the last pane had been removed, they just lifted the roof off, carrying it high above their heads and clear of the structure to lay it on the ground.

"It's one-quarter size, my lady. Seasoned pine for lightness and flexibility. The roof is shingles, but we can copper it or gild it if you wish." Seibt wiped his tall forehead with a cloth.

Thaler stepped inside and patted one of the uprights. "And you made this when?"

"Truth be told, Master Thaler, there's no other work. It occurred to me that without magical light, houses and halls were going to be so much darker. We built it in the hope that someone would want it, if not you."

Sophia crossed her arms around her ledger. "Mr Seibt, what happened to your master?"

"He . . ." Seibt stared at the ground, "he died, my lady. At least we think he did. After the, you know, emergency, there were a few of us who couldn't find a guild-accredited master, so we formed our own company. And someone had to apply to be the master of it, so I was chosen, except we don't have the money for the fees."

"Your guildmaster?"

"Master Emser, my lady."

"I saw him yesterday, along with the other guildmasters. I'll have to see them all again today: your situation won't be unique." She stepped inside the timber frame with Thaler. "Well, Frederik? Do you think it'll do?"

He slapped his hand hard against the wood and it hardly shivered. "I imagine there are advantages to being able to construct all the parts at ground level. Shouldn't we consider some of the other . . . ah . . . more experienced craftsmen?"

"We could. But if this will do . . ." She turned to Seibt. "How quickly could you build a full-size whatever-you-call-this?"

"A roof lantern, my lady, because it—"

"I understand."

"We can cut the frame in a week. The glazing will depend on the glassmakers. Two weeks? Three?" Seibt seemed to be having trouble breathing. "My lady, we're not properly even part of the guild."

"Leave that to me," she said. "You'll have your papers by tomorrow."

Thaler's gaze slid past Sophia to the crowd that had gathered around them. The other masters and journeymen looked less than pleased at being trumped by a few upstarts.

He leant in. "Sophia. The guildsmen."

"The guildsmen will be stealing this design and touting it as their own by nightfall. However, the original creators need both our encouragement and our money. And when they've put up their roof lantern on the library and shown it works, everyone will want one."

"We're trampling on every tradition we have," he complained.

"I know." She smiled brilliantly at him. "If we don't, we're doomed."

"There'll be a price to pay, though. And we can't make that price too steep, or there'll be rebellion along with it. Civil strife is worse than war." He felt a rumbling in his guts.

"Frederik, we've been paying through the nose for over a thousand years already, and those at the bottom of the pile always pay the most. The trick is how to raise them up without making those at the top feel like they're losing too much."

The rumbling got worse, and he clutched at his stomach, then realised that his whole body was vibrating.

He wasn't the only one who'd noticed something strange was happening: the window panes piled on the blankets were chattering and rattling. The very ground itself was shaking.

The crowd in the square grew tensely silent, with everyone looking either up in the sky or down at their feet to find the source of the ill-favoured movement.

A strange whistling noise rose over the rumbling, starting off low and building to a crescendo. Suddenly, a jet of water shot into the air, rising from the square's fountain like a javelin. The burst lost its shape, and started to fall back. Droplets sprayed into upturned eyes and wide-open mouths, and another, steadier stream started to fill the bowl around the base of the fountain.

From a distance came the faint echoes of a cheer, and Thaler felt a surge of relief and delight. He'd been proved right. They had water again. The town was saved. With the help of the dwarves, they could restart the machines under the fortress. They could build and adapt; not just survive, but grow and thrive without magic.

He'd doubted it up to that moment. Now, no longer. He felt quite faint.

"Master Thaler? Frederik?"

He waved her away and stumbled towards the fountain, a path opening before him, closing behind him. He held on to the stone rim and looked at the rippling surface of the deepening pool.

There was another noise, and when he turned, he found they were applauding him, every man there. Only then did he realise that his underground exploits had made him famous. He tried to wave them down, but they only cheered his name louder.

Crying with relief and with joy, Thaler raised his chubby arm and clenched his fist. "Carinthia!" he shouted. "Carinthia!" And all the people joined in.

68

Büber had no idea how long he'd been awake; they wouldn't let him outside to look at the sky, even though he could see the crack of grey light around the doors that led out onto the mountain.

Neither did he know how long he was expected to wait: when King Ironmaker had told him he'd have the dwarves' answer soon, he hadn't realised he'd be kept prisoner until then.

It was driving him to distraction, except there was no distraction to take his mind off the waiting. There was his horse, the dwarvish guards standing as still as statues at each end of the entrance hall, and that was it.

He'd done his duty: he'd delivered Felix's letter. He had thought it might be his final duty for Carinthia, but it was clear that the dwarf-lord didn't see it like that. The concept of being released from service wasn't one he looked prepared to even consider.

So much for the opportunity just to keep on going, into the

Franklands beyond the mountains, and the ocean's shore beyond that. In his wilder moments, he wondered if he could reasonably hope to take on the guards, batter them into submission and flee with his horse. He'd be free, but he couldn't hope to repair the damage to Felix's reputation once it was done. Trapped by the weight of expectations, Büber sat and stewed, paced and seethed, until finally the inner doors clacked and opened.

He wheeled about and saw Heavyhammer approaching.

"You kept me here," said Büber, "without a word."

"Did you have something more important to do than to wait on my king's word and take back my king's reply?" He held out a wooden box, long and flat, carved with intertwined serpents and chased with silver; just as an object, it would clearly command a high price, and Büber grew suspicious.

Beware of dwarves bearing gifts.

He purposefully put his hands behind his back. "I might be Carinthia's messenger-boy, but I'm not Farduzes'."

"Our ways are not your ways. The king demands that you take this back to Prince Felix," said Heavyhammer, thrusting the box into Büber's midriff.

"I'm sure he does." Büber stood his ground. "Why not take it yourself?"

"Me? I don't even know the way, human. None of us do." The dwarf tugged at his beard. "Our maps are a thousand years out of date, and we know little of the surface world. Where would we go? How would we navigate? We are blind and lost under the canopy of the sky."

Heavyhammer's doom-laden speech rang false to Büber, but he played along with it for now.

"You want me to hold your hand and care for you like wounded cubs until you're strong enough to cope on your own? How long do you think that'll take?" What was going on here? Heavyhammer had already shown himself to be a consummate liar, and although Büber was as straight as any given mile of Roman road, even he could spot this act of intended duplicity.

"What's in the box?" he asked.

"It is King Ironmaker's response to your prince," said Heavyhammer. He pushed the box at Büber again, forcing the huntmaster to take a step back.

"That doesn't tell me what's in the box."

"A message for the prince, clearly."

Büber took another step back, in order to give himself some room. "Can I see it?"

"The box is to be opened only by your lord, human. The message is for him alone."

"Yet you trust me to take it to Felix without peeking. That's" – he tapped his lip – "almost praiseworthy."

Heavyhammer tried to press the box on Büber for a third time. "You cannot open the box. Only a prince of your people can."

"Cannot, or should not?" Finally, and seeing no alternative, he took the box, and turned it over in his hands. It seemed . . . well, boxy. There was no hinge, just a thin line that chased around the edge, barely enough to interrupt the carving or inlay. He lifted it to his ear and gave it a little shake.

He could hear nothing: certainly no sound that might tell him what the box contained, assuming it contained anything at all.

"I think King Ironmaker forgot to enclose his message," he said, and went to hand the box back.

Now it was Heavyhammer who was having none of it: he stepped smartly away and was just as reluctant to touch the box as Büber had previously been.

"Everything is in order, human. Take my lord's reply to your prince without delay: he'll know how to open it."

"I did explain that Felix is a twelve-year-old boy, didn't I? If you're relying on any knowledge his father may have had of how to open the box, we'll end up just having to take a crowbar to it." Büber shook it harder, and saw a tell-tale twitch in the corner of Heavyhammer's eye. "Why don't you show me how to open it? I'll swear any oath you like to any god you like that I won't abuse the information."

Heavyhammer tugged at his beard. "The box is locked, human. You delivered a letter under seal: we reply in our way."

"I brought you a letter. I have no idea what I'm taking back." Büber decided that if the dwarf wasn't going to give in, then neither was he. He placed the box on the floor in front of him. "I think you should open it. My duty to my lord compels me to check its contents."

Büber turned his back and picked up his horse's saddle. Untying the reins, he lifted it onto the creature's back. It looked at him with a vaguely disappointed air. While he was busy with the girth strap and stirrups, he heard a faint snick from behind him.

"Look, then, and be satisfied."

Heavyhammer was holding the box open. The velvet-lined interior contained a folded piece of parchment. Büber strode over and, taking the dwarf by surprise, dipped his incomplete fingers inside and scooped up the parchment.

"Thanks," he said. "I'll make sure Felix gets this. Keep the box: it looks valuable."

Heavyhammer lunged forward, but Büber skipped away, spinning. As the dwarf repeatedly closed on him, trying to snatch at the letter, all Büber had to do was hold it up and keep twisting. In the few moments it took him to reach his saddlebag, the guards at the doors had hardly started their lumbering runs.

Büber whipped out his knife, caught Heavyhammer around the neck with the crook of his elbow, and stretched him against his own body.

The knife-point, so recently used to stick Teutons, tickled at Heavyhammer's beard.

"And that's far enough, friends."

The guards stumbled to a halt, tense and bristling. The hall echoed to the sound of their breath, and the horse shook its head, making its harness jingle.

Büber realised that, unless Heavyhammer was particularly important to the Lord of Farduzes, the stand-off wouldn't last long.

"Close the box," he said. He felt the dwarf stiffen, and pressed the knife harder. "Do it."

He was watching now, very carefully. Heavyhammer did something to the base of the box – held it in a special way as if he was pushing on part of it – and slowly, carefully, lowered the lid down. Only when it was safely shut did the dwarf change his grip.

The cavity inside the box was obviously only a small portion of the volume. There was something else there, something that was secret and lethal.

"Let's try this." Büber kept his knife at Heavyhammer's throat, and snagged the box with his other hand, still grasping the now-crumpled letter. When he had proper hold of it, he swept the dwarf's legs out from underneath him, then stamped on his descending back, pinning him to the stone floor.

The guards edged forward, but stopped again when he held up the box. "If I open this now, without using the hidden catches, what happens? Just how dangerous is it to everyone in this hall?"

He let the pressure off Heavyhammer's spine sufficiently to let him speak. "Do it, human. We will die in agony, but your prince will never hear of this."

What Büber really needed was a third hand. He needed the box, he wanted the letter, he had to get to his sword. Whatever trap the box held, he had no intention of falling victim to it himself: when it came down to the basics of life and death, he realised that agony wasn't for him.

They were going to rush him. He knew it. They knew it. So be it.

He dropped everything: knife, box and letter, ground his heel down hard on Heavyhammer, and reached behind to the scabbard hung on his saddle. The interval between the dwarf's scream and the song of his sword was an eye-blink's worth of time, but Büber found that was all it took for the white heat to boil up inside him.

He swung his arm. The very tip of his sword slashed the face of the first guard to reach him. The bloom of his crimson blood made Büber mad. Now an axe heading in an arc towards his chest, and he could see it and use his momentum to sidestep it and bring the edge of his blade across the exposed nape of the second guard's neck between helmet and mail coat.

The sword went straight through, and if there had been a spray of blood before, there was now a gout of it like rain.

The third and fourth guards had further to come but arrived at the same time. Büber wouldn't retreat. It wasn't in his nature any more. He thrust his sword through the open mouth of one and leapt at the other.

He was stronger, even without the berserker rage. His arms were longer and he was heavier too. His blunt fingers trapped the dwarf's axe-hand and he smashed it repeatedly down against the floor until he'd forced him to let go, and then Büber's hands were reaching for the sides of the helmet.

It took three blows against the stone pavement to roll the dwarf's eyes up behind his lids. Büber reached for his sword-hilt and drew it out between bloodied frothing jaws, and struck out from where he crouched at the injured first guard, whose descending axe split Büber's blade in two with a shock that should have numbed his whole arm.

He barely felt it. It was as if it were happening to someone else.

The cleaving blow had unbalanced the dwarf who'd made it. Now he was overstretched, axe scraping against the floor for support as he tried to lever himself upright again.

Büber reached past the head of the axe to the handle, and pulled. Since he refused to let go, the dwarf was pulled off his feet and came crashing down into the gore next to Büber. His wild-eyed struggle to free his weapon became weaker with every thrust of the shattered sword-stub.

When Büber felt the dwarf's grip on his axe fail, he rose roaring from the ground. In front of him, Heavyhammer. In his hands, the box.

Büber threw the axe at him. Instinctive, primal, savage.

It sliced into the wooden box, bursting it apart, and buried itself in Heavyhammer's chest. Springs and cogs and spinning blades sang out in a chaotic wash of noise, and, in an instant, the dwarf was cut to pieces. Hands, arms, legs, torso, face – all carved and sliced . . . and that was only part of the lethal armoury of the box. Steel glittered as it spun outwards. It passed to the left and right of Büber. Some travelled as far as the distant ceiling, some ricochetted off the floor in front of him and howled over his head.

What was left of Heavyhammer sank to its knees. Propped by the axe handle for a moment, it fell sideways and didn't move.

Now it was over, Büber could taste blood: he'd bitten his tongue, or the inside of his mouth. He spat it out. Not that he could tell where it landed, as he was all but wading in the stuff.

His horse was at the far end of the hall, spiky and skittering and flecked with white foam, clattering its hooves and dancing against the closed outer doors. It was hardly surprisingly; Büber was soaked in blood, so no sane grass-eating animal would want to go near him.

The inner doors clattered, creaked, started to open: he scrabbled on the floor for his knife and the half-soaked parchment, pushing both into his belt. He had to run, and found he could barely walk. He started slowly, lumbering, then speeding up as shouts and curses chased after him. His legs were longer. He could win the race. And his horse, even when he charged at it full pelt, seemed to smell him behind the iron taint that covered him, and didn't shy away as he threw himself at the lever embedded in one of the walls.

The outer doors swung apart and light flooded in. Büber squinted in the sudden brightness, barely able to see. His slippery, aching hands tightened around his horse's neck and refused to let go, even when the doors parted another fraction and the horse burst out onto the mountainside. Heedless of the path, it was mere luck that it didn't fall in the sharp rock shards or run off a precipice.

Büber held on, swinging his leg up and over and crouching low on the saddle. The cold air was like an ice bath, stinging and sudden after the heat of the fight, freezing the blood to his body and stiffening his clothes.

The horse would run and run until it was exhausted. He had no choice but to let it.

69

The key was heavy around Felix's neck and cold on his skin, though its weight and temperature were more to do with what it represented than with what it was. Fear and dread, mainly, a constant nagging reminder that they lived in a world where magic was still possible and was still shaped by it. The contour of every hill, the lie of each forest, every straight or crooked road, the position of towns and villages and their populations: everything was a legacy, and it was going to take time to change.

Even though he was in his own fortress, he felt like he was sneaking around in it. He checked up and down the corridor before fishing inside his shirt for the key on its leather thong. Its shape was crude, and the lock difficult to turn. As he leant into it, he felt the ache in his collar-bone, but he persisted and the lock gave.

He looked again along the corridor, then pushed the door open only just wide enough to ease his slight body through. He pulled the key back out and shouldered the heavy wood shut again.

Three windows pierced the wall high up on the south side of the room, giving little light to the space below. It was sufficient, though, to make out the long, still shapes of bodies laid out on the cold stone floor, arranged in rows and columns like beads on an abacus.

Some were partially dressed. Mostly, they were entirely naked. Some were without a mark, others had molten burns. Their grave-white forms lay exactly where they'd been placed. None appeared to be breathing. Their hearts were still. Yet their eyelids made an occasional traverse across their wide eyes.

This was magic. They were dead, but alive. It shouldn't be so, but it was.

There were seventy-two of them. There had been more, of course, but some had been burnt to a cinder in the fire that Mistress Agana had poured down in front of the novices' house, and more had been consumed in Eckhardt's chambers when she'd burnt them and him. The aftermath of the rebellion had been chaotic, but seventy-two of these . . . people remained, sequestered in the fortress, and he didn't know what to do with them.

They had families, most likely, who had first claim on them. How right would it be to send these still-living corpses back to wives or husbands, mothers and fathers, sons and daughters? There'd been no change in their unlife since Eckhardt had drained them – neither was there any prospect of them ever changing.

The door behind him opened again with the same care and quickness that he'd used. It closed, and he could hear her quick breaths and nervousness.

"My lord? Master Thaler said you wanted to see me."

"Yes, Mistress. You seemed the best person to ask about . . . about these."

She approached, her footsteps now slow and serious.

"This was Eckhardt's doing?"

"These are the ones that are left." Felix looked up at the black-cloaked woman. "I don't know what to do with them."

"I'm not . . ." Tuomanen said, then corrected herself. "I wasn't an expert on necromancy. None of us were. It was an art that was strongly discouraged by the masters. And, by strongly, I mean painfully."

She looked around the room, and at its inmates.

"Mistress, any help you can give." Felix felt their eyes on him. "We'd be very grateful."

"I don't recognise any of them. Are they all townspeople?"

"I think most of them are. Others are from the surrounding farms and villages."

"Have you considered that just killing them would be a kindness?" She crouched down to inspect a hollow-chested man, his ribs as obvious as they would have been on a skeleton. "What good is there in keeping them like this?"

Felix knelt on the floor next to her, aware of the black tattoos driven into her pale skin, the patterns they made and what they had formerly represented. But she wasn't like Nikoleta Agana, and he shouldn't make the mistake of thinking that she was.

"Because there might be some way back."

"From this?" She sucked air between her teeth. "Not now, not without magic. And even then."

"You used to be able to do the impossible. What about all the stories?"

Tuomanen sighed. "My lord, you know why you were told those stories. They were true, yes, but that wasn't the purpose of them. Our power has always been limited, but it has always been greater than anything the mundane world could do."

"And now it's not."

The corner of her mouth lifted slightly. "Quite. Although, because the fortunes of Carinthia have been so closely tied to the Order, that's little cause for celebration."

"My father couldn't have coped. He didn't." He reached out his hand and pressed his palm to the breastbone of the skeletal man. He could feel cold, dry skin, like paper. No rhythmic heartbeat. "I have to. I've seen what could happen. I saw it at Obernberg, just a taste of it, and I don't want that to happen to the rest of Carinthia."

"The young are often the most resilient of all," she said. "If the Norns break you, it won't be because you lack character."

She bent low over the man's body, and Felix drew back, giving her the space to work. She pressed and manipulated, but most of all she listened. She lay there, her ear pressed to the skin of the man's concave stomach, stretched as taught as a drum, moving up to rest on his chest, then his throat and finally against his skull, as if she was trying to read his thoughts.

"There's nothing," she announced. "Some vestige of the spell Eckhardt used is keeping him alive, and that's all. This man's dead. He just doesn't know it yet."

"There's no way to bring him back?" asked Felix.

She sat up. "If we still had Eckhardt's spell book, there might be something in it that I could use. I understand it's gone, and everything else he owned. In any event, you wouldn't let me use it, would you?"

"We can't . . ." Felix forced himself to look at the stricken man's face, at his wet eyes. "We know where that leads."

"The stories you were told were very different to the ones we used to tell ourselves. Armies of reanimated warriors, unkillable and never tiring; creatures made of flesh carved from the fallen and stitched together; skeletons held intact by nothing more than the hexmaster's will; soul jars; revenants; ancient kings who refuse to die and keep themselves alive by sucking out the lives of their subjects." As she spoke, the temperature seemed to drop, and Felix shivered. "We told such stories to each other in the freezing night while we were still burning from the day's humiliations and beatings, using them to give ourselves the courage to face the next morning. We knew that one day we'd wield spells of that magnitude, and all our suffering would be worth it."

"We were fools ever to trust you."

Tuomanen bowed her head. "My lord speaks the truth. So, no: there's nothing I can do for these people, even if I could. Have you tried feeding them?"

"One. Her lungs filled up with the broth we were trying to spoon into her."

"Did she die?"

"No. We emptied her out, and didn't try again."

"Have you," she said, "have you asked them what they want?"

Felix had. "They never reply," he said, "They can't move or speak, and I don't think they can see or hear either. I tried to get them just to blink a yes or no answer, but there was no pattern."

"Perhaps you're not asking them in the right way." She lifted the man's hand and hooked her thumb around one of his pale, worm-like fingers. She leant forward, pushing the finger up to an ever more contorted angle.

"Stop."

"My lord, pain is not just a good training aid, it's also a very great incentive to talk." She kept on pushing. "We don't even want to get information from him; we just want to know he's in there."

"Mistress, don't . . ."

"It's in his own best interests. If he's trapped inside this shell, he needs to find a way of breaking out. Mere discomfort won't do it." There was a popping sound, and she let go. The finger stuck out and away from the hand, clearly dislocated. "I can keep on until he does something."

Felix swallowed down the acid taste in his mouth. "Put it back," he said. "And don't do that again."

She shrugged, and gripped the finger hard, pulling it and pressing on the joint at the same time. When she let go, it was back in position. The victim showed nothing, not even a flicker of his eyelids.

"They're as good as dead. They show no sign of being aware of anything. Nor do they respond to pain. If they are awake in there, then I imagine they're all completely mad by now." Tuomanen stood swiftly. "They may well be immortal since they don't seem to be alive, and if that was me, I'd want to be burnt, then my bones ground into powder, just to make sure."

"There's no hope at all?"

"My lord, forgive me, but you are so very young. Now is as good a time as any to realise that some problems have no good solutions; just ones that are less worse than the alternatives. You need to embrace doubt and fear certainty." She smiled down at him. "I know that must sound strange coming from one of the Order, but there are no givens any more. We're feeling our way in the dark, and if you hear a voice calling out 'this way', distrust it."

"Oh."

"That includes me, for the avoidance of doubt. I'm just as likely to give you bad advice as the next person." She put her hands on her hips and gazed around at the not-dead bodies. "If you lack the stomach for it, I can deal with these poor wretches. I'll even promise to follow your instructions."

"I'm the Prince of Carinthia. I shouldn't ask things of those who serve me that I'm not prepared to do myself." Felix gathered his strength and dragged himself upright.

She laughed. It was a pleasant sound, but it had an edge to it. "Who told you that?"

"My father," he said.

"Ah," she said. "It's a fine ideal, but it wasn't done in Gerhard's day any more than it was done in his father's. The prince's hands have to be kept clean."

"Do they?"

"They thought so. Don't feel any compulsion to follow in their hypocrisy. If you get your hands dirty, a few will look down on you for it, but far more will respect you."

"I'll see to this, then. These unfortunates, whatever else they may be, are still my people." He mirrored her gaze, looking at each and every white-skinned form. It was going to be grim work telling their kin that their family members were still alive, and yet not; that there was nothing that could be done, and that every body needed to be burnt to free them from whatever trap Eckhardt had forced them into. Some would baulk at such an order; and he'd have to make sure it was done.

He'd better start ordering the firewood now.

He glanced at the witch. Former witch. She was studying him.

"As you wish, my lord," she said.

"Are you an elf?" he blurted.

She laughed again, and once more the edge was there, a catch of a blade at the back of her throat.

"Who says I'm an elf?"

"I . . ." No, no names. Master Ullmann would be left out of this. "I wondered. You're from the north, you have a northerner's name, but you're dark."

"Inside and out, my lord?"

"I didn't mean to offend you, Mistress."

She pursed her lips and narrowed her eyes. "Look at you: you haven't even learnt guile yet. Your statecraft is sadly lacking, Prince Felix, and from what I know of the Jews, with their strange notions of sin and judgement, it'll stay that way. You have to learn to lie, and lie well, or you'll lose your life and the palatinate to someone who can."

Felix raised himself to his full, insignificant height and tried again. "Are you . . .?"

"Yes," she said. "I'm a changeling."

Ah. "What happened to your human parents?"

"My differences eventually became too obvious to ignore when I turned from being a child to a woman. They wanted me to stay

– I was their daughter – but the rest of the village had other ideas. They chased me out, into the forest, where there were wolves and bears and worse. I was about the age you are now."

Had it always been like this, then? Had the Order been no more than the greatest collection of the most damaged souls in Europe? The greater the hate, the greater the power?

"What did you do?"

"Do? I cried. A lot. I cursed the wind and the trees. I walked south, expecting to be eaten every time I sat down to rest. Eventually, I reached the coast, and found a fisherman. He took me across the Skagerrak, and, on the journey, he told me of what he'd heard about the Order of the White Robe."

"Lucky," said Felix.

"Or not. I could have had a normal life, somewhere, if he hadn't put the idea in my head that, one day, I might break down the doors of Alfheim and demand my inheritance. So I don't know whether to find him again to thank him, or to kill him for it." She looked momentarily morose, as if she was remembering her loss for the first time. "And now, wherever the land of the Elves is, I'll never get there, and even if I did, there'd be nothing there for me."

"I'm sorry. I really shouldn't have asked." Felix pulled the key out of his shirt, feeling the warmed iron in his grasp. "I hope you decide to stay in Carinthia."

She looked at him differently. Still studying him, but less like a hovering hawk eyeing a rabbit.

"I thought," she said, "you were going to add: because Carinthia needs people like me. Rootless. Stateless. Violent. Expendable. But that's not right, is it? It seems I need Carinthia more."

She bowed, and Felix didn't quite know what to make of it all.

"If there are still gods, may they keep you safe, my prince," she said. "If there are none, and we have to rely on our own hands and courage, then you have mine. If there's nothing more, then Master Thaler has more book-work for me."

Felix nodded and, when she'd gone, made one last sweep of the room. There was nothing she could do, and nothing he could do.

She was right. Better to send them to the fire than leave them like that forever. And he'd see to the task himself, no matter what his father would or wouldn't have done.

70

At times, it was almost pleasant: the land either side of the Salzach was in its full flush of green, and cows were contentedly chewing on the fresh grass. It was much like home, and he looked at the beasts as a farmer's son would have done, judging their worth, their meat and milk and hide.

At other times it had been more a farce, as the drifting barge appeared to be inexplicably attracted to the river banks. The prow of the boat would slew across the channel, and as fast as Vulfar's crew scrambled to steer it away from overhanging trees and stands of closely packed reeds on one side, they'd have to scramble back to use their long poles on the other.

For his part, the bargemaster barked out orders in his barbarian tongue and swung on the tiller as though it were a child's toy. He'd convinced Mistress Morgenstern to part with a sack of cash, using his honeyed words and Frankish ways, but if she could have seen him now, cursing and swearing, she'd have refused to pay him so much as a penny.

Ullmann sat in the open hold with Horst and Manfred, who seemed enormously amused by the bargees' antics and shouted sarcastic encouragement to them at every opportunity. Ullmann wasn't the slightest bit amused, though. If Vulfar couldn't get the barge under control, then the crew would soon be exhausted. A tired man pushing against a pole would make a mistake, slip, fall in, and then there'd be a stupid rush to get him back on board, creating nothing but delay.

The only thing holding him back from leaping to his feet and wresting the captaincy from the Frank was that he knew even less about steering an unpowered barge down a river in spate than Vulfar did.

Bundles of spears weren't the comfiest perch, either. He gave up and swung himself out onto the barge-boards.

"Hey, Max: going to give the bargemaster a piece of your mind?" Horst grinned up at him.

"If I thought it'd do any good, I'd have done it while we were still in sight of Juvavum. As it is, we're going to make the best of it, and do our duty to Carinthia. If that means we have to walk to Simbach with two hundred spears, that's what we'll do." Ullmann held on to a strut and viewed the scene on deck. The barge was more or less mid-stream, although it was slowly turning to the right. The men on the starboard side plunged their poles in, and at the stern Vulfar steered hard.

"Master Ullmann, I think I've got it!" As Vulfar hung on to the tiller, sure enough, the bow came slowly around, and he applied a correction the other way. He shouted to the bargees: the poles on the right came out, while the ones on the left dipped in, briefly. They'd managed to avoid both banks.

Ullmann edged along the boards until he could step onto the stern section. "We've lost time, Master Vulfar," he barked. "Will we still make it to Simbach this evening?"

"Have some faith, Master Ullmann. I might not be able to will my ship where I want any longer, but godsdamn, I can still point it in the right direction." Vulfar shouted down the length of the hull again, because there was a bend in the river they needed to negotiate.

"You've spent most of the journey pointing it in any direction but, Master Vulfar. The coin isn't yours yet."

"Oh, you'd like that, wouldn't you? Watch me fail and lose my prize?" Vulfar held the tiller in the crook of his elbow and tightened the twists in his moustache.

"No, actually I wouldn't. What I'd really like is to get to Simbach at the right time, unload the weapons, find enough Bavarians willing to carry them, and chase Fuchs out of town." Ullmann gripped the stern rail. "If that's all right with you, of course."

"That's why we're all here, yes?" said Vulfar. He hauled hard and watched the direction of the bow intently. It started to swing into the slacker water on the outside of the bend. "No, no, no!"

He dragged on the tiller, mindless of where Ullmann was standing, and yelled full-throated instructions to the crew. Vigorous poling ensued, and slowly, slowly, the stern followed the bow into the curve.

"Do you have the hang of it now, Master Vulfar?" Ullmann rubbed his sore ribs. "Only, me and the other passengers would rather not have to get out and push us off a sandbank."

Vulfar muttered something under his breath, which, to Ullmann, sounded suspiciously like a threat to drown him sooner rather than later. He guessed, though, that any dislike the bargemaster held for him was more than outweighed by the prospect of a sack of silver coins.

"We'll get there, and in good order," said the Frank. But he was sweating and straining, his face a mass of lines; tension, concentration and concern all wrapped up in one fixed grimace. Ullmann clambered back to the hold and sat brooding for a moment.

"Everything all right up top, Max?"

"I wish I could say it was," said Ullmann, worrying at the ball of his thumb, "but Master Vulfar has no more control over this heap of shit than I do. We may have to change our plans."

Horst leant forward. "Can't he land us where we need to be, then?"

"Land us? We'll be lucky if we make it the next mile downstream without getting stuck sideways and overturning."

"Well, at least that's a mile we don't have to walk."

"Shut up, Horst. I don't doubt that Fuchs is nothing but a coward and a blowhard, ripe to be chased away by honest Carinthian courage" – Ullmann kicked the weapons he was sitting on – "but it'll be a whole lot easier if we can put these spears into the hands of friends rather than leave them at the bottom of the river."

"So what are you going to do, Max?" said Manfred. He opened his satchel and fetched out a long sausage and his paring knife.

"We have to be ready to act at any moment," Ullmann said quietly. He took Manfred's knife from him and leant down to cut the first of the cords that tied the nearest bundle of spears together. "If you count Vulfar, there are five of them, and only three of us, but if we can get Ohlhauser and the two Bavarians with us, that makes six. I'll have my sword, and you'll have spears – they only have clubs and their fists."

"They've got those long poles, though." Manfred watched as his knife travelled the length of the spears to the second restraining cord.

"Those are too long to be a threat," said Horst, "too unwieldy. Just step inside their reach. But are you serious, Max? I mean, these are a bunch of hard bastards who've fought and whored their way up and down the Donau for years."

"Yes, I'm serious: our duty's to Carinthia. These mummers might look the part, but without their magic they're just playing at being bargees. I don't want to end up on the wrong side of the river as we sail past Simbach, unable to do anything but wave at Fuchs as we pass by." Ullmann slipped his sword out of its scabbard and inspected it for rust spots. "If they can't get and keep control of this tub soon, we'll have to put them off and take it for ourselves."

Manfred frowned, even as he took back his knife and started slicing rounds of sausage for them. "I don't know. Perhaps we should leave it to them. A hundred florins is a big incentive to get it right."

"Which is what we hope. But, like I said, we have to be ready to act: we can't just assume that because someone has a title of master it follows they know what they're doing. Not any more." Ullmann looked at Horst's sceptically raised eyebrow. "I got my title *after* the change. That's the difference."

Manfred chewed, and used the point of his knife for emphasis. "But doesn't it make Vulfar as much of a chancer as you, Max? You took your opportunity when you saw it, and I'm not begrudging you your promotion in any way – you're sharper than I am, and you've always put yourself forward for stuff. This barge-master saw his opportunity too – he's looking to retire on the reward he'll get for this, and you can't deny that he's trying to keep his end of the bargain, can you?"

Ullmann hunched over. "It's like this: why did anyone get called master in the first place? It's because we weren't hexmasters and could never be hexmasters, but we still wanted the authority the title gave us. You could be a huntmaster like Peter Büber, or a guildmaster like Master Emser, but we all knew who the real masters were. No one questioned a hexmaster, not if you valued your life: we did what we were told or else. They're gone now, and there's no reason for us to call ourselves Master this or Master that any more."

"Especially not Master Vulfar, eh?" Horst licked his fingers. "He might know the river, but what good does that do him?"

"Exactly my point. Bargemasters might be tattooed with all the spells under the sun, but they've no magic to back it up." Ullmann looked at the brightness of his sword and tested its edge with his thumb. Not as sharp as it should have been; he really ought to have had it reground before setting off. "All Vulfar is good for is knowing the name of the sandbank or reed-bed we're going to crash into next."

"Steady on, Max," said Manfred. "You'll be saying next that princes and earls don't have a right to rule over their lands."

Ullmann caught sight of his warped reflection in the flat of his blade. No reason why a farm boy from Over-Carinthia shouldn't believe that he wasn't every bit as good as any earl. However, to say so would be dangerous, for now at least. Waiting until the grand council had abolished the position of earl and revoked their privilege would be much wiser.

So he sheathed his sword and affected a look of concern. "Someone has to be in charge, Man. We don't want chaos."

Horst scrabbled free of the hold and stuck his head out the side of the hold to check their progress. He looked like a farm-dog getting a ride on a cart. All he needed was his tongue lolling out.

"We're a bit close to the left bank, but at least we're going straight." Horst twisted around. "There's a lot of river on the other side of the boat."

Ullmann pursed his lips and picked his way over to Ohlhauser. "A word, if you please."

"Master Ullmann." Ohlhauser leant closer. "Is the barge supposed to do this?"

The farmer indicated a yawing motion with the flat of his hand, and Ullmann shook his head slowly.

"Do you recognise the land? Any idea how much further we have to go?"

"Difficult to say," said Ohlhauser, "this low down in the water. Let's climb up and take a look."

A plank's width of boardwalk ran the entire length of the barge on top of the hold, from the cabin to the bow. Ullmann scrambled up and dragged the older man up behind him, who then used Ullmann's head to steady himself as he stood on the narrow strip and faced eastwards.

"I know where I am," he said, and pointed. "See that shoulder of land, where the wooded hills dip out of sight? That's south of Simbach, on the edge of the plain where the Enn joins the Salzach. Simbach is another mile further than that, where the river turns and the bridge used to be."

"How far is that altogether?" The bargees were looking at them, wondering what they were doing. They certainly weren't concentrating on where they were going. The fast water was to their right; lazy was the only description of their progress.

"Fifteen, twenty miles?" Ohlhauser wobbled on his perch and gripped Ullmann's head even harder. "I don't come this way often, but you can see where the via runs. If I had keener eyes I could read the milestones."

"You'd better come down from there, Mr Ohlhauser. We're heading towards the bank yet again." Ullmann prised the farmer's hand from the crown of his head and started to help him down.

The bargees poled hard again as Vulfar yelled his obscure cant, and the barge pivoted about its midships: the bow struck out for the centre, while the back slewed further towards the tall cliff of brown soil knitted together with tree roots.

"I think we should take cover," said Ullmann, but it was too late. They could only hang on to the plank and to each other.

The barge shivered as it hit, and something cracked. Unable to tell what it was immediately because he had his face buried in Ohlhauser's armpit, Ullmann emerged to see the Frankish barge-master slump to the deck, finally free of the tiller arm that had pinned him to the stern rail.

"Oh, for fuck's sake." Ullmann climbed over Ohlhauser's shoulders and started along the centre board at a shuffling run. "Vulfar's down."

The back of the boat rattled free of the overhanging branches and into clear water. Ullmann leapt down onto the deck next to Vulfar, crouching to stop himself from pitching over the side. Grabbing the tiller, he found there was no resistance to his touch.

They'd lost the rudder, and from the look of Vulfar, who was gagging and gasping, eyes bulging and fingers clawing at the smooth wet wood of the deck, they'd lost their captain too.

Now they were heading into the middle of the river, with even less to steer with than before.

"We need to stop this thing!" shouted Ullmann. "Anyone got any ideas?" He looked at the bargees at the far end of the barge, who looked blankly at him. "Tell me one of you can speak German."

The barge was wandering across the river again, towards the Bavarian side.

"Horst? Manfred? On deck now."

They popped their heads out. Ohlhauser was still clinging to the top of the hold, looking desperate.

"Max?"

"We're adrift, and we can't afford to be. Get those bargees to pole us towards the bank. I'm going to see what I can do back here." He looked around for anything he might use. There were coils of rope piled up, already wound in a tight figure-of-eight around two bollards. If he could attach the other end to something solid on the bank, the front end would come into the side too.

Only if they were facing the right way, though. As the bow entered slacker water, the stern started to turn, and slowly but surely they started to go broadside down the river.

The bargees appeared incapable of doing anything except watch helplessly, and there seemed nothing that Manfred or Horst could say to make them do anything different. Ullmann realised it was his responsibility to salvage something from this disaster, yet his experience of boats was limited to the rowboat in which he'd crossed to the White Tower.

There was only one thing he could think of. He kicked his boots off, undid his belt, and wrestled out of his shirt. Taking one end of a length of rope, he tied it around his waist as quickly as he could, then pitched himself backwards over the side.

Gods, the water was cold. It wasn't long since it had been winter snow up in the high passes, and the chill took his breath away as the water closed over his head. He sank down until the pressure increasing on his chest reminded him that he had to break surface and breathe again.

A far cry and years ago: the memory of cracking the mirror-calm of a mountain lake, blue sky above and black water below, before crawling onto sun-warm stones to dry. Now it felt all so serious, but it was only his experience that had changed his perceptions. It always had been serious.

He kicked out, arms and legs, and made for the surface. As he filled his lungs with air, he remembered why he was there. The rope was paying out as he trod water, and the barge was sailing further away with every stroke of his hands.

He set off for the bank. Ahead was a sandbank, and the back of the barge was heading straight for it.

Swimming as fast as he could, he suddenly ran out of depth. His fingers plunged into the silt riverbed, and, using his hands and knees, he hauled himself up, streaming water.

The barge had grounded. The bow was swinging around, and

the grinding noise as the hull scraped along the stones sounded more than ominous. Ullmann ran across the saturated sand and onto the riverbank just as the barge started to drift again.

He didn't bother to untie the rope. He chose the thickest tree he could find and ran around it once, twice, three times.

The hemp rope tightened, rising across the river to make a straight line between tree and barge. It creaked and growled, and started to slip, stripping the bark in one big sheet as the coils shrank and bit deep.

Ullmann felt himself dragged inexorably backwards. His numb fingers pulled clumsily at the knot at his waist, trying with his nails to unpick the sodden fibrous mass. He was pulled ever closer to the tree, even as it made snipping and snapping sounds. The upper branches started to curl over towards the river.

With one last tug, the rope fell from around him, and he took what was left of the slack, jamming it between the trunk and the taut line. He leant against it, trapping it in position. As the barge pulled harder, the rope bit down against the free end. The tree shook, and Ullmann felt the ground quake as its shallow roots started to buckle and tear.

Either this would work, or it wouldn't. He closed his eyes and held on.

When he opened them again, the barge was up against the bank, and two of the bargees were leaping off, extra rope in their hands to secure the craft.

His hands were slick with blood, and when he tried to let go, he found that he couldn't.

He had, however, saved the cargo, and the barge. He grimaced and stretched out his fingers. The pain was exquisite.

Manfred came running up the bank and through the trees towards him. "Max, you really are a mad bastard, aren't you?"

71

He could see them, a mile or so behind him. It wasn't the kind of margin he was happy with, and he wasn't even certain it was the same group he was seeing each time.

There was no cover this far up the pass, so it was foolish to hope that he could stay out of sight and then duck down behind a boulder – his horse as well – and watch his pursuers pass by.

And even if that somehow succeeded, they'd then be ahead of him.

Any other time of year, he might have risked going over the top of the peaks to either the north or south. But with them still draped in slowly melting snows, he'd be dead under an avalanche before he ever made the summit. There was only one way out, and that was downhill all the way to Rosenheim.

At least he knew where they were, the little dark shapes picking their way down the path next to the river. They had no horses; dwarves were strictly, religiously, on their feet or not at all, though whether that taboo continued, given their changed circumstances, was anyone's guess. Their stamina, though, was legendary. He'd already witnessed Heavyhammer's ability to keep going over the roughest terrain, and still have the strength left to trick him at the last moment.

What was really getting to him, and worried him the most, were their horns.

Every so often, just when he thought they'd stopped blowing the damn things, a deep, sonorous note would echo from valley-side to valley-side, slowly fading away before sounding again. Two blasts, each time, then silence.

It meant that, as they got closer to Ennsbruck, the dwarves he'd sent there – like an idiot – would be waiting for him.

The tree line would start soon, but the chasing pack were simply too close. They were driving him on, knowing that he'd get caught further down. They didn't have to catch him up. They just had to keep him moving.

It meant that Büber had to think of something different, something unexpected, and he wasn't good at that. He knew what he knew. Nikoleta would have been able to come up with a plan. She'd been smart and ruthless, and she'd never shied away from what needed to be done, no matter the cost.

He hoped that by the time he got within earshot of Ennsbruck, he'd have his brilliant idea. For now, all there was was the chase.

In his more forgiving moments, Büber acknowledged that his escape from Farduzes had bordered on the heroic, the sort of story that as a young, barely civilised wild thing he'd have drawn closer to the fire to hear.

No one would ever know of it, though, if it didn't come from his own lips. The thought made him bitter and determined, and he kept up his punishing pace, switching his horse across the rough terrain, reassuring it when the horns sounded and cajoling it during the silences.

A few miles later, with the sun in the south and air smoky with early insects, he came to the lip of rock that marked the junction between mountaintop and high alp. There were stunted trees and low scrub below him, and further east, forest filled the whole valley floor.

The grey of the rock gave way to the green of leaf. It marked the edge of what the dwarves behind him knew, and what he, Peter Büber, knew. The path down was steep and narrow, but once there, it became shallow and broad. The subtle shift of advantages swung imperceptibly towards him. He might even stand a slim chance of escaping.

He took hold of the bridle, knitting his fingers between it and the horse's head, and curved his other arm under its neck to hold it fast against his body.

"Come on, then. Going down is much harder than coming up, but we can do this." He backed down the first part of the slope, and, by instinct, the horse resisted, trying to shake Büber off.

Dragging it wasn't going to work, and he had to persuade it down, step by hesitant step.

They were halfway when the horns began again. It could have been just a coincidence, but more likely it was planned: the dwarves were trying to spook the horse.

Büber kept tight hold, whispering in its ear all the time, trying to calm it. The beast rolled its wide eyes and foam dribbled from its mouth. The echo carried on, and seemed to come from every side. They were getting closer.

"Come on, you flighty fucker. We've been through all sorts of shit together, and I suddenly find that dying out here at the hands of those bastard dwarves is something I don't want to do. So ignore the horns, forget how steep this is, and concentrate on my voice."

Perhaps it was the familiarity that had grown between the two. Perhaps it was Büber's death-grip on the bridle. Or perhaps it was simply that the horse thought Büber was less likely than the dwarves to eat it. Whatever it was, the creature started moving again, with Büber keeping up a constant monologue in its ear.

The slope began to flatten, and they ran the last few feet to level ground.

They both shook themselves down, and the horns sounded again, seeming to come from just back over the rise.

"Right." Büber took a second to make absolutely certain the girth strap was tight before getting his foot up to the stirrup. "This isn't going to be good for either of us."

His backside hit the saddle and he dug his heels in. The horns bellowed once more, and the dwarves appeared at the top of the rock face, looking stern and purposeful. At least Büber didn't need to kick the horse twice: it started at a high-stepping canter and settled into a gallop for a stadia or two.

The dwarves lost definition as they grew more distant. Soon they were no more than squat stick figures against the blue haze of the mountains behind them, and Büber slowed the horse back to a canter.

The path grew closer to the river. It would have been a relief to stop, to cool down, but they had to keep going, and at speed. The ground was softer – less harsh at any rate – and the clattering of the horse's hooves dulled to a rhythmic drum-beat.

As the trees started to climb above them, the dwarvish horns rolled their sound down the valley once again. If they attracted giants, it would be some sort of justice, though Büber doubted there would be any within earshot, given the number he'd killed the previous day. Their bodies had been crow-food when he'd passed them earlier.

He eased down to a walk, and then speeded up for a gallop, alternating between the two, eating up the miles, aware that the dwarves marched inexorably onwards behind him.

Their horns called periodically; an initial blast, a sustained note, a long trailing away. The dwarves in Ennsbruck would have heard that sound already, but what commands did the notes carry? Would the dwarves understand what was being asked of them? He had to assume they'd be waiting for him, and would stop him if they could.

He kept up the cycle of walking and running, or rather he forced the horse to. It might have been punishing on him, but it was exhausting the animal he was riding. Every time it walked, it did so for longer. Every time it galloped, it was for a shorter distance.

It was killing the horse, and he knew it. What was worse was that he meant to do so. At some point, it would die under him, heart given out and lungs burnt. Büber would get off, take the things he needed, and carry on on foot.

That was his plan: to get as far ahead as possible from the following pack, and surprise Ennsbruck's new residents with his sudden appearance. Encountering one or two, or even three at a push as he broke through their picket line was doable. What he didn't want was to give them time to be properly organised.

The sun swung behind his right shoulder and flickered between the trees. To his left, the flank of the mountain swelled. There was a pinch-point ahead, where the river twisted to the north up against the valley-side, and the path squeezed through the gap between water and rock.

Across the river, on the other side, was a patchwork of field-lines, but he gauged that the water was too deep, too quick and too cold to cross. If he was a dwarf, he'd have made the same calculations and posted at least a couple of guards on the road.

Büber slowed the horse, and it all but stopped: habit was the only thing keeping it going now. Reaching for his crossbow, he pulled the string back with the lever, and laid a bolt against the wire.

His wasn't a quiet approach – the horse was making enough noise for two – so this had to be done quickly instead. The horns sounded again, but for the first time since the pursuit began, they sounded distant and indistinct. He dug his heels in and hoped.

Just as he was predictable, so were they. They'd heard him coming, were poised, braced for his charge, teeth bared and axes ready.

Except he wasn't charging. When he was still a distance away, several blade lengths apart but close enough to make a bow-shot easy, he pulled up and sighted along his arm at one of the dwarves.

They abruptly realised their mistake, but one of them paid for it with his life. The bolt pierced his chest, leaving only the flights protruding, and the impact rocked him backwards on his heels. He staggered, sank to one knee, and finally fell.

All the while, Büber was reloading.

An enraged dwarf ran at Büber, mouth open, voice raised in a bellow of anger. He drew his axe back ready for his swing, and Büber fired the second bolt down his throat.

It could only get harder from now on. He holstered the crossbow and took up the reins again, trying to coax one last effort from his horse. It responded feebly, only picking up speed when he kicked his hardest. The beast was trembling with effort, and clearly couldn't continue much longer.

The trees ended as the river swung away to the right. The black walls of Ennsbruck were closer than he'd anticipated, and the surrounding land was a maze of fields and gates.

He couldn't see any other dwarves, even though he knew they had to be there. They could have ducked down behind the rough dry-stone walls, but that would have made it hard for them to ambush him.

Büber hesitated. He ought to dismount, scout the way ahead, check for tracks and spoors – all the things that he knew how to do. Instead he drove the horse on, and that was when they sprang their trap.

It was nothing more sophisticated than a rope pulled taut across the road, but it didn't need to be fancy to bring the horse down and send Büber flying. The ditches either side were abruptly full of dwarves, swarming out, covered in soil and sacking and fountaining water as they emerged.

He hit the gravel face-first. It hadn't been his best feature, so he didn't give it a moment's thought. He flipped over onto his back, and skidded to a halt.

He was bleeding. Of course he was. And there were a dozen dwarves, filthy and stinking of sulphurous mud, running up behind him, weapons ready to make him bleed some more.

As they passed the horse, they hit it twice, breaking its neck and skull. It hadn't even tried to rise.

Gods, he was tired. He'd been going hard all day. If he chose to lie there, he could rest forever. Nikoleta might even be wherever it was he ended up. And yet the fight hadn't completely left him.

Büber hauled his lanky frame upright, and realised that he'd fallen between the dwarves and the town. He put his head down and started to run towards Ennsbruck.

He felt and heard the air cutting at his back. The axe-blade sang as it swung, and the draught caught his cloak. He was a hair's breadth from disaster, and somehow, despite his exhaustion, he managed to stay one step ahead. Then two. Then more. His long legs took great gulps out of the road, while the dwarves, with their much shorter limbs, struggled to keep up.

His heart pounded and his lungs burned. He was running on empty, with nothing left to fuel him except his pain and anger. They'd killed his damn horse as if they were swatting a fly, and that stupid kid he'd left in Ennsbruck – the one who tried to steal from him – was now hanging from the town wall, tied upside down by his feet with his hands cut off in case he should try to climb back up.

He had to escape from them, because this was what Carinthia could become, every town like Obernberg, their inhabitants nailed to the outsides of their houses. Worse than the Teutons, and that had been bad enough.

They were throwing their axes and hammers in an effort to stop him, but none hit their mark.

The gap between them widened as he put everything into his effort. No half-measures, no holding something back for later. There'd be no later otherwise. They were fresh, he was spent. They'd run him down before he'd gone a mile: but he didn't have to run a mile.

Only to the bridge.

The river was turning back towards him, and there was the twin-piered bridge. What he needed was not on the other side, behind the walls, but in the river itself.

He threw himself down the bank and into the water. Freezing, unspeakably cold. He plunged his arms below the surface to grab the edge of one of the submerged boats.

He had his knife and then he didn't. No use worrying now; he couldn't fight them all, and never could. Instead, he concentrated on the one thing that might save him. The effort just to get the boat moving was incredible. The water sucked at it, and his feet churned in the soft sand and loose pebbles.

The stones that kept it pinned to the riverbed rolled free as he turned it, and it rose. He lifted it above his head and the water poured out of it in a cataract over his head. He was blind and stung, gasping for air. One last act, born of desperation, because there were a hundred things he could have done differently but this was the only one he could think of: he threw the boat into the fast-flowing meltwater of the midstream, and himself after it.

His part-fingers clamped to the bulwark of the boat, which

started to fill with water almost instantly, but the current had both it and him. He was being washed away, and no matter how long and far the dwarves ran, they weren't going to catch him if he only could keep himself afloat.

But he'd freeze to death if he didn't do something about that, and quickly. The little boat sank lower in the water, and he tried to pull himself into it.

He couldn't get enough purchase. His few-fingered hands slipped against the wet wood, and he fell back each time. There were shallows, though, and he kicked out to try and guide his salvage towards them.

The dwarves weren't giving up. The hoom of distant horns, and close-by shouts of their strange words made that clear. He had bare moments to fix the situation.

His feet touched the bottom, and he pushed the boat up against the bank. Emptying it of water, he dragged his sodden cloak off his back and jammed it into the hole in the bilges, working the cloth deep down with his fist. Then, with one foot in the boat, he pushed off from the side, paddling frantically with his hands to put as much distance as he could between himself and the snarling, bearded faces assembling on the riverbank.

If any had been armed with a bow, he'd have been done for. Bows weren't dwarvish weapons, though, not like the axe or hammer. Dwarves preferred to meet their foe face to face, killing him like an honest man should.

Fuck that, thought Büber, as the river propelled him on. The bung he'd made of his rain-washed cloak leaked more than a little, and he bailed with his cupped hands.

At some point in his journey downstream, he realised that he might be dying. By that time he was too cold to care.

72

They were barely in any state to invade a beer cellar and order a round of drinks, let alone do more, but at least they'd finally arrived: it was just beyond dusk, a couple of miles upstream of Simbach, just past where the Salzach and the Enn met.

Ullmann had taken his turn tied to the barge like some draught animal, walking along the bank and helping to guide it along. Everyone had, except Vulfar who'd broken at least a couple of ribs and was lucky not to have pierced a lung. They'd laid him out in the cabin, and just got on with the job.

Ohlhauser had proved to be as strong as an ox, a lifetime of lifting and carrying, ploughing and reaping meant he thought little of wrapping a rope over his shoulders and leaning into the load. He reminded Ullmann of the father he'd left behind in Over-Carinthia, perhaps a little too much.

Crossing the Enn had proved difficult, but, once again, Ullmann had swum across and guided the barge to the other side.

With the boat safely tied up and not showing any lights, Vulfar felt he'd earned his florins. Ullmann wasn't so sure about the bargemaster, but his crew certainly had, as also had the Bavarians, and Manfred and Horst, who'd cheerfully done everything asked of them and more. He closed the hold doors, and lit one of the lanterns.

"Does everyone know their part?" asked Ullmann. "Mr Ohlhauser, you've already done your duty, and, if you wish, you're released."

"If you've something else in mind, Master Ullmann, I can lend an arm or two."

"Then stay with the barge and Manfred. The spears won't unload themselves, and we may have to do it quickly. If we can take the wharf, we'll do it there. If that's too risky, we'll send the towns-people to you. Be ready, and if you're attacked, cast off for Carinthia." He unfolded the map and pressed it flat with his hand. "Me, Mr Metz, Mr Kehle and Horst will enter the town from the north and go door to door. Fuchs never stays overnight in Simbach, but returns to his hall three miles to the north-east. He leaves some of his men behind, but if we gather enough townspeople, quickly enough, we can overwhelm and disarm them in whichever cellar they happen to be."

"That's clear enough," said Horst. "Are we taking spears with us?"

"As many as we can comfortably carry. If we can take the town without alerting Fuchs, we're half done." Ullmann counted out six spears to each man, and six for himself. "Our load'll soon get lighter."

They were ready, and Manfred asked: "What's the sign, then, that we're to come to the wharf?"

"Let's not get too pretty about this, Man. One of us'll run back and tell you. Just keep close watch, and if you see the town on fire, you'll know that things aren't going well for us."

"These are our homes you're talking about," murmured Metz in the darkness, "and our families and neighbours."

"Yes, Mr Metz, and if you didn't want our spears or our help, the time to say so would have been on the quay at Juvavum. Nothing's going to go wrong, and nothing's going to get burnt down – as long as everyone plays their part." Ullmann blew the lantern out and opened one of the landward-side hold doors.

The gusty night wind blew in, and Ullmann stole out onto the running board, then jumped up onto the soft soil of the bank. Manfred passed him his bundle of spears, doing the same for each person as they scrabbled ashore.

"Right. Man, you sit at the bow and keep watch. If you feel yourself dropping off, for gods' sakes swap with someone else – Mr Ohlhauser for preference." Ullmann slung his spears up on his shoulder, where they rattled against each other. "This should be straightforward, but it won't hurt to stay alert."

"The gods are on our side, Max," said Manfred. "Go on, get going."

Kehle took the lead, and they spaced themselves out, keeping track of each other in the dark by dint of tails of white cloth they'd tucked in the waist bands of their breeks.

The Bavarians moved quickly and surely. Fuchs's band of robbers didn't bother with wasteful effort like patrols; when the sun went down they started drinking, and when the sun came up again, they'd look for more people to intimidate. Dusk, then, meant a welcome respite for the town, when those who had somewhere else to go might take the opportunity to steal away under cover of night.

The band crept into the outskirts of town. There was no stone wall, narrow bridge or looming castle to mark the boundary – just buildings beginning to squash in next to each other. Glowing globes had hung suspended across a few of Simbach's major junctions, just as they had, in greater abundance, at Juvavum. Now the streets were dark, with most of the windows shuttered, and there was no edict in force, commanding that a light be shone from every house

Ullmann watched Kehle turn a corner, then abruptly reappear.

Working his way up the line, he pressed his mouth to the Bavarian's ear.

"What is it?"

"Fuchs's men. Beer cellar on München Street."

Ullmann crouched down and took a peek for himself. Drunken noise and dirty yellow light spilt out from one of the basements, and, across the road, someone was pissing up against the wall of a tailor's.

"At least we know where they are now. Is there another way across?"

"We'll have to back up." They trotted back the way they'd come, and took another side street that led them out further along.

This time, the beer cellar was an indistinct glow, and the figures visible in front of it were blind to their presence. Ullmann and his men crossed the München road calmly and quietly, Kehle leading the rest of the way to his brother's house, overlooking the market square – not by the front way, but down a narrow alley and up a creaking flight of wooden steps, difficult to negotiate carrying half a dozen spears each.

"Give me a minute," Kehle said, and handed his load to Horst before trying the latch. It rose, and he slipped through the door. A sliver of warmth, then darkness again. Ullmann shivered and looked up. The night sky was breaking apart to show the stars and the rising horns of the moon, the light of which risked exposing them to view.

He motioned for them to get down as best they could, and hide their faces from the moon-glow.

From somewhere inside the house came the sound of a woman's shriek – cut sharply off – and the shattering of a pot. Then the light under the door went out, and Kehle was standing there, beckoning them in. Quickly gathering up their bundles, they climbed up and in. The door was closed, and the candle uncovered.

"Sorry about the noise. My brother's wife." Kehle lifted the candlestick. "They came for my brother yesterday, and Juli doesn't know where he's been taken. She thought I was him."

"Does Fuchs know you went to Carinthia?" asked Ullmann.

"No, but he's taken Gerd hostage anyway."

Metz grew agitated. "I need to find my parents, my sisters."

Ullmann rested his spears against the closed door and bowed

his head. "Let's not complicate matters, gentlemen. Why don't we take a moment or two to work out what we want and how best to get it. I assume Fuchs is holding his prisoners in his manor?"

"That's what Juli heard," said Kehle. "There are others, too, taken in the last couple of days. In case there's trouble."

"He's a smart one, this earl of yours. Whole families start to disappear, and he's worried that they might band together into a force to challenge him. So he splits them every which way, even before they raise so much as a carving knife at him." Ullmann nodded at Horst. "Can you make sure the lady of the house isn't thinking of leaving for Fuchs's estates to try and trade her husband for his brother?"

Horst pursed his lips, piled all the spears he was carrying next to Ullmann's, and went through into the rest of the house.

"You see," said Ullmann, "that's where it leads. Divide and conquer, one part of the family against the other. You want rid of Fuchs, don't you?"

"Of course," said Metz, "but—"

"The cost." Kehle looked back at the door Horst had gone through. "It's too much to ask of anyone."

"We can get your brother back, Mr Kehle, and any relatives of yours whom Fuchs might have, Mr Metz. It's fear that's holding you prisoner just as surely as any chain." Ullmann looked at both the Bavarians. "How many men has Fuchs got?"

"Two dozen or so," said Metz. "Some will be with Fuchs, and when word reaches him that you're here, they'll kill the hostages."

Ullmann raised his finger. "How will word reach them?"

"One of Fuchs's men?" Doubt had already crept into Metz's voice.

"Not if we've captured them all. That part won't be difficult. They're steaming drunk, and even if they want to make a fight of it, my little sister could take two of them at once." He was bringing them around: the situation was difficult, yes, but not impossible. Far from it. "We can tie up any who don't want a scrap. I even know of a safe place to put them till morning."

"Then what happens when Fuchs comes with the rest of his thugs in the morning?"

Ullmann reached behind him for a spear-shaft, and held it out for Kehle to take. "If you want to get rid of Fuchs and run these lands as you see fit, now's your chance. If you're happy with the way things are working out for you and your kin, we can go back to the barge and Carinthia will have spent a hundred florins on a boat trip down the Salzach. Both me and Horst are here because you wanted this: if we go, that'll be that. If we ever have reason to come back, it won't be with offers of help. But it will be with weapons."

"I don't think you understand," said Metz, and Ullmann felt himself starting to lose his temper. Cowardice was cowardice, and it was embarrassing.

"We have a barge with two hundred spears on board. Fuchs will only have half a dozen louts left once we've done for those in the cellar. And there's no reason why we can't have half a century of spears waiting for him to leave his estate in the morning and sneak in when he's gone. This is not for Carinthia to do. It's for you, or have you forgotten why you ended up in Mr Ohlhauser's barn?"

Perhaps they had, but Ullmann's words reminded them. Kehle reluctantly took the brandished spear.

"We're just shopkeepers and tradesmen. We're not soldiers," he said. "We've had no training."

"Me and Horst were just ushers at the library. Why should that mean we're short on courage?" Ullmann set his face hard. "As for training? Use the pointy end. Now go and get your neighbours and bring them to the yard behind your house."

They moved the spears so that Metz and Kehle could leave the house, and Ullmann went in search of Horst, two of the spears in hand.

He found him in the kitchen, with Mrs Kehle sitting rigidly in a chair at the table.

"You were right," said Horst. "Caught her by the front door, off to tell Fuchs about us."

"You have no right to keep me here," she said. Ullmann passed one of the spears to Horst and laid the other across the table, among the crumbs and vegetable peelings.

"We'd be fools to let you go, though." He sat down opposite her. "You love your husband, yes?"

"Yes," she sniffed.

"Not every woman can say that, Mrs Kehle. Some would find benefit in a situation like this to be rid of a bad father or husband. But you'll get yours back quickest if you stick with us."

"I don't know that. You're from Carinthia, so how can I trust anything you say?"

Ullmann snagged a leftover crust of bread from one of the plates. It was dry and brittle, but he chewed on it anyway because he was hungry. "Fuchs is Bavarian, and he's been busy looting the town and taking hostages. We're Carinthian, and we're here with spears and men to help you overthrow Fuchs. Why don't you tell me who you can trust?" He leant back in the chair. "Take your time."

Mrs Kehle's face went through several contortions, and eventually she slumped her shoulders. "I just want Gerd back."

Ullmann pushed the spear towards her. "Then take this."

Horst coughed. "Max."

Ignoring him, Ullmann nudged the spear towards the woman again. "Can you leave your kids?"

"My eldest can look after the younger ones for a while." Then she shook her head. "You can't expect me to fight."

"My life was saved from Fuchs's spies only a few days ago by a woman armed with a broom. You can do the same for your husband."

"Max," said Horst again.

Ullmann looked at the ceiling. "Horst. What's the problem?"

"She's a woman and a mother. You can't expect her to take on a bunch of drunkards with a spike on a stick."

"If she was on her own, you might be right. She won't be on her own. And this is as much her fight as it is her brother-in-law's. There's no reason I can think of for not offering her the chance to hold her head up among her neighbours and tell them what she did this night." When Ullmann looked back down, Mrs Kehle had taken the spear and rested it along the arms of her chair. "Ideas don't stop at bridges," he said, appropriating Sophia's words as his own. "I'm guessing they don't stop at doors or walls either. Can we rely on the goodwives of Simbach?"

"Yes," she said, "if it'll mean our sons and husbands come back safely."

"Go on, then. We'll meet down by the wharf within the hour. Quietly, mind. Fuchs's men mustn't know what's going on until we're ready." Ullmann pushed himself back from the table and left her to get on with it. He found his way into the back room, and to the staircase.

"Gods, Max. You know how to take a risk, don't you?" Horst still looked sceptical.

"Remember the stories, Horst, about when we fought the Romans to a standstill on the banks of the Rhein? About how the women used to line up with the men in the order of battle and fight shoulder to shoulder for their tribe and their land?" Ullmann gathered up the spears and passed half of them to Horst. They made ungainly bundles, but they only had to carry them down to the yard below which was filling with the soft murmur of whispering voices. "The Romans made us different. We crushed them in the end, broke their walls and burnt their temples, but we so envied their civilised ways, we ended up adopting their attitudes."

"Not a bad thing, Max. We don't sleep in thatched huts in among the animal shit any more, do we?" Horst looked down into the little dark yard, struggling to keep control of his armful. "Gods, have you seen how many there are?"

"That was a thousand years ago, and we didn't need to take on Roman ways along with their stone buildings, did we? Sometimes I wonder who really won." Ullmann joined Horst at the top of the stairs. "Good. Let's get down there and start handing these out."

There were plenty of willing hands to relieve them of their load, and there were still unarmed men left over. It would be enough, surely, to take and hold the wharf.

"Right: Horst, Mr Metz. Back to the barge, as quick as you can and guide it down here. Go. The rest of you, follow Mr Kehle down to the river."

It was simple enough: the quayside was a series of wooden boardwalks and a couple of short jetties. A single large river barge was moored there, the whereabouts of its crew unknown: the half dozen smaller boats that should have had been tied up had, one by one, found their way to the Carinthian side until only a flat-bottomed skiff remained.

Fuchs had placed a guard on the boards to prevent its theft, or more likely, its use in transporting yet more people across the river in the dark. He was one man only, though, proving to Ullmann's mind that Fuchs was an idiot.

"What do we do about him?" asked Kehle, ahead of a knot of fifty men hiding in a side street. "Do we rush him?"

"He'll call out for certain if we do, Mr Kehle, and while I doubt any of his friends will hear him, I'm not going to say they won't, either." He lifted a few shillings from his purse and put them in his hand, also taking his dagger out of his belt and hiding it up his sleeve. "Let me do this."

He walked out into the open, but it took a while for the guard to spot him: a man in dark clothing, in the shadows, on a dark night.

"Hey there. Who's that?"

Ullmann affected a gruff voice to cover his own alpine-valley accent. "Don't let the others know. I've got coins, just for you." He rattled them together in his closed fist.

"You'll be after the boat then, eh?" The guard rested his spear point-down on the wooden quay. "The price has gone up since yesterday, mind. Let's see what you've got."

Ullmann drew closer, remembering to hesitate, to look over his shoulder. When he was within arm's length, he dropped the money into the proffered hand. The guard looked down to count the silver shillings, and all Ullmann had to do was take another step and drive his blade into the man's guts, in and up.

Air rushed from the guard's mouth as if he'd been punched, and Ullmann shoved him backwards over the edge of the boardwalk and into the river. Coins tinkled and bounced, and the body splashed into the water. The spear fell to the quay.

It felt a lot cleaner than when he'd stabbed Nikoleta. Easier, too. Where would they be now if he hadn't done that?

A black wet shape surfaced downstream, breaking the moonlit ripples, and floated slowly away. It was done. He turned and beckoned the Bavarians to join him.

"We wait for the barge now, so we need to put our own guard in place."

Kehle was the first to speak. He sounded incredulous, and not a little lost. "You killed him."

"This is not a game, Mr Kehle." Ullmann fetched out the piece of white cloth still tucked in his belt and wiped the dagger. "You're in the grip of a tyrant, all of you. Did you think you'd be free of him by asking nicely?"

"But you didn't even give him a chance."

"A chance to call all his friends from the beer cellar? No, because I don't want to have them descend on us mob-handed before everything's in place. Mr Kehle, that man, that neighbour of yours, made his choice: he chose Fuchs. He's seen Fuchs take hostages, take your property, take your money, take your livelihoods and your dignity, and he didn't just go along with it, he wanted it to happen. And he was still here, doing what Fuchs wanted, even when all his mates are somewhere else getting pissed." He bent down and scooped up the fallen spear, thrusting it butt-first at an unarmed man. "This is yours."

Kehle leant in with another objection, before realising it was futile. Their path was set and he was one of the reluctant revolutionaries. He turned to face his neighbours, and started to organise them into groups.

73

Ullmann looked over the wrecked beer cellar, the broken furniture, the sharp shards of pottery and crystals of glass. The odour was of blood and beer, and both had soaked into the wooden boards.

They hadn't surrendered. Quite the opposite: they'd come out fighting drunk and, being more used to casual violence than the spear-holders, had caused a number of casualties. Only weight of numbers and rising anger had driven them back inside, and then, of course, they'd had to go in and get them.

It had been disconcertingly messy, a brawl in a bar with lethal consequences. It turned out that Vulfar's bargees were actually very good at that sort of combat, where a spear had limited use, but a cosh, a cudgel or a fist came into its own.

Gods knew what the survivors from Fuchs's over-merry band would be like when they sobered up. All Ullmann knew was that they weren't going to be his problem. When they'd finally been subdued, they'd been trussed up like boars, knots tight and straining tighter.

He kicked half a stoneware mug aside and watched it spin into an overturned table, as Horst clumped down the stairs from the street.

"That's the last of them. They're in the barge, with Vulfar's lot staring down at them." He pursed his mouth and looked around him. "Bastards put up a struggle, didn't they?"

"It's difficult to say how much of their courage was found in the bottom of a bottle," said Ullmann, "and how much will remain in the morning. The Bavarians are blooded now, though. They know they can win against Fuchs."

"*You* might be confident, Max, but they're a bit flaky for my liking." Horst glanced back up the steps. "Speaking of morning, the sky's lightening. Won't be long now."

"Then we need to get ready." Ullmann turned his back on the cellar and climbed back to street level. The townsfolk were milling about, talking to each other in hushed voices about what they'd done, what they'd seen, and what would happen next. There was very little preparation for that and even less organisation: the one thing they couldn't afford to do was let Fuchs know of the uprising before they'd trapped him; nor could they let him escape once they had.

Ullmann could see that clearly. Why couldn't they?

"Horst? Get Manfred and go to the edge of town on the north road. If you see horsemen in the distance, one of you run to the town square and tell me. The other has to keep an eye on Fuchs. And don't be seen." Ullmann scanned the crowds. "Mr Kehle? Mrs Kehle?"

It took a little while, and he had to resort to pushing his way through the forest of spears in order to find them. Juli Kehle's weapon was dark and stained.

"It's time you went to get your husband and the other hostages. Take fifty people, go the long way around. If you can find someone who knows the inside of the manor house, then all the better." He wagged his finger. "Do not attack as soon as Fuchs leaves. Give him enough time to get to town, otherwise he might ride back and you'll be on your own."

Ullmann appointed marshals more or less at random, and got them to herd the townsfolk into the market square, opposite the Town Hall that Fuchs had co-opted as his headquarters.

There was a cart – a magic-powered one that had been abandoned against a wall and forgotten since. He climbed up on it and stared down. They were a mob, nothing more: the scene could have come from a hundred different stories where villagers gathered in a muddy main street with pitchforks and torches. Could Carinthia do any better at the moment? Perhaps not, and maybe he should lower his expectations. Then again, the stories always had the brave, good-hearted hero lead his kith and kin to victory over the lurking horror that terrorised them.

"People of Simbach," he started, "friends. A good night's work so far, but you're not done yet. There's Fuchs to bring down, ending his perverse rule over you. If you worked his land today, you'll work your own land tomorrow. If you paid taxes to him today, your purse will be heavier by morning. All it needs is for you to keep your heads and remember that you're stronger together than you are apart: that's what's brought you to this point. A single spear needs both luck and skill, but a forest of spears needs neither. By relying on your neighbour for your protection, just as they rely on you for theirs, you only have to stand your ground. We'll entice Fuchs into town, block his retreat and trap him right here. And this is where he'll answer for his thieving and plundering and kidnapping. He'll answer to you, and to no one else."

Gods, he was enjoying this. He'd always had a head full of tales, and now he was in one. His voice, despite its country-bumpkin burr, carried clear and far across the square, and they were listening to him.

"Each of you play your part, and you'll be free, just as the hostages Fuchs has taken will be. Three groups to guard the north, east and west of the town. When Fuchs goes past you, close in behind him, drive him on, and he'll meet another group coming the other way. There'll be no escape, though he'll try. You've already shown yourself equal to the fight. Down with Fuchs, up with Simbach."

It gained him a ragged cheer, and it was enough for now. Ullmann jumped down off the cart and started to divide the hundred and fifty or so people with spears into three half-centuries – he was tempted to send the unarmed people home, but they had as much right as anyone to be there.

Just as long as they didn't get in the way of the front ranks. He thought of a way to keep them out of trouble, and told them to find stones – tear up the cobbles on the streets if they had to – and use them as missiles over the heads of the spears.

Were they ready now? The sky was a dirty grey, and there'd be no sun to seal their triumph, just a cold east wind and the threat of rain. The last of the Bavarians trailed from the square, and he was alone.

There was nothing more he could do. Either the townspeople

could manage not to trip over their weapons or each other, or they'd rout at the first sign of trouble and he, Horst and Manfred would have to swim the river to Carinthia.

Perhaps there was one thing he could do. He drew his sword and followed the north road. There he found his countrymen, and Mr Metz, trying to hide fifty Bavarians up the side streets leading directly off the main road.

Horst shrugged at the futility of their efforts, and Manfred laughed nervously.

"Mr Metz, we have to do better than this. Whose houses are these?" Ullmann pointed to the four buildings on the corner of the junction.

"I . . . I don't know," stammered Metz.

"They're your houses, Mr Metz," said Ullmann, exasperated. "Open the doors, get a decade of men in each of them, and the rest of us will hide in that smithy there. There are windows through which you'll be able to see Fuchs pass by. When he does, form up here."

The sky was light. It was almost time.

Metz split his troops, as Ullmann had instructed, and hammered on the doors of the four houses until they were admitted. Those who were left, Ullmann led into the forge.

It was warm and dark inside, with the shuttered windows closed and only slits between the ill-fitting panels for illumination. The coals in the fire glowed a deep, charnel red that hurt the eyes. There were plenty of hidden obstacles to fall over, too.

"Just sit down where you can. Horst, can you see the road, or do we need to open one of the shutters?"

Horst worked his way over to the window, stubbing his toe on something that clanged. "Fuck. Piss. Shit. That hurts." He finally pressed himself against the crack of light and rested his hands on the frame.

"Well."

"My fucking foot. Yes, I can see, but we won't exactly be able to turn out quickly if we're half killed by the crap that's lying on the floor."

"It's not crap. It's work."

The voice was low and rough, and gave Ullmann some idea of the size of the man who owned it, which was confirmed a moment later when Horst unlatched the shutters and nudged one open.

Smiths tended to come in two sizes: short and barrel-like, and tall and barrel-like. This one, Ullmann reckoned, was half as tall again as anyone else in the room.

One of the Bavarians called him Bastian, though the way he said it, it may as well have been "bastard". He loomed into the half-light, moving his head from side to side to stop it knocking against the objects hung from the rafters.

"Who are you, and why are you here?"

It wasn't as if they'd been particularly quiet. They'd already had a pitched battle that night only two streets away. But smiths tended to be a little on the deaf side.

"We're getting rid of Fuchs," said Ullmann, and the smith slowly turned towards him.

"You're not from around here."

"No." Ullmann had his sword in his hand, but he needed more than a couple of lessons on defensive parries for it to be anything but an actor's prop. "We brought spears from Juvavum's armoury as a gift to the people of Simbach."

"Carinthian?" The wet slap was spit hitting the floor. "Since when did we need Carinthia to dig us up out of the pit we've made for ourselves?"

"Since our Bavarian neighbours started hiding in Carinthian barns."

Bastian had massive fists. They looked even bigger when clenched.

"You need to leave," said the smith.

Ullmann shook his head. "Why did no one tell me that coming in here was a stupid idea?"

"Because we didn't know Bastian slept with his anvil these days," was the hasty reply.

"We're here to pick a fight with your earl, not you. If you support him, there are still thirteen of us and one of you. If you don't, then you won't mind us borrowing your forge until after he's ridden past." Whether Ullmann would have been so bold without the others was something he wasn't going to think about too deeply. "There'll be no harm done, and your fellow Bavarians will be grateful."

"Grateful? Grateful? They've never been grateful yet." He took another step closer to Ullmann, who swore that the ground shivered. "I've asked you to leave. Do you want me to make you?"

"What is that you value, Master Smith?" Ullmann was aware of Horst's increasingly frantic gestures. He could hear horses. Fuchs was on his way. "If it's not the gratitude of Simbach, what else? Wealth? Love? Fame?"

Bastian bent low and breathed schnapps-flavoured breath over him. "If it were any of those, I would have had them by now. What I want, Carinthian, is a challenge. Something equal to my skill."

There were pots and pans and horseshoes and tools and hammers and vices and bars of raw iron all around; country-town fare, all of it. How often had Bastian moved his forge looking for his match?

"Very well," said Ullmann. "I'll find you your challenge. In exchange, let's all shut up, right now."

Horst shrank back from the window and pressed his back to the wall. Ullmann was very still, and the shadows flickered past the shutters. He counted them, each moment of darkness, reaching six before the light returned to constancy.

Everyone held their breath. Horst leant forward slightly, and gave them the nod. It sounded momentarily like a windy night on an alp.

Ullmann shifted from his perch.

"Thank you, Master Bastian. Expect to hear from us soon. Men? Remember your spears." He moved to the door and opened it a crack. The road was clear, and he tiptoed out.

He ushered his group out and made sure they were all armed and facing the right way. The corner houses emptied rapidly once the men there saw the first phalanx forming up. Down the road, Fuchs and his troop were idly clopping along, unaware of what was happening behind them.

"Tight packed," he hissed, "shoulder to shoulder." He pushed the spear-carriers forward, and let the stone-throwers arrange themselves behind. "Not," he warned them, "until I say so."

When he'd finished, he found that the knot of spears weren't advancing as he'd hoped – they were still fixed at the junction, looking severe but static. The trap would only work if they were moving.

He turned himself sideways and eased through them, snagging Manfred's collar as he went. The two of them popped out the far side, and he just kept walking. Horst nudged his immediate neighbours, and, slowly, the Bavarians caught on. They clattered and rattled, less a column and more of a rabble, but at least they were moving.

Still neither Fuchs nor any of his entourage looked in their direction. But the townspeople's now purposeful marching was faster than the ambling of the riders' horses: they were catching them up.

The trailing horseman glanced over his shoulder, looked back, pulled hard on his reins and wheeled around. His eyes were wide and white.

Ullmann stared at the man, while Manfred lowered the point of his spear. Neither of them stopped their advance, and after a few broken steps of uncertainty, the Bavarians' spears dropped to form an impenetrable, still-moving, barrier.

"My lord," shouted the man, "an ambush."

All six riders looked their way. The horses were big, and snorting, and they filled the street just as much as the spears did. If they'd have charged them there and then, it could have gone terribly wrong.

"Stones!" called Ullmann. He raised his sword, and inaccurately thrown cobbles arced over his head, accompanied by grunts and cries of effort. Most of them missed their targets, falling short and clacking against walls and the road, but hitting Fuchs wasn't what they were for.

The effect was almost instant. The ground was covered in loose, spinning cobbles, and the one or two that covered the distance so rattled the rearguard rider's horse that it bolted. And where one went, so did the others with only slightly more control.

The spear wall started to break as some at the front started to run after them. Ullmann didn't want that at all. "Hold. Keep the line. Think as one. Act as one."

They fell into line again, and were ready.

"Forward."

The horses were regrouping at the end of the street, just where it joined the market square. They were wondering what had happened to the men they'd left behind, because they rode backwards and forwards, shouting names and getting no response.

Fuchs – the man that had to be Fuchs, because he wore a polished breastplate and the fanciest red cloak, his hair in a Roman cut and his cheeks smooth – fought to keep control of his nervous, high-stepping horse. He looked straight at Ullmann, and the Carinthian felt a thrill.

Even earls feared him now.

There were four ways out of the square: one ended up in the river, leaving just three. They took the Passau road, and vanished out of sight, hooves sparking on the cobbles.

Abruptly they were back, streaking across the square, stones flying after them, heading for the road that led to München. Fuchs, in the lead, pulled up hard, horse rearing up at the crowd facing him. He cast about wildly for somewhere, anywhere, to run to. The groups from the east and west burst into the square, and Ullmann aimed his vaguely disciplined spears at them, to press them from the north.

More stones came over the top, and the throwers were so close now, they couldn't avoid hitting something. One rider went down, caught on the crown of his head, and his horse backed away down the street towards the wharf.

The Bavarians were spear-point to spear-point. Fuchs drew his sword, but did nothing with it but hold it high.

"Do you surrender?" called Ullmann.

Fuchs searched the faces for the one who addressed him. "Surrender? Your lives, your families, they're all forfeit. I am your lord."

"The time of earls is over, Mr Fuchs, and the gods know you haven't been an earl to these people for a while now." Ullmann had Manfred by his side, spear angled, foot on the butt to brace it. "Put down your sword and order your men to do the same. There's no help coming for you today. Just us and those you've been robbing."

Fuchs's eyes narrowed. "You're a fucking Carinthian," he said; then, louder: "You're following a Carinthian spy."

A spear drove into his side, between breast and backplate, under his sword-arm. The leaf-shaped head went in halfway.

"This is a Carinthian spear, so I'm told," said the woman who'd thrust it there. "But this arm is all Bavarian."

She jerked the blade out, and blood welled up, down Fuchs's side, staining his undershirt and the top of his breeks. His expression was not just of surprise but of incredulity. Perhaps he'd deluded himself that he could go forever.

The sudden silence that followed his initial grunt of pain

stretched on. Fuchs lowered his sword and pressed his forearm against the wound, staring with total concentration into the distance. It looked for a moment as though he might rally: the cut wasn't deep and nothing vital had been pierced. Then a cobblestone smashed into his face. His nose broken, blood in his mouth and eyes, he lost his grip on both his saddle and his sword. He rolled off backwards with one foot still in the stirrup.

There was no shortage of people to finish him off, and while they did their savage work, Fuchs's men were dragged down screaming off their panicked mounts and butchered where they lay; trampled, stabbed, stamped on and crushed.

Arms and feet rose and fell in a perverse parody of a wine press, rhythmic and deliberate, and it was over a long time before they stopped.

Ullmann withdrew, along with Manfred and Horst, and stood a way off.

"Gods, Max," said Horst. "Gods." He was at a loss for what to say.

A loose horse skittered past, and Manfred hooked its bridle. He distracted himself with the act of calming it down. "What happens to the poor bastards we've got on the barge?"

"It's not up to me, is it?" Ullmann shrugged. "Whatever, it's not like they don't deserve it. You can't go around kicking in people's doors, beating them up, stealing their things, day after day, and expect there not be retribution at some point."

"You don't feel the least bit sorry for them?" asked Manfred. He held the horse's head close to his own.

The residents of Simbach were starting to back away from the bodies, forming a circle around the scene, spears no longer directed at the ground but at the sky. They were regarding what they'd done, weighing its significance and meaning.

"I think we should go," said Horst. "We don't need to be here any longer, right?"

Max Ullmann sheathed his sword. He hadn't had to use it once, and yet they'd taken the town. There was a lesson there, somewhere. "Back to the boat," he said.

74

Sophia had sworn never to get back on a horse, and absolutely never to go any distance on one. Necessity dictated otherwise.

It might have been the quickest way to get from one place to another – always had, probably always would – but she'd still have preferred to have walked. It wasn't far to Rosenheim: a day, sunrise to sunset, if taken at a brisk pace and no stops. She'd almost begged Felix to allow her to make the journey that way; almost, because it was clear that he wouldn't countenance a noble lady going on foot.

What he meant, of course, was that she was *his* noble lady, and it'd make him, and by extension, Carinthia, look bad. So they emptied the stables for her and for what he called her retinue, which was ironic since it consisted of an elderly Mr Kuppenheim and the four out of the newly recruited fortress guards who could actually ride.

Mr Kuppenheim, being the Jewish doctor, was the best horseman of all of them. Used to turning out in all weathers to one remote shtetl or another, he managed to look both assured and relaxed, while she winced and groaned with every jolt.

She'd have done better in the back of a horse-drawn hay cart. Unfortunately, that had also been deemed not lady-like.

There was another rider with them: Gretchen, older than Felix but a girl all the same, from the upper reaches of the Enn where it ran out of the steep valley and onto the plain. She'd turned up at the fortress breathless, holding out Peter Büber's seal and asking for someone to come. Breathless, because she claimed to have run all the way, which was quite a feat if she had, and wild exaggeration if she hadn't.

Even the Rosenheim farm-girl was a better horseman than she was, thought Sophia, which didn't improve her temper.

She was sure that part of the reason Gretchen had come directly to Juvavum was in the hope of a reward. A Carinthian seal denoted a prince's man, and giving aid to its bearer would earn gratitude of a spendable kind. The bag of coins Sophia carried would be used to express various permutations of that gratitude, depending upon whether Büber was alive, whether he'd been cared for well, whether he'd received treatment from the local doctor, whether he could be moved, whether his belongings were still together and not stolen.

It was three days since Büber had been found, two days since the girl had left her river-bank farm, half a day since they'd set off back down the road. When Sophia had asked what state the huntmaster was in, Gretchen had remained grimly mute.

Would HaShem be merciful to this gentile, who was His servant whether he knew it or not?

Büber was tough, and, like the forests he loved, he bent before the wind without breaking. At least, he always had done before. But even a bruised reed might eventually snap. Perhaps they were hurrying because Büber might die.

"How far?" she asked.

"Not far," came the answer, which was progress of sorts, because the last time she'd asked, it had been "a way yet". There weren't any milestones on this road, and it was certainly no via with free-draining surface and wide ditches. What they had was a green lane, with ridges and puddles between the ridges. The land itself served as waymarkers: the rivers they crossed, the lake they passed, the steep alpine hills that yearned to be mountains.

Sophia wasn't used to the openness of the sky, the darkness of the forests, the roughness of the road. She was a child of the city, the polis. She could bargain in the markets, navigate the alleys, use the tools and skills of her culture. She didn't recognise this place, which was not just beyond the walls but out of sight of them completely: over the horizon, the place where magic was wild and untamed.

Or, at least, it had been. Now it was just the mundane that was wild and untamed. That should have meant there was less to be frightened of, but she wasn't so sure.

She could see a square stone tower in the distance, an old Roman one faced in white stone.

"Is that it?" she asked Gretchen.

"Yes, my lady. The tower's before the bridge, and the town's on the other side."

"And how far from Rosenheim do we have to go?"

The girl squinted as she thought. "Five miles south?"

She had the blondest hair and bluest eyes Sophia had ever seen. She was young, strong and capable. And one day she would grow up and know pain and become frail and old.

The wise man, no less than the fool, must die.

No matter that her zitser hurt with an agony beyond description. Life was short, and a sore arse wouldn't kill her.

"We should try and go faster," said Sophia.

Old Kuppenheim smiled. "My child," he said. To him, everyone younger than him was "my child". "Is there a reason for our haste other than your pride?"

"Yes," she said, and came up with another reason. "My lord expects it of me."

"Ah, Felix." He let go of his reins long enough to tug at his beard. "You can't marry the shegetz, you know that, don't you?"

"The . . . what?" She coloured up. "You can't call him that."

"And you'd be a—"

"Don't you dare, Avram Kuppenheim, don't you dare use that word on me."

"Find a good Jewish boy and put all this nonsense behind you."

She clicked her heels, and the horse actually responded by moving more quickly up the line past Gretchen to the leading guard. She was fuming – no, righteously angry. She'd have this out with him when she'd calmed down. No one likened Felix to an abomination. No one.

Of course the Jews of Juvavum were glad she was the prince's consort. They were also glad that she was Aaron Morgenstern's daughter, and not theirs. It wasn't as if she'd taken to dancing around the irminsul on Wotan's day. She still joined the women in the synagogue for the Sabbath, and still kept kosher. But even with the story of Purim ringing in their ears, they looked down on her.

She'd saved them; rather, HaShem had used her to save them. Now they had freedoms and rights they'd never had before. Hers was a sacrifice willingly made for the good of everyone. When she felt their ingratitude, it burnt her.

The guard nodded to her. "My lady?"

Why did she get more respect from the Germans than from her own people?

"If we're to be of any use to Master Büber, we need to pick up the pace."

The guard looked behind him. "Will your doctor be able to keep up?"

"Oh, don't worry about him. I'm sure he'll survive more or less anything." Sophia goaded her horse on until she came to the river, and the via that ran from the high Enn valley down to the towns of the wide northern plain.

There was the bridge, down the hill from the tower, and there was little Rosenheim beyond. Barely big enough for a market, more a straight road with houses on the way to München.

Sophia stood up on the stirrups to relieve the pain in her back, then started along the via. The tower was deserted, and close to she could see it was missing some of its limestone dressing, at below head height, the rock having been taken for building.

The bridge was Roman, too, its parapet foxed, and she dared not look under it in case the mere act of investigation collapsed the arches. The water ran cold and deep, the same water that flowed past Simbach, from where word had reached them that Fuchs was dead and the future was both more hopeful and uncertain.

Gretchen caught up with Sophia. "My lady, wait. I should ride with you when we go into town. They know me, and they don't know you."

"Do they still throw stones at Jews in Rosenheim then?"

The girl looked away, then looked back, and Sophia recognised her confusion. She was both a princess and a Jew. How did that work?

"Ride with me," she said, and they went side by side down the main street.

It was muddy and it smelt, and anxious, dishevelled people stepped out of their houses to watch them pass. Two women on horses, followed by five men, four of them soldiers: it would have been difficult for the townsfolk to tell who the important travellers were. If they recognised Gretchen as one of their own, they didn't show it. Their suspicion extended to her just as much as it did to Sophia.

"Did you use much magic?" asked Sophia.

"Bits and pieces. For trade we had boats and carts: that's what hurts the most. Everyone we buy and sell from now feels further away and more likely to forget about us."

"But up on your farm?"

"We had a plough, which doesn't work any more. At least the

animals do mostly what they've always done, and we can eat, at least until the next winter."

"And after that?" She knew the answer already. If farmers didn't plant enough for themselves, they'd starve. If they didn't plant enough for everyone else, the towns and cities would starve.

Gretchen shrugged. Despite her youth, she could tell what the future might hold. "We'll see."

"You and your family should visit a Jewish farm to see how they do it. Use cattle to pull a plough, the wind or a donkey to turn a millstone. Oil for light." Sophia wanted her to accept the offer, wanted her to persuade the girl's father it was something worth doing. "I can write a letter of introduction if you want."

"We'll see," said Gretchen again.

They were Bavarian. Perhaps when they saw what was happening in Carinthia they'd come around, if it wasn't too late.

A track threaded its way between two houses, heading south towards the mountains. Gretchen steered her horse, more expertly than Sophia – perhaps it was being around animals that made her more confident – up the track, with a call of "This way, my lady."

Sophia almost overshot the turning, allowing the gap to close between her and that wicked old doctor. The horse finally realised it was supposed to be following the one ahead, and shuffled its hooves sufficiently to complete the manoeuvre.

On her left, there was marshy ground between her and the river, with standing water and last year's reeds rattling in the wind. Ahead of her, there were fields and trees, then trees with a few clearings, then only trees.

Five miles later, the trees parted, and the Enn valley opened out like a flower. Mountains rose up distant-blue either side of the river plain, and cold air fell from the gap like a reminder of the weather a month past. A steep-roofed alpine house sat above the river, and a curl in the bank made a natural harbour of sorts. The fields were tiny, and grass grew and flowers danced on top of the high protecting walls infilled with soil.

Gretchen casually took her feet from both stirrups and swivelled on her saddle until she sat sideways. From there, she jumped lightly to the ground and ran on.

"Dad, Mum, they're here."

Her horse, free of its slight burden, looked around at Sophia, and kept on walking up to the farmhouse.

Sophia found that dismounting gracefully was something she wasn't good at, along with all the other things she wasn't good at on or near a horse. She ended up on her back, one hand still holding her reins.

One of the guards made to rescue her, but she growled, "I'm fine", with such venom that he remained mounted. Slowly, she reached up the nearest wall, jammed her fingers in between two pieces of stone and hauled herself up.

It would be miracle, she thought, if she ever walked again without bow-legs.

Kuppenheim slipped wearily from his own horse and started unlacing his surgeon's box from the back of the saddle. It gave time for Sophia to adjust her clothing, straighten her sword, and walk the last few feet to the farmhouse door.

She was about to knock, when a round-faced farmer with no hair on his head but plenty on his face opened it to her.

"Mr Flintsbach?"

"You'd better come in," he said. Naturally dour, he gave nothing away.

It was dark and warm in the kitchen – the warmest place in the whole house, no doubt, because they'd made up a mattress of straw and sacking right there in front of the deep fireplace, and Büber was lying on it, propped up on one elbow.

"He wasn't like this when I left," said Gretchen, breathlessly. "He was near death, and now look."

Strange that she was breathless again, but perhaps the sight of Büber's lean, muscled torso, showing every scar he'd ever won, might have been enough reason.

Sophia moved around the table to see him better, and smiled. "Hello, Peter."

Büber tried to cover himself up. "Sophia. I mean, my lady. When they said they'd brought help, I—"

"Peter, shut up." She knelt down beside him, scabbard clattering against the floor. "How are you? I wasn't certain we'd ever see you again."

"There's something I need to tell you," he said, ignoring the question. "In private."

She reached out and pressed her hand against his forehead. He

547

pulled back, and she frowned, then firmly applied her palm to his head once again. Warm, which, given his closeness to the fire, was reasonable; and he was neither dry nor excessively sweaty.

"Can it wait?"

"No," he said.

"Peter, what happened to you? You should be miles away from here, drinking Frankish wine in the sun and eating olives straight from the tree." She pulled at his blankets, and he only half resisted. There were fresh roads across the map of his chest. "Some of these wounds are new."

"Clear the room and I'll tell you," he said.

"Is that really necessary?" she started, but it was her turn to relent. "I'm sorry about this, Mr Flintsbach. Affairs of state."

After they'd all reluctantly left, and she'd issued instruction for the guards to keep everyone away from the walls, windows and doors – especially Kuppenheim – she sat cross-legged by Büber's feet, sword across her lap.

"Talk to me, Peter. Tell me good things."

"Wish to the gods I could." He scratched at his chin, making his stubble rasp. "I did as I was asked. I took Felix's letter to the dwarves. Except I met the dwarves coming down the valley towards me. They've closed the passes, and told the people of Ennsbruck to leave. They're changing, Sophia. Growing. We were attacked by giants, too, and they're shrinking. It's all going wrong."

"The letter, Peter. What happened to the letter?"

"I handed it to King Ironmaker myself, deep in the halls of Farduzes." He looked around him. "My clothes are somewhere around here."

She got up stiffly and searched them out, bringing them to him and laying them on his lap.

Büber rummaged around until he found a crinkled wodge of vellum. He lacked the fingers to open it carefully, so he handed it to Sophia.

"This was part of Ironmaker's reply. The rest of it was a box that would have killed Felix, and probably everyone else in the room at the time."

"Oh," she said. "I take it you decided to leave that part of the message behind."

"They insisted I took it. We fought. I escaped. I made it as far as Ennsbruck, where they'd laid an ambush for me. They killed my horse. I managed to refloat a boat with no bottom, and the Flintbachs fished me out of the river just outside here, more dead than alive." He stared into the distance for a moment, before his attention snapped back to the present. "They're coming, Sophia. They're coming out of their stronghold and they'll take whatever they can. The Enn valley is just the start of it: they want to carve out a kingdom above ground, because they can't bear to be under it any longer."

She examined the vellum, and began to tease apart the layers of skin joined together by blood and water. She worked carefully, and eventually was able to press the sheet against the floor; the ink had been damaged in places, but most of it was legible despite the smears and deletions, if only she could read Dwarvish. She knew better than to ask Büber.

Rather than refolding the parchment, she rolled it up. "Will they parley?" she asked.

"When I gave Ironmaker Felix's letter, he asked me if Felix meant what he said. What was the invitation he gave them?"

"That as many who would come were welcome." Sophia settled back down, and reached instinctively for her sword again, dragging it across her knees.

"He was asking me if Felix could have meant all of them. I said yes."

"You said yes?" Her voice rose sharply.

"I did, because it was what Felix would have done. He wouldn't have changed his mind." Tired of sitting up, Büber lay back down with a grunt. "And the dwarves still wanted him dead and our land for themselves. They don't mean to share Carinthia with us. They mean to drive us out."

While he stared at the ceiling, she stared at the floor. "How many of them are there?"

"I don't know. They kept their strength hidden. You know I'm not good with numbers. Thousands, tens of thousands, they're just words to me. I don't know what they mean. They'll fight, though. They'll be cruel and tenacious, and that I do understand." Büber looked at his few-fingered hands, holding them up in front of his face. "Gods, they'll fight."

"So will we," she said.

"It'll be the hardest thing we've ever had to do. For a thousand years. It'll make Obernberg seem like a squabble between two drunks." He turned his head to look at her. "Even if we win, chances are that you, me, Felix, everyone we know, will be dead by the end of it."

"Yes, there is that chance." She lifted up his blanket at the feet end. Some of his toes were blistered and the skin on his hard soles was peeling off in sheets. "I've a doctor with me. He won't kill you. I might kill him, but that's a different story."

Sophia lowered the blanket gently over his feet again, and made to stand, but Büber reached once more into his clothing and pulled out a small metal case.

"Take this," he said, and pressed it on her. "They use this to light fires."

"What do I do with it?" She rehung her scabbard and opened the little box. She sniffed it and made a face.

"Give it to Frederik Thaler. He'll . . . know what to do with it." The effort of talking to her had worn him out. "Gods, I'm tired. I'm tired, and there's so much to do."

"Get well, Peter. We'll get you home somehow. And then" – she shifted her shoulders, as if squaring up to the enemy – "prepare. How long do you think we have?"

"It'll be over, one way or another, by winter."

He sounded more than tired. She nodded slowly and, taking the scroll and the case, she left, closing the door quietly behind her. Outside, the soldiers were keeping the Flintsbachs and Kuppenheim at a discreet distance from the house.

Sophia went straight to her horse and stowed the items Büber had given her. She collected the purse and held it out to Mr Flintsbach without subtracting from its contents.

"Take this," she said. "You'll need every red penny of it."

"Why?" he asked, even as he closed his fingers around it.

She thought about lying, or at least of not telling him the truth. "You're going to need to buy another farm, a long way from here. There's a war coming, and this little house and these fields are going to become our battlefield. That river will run red and the first snows will bury the dead."

She fastened her saddlebags again and, reluctantly, awkwardly, raised one foot to the stirrup.

75

He always seemed to end up back in the refectory when something significant happened: some setback, some triumph, some event large enough to shake him, and he'd suddenly find himself at one end of the long table, drinking or eating, or both.

To explain the size that he was, his whole world had to be changing daily.

Take now, for instance. The princess consort, or Sophia to give her the name that Thaler had known her by all her life, had ridden – ridden, mind: she'd barely sat on a horse before – all the way to Rosenheim and back, just to press a small box of grey-black powder on him.

The box sat on the worn and scrubbed table in front of him, right next to a cup of short beer and some middling cheese he'd managed to procure. What he wanted was a good thick slice of sausage, and preferably several thick slices of sausage, some bread, and perhaps some sauerkraut. It was too early for anything like that, so beer and cheese had to do.

"She said I'd know what to do with it," growled Thaler. He liked his sleep almost as much as he liked his food. "Or rather, Peter said I'd know what to do with it."

He drank his beer and cut himself a generous slice of cheese. While he was still chewing, he snagged the box and inspected it for what felt like the tenth time that morning. This time was no different to the others, so why should it yield any more information than before? It was lighter in the hall, certainly, and there were hopeful sounds beginning in the kitchens, but the box was just a box: silver, finely made, carefully carved with dragon-things looping in and out of their own coils, clearly dwarvish. Nothing but a container for the powder.

So it had to be the powder itself that was special.

The lid was tight fitting, like Thaler's breeks, and had to be dragged free by opposing motions of fingers and thumbs. It struck him that perhaps the box was intended to be water-tight. The powder inside wasn't really a powder, more a grit, like sand. It smelt . . . odd. Of anvils and the cloud of dust made by the strike of a mason's chisel.

He took a pinch of it, felt its coarseness between his fingertips and made a little pile of grains on the table. He peered at them. If the case was designed to keep out water, what would happen if he deliberately got the powder wet?

Thaler still had dregs of beer in his cup, and he dribbled them onto the pile. It turned to mush, and nothing obvious happened, even when he poked it with his finger. The mixture ran up inside his carefully clipped nail and stained it black, and he was left rubbing and smelling his fingers. The odour of broken stone grew strong.

"Master Thaler?"

He turned, expecting to see a cook because it was a woman's voice.

"Mistress."

The Order wore white, the library wore black. She'd chosen to dress in grey, all in grey, as if she'd taken the robes of her former profession and washed them with ink.

He'd also learnt that she was a changeling, an elf-girl who'd been left in a newborn's cradle. Felix hadn't known what to make of that, and neither did Thaler.

He remembered his manners long enough to stop staring and wave at the space next to him.

"Please, sit. I don't think breakfast will be long."

Tuomanen perched on the bench beside him, then swung her legs over so that she was properly at the table. Her sleeves fell as she steepled her fingers in front of her. Her tattoos, two full forearms of disturbing patterns, were on view. There was a design on her neck, too. He could see it rising towards her jaw-line.

She looked tired. More tired than Thaler, even.

"Not sleeping?"

She pursed her lips. "You were up before I was."

"Ah, but I was woken."

"Whereas no one dares to wake me." She scrubbed at her face with her open hands. "I have nightmares, Master Thaler. You wouldn't want to know what happens in them, but screaming your throat raw every morning clearly isn't the best way to start your day."

"There are things you can take," he offered. Simple hedge

remedies, relying on the amount of distilled spirit in them for potency.

Tuomanen sighed. "Then I wouldn't be able to wake up when they come for me. At least I know that, when I open my eyes, what's gone before is only a dream." She reached out and took the box from in front of Thaler. "Good craftsmanship. Silver. Dwarvish?"

"Yes."

"A pretty gift. Dwarves don't normally give anything away." She rattled the box next to her ear and frowned.

She didn't know they were at war, thought Thaler. The only people in Juvavum who knew that were himself, Sophia and, by now, Felix. He mashed at the splodge of powder-slurry. "No, apparently not. I'm not sure they gave this away."

"Then . . .?" She gave the box another shake, then inspected it to see how it opened.

"Peter Büber sent it to me," said Thaler. "Apparently, I'd know what to do with it."

"And do you?" She pulled the two halves apart carefully.

"Not a clue." Together, they looked at the contents.

He felt, rather than saw, a change in the hexmaster's demeanour. She turned from being open and expansive to guarded and precise. She took a pinch of powder and sniffed at it, then carefully removed the grains from the ends of her fingers so they fell back into the container.

She said nothing as she replaced the lid.

"Do you know what it is?" he asked her, and felt a sudden surge in his heart. Büber was right. He did know what to do with the powder: show it to other people and ask them. There was no reason, no reason at all why he had to have all the answers himself.

Tuomanen stayed silent. She looked to the door, way down at the far end of the refectory. She wanted to run. She certainly didn't want to answer Thaler's question.

"Mistress," he said. "I've made vows of obedience to my lord Prince of Carinthia. You've given your own promises to me."

"I have to go," she said, and started to get up. Thaler instinctively put his meaty hand on her shoulder and brought her down again. Both of them were so surprised that it worked.

She sat heavily, and Thaler pried the box from her grasp. "What is this?"

He brought his face close to hers. He was angry. At her, at the dwarves, at being woken before sunrise, at everything. Normally, he would have apologised for his intemperance, but not today.

"I . . ."

"Let me explain something to you, something I thought you realised without me having to spell it out as if you were some neophyte apprentice. The library works by cooperation. We don't own the books we care for. We are their slaves, their serfs, if you will. Our knowledge is open for all to share. If I keep a secret, and the gods know I've done this and suffered the consequences, then we are all less for it." Thaler sucked air through his teeth. "In the Order, you guarded everything, yes? Nothing was given away, and in any trade of knowledge, advantage was sought. The strong took from the weak."

Tuomanen nodded, dry-mouthed.

"I have no intention of beating this information from your tattooed skin, or threatening you in any way. That is something I would never do. I would, however, be very, *very* disappointed in you should you fail to share it." He sat back, folded his arms and waited.

She seemed shocked, unable to respond, and Thaler thought he'd lost her, her trust and her confidence in him.

Then she laughed, loud enough that one of the round, red-faced cooks peeked out of the kitchen to see who was killing whom.

He took affront. "Mistress Tuomanen, I see little to amuse either you or me. These are serious matters for librarians and, may I say, the palatinate."

She grabbed his head in the crook of her elbow in a movement fluid and fast, but instead of visiting violence on him, she planted a kiss on the side of his head, right where his thinning hair met his rising forehead.

"Gods preserve you, Thaler. You're a prince among men, and worth more than a dozen hexmasters. If I'd defied the Order like I defied you, they'd have flayed me, torn the muscle from my limbs and ripped my heart from my chest, all the while keeping me alive, with everyone watching and making suggestions as to which part of me to mutilate next."

Which was all too much information for Thaler.

"And you try to control me with your stern looks and

down-turned mouth." She let him go. "You've disarmed me, my lord. I apologise."

The refectory door creaked open, and a gaggle of apprentices burst in, all talking at once.

Thaler was at a loss. He seemed to be swinging from one emotion to another with no visible means of support. What did any of this mean?

"Will you tell me what the powder does? Do you even know?"

She met his gaze steadily. "I know what it does, and yes, I'll tell you. There's something else I need to tell you first, though. Just not here. Somewhere we can't be overheard or spied on."

"They are your brothers," said Thaler, "as they are mine."

"I'm hiding something from you, my Master. It's about time I told you."

From hungry to sick in a moment. Gods, he couldn't keep doing this. "Is it something my lord Felix needs to be present at?"

"It'll sound better coming from you."

"Will it?"

"I'd rather not be there, and you have a way with words. Perhaps you can stop the prince ordering my immediate pressing."

She was serious.

"Mistress, I appear to have lost my appetite anyway. I know just the place." Thaler pocketed the dwarvish box and swung his legs out from under the table. He remembered to greet his apprentices, but was in too much of a daze to remember any of their names.

He led her through the corridors into the library. It was silent, though full of scaffolding. Soon it would be noisy with the rasp of saws and creak of wood and ropes. Outside, the workmen were beginning to gather, but where he and the mistress were going, they wouldn't be disturbed. He snagged a lit lantern as he passed the entrance hall, its candle burnt almost to a stub and the melted wax a white pool on the plate underneath, and carried on to the little door that opened directly into the wall.

The staircase was dark except for the thin window halfway up. He ushered the hexmaster in, and pulled the door firmly shut behind him. There was no room to push past her without getting far too close: he handed her the lantern and shooed her on until they reached the window.

"Here?" she asked.

"Can you think of a better place?"

"Several." Tuomanen put the lantern on the floor and squeezed as much of her as would fit into the window niche, managing to get far enough in to be able to look down at the alley below.

"You had something important to say?"

Her shadowed face looked down. "We – the Order – deliberately kept secrets—"

"Hardly a revelation," interrupted Thaler.

"Knowledge that was useless to us. But not to you."

She gave him time to think the concept through.

"Ah," he finally said. "Knowledge that would have allowed us mundanes to challenge your power?"

"Yes. We found things out, by accident mostly. Other things we learnt from outside the Order and decided it'd be better if such matters never came to your attention. We killed people where we had to, but, for the greater part, we didn't have to do anything but let the discovery wither and die. No one was really interested because it wasn't magic."

Tuomanen looked small and unthreatening, almost merging with the stone on which she sat.

"What sort of things?"

"Alchemy, mainly, because it was so close to magic. We have books on it, all written in code. Our maps of the human body are, shall we say, worryingly accurate. Metal and glass working techniques that are beyond Juvavum's best smiths. Or Firenze's, for that matter. If it could be mistaken for magic, then we probably know about it already." She shrugged and looked up at Thaler. "It's all written down, but just telling you that this knowledge even exists breaks one of the Order's most rigidly enforced rules."

"And the books?" asked Thaler. "The ones we've been pulling out of the White Tower and locking away in a separate room? What an idiot I've been. A naïve, trusting fool."

"Deceit is at our core," she said. "It's a habit we learnt throughout our training, and its full expression is seen in the masters. If I'd lured you here, where there are no witnesses and no one to overhear us, my next step would be to push you down the stairs and take the dwarvish box from you, and then simply to close the door. I'm sure they'd find your body, eventually, but I'd be innocent of everything."

Thaler didn't have so much as a knife on him. "Is that what you're going to do?"

"No. But I don't think you'd get the same response from . . . well, some others. I don't know what they'd do." She gnawed at her lip. "If I throw my lot in with you, can you save me?"

"Save you? From what? From whom?" He reached into his robe and held the box tightly, so that the corners dug into his palm. "I've already said you are welcome to stay for as long as you wish, and, perhaps in time, you'll choose to become a librarian."

"Save me from myself," she said. "I'm a bad person, Master Thaler, used to doing bad things."

"The gods offer no more salvation than I can, Mistress, but you're as safe as anyone can reasonably hope to be in these troubled times." Which was scant comfort, he knew. How bad could it get, and how quickly? Here she was, telling him all the Order's secrets, while he was keeping his own. "We, that is, I . . . the box. Apparently, we're at war with the dwarves of Farduzes."

She blinked in the gloom. "Since?"

"Since we can no longer defend ourselves. Or rather, since you can no longer defend us and we are like sheep in the face of wolves. We have some things in our favour: the Bavarians seem content to tear each other apart, and Byzantium will fall to a slave revolt. Felix is a Frankish prince as well as a Carinthian one, so we may be able to count on their support. On the other hand, Over-Carinthia is vulnerable to the Doge, and our eastern quarter to the Protector of Wien. But it seems that the dwarves have first claim on our land."

Put like that, it seemed hopeless. In a year, in five years, with all the reforms in place – local militias and palatinate cavalry, training and better weapons – they might have been able to give a decent account of themselves on the field. Instead, they had to fight a war this summer.

"Why the dwarves?"

"Now you know as much as I do, Mistress. I was woken in the night and told we are at war. I was given the dwarvish box with no more comment than that I would know what to do with it." He held it out to her again, and she reached out to collect it. "That's the only part of this that makes any sort of sense. I do know what to do with it."

He dropped it into her hands.

"Where does this staircase go?"

"To the roof," he said.

"Good. Bring the lantern." She scrambled off the window ledge and walked purposefully up. She didn't appear to need light: either it was younger eyes or elvish eyes that allowed her not to stumble. She even worked the door without assistance.

After the dark of the staircase, the open expanse of the roof was blinding. Thaler stayed still and squinted until he could see. The parapet was low, and accidents likely.

Tuomanen judged where the wind was blowing from and crouched down on the stone to shield the small mound of grey grit she poured from the box. Thaler lowered himself down with difficulty next to her.

"They use this to light fires. Underground, they have their black rock, but not kindling." She opened the lantern door and, heedless to the closeness of the flame or the molten fat dripping onto her fingers, she worked the candle stub free.

She touched the flame to the powder. For a moment, nothing happened, then she jerked her hand back as orange fire blossomed. It grew as it consumed the whole pile, then winked out just as quickly. Smoke roiled away into the newborn sky.

Thaler had felt the heat on his face, and the brightness of the fire was still with him when he closed his eyes.

"Remarkable," he said.

"No, no. You don't understand." Tuomanen sheltered the guttering candle with her curved palm. "That it burns is not the interesting thing about it. Otherwise it'd be no more than a curiosity."

She refixed the candle inside the lantern and rose to search through the debris left by the workmen from the day before. Picking out a metal canteen and an off-cut of wood, she came back and sat cross-legged.

She opened the box, and tipped out a third of the remaining powder into the lunch-pail. She noticed Thaler's pained expression.

"We can make more of this," she said.

"Can you?"

"Yes. We have the recipe. It's not hard to make, just difficult to control." She tapped the side of the tin and peered inside. "We're told what it is so that we don't create it by mistake. It's not just a pretty flame. And you might want to stand at the doorway."

Thaler, unnerved already, backed away and lurked. He could see her clearly, though, and what she was doing. She went back for the candle, and, holding the pail almost sideways, slid the lighted tallow inside. Then, in one quick motion, she held the wood to the open end and turned the pail upright again, placing it down firmly on the stone roof.

She ran, crouching low, until she was by Thaler's knees.

"Down," she said, pulling at his robe.

As he dropped, the square of wood flung itself on a pillar of smoke high into the air. The canteen bounced up and fell clattering on its side, steaming as if it were a cookpot.

Ah, but the noise. Not the sharp crack of a whip, nor a pop of a beer bottle. It boomed, and its echo would be heard all over Juvavum.

The smoking wood hit the roof near the open oculus, spinning as it landed and running like a wheel down the slope. It ended up more or less in front of Thaler, and he stooped to pick it up. It was scorched on one side, blackened and still smouldering.

After a long while, well after the first workmen had scaled the scaffolding on the outside and were standing mute on the far side of the pantheon roof, Thaler turned to Tuomanen.

"The prince will need to know about this."

She looked up at the White Fortress, its walls and its towers dominating the town below.

"He has ears. He already knows."

PART 4

Ignite

76

Büber crawled on his belly along the rock slab and looked down. Ennsbruck was a long way below him, caught in the curve of the river just as he'd remembered it: black walls and black roofs, the Enn a black ribbon on the valley floor.

He knew that fog could sometimes collect in the valleys, where the uplands were bathed in bright sun and the lowlands wreathed in cold mist. With midsummer past but winter still months away, it was smoke from the chimneys that obscured some of the detail; although it had many sources, it coalesced as a single hazy cloud that spread between the steep Alps.

Never mind, he had something to help deal with that. He pulled his satchel up to near his head and worked the straps open. Delving inside, he pulled out a leather cylinder.

It came in two parts, one tube fitting snugly inside the other. At one end, a circle of glass fatter in the middle – like Thaler – than the edges, and at the other, another smaller piece of glass, just bigger than a full dewdrop. Büber eased the halves apart so that the apparatus grew longer, and rested it on the stone ledge in front of him.

He had no idea how it worked, just that it did. Thaler had drawn all sorts of pictures for him, but hadn't quite managed to explain how things that were distant were apparently brought close enough for him to see them.

Büber put his eye to the narrower end and suddenly he was floating over the town below. The image was sharp enough that he could count individual chimney pots and windows. Chimney pots which were inexplicably upside down.

He moved the distance-pipe, as Thaler called it, so that it pointed into the fields beyond the walls where a camp had grown up, canvas sprouting like mushrooms on the green grass.

Were there more of them than before? It appeared so. The temptation to move the pipe in the exact opposite direction to that needed was almost overwhelming: in the image, up was down, left was right. Ignorant on the finer points of optics, he struggled to use the apparatus.

He carefully tracked up the road. There was dust in the distance, so far off that when he looked with the naked eye to get a truer perspective, he couldn't even tell it was there. He resighted down the valley, in the direction of Rosenheim. He could see evidence of clear-cutting, a swathe of forest having been hacked down and stacked in log piles, ready to feed the growing dwarvish army.

Army? An army implied that some would be left behind, whereas here it was an entire people on the move, like in the days of the Hun. They were a horde, looking for new land to settle.

"Wulf?"

The northman crept up beside Büber and lay down next to him. "Gods. Look at them all."

"That forest has stood since we were trees ourselves. Now look at it." Büber tried to pass the distance-pipe to his companion, but he refused it.

"You're telling me it's not magic?"

"It's not magic."

"I don't believe you."

Wulf Thorlander was young. Not a child, but barely old enough to grow a moustache. Yet he acted as if he were an old man, full of lore and superstitions. He lacked a certain wildness. Torsten Nadel hadn't. He'd been cunning, raucous and foul-mouthed.

Thorlander still had all his fingers and toes, too. Büber was running out of them.

"But you can count," said Büber. "Felix needs to know, to the nearest century, how many dwarves are camped out here."

"I can see well enough for that, Master." He pushed his blond hair out of his eyes and grew still. His lips moved, adding up as he went.

Büber put his eye back to the brass viewing piece and scanned the river. He could see no evidence that they were boat-building. Dwarves didn't build boats, though they appeared to need a prodigious amount of wood for something. They had constructed a crude palisade from some of the timber at the pinch-point just short of where the Ziller flowed into the Enn; a place where the valley was just a mile across.

What else were they making? He couldn't see it, no matter where he looked. They might be carrying out construction in the town, but they still needed to stockpile the completed articles somewhere.

He rubbed at his right eye, and switched to his left, twisting the tubes slightly so that the image was as sharp as he could make it. Everything had a little rainbow fringe to it, which was distracting, but more so was the fact that he still couldn't find what he was searching for. He could see almost all of the valley, except the part which lay directly below him, the north-facing side.

Ah. There was something he'd missed. A wide, flat bridge, apparently balanced on stone piers and topped with whole trunks. It wouldn't stand up to the spring meltwater, but if it only had to last a season, it wouldn't have to. And there was traffic across it: a cut and trimmed log was being carried across and out of sight as he watched.

He waited for Thorlander to finish counting before he broke the news. "I'm going to have to go down."

"You're not joking because you never joke. No good will come of this." Thorlander rolled on his back and looked up at the sky. "There are, allowing for four to six dwarves to a tent – if you can call them tents – between two and three thousand of them down there in the temporary camps alone."

"There are more coming from Farduzes. You can just about see them in the distance." Büber rolled over, too, letting the sun warm his face. "They've got some sort of construction yard below us, and I need to find out what they're building."

"Add the thousand that are in Ennsbruck, and the two thousand who're down by the wall: if it were easy to kill them all, the prince would have attacked by now."

"Felix needs a full report." Büber closed his eyes. "Go back to the others. Get a runner to pass on a message about numbers, and that they're felling the forest. I'll meet you where the Gerlos flows into the Ziller. By nightfall if I can make it, by dawn otherwise. If I don't come back, go back to Kufstein, and for gods' sakes don't send out search parties."

"I'm sure my lord Felix would never do such a thing."

"Good."

"Or the Princess Sophia."

Büber lazily reached out and grabbed the man's hair tight in his finger-stubs. "Don't cry out. You'll attract the thousands of dwarves you say are down below. Let me explain. Kingdoms fall with such gossip. Felix is a boy of thirteen, so we're already finely balanced. If you push too hard, in the wrong way, lots of people will die. I'd rather *you* died than them. I'll forgive you this once, but I won't forget it. Tell me you understand."

"Master," gasped Thorlander, and when Büber released him, he scrambled away, clutching his scalp.

"I won't have such talk from my men. If you can't control your tongue, find someone else to serve under." Büber seemed to be having this talk with wearying regularity. "I have to trust you completely, because there might be – more likely *will* be – a moment when my life's going to depend on you. Now fuck off and go and do what I said."

At least the man didn't argue, or worse, apologise. Thin-lipped, he looked away, before slithering back down the rock slab. When he was in no danger of presenting a silhouette to the skyline, he stood up and carried on, angling his descent down the sharp frost-shattered ridge that Büber was still perched on top of.

Büber had no idea if he'd made the situation better or worse. And he ought to have sent the distance-pipe back with Thorlander for safe-keeping. Thaler and Sophia's father had presented the first one they'd made to Felix, the second to him.

He turned the two ends to shorten the tube again and pressed the lens covers back in place, before slipping the instrument back inside his satchel. Back on his stomach again, he wondered at the best way to approach the hidden part of the valley.

What unsighted him was a wooded spur that dropped from the ridgeline down to just above the town. He could try to traverse the ridge, but then he'd lose too much height, and there'd be no guarantee he'd have a clear view.

Simpler to just go to the spur and take a look. Would the dwarves have pickets that far up? He hadn't been spotted so far, despite his group spending a week in the next valley along. The dwarves might be so new to being above ground that it hadn't occurred to them they might need to stop people from spying on what they were doing.

There was a stadia or two of clear ground from the summit of the ridge to the first scrubby bushes, and the slope of the ground was such that this was in full sun. His moving shadow would be obvious, but he certainly didn't want to wait until dusk.

Nothing for it but to make for the tree line on the south side of the ridge and go around it. A cross-cutting valley was just to his left, and then he'd be in cover all the way down.

He checked his position one last time, then slipped back the way he'd come, scrabbling down the steep scree – which had taken him hours to climb – running even as the ground under him slipped and slid under his feet. His scabbard rattled against the stones and his satchel banged against his hip, but he was in control, all the way to where the scree stopped and the ground flattened out.

After that, things took longer. He would walk, stop, listen, and only then move again. Sometimes he dropped lower, just to check whether any patrols had passed that way and might be likely to do so again. There were no signs, and it appeared that the dwarves genuinely believed they'd driven all the humans out, and that this was now their land.

Büber was going to take advantage of that.

There was a dip before the next rise. The trees – proper trees, not stunted, cold-damaged specimens – hid his approach, and he was able to walk on rock, soil and needle-strewn ground as silently as he could in the depths of the forest where everything was green and cool and still.

He topped the ridge, and made his way down the other side. The next time he stopped and listened, he could hear the sounds of sawing and hammering. Lots of hands were at work, not just a few. Their noise would cover his approach.

Slower and slower. The trees were obscuring his sight-lines even as the downhill gradient steepened for the last part of the drop to the valley floor. He held himself up against one trunk, then crouched and slithered to the next. His rough fingers smelt of moss and pine where he'd pressed them into the bark.

Gods, they made a racket with all their industry. It was as if all the metal-workers on Coin Alley had taken their forges and set them up next to the saw pits and lathes of the carpenters. The noise, previously useful, was now a hazard. He might stumble into an individual dwarf, or a whole group of them, and not have any warning at all.

The light between the tree-trunks grew brighter, and he could start to see shapes through the gaps. He twisted his head to try and make sense of what he saw: a wheel here, a wall of planks there – such things were outside his experience. He risked going forward another few feet to get a clearer view.

Now he could see better. There were lines of wagons, too many to count. Some had four wheels like carts; some longer ones had six. Each was completely covered – sides, front, roof – with a gently pitched roof and a pointed front. There were doors at the back.

Büber wondered what they might be for, and what might pull them. Dwarves didn't use horses. They couldn't be mobile barracks, surely, because tents were easier to carry and more versatile.

They were big, too. What were they meant to carry?

Perhaps Thaler would be able to make more sense of them. Whatever their intended use, the dwarves' unstinting labour and resources were being poured into making as many of them as they could. They were clearly important, so it was vital to Carinthia to understand what they were.

Closer still, then. He ducked down and crept to the last tree. Beyond that was clear ground, then a stone-and-turf wall. There seemed to be no gate or gap in this for him to slip through, and the grass in front of the wall showed evident signs of wear. Booted feet had passed that way, and often.

He might have got past it at night, but not by day. It was time to go. He edged backwards, keeping a wary eye on the wall. A group of dwarves ambled past, speaking casually, making no attempt to look for intruders. They seemed to be craftsmen; one carried a bucket, and they all had hammers.

They passed without so much as glancing in Büber's direction, though, had they done so, what would they have seen? Just another shadow in the trees, green and brown, perfectly still, perfectly silent.

He watched their backs recede, then started up again.

77

Felix's forebears had faced down the might of the Roman legions with nothing more than their courage, a stout spear, and sufficient drilling to make them stand in line and face the enemy. That and their priest-kings' wild magic.

A thousand years of peace, and Felix knew nothing of magic, while his subjects seemed to have lost the ability to even stand in line.

Sophia pretended not to look, keeping her face down at the pages of the book in her lap, but she could see the problems. The sergeant had them ten abreast, eight deep, with their spears resting upright on their shoulders, except that they were ragged and disorderly. When they lowered their weapons, they hit each other rather than forming a wall of spear-points.

"Again," Felix said wearily to the sergeant, who was newly promoted to his post after Reinhardt had gone to command the troops at Rosenheim. As the man shouted and swore his way back to the start line, Felix walked over to where Sophia sat. She wedged her tongue between her teeth and pretended to concentrate on the words in front of her.

"It's hopeless. They all have two left feet and two left thumbs." He sat on the chair beside her. "If we have to take the field now, we'll be slaughtered."

She looked up absently, "They're good men. Remember that."

"They'll be dead men soon enough if we can't get them to keep a formation." Felix snatched up his mug of small beer, only to find it empty. "We lost what martial strength we had at Obernberg. No one knows how to do this any more."

"Hire soldiers. We've got the coin."

"I refuse to hire mercenaries. They'll be on us like wolves."

She turned the page. The vellum was old and crisp, and the binding creaked. "Just enough to train our militias, Felix. Send to Milano, or Lutetia. Your cousins will help."

"We don't have time."

She made that noise, with her tongue behind her teeth, that he didn't like.

"Don't tut me."

She couldn't deny it. "Have none of the stories you've heard ended with, 'So the brave prince, having previously gone with a sack of gold to his neighbours to beg for veterans, was able to defeat his foe's army so thoroughly that they all lived happily ever after'?"

Sophia could tell by the look he gave her that they hadn't. She closed her copy of Tacitus's *Germania*, and passed it to Felix.

"Neither have I. My stories depend on the faithfulness of the people of Israel to HaShem. That doesn't always end well, either." She got up, adjusted her clothing and strode out into the courtyard. She walked along the line of men, and they grew silent under her gaze.

"My lady," said the sergeant. "Do you wish to address the troops?"

"Troops?" She pursed her lips. "Yes."

"At ease, lads. M'lady wants a word."

"A word?" she said under her breath. "I'll give them more than a word." She unsheathed the sword on her belt and held it point-down on the flags. Now she had their attention. "Tacitus tells me that in the days when the Romans fought your grandfathers' grandfathers, the wives and mothers of the tribe used to go into battle with their menfolk. Perhaps we should revive this tradition. Perhaps we should put them in the vanguard of the Wild Boar's Head instead of you, because, despite your sergeant's clear instruction, you're all determined to be worm-food come battle."

She was shaming them, and she didn't care.

"Your homes, your families, your land – you can say that now, your land – will be taken from you if you carry on like this. Once you pick up that spear, you're no longer a farmer or a carter or a cook or a butcher. You're a soldier. Act like one. Have some discipline. " She dragged her spatha up and onto her shoulder, and paced to the end of the line. "Tacitus also said that the German tribes were renowned for their ferocity. So be fierce. I'm standing in front of you, and I'm not scared. First rank, hold your spears out."

Some complied quickly. Others hesitated and presented their arms slowly. She dropped her shoulder and swung her sword, hitting with the flat against the spear-haft of the nearest man in range. His spear flew out of his hands and clattered away. He was left with stinging palms and still she went at them.

"If that had been a dwarvish axe, you'd be dead by now. That spear is there to protect you and the men either side of you. They'll be killed next, and the whole line will fail because *you* can't keep hold of your weapon." Her sword went back to her shoulder. "You're not a phalanx either: you're not carrying a sarissa, and you've no shields. You're too deep. The men at the back can do nothing but watch the men at the front die." She pushed through the forma-tion. "Back four rows, form up next to the front four."

Sophia had to push and slap the tardy ones into position. They stretched from one side of the inner courtyard to the other now. It made them look twice as many.

"Front row, put the butt of your spear under your foot. Now crouch down. Second row, two-handed grip over the shoulders of the men in front. Third row, over the shoulders of the men in front. Fourth row, the same." She walked the line again, picking on the man she'd disarmed before.

This time, with his spear properly held and braced, the spear shivered but didn't fall. He smiled grimly at her, and she nodded her satisfaction.

"Now I'm scared." The men had transformed themselves into a hedge of spear-points. They were still static, vulnerable from the sides, but with what little time they had they could do something about that. "As you were, sergeant."

She sheathed her sword and sat back in her chair. She'd have to move in a little while, chasing the sunlight around the enclosed courtyard, but for now it was bright enough to read by.

"What else does Tacitus say?" asked Felix.

"It'd be more encouraging if he didn't keep on about what superb individual fighters the Germanic tribesmen were in the same breath as decrying their lack of unit cohesion." She took the book from him and found her place again. "He was Roman. The dwarves aren't going to be using Roman tactics to fight us any more than we're going to use Greek phalanx tactics to fight them."

"Does anyone know what tactics they *will* be using?" Felix was momentarily distracted by the upheaval in the yard as the line dissolved and reformed as a marching column.

"The last people to fight dwarves were the Gauls, during Julius Caesar's campaign. The library has copies of *De Bello Gallico*, but the caesar was a consummate liar and self-propagandist. How much we'll learn from him is debatable." Sophia turned her attention back to Tacitus, despite the noise. "This is a better history, written by a better historian."

The column marched the length of the courtyard, then back again. It took them a little while to replicate the spear wall, but they were better the second time than they'd been the first.

"You said something about a boar's head," said Felix.

"Wild Boar's Head. You put your elite troops in the vanguard and pile them a hundred deep, then bend the rest around either side like the limbs of a bow. Your weakest soldiers aren't even meant to fight, simply discourage flanking attacks on the main thrust."

"Except," said Felix, "we don't have any elite troops. All we have are bakers and butchers."

"Either it'll be enough, or it won't. If you won't hire anyone—"

"I will not."

". . . then you're telling me and everyone else that Carinthia can defend itself. You've trained a hundred swords. They're training hundreds more. These men, even after an hour, are on their way to becoming competent." Sophia closed the book again. Clearly, she wasn't going to get any more reading done. "If you don't think we're doing enough, what else do you think we should be doing?"

"I don't know. There's Master Thaler's powder."

"Which is tying up half the smiths in Juvavum, when they could be making war hammers and maces to batter dwarvish armour. And this insistence that we all piss into barrels." She didn't say what she thought about the witch Tuomanen, and her unhealthy influence on both Felix and Frederik. "The smith from Simbach, Bastian?"

"The giant?"

"Has used enough iron in one of his pots for a hundred swords." She watched the would-be soldiers as they attempted to march forward in line, spears ready. She pulled a face. "The dwarves don't ride, and they might throw axes, but they don't use bows. We know that mixed spear and bow formations will work against them. Yes, we're fortunate to have the library, and yes, there are great benefits to be gained by reading old books, but Master Thaler isn't offering you a substitute for magic."

"I know he's not, but" – he screwed his face up – "I can't just ignore him. He's so enthusiastic."

"And so are your boar hounds. I worry, Felix. I worry for the fate of the palatinate: you, my father, and everyone in it. Those powder weapons are a distraction. They need a drum." She started to get out of her chair again.

"Who?"

"These," and she waved her hand at the troops in the yard. "They can't march in time. It's unnatural, and there's no reason why they should."

She stopped a pot-boy on his way to the midden with a bucket of peelings, and told him to come straight back to her. The boy dodged away through the ranks and disappeared.

"They have promise, Sophia."

"Who?"

It was Felix's turn to tut. "Master Thaler's powder weapons. And Mistress Tuomanen . . ."

"What about her? Has she still forsworn magic?" She frowned. "I've seen the fires in the jars that don't go out."

"It's entirely natural. Master Thaler says so." He looked petulant. "Your own father says so."

"Yes, well. He's had his head filled with all sorts of nonsense recently."

They stared at each other. He might be the prince, but sometimes, she thought he should just listen to her. They didn't need things that spurted fire and smelt like Sheol. They needed steel and enough men to wield it: HaShem would see to the rest. They were faithful, so they would be saved.

Felix slumped in his seat, looking away. "If I send to the Franks for help, will you let Master Thaler continue?"

"You're in charge, you can do whatever you like." That was just mean. Felix was in charge, and he had other advisers besides her. Thaler was like a child in a pastry-shop with his new-found knowledge, never quite knowing which sweetmeat to pick and taking a bite out of each in turn: but he did know what he was doing most of the time. "If Master Thaler thinks his investigations will produce something that works, then he can continue. Meanwhile, we'll send a messenger to your cousin the Frankish king, asking for some people who know how to drill spearmen."

The pot-boy ran up to her with his now-empty pail and presented it to her.

"Because otherwise," she said, "I'll be stuck banging on the bottom of a slops-bucket until winter."

She got to her feet again and unsheathed her sword. The men thought they were going to get more schooling from the mad Jewish woman, and they were half right. She struck the wooden pail with her sword pommel in a steady rhythm, as though she were clapping in time with a song.

Effortlessly, the soldiers fell into step. It was that simple. Once they worked out which leg was which, they stopped looking like a rabble and started behaving like a strange creature with many heads, arms and legs, but one mind.

When the sergeant gave the order to turn, they mostly managed it in one movement. When he ordered them to speed up, she picked up the pace along with them. After another two circuits of the courtyard, she handed the bucket over to the sergeant with the suggestion that everyone needed a rest, a drink and something to eat.

She was tired, too, and she had to go riding with Felix later, because she still wasn't very good at it and needed to get better.

"We need to recruit some drummers," said Felix.

"One for every century. Those who can keep a beat would be a good choice." She poked at the ground with her sword-point. "We're not going to be ready, are we?"

"We'll be as ready as we can be. When they come down the valley, we'll meet them with everything we have. We'll win, and all of Europe will talk about us the same way they talk about Alaric."

"The dwarves aren't ready yet, either. We should be making sure they never are, rather than wait for them." She reached out her right hand and found his left, catching his fingers in hers. "How can we harry them, when we don't have soldiers to spare?"

"Perhaps we do. That night in the library; remember those who attacked it?"

"You marked them, and then arrested them later."

"I'll free them from the mines if they'll fight for me. They can go back to their families – if they want them – and wear their crosses with pride rather than shame." Felix looked pleased with himself. "Two letters to write, then. One to the Franks, and one to the mines. Master Wess can make copies of the second with his press printer thing."

"Who will you send with the first?" she asked. "We can't spare Peter Büber."

"Master Ullmann? Or some of his men? There's the two he took with him to Simbach." Felix played with the ends of Sophia's fingers. "Have you seen a woman around Master Ullmann recently?"

She thought it an odd question. "No, I don't think so. Apart from the witch, on occasions."

"He needs to tell me everything: that's part of his job. I shouldn't have to find out from someone else."

"Then ask him," she said. "You can't have your spy master hiding things from you."

78

"Aaron," said Thaler. "Be careful."

"The devil take your care. My hands are perfectly steady."

Morgenstern stood at the trestle with a funnel and bored-out wooden tube. "And your chattering won't help one jot."

It didn't stop Thaler from fussing. They'd set up a system to try and stop stray sparks from igniting the mixtures, from the grinding to the mixing and the graining and the storing. For more delicate operations, trestles like Morgenstern's were surrounded by hessian screens, but were otherwise open to the sky. As a result of all their caution, they'd lost only one of their sheds, and none of their millers. It helped that they knew what they were dealing with: the books salvaged from the hexmasters made the powder's quixotic nature quite clear. But an accident was inevitable, the further they went. Everything was an experiment, every time was the first time.

They were making fuses. Paradoxically, these would make their detonations safer, but only if the fuses were reliable, and burnt at the same rate. Mistress Tuomanen could be of no further help. They'd outstripped her knowledge weeks ago: she knew what she knew. Trying something to see if it worked hadn't been a habit the Order had encouraged, and there was a lot of unlearning to do. She was mortally afraid of making mistakes.

Unlike Aaron Morgenstern, who revelled in novelty and flew the flag for danger.

"All the same," said Thaler. "Please be careful."

"Is this what being married to you would be like?" countered Morgenstern. "Let me get on with it."

Thaler knew that Morgenstern only had a few ounces of powder – enough for his task. Perhaps he was worrying unnecessarily. "Call me when you're done."

The field in which they were working was across the river, under the shadow of Goat Mountain and the White Tower. It was close enough to the Witches' Bridge to make access easy, while being far enough away to . . . well: if they were going to lay waste to Juvavum, they'd need a lot more powder.

The meadow was dotted with flapping hessian screens and small sheds. Every once in a while, a door would open and a man or woman would come out, carrying a small pot of something or other, and take it to a storage area. At times, someone would go and collect some ingredient, or draw another bucket of water. Otherwise, everything was quiet.

Bastian's great iron pot sat on a series of boards at one edge of the field, pointing northwards. Next to it were smaller versions in the same style, resembling not only the mortars found in every kitchen, but the mortars in which they combined the white, the yellow and the black to make the powder itself.

They may have been small, but these little ones worked; honest-to-gods worked. They could lob a ball of iron high into the air and across the width of the practice range. It took an age to load them, though, and aiming them was painfully slow. Also, the projectiles would only kill a dwarf if they hit one square on the head.

In other words, they were next to useless. Thaler wasn't in the business of producing a curiosity. He could picture in his mind what he wanted, how it would work if only they could build one not just bigger, but better. Which is where Bastian's latest pot came in, and where the next in the series would come, too; a real beast of war, he hoped.

"Mistress?" he called, and was answered by a wave, a tattooed hand that appeared over the top of a screen.

He stepped around it and inspected Tuomamen's work-bench. She wasn't working with the combined black powder, just the white nitre. She had lengths of wick hanging from a frame, and various bowls and jars set out in front of her. There were stains down the front of her grey robes, and Thaler discovered how they'd got there: her first instinct was to wipe her hands down her front.

"Master Thaler. Success, of sorts."

"Ah, that is good news. Show me."

She took one of the long wicks and opened the lantern she had on the table. "It's not what you wanted, but it's useful all the same."

She applied one end of the wick to the flame, then withdrew it, holding it out to Thaler.

He took it and held it close to his face. The very end of the wick was alight, not with a flame, but with a tiny red coal. He waved it around, then looked at it again. The glowing ember was still there.

"It won't go out," Tuomanen said. "You can pinch it off, or wet it, but it'll burn otherwise."

"Just not quickly," he noted. The wick wasn't noticeably shorter than when she'd first lit it.

"A length of your height will burn for half a day."

"Impressive." Thaler handed the cord back. "But, as you say, it's not what we want."

"It is, however, enough to light the black powder." She squeezed the lit end between her fingertips, making a rubbing motion as she did so. It must have hurt, but she showed no pain. "It won't blow out like a taper, and no one will have to carry a lantern along with the powder."

She was right. It wasn't what he'd hoped for, but it was useful all the same.

"We know that we can make a line of powder, set it alight at one end, and the flame will travel along it until it reaches the other, but" – he wagged his finger – "it burns too quickly; which is the point of Aaron's wooden quill fuses. Packing the powder in tightly makes them burn slower. It makes no sense at all, but we'll have to work out why later."

"I've tried soaking the wicks in a slurry of black powder. The fuse just flashes to ash no matter the length." She shrugged and turned back to her table to pack away her jars.

Thaler was left with his chin on his chest, thinking aloud.

"Wood isn't flexible, though joining quills together would allow us to change the timing quickly. We'd need half a tree-trunk for a long fuse, though." He huffed. "Sausages."

"Master Thaler, it's mid-morning."

"Sausage *skins*. No, too big. Like sausage skins, but thinner, like cord."

Tuomanen put down her alchemical equipment and turned to Thaler, a strange expression on her face. "If I was to take a knife, and cut you here, and here" – she touched him twice, once on the inside of his arm, under his arm-pit, and again on the fold of his wrist – "I could draw out one of the vessels along which your blood flows. It's the whole length of your arm, and as thin as a quill."

"I'm rather attached to my arm, Mistress," said Thaler. He clasped his hands behind his back.

"The same vessels exist in pigs and cattle." She smiled. "That was all I meant."

There were times when he forgot who she used to be, *what* she used to be. Then she would remind him. "I'll call on the butcher's shortly," he said, and blinked away the image of himself, prone on the floor, and her, astride him with a bloody knife, opening him up like a side of beef.

Aaron Morgenstern, clutching his fuses, came across them, and wondered why his friend had grown so pale. "Frederik?"

"Nothing, it's nothing." Thaler applied a mask of calm. "Are you done, Aaron?"

"I am. Let's light up these devils and see how they burn."

Thaler took one from him: the drill hole in the cylinder of wood was packed tight with fine powder, tamped down and pressed in. There was very little actual powder in the device, but if it worked, then they would be on their way at last.

All three of them went to another hessian-shrouded table, one supplied with black powder, and the mistress brought one of her slow-burning wicks rather than the lantern. Thaler poured a small pile of loose powder onto the table, enough to support the upright tube, and Tuomanen touched the tiny coal to the end of the fuse.

It sparked and fizzed. Smoke jetted from the open hole. And the loose powder did not immediately flash into flame.

Thaler counted, and reached five on the first attempt, before fire and smoke belched out. Morgenstern did a little jig, and looked uncommonly pleased with himself.

"Again?" he grinned.

"Oh, most certainly." Thaler swept away the residue and reset the experiment. "We need to be certain of the burn rate, or we'll be losing our lives soon enough."

Each one they tried burnt through between a count of four and six. Morgenstern skipped away to make more, his speed belying every year of his age.

"This is progress," Thaler announced. "We should try and test-fire a shell."

He hadn't dared do so before, as he'd had no reliable way of setting it off from a distance, even though the idea was one of the first things he'd thought of: to deliver a charge of exploding powder, right into the heart of the enemy. He wasn't martial, like Sophia. He wasn't cunning, like Max Ullmann. He wasn't, gods preserve him, like Peter Büber. The only contribution he could make to the war lay in this field.

At a push, he could hold a spear, and blunt an axe with his bones which seemed a waste of his life, and indeed of anyone's life. The dwarves hadn't needed to pick a fight with them; Felix had offered them a share of both land and gold, but they, greedily, wanted it all.

"Master Thaler?" said Tuomanen.

"Sorry. I'm angry. Angry with having been put in this position, of having to design machines that kill rather than ones that save. Everything we do is bent towards war: if it has no military application, we have to put it to one side. But do you suppose this'll be the end of it? We'll fight the dwarves of Farduzes this year, the Protector of Wien the next, and the Doge the year after."

"You're a peaceable man, Master Thaler, because a thousand years of peace breeds a peaceable people." Tuomanen glanced at the wick she was carrying, still smouldering away. "It was a peace that was won with fear. Fear of hexmasters like me."

"Yes, but—"

"There are no buts here. You're trying to do with these powder weapons what we did with our spells; make your enemies afraid to face you, and leave you alone to your books and your brass." She pinched out the ember with no more thought than before. "Peace is not the absence of war. I understand this – this world of fire and smoke – far better than you do, and King Ironmaker is an idiot for risking everything on a single throw of his dice."

"He tried to kill Felix, Mistress. In response to a friendly treaty."

"So we are at war. What happens if we win? News of these great powder-driven monsters will be broadcast from Hibernia to Persia. Everybody will have them soon enough. We'll build better weapons and have more of them, of course. We'll have exchanged the white robes of the Order for the black robes of the library. That's all."

"So what do we do?"

She shrugged, and went back to packing away her materials. "Prosperous people, content with their lot, never went to war willingly. What can you do about that? Can you abolish famine and disease? Can you say when the rivers rise and the snow falls? Can you meddle in the affairs of kings and princes so that they don't cast envious eyes on their neighbours?"

"Perhaps." He answered without thinking. "Yes. Why not?"

She laughed, and she rarely laughed. "Hubris, Master Thaler. The gods have made you mad."

"Why not?" he repeated. "It's not me who shoulders the burden alone, but us and all Carinthia. All are equal before the law. The earls' estates are broken up. We hold no slaves. We choose our civic leaders. We haven't even pressed anyone since Felix came to the throne."

"You believe it." Her laughter died. "Yet Ironmaker will sweep you off the map, and you'll either flee or be enslaved. Resist and you'll be killed. Within a generation, Carinthia will be forgotten, except in old maps."

"He won't win."

"Which is why we devise ever more intricate ways to kill. See why I wear grey robes?" Tuomanen looked down at her stained and burnt front. "It doesn't matter what we aspire to. This is the way things are from now on."

Thaler tasted sourness, and screwed his mouth up. "I believe it does matter. I believe it matters a great deal."

A cry went up from across the field, and they both turned, expecting to see a roil of smoke and hear a crack of thunder. Instead, it was Bastian and some carters, dragging his latest piece to the proving grounds.

"We have a new toy," said Tuomanen, going to join the crowd that was gathering around the cart, and Thaler had to accept that she was, at least for the time being, right.

He eased his way through his powder-makers and called up to the smith, who rode on the cart with his new creation. "Come on then, sir, unveil it. Let's all see what you've brought us."

A waxed cloth sheet was draped artfully over the piece, and Bastian gripped one corner of it.

"Master Thaler. I beg your indulgence," he started, and Thaler's gaze went straight from the blond-haired giant of a man to the shape of the hidden pot. It was too long, like a felled tree. Certainly not squat and fat as it should have been.

"Gods, man. What have you done?"

"I've found my destiny, Master Thaler. *This* is what I was born to make."

He pulled the cover free, and Thaler didn't know whether to be horrified or excited. The tube was as long as he was tall, and he could just about manage to fit his fist in the muzzle.

It was made from black iron, with bands of steel.

"This . . . this isn't what we agreed. This isn't the design I showed you."

"No." Bastian kicked open a box at his feet, and inside were iron balls, made to match. He dropped one into Thaler's hands.

"Think of this, not falling from above, but charging straight at the enemy."

Thaler felt the weight of the shot, and slowly realised that everyone was waiting for his judgement. He looked at their faces and weighed their expectations, together with his own.

He came to a sort of decision. "Let's get this unloaded and set up. Preferably before the Lady Sophia finds out."

79

Ullmann's table was covered in little slips of paper. Each one was a message, sent back from his spies. They needed to be sifted, ordered and collated. They needed action.

The news from Bavaria was simply confusing. With Leopold's death, every earl seemed to be taking it as his right to follow him down the same road to madness. Some, like Fuchs, were uncomplicated robbers, accumulating wealth for themselves from their own lands. Others had larger ambitions: München had swapped hands twice already, each of the usurpers styling themselves Ruler of all Bavaria, and the Earl of Augsburg was now marching on it – at least, he had been at the time of the message. Ullmann hadn't received another, either from his agent inside München, or outside it.

The Austrians were as broke as the Bavarians. People were leaving Wien by the cart-load every day to return to their distant kin still in the countryside in the hope of bread and beer. Some of them were inevitably moving into Carinthia because of family ties, but he judged it wouldn't be long before what the situation at Simbach had presaged wasn't written large on the east of the palatinate. Felix had parcels of land that he could give away, taken from the defunct earldoms, which would absorb some of them. There would come a point, though, where it might be necessary to tell the Protector enough was enough.

The situation beyond the mountains of Over-Carinthia was a confused jumble of contradictory noises. This duke was fighting that duke, alliances were made and broken in the space of a day, cities were besieged, crops burnt, fleets of square-sailed ships vied for control of the seas. Just as long as they didn't look north: he'd given orders to close the high passes. Over-Carinthia would have to take its share of refugees and use them as a buffer against any army that wanted to march over the mountains.

Further afield, it was nothing but a cloud of rumour. The dwarves had taken the Enn valley, but no one had any idea if they had also gone north and west to the plains. Perhaps Horst and Manfred might send news when they reached the Franks, but their route might just as likely be cut off. Was that why the Earl of Augsburg was marching?

He had thought that he'd feel powerful, sitting in Juvavum, being able to see and hear everything that happened in courts near and far. What he did feel was impotent. His network was as ill-prepared as the prince's army, both consisting of amateurs who had to learn the job as they went. Inevitably, some of them were quickly out of their depth.

If that wasn't enough, there was Carinthia itself to deal with. He had to know what was being said in the beer cellars and across the market stalls throughout the whole length of the palatinate. The people were fearful, and there was little he could do about that. There was plenty to be afraid of. At least they weren't rioting or planning insurrection. Yet, Eckhardt had shown that rebellion could come suddenly, from unexpected directions.

How could he best serve his prince? Not by merely telling him who sat on which throne, but by placing Carinthian arses on those thrones and making the people regret he'd not done so sooner. That was the lesson of Simbach, and later of Rosenheim, which they'd taken over after the earl had fled with his household and the little treasure he could scrape together.

A mayor now sat in his place, and the farmers of the manor found themselves owning the land they'd once inhabited as serfs. It was a tactic Ullmann was eager to export, Felix less so.

As far as Ullmann was concerned, now was the time to do it, when kings and princes – other than the Carinthian one – were weak, and earls isolated. Introduce Carinthian law and Carinthian practices to unseat a foreign earl, and there was another century or two of fighting men to call on.

He needed to prepare the day's report, ready for Felix, Sophia, Thaler and Wess to debate with him. And, more recently, the hexmaster Tuomanen. He didn't like that. Neither did Sophia, he knew.

The witch had pledged her allegiance to Felix, and promised to inform on her former Order to Ullmann, He couldn't shake the suspicion that she was playing a game which involved both the fortress and the library. He watched her closely, and wondered if he should have her killed.

It definitely wasn't because she reminded him of Nikoleta Agana.

Then there was Aelinn.

What was he to do about her? He thought of her all the time – all the time his life wasn't in mortal danger, at least. As for her, she didn't seem so bothered. She enjoyed his company when he called. She shared his bed when the mood took her. But she continued to keep house for the Odenwalds, and nothing he could say to her could tempt her away. He had offered her handfasting more than once, and she'd laughed it off. He'd offered her her own house, with her own servants. She'd kissed him and told him he was being foolish.

He was a farmer's son from the banks of the Mur. She was Juvavum born-and-bred. He had ascended to the prince's court. She seemed content to sweep floors and wash pots. He simply didn't understand.

Gods, he couldn't concentrate.

He forced himself to sit down. Cracking his knuckles, he moved the pieces of paper around – placing them according to the area they related to – so that they resembled a map: Bavaria to his left, Wien to his right, Over-Carinthia and the Italians closest to him, Carinthia proper in the middle. That left a small handful of messages that came from further north.

One of those mentioned the Teutons.

Ullmann hadn't been at Obernberg, but he'd heard all about it. How a few hundred Teuton horse had ambushed, then destroyed the Carinthian line, killing Gerhard in the process. Only Nikoleta Agana had managed to salvage anything. Why did it have to be her?

Now the Teutons seemed to have left their frozen, fly-infested swamp and taken a swathe of land along the Baltic coast as far as the Mark. That news had to be passed on to Felix, even if it might be something to worry about next year rather than this. It wouldn't do to leave them unopposed for too long. The south traded with the north through the Baltic ports, and using the Teutons as middlemen wasn't something civilised people did.

Out of the whole of Europe, it looked as if only the dwarves were capable of fielding a sizeable army. And it was Carinthia's bad luck to be first in the way. One thing was certain: they couldn't field a sizeable army for themselves. Not yet.

Ullmann drummed his fingers on the table. There were two small forces, relatively intact, close by – those of München and Augsburg. If they'd stop fighting each other, and join Carinthia . . . there was a core of an effective fighting force right there. What would that take? The death of the Bavarian pretender, perhaps? So that when the Earl of Augsburg reached München's gates, they were already open?

Felix would never sanction that. He would talk about his brother princes again, and Sophia would simply gainsay any murder, no matter how necessary.

Did either of them need to know, he wondered? It was for the good of the palatinate. It might even be necessary for its survival. He'd stabbed Nikoleta for exactly the same reasons.

He'd do it again. He wasn't some sort of monster who delighted in death, but he hadn't become Master Ullmann through ducking difficult decisions.

He had a book of codes, given to him by Thaler. He leafed through it until he found the one used by his München contact, and wrote out on a scrap of parchment a brief, unambiguous message: kill pretender-king, open gates to Augsburg. Then, using the code to work out the encrypted form of the message, he wrote out those out onto a second slip of paper. The first copy, he consigned to the flames of the fire, and made certain that the whole thing was ash.

The message could go as soon as a rider was ready. It was a short journey, forty miles, no more. He toyed with the idea of sending a second message to Augsburg to see if there might be the opportunity to finish off the earl and have two ripe plums fall into Carinthia's hand.

Best not. Carinthia needed someone in charge for them to deal with; someone to hold the troops together and commit them to fight against the dwarves.

He picked up the slip of paper he'd written on. The ink was dry. He only needed to roll it up and seal it in wax. The messenger would secrete it about his person – even inside his person, as the wax coating would pass through the gut undamaged – and deliver it to his man. Would he baulk at the order to kill? If so, would he still do his duty?

He screwed it up and dropped it into the fire.

Someone would guess that the death wasn't merely a happy coincidence for Carinthia. They'd openly blame Augsburg, but, in secret, they'd know. Thaler and Wess would be appalled, and all their disappointment and squeamish horror would be on show. Sophia, incandescent with rage, would demand that Ullmann be thrown into the same tower cell as the two hapless fools from Simbach, who still languished there, despite the cause that had brought them to Juvavum being long gone.

Felix wouldn't overrule them. Ullmann would be dragged away, protesting not his innocence, but his guilt in an earlier, equally significant death. Thaler would feel himself obliged to tell Peter Büber, and no jail door in the palatinate would be thick enough, no dungeon deep enough, to spare him from the wrath of the berserkergang.

His hands were tied. He was impotent. The things that needed doing couldn't be done because everyone in charge was infected by scruples. If his prince commanded it, he'd do it. Gods, he'd do the deed himself. But Felix wouldn't allow him free rein. Was that the lesson of Nikoleta Agana? Not that he was trusted with running the Carinthian spy network, but that he'd been chosen to run it because he was the one person who *couldn't* be trusted. Wess would be useless at the job, Thaler too distracted, Sophia too honest.

Thaler was an idealist, a loyalist, intelligent and ardent. So was he. What made the people love Thaler so, yet fear Ullmann? They loved Thaler even though he stank of sulphur and smoke, and despite the fact that his explosions echoed across the rooftops of Juvavum from early morning to late evening. "Good old Master Thaler," they'd shout as they made way for him in the streets and alleys. He couldn't buy a drink anywhere in town without rich or poor slapping their coppers down on the bar ahead of his fumbling fingers. He even made the witch Tuomanen respectable by association.

Thaler was making killing machines in the shadow of the White Tower and was a hero as a result. Ullmann was organising inform-ation from all corners of the map and was entirely reliant on decent, upright Carinthians who'd chosen to put themselves in mortal danger every day, yet he was treated with suspicion.

The last curl of his coded message fluttered away up the chimney, and his shoulders sagged.

Was there another way to achieve the same goal? Could he get Augsburg and München to stop fighting long enough to realise that if the the dwarves escaped the Enn valley, there'd be no Bavarian crown to claim? The fact that they were arguing about a worthless symbol made their quarrelling all the more pathetic. Bavaria was broke, and unless its serfs had planted in the spring, there would be famine by winter.

By seizing Rosenheim and Simbach, Carinthia had taken over a full third of historic Bavaria. Carinthian administrators, wherever they'd travelled, had carried with them copies of the first book off of Wess's printing press: *Of the Theory and Practice of Mundane Farming, as Practised by the Jews of Carinthia*. There would be shortages in the palatinate's storehouses, but no one would starve.

See? They were doing good things. They weren't burning houses, killing those who fought and enslaving those who didn't, stealing their goods and their livestock. It was likely that if Augsburg and München didn't join with Carinthia this summer, by the next they would be begging for any crumb that might fall from Felix's table.

Better that one man die than thousands.

Ullmann gnawed at his fingernail, staring into the red, shimmering glow at the heart of the fire.

He could see clearly. It wasn't just in Carinthia's interests that the fighting between men ceased. It was in everyone's. The German people didn't want to end up like Italy, with city states constantly at war with their neighbours, year after year, pissing their treasure away over the same scrap of ground. They were a peaceable, civilised race, descended from gods-fearing Goths, so unlike the hotheaded Romans.

No. The Carinthian leopard would become a rallying point for Bavarians and Austrians alike. After that, Saxony and Bohemia, and together they would once and for all drive the Teutons into the chill embrace of the Baltic.

He tasted copper. His worried nail had split, and blood was seeping out from underneath. He sucked at his fingertip, and turned back to his desk. He picked up his pen, and pressed the code book open again at the right page.

He began to write.

80

It was late when Büber arrived at Rosenheim, late enough for it to be on the edge of darkness, the sun slipping away off to the north-west. He'd left his men to camp outside the town, where there were many circles of tents and bright fires burning. Thorlander was there, and neither of them mentioned what had passed between them earlier.

He ought to have whipped the man all the way down the valley for what he'd said, but he'd come to realise there was a certain prestige in being part of Büber's scouts. Getting kicked out would probably mean not just temporary embarrassment, but permanent shame.

Rosenheim was out of bounds to ordinary Carinthian soldiers, although some slipped in for a crafty fuck with a willing local. Felix wanted the Bavarians left alone, but it wasn't just Carinthians doing the sneaking: Rosenheimers would tour the camp, selling everything they possessed for whatever coin the soldiers carried. As a consequence, half the houses and shops had closed up, and their inhabitants had fled somewhere safer.

The market square at the end of the muddy main street was overlooked by a row of houses, as might be found in the oldest part of Juvavum – tall, thin and protruding over the road. One of them had a limp leopard banner draped from a first-floor window, and a lantern hung by the front door.

Büber entered without knocking, and the guard who sat on a chair by the bottom of the stairs glanced at him once before resting his chin on his chest again.

The huntsman had spent the last week permanently alert for any sign he'd been spotted. The laxity of the guard worried him. He was reasonably certain there were no dwarves within thirty miles of them, but where previously one glance would have been enough to tell the difference, even Büber now had to double-check it was dwarves he was seeing, and not short men.

He kicked the guard's chair as he went past.

"Wake up, you lazy fucker. I could be anyone."

The guard jerked upright and staggered to his feet. His hand was on his sword, but he found himself faced with quiet contempt and an awful lot of scars.

"Master Büber," he said, and used his sword-hand to touch his brow instead.

Gods, the dwarves were going to roll right over them. Büber scowled and started up the stairs, taking two at a time.

Reinhardt was eating and reading at the same time, holding a slice of sausage, pinched between a greasy thumb and forefinger, in one hand, and a scrap of parchment in the other. Without looking up, he extended a leg and pushed a chair towards Büber. "Peter, what news from Ennsbruck?"

Büber sat in the chair. It felt almost odd to him. It wasn't a saddle and it wasn't a rock; pretty much the only two places his arse got to rest these days. Still reading, Reinhardt used the back of his hand to slide the plate of unsliced sausage across the table. "Help yourself."

His men would be eating. No reason for him not to. He cut off a round and popped it into his mouth, chewing slowly.

Reinhardt put the parchment down with a sigh. "We've trained another two centuries of spears, and two of bows. Juvavum wants to know if we need them or not." He pulled at his moustache before reaching behind him for a jug and two mugs.

It was expensive to keep an army in the field. Sometimes it was all but impossible. "How many have you got out at the moment?" asked Büber.

"Six hundred spears, four hundred bows, who can also use spears when they're called to. What cavalry I have is posted up near the dwarvish wall. Three centuries are at Kufstein, and I swap them over for fresh every couple of weeks. It gives them something to do, at least."

"My man reckons around ten to twelve thousand dwarves are now camped in and around Enn valley," said Büber. "There are more arriving from Farduzes every day."

Reinhardt poured both of them a mug of beer, and they drank in silence.

"That's a lot of dwarves," he said finally.

"They mean to attack. That's certain. They've built covered wagons by the dozen, and they're still building them. The forges of Ennsbruck are busy at any hour, and they're using the forest up at a fearsome rate." Büber rasped his stubble. "They have a plan and they're getting ready. It seems stupid just to sit around and wait until it's ripe."

"Yet if we were to spend our soldiers on raids across the wall, it would hurt us more than it would hurt them." Reinhardt, like Büber, was a veteran of Obernsberg and of Gerhard's funeral, and neither of them was under any illusion as to how green the new men were.

"My lot – though I could always do with more – could harry them," said Büber. "All their supplies are coming from Farduzes, and the road from there's long. They've no idea about growing crops or things like that. If we can just keep them bottled up until the winter snows come, we've won. They'll have to retreat. Look, we don't even have to win every battle, just the last one."

"Put it to Felix," said Reinhardt.

Büber leant across the table. He and Reinhardt both answered to the prince, but neither knew who was in charge out here. "I'm putting it to you. Thirty men, mounted, with crossbows and swords. We'd cause havoc."

"I'm not denying that it's an interesting idea, but . . ."

"We can't just sit here darning our socks until twenty thousand dwarves decide that they're ready. Gods, man. Attack them before that."

"Peter, what if you provoke them? What if they come across the wall early because of it?" Reinhardt flipped at Büber the piece of parchment he'd been reading, knowing full well that the huntmaster couldn't read. "We've got two thousand trained men, none of whom have been in a battle. We can dress another two, three thousand more with spears and tell them to stand there and look impressive. We can muster only a couple of dozen horse. We're less ready than the dwarves. All that we can hope for is that by the time they decide they're ready, we are too."

Büber threw himself back with a growl. "You didn't see them, working away, walking around like they own the place. They're cutting the trees down, Wolfgang. Clearing them completely. If they win, that's what they'll do to Carinthia."

"Then we have to be smart and not stupid. There are some things we can do now, things that'll buy us time to bring our forces up. See here." Reinhardt lifted up several sheets of paper on his desk, and slid a map out from underneath them.

It was crudely drawn, but it was accurate enough. There was the Enn valley, heading north-east, and doing a dog-leg when it reached Kufstein. It was incredibly narrow there, the mountains coming right down to the river's edge and permitting passage only on the eastern bank.

Beyond that, the valley broadened, splitting into two. One went downstream, due north, straight at Rosenheim. The other headed east, up various tributaries and thereafter becoming lost in a maze of spurs and cols.

"They have to get past Kufstein with their main group. Even if they try to flank it, gods, you know what it's like up there. Some of those tracks are barely wide enough for a goat. There's one bridge from one side of the river to the other. That's below where the old Roman fort used to be. It's only so many stones piled on top of one another now, but the earthworks are still there. I've strengthened them a bit, but what if we dug them out and built them up, put a palisade up and a parapet? We could make the river run red." Reinhardt stabbed the point with his finger. "They do bleed red, don't they?"

"Yes," said Büber. "As red as yours and mine. But why would they cross at the most obvious point? They could build a bridge of their own, further up, and come at Kufstein on the south bank, take it, and that would be that." They're dwarves, not idiots, he almost added.

"There's a river that comes down from the south here, just before Kufstein," said Reinhardt. "The . . ." – he squinted at the map – "Weissach. It cuts through the middle of two big hills, both heavily wooded. You could hide an army on them, and no one would know. If the dwarves sent a raiding party that way, we'd fall on them like wolves and push them into the river. If we were ready."

Büber pulled the map closer, and turned it so that he could look at it as if he was facing upstream. Reinhardt's idea wasn't as bad as he'd first thought.

"We could defend this," said Reinhardt. "Not easily, but it's better than meeting them out on the plain. A series of ditches and ramparts arranged across the valley floor. Spears and bows on each one, and we could retreat from one to the other as they pressed forward. We'd hold the high ground on both banks, and the bridge."

"We'd still be outnumbered," said Büber.

"If they come in the autumn, when we've trained everyone we can, it'll be two to one. If they come now, three, four, five or more to one." Reinhardt raised his eyebrows. "Pray to the gods they don't come now. If they knew how weak we are, they'd be all over us like the pox."

"I won't be telling them." Büber retrieved the note about the extra spear and bow centuries, and passed it back to Reinhardt. "Say yes to this. Tell them all to bring a shovel and a bucket. How far away is Kufstein from the Ziller?"

"Fifteen miles, and no line of sight." Reinhardt took the parchment, and placed it in front of him. "Do you know how to build ditches and walls?"

"No. No idea. We've never needed to do anything like this before."

"I'll get the prince to send some builders. I'm not looking for a palace, just something that'll get in the way of whatever the dwarves have planned for us." Reinhardt poured more beer from the jug into the two mugs. It was empty when he'd finished, and he put it behind him. "I'm fucking terrified of this. This whole thing. We've nothing in our favour, Peter, and everything against."

The grumbling in Büber's stomach had no cause in either the beer or the sausage: he had his own fears. "They have to come down the valley. I suppose if we can't choose when, we can choose where. The dwarves: they don't fight like they used to. They've grown lanky like us, ungainly and unbalanced, while our men know the length of their own arms." He scratched at his face again. "I'll give up any idea of harrying them, at least until the defences are dug."

"Yes, that's good." Reinhardt drained his beer. "Then would be the right time to poke them with a stick until they lash out. Make them angry and careless. I'd drink to that, but I seem to have finished mine already."

Büber raised his mug. "To Carinthia, then."

"And may we still have it come Yule." Reinhardt clanked his empty mug against Büber's full one. "I'll write my response. Tell me about these covered wagons."

"Not covered as a carter would do, to stop his load getting wet. Enclosed. A wood roof, and a prow, and a stern. Like an

upside-down boat, I suppose. Wheels. Big enough for ten at least."
Büber shrugged. "They looked heavy."

"Rams for the gates used to be covered with a roof. But they'd be left open at the sides." Reinhardt's hands wandered across the table, looking for his pen and ink. "I'll put it in. Whether your friend Thaler can make anything of it, I don't know."

Büber was done, and he walked back out into the night. The guard made a point of looking alert, which was something, thought Büber: it might even help to keep him and Reinhardt alive. The fields beyond Rosenheim were now covered in sparks of light and the ghosts of tents.

He should have been hungry and thirsty. A couple of weeks in the high mountains, eating only cold dry food and drinking nothing but stream water, should have given him an appetite for a good roast and some decent ale, followed up by sleeping warm and safe next to the fire.

All those things were already pale, and growing fainter by the day. The only experience which captured and held him was his rage. The prospect of – sword in hand – cutting at his enemies until his arm ached, until he was bloodied and bruised and still wanting more.

Everything else? He'd eat and drink when he needed to. Sleep when he had to. Ride and stalk, observe, command and report as necessary. But what he wanted, even as he feared it, was the hot rush of sweat as the change came over him.

He tramped through the perimeter of guards into the dispersed sea of tents, looking for his men. It was his duty to try and keep them alive, and it was their duty to do what they were told so that they didn't get themselves killed.

Also their duty not to piss off their commander by suggesting he's fucking the princess consort.

He found them eventually, and they made room for him within their circle, passing him the flask of schnapps that was doing the rounds. The fire in his mouth and belly was only temporary, and soon faded.

There were two chickens over the fire on a spit.

"So, will there be raiding?" asked one of his men.

"Yes," said Büber, "but later. Master Reinhardt has made the point that if we're too successful, the dwarves may decide they've nothing to lose by attacking early. Tell me whether you think this lot" – he jerked his head at the rest of the sprawling camp – "are capable of holding back ten thousand dwarves. No. We're going to dig in at Kufstein, and only then will we try to flush them out. Our hammer, Kufstein's anvil. If it works, we'll be heroes and our victory will be toasted for a thousand years."

"And if it doesn't?" The man tugged at his thick moustache. For Büber, who'd shaved, albeit sporadically and inexpertly, since his balls had dropped, this sudden fashion for facial hair in the style of their ancestors bemused him.

"I doubt there'll be anyone left to worry about that. Least of all us. We're the dogs who protect the sheep. We win or we die. That's what I expect from each and every one of you. The dwarves won't take your surrender, and gods protect you if you run." He took another nip of schnapps and passed the flask on. "Because, if you do that, I'll kill you myself."

81

Felix felt useless, despite all the things he managed to cram into a day. Perhaps his father had had days like this, when he was busy with trivia but not actually doing anything important. Perhaps his father's whole life had been like that, which was why he'd been so rash and thrown himself heedlessly into his first and last battle.

At the age of thirteen, Felix had seen more fighting than Gerhard ever had. Not that this was any great feat: Sophia had seen more fighting than Gerhard, too. Yet now, thought Felix, he had an army in the field – of sorts, anyway – but he wasn't at the head of it.

That's what princes of Carinthia were meant to do: they led their armies from the front, even if in the past that had always entailed simply standing by and letting the hexmasters blast the opposition with fire and ice, rock and wind, blinding lights and utter darkness. The prince led them out and brought them back.

The Armour of Carinthia had been charmed. No sword or axe could part its skin or its plates, and no arrow could pierce the shield – so he'd been told, though that had never been tested in anger until Gerhard had worn it to Obernberg. By then it had been too late, and it had been battered and broken under the blows of the Teutons. He had his own armour. It fitted, and he knew how to move in it. The Sword of Carinthia was a fraction too big for him, a little too heavy. He'd still carry it, though, and he'd use it as well.

Sophia wasn't going to like the idea. She kept him close. Tried to keep him safe, even. The fortress walls weren't a prison – except for, that is, the two spies from Simbach – but it was where he returned every day, no matter what he was doing elsewhere. He'd not seen Over-Carinthia, or Styria, or stood by the banks of the Donau to view the towers of Wien.

Ullmann assured him that everything was going well. His other army, the one with pens rather than spears, had calmly and efficiently divided up the land and made records of those divisions. They'd put mayors in place to run the towns and their surrounding farms, given the foresters the right to live in and off the forests forever. No one had complained, except those earls who'd survived or had inherited after Gerhard.

Felix had unashamedly bought them off. He had gold, and that was no use sitting there in a chest. Better to hand money out generously than grasp after every last copper, and it wasn't as if he lacked coin. The sheer amount of wealth that had poured out of the White Tower had astonished everyone. A suspicious man would have suspected the Order of keeping the palatinate just too poor to keep a standing army.

He called for his arms, and went to find Sophia.

She was on the Bell Tower, staring out over Juvavum, and specifically at the field across the river where Master Thaler was conducting his tests. Her father was there, of course, and the elf, and the growling, angry smith from Simbach.

A pall of smoke hung low over the river, drifting idly towards the quays. Felix had had complaints about the smell, not least from the Frank Vulfar, whose boatyards were on the opposite bank. The last time he'd been down to inspect the bones of the barges he made, the whole place had stunk of boiling pitch. Any alchemical odours were merely notes to its overpowering bouquet.

"He used to be so passionate about books," she said.

Felix wasn't sure whether she meant Thaler or her father. At least they were doing something. Making holes in the ground and creating a lot of noise, perhaps, but they were so incredibly keen in the way they went about it. He couldn't quite see what they were currently up to, and he'd left his distance-pipe back in the solar, but they seemed to be busy arranging ribbon-decked poles at various distances from a rampart of earth.

"They still are. They just know that when war comes, pleasures are put aside for a season."

When she looked down at him, it was with that expression of hers. "Those are Frederik's words, not yours."

"Yes. Well. He's right, though." He blushed a little at being so easily caught out. "And they have such . . ."

"Promise?" she finished for him. "That's his word, too. Now is not the time for weapons that we don't know will work. Spears and bows, cavalry and swords. If he wants to spend his time building machines, why doesn't he make siege engines we know will work: scorpions and ballistae, mangonels even?"

"Because we don't know how to make those things either, and it's not like we're besieging anything. We'd have to hire Byzantine or Italian engineers, and . . . Oh, let Master Thaler be, Sophia. He's a good man trying to do his best for me." He leant over the parapet and looked down at the town. Everyone appeared properly busy, with not an idle hand in sight. "Master Thaler reminds everyone who thinks that war is far away and may never happen, that it's real and it's here."

The smoke had dispersed, and the poles had all been poked upright into the ground, ribbons fluttering. The tiny figures had retreated back to the maze of sacking screens and rough sheds, and appeared to be waiting. The only activity came from around the mound of packed earth.

Sophia turned her back on the town and looked to the mountains. "And we're absolutely certain the dwarves don't . . .?"

"So says Master Thaler. He supposes powder weapons are worse than useless underground. For the same reasons they don't ride, and don't use bows. We wouldn't have Master Büber with us if they did either." There was no point in putting it off any longer. "I want to go to Rosenheim," he said.

"That's a good idea," she said, after a moment's reflection.

"I . . . yes. I thought so too."

"Did you expect an argument?" She wore a smile. "A prince should be with his army."

"Yes. He should." Was he missing something? "I thought I could go with Master Reinhardt's reinforcements."

"And their spades."

"I could be there in two days, and nothing will happen to me on the way."

"I know," she said. "Go, with my blessing. Talk to Peter Büber and Wolfgang Reinhardt, inspect the troops, and don't interfere. Spend a few days with them and then come back."

Thunder rolled across the river again, and a fresh cloud of smoke was billowing into the air. Felix squinted at the field, and couldn't make out anything different.

"I'll go and get ready then." He was discomforted. "Are you sure?"

"Felix. You're thirteen now. You're the Prince of Carinthia, and I have to stop mothering you. At least, that's what my father says. 'Don't mother the boy', he tells me, 'or he'll grow up farmisht.'" She tilted her face to the sun. "We can't have you growing up farmisht, can we?"

"No," said Felix with absolute certainty. "No, we can't. It'll take a day to get everyone and everything together. I'll leave tomorrow."

"Then go. Lots to do." She dragged him in and hugged him tight enough to leave him breathless and not a little dizzy, then released him, almost pushing him away.

With a last glance at Thaler's proving ground, he went to ready himself. He'd need his armour and his sword, and a horse, and . . . what? What had his father taken with him? A tent. Servants. Food and drink. He had no idea how any of this worked. Trommler would have done: he knew everything that a prince had to do. For Felix, having to make it up as he went along was fantastically wearing.

There were a few people he could ask. The centurions, for a start, who were camped out to the west of the town wall with their men. He strapped on his sword and rode through the streets to find them.

The townsfolk stopped and stood aside as he passed. They greeted him respectfully, offering up comments like "fine day, my lord", and "make way for the prince". Some rulers, like the false earl of Simbach, needed to assemble a guard before they stepped from their keep. The prince of Carinthia didn't, and that was the difference between them.

No doubt, Master Ullmann would have raised his eyebrows and insisted that he was protected by his recently formed Black Company: men he'd drawn from the library ushers and elsewhere, and formed into a guard. Instead, the townsfolk were his guard, and they were everywhere.

He rode out of the gate and across the fields to the camp, and arranged with the centurions to travel with them to Rosenheim. Nothing was, apparently, going to be too much trouble. They would make sure that he'd be provided for: a tent of his own, a groom from amongst the men, his own cook.

Felix had been grooming his own horse since he'd been first able to ride, and more often than not, he'd eat kosher with Sophia and fill up on a variety of cooked pig products when she wasn't around. He agreed to the tent, and refused the rest. He'd eat with the men, whatever the men would be eating, and if they'd room for his kit on one of the wagons, then he'd not have to ride all the way in full armour.

He found himself winning their approval and respect, only recognising that as he rode away. Perhaps it would work out after all, small as he was. His father and the earls had ridden to war with great tents and banners and squires and servants. Felix would do it with as little fuss as he could manage.

And while he was out and day not yet over, he thought he might see what all that noise from Master Thaler had been about. He rode back along the quayside, past the first of Vulfar's new barges tied up beside it – smaller, narrower, pointed at both ends – and across the bridge.

The White Tower glistened in the sunlight above him. The tunnels beneath it had been mostly emptied, but even the most experienced of miners quailed at the prospect of exploring the few that went deeper.

Why didn't the stupid thing fall? The magic had gone, and still it remained. Oh, he knew the explanation, that people still believed in it. If only they didn't, it would be gone rather than looming over the town like some scabrous finger.

Then there was the bridge itself, from which he'd thrown the torch to light his father's funeral barge, and over which his ever-loving people had stampeded to see Eckhardt's brilliant light. They'd killed half his guard, his stepmother, half-brothers and sisters, together with Trommler and those few earls he'd had left.

That soured him. Perhaps Ullmann was right to be suspicious: while the gold was flowing and fresh marvels were coming out of the library seemingly every day, he was "Good Prince Felix", but he'd already seen what would happen if times turned difficult. He'd be bundled head-first into a sack and carried away for sacrifice.

He hoped those weren't the only two options open to princes.

By the time he arrived on the practice field, they were setting up again. Men and women were wrestling with the ribboned poles – paired up this time with a screen of sacking between them – taking them up the pasture towards the edge of the forest.

Sitting at a table, Aaron Morgenstern was engrossed in his calculations, clicking the beads across an abacus with practised agility and occasionally peering at a finely written table in a book. Thaler was at his side, writing down numbers, and Mistress Tuomanen was bringing a charge of powder out from behind one of the screens.

"Good afternoon, my lord," she said, loud enough to alert Thaler, but not the deafer Morgenstern. He started to badger Thaler for the next part of the sum.

Thaler tapped Morgenstern's arm and raised himself from his stool. "Ah, my lord. Welcome again. We are, as you can see, working for the safety and success of the palatinate as diligently as we know how."

Felix leant onto the pommel. "I've talked to Sophia, Master Thaler. She may leave you alone now, at least for a while."

"Right," said the librarian, and looked momentarily perplexed. Felix hadn't been the only one expecting to have an argument. "Is my lord wishing to see anything in particular?"

"No. I'm going with three centuries to Rosenheim tomorrow. I just wanted to tell you to keep up the good work, and that I'll see how you're doing when I get back." Felix glanced over to the earth rampart. There was a long black cylinder embedded in the packed soil. "That's interesting, Master Thaler. I haven't seen that design before."

For a moment, it looked as if Thaler was going to stand in front of it, spread his gown out and deny all knowledge of its existence. "Yes," he finally said. "Bastian has gone off on a frolic of his own, it seems."

Felix narrowed his eyes, and slipped from the saddle for a closer look. He kicked the iron tube and peered down its muzzle. "What happened to your pots?"

"They're all very well, thank you, my lord." Thaler turned to watch those down-range start setting up the poles, hammering them into the ground with mallets. "I . . ."

"What is it, Master Thaler?" Felix followed his gaze. "Those last few markers are a very long way away."

"Yes, my lord. Yes they are. I just hope they're far enough. We, er . . . we lost the last ball." He looked about him with mild embarrassment.

"Lost it, Master Thaler? Where?"

"Either it disintegrated with the force of the explosion, or it travelled into the forest. We've adjusted the elevation down, and erected those screens to help us find it this time."

Felix shielded his eyes and tried to judge the distance to the trees. "That's . . ."

"Five stadia. And thirty-two feet." Thaler pursed his lips and sucked in air. "I don't quite know what to make of it. We searched, but couldn't find it."

"Five stadia. Gods, Master Thaler!"

Thaler shrugged. "My lord is welcome to stay and watch us lose another."

One of Thaler's crew had a builder's level, and was tamping extra earth under the back of the iron tube. "It's now horizontal," he said, "as near as I can make it."

"Right. Positions, everyone. Powder team advance. My lord, it would be best if your horse went elsewhere. From bitter experience, we've found that they don't like the noise." Thaler waved at one of his pole team. "Gertrude, please be so good as to take my lord's horse to the back of hut four."

That seen to, the powder team pushed a measured charge of powder, sewn into a cloth bag, into the muzzle, and rammed it to the back of the closed pipe with a wooden tamper. An iron ball was rolled in after it, and then a circle of felt.

They retreated and Thaler ordered his firing team into position. One man poked a slender wire into the thin hole in the top of the weapon, a second filled the hole with loose powder, and a wooden tube was screwed into place on top of that.

"Ready."

"My lord. This might be slightly undignified, but if you care to join us in the trench, we can commence."

"Trench?"

Thaler indicated the way, behind a set of screens. The trench was four feet deep, and wide enough to crouch in, but with all of them packed into it, it was a tight fit. The final two in removed the front screen, and jumped down, leaving only Mistress Tuomanen by the rampart.

"Why are we in a trench, Master Thaler?"

Thaler coughed. "The device might shatter, and send shards of red-hot metal in all directions. Bastian assures me that using bronze will solve that problem, but the castings aren't yet cool. I wouldn't want to be responsible for the deaths of any of my warband, nor of my prince: hence the trench. The pots are much thicker, and the shorter barrel confines the hot gases for much less time. No problem there. No problem at all."

Felix blinked. "How dangerous is this, Master Thaler?"

"To us? Hardly at all. What we're trying to quantify is how dangerous it might be to those on the receiving end." He raised his hand. "Ready for firing, Mistress?"

She held up one of the slow matches, smoke idly curling from its end. "Ready for firing."

"Firing now."

"Firing," she said, and applied the match to the end of the fuse, making sure it had caught. "Now."

She ran, covering the distance in no time at all, and dropped into the space on Thaler's right, between him and Aaron Morgenstern.

Everybody ducked, except Felix; Thaler pressed his hand on the prince's head and pushed it down.

When it came, the sound was incredible. Felix felt rather than heard it, the ground jerking as though it had been struck. Little motes of dust leapt from the wall of the trench, and hung in the air, frozen.

Then the smoke roiled back in a thick white cloud. It drifted over them, and it was safe to look up again.

The first screen had gone. Burning tatters of cloth hung on each of the supporting poles. The second, a hundred feet further on, was still on fire, with thick orange flames busily consuming the sacking, which had been torn in two. The third was leaning drunkenly at an angle, and there was smoke rising from just behind it.

Felix clambered out, as did Mistress Tuomanen. While he stared, she pulled Thaler and Morgenstern from the trench with practised ease, and a team went over to inspect the still-smoking pipe, douse it with water, and rake out the soot from its insides.

"That settles that, then," said Thaler, wiping the soil of the trench off his gown. "The ball didn't fall apart. Call it three hundred and twenty feet, at no elevation. Aaron, the calculations, if you please?"

Morgenstern went back to his table and his books as if nothing out of the ordinary had happened, but Felix caught Thaler by the arm and wouldn't let go.

"What did I just see?"

"Well, it's all very simple," said Thaler. "If we know how fast the ball leaves the barrel, we can work out its range. By placing the device on a mound of earth of a known height, we know how long the ball takes to fall to the ground."

"You do?"

"Most certainly. From there we can derive its maximum theoretical range, and, more importantly, the range at a given angle. The real range won't be anything like that, of course, because of the resistance of the air and other factors. We shall, however, attempt to work out those equations at a later date. Aaron?"

"Two and a half miles," said Morgenstern, still scribbling feverishly. "And for a ten-degree elevation." He paused, then finished, "Seven and a half stadia. Roughly."

"Which would explain why we never found the first ball." Thaler raised his voice and clapped his hands. "Thank you everyone. Let's get ready to go again shortly."

They dispersed to their own work, leaving Felix with Thaler. "Are you saying you could hit the fortress from here?"

Thaler judged the distance, then nodded. "Yes. Not accurately, perhaps, but there's a lot of fortress to hit."

"Gods," said Felix. He let go of Thaler's arm, and found himself adding, "Carry on, Master Thaler. Carry on."

82

Saying goodbye to Felix gave Sophia an odd feeling. She knew it needed to be done, though. It was important for the people to see their prince and understand that he made his own decisions – and the townsfolk seemed to approve, as reported by Master Ullmann. All well and good. It wasn't as if she didn't have plenty to do: her role as princess consort was ill-defined, but she very much doubted that other princesses had to school spearmen or debate tactics with their centurions.

She realised that her fear was neither right nor reasonable, which then made her feel stupid. Still, the dragging tension in her stomach made a lie of her open smile and warm words.

"I'll be back by midweek," he said, patting his horse's neck as it stamped at the road.

"I know. Make sure they look after you. No wild hunts or bragging contests."

His shoulder had healed: the ends of the collar-bones had knit together well, leaving only a knot beneath the skin.

She rubbed her thumb through his shirt along the line of it, silently reminding him of the day he'd broken it.

She looked around at the men he'd be marching with. Not quite raw recruits, but untested even with shovels, let alone spears. Battle-ready all the same, and road-ready too. The carts had been loaded up, and the bullocks tied into their yokes. The centurions were waiting with their men, and family members stood in a group by the side of the western gate.

All they were waiting for was for her to finish flapping at the prince.

"My lord," she said, and stepped back.

Felix put his foot in the stirrup and swung himself into his saddle, making what Sophia still found difficult look so very easy. He smiled down at her, and she forced herself to smile back up.

He had nearly three hundred men behind him and the Sword of Carinthia at his side. And still she worried.

Felix walked his horse to the front of the column, raised his hand, and set off down the road. The men's kin clapped and cheered, shouting for their gods to take care of their fathers, brothers, sons. She couldn't do the same, of course. Her God was not theirs. There would be earnest prayers tonight from her to Elohey Tzevaot, the Lord of Hosts, but nothing in public, nothing to make the good folk of Juvavum think that Felix had converted.

The soldiers marched away, three yellow standards bearing the black Carinthian leopard twisting in the wind, a haze of dust kicked up by their feet. The crowd had started to disperse – the Germans were an unsentimental people compared to hers – but some lingered: two children, staring down the road, an old man leaning on his stick and letting the crush clear from the gate, and a woman who she recognised.

Sophia had dressed in finery, rather than clothes that allowed her to swing her sword, so, when the woman finally turned and stepped under the shadow of the gate, she had to pick up her skirts in order to hurry after her.

"Mistress," called Sophia. "Wait."

The woman looked around. Yes, it was as Sophia had thought: she'd spotted this woman and Ullmann together while on her way to the mikveh a day or so before.

"My lady," said the woman. She was younger than Sophia, with a strong face and bright eyes.

"You've someone among the soldiers?" asked Sophia.

"My brother. He carries a spear, and hopefully knows how to use it too." She frowned. "Can I do something for you, my lady?"

She had no qualms about being direct. Some would bow and stutter, and rather than finding it amusing, Sophia would be sad since she was only Aaron Morgenstern's girl from Jews' Alley, and no better or worse than anyone else.

"You can tell me your name, Mistress."

"Aelinn, my lady. Maid to the Odenwalds, in the main square."

She knew the Odenwalds. Not great readers. "If I said 'Max Ullmann' to you, would you know what it was I wanted to talk to you about?"

Now Aelinn looked anywhere but Sophia. "Whatever my lady wants to discuss."

"Walk with me, then," said Sophia.

"My lady, I'd . . . the Black Company are everywhere. If I'm seen with you, Max will want to know what we talked about."

"Not through the town then. Outside the walls. Up the hill and into the woods, where there's no one to spy on us." She didn't want to take no for an answer, but she couldn't force Aelinn to come with her. Or rather she could, but it was doubtful she'd hear the truth if she did.

"I have to be back to prepare lunch," the woman said, then finally nodded.

Sophia, in her stiff skirts and tight bodice, found the climb difficult. The path was narrow and not often used, while summer's growth pressed in around her. Her own maid would look later at the ticks and catches in the fine cloth and despair.

Even though they were quickly hidden, Sophia had the urge to keep climbing, and Aelinn dutifully followed. Near the top was a clearing, bright with sunlight and flowers, and a fallen tree made a good bench. She sat down, facing the sun, and Aelinn sat hesitantly next to her.

"My lady," she started.

"You're allowed to call me Sophia. Or Mistress Morgenstern if you feel you absolutely have to."

"Yes, Mistress."

This wasn't going well. "Aelinn, you're not in trouble. No one's hauling you off to the Hare Tower. I – both me and Felix – want to know why Master Ullmann hasn't mentioned you to us at all. We're going to ask him, of course, but seeing you today, I thought I'd ask first. You are . . ." – and she realised she didn't have the language for it; German etiquette was very different to Jewish – "seeing each other?"

"We see each other often, Mistress." She looked at her shoes. "I don't think that's what you mean, though."

"Do you take him into your bed?"

"Yes, Mistress. And I go into his, too."

"You saved him from a beating and worse at the hands of the Simbach spies. That was, what: three, four months ago? And you've been seeing him since?"

"Yes, Mistress." She swallowed. She knew what question was coming next, and so did Sophia. She was going to ask it anyway.

"You haven't got two heads, Aelinn. Why hasn't he asked to marry you?"

She stayed silent for a while, then gave a little grunt. "He has. More than once."

"But you said no. And you keep on saying no." Sophia laced her fingers in front of her and squeezed her hands together. They were callused. They'd always been callused, but now the calluses were in different places than previously from horse-riding and sword-fighting. "Why? You don't have to answer, but I am interested."

Aelinn was quiet again. "Mistress, it's not that I don't love him. I do: he's funny, and clever, and kind. He treats me right, never a harsh word, and he's a good-looking boy, too. Strong, and brave with it. And some men only think about themselves, in and out of bed, but he's not like that."

"He sounds perfect, Aelinn. He's very diligent in his work, as well; always looking ahead to see what needs to be done, rather than simply reacting to events. The palatinate is very lucky to have someone like him as a prince's man." Sophia cracked her knuckles. The noise startled her, and she put her hands firmly down by her side. "Is it what he does for the prince that's putting you off?"

"No, not at all. He's even suggested to me that I should become a spy too. I have my wilder moments, but I'm not a very good liar. A spy for the prince needs to be that."

"Yes, you're right. But not *to* his prince. So, is it your parents?" Sophia knew that there was very little in law or custom that that might mean a girl's father could reasonably object to a marriage, above the weight of his words.

"It's not that." Aelinn put her head back and groaned at the sky. "My mother told me never to marry a man who didn't sleep well at night."

Sophia almost fell off the tree-trunk. "That . . . is a strange reason."

"Yes," said Aelinn pointedly. "I know. But that was what she said when I was young, and it's stayed with me. Max, he doesn't sleep well at all."

"Is it that he doesn't sleep, or that he does?"

"He sleeps, and he dreams. They're not good dreams, Mistress. If there was still magic, I'd call him hag-ridden and have him make sacrifices at the irminsul in order to drive it off." Aelinn lowered her head. "He moans and talks, and then, just before he wakes, he screams. It's . . ."

"Disconcerting?"

"More than that. I calm and comfort him, but he's scared to death in those first few moments. He clings to me. Then it's over, and he's back to his normal self again." She turned to Sophia. "It's not all the time, but it's often enough that I wonder what he saw, what he did, to give himself such terrors. He won't talk about it to me, denies he ever has them. Do you see, Mistress, why I won't consent to the handfasting?"

"Yes, I see. And I'm sorry I ever intruded. This isn't really anything to do with me: I thought I might help Felix, but all I've done is embarrass you."

"No, no, Mistress. It's a relief to finally tell someone. Even if it is the prince's consort." She made a face that suggested she wished it had been anyone else but her.

"What does he cry out?" Sophia blurted out. "What's he so afraid of?"

"Fire, Mistress. It's always fire." Aelinn shrugged. "I don't know why, because he hasn't got a mark on his body except for a few tiny ones on his chest, and he's not scared of flames in the hearth."

"Just in his dreams," Sophia said. She picked at the bark beneath her fingers. It peeled off easily in thick flakes, and beneath were a myriad of tiny crawling creatures. "These marks . . ."

"Just little silvery patches of skin. I asked about them, but he said he'd been born with them. Five there are, one for each finger." She stopped and blushed deeply.

"I've kept you long enough, Aelinn. You should go, before anyone misses you. And if, at any point, you want Master Ullmann to leave you alone, I find myself not without influence."

"Thank you, Mistress."

"That goes for any of the prince's men, or any of mine, for that matter. I won't have them abusing their positions for any reason. One last thing: can you read, Aelinn?"

"A little," she said, pushing herself up and away from the tree-trunk. "Enough to tell who a message is meant for."

"You should learn. Master Thaler's school shouldn't be just for the children."

"Perhaps, Mistress." Aelinn batted at her clothes to remove most of the lichen and wood fragments. "I'll be off, with your permission."

"You're freer than I am, and you don't need my permission." All the same, she nodded at the maid, and watched her leave the clearing, early summer seed-heads clinging to the swish of her skirt.

Their words concerning marriage set Sophia thinking about the possibility of her own, and the complications that might arise.

When – if – she and Felix married, and no matter what tradition said about his age, he was still a boy, their children would be Jews. So said the Mishnah. And she would raise them as Jews, meaning that, in time, a Jewish boy would inherit the throne of Carinthia. And then, this Jewish boy, this son of hers, would look down from the fortress wall, as she had so often done, and see the tops of the circle of trees in the town square, and the irminsul rising at their centre.

What would he do? Would he tolerate these northern gods, and bow his head to them as necessary? Or would he have the trees and the pole cut down and burnt, and in their place build a temple of white stone and a gold roof to rival Solomon's?

Would her own people accept him, or reject him as a mamzer? He could end up hated by both the Germans and the Jews.

It might be better for everyone if she simply slipped away in a year or two's time to somewhere well outside of Carinthia's reach and Felix's ability to call her back. Alexandria even, where there were both Jews and a library.

A Jewish queen anywhere was an anomaly. A Jewish prince anywhere but Jerusalem was unthinkable, and the Byzantines, Egyptians and Persians seemed to take it in turns to stir the rubble of that great city on a yearly basis.

Better that Felix should wed someone like Aelinn than someone like her. Doctor Kuppenheim was right: she should find some nice Jewish boy. Except, except.

And then she remembered what it was that had been bothering her all the while she'd been descending into self-doubt and pity. She had an idea where Max Ullmann might have encountered fire strong enough to breed such fear.

83

"We should still destroy the bridge," said Reinhardt.

"But your plan requires that it remains standing so that we can retreat across it." Büber leant on his shovel for a moment's rest, while those around him dug and threw, dug and threw, in time to the slowed-down chorus of "The Rheinmaid's Daughter".

When they'd started that morning, they'd sung lustily and wielded their spades enthusiastically, but, despite regular breaks and a long rest at midday, they now worked with a dull monotony that spoke of exhaustion.

He turned back to his part of the earthwork. The task was simple enough: dig a ditch and use the soil as a rampart. The deeper the ditch, the higher the rise, which was why he was standing ankle-deep in a pool of water. It hadn't rained for two, three weeks, but this close to the river, the ground below was saturated.

On the finished part of the wall, men were tamping the lee side of the earth ridge with planks. They stamped in time with the singing, their weary feet driving the tune slower with each repeat.

Büber dug down into the watery sludge, loosened the soil, then flung it at the crest. Some of it ran down again, splashing in the puddle. The rampart was as high as it was going to go, and it was time to move on; he found another place in the line, close to the crag of Kufstein itself.

The ground here was untouched. He looked across to his left to make sure of his mark. Then, he put his boot on the shovel, and turned the first sod.

The singing was a necessary distraction, but he could have done without the talking. Everyone knew what needed to be done that day. Perhaps tomorrow, they'd do something different – make stakes and build walls of stone. The day after that, there'd be more digging for certain.

Reinhardt followed him up the ditch. His shovel was barely used, his boots free of sticky mud and trampled grass.

"If you've come to bend my ear again, direct some of that effort into spadework. If you've breath enough to talk, at least dig at the same time." Büber fell into the rhythm: thrust, lift, throw, return.

"We're done with that, Peter. You're as stubborn as the mountains themselves." Reinhardt plunged his shovel into the soft ground. "Just tell me that you'll keep the bridge in mind, if it comes to it."

"I don't know *why* Felix decided to put me in charge all of a sudden; just that he did. It's not as if I know more about battles than you do." There was rock a spade-length down, and Büber's foot now ached with the jarring impact. He took a step back to dig a fresh patch of earth. "But it was your plan we agreed on, and it's a little late to change it now. We've more than enough work for all of us."

There was. While a century toiled east of the river, there was another on the west, digging across from the hill that the locals called Zellerberg towards the valley-side. The ground was marshy there, and the ditch was forming quickly. The embankment was more disappointing, but it couldn't be helped: the men building it were amateurs, and had no expectation of being fêted for their siegeworks. Another group was piling stones on top of each other at the top of the col, making a barrier that they could use both to hide behind and to sortie from.

On Kufstein itself, walls were being built up and rammed with earth. The Romans had built defences here, but they were a thousand years in their graves, and the tower was now little more than a ring of soil on top of an isolated rock. There was no time to build a new stone structure, but the crag still managed to dominate the bridge crossing, and importantly it was within bow-shot of it.

The picket line up near the Ziller hadn't seen any dwarves beyond their valley-spanning fence. Büber's scouts patrolling the neighbouring peaks reported there'd been no attempts at infiltrating. It seemed the height of arrogance, over-confidence and complacency for the dwarves not to have at least tried to see what the humans were up to. Yet their very failure to do so concerned Büber more than if there'd been a flood of spies.

He worked himself hard, on the premise that men far younger and with more fingers than him would be shamed into putting in as much effort. He grew tired and sore and sweaty and dirty. He forgot, for a while.

The sun slid around in the sky, and as it dipped below the first distant mountain peak, he called for the horn to sound. There was plenty of daylight left, but there were tents to pitch, firewood to gather and meals to cook. And gods, his bones ached.

Upstream of Kufstein was a sandbank, where the Weissach joined the Enn, and Büber made his way there, pulling off his clothing as he walked. By the time he reached the grey shingle slope, he had only his breeks left on. He dropped his boots and waded in, still holding his shirt and necker. The water was cold, though not cold enough to take toes as it had been in spring. When he'd reached waist-deep, he ducked down and let the water flow over and through him.

He opened his eyes. Everything was green and glassy. Light flashed bright on the surface above his head, and the riverbed as dappled as a forest floor. Silver fish scattered from him like birds, and fronds of weed danced in the wind above.

He rose with a shout, and started back to shore.

There was a man on a horse watching him. Büber wiped at his face with his clothes. No, not a man. Not yet.

"My lord," said Büber. "If I'd known you were joining us, I'd have found something more suitable to wear."

Felix, leaning over the front of his saddle, grinned. "I'll take honest sweat over Byzantine robes, Master Büber."

"Have you brought more men?"

"Three centuries. I left them at Rosenheim – they walked while I rode. There was time enough for me to get here, but not them."

"As long as we have them in the morning." Büber wrung out his shirt and used it to dry his hair. "Did they bring shovels?"

"By the cart-load. Good iron ones, too." Felix's horse seemed interested in the water. The prince dismounted and led it down, where it dipped its head and drank deep. "Did Master Reinhardt mind that I put you over him."

"Mind? I think he'll get over the disappointment, and I still haven't managed the trick of being in two places at once." He squeezed his shirt out again and struggled into it, covering up his scars. "He'll have plenty to be in charge of, and once the battle starts? I don't know of any plan that survives meeting the enemy."

"I wanted someone who knows what fighting dwarves is like," said Felix, his hand on his horse's bridle. "That's why I chose you. Master Reinhardt's a good man, but—"

"I know why, my lord." Büber tied his necker back on. "But we were both at Obernberg." He looked away. He would have to go and remember it all over again, wouldn't he?

"And you've done more than that, Master Büber: giants and monsters, too. Sometimes I think you're the only veteran we have." Felix pulled at the horse's reins, and led him round in a broad circle.

Büber carried his boots to the bank and sat on the grass, pulling them on. "We're unprepared for war. I can't deny that. So are they. Some battle-hardened soldiers wouldn't go amiss, though. If the people of Augsburg and München decided that fighting each other was mad and threw their lot in with us, I'd be a happier man."

"We've asked. We haven't had a reply from either side yet."

"A shame." Büber stamped his feet. "We're stretched thin."

"I know."

They both turned to look up the valley.

"Another month, or two," said Felix. "It'd make all the difference."

"Half these men are farmers or their sons. They'll be needed to get the crops in before the snows come. But if Ironmaker waits that long, he runs the risk of getting snowed in himself, no matter if we've made harvest home or not. No," said Büber, "he'll attack sooner than that."

"I read your report—"

"Reinhardt's report," said Büber.

"Your words, his pen. These carts of theirs. I'd like to see them for myself."

Now he was washed and wet, Büber felt the need for a fire and some food. With the sun occluded, the summer air was cooling down. He suppressed a shiver.

"It's a dangerous journey, my lord. They're on the south side of the town and there's no easy approach. You have to get right down into the valley, and that's full of dwarves."

"You're trying to put me off, Master Büber."

"I'm not going to lead my lord prince into the heart of the enemy's camp unless there's a very good reason for doing so. Sightseeing isn't a good reason." He kicked at a stone. "I didn't fight shoulder to shoulder with you at the library just so I could watch you throw your life away on a whim later."

That should have settled matters, but Felix still glanced up towards the dwarvish wall, hidden by distance, shadows and trees.

Büber shrugged. "We'll talk about it over dinner, such as it is."

Kufstein didn't have gates. It didn't even have a proper wall yet to fix them to. Büber showed Felix what the defences would look like when they'd finished; the earth ramparts, fronted by a palisade, which would command both banks of the river as well as the bridge. From the edge of the crag, he pointed down the river bank at the ditch they'd dug, and, a stadia further inland, where the next one would go.

Across the water were more works, all designed to keep the dwarves bottled up within range of their bows. The longer they had, the more defences they could build.

"I'd rather attack," said Büber. "Wolfgang's persuaded me not to, but I don't know that he's right. The dwarves' supply route's stretched tighter than a lyre string, but no one's strumming our tune on it."

"If you want me to take your side, you'll have to at least take me as far as the wall tomorrow."

"That might be possible." Büber worried at a knuckle. "My lord, you don't need me to remind you that you're the last of your line."

Felix turned away and looked at the scattering of tents and fires thrown up on the meadows below. "If something were to happen to me, then you'd choose another prince among those worthy of the honour, like in Alaric's time. It hasn't always been father-to-son, and there's no reason why it should be. For all I know, my sons might be idiots."

"I'd have to explain to Sophia how I lost you. That would be difficult." Talking about death and succession was difficult too. "I intend for you to live through this battle, this war."

"I don't intend to die, Master Büber. If we can manage that, and turn the dwarves back, then it'll be a job well done." When he turned away, he looked like his mother, just for a moment.

It had been thirteen years since the Order had killed Emma. Gods, she'd been dark and beautiful; he'd found himself almost incapable of speech the few times she'd talked to him. Thirteen years ago, Büber had been in his wild youth, leaping from mountain to mountain as though he had wings, running through the forests and diving into the lakes without pause or heed.

Now, this was her son, almost grown, and he was a man in charge of the prince's army

"Master Büber?"

"My lord. Lost in the past for a moment."

"We need you in the present. If you can see into the future, all the better."

They left the Kufstein crag and walked among the tents for a while, and Büber could see the effect that Felix's presence had on the men. Whether Gerhard would have inspired them the same way was moot: he'd had one battle to fight, and had lost it.

Büber was chilled inside and out by the time they found Reinhardt's fire. Even while they sat around a pile of burning wood, eating mutton stew and discussing the best way to skin a rabbit, he thought they should be out there, digging by torch-light and praying to gods seemingly both deaf and blind that dawn would not reveal their inadequacies.

The sun would rise all the same: the dwarves would swarm out and overwhelm them. Carinthia would be broken, and its army swept away.

He found he'd lost his appetite, but shovelled in the food all the same. The beer tasted like piss, but he swallowed.

The problem was this: the prince of Carinthia had come to lead his troops.

No matter that Felix was due to go back to Juvavum in a few days, that there was no reason for an attack tomorrow – nothing to separate it from yesterday or the day after. They might even get the couple of month's respite they wanted.

But the Prince of Carinthia had come to Kufstein. This was Fate. The Norns had spun their wyrd from before they were born, and the ends unravelled here.

Their only hope was that with the passing of magic, what might have been certain was no longer necessarily so. Their destiny was in their own hands. Büber realised with a snort that if there were any gods left, then he'd spit in their faces and defy them to do their worst.

"What's so amusing, Master Büber?" asked Reinhardt.

"Nothing. Just an idle thought."

His head came up, and with it, the bottle he held in his hand. "To Carinthia," he said. "And victory."

84

It was always coldest just before dawn, and Felix had shivered himself awake under a pile of blankets. As he lay there, staring up at the white canvas rippling lazily above his head, he listened to the sounds around him: the creak and stretch of ropes, the distant coughing of men and barking of dogs, and, closer, someone snoring as if they were sawing logs in their sleep.

He absorbed the sounds; the last time he'd lain like that, not quite warm enough to go back to sleep, pale light leaking in through a pale ceiling, had been the night before Obernberg.

There were voices, low and muttered, indistinct, whispered almost. There were guards outside his tent – Reinhardt had insisted on that, stating baldly that being gutted from neck to navel by the Lady Sophia wasn't his preferred method of passing to the afterlife.

What Felix was hearing wasn't the exchange of conversation between two men passing the time. He stretched and stirred, poked his head out of the flap, then emerged, his bare feet chill on the dew-drenched grass. He reached back in and grabbed a blanket to wrap around himself.

The guards had gone. In their place was Peter Büber, hooded in his cloak, talking to a sweaty-faced man in a mail shirt.

"Master Büber?"

Büber stiffened, and looked askance at Felix. Then he nodded at the other man, who turned and ran back through the still-quiet camp.

"My lord. You're up." The toes of Büber's boots were already dark with water.

"There's something wrong?"

"Wrong? No. Entirely expected. The dwarvish wall, it appears, has gates. Those gates are now open."

"Are we under attack?" Felix felt his heart beat hard under his shirt.

"It's twenty miles to the Ziller. We have at least the rest of today. I'd rather everyone was rested before we see what defences we can strengthen in the time we have left, than rouse the camp and have them work without breakfast." Büber adjusted the strap on his swordbelt. "We have pickets who'll tell us where the dwarves are."

"You're riding out to see, though."

"Yes, my lord."

"I'll come with you." Before the huntmaster could say yes or no, Felix darted back into his tent. He threw the blanket aside and started to dress in his damp, cold, day clothes. There was only enough room in his simple ridge tent to sit and kneel, not to stand, but he still managed to tie and tuck himself in quickly enough. "Master Büber?"

"My lord?" came the voice.

"Are we expecting to fight?"

"My lord, if you're asking me whether you should plate up, then the answer is ten thousand times yes."

Gods, that made his heart beat all the faster. At Obernberg, he hadn't known what to expect. It had been thrilling, the fear of the unknown, the fear of soiling his breeks at the first sight of the enemy. Now he knew, and his courage was as small as his stature.

I am the Prince of Carinthia. I am thirteen. I have a hundred good people who could lead the palatinate after me.

He picked up the Sword of Carinthia and ducked back out of the tent.

His armour was hanging from a mannequin under an oilskin. He pulled off the cover under Büber's watchful gaze, then lifted the harness off the wooden shoulders and onto his own. There were straps and buckles, which his tremulous fingers made hard work of fastening. The sword went into his belt and the shield onto his arm.

Büber lifted the pot helmet off the mannequin's head and dropped it on Felix's. It went snug over his ears, the padding gripping him in an unfamiliar embrace.

"Most lords couldn't dress themselves in breeks and shirt, let alone their own plate."

"Is that approval, Master Büber?" It wasn't something he felt he needed to seek any more, but it was good to know, all the same.

"At least Carinthia has a prince who can piss in a pot and not get it down his leg. Would that the rest of Europe were so lucky." Büber rapped his knuckles on Felix's breastplate. It sounded reassuringly solid.

"No mail for you, Master Büber?"

"Can't say I've ever held with it. Better to avoid being hit in the first place." He looked out towards the blank black shape of Kufstein's crag. "Our horses are being saddled. We may as well see to our stirrups ourselves."

Büber set off across the camp, and Felix caught him up. "You knew I'd want to come."

"Knew, no. Presumed, yes. You've that much of your father in you." The grass hissed against their feet. "Let's just hope you've the better sense."

"This is my father you're talking about," said Felix. He realised that Gerhard had been too slow to change, and that it had cost him his life and those of the men he'd led into battle. It was still his father.

"And if you were to give me the choice between the man and the boy, I'd still choose the boy, even if the man did come with his earls. Mind, armoured cavalry is something we're missing."

"If we had earls, we'd have nothing but levies." Felix embraced the whole camp with a gesture. "These men are now fighting for their homes and their land. What do you want from me, Master Büber? A few more horsemen or a host of militia? It's one or the other. We have what we have, and we are where we are. You may as well wish for hexmasters and be done with it."

Best not to have said that, he thought afterwards. He was sure Büber didn't wish for any hexmasters, save for one in particular. He glanced at the big man.

"We're fighting infantry. A few more horsemen could turn the battle for us, used at the right time."

Either Büber hadn't noticed, or he'd ignored the comment. Felix kept on the subject of horses. "How many do we have?"

"Too few. People don't keep horses except for pleasure, and then only the rich. The Jews have a few horses, but they use mostly bullocks to drag their ploughs and their carts. I can't see riding a cow into battle catching on." Büber pointed to the far bank, up by the col. "I'll put what we have up there, most of them. They can ride down the side of the valley, strike hard, then away again. It'll keep the flank occupied during our retreats, and perhaps they'll sting a little. I'm told that Byzantium has horses covered head to foot in scale, their riders too, and that when they strike, they ride over their enemies as if they were nothing but a field of rye."

"The kataphraktoi," said Felix. "I don't know if it's true."

Their horses arrived, ready for riding, held by two of Büber's scouts.

Felix swung into the saddle, and waited for the others to mount up. The jingling of tack and stamp of hooves did nothing to calm him. It felt like his heart was only still behind his ribs because of the breastplate strapped across them.

"Across the bridge to the road," said Büber. "We've already sent a messenger to Rosenheim, and someone else will ride to Juvavum."

Horses, carrying messages. This was how both war and peace were conducted now.

They rode off at a steady trot, past the sagging canvas and drooping ropes, the still-smouldering fires and the blinking eyes of the morning watch. When they returned, the camp would have been struck. Every man would be armed and armoured. They were Carinthia just as much as the land was: every man they lost diminished the palatinate. It brought a sour taste up into Felix's mouth.

The bridge seemed less significant the closer they got to it. It was narrow, enough room for a single cart and no more, stone parapet up to waist-height across its three spans and two piers. The river below didn't seem to be flowing that fast, or appear that deep. The banks were straight down for the most part, but it was hardly the insurmountable obstacle around which to base all their defences.

There might be some overarching reason, thought Felix: perhaps dwarves didn't like getting wet. He hoped so.

They passed the limits of their earthworks, a mostly finished ditch from the Zellerberg hill on the left to the valley-side to the right, then they were into the area beyond, of quiet woods and little abandoned farms, and the road wound up the north side of the river all the way to Ennsbruck and beyond.

The pickets were ahead of them, groups of two or three horsemen who were under strict orders to keep a watch on the dwarves but not to fight, even if it seemed likely they could score an easy win. What might look like a gift one moment could so quickly change to an irrecoverably dire situation the next – and they needed the horses more than they needed the men to ride them.

Twenty miles. In any other circumstances, it'd be a decent morning's hack, with the prospect of a good lunch at the end of it, and a pleasant feeling of fatigue afterwards that might last until bedtime. The scenery was stunning, with blue mountain peaks in the distance, the forest a deep, almost black green, and the constant companion of the river washing by.

This valley, these trees, were not really his either by custom or right, but it fell to him to defend them, to keep the dwarves at bay from the pastures and cornfields of the plain.

It struck Felix that peace was far better than war, and that he'd rather be remembered for his land reforms than for his prowess on the battlefield. He'd not asked to be prince, but gods, if prince he was, he'd see his people well fed and content. There was just the small matter of the entire population of Farduzes to contend with first. Curse them, and curse King Ironmaker. He would have welcomed them all as friends, and Carinthia had room for them, no matter how many there might be. Perhaps, when all this was done and Ironmaker had yielded his axe and his crown, there could be some sort of treaty between them.

A picket from further up the line took over from the two who'd escorted them thus far, and Felix and Büber went on with the new man, further and deeper into the mountains, which now rose around rather than only ahead of them.

The closer they got to the dwarvish wall, the more nervous he grew, but Obernberg had taught him that he was braver than he'd thought. After spending the first half of the battle running away from the Teuton outriders, it had been Felix and not Allegretti who'd stood his ground, and his refusal to run any further had forced the swordmaster to fight. He would carry on, no matter that his throat was dry and his stomach churning like a butter-tub; he'd not disgrace himself.

They left their horses by a narrow forest path and climbed the rest of the way up to past the tree line. Büber went first, then Felix in his armour, and the picket third. It was hard, and Felix was out of breath soon enough. But then they came to an outcrop of rock that seemed to hang over the broad valley. They could sit in its shade and see everything.

Büber had his distance-pipe, and so did Felix. Once he'd accepted some water, warm from the flask, his hands were steady enough to hold the tube and sight at the line of wooden stakes below.

There were gaps in the wall, that much was obvious, places where pre-cut sections of palisade had been dropped to the ground. Through these gaps rolled a stream of the dwarvish wagons, arranged in long lines behind and forming up into two columns either side of the river.

"What are they doing?" asked Felix.

"Gods only know," said Büber. He lowered the tube from his eye and blinked hard. "The only road suitable for those beasts is on this side. If they try and take them along the south side, they'll find it not just heavy going, but all but impossible."

"And there are dwarves inside each one?" said Felix, twisting his distance-pipe to give him the best view."

"There aren't any outside, pushing. So unless they've magic and we don't, yes: ten or more to a wagon." Büber rubbed at his eye. "If they've magic, we may as well go home."

The covered wagons were moving ahead relatively easily on the road, where the surface was hard and dry. On the other side, where there was barely a footpath, their progress seemed painfully slow.

Felix kept watching. Yes, he could see dwarves now, cutting axes in hand, flanking the wagons as they disappeared into the forest. They looked somehow odd. Not the dwarves of legend, short-legged and barrel-chested, vast beards and dark-coal eyed: more half-made, pale worms wriggling out into the light.

"Can we try and stop them?" he asked. "Or slow them down at least?"

"We could. But we haven't the men to make it count. If we cut trees across their path, they'll have to get out and move them. We could kill a few before they drive us off. We've committed to Kufstein, though." Büber put the tube to his eye again. "No sign of any flanking forces. They're doing what we expected, at least. We'll need to pull back ourselves soon, or we'll get cut off."

"There are a lot of them, Master Büber," said Felix.

It was true. A stream of wagons continued to rumble and roll through the gaps in the wall, and behind them was an inchoate mass of figures, so large that it lost meaning.

"And they're all coming our way," he continued.

Büber took one last look, and slid his distance-pipe away. "If they use those wagons to attack us, our bows – our advantage – is lost until they climb out of them. The ditches will force them out, at least while they take the embankment behind. But then it'll be spear against axe. We need a way of stopping them well ahead of our lines."

"Then we'll have to do just that."

"Easier said than done, my lord." Büber looked troubled as he touched Felix on the arm. "Unless we intend to be trapped here, we need to leave now."

Felix folded his own pipe away and took a last look at the horde. The next time he'd see them would be in battle.

85

The whole town was hurrying, as if it was an ants' nest and had been kicked hard. The dwarves were on the march, and thus, by necessity, so were they. There was no time for drilling, or reflection. The Lady Sophia had rung the Bell Tower's bell and those able to pick up a spear and wear a helmet, and who were willing to do so, were collecting by the West Gate.

Messengers had gone further into Carinthia, and up to Simbach. The message Ullmann had been sent had spoken baldly of the odds: they were outnumbered seemingly ten to one. He stared out of the window and over the roofs. Everything he'd worked for: his parents owning their own farm, his brothers and sisters equal before the law with some lordling's issue, their – his – ideas spreading out like ripples, subverting the former order from within and without: it was all in danger of being swept away by a bunch of bastard dwarves too stupid, too hidebound to the past, to negotiate with reasonable people.

Nothing yet from München, either. A thousand, two thousand spears could make all the difference. Another message had been sent, but Ullmann still secretly hoped that his own, earlier message would be acted on. With one Bavarian pretender dead, the Earl of Augsburg would be much more likely to throw his lot in with Felix, if only to protect his recent gains.

His sword was on his desk. He reached out and picked it up, weighing it in his hands, surprising himself as to how light it really was. He drew it from its scabbard, looked at the way the light shone down its edges, then resheathed it.

He turned at a knock on the door, and a man was there. "The Black Company are assembled outside."

Ullmann nodded. "I'll be down in a moment."

The man left again, leaving the door slightly open. Voices drifted up to him, indistinct and echoing. Ullmann scanned his desk for anything that really ought not be left out in the open. He'd locked his code books away, along with his lists of agents and their reports. No, everything was as it should be: he'd been thorough.

Would he see this place again, this tower room in the fortress wall? He hadn't made it homely, because that hadn't been the effect he'd wanted, but it had become his space all the same.

He strapped on his sword. It didn't feel so light now. Then, taking one last look, he closed the door behind him. Down the stairs, across the drawbridge to the courtyard beyond. Forty men in the Black Company, dressed like him, with no insignia of rank or identification. They looked like ushers, but instead of carrying canes, they had steel, and under their robes, they wore chain.

As Ullmann approached, they formed up, and, without ceremony – that was how lords and ladies acted – they marched off through the Chastity Gate, and into town.

The people they passed stood aside for them, even as they were organising coats and capes and boots, and food and drink for themselves. Down Stable Street, where the last of the horses – anything that could be ridden – were being turned out and tack hoisted onto them; then into Coin Alley, where the smithies had fallen silent but the hammers were still in the hands of those who wielded them.

The Black Company collected on the muster field. Sophia was already there, with two centuries of Jews, and companies of builders, carters, boatmen and farmers keeping nervously to their guild banners. None of them were ready for a twenty-mile hike to Rosenheim, let alone what faced them there.

Where were the gods? Had they left Carinthia at the same time the magic faded? In which case, it was Ullmann's own hand that had finally brought them down. Max Ullmann, Max Godslayer, Max Hexkiller. What name would he have when all this was done?

Then he spotted Aelinn in the crowd. He slipped between the boat hooks and cudgels of the bargees, and into the midst of stable boys, messengers and maids. He tried to find her: surely she wasn't thinking of marching on Rosenheim? The thought made him queasy, but, try as he might – calling her name, asking after her – he was unable to spot her again.

Had he imagined it? A fleeting glimpse of a bob of blonde hair in the mob, and perhaps he'd jumped to conclusions. Aelinn was brave for sure, but she must have more sense than this. Let others take the risk and either win the glory or suffer the defeat: Aelinn had to be kept safe.

If she was here, he vowed to send her home, back to the Odenwalds' house on the main square. He returned to the Black Company angry and troubled.

It was obvious that Sophia, now mounted on her comfortable old nag, wanted to be off as soon as possible. She rode back and forth impatiently, counting heads, and didn't – for once – look like she was going to fall off.

It was close to midday by the time she decided that their ranks were large enough to make it worthwhile setting off. Ullmann would have gone sooner, but with Felix absent, it was clear that she was deemed to be in charge: not Thaler, not Wess, and not him. Someone brought her out a banner, a fine yellow cloth with a black leopard. She lifted it up and received a ragged cheer, her name being shouted along with Felix's.

Then she wrapped the cloth around her shoulders as if it were a shawl. The leopard rose up her spine, paw extended out the way they had to go.

She twisted in her saddle as her horse walked slowly out onto the München road, and she appeared to be smiling and crying at the same time. If anyone else noticed, they didn't say, but Ullmann had. She wheeled about at the head of the column to face them. She looked down from her height, and she most definitely caught sight of him at the head of his company, which was at the head of the host.

Her mouth pursed. If she had been going to address them, she decided in that moment not to. She turned the horse again, and started up the road. Other riders trotted up the sides of the road, some of them showing off, others deadly serious, to gather around her.

The Black Company was still waiting for his word. Him, a farmer's son from Over-Carinthia. He'd achieved his position not because he'd been born to it, but because he'd won it for himself.

Ullmann pointed to the sky, then at the east. "Move out," he called. His company started walking, and everyone followed: the guilds, the trades, the Jews in the rearguard, and everyone in between.

After a while, Sophia left the vanguard and rode down the line. She smiled at him as she passed, but it seemed forced. Then a long time later – they were stretched out over a couple of miles – she rode back on the other side, still wearing the Carinthian banner as a cloak. Now she looked at him differently again. Her cheeks were white, and her jaw was set hard. An argument, and the only ones who'd dare do so were her own; they would talk and argue and call each other names from sunrise to sunset, and still they seemed content to live together all on one street and cram shoulder to shoulder into their temple to worship their god.

"My lady," he said as she ground her teeth. She was so distracted that she looked through him for a moment, before blinking and realising that she was being addressed.

"Master Ullmann."

There was something else, more than having just argued with her rabbi. Gods, the rules they lived under. "My lady, do you want to talk in private?"

Her face underwent an unexpected number of contortions. "Not now, Master Ullmann. After we've secured the safety of both Carinthia and Felix, then we'll talk."

What was this? "My lady, if we need to discuss matters of state—"

She cut him off. "Not. Now." She drew in a deep breath. "There'll be no distractions. We have one goal, and one enemy. Nothing else matters for the moment."

She jabbed her heels into her steed's flanks, and it picked up speed. She only slowed when she was well ahead of the other riders, alone, the banner of yellow and black fluttering like an angry wasp.

"Master Ullmann?" asked the man to his right. "Is there anything that needs doing?"

Ullmann wasn't sure. Sophia was their lord's consort, but she was ultimately only a figurehead. Felix was the source of all authority, and he was at Rosenheim.

"I'm going to talk to Cohen. If he's been causing problems, I'll get him to button it. My lord Felix decides whether his lady's behaviour is proper, not some funny-hatted priest." He glanced behind him. "We need to pick up the pace and keep together. We're scattered; more a festival crowd than an army."

He dropped out of the line and and attempted to move back against the flow. It was all but impossible, so he jumped a ditch and strode through the grazed grass until he could see the back of the column.

The Jews were in their town-guard garb, a mixture of swords, spears and maces, shield and helmet styles, shirts of mail, scale and leather. They walked together as if they were still squashed in one of Juvavum's narrow alleys, their braids and tassels swinging in time with their steps. They were a jostling, happy crowd that had brought its own ram's horn trumpets.

Ullmann jumped the ditch back to the road, and fell in with them. Cohen, his beard striped with grey, welcomed him.

"Master Ullmann, to what do we owe this pleasure?"

He got to the point. "My Lady Sophia."

"Oy," said Cohen, and pushed his helmet back far enough to wipe his forehead. "One moment she's chasing us to battle, the next she's chasing us away. The woman can't make up her mind."

"Please explain."

Cohen gestured to the people around him. "We had a good shake-out of Jew's Alley, shaming those who'd rather have stayed in bed. Every man of fighting age is here, a century and more, and Sophia's worry is that, having saved ourselves from the mamzer Eckhardt, we'll throw ourselves away on the blade of a dwarvish axe. No Jews left in Juvavum except widows and orphans."

Telling part of their army to abandon their duty was, what? Treason? She'd rather Germans die than Jews? Ullmann had to get to the bottom of this. "And still you march?" he asked.

"Gehenna isn't as bad as the way to it. And our father Abraham promised we'd be as numerous as the stars in the sky. The world's not going to run out of Jews any time soon."

"Perhaps," said Ullmann, looking at the empty road behind them. "What did she tell you to do? Stop and turn around?"

"Just the boys. Those under their sixteenth year. They refused, of course. HaShem is with us, and we all want to be there when He hands us our victory." Cohen nudged the man next to him, who raised his horn and let off a long two-tone blast. "O Israel, trust in HaShem; He is their help and their shield."

And those around him answered: "O House of Aaron, trust in HaShem; He is their help and their shield."

"The ones fearing HaShem, trust in HaShem; He is their help and their shield." Cohen tugged at his beard. "You see, Master

624

Ullmann? We make common cause with you, our neighbours and our friends. This is our fight too."

Ullmann frowned. Would that the Germans were as enthusiastic. "She still shouldn't have said what she did."

"She feels responsible for us, our Esther. She needs to trust HaShem for our deliverance instead."

"I understand," said Ullmann.

He didn't really. He didn't understand at all. He could see why Sophia would want to protect the small Jewish population, but to do so at the expense of the German one? To try and deny Felix the iron and the blood they'd bring to battle was most certainly treasonous. They couldn't have too many soldiers; only too few. The Jews themselves were fanatics. How could he have not realised they had a warrior god and no fear of death? Hadn't they used to meekly complain when the German children threw rotten fruit and vegetables at them, and the adults tried to cheat them in business?

"I'll rejoin my men now, rabbi."

Ullmann trotted forward a few paces, then began to walk briskly, overtaking the carpenters with their adzes and axes, then the bargees, a rough and unreliable company. By the time he was level with the farmers and woodsmen from north of Juvavum, he was starting to tire, but suddenly, up ahead, he caught sight of a flash of blonde hair again, moving in exactly the same way that Aelinn's did when she walked. Determination sped him up, and he started to close on the rag-tag band who walked with her.

It *was* her. She didn't even have a weapon, not even her broom, and she was marching to war. This was surely madness, and he had to put a stop to it.

Except. Except he'd be doing the same thing as Sophia had done. Preferring that someone else should take her place in the line, perhaps to die, just as long as the person most important to him was out of harm's way.

Of course he'd prefer that. He'd have to be an unfeeling monster to think otherwise.

And Aelinn would argue with him, in exactly the same way that Cohen had argued with Sophia, and in exactly the same way as Cohen had, she would win that argument simply by refusing to turn around. He couldn't make her go back. He couldn't order her. There was nothing he could do. He didn't own her or have any hold over her.

He could beg. But what did he imagine Sophia had done? And with what result?

Gods, if the armies at München didn't come over to them, then she'd – eventually – have to fight. She wouldn't run. Aelinn was brave.

With treasonous thoughts all of his own, he ran past her group. He didn't try and speak to her, nor did he turn round once he knew he'd overtaken her. He ran all the way to the front of the column, tasting bitterness with every footfall.

86

Agathos came running onto the practice field, waving his hands around and shouting. Thaler stood up from behind his desk, remembering to place a weight on the loose papers, and called him over.

"Master Thaler," he said, "they gone. They all gone."

"Good," said Thaler, "well done, boy."

"Do you still intend to go through with this ridiculous idea?" asked Morgenstern, looking up from his calculations.

"The idea is not ridiculous, Aaron. What else are we doing here, if we can't make a difference?" Thaler turned back to the Greek boy. "Tell everyone to get ready."

"I should have told Sophia," said Morgenstern. He blew on his freshly inked work and held it up to the sun to make sure it was dry before he closed the book. "She would have forbidden this . . ."

"Yes, yes, I know. But you didn't, did you?" Thaler put on his secret smile, the one he wore when he knew he'd won an argument.

All across the field, people were emerging from inside huts and behind screens, carrying all manner of paraphernalia. Iron tools and barrels, buckets and long cleaning rods, brass sextants and coils of slow fuse.

From the woods, Bastian emerged at the head of a caravan of ox-pulled carts, empty now but not for long.

"Mistress?"

Tuomanen was by his side like a grey mist, her sleeves rolled back almost to her shoulders. Her tattooed arms were long and lean, and her patterned hands carried a rough wooden crate. "Master."

"Put it with the powder kegs, then can you supervise the loading of the pots? They're not going to break if we drop them, but the carts most certainly will."

She walked over to where the powder barrels were piling up and gently lowered the crate next to them. They'd all had to learn how to behave around the stuff, which they'd been accumulating in increasingly large amounts. "Carefully" was a word that was repeated often, and meant seriously.

Tuomanen gathered a group of workers and they started to dig out the pots from their emplacements. Carved wooden cradles appeared from behind a screen, and the ironware was lifted onto them, one by one.

Morgenstern was watching him rather than helping, and Thaler frowned. "What?"

"You're not too old, you know," said Morgenstern, "and she's not too young."

"What are you talking about?" Then he realised and spluttered. "Good gods, man. I don't . . . I can't . . . I mean . . . a man in my position?"

"Oh, stop your kvetching. You stare at her tusch as it sways."

"I do not. It's simply preposterous. I'm the master librarian. Librarians don't marry."

"You mean like Thomm? Or like the Jewish men you took on." Morgenstern tucked his book under his arm. "You've thrown all the old rules in the midden, Frederik. Jews, women, old men, foreigners, they're all welcome in the library now. When all this is over, I could get the matchmaker to introduce you."

"I'll tell you what's ridiculous, Aaron Morgenstern: this conversation. We have far more important matters at hand, as do you. Now, hand over that book: our crews will need your tables."

Morgenstern looked at the book, and crossed his arms over it, holding it to his thin chest. "You'll just use it wrong, and waste all the work I've done. I've a mind to come along too."

"Gods, man. Are you determined to make my blood boil today? I'll get Bastian to rip it from your cold, dead hands if that's what it takes." Thaler took a step forward, and Morgenstern took one back.

"As you say, there are far more important matters to worry about. I'll sit on a cart. I don't weigh much." He took himself away, and pointedly climbed up next to the teamster on the lead wagon. They were using Jewish carters, and he fell into conversation quickly.

Thaler balled his fists and grunted with frustration. If the old man wanted to put up with the hardships of travel, and to rough it in a tent at the other end, then who was he to dissuade him?

The first of the pots was hefted into the waiting cart, and the loaders took time to make sure it was positioned centrally between the two axles. Nothing broke, so Thaler assumed they were competent to load the others, and went to help with stacking the powder.

His powder team seemed more than capable, too. They lifted the kegs one by one, made sure that the metal bands around the barrels were padded with scraps of canvas, and listened to the rattle they made, before moving onto the next.

The fuses, both slow and quick, and the tools and buckets, were loaded with equal care. And the long-barrelled iron pot they'd named Gunnhilde was already safely lashed to the flat of another cart, next to one of Bastian's new bronze castings. There were two more of these in a different wagon.

"Is there nothing I can do?" he complained loudly, throwing up his hands.

Apparently, there wasn't. He had managed to delegate all the jobs to people who knew how to do them quickly and well. It didn't stop him from fussing over them, and it took them until mid-afternoon to load up, strap everything down and cover it all with oil-cloth.

Before they set off, Thaler called them together.

He was surprised at how many people there were. He'd collected a half-century of his own, except his consisted of boys and women, old men and magicians. He knew all their names, and where they came from.

"Good Carinthians and honoured guests," he said, then climbed up onto a cart and started again. Now he could see them all properly. "The time has come, sooner than we'd have wished, for us to put our knowledge to the test. From what I've gleaned, our little force at Kufstein is woefully outnumbered. There will be at least five dwarves – possibly more – to one of us, and we are a peaceable people, unused to war. What we have in these wagons may well be insufficient to turn the battle in our favour, but what use are they sitting here in a field in Juvavum when they could be in the west, bolstering our troops' resolve and aiding them against the enemy?"

He had meant the question to be rhetorical, but some of them shouted back at him, "No use at all, Master Thaler," and "The dwarves will turn tail and run at the sound of us."

"That they might. We have to be prepared to keep going until the last keg of powder is cracked, the last ball and shell sent, until the barrels overheat and melt with the fury of our bombard. We will fight for our homes and our honour, as any freeborn man or woman is bound to do. If we fail, we go to our deaths knowing we did our best. If we win, we will be able to hold our heads high among the host and say we were the pivot about which the battle turned. I hope that these weapons of war stay silent forever afterwards, that we'll be able to turn them back into frying pans and ploughshares. But, for now, they'll bark our displeasure and show our foes that ordinary people, people like us, can control the very elements of nature when roused.

"So be glad that we live in times like this. Our investigations of the natural order have only just begun. Who knows what marvels we'll have by next week, next month, next year? We have some already, and many more wait for our return. So if you want to fight for something, fight for the future, the time to come. Carinthia has been reborn, and it takes its first steps in the world. Let us not be the cause of its stumbling."

He rested his hands on his hips. Had that gone well? They were silent, open-mouthed even. Or was that boredom? He'd better get on with it.

"Some of us will ride for a time while some will walk. All of us will help. The road is, I'm told, a little bumpy, so pushing may be needed. Organise yourselves as you see fit. Aaron? You have the lead."

Morgenstern looked unduly pleased with his duties, even if all he had to do was nudge the carter next to him. The man flicked his whip, and the pair of oxen deigned to stop chewing the grass long enough to put one hoof in front of the other.

The cart creaked and rumbled on, heading towards the bridge

over the Salzach. Some of the wagons needed a shove to get them going, but none had sunk irrevocably into the soft pasture. Thaler watched with satisfaction as the last cart clattered into the life, and the last powder crew followed it.

"Master Thaler?"

"Gods, woman," said Thaler, clutching his chest. "I should have learnt to expect this by now, but please, make some sound when you approach."

"Apologies, Master," said Tuomanen, her expression one far removed from apologetic. "Are we going, too, or were those fine words just for others?"

"You impugn my honour, Mistress." He strode off behind a screen, and came back with an ash walking-stick and a little felt hat. The hat was green, with a short brown feather stitched onto the side. He slid the hat onto his head and pulled its brim down. "Now we're ready."

They set off, behind everyone.

"I've done what you asked," she said, looking to see if there were any eavesdroppers.

"Ah, that. Excellent. Any problems?" His walking-stick was just the right height for him, its horn handle smooth and dry in his hand.

"No. The shelves look a bit bare now, but if anyone checks the missing titles against the catalogue, they'll see they're all lent out in different names."

"And Master Wess has them all under lock and key?"

"Better than that. He was aware of a certain room in a certain house that had often been used for hiding contraband books. That's where they are."

"Aaron's? I take it he doesn't know?"

"I don't think he's been back to his house in weeks. No one saw us, and we can retrieve them the same way." Tuomanen smirked. "I never took you for sneaky, Master Thaler."

"Sneaky? My dear lady, it's merely a prudent precaution. There will be casualties, it is quite inevitable, and just as inevitable that some, if they're desperate enough, will want their loved ones to be, how do we say, restored to wellness." He tutted. "Better we remove temptation before it becomes an issue."

"I thought . . ." She looked at him. "I thought you meant something else."

Thaler coughed. "Else? What else could there be?"

"An army of the dead, doing the will of the spell-caster, howling their pain and desolation and not stopping until each one has been all but dismembered. That's not the temptation of a parent who's lost their child, but the temptation of a king who's about to lose his kingdom."

"Felix would never consent to that."

"I wasn't thinking it would be others begging him to do it. It would be him demanding it was done."

Thaler gave her a sideways glance. "Would you do it?"

She bent down and picked a white meadow flower, all without breaking step. "I've sworn my oath of obedience," she said.

"That wasn't what I asked."

Tuomanen tucked the flower behind her ear. She usually wore her hair so it covered the slightly pointed tips of them, far more self-conscious of that difference than she was of the tattoos that covered her. But there it was, the white flower caught between her elvish ear and her tucked-in dark hair. She considered her words.

"If Felix demanded I practise necromancy and raise a horde of unthinking, unfeeling dead to fight for him, I'd spit in his face and tell him he was no prince of mine."

"And your former colleagues?"

"Oh, they'd do it, and not even reluctantly." She snorted a sarcastic laugh. "You're wiser than you know."

"As long as no one asks Master Wess where the books are. I'm not certain of his firmness under interrogation." The first cart with Aaron Morgenstern on board was climbing the rise of the bridge. "Are there any guards left?"

Tuomanen squinted into the distance. "A couple. I'm certain Mr Morgenstern can handle them. You could always destroy the books."

"I have never done such a thing, and I will never do so."

His indignation was fake, and she saw through his act.

"What did you tell Master Wess?"

"Just to make certain, if the circumstances warrant it." Thaler puckered his lips. "How very distasteful."

Up ahead, the carts breezed through any administrative objection that might have been raised. The oxen turned right and headed along the quay towards the West Gate. Some of the more heavily laden wagons needed help up the bridge, and extra braking on the way back down; everyone did their part without asking. By the time Thaler and Tuomanen strode past the guard post, the way was clear and all Thaler had to do was doff his cap to the spearmen and wish them good day.

The head of the caravan was already out of the gate on the München road. Their way was set, their destination fixed.

Thaler looked up at the stone arch of the gatehouse as they passed under it. She had called him wise, but what about this expedition? Aaron thought it was nothing but a folly hat worn with a hubris coat, yet he was still coming with them, along with the entirety of his crew. Not one had backed out: that had to count for something, surely.

"Is that," Tuomanen asked, pointing at Thaler's walking-stick, "is that handle carved from unicorn horn?"

"Yes," said Thaler. "Yes it is. I happened to have one lying around and thought I'd put it to good use. Since, well, you don't need it any more."

He stepped out from under the shadow of the gate, and felt strangely calm.

87

A rider galloped towards her across the Rosenheim bridge, and Sophia instantly thought that she was too late, that the dwarves were already on them, Kufstein overrun and Felix killed.

She'd no idea what she'd do if that was the message. It was already dusk, and the road was barely visible in the dark. They had nowhere left to go: if the enemy was indeed on them, then they'd have to fight where they were, no matter how exhausted they might be.

"My lady," called the rider, and pulled up next to her.

Her heart stopped while she waited for the next few words.

"My lord Felix sends his best wishes and, if my lady can manage another ten miles, wonders if she cares to join him for dinner."

Her relief was like ducking down into the freezing waters of the mikveh, then surfacing with a shout.

"Are we fighting yet?"

"Skirmishing only. The dwarves are some ten miles from the crag at Kufstein, and have halted for the night. We've had the better of it today, for certain." The rider looked past Sophia at her strung-out, rag-tag army. "There's tents – probably enough for everyone, as long as they don't mind lying on their sides – and cook pots and firewood, in the field south of the town."

"I'll leave Master Ullmann in charge," she said at once, and knew it to be the right decision. She needed to talk to Felix, and she needed Ullmann not to be there when she did.

"As soon as you're ready, my lady. The way up the valley's not easy in the dark, and I'd rather not have to explain to my lord why we broke both our own necks and those of the horses."

"Thank you, sir," she said, and rode back the short distance to Ullmann. "I'm riding on to Kufstein. You're in charge, both tonight and in the morning. Make sure that everyone's ready to move off at dawn. The dwarves will attack tomorrow, and I want us to be ready and to know our parts."

Ullmann seemed strangely subdued. He looked up at her, and agreed with a simple "My lady."

Sophia frowned, but there wasn't time to worry about what the problem was; it would have to wait. She wheeled around again to meet her escort, and they trotted on across the bridge, along the road crossing the marshy wetlands, and then south towards the mouth of the valley.

"Tell me about the fighting," she said.

"Not much to say, my lady. The dwarves have these covered wagons that they're pushing down the valley. We've been felling trees in their path; when they come out to clear these, we shoot a few of them. They chase us off, and we get to shoot a few more; then we do it all again a few hundred feet down the path. Gods only know what they're doing, but their tactics are costing them dearly so far."

"We should be grateful. How long is it since the dwarves have fought a battle?"

"Not since Roman times, if the stories are anything to go by."

"Well then," said Sophia, "perhaps they're even worse at this than we are. What's happening on the east side of the river?"

"There's barely a cart track on that bank, but they're still pressing down with their wagons all the same. More dwarves in the open, cutting their way through. We've popped a few bolts at them, but their progress is slow already, and they can't match the progress of those on the west side of the Enn. They may even reach Kufstein too late to join the fighting."

"Unless it's their plan to come at us when we're all but spent. Who's in charge of the east bank?"

"Master Büber. Master Reinhardt has taken the west, and the prince is leading the cavalry."

"And is there any way the dwarvish west side can reinforce their east?"

"The river's wide and deep – not as deep as it is in spring, but the banks are cliffs. They could swim across, but they've shown no sign of wanting to do so. Unless they have a spare bridge about them, no."

"So why wait? We could concentrate all our forces on the west bank, then bring them back against the east."

"I . . . I'm not in charge, my lady." Sophia's escort turned away from her. "I don't have the knowledge about how these things are done or the authority to order anyone to carry them out. All I can do is trust that those who do, make the right decisions. Otherwise they'll end up throwing my life away for nothing."

Now she was ashamed. "Apologies, sir."

"Groer, my lady. Oktav Groer. From Hallein," said the man. "Whether I ever go back home is in the hands of the Norns. Whether I'm remembered as part of a victorious army is in yours and the princes."

"If we don't win, no one will remember any of our names, except in a story to frighten their children."

It was almost properly dark. Light from the half-moon made the brown road appear only slightly different to the green verges. At some point, they must have passed the Flintsbachs' old farm, but she'd not seen the boarded-up windows or the cold byre. Fortunately, the horses seemed to know where to go better than they did.

The forest was darker still, pitch black with only a slit of indigo for sky. The southern summer stars turned in that gap, shining weakly and cold.

They kept going, silent as the night demanded, and, at the point where the peaks retreated from the valley sides, a voice leapt out at them.

"Who goes there?"

"Groer, and the Princess Sophia."

A shuttered lantern opened and, feeble as it was, the difference between the light and the dark was more than enough to show the group of four spearmen emerging from one side of the path, and another group of four stepping out from the other.

One of them held the lantern high so that it showed their faces, though none of them had ever heard of dwarves on horseback before.

"Evening, my lady. That sword of yours sharp?"

She pulled it half out of its scabbard so that it caught the yellow light. "As sharp as your wits, soldier. I suppose we'll need both in the morning."

Another of the guards laughed. "Pray the gods your sword's sharper; Heinrich's wits are as dull as brick."

"You can't make a home out of steel, good sirs. For that you need . . ."

"Brick," crowed the first man. "You see?"

Groer's horse stamped its hooves. "Are you letting us pass, or are you showing off to the princess all night?"

"We'll let you pass, horseman." The lantern and the shadows surrounding it moved aside. "Give us a blessing, my lady. For tomorrow."

She stiffened. "But your gods are not my God," she eventually managed.

"So I've heard. But if there are Jews in the line with us, perhaps he might want to protect us as well as them, seeing how we're all on the same side."

Sophia took a deep breath and blinked away her tears. "Yes, yes of course." But what to say? A psalm, a fragment of a psalm. "HaShem is my light and my salvation; who then should I fear? HaShem is the fortress of my life; of whom should I be afraid? When the wicked, my enemies and my foes, came at me to devour my flesh, they stumbled and fell. Though an army should encamp against me, my heart shall not fear; though war should break out against me, in this I will be confident."

The words, familiar to her, foreign to them, seemed to pass muster even though she had to take both the cantor's part and the responses. The guards murmured, and the lantern faded from sight as the shutter closed.

They rode on a little way further. The forest ended, the fields around Kufstein twinkled into view, bright with a constellation of camp fires.

"Where's the prince?"

"On the Kufstein crag, my lady, with Masters Büber and Reinhardt."

There was a gap in the pattern of fires, where the black river ran, and another where the walls of the fort blocked out the light. The bridge across the Enn was marked out with lanterns and guards on both sides, and Groer guided them down to it and across.

It seemed so happy. Laughter and music drifted up with the wood smoke and the cooking smells. Lyres provided the melodies while the rhythm was maintained on marching drums or pot helmets. The lyrics were raucous and bawdy, and the atmosphere was that of a festival night in Juvavum.

"Everyone's in good heart," she said to Groer.

"We've won some small victories today, for no loss. They take it for an omen."

"And you, Mr Groer? What do you think?"

"I've seen the dwarves, in their thousands and tens of thousands. I'd rather not fool myself into thinking this'll be easy."

Their horses wound their way around the crag and through a rough but functional gate set into an earthwork faced with a palisade. The ground inside had one large fire, and a tree-trunk bench next to it, just like the one she'd sat on with Aelinn.

Except it wasn't Aelinn's face reflecting the firelight, but Peter Büber's freshly shaved head, Reinhardt's whiskered cheeks, and, between them, Felix, with the Sword of Carinthia resting across his knees.

When it came to it, she found she couldn't dismount. Everything, the effort of riding, the effort of appearing to be able to ride competently, the effort of not showing any sign of pain, had overwhelmed her. Her legs had locked into position, and even though she was able to kick free of her stirrups, she was quite incapable of even falling off.

"I seem to be stuck," she said, and only Büber was tall enough to lend any sort of practical assistance. His strong hands gripped her waist and bodily lifted her clear of the saddle, then tilted her almost horizontally to slide her free.

Neither could she stand when she was on the ground, and had

to be helped onto the tree-trunk. Sitting was all but impossible too; instead, she lay face-down on the ground, the Carinthian flag draped across her like a blanket.

"Hello, Sophia."

"Hello, Felix," she grunted into the grass. "Everything hurts." It did, too. Quite exquisitely.

"It'll pass," he said. "You'll have to do it all again tomorrow."

Was now the right time to have that particular argument, or would it wait? She decided it would be better if she just presented it as fact in the cold light of morning, when he couldn't afford to spare any riders to make sure she left.

"Wine or beer or water?" Felix asked. "We have some of everything."

"Is the wine kosher? No? Then beer."

Reinhardt went to the barrel to pour a mug for her, and she'd started to roll onto her back, as a preliminary to at least sitting upright, when she realised she'd make the banner dirty. She undid the knots that tied it around her neck, and passed it up to Felix.

"A present for you. You should fly it from the walls."

"My lady," said Büber, "if we don't know who we're fighting for by now . . ."

"Hush, Master Büber. It's a fine idea. Thank you." Felix folded the banner carefully and put it on his lap beside his sword.

Sophia propped herself up against the log with her feet splayed in front of her in the direction of the fire, and accepted the beer from Reinhardt. "So," she said, "why aren't we attacking?"

She could hear, rather than see, Büber and Reinhardt look at each over Felix's head.

"We chose not to," said Felix, taking the responsibility for the decision away from the two men. "We don't have enough spears and swords to do that properly. Our whole army is based around spears and crossbows. Bows aren't a melee weapon, and our cavalry is limited, so we can't rely on them to cover our flanks. We have to let them come to us. The terrain suits that sort of deep defence, all the more so now that we have ditches and ramparts dug. We can hold this place, but if we attack, we'd always run the risk of getting caught up in a battle that might turn on us in a moment."

"Let them make the mistakes," said Reinhardt. "Let them get desperate so that throw themselves at our spear-points. Every step they take towards us we'll be shooting at them. As plans go, it's not very finessed, but I'll take dull and slow over something flashy and risky."

"You're very quiet, Master Büber," Sophia noted.

Büber rasped at his chin. He'd shaved his head, but not his stubble. "I don't like this waiting any more than you do, and if there was a chance of breaking them and routing the whole horde, then I'd be at the front of the charge."

"But?"

"There are too many of them, and, like us, they're piled deep. Even if we chased the first few thousand off the field, we'd still run into just as many coming the other way, all with fight in them. And fight they will. They might not be the dwarves of old, but they can still swing an axe."

She clicked her tongue. "Can't we can keep engaging them at a distance, then? Keep shooting at them with crossbows all the way to Rosenheim, and beyond."

"We didn't know what the covered wagons were for," said Felix. "We do now. If they get on open ground, they'll spread out. Beyond here, after the valley widens again, they're on the plain and they'll have such a broad front they'll surround us if we stop."

"So it has to be here."

"It has to be here. We should count ourselves lucky, because we couldn't have chosen a better place. They'll have to come out from under their wooden shells to engage us, and when they do, we'll shoot them down."

She sighed. "If only—" she started, but Büber interrupted.

"My lady, this enemy isn't some mob with clubs. They haven't come to take us alive, and they won't be put off at the sight of spears and bows. This isn't the library. Not this time." He flicked his wrist, launching some crawling thing he'd caught into the fire. "I don't like it either. But it seems it's the best we can do."

Sophia sighed again, and wondered, just for a moment, what a mess Nikoleta would have made of the oncoming army: each wagon burning brightly, dwarves spilling out, on fire, dead and dying, struggling on while bowmen crowded the top of the embankments to make sure that not one of them reached the first ditch alive.

Nothing but a bloody massacre. The Enn would have run red for a year.

And that was the temptation, the sin of covetousness. If Nikoleta had been there, it would be all so easy. There'd be no need for

Felix to be in harm's way: he could safely oversee the slaughter from the baggage train. No need for Büber to put his life in peril again in the service of his prince. No need for the Jews to be camped out at Rosenheim.

No need for her sword-arm, her prayers or her God.

She drank her beer in silence, brooding. It was something she didn't want to consider – that this was meant to be, rather than something to be avoided at all costs. HaShem would be with her, and all the Carinthians. Their victory would be divine, not mortal. They'd build an altar here, like her people had done in the time of the prophets, and they'd sound their shofar and chant their psalms of praise so loudly that the sound would echo all the way to Ennsbruck. HaShem would deliver them.

At some point, by unspoken agreement, both Büber and Reinhardt got up and left, but she didn't notice them go. Only when she blinked away the after-image of the fire did she realise that she and Felix were alone, and that he was sitting next to her, leaning back on the log.

"I think . . ." she said. She stopped and swallowed. "I think Max Ullmann killed Nikoleta Agana."

Felix said nothing, and Sophia wondered if he'd heard her or not.

"Felix?"

"I . . . know."

"You know? You know I think he did, you think he did too, or . . .?" She looked sideways. "You know he did?"

"I don't know for sure," he said quickly. "Why do you think he did?"

"His . . ." She still didn't know how to describe her. "The woman he's seeing. She works for the Odenwalds. I had a chance to talk to her. And it's not like Nikoleta hadn't already beaten Eckhardt. She had him trapped in his room and he was on fire: Peter told Frederik as much."

"Perhaps Eckhardt caught her off guard."

"But then why does Master Ullmann wake up screaming about flames?" She stared into the fire again and wondered what it must have been like. "He was there, in the White Tower, before Peter. She'd not have suspected anything."

Felix nodded slowly.

"He said to me something, a week or two afterwards, about

how her death made things more simple, and how no one would be expecting the magic to return. How we could do things differently from then on." The prince shrugged. "He was right, of course. It was more simple."

"Did you ever say he should kill her? Even as, I don't know, a joke?"

"No!" He lowered his voice. "No. She was one of us. She'd pledged her allegiance to me. I wouldn't have done that. Sophia, you have to believe me."

"Then why is she dead?"

"I didn't order her killed. I'd never even met Master Ullmann until that night in the library, and I was never alone with him. Master Büber and Master Thaler were there the whole time. I even gave him my dagger so he'd be armed against Eckhardt."

She worked her jaw slowly. "And he killed her with it."

"We don't know that, do we?"

Sophia rolled back against the log, and banged her spine hard against the rough bark. "You're going to have to ask him."

"Can it wait until we've won this battle?"

"Don't you want to know the truth?"

"Do you think he's going to tell either of us he murdered the mistress? Sophia, please. I made him a prince's man and put him in charge of my spies because I thought he was someone who could keep a secret." Felix pulled out some tufts of grass from under his legs and threw them fluttering in the air. "I need him. I need his spies and, right now, I need his Black Company."

"They're your spies, Felix. Not his. Your Black Company, too."

"Master Ullmann is loyal to me. He wants to protect me from my enemies. He wants what's best for Carinthia. He just has a . . . a different way of doing it than you."

"Nikoleta Agana wasn't your enemy."

"She would have become one."

"Is that you or Ullmann talking, Felix, because I can't tell the difference any more." There was no doubt that having a hexmaster around would have complicated everything they'd done in the short spring and long summer. In that, Ullmann was absolutely correct: Nikoleta's dying with Eckhardt had meant that the age of magic was clearly over, and the Germans had no choice but to leave it behind. And for her people, they'd no longer had to watch their taxes going towards the upkeep the Order. But what if Ullmann had killed her? "No one's above the law. That's what you said. That's what you wrote. I want him investigated."

Felix pulled his knees up and rested his chin on them. "Who's going to do that?" he asked. "Who could I possibly ask who'd say yes?"

"It has to be you, Felix." She slumped against him. "Ullmann's too powerful already. We should – no, *I* should – have realised something like this might happen at some point. Spymasters."

Felix picked up a twig and flicked it towards the fire. It fell between the logs with a puff of flame. "Once the huntmaster finds out, well: I imagine Master Ullmann's innocence won't count for much."

"When this is done," she said, "there will have to be a reckoning. Nikoleta Agana was a loyal Carinthian, and she died defending the ordinary people from a great wickedness. Her blood cries out to us for justice, and we've been deaf for too long."

She felt Felix's shoulders drop from a tense knot of bones to something more at ease. "When this is done," he agreed.

88

Pre-dawn mist had settled over the fields and ran damp streamers between the tents. Büber, wrapped in a blanket, had slept out under the stars and fallen asleep to the sound of men talking low and late into the night. The music and singing had eventually died away, and more serious discussions had taken place: who would take care of whose family, who would inherit newly acquired land, or tools or a business. Fatherless children were apprenticed, widows were taken in, brothers were made.

He couldn't remember falling asleep, and neither could he remember waking up. He was simply aware of the glimmer of light above him, and the last of the stars fading away. He lay there for a while, watching the light creep across the sky, listening to the snores and the coughing, the river running by and the wind in the trees, smelling the faint drift of ash as a breeze stirred the white embers of the cook fires and the stronger scent of pine and crushed grass.

It was time. He pulled the blanket aside and made his way quietly to the gravel bank to splash water on his face and pour it over his head. He could eat something, drink something else but water: he had a knot in his stomach that would be found in many a man that morning. If they won, then there'd be feasting and drinking. Today, that morning, better to go hungry and keep keen.

A rider trotted over the bridge, and he went to meet him.

"What's the news?"

"They're on their way, Master Büber. Started moving just before first light."

"Same as before. Harass them, but don't get caught. Do they know where we are yet?"

The rider shrugged. "Unless they've spies in our camp, they'll come at us blind."

"Let's make it a surprise, then. Don't stop just because you're almost on our own lines, otherwise they'll get suspicious." Büber lifted his hand up to the rider, and the rider reached down to grip the huntmaster's forearm. "Good hunting. When you get back to the col, my lord Felix will take command. Look after him."

"It'll be our honour, Master Büber." The rider turned and headed back the way he'd come, and Büber turned to the guards. "Sound the horns. Everyone needs to be up. Send word to Rosenheim: if they're not already on their way, they'll miss all this. If anyone needs me, I'll be with the prince."

He walked behind the first earthwork and round to the gates. The guard stood aside for him, and he found Sophia sitting on the tree-trunk, Felix asleep at her feet under the banner of Carinthia.

"My lady," he said quietly.

"Good morning, Master Büber." She looked down sadly at the huddled form under the yellow and black. "If we can call this morning good."

"Ask me tonight," he said, and then the slow ululation of the war horns breathed out across the camp, low and insistent. "The pickets say they're on their way. We should get ready."

"Ready? Ready? Give us a year, two years, then we'd be ready." She clamped her hand over her mouth, and only released it when she thought she could trust herself. "Sorry. Do you remember that night in the library? When you found Felix asleep next to me and you called me 'my lady'?"

Büber nodded. "And you said you were a lady of nothing. I disagreed."

"We've been desperate before, and we've come through. We'll come through this, and we'll earn ourselves some peace."

Felix stirred at the second blast of the horns. Perhaps he'd thought he was dreaming them, or that he was already strapping on his sword and fastening his helmet.

"Pray to your god, my lady. Even I'm afraid."

He almost ran back to the gate, but checked himself. He was a berserker. When the battle lines met, he would lose all sense of himself and throw himself at the enemy. Sweet darkness would fall on his mind and he would either come to surrounded by the dead, or open his eyes to the roof beams of Asgard. Perhaps the gods had been kind to Nikoleta; she would be the first face he'd see, and she'd bring him a silver-rimmed horn of honest beer to share with her.

So be it.

The Carinthians were mostly awake. He watched them from the top of the earthwork as they struggled into their armour and picked up their weapons, then he went down to meet his men.

The leader of one of his spear centuries was called Taube. He'd been a carpenter – apparently quite a good one. Then he'd had a diagonal cross cut into his face by Felix, and been sent to work in the salt mines as an alternative to being pressed. All the other men of Taube's century could tell a similar story.

Their scars looked ugly, uglier than Büber's own. He'd won his honestly and each was a badge of something other than murderous intent: some would call it bravery, but he preferred simply to call it life.

"Mr Taube. Line them up."

He had another century of spears – regular militia he was going to use to screen his crossbowmen. Three centuries against the whole eastern column of dwarves. He was to throw the enemy into such confusion that they were to believe there were ten times his number in the woods. Then he was supposed to push them into the Weissach, or hang them from the trees, whichever was more convenient.

The Crossed, those who Felix called the damnati, could win their freedom – but only if Büber lived. Their liberty was down to his good report, so they had to fight. That was the bargain:

otherwise it would have been too easy to kill him first, then escape.

It still might be a choice they made. But they weren't brigands, hardened by years of living outside of the law. They weren't mercenaries, either, selling their skills to the highest bidder. They were ordinary people who'd made a poor decision, had paid the price for that, and were still paying.

If they played their part today, they'd have paid in full.

They were ready. So were the other centuries.

Büber took delivery of a crossbow and a quiver full of sharp black quarrels. He slung them over his back, and there was nothing else left to do. "Let's move out."

He led them – in loose order, because marching didn't seem right for the war he wanted to wage – across the fields and pasture at the back of the Kufstein crag. Ahead was the narrow gap between the two steep hills through which the Weissach passed on its way to the Enn. Both hills' sides bristled with trees, dense and dark. It was almost too perfect a place for an ambush, for a few to hold out against many.

The track met the tributary, and followed it into the foothills. The trees closed around and over them. They were hidden from view, and Büber forged ahead to the rickety wooden bridge that crossed the river.

It was summer, and the water was low. The banks were still sharp and deep, though, carved by the spring melt. Once they'd crossed, they'd knock the bridge down; not that it would take much effort. It would serve as another ditch, another obstacle, and one they hadn't had to dig with their hands.

He crossed it and stepped off the path, into the forest and up, along the flanks of the hill, moving from trunk to trunk, feet barely whispering on the needle-rich ground, brackens and grasses bending before him and springing back behind.

Now he could hear them: a steady chop-chop of an axe at the base of a tree, the rattle of their wagons, their voices calling to each other. A few paces more and he could see them, edging forward. A tree fell away from the side of the track, and the line of wagons rolled on. There were perhaps as many as ten on clearing duty, if Büber had marked them off on his fingers and stubs right.

They'd be the first to die. Then he'd set about the lead wagon. He'd been told there were a hundred such wagons, stretched in a long line up the valley, and still he wondered why. They were so ungainly and slow. They gave protection against bow fire, but, at some point, they had to come out and fight. Perhaps they feared the sky, and a vault over their heads gave them comfort.

Büber wasn't there to give them comfort.

He pulled back and met his troops at the bridge, telling his Crossed to destroy it, while he led the other two centuries up and over the hill before spreading out along it. They knew to move as quietly as they could, not speaking. They knew to form up, crossbowmen behind on the slope with a clear view of the track, spearmen in front, crouched down and weapons ready.

He raised his finger: wait. They looked back at him. Scared as they were, they nodded, and they waited.

The bridge had gone when he returned. Taube had his spear, and something else besides: he part-carried a long, thin tree, its branches lopped.

"Are you ready to ransom yourselves?" asked Büber.

"It's not often a man's given a second chance," said Taube.

"We take them when they're offered. Let's send these bloody dwarves back to their caves."

They carried three trees in all, the ends already tied with thick rope, and there were three half-logs too. Büber had eaten crayfish on occasion, and supposed that winkling the dwarves out from under their wagons was going to be as difficult as shucking one of those sharp-shelled creatures.

Büber positioned the Crossed in knots of ten alongside the track, poles ready, blocks ready, encouraging them to cover their white faces with forest dirt and lie down in the undergrowth with green branches over them. When he looked up the slope, he couldn't see either his spears or his bowmen. Then one of them moved, just a leg to shift position. When he'd finished, he vanished again.

The trap was set. All they needed now was prey.

Büber cocked his head to one side, listening again. The low rumble of wheels, the break of a stick under foot, the incoherent bark of voices, the rushing water hissing down to his left.

He lifted the crossbow off his back. Not as good as the one he'd lost, but decent all the same. He worked the lever and the arms of the bow creaked. The string clicked into place. He slid the quiver around so that it was in easy reach, and plucked a bolt out. Laying it carefully on the stock, he raised the tiller to his shoulder.

He was one man, standing in the road. That was what they saw. A dwarf reached out and banged on the side of the lead wagon. It stopped, and the dwarf shouted to whoever was inside.

He was well within range, and Büber killed him, punching the quarrel straight through his breastplate. While the rest of the clearing party took cover, he reloaded.

The wagon started to roll forward again, with dwarves behind it, huddled to its rear axle so as not to show any part of themselves.

But it wasn't Büber they should have been worried about.

Most of them took two or three bolts, which was wasteful and their centurion should have prevented that, but gods, it was quick. A single volley and they were all down, most of them dead, the few who weren't left shrieking and trying to drag themselves away.

The wagons stopped, then started again, rumbling towards him. There was only so much he could do now, but what he could do was this: he walked towards the lead one, right up to the narrow eye-slit in the front of its angled face, and loosed his bolt through it.

He hit someone for certain, and he stepped aside as the wagon faltered, then carried on past him.

From the undergrowth, three long poles clattered out, pushing right beneath the hem of the wagon's wooden skirt. Men leapt out and, as the poles lifted up high, they slid semicircular blocks underneath them.

Then the poles were hauled down again, aided by the ropes that the men had tied to the ends. The poles caught the rim, raised it up so that the wheels all along one side spun uselessly to a halt, and still they kept lifting. The levers opened up a gap of two feet, three feet, more, tipping the wagon up to expose the dwarves inside.

The Crossed rushed the wagon. They jabbed furiously with their spears, roaring out of their own pain, and again, within moments, every dwarf was down, dead or dying. The levers loosed their hold and the wagon banged back down, partly breaking in the process, the green, unseasoned timber and crude construction failing at the first test.

Limbs sprawled out from underneath, and the mud and stones of the track were stained red.

"The next one," ordered Büber.

The teams with the poles briskly picked up their equipment and moved to the next in line. There were a full century of wagons, and it would take the better part of the day to work their way through them at this rate. Not that the dwarves were going to let them do that, sitting mutely and meekly until it was their turn.

They had the second one over in short order, being more confident now in their lifting, certain of the weight. They cut down the dwarves inside, and, with a final shove, sent the wagon crashing down off the track and half into the river below.

The third wagon beckoned. The doors at the back opened, and the dwarves spilt out. A score in each, guessed Büber, as bowstrings hummed and bolts hissed. The Crossed hung back, waiting for the arrows to do their work. Some of the dwarves tried to retreat, others to attack. None made it more than a pace or two.

The next wagon. Fourth? What did he care? He needed to see to them all. Above him, on the slope, the bowmen were moving, getting into position for the next volley, while below, they picked up their poles.

Now word had reached the nearest wagons down the line that there were men outside, attacking with impunity. The rear doors burst open, dwarves rushed out. Some were brought down. Others took shelter behind the wagons, but the Crossed formed up in squads and flushed them out.

Wagon after wagon emptied and was abandoned, its occupants killed or chased away. Behind them all stood Peter Büber, crossbow in hand, urging his men onwards. He could feel himself grow bolder at the scent of blood in his nose, the sound of a grunt a man makes when he pushes a spear deep into the stomach of another, the gasp he makes as he takes the blow. The dwarves didn't look so different from men now, though they were short and stocky, they had beards and long braided hair, they wore armour too tight for them and held weapons a fraction too small. Call them men and have done with it.

He reached down and touched the pommel of his sword. Not yet, not yet. But soon.

The whole line seethed. Dwarves poured out and ran back, far enough to be out of range, to regroup, to form ranks and files. Büber called his Crossed back, and they trickled towards him, reluctant to break off from their duties. Carpenters, bakers, butchers and vintners they may once have been; killers was what they'd become.

The dwarvish army had formed up, and they began to advance.

"Into the woods. Get to your positions." He shooed them up the hill, and was the last up behind them. He climbed strongly, taking big strides; when he judged he was halfway up, he turned and sat down, bracing his legs against a tree-trunk. The rest of the Crossed crouched, waiting.

Their enemy couldn't pass them by; their rear would be insecure and vulnerable. Neither could they split their force into two, with one half carrying on towards Kufstein, because they had no idea how many Carinthians there were.

They hesitated. The forests were alien to them, and wild things lurked there. They'd much rather put their axes to the trees. But here, on the hills outside Kufstein, there were far too many of them to clear; they'd have to go into the woods, and try to find the men hiding under their vast green canopies.

89

"Sophia, you have to leave now," said Felix. He'd put his armour on, mounted his horse, and collected his shield.

"Do I?"

For a moment, he was nonplussed. "Yes. You can't stay here."

"Why not? You are."

"But I'm the prince. It's my duty, my people, my palatinate." He checked that everything was buckled on tight. It'd come loose soon enough if it wasn't, and getting killed because his helmet had slipped over his eyes at the wrong moment wasn't how he wanted to be remembered.

He didn't want to get killed at all, but he realised he might not have a choice.

"It's *my* duty too, Felix. And my people." She unsheathed her spatha, tried a few practice swings and rested it on her shoulder. "I'll stay on the crag if you prefer, but I will stay."

She planted her feet and looked determined as only she could.

"If the last wall falls, I want you to ride back to Rosenheim."

"And what will be waiting for me there? You won't. Unless you have another army you're not telling me about, I can't see how running away will help."

Felix leant low from his saddle. "Gather the survivors together, see them safe back to Carinthia. Something might happen between now and then. München and Augsburg might come to our side. Or my Frankish cousins. Promise me you'll do that."

She swallowed, and looked down at the ground for a moment.

"You can't promise me anything," she said, and it was true. He couldn't; only that he'd spend his short life of thirteen years as expensively as possible.

"We can win," he said, "and it's not like we want to lose."

"No one takes the field wanting to lose, Felix, but, more often than not, one side does."

"I thought that if your HaShem is for us, none could stand against us." That was what she'd told him last night. He had his doubts, but she seemed to believe it.

"I'd rather we won, and you lived." She looked up again and reached for his hand. "I want them both."

"Then pray for both," he said. Her fingers were cold, as if she were dead already. He couldn't countenance that thought, no matter what. "I have to go. I'll leave orders so that if it looks as though things are going badly, you're to be taken to Rosenheim first, then Juvavum. By force if necessary."

He dragged his hand back and, before she could answer, rode for the gate. If he couldn't save *her*, who could he save?

Through and round and across, gates, earthworks, bridge. Master Büber had already marched away with his small force towards the Weissach. Whether any of them would come back was something only time would tell: there were lookouts in place, but no reserves to call on, not yet. Master Ullmann was marching from the north with the reinforcements. The dwarves on the west bank were just broaching the edge of the forest. They'd reach the first earthwork soon enough.

The camp had been roughly put down. There were piles of tents, and the pale, trampled rectangles of where they'd been. The men who'd slept in them were already in position, spear and bow ready.

He rode up to the rear of the two earthworks they had in the way of the main advance, squeezed between valley-side and wooded hill. Four centuries of spears stood nervously behind it, watching him from under the iron brims of their helmets. He ought to have prepared some stirring words before the battle, something to stiffen the resolve of his ill-trained troops.

He had nothing beyond what they already knew: that if they lost, Carinthia would be lost, and, along with it, their homes, their land, their livelihoods and their kin.

Felix drew the Sword of Carinthia, and held it high as he rode by. If a boy of thirteen was at the very front, then his troops might consider proving themselves at least his equal in courage.

The forward earthwork was manned by spear and bowmen. Master Reinhardt was already there, standing on top, with his horse below held by a spearman. Felix dismounted and joined him. There was little point in opening up his distance-pipe, as the trees obscured everything.

"How far away are they?"

Reinhardt peered down the road, turned into a green tunnel by the over-reaching trees. "Four, five stadia. We've killed a good number, but there always seem to be more to take their place." He pulled at his moustache. "Any news from Master Büber?"

"I'm sure he's got better things to do than send us messages, Master Reinhardt. He'll hold the line, even if he has to do it all on his own." Felix saw movement ahead, and he stiffened, but it was only Carinthian horsemen tracking back. "I've no intention of letting him down on this side."

More horses trotted out into the cleared area, almost a stadia deep and deliberately covered with rooted, knee-high tree stumps. The road was covered with logs, all the way to the ditch in front of them.

"This looks like it," said Reinhardt. He raised his voice. "Don't waste your shots on the wagons. Make every bolt count. Listen to the horns and the drums. Remember, we want to pull back to the next defence, and the one after that. When the time comes, we retreat in good order and leave time for our bowmen to cut the bastards down. Stay with your century. Act as one. We're going to grind this one out, so no stupid heroics: your spear and your bow, with you behind them, are more important to us than killing that beardy fucker right in front of you. He'll die soon enough."

A bowman laughed, braced his bow and cranked the lever. "Back to Svartalfheim with you, Master Dwarf. Midgard's no place for you."

"That's right," called Reinhardt, "sound the horns and bang the drums. Let them know we're here. Carinthia!"

The Carinthian lines burst with noise, so loud that Felix could barely hear himself say to Reinhardt, "Get the horses back over here and leave the field clear. You have command."

Boy and man clasped arms, and Reinhardt pulled him closer.

"You've done more in a year than your father did in ten, my lord, and what's more, you're the better man. Gods' speed."

Felix struggled for something to say. "Master Reinhardt. Rather you here than any number of earls. Make them pay for every foot of ground they take. Make them pay dearly."

"My lord," he said. "It'll be an honour." He went back for his horse, and left Felix with the men on top of the earthwork, watching the first wagon roll sluggishly into view.

It trundled along, then banged up against the first log in its path. It stopped, then eased forward further. The log rolled a little way before clattering into the next. It was much harder to make progress now, with two tree-trunks to push along the ground. When the wagon hit the third, it stopped altogether. It was a hundred or so feet into the stadia. Within range. Felix waited to see what would happen next.

The rear doors of the first wagon were thrown aside with a bang. Carinthian bowmen raised their weapons, and those who hadn't already nocked a quarrel did so now in a whisper of hissing and clicking. The second wagon collided with the back of the first, its pointed prow lifting up to rest on the roof of the one in front. The third locked with the second, and so on, until there was an unbroken line of them all the way back to the trees.

And if they hadn't blocked the road, that line would have come right up to their defences. That was how they'd wanted to do it. Now they'd been thwarted.

Felix walked along the top of the earthwork, waiting for the dwarves' next move.

"My lord," asked one centurion, "I thought we'd come here to fight."

"So," said Felix, "did I. Sound the horns again."

The low, vibrating roar of the animal-headed horns echoed across the field. They were answered by higher-pitched ram's horns from down the valley. The Jews were coming, and with them the troops mustered by Sophia.

Then came a sound like a slap in the face, harsh and uncompromising. The dwarvish horns bellowed, and emerging from the tree line, a trickle, a seep, then a flood of armoured dwarves. The nose of the front wagon popped, and the vanguard charged out.

"Aim at the targets in front of you," bellowed Reinhardt, wheeling his horse about. "Loose at will."

Three hundred crossbows all sounded at once, and the air hummed. The first row, the first two rows, were cut down. Those in the front of the vanguard fared particularly badly: every single one of them fell.

Felix stared at the dwarves as they ran across the open ground, around the sawn trunks, their awkward strides slowly narrowing the distance. Weighed down by armour, axes and hammers, they got no further than halfway before the fastest bowmen were ready to shoot again.

Those remaining in the vanguard had climbed over the bodies of their kin, and were closer still. And behind them, there were more. There was no let-up. They poured out of the forest like spilt water from a breached dam.

"Spears," called Reinhardt, and the drums beat urgently. "My lord, get your arse on your horse."

The crossbowmen stood their ground as the spears formed up in a wall in front and down-slope of them. The latter pointed their weapons towards the ditch and braced themselves.

"My lord. Your horse!"

Felix turned to see the lone spearman still holding his horse's reins, then glanced back at the dwarvish van as it struggled through the hail of bolts to get to the Carinthian lines. Gods, they were being slaughtered in their tens and hundreds, but there were so many of them it didn't seem to make any difference.

He ran down the reverse slope and took the reins for himself. "Stand with your brothers," he said, sheathing his sword for the brief moment it took him to hoist himself up. Then he drew it again and galloped to join the other horses, gathered at the steep valley-side.

Reinhardt rode up and down the line, roaring his orders, his defiance. The hum and slap of crossbows was constant. "Hold, you brave men, hold."

The groan as the front lines met was a ghastly sound. Spears jabbed forward as if hoeing the ground, and the formation the Carinthians had practised and practised again in the fortress court-yard stayed firm.

Crossbowmen loosed their last shots. Horns called them back, and they slithered and slipped off their perches to run the half-stadia to the next earthwork in line.

Felix held his sword in his shield-hand, and wiped the sweat away. "We have to time this charge right. Get ready." He moved the sword back to his right and watched.

Reinhardt judged it was time the spears pulled back. The crossbows were in position, ready and loaded. The horns sounded again, and each man peeled away up and over the top, down the slope, across the grassy pasture, looking for their century's mark.

Not everyone succeeded in withdrawing. Men gained the top of the embankment, only to be dragged down with a cry. Reinhardt raved and yelled at his troops, but it was now him who needed to get out of the way. The last man stumbled and fell at the base of the earth bank, and his commander hesitated.

Dwarvish hands and heads rose above the ridge.

"Up, man, up."

The spearman got his feet under him, scooped up his weapon and ran as if trolls had smelt his blood.

Reinhardt tracked with him all the way, urging him on, and the dwarves swarmed over the embankment.

The air was abruptly full of rushing, and the volley of bolts burrowed home. They could hardly miss, but it took time that they didn't have to reload.

"Now," said Felix, and his horse dashed forward. Hooves thundered against the turf, and, in moments, the cavalry were at full tilt, riding down the line and thrusting with their short spears.

Felix pulled back his sword-arm, and cut forward. The Sword of Carinthia sliced a dwarf's neck so deep that it separated head from shoulders, and it was done so quickly that he barely felt the impact in his hand. Another strike, slashing up, blade flashing between forearm and wrist. And again, overhead to slice through shoulder and chest.

He was at the river, and he wheeled about. Here they came, his riders, and they all seemed to have made it through. Some had lost their spears and had drawn their swords, but they were ready to go again.

It wasn't as easy this time. The dwarves were ready for them, thicker on the ground, and rather than being on the sword side, they were on the off-hand. Felix used his shield as much as his sword, punching hard at faces twisted with effort, using his speed to carry him through. He brought his sword down point-first, thrusting through gaps in their mail, hacking at their arms and faces.

He was back where he'd started, but not all of his riders had survived. One man was still upright on his horse, in the midst of the dwarvish host, surrounded, lost, still stabbing and hacking away at the determined hands that had hold of his legs.

His horse whinnied and fell, and that was the last anyone saw of him.

The Carinthian horns blew again, and another volley of bolts hammered into the enemy's lines. Still they pressed on, trampling the bodies of man and dwarf alike.

"Again." Felix turned and levelled his sword at an axe-wielder who was huffing up towards them. They'd done enough damage to attract a dwarvish commander's attention: others were following behind him.

His axe swing was mistimed; unlike Felix's underhand thrust, which caught the dwarf in the throat. He pulled his blade out straight as he rode by, and charged at another, swinging his sword overhand, past the held-high hammer half and against the side of its helmet, which buckled. The blow made his fingers sing, and he flexed them to adjust his grip.

Down the line again, cutting right, right, right, as often as he could manage, and he was riding along the foot of the second embankment. That shouldn't be happening – they needed space to ride back and retreat to the col above the valley floor. Reinhardt was already ordering his spearmen into position, and the closeness of that wall of spikes unnerved his mount.

He wheeled away from the Carinthian line and started to carve his way to the muster-point. The second charge had been a mistake. He'd been too eager, too pleased with the first attack and wanting more. The bowmen were ready, and it was him who was delaying them.

The other riders saw him change direction, and they pulled up and turned. They were in a better position, not so deep, not so pinned against their own defences. Most of them would make it, except the one who at that instant took an axe to the leg, and such was the force of it, it cut through the horse's flank that they went down and died together. Or that other rider, now on foot, who was backing towards the spear wall, parrying axes, hammers, mauls and maces. Respite came from the crossbow bolts that drove through dwarvish mail and plate and leather and skin and bone, giving him the time needed for friendly hands to reach out and pull him to safety.

Felix suddenly realised he was on his own in a sea of foes, and the tide was strong and fast.

90

Ullmann's Black Company were first to the earthworks at the approaches to the bridge. They stopped and formed up along it, and wondered why the bowmen weren't streaming back past them to the Kufstein crag, a hundred feet above them. Ullmann wanted to know why, too. He joined his men and put his hand above his eyes to shade them, trying to see what was happening.

There were horses, some with riders, some loose, scattering in the fields behind the Carinthian line on the other side of the river. There was a thick ribbon of men on the embankment, bowmen and spearmen alike. They seethed like boiling water, and the sound was of drums and horns and the bright clash of metal.

"Forward," he called.

The Black Company obeyed as one, Ullmann leaping down into the ditch to chase after his men. The ten-mile march from Rosenheim had been demanding, recrossing the Enn and coming down the east bank. He'd hoped for a few moments' rest before they joined the battle, and his legs ached as he ran.

It wasn't that far – less than a couple of stadia – but it felt much further, running towards the roar of battle while riderless horses panicked and darted in front of them. A man on a horse was galloping backwards and forwards behind the line. It had to be Reinhardt, but why wasn't he ordering the bows back? His front was clearly engaged, and that was the signal for an orderly withdrawal to begin. Had he lost sight of the battle plan already, a plan that so clearly depended on getting as many bows behind the wooden walls of Kufstein as possible?

"Support the centre," shouted Ullmann, as he tried to flag Reinhardt down. "Master! Sound the retreat."

"Gods, Master Ullmann. It's the prince." The man was close to breaking.

This wasn't how it was supposed to be.

"Sound the retreat, now. Or we've lost the bows." He drew his sword and struggled breathlessly up the embankment.

He understood when he reached the broad top why Reinhardt couldn't decide. The entire ground between the first and second defences was thick with figures. Helmets and raised weapons bobbed like a mass of floating corks, those at the front separating themselves from the mass to throw themselves at the Carinthian spears.

The crossbowmen were firing as fast as they could, a cataract of bolts pouring down over the heads of their kin into the dwarvish host. It was the only way the spears were holding the line, the ranks of enemy axes and hammers being thinned as the dwarves waded through their own dead to reach the men.

The prince.

Still on his horse, with three, four, five other riders around him, trying to cut and slash their way through to the tree line on the right of the field. They shouldn't have even been there; they should have been up behind the second bank to cover the spears' backs while they made for the bridge.

The horses were crazed, the riders exhausted, the situation hopeless.

"Black Company, with me. Carinthia!"

Ullmann pushed his way through the spear wall and started towards Felix. The dwarf in front of him raised his spiked hammer, but it was almost ludicrous the amount of time Ullmann had to execute the most simple of sword-thrusts into his exposed throat. He pulled his blade back, and the dwarf crumpled forwards, blood pouring out.

Then another: an axe, swinging sideways towards his ribs. He turned to avoid the sweep, then stepped in behind it and brought his own blade down on the dwarf's half-turned back. And then another, except this one was cut down by someone else even before he could steady himself.

The Black Company had taken the field, pushing the dwarves back, making a space before the spear wall as they pointed them-selves like an arrowhead at the surrounded horsemen.

It was only as he stepped on a body that grunted, on his way to engaging his next opponent, that he questioned what he was doing. He wasn't following the plan, either. The Carinthian horns blared for the bowmen to retreat, and the steady hiss and thud of bolts tailed off to nothing. The spearmen began to turn and run for the earthworks behind the bridge.

In moments, he and his men would be isolated and the only thing that could possibly follow was their annihilation. Even though they might hold, they'd be flanked left and right, then engulfed.

He sidestepped an axe swing, kicked onto his back the dwarf who'd made it, and pushed his blade between breastplate and groin: in, twist, out. They were still twenty feet away from Felix, and the five horsemen had been reduced to two while he'd been wading knee-deep in corpses.

So it had come to this. Ullmann judged that even if he reached Felix's side, they'd be facing the entire dwarvish host on their own. Better that one leader of the Carinthians should die than two. Better the privileged son of the idle nobility than a man like himself.

Felix looked up from his increasingly weary swordwork. Hope flowered and died in the same breath.

"Pull back," shouted Ullmann. "Back to the bridge."

Two of his men died simply because of their incredulity. They turned their heads at his call, and let their guards down. The rest took a step back, then another. Dwarves filled the gap, looking for them to either break and run, or suddenly charge forward again.

The Black Company moved ever backwards, chopping at any who dared come close enough, and then finally, with their feet in the ditch and heels on the bank, they turned and scrambled up and over the earthwork.

When Ullmann paused to look behind him, Felix had gone. Had he fallen, or had he somehow escaped? Ullmann didn't dare ask one way or the other, and there was no time to do so anyway. The horns were sounding, loud and long, and they were the last on the wall.

They'd have to run as fast as they could for the bridge, with the dwarves free to chase after them: there'd be no sudden attack from mounted swords or storm of crossbow bolts.

"Come on, come on," he urged his company. The bridge was narrow, and there were a lot of them to get across it.

He glanced over his shoulder, to see how close the enemy were. They'd stopped. They weren't giving chase at all.

He looked again, slowing. The dwarvish fighters had crested the bank and advanced as far as the base of the lee-side slope, but they weren't pursuing them across the field. They seemed content with the gains they'd made, and showed no inclination to assault the bridge directly.

Those on the crag had seen what was happening. Carinthian horns ululated across the valley, and the army's headlong flight eased into an exhausted walk.

Ullmann's men collected together as they headed for the bridge: there were fewer of them than before, and there were one or two present who wouldn't fight again that day. He didn't have the breath for conversation, which would have been redundant anyway. His men knew they couldn't have reached Felix, no matter what. If the prince was dead, it was because of the boy's stupidity. Ullmann had saved them from throwing their lives away in what would have been nothing more than a futile gesture. Carinthia needed them. Carinthia needed *him*.

They started to cross the bridge, but Ullmann hung back. Leaning against the parapet of the the bridge, he rested his blunted, bloody sword on its stonework.

"Master Ullmann? What're the dwarves doing?" One of his company, just as tired, crouched on the ground next to him, and spat phlegm.

Ullmann coughed, and once he'd started he found it difficult to stop. It left him breathless all over again. "Don't know," he managed.

"The prince?"

"Don't know," he repeated.

Straightening himself, he hooked his arm under his colleague's and pulled him up too. In the brief moment they looked each other in the eye, shame and regret were plain in each man's face. And fear.

"We did what we could," wheezed Ullmann. "I'm sure he lives."

The man nodded and limped away. Ullmann picked up his sword and wiped it on his breeks, though whether that made it cleaner or more filthy was questionable. Now that the stuff was drying his clothes stiff, he realised he was caked in gore.

He raised his head quickly at the sound of hooves, but it was only Reinhardt.

"Did you see?" Despite being on the back of a horse, and taller than the embankment, he didn't know either. "My lord prince?"

"He must have got away." If he said so often enough, thought Ullmann, people would believe him. They'd seen him lead his company over the embankment to Felix's defence. They weren't to know what had happened after that, or suspect what thoughts he'd had.

Reinhardt passed down his flask. Ullmann took it and swallowed some of the warm, brackish water.

"They're supposed to attack us," said Reinhardt, wheeling his horse around.

"Perhaps they expect us to attack them." Ullmann was about to wipe his mouth with his sleeve, but decided against it. In comparison, Reinhardt was spotless. "Give me a moment and I'll be ready."

"Gods, man. You look like someone bled a pig over you."

Ullmann drank again: the last of the water swilled into his open mouth and down his chin.

"Killing dwarves is thirsty work. How many do you think we did for?"

Reinhardt pulled at his moustache and stared across at the enemy line. "A good thousand or two. More, even. Each bow-century must have seen off five times their number, and they were piling up at the foot of our spears."

"And our casualties?"

"More or less all our horse." Reinhardt clenched his jaw and gritted his teeth. "Bowmen, none. Spears, two dozen or so. Those who couldn't stay on their feet and were run down."

"Two thousand killed for the loss of forty men?" Ullmann sheathed his sword, uncleaned or not. "Are you sure of your sums, Master Reinhardt?"

"That's what my centurions tell me. There was a whole century on the right that went into the woods. Assuming they can swim the river, or join up with whoever's up on the col, I'll still count them able to fight." He reached up and unbuckled his helmet, working it loose and dragging it off his dark, damp hair. "Victories are carved out of numbers like this."

"Then why aren't we singing, and blowing our horns? Freyja's tits, we've got something to cheer about."

"It feels like a defeat," said Reinhardt. "We were pushed back too easily. There are too many of them. It doesn't matter if we kill two or ten thousand of them, they still outnumber us."

Ullmann kicked at the ground. "If every Carinthian life is worth a hundred dwarvish ones, most of us will get to go home. That's news worth spreading, so let's not keep it to ourselves."

Reinhardt declined the return of the water flask. "If that's the end of fighting for the day, I'll spread it far and wide. I'll set a watch, the centuries can rest at their posts, and we'll wait for Felix's return. There's no word yet from Master Büber, though."

Ullmann pushed an unruly thought away. "I'm sure he's doing his duty."

"I've sent some reinforcements to the Weissach bridge. If he needs them, they'll be there." Reinhardt turned towards the bridge. "Clean yourself up, get something to eat, and we'll sort out with my lady exactly where we stand."

"Lady Sophia's here?" There was no reason for her not to be, but he'd assumed Felix would have sent her back to Rosenberg via the west side's horse track.

"Standing on the walls of the crag." Reinhardt pointed out the Carinthian banner draped over the wooden palisade, and the dark figure resting her elbows on the top, distance-pipe in hand.

Ullmann looked and looked again, judging angles and distances. "She couldn't have seen what happened to Felix from there, could she?"

"The shoulder of the hill opposite gets in the way," said Reinhardt. "From the crag, it's only the far end of that second wall that's visible."

So she hadn't seen his abortive attempt to rescue her consort, nor his subsequent retreat. That was something, at least.

"That's . . ." – and he tried to find the right word – "unfortunate for my lady."

"I'd rather her not be here at all," said Reinhardt; "it's too dangerous. But she is who she is and, what some people think she is too, a seer of her god. Strange days we're in, Master Ullmann."

He rode off, back through the lines, and Ullmann followed wearily. On the other side of the bridge, every spare blade of grass, every turned sod, had someone lying on it. Half of them looked stunned by what had happened to them, and the other half looked dead, eyes closed and still.

Further back, though, were the volunteers he'd brought. They were fresher but more anxious. Their only experience of battle so far had been watching the Carinthian line run from its defences as fast as possible. It hadn't been like that at all: those who'd fought had acquitted themselves magnificently and when the dwarves approached them again across the open ground and funnelled themselves across the bridge, they would do so again. Dwarves would die in their thousands, except this time, the spears would hold the earthworks while the bowmen above shot at them until every quarrel had flown and even the bows were thrown down on their treacherous dwarvish heads.

Suddenly, he was staring at Aelinn, and she at him.

She blinked roundly at him, and rather than taking a step towards him, took a step back.

He pressed his lips thin, and gave a short, stiff bow.

"I have a . . ." – he took a breath – "an appointment I have to keep."

She nodded, mutely, and he turned aside to avoid walking any closer to her.

91

It had degenerated into a series of skirmishes, but each one followed the same pattern. The dwarvish line would advance cautiously uphill, clearly hating the terrain, and slowly collect in knots rather than form a continuous chain. The shadows under the trees would shift subtly, and a sudden harvest of half a dozen bolts would sprout from mail-clad chests and bellies. The dwarves would fall, and their brothers would race to where they thought the shooters were.

And when they arrived, out of breath and aching from the run, spearmen would pounce and momentarily outnumbering them, overwhelm them, leaving them dying on the prickly, thirsty ground.

Then the spears would be gone, further upslope, and any pursuit would be met with more crossbows from a completely different angle.

It could have gone on all day until the last dwarf dropped: it might have surprised Ironmaker as much as it had Büber, but the

Carinthians were simply better disciplined. And while each dwarf was likely to be more than a match against a man in single combat, when the Carinthians acted together and played to their strengths, they were the better fighters, too.

The problem was that they were running out of hill. They were halfway up now, and behind him, Büber could see the daylight over the long ridge. They'd retreated from the track and through the forest, and unless they wanted to defend the reverse slope, fighting with their backs to the river and facing uphill, they'd have to do something different when they reached the top.

It was his turn to skirmish. He twisted around, rested his back against honest pine and selected a target downhill. There was a flurry of fighting, a crowd of men stabbing down hard and fast, then scattering. The next group of dwarves half-heartedly tried to respond in kind, and Büber's bolt looped through the tree-trunks to bury itself in the shoulder of their leader.

The dwarf gave a cry and spun away, and the others faltered, giving up almost as soon as they'd started. Büber reloaded. The lower slopes were crawling with dwarves, still too many for his comfort. Forming up and slugging it out wasn't going to be a good choice. The enemy would push him and his men into the Enn.

He turned and used his long legs to gain height. Another scrappy fracas broke out below him, and was over just as quickly as all the others.

What was he going to do? All he had was what he knew, and he knew that in a stand-up fight they'd lose what little advantage they had.

He faced them once more, waited for his moment, put another dwarf on his back, and climbed the hill again. These men were relying on him not to throw their lives away, but he wanted more than that: he wanted a way they could win. He hadn't thought this far ahead, though, thinking he'd force them out of their wagons and hold them up for as long as it took. When the main dwarvish force had spent itself against the Kufstein crag, then the Carinthians would simply turn around and crush the flanking group.

In the meantime, he could have everyone melt away and leave the dwarves with no one to fight. What then? Regroup, and hit them again. From where? And the answer was suddenly obvious. Behind the dwarves. While they were searching ahead, jumping at every flap of a fern or snap of a twig, his men would be at the bottom of the hill, pushing the dwarvish wagons into the Weissach.

Of course, the dwarves would come after them again. And the Carinthians would vanish back into the forests.

He'd been thinking too small; it wasn't about this hill, this high ground. All of the valley was his. He could torment his enemies until those that were left alive broke and ran.

How stupid to rely on earth walls and open ground for their main defence, when that was exactly what the dwarves wanted: something solid to attack, with all the men conveniently all lined up behind it, so they didn't have to go looking for them amongst the vast green silence under the trees.

He should have insisted that Felix had done it that way. He should have done it regardless, raiding behind the dwarvish wall, striking and withdrawing, then appearing somewhere else to strike again. Gods, the tactics were obvious, except they were learnt too late.

"Centurions, to me," he called, and while he waited, he reloaded his bow. The berserker rage ebbed and flowed in him, but he thought he could control it for a little while longer.

Another fight, and more dead bodies rolling back down the steep hill, catching on tree-trunks, sliding over the rocks protruding between the roots.

Sweaty-faced centurions gathered around him, one of spear, one of bow, and Taube.

"Are we strong? The men holding up?" Büber asked them.

"Even with the double-share of quarrels, some are starting to run short."

"Doing well enough," said the second centurion. "No more than four, five lost."

Taube grunted. "They come at us, we kill them. It's what's asked of us."

Büber was satisfied. "Get the bows on the ridge, waste some bolts if that's what you have to do. When the dwarves get too close, just turn and run, nothing fancy. They're exhausted already and they won't follow for fear of ambush. Spears over the top and head south, out of sight and as quiet as you can. I mean for us to disappear as well as any hexmaster could manage. Come back around the rear of the wagon train and kill any guards they left, and quickly before they can call out. Start turning them over, break their wheels, anything to make sure they can't be used again. Got it? Go."

The men went back to their centuries, moving from group to group, repeating the orders, while Büber looked down the slope at the dwarves struggling up the hill to meet them, weighed down by their armour and weapons. Every few moments, one more of their number gasped as a bolt plunged through metal and cloth into the weak flesh beneath.

Should he just charge them? Should he raise his naked blade and barrel down at them, two centuries of spear at his back, and tumble them all broken at the bottom of the hill? The roar of his kinfolk's war-cries, the pale bleating of his foes' fear. It would be over so quick he wouldn't even remember it.

He took a breath. He took two. He lifted his hand from his sword grip. Soon, soon, but not now.

He looked again. His own lines had withdrawn like he'd told them, and he was now between them and the dwarves. He ought to set an example and obey his own orders.

He turned back up the slope, using one hand to steady his climb, until he was at the crest of the hill. The spear centuries had all but melted away down the other side, the browns and blacks and greens of their clothing blending with the forest colours. The bows were crouched in a long line, shooting steadily, picking off their targets when they were certain of a hit, waiting if they didn't, calling among themselves so that they didn't all aim for the same dwarf and waste their quarrels.

He glanced to his left, and saw movement on the broad ridge. Armoured figures had reached the top, far away from any Carinthian.

Büber tapped the nearest man on the shoulder, pointed, and shouted so that others could hear. "Pull back. Now."

The bowmen peeled away, holding their bows by the stocks, running through the forests they'd seen since they were born and had played in as children. They knew to duck under branches and dodge tree trunks. They knew how to run downhill with their feet in the soft needlefall.

Büber would have been the last the dwarves saw of them, his shoulders shifting as his arms balanced his body in a way they'd yet to learn. Whisper-quiet and wordless, they all climbed the second smaller rise and descended over it. The woods were dotted with men, crouched, catching their breath, and ahead of them was the track and the evidence of dwarvish axes: fallen trees and the scent of fresh-cut pine.

He stopped for a moment, listening for sounds of pursuit. Gods, he'd spent half his life doing that, running from one eldritch beast or another that was trying to kill him, and now it was dwarves.

He heard calls, faint and incomprehensible. They were coming from the top of the ridge, half a mile away, and beyond it, too. They didn't know the signs to track even three hundred men through the forest, and perhaps they thought they'd gone down to the river and from there, headed towards Kufstein.

The Carinthians had pickets, but he didn't want the dwarvish flanking move to come anywhere near the crag. He looked again at the track, and off to his left he could see the creamy pale planks of a wagon. It was the last in line.

He was just where he wanted to be, then. He crept forward through the silent Carinthians, gesturing that the spearmen should follow him. They unfolded from their rest and formed up behind him, moving towards the tree line at the edge of the track. Büber went closest of all, and saw that they'd left two guards with each wagon. If there was a century of wagons, that was . . . what? Fewer soldiers than he had? Probably.

Save the bowmen's shot for later. It was time for the spears. He raised his hand, hidden from the road by a tree, and pointed at the rear wagon. He dropped his hand, and the Carinthians rose with a shout and rushed the dwarves.

They were so startled they barely had time to realise they were being set upon, let alone to assume a fighting stance. Men raced down the track, either side of the wagon train. Everywhere they met the enemy, they outnumbered them enormously. They were a moving wall of spear-points bearing down on whoever got in their way, and it looked like they could go down the whole line, all the way to the front again.

"Bows, get their weapons. Every man arm himself with more than a knife."

He left the forest and started down the track himself. What he realised was that they were winning. They could wreck the wagons at the rear with impunity, and a few more at the front to prevent the ones behind ever moving again. The dwarves had no answer against him. None of their engines would make it to Kufstein because he'd killed so many of them. Half of them at least, and the ones left he'd run ragged across hill and vale.

No point in getting over-confident, but none in timidity either. It was almost time.

He was back where he'd started, all those hours ago, at the front of the wagons. Taube was there, with his Crossed men, bloody and mean. "Break this one," said Büber, slapping his hand on a wagon. "Leave it on the road. Spears, take the bows and hide on the east side of the track, a stadia or two deep in the forest. Wait for us there."

The spear centurion nodded and retreated again, leaving Büber with the Crossed, who were already putting dwarvish axes through dwarvish wheel hubs.

Straining with the effort, Taube kicked one of the wheels free and sent it rolling away in the direction of the Weissach. The wagon tilted, and there was a splash from the river below.

"What are we still doing here, Master Büber?" asked Taube.

"We're the bait in the trap, Mr Taube. As if you needed to ask."

"If we win here, are we free?" He pulled his purloined axe free of the split green wood and hefted it.

"You won't be under any sentence, that's for sure. You may still want to fight for your homes and your families."

Taube walked to the next wagon and started chopping. Between axe-blows, he grunted. "Our homes and our families. Of course."

Older, more capricious princes would have seized these men's property and shown their household the road, but Büber knew that Felix had made certain that whatever the men had done, their wives and children hadn't suffered for it.

"If you don't know shame, how about duty?" Bait or not, he was offering himself in the same way.

"And you suppose my precious wife has the same notions of duty?" He'd all but reduced the axle to kindling, and the wagon sagged to the ground. The scars on his face twisted. "Take me back, will she?"

Büber shrugged. He knew all about scars, and lost fingers and toes. If Taube had been this much of a bitter little shit in his previous life, perhaps sending him down the mines had given his family a freedom they hadn't looked for or expected.

"You could always beg," he said, and turned his attention to the dwarves up the hill.

They were massing near the crest, above the slopes that were strewn with dwarvish dead: everywhere he looked there were bodies, in ones and twos and mores, face up, face down, wrapped around tree trunks and in the hollows of roots, at the end of long scrapes where they'd slid and at the bottom of rocky outcrops.

Led by an idiot king to their deaths. Gods, that made him angry – that none of this was even necessary. Was Ironmaker even here to see what he'd done?

There was more movement as the dwarves started to descend. It was time they ran again.

"Taube, with me."

Büber took the river-side of the track and ran down the long line of wagons. The Crossed followed, some having permanently exchanged their spears for axes and hammers. That they'd made a stupid decision to fight with a weapon they hadn't trained with was up to them. But they had a history of ill-discipline and making bad choices, and it was too late to change them back or castigate them. The dwarves were slithering and sliding down the hill towards them.

Büber reached the end of the wagons, and started to shove men towards the Weissach, through the trees. "That way. Keep going." He stayed long enough to make certain that he'd been spotted, and that when he plunged through the green ferns by the side of the track, he was being followed.

Of course the dwarves wanted to keep sight of him, in case he disappeared again into the green mist, only to come at them from a different direction. They struggled after him, exhausted, savaged, scared of the bright sky and the tall trees.

He ran on, through the hidden spearmen, the crouching bows. As he passed the bowmen, they rose up and fired, and still the dwarves came at them. Then the wood erupted with men, charging forward, spears thrusting, twisting, charging again.

Now.

Büber stopped, turned and drew his sword.

92

When she asked them straight, no one would tell her.

She was given hints, and veiled elisions, but when her patience for such verbal circumlocutions had worn thin and she'd finally demanded, "Is Felix alive or dead?", she couldn't find anyone who would admit to having seen him being either dragged off his horse, or ride away free.

"But he was right in front of you. Master Ullmann, you were there, on the earthwork. How could you not have seen what happened to him?"

She looked at Ullmann carefully, watched him glance sideways at Reinhardt. Was he worried that Reinhardt would deny his story, she wondered, or were they both hiding the same thing?

Ullmann was wet, not from sweat, but from river water. She could smell its weedy taint on him. "My lady, I didn't see. I was fighting for my life and the life of the men around me." He ran his fingers through his damp hair. "There were loose horses, I know that. None of them were Felix's."

"Master Reinhardt? If I go down and speak to the centurions, what will they tell me?" She put her hands on her hips and speared him with her gimlet eye. She'd have liked to have speared him with something more substantial.

"They'll tell you what we've told you, my lady. That he was on his horse, and then he'd gone, and no one can say where."

She howled with frustration.

Ullmann pulled out his sword, and it was filthy. She knew what a sword looked like when it had gone through a man, and it didn't look that much different when it had gone through a dwarf. He set about cleaning the blade.

"You've lost your prince," she accused them, stamping her feet.

"He's not lost—" started Reinhardt, but she cut him off.

"Then where is he? Is he hiding? Has he run away?"

"He is not dead," said Reinhardt. He stood up to face her. "He is not dead, because no one saw him die."

"People die all the time without being watched."

Reinhardt took another step closer, and lowered his voice so that only she could hear. "When a prince of Carinthia leads his army into battle, his troops will win the battle, not least because they know the prince still lives. If he dies while there is still fighting to be done, they might lose heart. Their courage might falter. They might decide to run away."

"But we—"

It was his turn to interrupt. "They have not lost heart, and their courage is still strong. Felix is therefore alive. Does my lady understand?"

"Yes. I understand." She did, but it didn't help. She needed to know the truth.

"So my lord Felix's commands still stand," said Reinhardt. "He'd be angry if we changed them now."

"He might be angry if we change the order of battle," said Büber, arriving as silently as a ghost and as bloody as a butcher, "but he'll be livid if we throw the war away doing something we know won't work."

Sophia's eyes widened at the sight of him, and Reinhardt managed, "Gods, Peter," before he was struck dumb.

Büber ignored him for the moment. "My lady, the eastern side of the river is secure."

She recovered. It wasn't like she hadn't seen him covered in other people's blood before. "Secure?"

"All the dwarves there are dead, my lady, save the few who had the wit to run away." His arms were red up to past his elbows, as if he'd purposefully washed them in gore. "I've lost twenty-five men. So I've been told, anyway. And I've gained as many axes, hammers, mail shirts, helmets and the like as you might want."

She couldn't celebrate. She wasn't even sure of the reaction Büber wanted, since his winning a battle against overwhelming odds clearly wasn't what he wanted to talk about.

"Thank you, Master Büber," she said; then she left them for a moment, and went to the barrel that they'd drunk from the previous night. There was still some beer left inside, so she heaved the barrel to the log where they'd sat the night before, and poured him a mug.

She presented it to him, and he took it from her. She was left red where his fingers had momentarily touched hers. Büber drained the mug in three gulps and tossed it empty back into the grass.

"You say we're going to lose the war," she asked him, "despite what you've just done."

Büber sat down on the log. She'd seen him like that before too, after the library, when he'd gone berserk for the the first time. After she'd manage to convince him that she, Cohen and the others were on his side, he'd subsided into a melancholic flatness that was the opposite of rage.

He'd done his fighting. He'd won. And now, even though they might be pitched back into the fray at any moment, he'd stopped.

He stared at his hands. "We beat them because we kept moving.

They hate the forest, the sky, the grass, the wind and the rain. But they hate the forest most of all. If we'd fought them between here and the wall, we'd be packing up our tents and going home already."

"What did you do, Peter?" she asked. "Tell us what you did."

"Just let them chase us, up the hill, down the hill, through the trees. They move as a mass. If you can split them up, they don't fight so well . . . it's like eating a cow."

"One bite at a time," she said.

Reinhardt scowled. "All credit to you, Master Büber, but we've killed a couple of thousand of them too."

"That doesn't matter," said Büber. "They know where you are, and they're coming to kill you. Even if we build walls of stone as high as this crag, they'll still eventually overwhelm us. There are, how many of them left?"

"Ten thousand," said Sophia.

"We won on the Weissach because we had nothing to defend and they had nothing to attack. If we stay here, we'll lose."

"But you built these ditches with your own hands, man," said Reinhardt. "Are you now saying they're useless?"

"Yes," said Büber. "It was the wrong plan, and we wasted our time. We need to change it now. They'll crush us if we stay still."

Reinhardt spun away, then roared back around. "This is the place we decided we'd make our stand. This natural fortress. One bridge to cross. Open land for our bows. Ditches and ramparts for our spears. And you want to change all this on a whim?"

Büber sighed. "It's not a whim. You'd never even fought a dwarf before today. Don't you think you should at least listen to me?"

When Reinhardt took another step closer to Büber, Sophia stood between them. "Stop this. Now," she said. She looked over her shoulder. "You're very quiet, Master Ullmann."

Ullmann was rubbing at a spot of congealed blood caught inside a fuller on his blade. He looked up, and she couldn't read him at all.

"My lady," he said.

"Give us your wisdom. Master Büber wants us to fight in the forests, where there's a chance we'll get separated from one another. Master Reinhardt wants us to fight behind our walls of earth, which if we defend, may well break us. You've fought the dwarves: what do you say?"

Ullmann gave up his cleaning, and slid his sword back into its scabbard. "There are too many of them to face at once." He looked at his feet, anywhere but at Reinhardt. "It doesn't matter if we kill another two thousand, or five thousand, or seven thousand. If they destroy our army, then . . . if they mean to take Juvavum, they will. Over-Carinthia, or the east of the palatinate near Wien haven't had a chance to provide any militia, and perhaps they could retake the town. There are woodsmen in the north and miners in the south, too. They own a stake in their forests and salt now, and King Ironmaker will have to pry those out of their dead hands. The dwarves probably wouldn't be able to hold on to any of the gains they'd made, and we'll probably win in the end, whatever we decide here."

"And afterwards Carinthia would be too weak to resist being carved up between Bavaria, Wien and the Doge. Everything would be lost." Sophia stared bleakly in the direction of the dwarves, where she hoped Felix also was, up on the col by the lake with the remains of the Carinthian cavalry.

Büber, Reinhardt and Ullmann were looking to her to decide what to do.

"If . . ." she asked, "if we stand and fight, as we intended, can we kill enough of them to allow some other army to finish them?"

"We don't have another army, my lady," said Reinhardt.

"If München and Augsburg turn up, we do," she said.

"There needs to be some Carinthian force left in the field." said Ullmann, "or there'll be nothing to stop the Bavarians from taking Juvavum."

"The Bavarians should be here with us, shoulder to shoulder on the walls," said Reinhardt. "It's a disgrace that they're not."

Ullmann nodded. "I don't disagree. So why not let the dwarves take München instead of Juvavum?"

His words lodged in her heart like a hook. She looked at Reinhardt, at Büber, at Ullmann. "Can we do that?"

"We can talk to them under a flag of truce – we don't have any Dwarvish speakers, but they'll have some German ones. Or Latin. My lady knows Latin." Ullmann picked at his nails. "We promise to retreat to our borders; they promise not to cross them."

"We've destroyed a third of their army," said Reinhardt. "Do you think that's enough of a message for them to comprehend?"

Büber sighed loudly, and Sophia sat down next to him. "Peter? What is it?"

"Let's not do this. Let's not pretend to ourselves that Ironmaker will keep his word. Let's not sell our neighbours as worm-food as the cost for saving our own skins. Let's not overlook the protection we've extended to Rosenheim and Simbach. Let's not take the fucking cowards' way out of hiding behind a line on the fucking map while everything around us burns."

He got up slowly, leaving the place where he'd been sitting damp and stained with blood. "We've been here before. We've been here so many, many times in the last thousand years that you'd have thought we'd have learnt something from it by now. This is our business. Ironmaker has to be stopped, and I don't see the lords of München or Augsburg or the King of the Franks or the Protector of Wien lining up to do this. No, it's a thirteen-year-old boy instead. And if he were here, he'd want us to fight on in whichever way we can until we've finished what we came here to do. You know it, all of you."

He was right. Of course he was right. Anything else was unworthy of them, of her. She had to trust. To believe.

"How do we do this, then?"

"We destroy the bridge, swim the Enn, and we drag them one by one into the forest."

He was serious, absolutely and utterly serious; deep conviction written across his scarred face.

"What if they cross too? What if they march on Rosenheim, or Juvavum, while we're still pecking away at them?"

"My lady, they won't be able to march on anywhere because they won't be able to turn their backs on us. The reason they're still in this valley is not because of the walls we've built but because of the army we've raised, and it's not our walls they have to take, it's our lives. Deny them the chance to do that, and they're still stuck here." He held out his crusted hands imploringly. "Our strength is in our arms and our hearts. I see that now. Please see it with me."

He so rarely asked for anything. She couldn't even remember the last time she'd heard him say please.

"Can we bring down the bridge?" she asked. It wasn't that wide, but it had spanned the river solidly enough to take the annual spring flood for at least a hundred years.

Reinhardt gritted his teeth. "Given a century of men with crowbars and a full day, I could reduce it to rubble. We came to build, though, not tear down. I think it's too late. Which is why we should stay with Felix's plan."

That was just a little bit cunning, invoking Felix's name. Sophia bit her tongue at its mention and blinked away the tears.

"How many men could you spare, Master Reinhardt? If Master Büber was going to take part of our army across the Enn and attack from behind, how many centuries do we need to defend here?"

"All of them, my lady," said Reinhardt. "All of them, and more."

She buried her head in her hands. They could make their stand here. They could fight in the woods. They could sue for peace. If she chose badly, Carinthia was lost.

She stayed still for the longest time, so much so that she only moved when Büber's shadow crossed her. She looked up to see him beside the palisade, looking out through a distance-pipe over the valley.

"What are they doing, Master Büber?"

With the lens at his eye, he tracked between the far bank and the valley-side.

"Taking apart our earthwork, my lady. They mean to use their wagons again, and my guess is they'll be able to bring them up all the way to our lines this time."

It suddenly became simple.

"Master Büber. Go and talk to the centurions. Take whoever will go with you. The rest of us will hold out here as long as we can, then turn and run." She turned to Reinhardt. "Put no more than two centuries of spears on the first embankment facing the bridge. The bows will be up here with me."

"Two, my lady?" His voice was weak, uncomprehending.

"No more than that, yes. When they fail, the crag will be surrounded quickly. Everyone else will be behind the second embankment, and you'll have to lead as many of them as you can save back to the bridge at Rosenheim, and try and protect that from the dwarves as best you can. Put pickets on the west bank, too, in case they cross the hills rather than follow the road."

Then she looked at Ullmann, who must have realised she was keeping something special for him.

"My lady?"

"I need your Black Company. I have no intention of sacrificing the lives of the bowmen for nothing. Nor yours. But we will have to fight our way out. Do you understand?"

She was certain he did. She wanted him separated from his own personal army. Whether he agreed with her was, for the moment, irrelevant. He couldn't refuse her openly.

"You have your orders, and you need to hurry," she said. Ullmann and Reinhardt realised they'd been dismissed, along with their advice, and Sophia thought it was better that Büber got among the troops now, rather than staring up the valley through his distance-pipe, looking for a likely crossing point.

"You can do that later," she told him. "Go and collect your men, while we still have some."

Büber closed the tube and carefully replaced the covers over the lenses. Everything he touched was left with a rime of bloody fingerprints. He walked past her on the way to the gate, and she whispered, "HaShem go with you, Peter."

He paused, nodded, then carried on.

93

The sun crawled across the sky until it lanced straight down the valley, turning the dark river into a white-gold line too bright to look at. Across on the west side of the valley, the dwarves were lining up their wagons on the flat ground. They'd all but demolished the embankment – at least the part Ullmann could see past the shoulder of the hill – and they'd taken out a few of the small drystone walls that divided the farm land, all outside of bow-shot.

Büber had marched off before midday, taking two-thirds of the centuries with him into the forest behind the Kufstein crag. He'd taken the Crossed, despite Sophia's releasing them from their sentences. Or perhaps because of it. He'd also taken both centuries of Jews, and Aelinn's mob of domestic servants, stable boys and porters. There'd been nothing he could do about that.

He'd watched the trees swallow them, one by one, until none were left. If they were out of his sight, they were out of Sophia's too.

Büber could take his army wherever he wanted: over the mountains and back to Juvavum if he chose. He could leave them all here to die, and rude, rough Peter Büber would be prince.

Ullmann glanced over his shoulder at Sophia, who was adjusting her skirts so that she could fight and run in them better. There were rumours about her and Büber. He knew them false, because he'd started them: but with Felix gone, he'd be using those rumours differently now.

Below the crag were the remnants of their spearmen: two centuries on the first wall, two more on the second one, which didn't stretch any significant distance. The dwarves could go around the end. Everything appeared small and weak in comparison to the force massing opposite them.

The top of crag itself was covered with crossbowmen, slowly lining up at the palisade and checking their angles. The bridge, both ditches, and the ground either side were all in range. As in the earlier engagements, it would be a bloody slaughter, except this time they knew it wouldn't be enough.

There was still time for him to walk the short distance between the two armies, and talk terms. Considering their own small losses compared to those they'd inflicted on the dwarves, they should have the upper hand in any negotiations. What was wrong with setting the dwarves on Bavaria, as long as they left Carinthia alone? If München wasn't going to send anyone to fight on their side, then they deserved to be besieged – again.

Then he remembered he'd ordered the ruler of München to be killed. Had it been done, and, importantly, had it been done secretly? Where was Augsburg? Most likely relying on Carinthia to sort out its problems like the Bavarians had always done.

They'd be next, the proud, vainglorious lords of Bavaria. They'd go the way of Fuchs, stabbed with a Carinthian spear in the hands of a Bavarian housewife.

His anger was directed in all directions at once. It was the dwarves' fault for going to war, Felix's fault for refusing to hire mercenaries, Büber's fault for taking away the best part of their army, Sophia's fault for allowing him to do so. He needed Carinthia intact if any of his plans were to ripen and bear fruit.

If, if, if. If he'd been in charge now, those mistakes simply wouldn't have been made. He gripped the top of the palisade and watched the play of light and shadow across the valley.

The first wagon rolled forward. He thought he might have imagined the movement, but it was followed by a second, then a third.

The bowmen had noticed, too, and were growing quietly serious, pointing.

"My lady?" he called. "They've started."

She stopped her impromptu cutting and lacing and ran across, darting between the bowmen to press in next to him at the palisade. Her mouth made a thin, grim line.

"Regrets, my lady?" Even now, she could send out the white flag of truce.

"Plenty, Master Ullmann, but none about the company I keep."

The men around her cheered at that, and Ullmann thought them fools. Better they had ten times the spears and five times the bows; a proper army, silent and disciplined, swift and deadly.

The good humour started to drain away, and he looked out again over the river. A murmuring started, and Sophia's eyes narrowed.

"The distance-pipe," she called. "Bring me the distance-pipe."

It was passed forward, and by the time it was put into her hands, she was visibly trembling. She held it to her eye, twisting the tubes for focus. She grew still.

Then she was thrusting the apparatus at Ullmann and stumbling away. The bowmen parted before and closed behind her.

Ullmann lifted the unfamiliar device to his face. Everything was blurred, and green, then blue, but eventually he got it under control. He scanned the advancing wagons – gods, they looked so close – and finally lighted on the lead vehicle.

A thin, sharpened stake had been crudely nailed to the front of it, and impaled on top was a head, bouncing and jolting with every imperfect revolution of the wheels.

The spike came out through a crown of matted dark hair, and, despite the blood and mud, it was obvious whose head it was.

How they'd recognised him was anyone's guess – none of the dwarves had seen Felix before, and he'd carried no distinguishing tokens, no crown, no seal. Even the armour he'd worn was plain, and the Sword of Carinthia . . . ah. So they had long memories, and the ancient, once-magical weapon had given him away.

The prince was dead, and there was no one to take his throne after him. He slipped down from the palisade, and went to find Sophia.

She was white, her eyes large and dark and staring. Her whole frame rose and fell in time with her deliberate, deep breaths. He wasn't even sure that she was aware of his, or anyone else's presence, when she suddenly hissed: "And you'd have me make a deal with these, these creatures?"

Ullmann thought of a dozen different replies, none of which would help, so he stayed silent.

"They cut off his head."

They had. No one could deny it, because the head was there in plain sight, stuck on a pole and getting closer with each passing moment.

"They will pay for this."

But not today, not with the army she'd purposefully split in two. Ullmann would remind her of that.

"My lady, I think we need to retreat. Save what we can of the men."

"No," she said baldly. She started towards the palisade, every step agony.

"My lady, I insist." He reached out and pulled back on her sleeve.

She drew her sword and, in one fluid move, swung it down to where his neck and shoulder met. It stopped at the collar of his mail shirt.

"You insist? Or what? You'll rid yourself of another troublesome woman?" Her knuckles had turned as white as her face. "A dagger through the ribs maybe?"

She lifted the sword-blade away, holding it high.

"We both have our parts to play, Master Ullmann. See that you play yours." She strode off to be among the bowmen, who were sombrely going about the business of cocking their bows, pressing bolts onto the stock, saying their last prayers to whichever of the Aesir they thought might help them best.

Ullmann closed his eyes and raised his own entreaty. Gods, she knows. How could she know? How long has she known? With Felix dead, there'd be nothing to stop her doing whatever it was she wanted to do to him, because she was all they had now. The people loved her despite all the reasons they had not to. They would, quite literally, follow her to the gates of the underworld if she asked.

How had it turned out this way? His chest constricted as he imagined the weight of the huge stone used in pressing settle on him. He turned away and leant forward, hands on knees, in an attempt to get more air in.

It wasn't over yet, though. A hundred different things could happen in battle, and almost all of them unexpected. There was no reason – no good reason – to give up hope. She was the only person who knew. If, may the gods forbid it, something was to happen to her, then that was that. The secret would be dead.

He took another breath and found that he'd recovered enough. Going through the still-open gate, he went down the lee side of the crag to find his men.

"Form up," said Ullmann. "No one's going to find us unready."

They lined up, four ranks deep, and did it quickly. He could take pride in that.

He paced in front of them. "When the time comes, it'll be hard fighting. The bowmen from the crag need to run the four or five stadia to the trees, and we're to protect them until they're safe. When we're certain of that, we retreat, too. Anyone gets separated, we'll regroup at Rosenheim. It's more than likely that the dwarves will stop for the day here, but if they pursue us, we have to stand in the way. Any questions?"

There was silence, then a voice piped up from the back. "Prince Felix. Do we try and take him back?"

"Ah, lads. Would that we could, but don't you see what a trap they've made for us, and what fools we'd be if we fell into it? I don't like what they've done any more than you do, but we can all see why they've done it – to provoke us into doing something stupid. There'll be other times, and yes, a bag of florins to the man who brings him back home. But not now. Let's worry about the living, not the dead, as cold as that may seem."

The Carinthian horns sounded, the dwarvish horns answered.

From where he stood behind the crag, Ullmann's view was limited to the rear of the first earthwork. The spears had lined up to receive the lead wagon – with Felix's head displayed banner-proud – as its front wheels fell into the ditch. The second would come up behind it, then the third, just like they'd seen earlier that day. The doors fore and aft would open, and there would be a ready-made tunnel stretching across the bridge all the way to beyond bow-shot where the dwarves were mustering.

There came a roar, and the spears braced to receive the charge. They stood firm as dwarf after dwarf hurled themselves out of the narrow opening in the lead wagon, almost directly onto the Carinthian spears. It was insane to fight like that, sacrificing so

678

many, but soon enough there was a bulge in the Carinthian line, where the dwarves had forced them back with the sheer press of their bodies and ferocity of their blows.

Bows were useless at this stage, their bolts more likely to hit friend than foe, and, worse, more than half the spearmen at the earthwork weren't even engaged. They were keeping their positions along the rampart rather than crowding the wagon's opening.

Reinhardt rode back and forth as before, exhorting his men to hold. To Ullmann's mind it was exactly the worst thing he could have done.

The line suddenly broke. A dwarf made it to the top of the embankment, was cut down, only to be replaced by two more, then several of them. The spears were were now split. And they were fighting not downhill but on the level.

Reinhardt rode into the melee, slashing with his sword, rather than calling for the retreat. And without waiting for the order, those on the limits of the line started to run back. A trickle became a flood, and the Carinthian line burst asunder. Reinhardt looked for a moment like he'd lose his own head, but used his rearing horse to clear a path ahead of him before bolting to the temporary safety of the second and final earthwork.

The bows all fired at once, and the battle suddenly flowed the other way. Dwarves were riddled with bolts, two and three to a body. Where there had been a score or more, now there were none, cut down by the hard rain from the crag above them.

More took their place, though, and in the time it took the bowmen to reload and resight, the ground between the first and second embankments was lost. The dwarves ignored the spears on the earthwork. They turned and made straight for the crag.

Of course they would. Getting rid of the bows was their priority. Ullmann barely had time to join the Black Company's line and draw his sword before their fronts met.

The dwarves threw themselves at the swords with the same delirious vigour as they had at the spears. Leaping, they held their axes and hammers high, then drove them down. Most of them died in the air, impaled, but their momentum carried them onwards, knocking men over, breaking the ranks, leaving undefended gaps that were impossible to close.

Even though the bolts whirred and hissed, thinning the enemy, there were simply too many to withstand. The spears on the earthwork remained where they were, when they should have attacked. Reinhardt had it wrong again.

Ullmann's arm ached from the parry and thrust, and his legs from the continual backstepping over uneven terrain. They had started with four ranks; now they could barely muster two. No matter how many they killed – and the ground they were slowly yielding was thick with corpses – there was always another dwarf hurling himself at their line.

The Black Company was being hacked to pieces, and soon there wouldn't be enough of them to shield the crag, let alone to cover any retreat by the bowmen. Amid the forest of raised axe-blades and hammer-heads, he could see Felix's head, still on its pole, bobbing and yawing, being passed from hand to hand.

And still the spears didn't engage. Gods, Reinhardt. Do something.

It was Sophia who saw that the battle had tipped again. She came riding out behind the Black Company, ahead of a stream of men, each clutching their bows and running for the tree line.

"Pull back," grunted Ullmann, defending himself against an inexpert hammer-swing that would have nevertheless caved in his skull. "Pull back."

The call rippled up the line. The rush of bowmen trickled to nothing, and Ullmann checked the distance they had to cover. The remnants of the Black Company needed the right moment to break, or they'd be cut down to a man.

Finally, and far too late, Carinthian horns blared and the spears surged forward, down the embankment, across the ditch, into the dwarvish flank. They struck hard, then pulled back at once.

Heads turned, and Ullmann thought that might be the time, but they were still toe-to-toe. Again, the horns, again the charge, and the relentless advance on what was left of his men faltered.

"Go. Run."

He'd have been a fool not to take his own advice, and Ullmann was no fool. He spun on his heel and started to put one foot in front of the next as quickly as he could. He daren't look around, even though he knew that some of his men weren't going to be as fast as he was, and were being brought down behind him.

All he needed was a lead, a little bit of distance between him and them to get him to the point where their weapons couldn't reach him and they'd have to chase after him on those stunted legs of theirs. Six feet, the height of a man, would do.

Gods, the trees looked as far away as when he'd started, though that couldn't possibly be true. To his left and right, men in black surcoats were running level with him, and out of the corner of his eye, he could see a dark swell, a grey metal wave, following him across the trampled pasture.

It wasn't easy. He'd already been tired. Now his chest was starting to burn and his mouth tasted acid. His sword was balanced and light, but his scabbard swung awkwardly, waggling like a tail. His mail coat could turn a blade, but he wasn't facing blades now.

He felt himself slowing down. He gritted his teeth and tried harder. He had to outrun the pack. He had to beat them to the trees. Halfway there.

Sophia kept pace with them. She couldn't ride that well, and she was on a horse that wasn't a trained warhorse, more a half-bred carthorse suited to the learner she was rather than the warrior she pretended to be. She was there, though, a distraction, and more so as she angled her horse between the Black Company and the dwarves.

The metal-shod hooves and her sword gained his men a few extra feet. It might be enough, and he risked turning his head to see just how far ahead he was.

His eyes went wide.

Not far enough. Thirty feet or so. If he could lose the mail, the sword, the scabbard, he'd make it for certain. With them, he wasn't sure. He was starting to fall behind the rest of his men. But he was young, he was active; he shouldn't be being beaten by his men, some of whom were twice his age.

His breathing was ragged, his throat closing up. This wasn't exhaustion: this was fear. He could do it. He could make the trees. They were closer. He was in front. The dwarves had to be more tired than he was. They had to be more unused to running on their strangely lengthened legs than he was on his that he'd had from birth.

Sophia rode behind them again, tracking from right to left. Those dwarves that were closest to her tried to strike at her. They stumbled. Some of them fell. See, they were tired. They'd had enough. They'd stop soon and let him slow down.

The acid in his mouth swelled suddenly, and he was vomiting

even as he was running, spitting it out and hauling air before the next contraction of his stomach.

It was her fault. That was it. It was her fault because he knew that it didn't matter if he reached the tree line, even if he managed to evade the dwarves that would inevitably run in after him, she was going to have him pressed anyway. He was running towards one doom as fast as he ran away from the other.

He had vomit down his front, stinging tears in his eyes, burning pain in his legs, agony in his chest. He was going to die like this.

Then there were trees, right in front of him, and the heels of the men ahead were disappearing through the ferns. He'd run all that way, the Kufstein crag now small with distance, only to fail at the last.

Sophia came galloping towards him, crouching low over the saddle, her head almost pressed against the white foam on the horse's neck. She held her sword against her leg. She started to slow, to pull back on the reins, to rise up and raise her sword, ready to strike at dwarves at Ullmann's back.

And as she passed him, he slashed at the horse's legs.

It screamed in pain, and he heard it go down. He kept on running and choking, choking and running. Almost there. He tried to blink away his blurred vision, trying to pick a path into the forest before he reached it.

He could hear footsteps behind him. Gods, so close behind him. He waved his sword again, a desperate effort to fend them off, and it sent him stumbling to his right. Somehow, he managed to keep his feet.

Sophia appeared on his off-side, running strongly, her legs devouring the distance left between her and the first of the trees. Her old cavalry spatha was still in her hand, and she didn't even break stride as she back-handed him in the face with the blade.

His world went abruptly dark.

94

The first they saw of it was the old square Roman tower, a dilapidated shadow against the setting sun. Aaron Morgenstern called his wagon to a halt, and the rest of them slowly rumbled to a standstill in a long line behind.

Thaler climbed stiffly from his wagon at the rear, and they met halfway.

"Gods," said Thaler, "my arse feels like I've sat on a wasps' nest."

"You should worry," said Morgenstern; "at least you have padding on your tusch. My bones have rattled free and the only thing holding them together is my skin."

"Yes, well: let's not make it a competition, shall we?" Thaler put his hands on his hips and scanned the horizon to the south. The Enn valley was a deeply incised blue notch in the blade of the golden mountain peaks.

There was no sign of battle, but it occurred to him that he had little real idea of what he should be looking for. He didn't see smoke, and he didn't see crows. That was about the limit of his knowledge.

"Do we keep going south, or should we stay here tonight?" asked Morgenstern.

"I have absolutely no idea." Thaler frowned. "It all depends, doesn't it? Do they need us now?"

"And just how are we supposed to find out? Ride a bullock up to this, this place where they are —"

"Kufstein," said Thaler.

"It'll be the middle of the night by the time we get there. We may as well camp and start again in the morning." Morgenstern, satisfied with his logic, stretched his spine and began to walk back to his wagon.

Thaler, thoughts suddenly on bread and sausage and beer, shook his head. "Aaron, you're right. It'll take too long to see how the land lies. Which is why we must press on. It's taken us two days to get here as it is, and we absolutely cannot delay any further. If we turn up and we've already won, we can join in the celebrations. If we turn up too late, well: that's that, isn't it? But what if we turn up exactly when they need us? The longer we wait, the more likely it is we'll lose."

Morgenstern stopped. "And how do you make that calculation?"

"Because if we assign a third to each probability, it's quite clear that two-thirds of the time we haven't won yet."

"But half of that two-thirds means we've lost already."

"Ah," said Thaler. "If we carry on now, we'll win two-thirds of the time."

"I . . ." Morgenstern stared at the ground, deep in concentration, then finally back at Thaler. "That's drek and you know it."

Thaler smiled and gave a little bow. "Nevertheless, we'll continue. Left, if you please, Mr Morgenstern."

Morgenstern muttered his way back to his wagon, and Thaler returned to the rear cart. Tuomanen had been asleep in the back, and she looked up over the side.

"Where are we?"

"Rosenheim," said Thaler, bracing himself to mount up next to the teamster.

"Are we stopping?"

"No." He heaved, and fell into the lap of old Kaleb. "Apologies."

She curled back up like a cat on the sacks of grain they'd bought as cattle feed. "Wake me when we get to wherever it is we're going."

The line of carts started moving again, rattling and bouncing up the potholed track. Up ahead, Thaler could see Morgenstern's wagon turn and plod away up the Ennsbruck road. It stopped after only a short distance, and Morgenstern stood, using the driver for support.

"What now?" His own wagon shuddered to a halt.

Morgenstern was waving at him, and pointing due south. Thaler leant back over the wagon to retrieve his bag, and found that Tuomanen was lying mostly on it.

"Mistress, I need my distance-pipe."

She lifted her head, and Thaler pulled the bag free. Retrieving the instrument, he stood up to gain height, and held it to his eye.

There was the swathe of forest in the valley's mouth, cloaking its sides up to the bare rock. There was the pasture land east of the river, good grazing all of it. And there, in between, was the via. On it was a rider.

At first, it seemed that the man was alone, but after a little tweak on the focus, Thaler could see a long, ragged line of figures on foot behind him. At least, he assumed it was a him. At this distance he couldn't tell.

"We have company," he said, and Tuomanen was instantly on her feet. She took the distance-pipe from him and peered down it.

"I can't tell if that looks like a defeated army or a victorious one. One thing: they look tired." She put her foot up on the side of the wagon and rested her elbow on her knee, seeking a steadier view.

"There doesn't seem to be that many of them, either." Thaler groped for his walking-stick. "I appreciate that this suggestion is somewhat redundant, but would you be so kind as to stay here until I return?"

He struggled down from the cart and walked along the via, apprehension rising in his craw. Morgenstern watched as the librarian passed the lead wagon, saying nothing but pursing his lips and frowning.

Slowly, the approaching figure on horseback resolved in detail. Yes, it was a man. Yes, he was in armour with a sword at his waist. Yes, his expression was dour.

"Gods, Master Thaler. What are you doing out here?"

Reinhardt. "Good evening, Master. We've come to offer you our assistance, in whichever way we can."

"We?" Reinhardt shielded his eyes against the low sun to take in the line of ox-carts. "Are you quite mad, man?"

"Never saner, Master Reinhardt. Tell me how the battle went. Or goes. You're here, so there has to have been some sort of resolution."

"We've been . . ." he started, then chewed at his lip. "Ah, there's bad news. Our lord Prince Felix has fallen."

Thaler steadied himself on his stick. "Oh."

"He died bravely, charging the foe repeatedly, but . . ." – he looked down sadly – "you'll hear this from others, so I may as well tell you first. The dwarves mounted his head on a pole and carried it in their vanguard."

Thaler rummaged in a pocket for a handkerchief, and dabbed at his eyes. "Are we lost, then?"

"No," said Reinhardt, "and no one's more surprised than I am at that. We held firm. We changed our tactics. Master Büber won a famous victory against their left flank, destroying it utterly with few losses, but their main force managed to overwhelm our defences each time, no matter how many of them we killed. What you see here is a planned retreat. Master Büber still has a large part of our forces in the field, and will skirmish with the dwarves' rear as they try to advance down the valley."

"So are you . . ." – Thaler struggled to find the words – "in charge now?"

"The Lady Sophia is our war-leader. Assuming she's still alive. And can make her way back here. She has the bowmen and Master Ullmann's Black Company with her, so our hope's not without foundation." Reinhardt leant forward onto his saddle's pommel. "Gods, Master Thaler, it's a mess. We're scattered to the four winds and no one knows where anyone is any more. After chasing us off, they may well have turned around and crushed Büber's forces, and we won't know until they come howling at us again and burn Rosenheim down around our ears."

Thaler blew his nose. "Sophia. I mean, Lady Sophia: was she there when they paraded Felix's head?"

"She had one of your distance-pipes. I imagine she'd have been among the first to see it."

"And?" wondered Thaler.

"She held. She held like a true Carinthian. I was never for her, Master Thaler, not like some. I'd entertained thoughts of Felix choosing a German bride when the time came, and shooing these Jews out of the fortress and back into their own alley." He shook his head. "But the woman has steel in her heart as well as in her hand, and as irregular as it might be to have a Jewess lead us into battle, I can't think of anyone else from among our number more suitable than her."

Thaler was lost for a moment. There'd always been one of Alaric's sons on the throne, no matter how tenuous the genealogy had sometimes been. "What will become of us?"

"I don't know, I'm afraid. I simply don't know." Reinhardt looked behind him at the spearmen he'd brought from Kufstein. "Everyone is tired and angry and not a little hopeless. We haven't lost yet, but gods, we're close to it. Unless Büber can win five battles like the one he already has, then that's it. The dwarves could even choose to ignore us, and there's little we could do to hurt them."

"We haven't lost yet? Well, that's good, surely, because it means we can still win." Thaler pulled himself together. "I'm sure we can sort something out in due course. It sounds like most of our army is still intact, yes?"

"Yes—"

"And you've made it back to the muster-point without

incident, so there's no reason to suppose that others can't do the same." Thaler smiled uncertainly up. "Courage, Master Reinhardt. Despite our tragic loss, we can still leave him a legacy to be proud of."

"We need to rest. The field south of Rosenheim should still have tents. Bring your wagons." Reinhardt sat back up and frowned. "What exactly do you have in them?"

"Gunnhilde and her three sisters, five pots of various sizes, ammunition, a great deal of black powder, and, frankly, whatever else we could find."

"Not food, or crossbow bolts, or anything useful then."

Thaler stroked his chin. "I shall take that as a reflection of your grief, Master Reinhardt. Lead your men into Rosenheim, and I shall join you shortly."

Reinhardt ground his teeth together, but rather than saying anything more, he dug his heels in his horse's flanks and slowly plodded on towards the bridge over the Enn. Thaler raised his stick at Morgenstern and jabbed it in the same direction, then walked back to his cart.

"Nothing useful indeed," he muttered to himself over and over again, and he was in a sour mood when he climbed back up next to Kaleb. "A change of plan," he announced. "To Rosenheim."

"What news?" asked Tuomanen.

"Felix is dead," he said baldly.

"Does that mean . . .?"

"No, it does not. Perhaps with lesser peoples it would, but not Carinthia. We can still put an army in the field, and we will still fight."

Tuomanen dragged her fingers through her sleep-squashed hair, and left it spiky. "So who's . . .?"

"Sophia."

"A woman."

"Well, she was the last time I looked." He turned in his seat and narrowed his eyes at her. "I would've thought you'd approve of this development."

"Felix was nice," she said. "I liked him. He seemed very concerned about doing good."

"He was. He'll be greatly missed. Not least by Sophia."

Tuomanen shuffled forward on her knees and leant between Thaler and Kaleb. "Will you dissolve into civil war now, with two or more claimants for the throne? Or will you take a Jew as your queen?"

"This isn't the time for such singularly inappropriate talk, Mistress. We narrowly avoided one civil conflict. I trust that whatever solution we arrive at, we do so peacefully. Such transitions from one ruling house to another have happened before, as our histories testify." He turned to the front again, and folded his arms.

Tuomanen whispered in his ear. "Except that you've got rid of all the earls, and now every man and woman is allowed to own their own land. Who'd want to rule a palatinate like that?"

"Someone who doesn't aspire to be a despot, perhaps." He huffed. "There are other forms of government, you know. Just because you've lived half your life under a tyranny."

The cart in front jerked forward, and after a suitable gap had widened, theirs started to follow.

"The strong rule, the weak are ruled," she said. "It's natural law."

"For an educated woman, you do speak all kinds of nonsense sometimes."

"Prove it's not so."

Thaler puckered his lips as he thought. "Well, then. Perhaps you can explain why you're here to debate such matters with me? Were you forced? Were you obliged? Or did you choose to come of your own free will and be among a company of free men and women, to fight for something that is little more than an idea?"

She laughed, tossing her head back and showing her teeth.

"Well played, Master Thaler, very well played indeed."

"I thought so too," he said, and allowed himself a certain smugness. "Oh, for certain, tyranny is our natural state – you'll have no argument from me there – but it's a mean, brutal and unstable state for both ruler and ruled. Civilised people will always aspire to greater things, and here we are, on the cusp of change again. Do we go on or do we fall back?"

"It'll be interesting to watch," she said.

"Watch? Watch? Good gods, Mistress. You're as much part of this as I am." He turned to look at her again. "All kinds of nonsense, I say."

Kaleb just shook his head and concentrated on getting the cart wheels between the bridge parapets.

95

Sophia was determined to lead them in with something approaching dignity, but all she could manage was a bone-weary limp. The rush of battle had been one thing, but once its numbing effect had worn off, she'd hurt: all over for certain, her right ankle in particular, where she'd tried and failed to extract her foot from her stirrup as the horse fell underneath her. She'd ending up wrenching it free, and it gnawed at her like the everlasting worm.

They hadn't been followed: Peter Büber's intuition was proved right when the dwarves had refused to enter the forests after them.

And she'd killed Max Ullmann, who'd tried to kill her.

It hadn't even been hard. A flick of her wrist, barely aimed. One moment he'd been next to her, and then he wasn't.

Then she'd been in the trees, crashing through the undergrowth, putting as much distance between the dwarves and herself as possible, climbing up the valley-side and only stopping when she was all but pulled down by several bowmen.

She'd wept after that, and none of them had dared comfort her, though they consoled each other well enough as they cried their own public tears of loss.

Hidden by the forest, they turned north, and here they were again, at Rosenheim.

Across the river, she could see the camp fires Reinhardt had raised, and the reflection of the flames against the white canvas of the tents. She hoped that there'd be food and rest for her men, even while she knew there'd be precious little for her. She was in pain, inside and out.

Sophia saw the first wagon, sitting on the road, and wondered what it was doing there. She didn't recognise it, and what it carried just looked like supplies. She passed the second one, and on a whim, lifted up the waxed canvas cover that was tied down over the goods. It was too dark to see anything. Barrels perhaps? Beer? Sauerkraut?

When she got to the third one, and saw that there were more ahead of her, she started to grow suspicious. She told her centurions to take the men down to the camp, while she dragged herself up onto the wagon bed to take a closer look. Her hands found rough, unplaned wood turned into packing crates, and her probing fingers cold, hard, metal balls the size of her fist.

"Frederik?"

She scrambled back and overtook half her army, limping ridiculously and growling at anyone who got in her way. When she reached the camp perimeter, she spoke to a weary guard.

"Is Master Thaler here?"

"He's" – and he pointed – "over there with Master Reinhardt."

"Have you eaten yet?"

"My lady?"

"It's a straightforward question, man. Have you eaten?"

The man stopped leaning on his spear and looked alive for the first time in hours. "Yes, my lady."

"Good. Just making sure. Now out of my way."

She was almost to the point of dragging her right leg behind her through the camp when she came across Thaler, Reinhardt, the witch Tuomanen, and –

"Father?"

"Ah, my girl. You're safe." Morgenstern smiled broadly at her. "I was worried for you."

"I'm safe," she echoed. "Yes. Father, what are you doing here?"

"Helping?"

She managed to convey that the emotion boiling up inside her wasn't over-brimming joy. "Master Thaler, what have you done?"

Thaler hastily put down the bowl of stew he'd been ladling into his mouth, and got up off the little fold-up chair that he was somehow failing to break. "If I might explain," he said.

"You've brought my father into the middle of a battlefield. Why are you here? Why are any of you here?"

"My lady," ventured Reinhardt.

"Shut up. I'm not talking to you at the moment. I'm talking to my fool of a father and this great tub of lard that masquerades as a librarian." She was vaguely aware that she shouldn't be behaving like this, that her voice was carrying across the camp and that conversations were drying up like sheets in a gale all around her. But she'd had enough.

"Your father can calculate angles and distances more accurately and faster than any of us," said Thaler. "And he wanted to be where we were."

She turned on Thaler. They were more or less the same height, and his face was well within spittle-flecking distance. "Then why didn't you all stay at home?"

Thaler didn't answer straight away. He got out his handkerchief and dabbed at his face. "My condolences for your loss," he said, then went back into his voluminous pockets for something else. "You may have my immediate resignation as master librarian. We'll turn around in the morning and head back to Juvavum."

He pressed something into her hands, and walked out of the firelight.

She looked down at what he'd given her, and angled it to the flames to see it better. It was the library seal.

"Master Thaler?" she called after him. "Frederik?"

He didn't answer, and both Tuomanen and Reinhardt stood.

"I'll—"

"Go."

They looked at each other. "Why don't we both go?" suggested Reinhardt, and the witch clearly agreed with him, because a moment later Sophia was alone by the fire with only her unexpected father for company.

He patted the vacated seat next to him. "Why don't you sit down and tell me all about it?"

She gnawed at her lip. "Will you use sarcasm?"

"Oh, I expect so. Irony, too. Later, though. Sit with me, my daughter." He tapped the chair again, and she gave up trying to fight everyone. She sat, still holding the library seal in her writhing fingers.

"I lost him," she said.

"I know," he said. "Frederik told me."

"They—"

"I know that too. It's a bad business, Sophia."

"It wasn't supposed to be like this."

Morgenstern rested his hand on her shoulder. "I know."

"You shouldn't even be here."

"That? I also know. Your father is very wise and knows everything."

She leant into him. He was bony and small and uncomfortable,

691

and she didn't care. She was his. He even smelt of home. "What do I do now?"

He rumbled deep in his chest. "How about you listen to your old tateh for a while?"

She nodded, and he continued.

"Felix was a good boy, and he was a friend to us. That was your doing and I'm proud of you, whatever that fool doctor says. And look, you stayed strong when it mattered, you led the Germans into battle – my girl, Sophia Morgenstern."

"We lost, Father."

"Hush. You don't know what you're saying. What would you do differently? Your army's intact, and all you've lost is ground. HaShem made plenty of it, so why should we care?" He gave a little grunt of satisfaction. "And this Ironmaker, you suppose he's sitting comfortably on his throne with half his soldiers dead and little to show for it? If he counts that a victory, then he's an idiot and we've nothing to fear. So far, you're better than Joshua, David and Gideon."

"But Felix is gone."

"Yes, but why are all these Germans around you? Why is Cohen – Cohen, of all people – following that goy Peter Büber through the forests? Do I have to spell it out for you like when you were a little pitseleh? Things will sort themselves out one way or another, but don't you think today has enough worries of its own? Why make more of them by insulting your friends and your own flesh and blood? They put you in charge, Sophia. It doesn't have to be forever, but it does have to be for now: don't make them curse the Jews all over again."

"I can't even sit Shiva for him."

"We'll get him back, and we'll . . . well: they'll put him on a boat and set fire to it like the heathens they are, but we can mourn the way we know how. And we can say the Kaddish later. After you've eaten." He moved her aside and collected Thaler's half-eaten dinner. "Here."

She took it from him, and frowned at both it and him. "This is treif."

"Listen to the ungrateful girl. I made it myself. It's as kosher as you're going to get out here, and besides, you look like you need a meal or two."

"You made this? You?"

"Oy, what did I do to deserve this daughter? Yes. When Frederik devised this plan to get us all here – and that's something that mamzer Ullmann never heard about – he knew he couldn't get Germans to drive his wagons, because they were all busy catching up with good Jewish farming practice. So he went to the shtetls, and they came when we called. Jews grew this food, cooked this food, served this food. All you have to do is eat it." Morgenstern folded his arms and waited.

"I'm not hungry."

"Then I'll give it to someone who is." He made to take it away from her, but, despite everything, she hung on to the edges of the bowl. He relented and let her keep it. "They need you to be strong," he said.

She was still eating – thirds, by her counting – when a spearman came running.

"My lady, horses." He took a shuddering breath. "Lots of horses."

She put the food down by her feet and glanced at her father. "It can't be the dwarves. Do they have a banner?"

"It's too dark to see what's on it, my lady. They're coming from the west."

"Call the muster, sir. I won't be caught asleep." She patted her hip to check she still had her sword. "Pray it's not Teutons," she said, then half ran, half walked towards the black outline of Rosenheim's roofs, feeling the bright pain in her ankle with every jarring step she took.

She gathered as many as she could as she passed through the camp and they followed her out onto the Rosenheim road. Some carried lanterns with them, and the sparks of light they shed drew a shout from the distance.

She approached warily, making sure that her men were close behind her. With the lantern-light at her back, she could just about make out the outlines of Thaler's borrowed carts and the shadows of mounted figures.

"Who goes there?" Her voice was swallowed up by the night, but, after a delay, it was answered.

"Prince Clovis for the Franks, Mistress. We're looking for Carinthia."

HaShem be praised. It wasn't more foemen, but friends.

"You've found it, my lord. Welcome."

"I was under the impression that Carinthia lay further to the east, beyond the Enn. My native guides have failed me." He laughed, and the sound was both kind and generous. She could hear him dismount, and his horse shake out its mane.

"Horst? Manfred?"

"Here, my lady. But what are you doing out here?"

"I . . . the situation is complicated, sirs, and I'd much rather only explain once." She squinted into the night. "How many have you brought?"

"Two hundred horse," said Clovis. His blond moustache glittered with forming dew as much as his mail shirt and horse-head cloak clasp did.

"Two hundred." She felt numb. They couldn't have found two hundred horses, let alone two hundred riders, across the whole of Carinthia. "You are very welcome."

Clovis dragged his half-helm off and bowed. "You must be the Lady Sophia. My father, King Clovis, sends his fraternal greetings to his cousin Felix. Surely you didn't come out all this way to meet us, though."

"We've fought two battles today, and we'll be fighting a third here tomorrow. That, I think, will decide the fate of Carinthia one way or the other." She bowed her head briefly, then realised what she was doing and how she must look. She raised her chin again. "We've killed perhaps a third of the dwarves so far, and it maybe as many as half by the time they reach us. We're not defeated yet, but we are still outnumbered."

Clovis pulled at his moustache. "I see. I came with experienced men to help train your armies. I didn't expect to be in one."

Sophia looked to heaven for inspiration. "My prince, I'd say that a man skilled in teaching others should be an expert in what he taught."

"All the same," said Clovis, shifting his weight and looking past her and her spearmen at the camp stretching out across the fields of Rosenheim, "I have no authority to go to war. The King of the Franks takes his responsibilities seriously, and our land borders Farduzes. I'll need to speak to Felix about this."

Her stomach shrinking to a knot, she steeled herself. "Felix is dead."

Clovis thinned his lips and stared for a moment at the reflections in his burnished helmet. "Then who leads?"

"I do," she said. "I am strategos and war-leader of Carinthia, by

694

divine fiat and popular acclaim. Does the prince have to inspect my sword for battle damage, or will he accept my command on my word?"

The Frank struggled to contain his surprise. "Your command?"

"My lord Clovis, I've no time for fine words, an exchange of gifts or other diplomatic niceties. I have a battle to fight in the morning, with or without you. I'll just say this: would you rather be known by your subjects as Clovis, Hammer of the Dwarves, or Clovis Pissbreeks?"

He reached for his sword, and so did she. The spearmen behind her lowered their spears around her, forming a wall of defensive blades.

Clovis let his half-drawn sword fall back into its scabbard. "My lady presumes an awful lot."

She sheathed her own spatha and waved the spears back. "We can argue into the small hours about this, but we both know by your finely waxed moustache that your Frankish pride will prevent you from leaving for home in the morning. You can claim the victory, have a triumphal column raised on this spot in your name, and loot Farduzes of all its fabled gold and gemstones. Everything is yours. All I want is to win, and in order to do that, I need your cavalry."

"I should, by rights, turn around," he said.

"I've offered you everything you could possibly want, my lord, and for that, you'll stay. Rosenheim is deserted: there are rooms for your men, and there's grass for your horses. I'll send someone before dawn: we'll need to discuss tactics before we fight."

Clovis reached up and pulled at his moustache again. "Discuss tactics? With a woman?"

Again, she didn't need to say anything. The spears bristled like a hedgehog around her. She waited.

"Apologies, my lady."

"Accepted," she said. "You're very gracious, my lord."

He pulled a face, but he knew he'd been thoroughly beaten. "In the morning, then."

He bowed to her, and she to him; then he went back to his horse, muttering under his breath.

She cleared her throat. "Horst, Manfred. To me."

They came towards her, leading their horses, uncertain of their reception. She hugged them both, with a whispered thank-you in their ears.

"My lady, we just did as we were told," said Horst.

"And you were faithful in your service to your prince, for which I'm profoundly grateful." Sophia rested her hands on their shoulders. "Stay with the Franks tonight. If they look like moving out, come and tell me straight away. I won't have a Clovis Pissbreeks on my conscience."

"My lady. We're sorry about Felix."

"Thank you," she said. She genuinely needed to tell them, and wondered if it was the right time: they'd find out, sooner or later, and it was probably better done now. "The Black Company lost half its number in the rearguard at Kufstein, but it was their sacrifice that meant we could all escape. Master Ullmann was . . . killed."

"Oh," said Manfred.

She wanted to sit them down and explain exactly why. What she'd found out about him, and how she'd confronted him with it, and how, despite that, she'd ridden repeatedly behind him to keep the dwarves off his back. How he'd slashed at her horse's hamstrings and left her for dead. How she'd miraculously survived the fall and brought him down instead.

Not the right time for that, she decided.

"Go on, gentlemen. I'll see you both in the morning, too." She was tired, and there was still much to do. She limped away, and the spearmen parted for her, forming an escort to take her back to the camp.

96

Cohen crouched down next to Büber, said nothing, and gestured with his hand. Three, to the front and right, a little way off but not so far. Büber nodded, and circled one of his maimed fingers in the air, gathering together the little band of Jews around him, and pointing so that half would go straight forward, and the other half go hard right, then come around.

They moved out as silently as they could manage, making only the sounds they couldn't avoid: the soft hiss of a branch, the dull snap of a buried twig. Büber had always thought – when he'd given them any thought at all – of the Jews as a peaceable people, the first to apologise in any argument, the ones who'd always back down and retreat.

He'd been wrong. Or at least, there were two sides to them. He didn't know if Cohen was a good priest, but he was a good soldier and a decent leader.

When they were in position, indicated by the slightest of signals, Büber levelled his crossbow and crept forward. The forest canopy leaked the grey light of dawn, but, beneath, the shadows were still as black as night. There was a wind-felled tree, its roots making a woven earth and wood shield, and in the hollow beneath it were three figures. One was standing, the other two were lying down, and while all he could see was the contrast between black beard and white cheeks, it was enough.

He aimed, and the bowstring slapped as he pulled the trigger.

The dwarf heard, his head snapping around to look in completely the wrong direction. He took the bolt in his chest, and gave a gargling cry that woke the other two.

The forest was full of rushing, and they lasted only moments longer than their dead colleague.

Büber had been doing this all night, taking out small groups to hunt down and kill more of the fractured dwarvish rearguard. By his unreliable count, he'd seen off several centuries, and, more importantly, kept them all moving and afraid while he rested his own men in shifts.

In the dark forests, dwarves froze. He almost felt compassion for them, but they were both there to see each other to the afterlife, and gods, they'd started it. They could finish it just as easily by marching back up the valley and leaving Carinthia the fuck alone.

The main force was ahead, but he'd niggled and niggled at the rear until, more in desperation than anything else, part of the dwarvish army had split off to deal with his skirmishing.

And, once they'd separated, Büber had split them, then split them again, and chased them up blind valleys and against cliff faces and broken them. When night finally came, he started picking off the remnants.

He brought his men together by the base of the fallen tree.

"We need to get back. Ironmaker will be on the move soon, and we need to be there to make it difficult."

They left the bodies, unburied and unremembered, where they

lay, and tracked downhill, following the course of one of the mountain streams that flowed into the Enn. The dwarves were north of it, his army to the south, though they'd raided across it during the hours of darkness, killing the watch with bows and blowing the Jewish ram's horns before vanishing back into the night.

Büber was certain the dwarves were far from comfortable with their lot.

When he was back in his rough camp, he told those already awake to rouse the sleepers, then went to look for himself at what was happening.

The stream was sharp and cold: there was a bridge, a simple stone one with a narrow arch, but he ignored it and waded across further upstream. His picket line watched as he emptied his boots on the far bank and sat down to put them on again. There was no corresponding dwarvish line – those that had been posted there had met their ends under the green canopy, so, after a while, the dwarves had stopped sending replacements. The only remaining guards stood on top of the circle of wagons, in an open space barely large enough for them all. They were crammed in like cattle, and it would take them time to extricate themselves.

He could almost reach out and touch the sides of one of the wagons before he had to stop. It was difficult to see inside the corral, but he could hear the great weary mass of them rumbling into life there.

If they wanted to roll along the Roman via, then they'd have to go past Rosenheim. Otherwise, there was the cart track to the south of the lake. He didn't want the dwarves to take that route. It cut off before Rosenheim, and Sophia would have to leave the town and chase after them across open, flat ground.

He'd have to force them north, then. If he could get his army in front, and block the track, then north would be the only direction they could go. Bounded by the Enn on one side, and the hills and Büber on the other, the dwarves would join the via to Juvavum where it crossed the Rosenheim bridge.

He knew a way around that his enemies didn't. The dwarves were marching blind. They'd shown no sign of scouting ahead, and all their maps dated from Roman times.

Good enough. He took one last look at the dwarvish sentries, then slipped away, stepping over the small corpses of dwarves who'd ventured outside the circle.

Back across the river and, with his legs goose-bumped with cold, he gathered everyone to him. They'd found a natural bowl in the land, and it acted like an amphitheatre. Six centuries sat close by, or stood nearer the lip, while he occupied the stage.

He studied them all, men and women from all walks of life and position, from stablehands to guildsmen. As difficult as he found it, he felt a belonging that he'd never encountered before. When magic had reigned, he and his fellow hunters had been the bastard offspring kept isolated beyond the gates of civilisation.

"One last push," he said. "We need to put them on the field at Rosenheim, and make sure they don't try and strike across the foothills. That means a bit of marching: up this valley to the head of it, then around to the north and down the next. It's not difficult, nor is it long, but we need to get there before they do. They're breaking camp, but they have their bloody carts to push. We don't even have to hurry if we leave now."

He scratched at his stubble and searched for the Jews among the sea of faces; they were less recognisable in their armour than they were on the street.

"Rabbi. Not you. You've shown you're more than worthy of this: keep at them. Make them think the whole army is still snapping at their heels. I want them looking over their shoulders every step they take, so that they're not looking ahead at what the rest of us are doing."

Cohen nodded, and that was the end of what Büber wanted to say. People stood up, gathered up anything they might have left on the ground, and started walking uphill. Barely moments from receiving his orders, they were gone: that was something the dwarves couldn't match, even if they tried.

The Jews formed up below. As Büber climbed through the empty, open forest, their shapes merged with their surroundings, and he lost sight of them. He gradually overtook the rest of his troops, and was soon out in front, following the river upstream. To the north was a particularly steep and savage hill, with scree and bare rock on the lee side, but it was compact and straightforward to go around. They'd meet it on the east side, and follow the low ridge for a while before dropping down onto the plain.

He went on ahead, and doubled back on himself, going to the

end of the ridge where it overlooked the Enn. There was the Flintsbachs' farm on the opposite side of the valley, where he'd washed up and been cared for by Gretchen. He had a fleeting memory of her, and of her warm, strong hands that seemed to not mind his scars and deformities. She'd gone, of course, with her parents, well away from there. Perhaps they'd come back when the fighting was over, and he could thank her . . . well, he could thank her, at least.

The dwarves were below him, struggling through the forest, harried by Cohen. He traced the route they'd have to take, to where the trees ended and the farmland began. There were still stands and strips of the old forest, especially on the low line of hills that faced across the river from Rosenheim, but much of the land had been cleared and turned over to grass.

Some places were greener than others, though, where the Enn slowed and started to meander as it flowed out onto the plain. The ground was marshy there, and the road north threaded between the river and the hill.

He looked closer, and wished for the distance-pipe Thaler had gifted him. The woods on the hill would be good for an ambush, but the land around it was clear. If his forces were chased out of the trees, they'd be vulnerable in the open. But with the other flank covered by marshland on the left, and a narrow front that could be held by a small number of troops to block the advance . . .

It was probably the best they were going to get, and he hoped that Sophia had seen it in the same way. He'd dearly love to get a message to her, but they had no horses, and the only alternative was a runner.

He had six hundred men and women at his command. One of them ought to be able to run that distance and still remember a message. He headed along the ridge and caught up with the others.

"I need a runner," he said to those around him. "Someone with the sense to evade the dwarves and get to Rosenheim."

They all volunteered, every one of them, and he had no way of telling which might be best suited. Someone small and slight and fast. No lumbering oxen, or the plain of wit. He needed sharp and cunning and reliable.

"You," he said.

She'd armed herself with a dwarvish war hammer, its head tucked in her belt. She had a knife, too, one she'd brought with her, and she'd cut her skirts short with it. She looked shrewd and capable.

"Master?" she said.

"You have a name?" He wanted to check she'd not volunteered out of enthusiasm or duty.

"Aelinn, Master Büber," she said. Her expression was serious, but confident.

"Aelinn." He frowned. Did he know her? He looked at her again, leaning back slightly. He wasn't sure, and it didn't really matter. "Will you go?"

"If you send me," she said.

"Good." That was settled, then. "Can you repeat, word for word, what I tell you to say?"

"Yes."

"Then come with me."

He led her up the ridge while the others crossed onto the plain, to work their way up the Rosenheim road until they came to the via. Büber stood with Aelinn on the top while he pointed out the features of the landscape, and from there, with the extra light, the Carinthian camp was visible with its haze of wood smoke.

"The dwarves are directly below us. Go down and north. You'll need to put the hills near Rosenheim on your left. See the tower?" He pointed, and she nodded. "That's just before the bridge. We may have posted a watch there, and they may have twitchy fingers. Tell me why I chose a woman?"

"Because I look less like a dwarf, even from a distance." She took a couple of steps towards her destination, then stopped. "Aren't you going to wish me luck?"

"I don't trust luck where a sharp mind and a pair of strong legs will serve us better." He relented with a snort. "Good luck, Aelinn."

She was gone, skipping down the slope, over a rock, into the trees. Her shortened skirts rose and fell, revealing her well-muscled thighs and taut calves, and she held her arms out for balance, making her appear more a dancer than a warrior. Even when she had disappeared from view, he ruminated over the space where she'd been.

Not dead yet, then.

He rejoined his army, who were busy spreading out in the woods on either side of the cart track. Telling them to wait, he gathered up half a dozen pickets to come with him. The object was not to engage the dwarves, but to make absolutely certain they carried on towards Rosenheim. He could block their path if they tried to come his way; it wasn't as if the Carinthians lacked axes now, or the trees to use them on. After the dwarves' experience on the road down from Ennsbruck, Büber hoped that they'd want to take the easier route.

He slowed down, and waved at the others to halt. He could hear wagons approaching, and he stepped lightly into the undergrowth. The pale wooden planks of a wagon prow edged into view, and he stayed perfectly still. Even though he was in plain sight, he was certain they wouldn't see him. Their eyes hadn't adjusted to the shift and shadow of the day, just as their bodies hadn't finished changing to suit the overground.

The wagon stopped as it reached the turning. The dwarvish train could either go on up the via, or head east now. The Roman road was inviting, with its smooth, well-drained surface and solid construction; the cart track south of the lakes less so. It was pocked and pitted within feet of the junction, deep ruts holding out the promise of broken wheels and cloying mud if it rained.

He could hear the sound of dwarvish voices raised in argument. Their maps didn't say where this road led, as it hadn't existed a thousand years ago. It might be nothing more than a spur to a farm, a dead-end up some uncharted valley.

No, the via was a much better bet. They knew where it went, north of the lakes and back around to Juvavum.

Still they argued, the swell and timbre of their words strange and foreign in his ears.

Take the via. Take the fucking via. It was almost too tempting not to overturn the lead wagon and shout at the dwarves inside, pointing north and shaking them until they complied.

He remained motionless, only the blink of his eyes to give him away.

The wheels started to turn again, and the cart continued north.

Büber could breathe again. Everything was in place. No matter how many of them there were, there had to be an end to it now. He twirled his finger, and slipped away with his troops.

97

Thaler kicked the mound of earth to make sure it was solid, and was satisfied. He stepped back to allow the pot to be lowered slowly on top of the flattened base, and when the carrying poles had been removed, he gave it a good shake.

Nothing moved that shouldn't.

"Very good," he said. The smith didn't like being called either master or mister – he regarded all titles with suspicion. "Bastian, would you be so kind as to join this fire team? They'll give you a role."

Bastian, mud smeared and sweaty, nodded and heaved a crate of shot off the back of the nearby cart, carrying it by himself to behind the black iron pot. "Are they coming now, Thaler?"

"It won't be long. I'll check."

They'd set up a table for Morgenstern, and built a somewhat rickety tower next to it. Thaler didn't dare climb it, but he'd positioned the boy Agathos on top, carrying his distance-pipe.

"Agathos? Any sign of movement?"

The boy rested the tube against one of the unfinished uprights and, with a practised eye, he looked south.

"Ochi," he said. Then, "Nai! They come."

In the absence of anything else, Thaler had a bell on Morgenstern's desk, and he gave it a vigorous ring.

"Do stop that, Frederik," said Morgenstern, clapping his hands over his ears, "you're like a child with that thing."

Thaler ignored the complaint. "Places everyone. Load."

He watched with satisfaction as his crew went about their work: placing the charge in the barrel, tamping it down, rolling the ball into the muzzle, fixing it in place with another piece of cloth, priming the touch-hole.

Behind him, Morgenstern opened his books up and made a few practice calculations on his brass wheel calculator. "I'm ready, too, if you're at all interested."

"I had no doubt, Aaron. If you could lay in an angle for the pots, I'd be grateful. Do you think Gunnhilde and her sisters are almost too close?"

"We're three stadia from the road. Eighteen hundred feet."

"The trajectory is almost flat," said Thaler.

"Why don't we find something more difficult for us to shoot at later? For now, the dwarves are going to parade a series of targets before us that we can barely miss. I know I complain a lot, Frederik, but honestly. This is war." He huffed at the surface of his calculator and rubbed at it with his sleeve.

All Thaler could see of it were the little cogs and gears on the back surface. "You're right, of course."

"Yes," said Morgenstern, peering over the top. "There are an awful lot of them, though."

The line of wagons was being added to. Each time one came wholly into view, another started to grow after it. They were twenty, thirty wagons so far, and there seemed to be no end in sight.

"We could hit them from here." Thaler picked up the cross-staff from the table and sighted down it, adjusting the crosspiece until he'd found the angle. "Eight stadia. Well within range."

"And you're just as likely to kill Büber and his men hiding in the wood. Sophia gave us our orders and, for once, I'm going to do what the girl tells me."

Thaler looked up at the tower, where Agathos was almost hanging off the platform, agog at the sight of so many enemies. "Careful, boy. Especially careful with the distance-pipe."

The boy glanced down and grinned.

"He thinks it's all a game," said Thaler sadly. "For him, it prob-ably is. He's used to being part of the spoils rather than one of the victims. I've tried, the gods know I've tried, to explain he's not a slave any more. He seems to think apprentice is just another word for it. We are ready, aren't we?"

"We're ready. This is what you wanted, yes? To make a differ-ence? Then stop kvetching and light some fuses, or something." Morgenstern put down the brass disc and flexed his fingers. "They're almost where they need to be."

They were. The road cut off the bend in the river and ran right next to the water opposite their position, raised on an embankment to lift it clear of the marshy ground, which meant that they could see everything: sides, wheels, even the shadows of feet underneath.

"Thank you for talking to Sophia for me. I . . . well, none of us behaved perfectly last night." He fetched out the library seal and placed it on the table in front of Morgenstern. "I'll just put this here for safe keeping."

Morgenstern waved him away. "Light the fuses, Frederik. The horns will sound soon enough."

With one last anxious eye on Agathos, Thaler collected the lengths of slow fuse from the back of one of the now-oxless carts and opened the door on the single, lit lantern. He held the cut end of a fuse against the flame, and it began to smoke. He did the same with the other fuses, and then walked to each widely spaced position in turn and handed one over to the crew's leader.

Last of all, he passed one to Tuomanen.

"Mistress," he said, presenting it to her.

"Master Thaler." She took it from him and turned to watch proceedings on the far bank. "This will work, won't it?"

"The dwarves are irresistible as one horde. Divide them in two, and they are less than half as effective. The more we split them into parts, the weaker they become and the stronger, relatively speaking, we grow. The logic is quite sound, not just in theory but in practice. Did you hear that Simbach sent us two centuries of spears this morning?"

"But nothing else from Bavaria?" She looped the slow fuse around her neck and shoulders, the lit end leaving a white trail in the cool morning air.

"We have two centuries we didn't have last night. Then we have the Frankish horse, and there's still time for more. München's not that far away." He patted himself down. "Now where did I put my walking-stick?"

"You left it in Mr Morgenstern's cart when we were setting up the calculating table." She blew on the fuse, not in case it might go out, but because she loved to see it spark. "You don't really need it, do you?"

"I wouldn't want to be without it when I do need it." He checked across the river. "I wonder what they're thinking?"

"Most likely? That we can't hit them from over here." Tuomanen moved slightly to her right. "The first wagon is passing in front of the Gunnhilde."

"A few of them have to go past before we fire." He patted his pockets again. "The speaking-trumpet?"

"In the wagon with the quick fuses," she said, and Thaler hurried off to find it. He moved a crate or two, and there it was, a great brass funnel with a little mouthpiece at its apex.

He heaved it up by its handle and pressed it against his face.

"Testing, testing." He swung it around. "Can you hear me, Aaron?"

Morgenstern clapped his hands over his ears and feigned violent death.

"I'll take that as a yes. Right, everyone." He swung it back to point towards the five pots and the four Gunnhildes. "Gunnhilde One?"

Tuomanen waved back.

"On my mark."

Gods, the speaking-trumpet was heavy. He ought to have a little pole, or better still, a tripod to balance it on. Thaler let it fall by his side while he waited. It had to be soon. More than a few dwarvish wagons had already passed, and they were still emerging from the forest to the south. He quickly counted them: fifty, sixty, seventy at least. How many did they have?

The horns set up on the Roman tower called, a single vibrating rasp echoing across the plain. The lead wagon was no more than a stadia from it, and too close to Carinthian troops to target. They had their arc of fire. They were going to stick to it.

"One," he called, then again, through the speaking-trumpet. "Sorry. One."

The crew around the first Gunnhilde swung into action, using crowbars to adjust the weapon's horizontal angle, and wooden wedges to change its vertical. They stepped back when the aimer was satisfied, and Tuomanen ran forward to poke the slow fuse into the touch-hole.

The powder smoked, and everyone held their breath.

There was a great crack of thunder and a billow of dirty white smoke. Almost instantaneously, the rear of one of the dwarvish wagons lifted up and slewed sideways. A cloud of splinters burst into the air behind it, and, on Thaler's side, one plank, then another, dropped away. As the wagon fell back to the road, its rear axle snapped, and the wheels pointed upward.

"Gods. It works." Thaler raised the trumpet. "Two, fire when ready."

Tuomanen's team were already busy dousing the barrel with water, scraping the soot from the inside, preparing a new charge and shot, when the second Gunnhilde spasmed. The shot punched through the side of a wagon three down from the first that they'd hit. It stopped instantly.

"Three! Fire!"

The third Gunnhilde was aimed too low, or the charge too light, or it had burnt too slow. The ball hit the marshland before the road, sending two sheets of mud and water flying into the sky. But before Thaler could even raise his foot to stamp in frustration, the ball bounced. It caught another wagon just under the roof, and the roof panel spun away in two pieces. The wagon itself was rocked on its wheels, lifting up, then crashing back down.

This was better than he'd hoped.

"Four."

The old iron Gunnhilde boomed. It had a lower muzzle velocity than the newer brass ones, but it was still at point-blank range. The wagon it was aimed at shattered – disintegrating into chunks and sheets and boards and fixings – with the pieces pinwheeling away.

Each firing position had a flag they'd raise while they were preparing for the next shot. He had four red pennants, but the pots were still ready. He turned the speaking trumpet towards them, a line of five emplacements fifty feet behind the Gunnhildes.

"A ranging shot from each of you, please."

They fired in quick succession, a series of short, sharp concussions that made Thaler's clothes stiffen. Five black specks rose out of the smoke, trailing vapour behind them, marking the arc of their flight. Each soared up into the blue sky, and froze for a moment at their highest point.

Then they fell.

One exploded in the air in a flash of flame that transformed itself instantly into a blossom of sharp smoke. The others buried themselves in the soft ground on the far side of the via, and great gouts of steam and soil vomited upwards.

The pots were more affected by windage than the Gunnhildes, and had clearly overshot for one reason or another. When Thaler looked around, Morgenstern was already spinning his calculator and reading off values in his books. A runner from each pot crew was hurrying towards him, and they'd receive a thin slip of paper with the new angle scribbled on it.

Everything was decidedly hazy. Smoke hung low over the river and drifted out over the far bank. The broken wagons had halted the rest of the column behind them. The dwarves had to emerge to try and clear them out of the way. They did so, slowly, fearfully, staggering and reeling with shock. Some were dragging the dead and injured out, and some were injured themselves.

Thaler pursed his lips. This was like being a hexmaster, being able to reach out and kill your enemy at a distance, without them being able to strike back. Killing with impunity. Never mind the maimed and crushed and the torn-asunder: the Order had never minded. They'd turned whole battlefields to molten glass that had swallowed up entire armies, leaving no trace of them but whitened stains on an obsidian floor.

Except he hadn't trained as a hexmaster. He didn't have that level of disdain for others or hatred of his fellows. If anything, he felt sorry for the dwarves, so very far from home, lost under the shield of the sky, desperate to find their place in this new world. Desperation led men to desperate measures, and he had no reason to assume that dwarves were exempt.

The flags were going down, one by one. The Gunnhildes were primed and ready to fire again.

Gods, why didn't they surrender? They had to know they were beaten, despite their vastly superior numbers. Fighting Carinthia was like fighting . . . Carinthia. It had always been that way. When they'd had the Order, they'd won every battle. Now they had the library, they'd win this one too.

The dwarves were frantically wrestling with the first disabled wagon, the others ahead of it still rumbling uncertainly on towards the tower. They didn't look like an army on the brink of surrender. They still looked like they wanted to roll all the way to Juvavum, and drive everyone out before them.

He lifted the speaking-trumpet. "Number one. Fire when ready."

And his sound and his fury were very great indeed.

98

Sophia watched from the tower, open-mouthed. The wagons they'd struggled to overcome were being smashed to kindling by Thaler's toys. There was smoke like clouds drifting across the battlefield, and a strange scent of cleaved slate hung in the air, giving the scene a dream-like quality, indistinct and distant.

"My lady," said Aelinn, "how is that even possible?"

"It's not magic." Sophia let her distance-pipe hang by her fingers. She needed to see the whole picture, not just parts of it. "It's not."

The devices Thaler called Gunnhildes barked again, and the dwarves lost another three wagons: one left a splintered ruin, one fallen apart, and one seemingly undamaged but for two holes punched through the fore and aft of it. She couldn't see inside, but could only wonder at the devastation it contained.

The dwarves were trying to clear the road: they'd managed to push one wheel-less wagon off the via and into the river, and another group was heaving debris – which included bodies – into the ditch, but Thaler was creating chaos faster than they could restore order.

The pots – their sound different to that of the Gunnhildes – erupted in gouts of flame, and their projectiles streaked into the sky. They slowed, and started to fall. Loud reports, flowers of smoke, and the dwarves under the blooms shuddered and collapsed.

Only half got up again.

"Gods," said Aelinn, clinging to what was left of the battlements, "it's bloody murder."

"Yes." Sophia pushed the two halves of the distance-pipe together and handed it to Aelinn. She looked down at the wagons almost at the walls of the tower. "Sound the horns," she said to the man with the carnyx. "We're attacking."

The via ran between the tower and the bridge, the tower sitting on a rise in the ground made taller by a man-made motte. She had five centuries of spears behind it.

She limped and scuffed her way down the ladders they'd put up between the floors. Her ankle, bound tight with strips of cloth, protested all the way. Tomorrow, Kuppenheim could chop the damned thing off, as long as it held out long enough to keep her standing today.

The horn blew again as she descended: the first blast had been for Thaler, the second was for her. She hurried, and emerged from the gap where there'd once been a door. She adjusted her skirts – she should have cut them short like Aelinn had, but shame had stopped her – and drew her sword.

Her centuries were there, ready, waiting. She bowed deeply to them all, and turned. They all ran forward, with what armour they'd been able to muster rattling as they passed, and formed up along the edge of the motte and out across the via. They lowered their spears and braced them.

Sophia walked out behind them to assess how they'd do this. The dwarves in the vanguard stopped their wagon. Twenty-five wagons in all had been separated from the head of the column. Büber's men had reported twenty in each: five hundred dwarves, five hundred Carinthians.

The lead wagon started again. Her troops lacked the ability to turn the wagons over – they should have had poles and the time to train with them, but they did have alternatives. Thaler had offered up two of his crew who'd try something different.

The wagon started to bull through the spears, and there was nothing they could do save jab ineffectively through the narrow slits either side of the prow. It looked like it could simply break through the Carinthian line, and to stop it, they'd have to try and push it aside with their bare hands.

Hidden from view behind the crowd of jostling spearmen, Thaler's smock-clad laundrywoman held an old stoneware beer bottle. A quick fuse had been hammered into the neck. She crouched down and waited for the nose of the wagon to push aside the yelling men who stood hammering on the green wood sides with the butts of their spears.

Here it came, and she touched the slow match to the fuse. Timing was everything.

The powder caught with a hiss and a flare, and she rolled the bottle under the wagon with a banshee shriek that warned the spearmen to scatter.

The bottle ticked and tacked under the dwarves' feet.

Then the wagon seemed to stretch upwards. Fire squirted from its skirts and out of the viewing ports, to be quickly replaced by grey smoke as thick as water. Even a dwarf's scream was high-pitched and penetrating, and there were enough of them to carry on making that noise long after the crack of concussion had trailed away.

The front opened, the back doors swung wide. White smoke billowed out. The few dwarves to stagger out were blind and deaf, and their legs were burnt and bleeding. It was, as Aelinn had rightly called it, bloody murder, but the spears still went about their task with grim efficiency before closing ranks across the via again.

There seemed to be a paralysis of mind infecting the dwarvish column. As the spears advanced on the next wagon, Thaler's other volunteer dug around in his satchel for a second bottle. Again, the spear butts pounded against the wagon, creating a disorientating cacophony inside, while the charge was lit and slipped under the wagon's base.

This time, it burst almost immediately, and caught several Carinthians in the blast. They reeled away, and the bottle-thrower stumbled back, dazed and bleeding. A short fuse, or he'd held on to it for too long. The wagon doors broke open: the dwarves near the back were choking on the fumes, their mail smoking with still-burning fragments, but they did at least look like they could fight.

The spear wall closed around them just the same. No matter that they hacked and hammered, severing leaf-shaped spear points from their shafts, they didn't last more than a few moments.

The pattern that had been set on the banks of the Weissach repeated itself: the wagons that hadn't been directly attacked emptied backwards, and a hundred, two hundred, three hundred dwarves collected at the rear of the severed column, ready to strike forward. But, unlike at Büber's battle, they had no forests to retreat to, no hills to climb up.

"Form up," shouted Sophia. "Ready to receive a charge." Once the smoke had cleared, her wounded numbered only three, and the injured bottle-thrower, breeks black and shiny with blood, was intent on carrying on. This was the test, then: for every Carinthian or ally on the field – they had allies, HaShem be praised – there were ten dwarves. If Ironmaker managed to concentrate his forces, hers would be crushed like a nut.

The balance was so fine. They could win every encounter except the last one, and still lose.

Then the dwarves came, swarming forward to throw themselves on the spears, bared white teeth framed in black beards, hammers and axes raised above their iron-covered heads.

Sophia cupped her hands around her mouth. "Aelinn, the third horn."

The lines met with a shout. The Carinthian spears shuddered with the impact. They held and started to push back, and Thaler's laundry maid bent over her bag of bottles again.

The carnyx sounded again, part of its call lost in among another volley from the east bank of the Enn.

Her centre was starting to bend. The flanks, bounded by the marshy ground and the river on one side, and the tower motte on the other, were unengaged. It was like Kufstein, and she wouldn't make the same mistake as Reinhardt had.

She ran to her left, to the centurion of the spears at the end. "Charge them, sir. Charge now."

He nodded, and shouted his orders over the groan and grind. The drummer hammered out a double pace as the spears wheeled about, and when they were in position, they roared and ran.

The effect was instant. Instead of going backwards, the centre started forwards. There was another noise, too, a distant rumbling thunder like an avalanche. A field of pennants as bright as a summer meadow fluttered into view, the white bird of the Franks on every one.

The pennants dipped with the spears they were tied to, and Clovis's cavalry came galloping up behind the dwarves, already penned in on three sides.

It broke them. They died with blades in their fronts, in their backs, and it didn't matter where they turned, there were always more. The Franks, after the first shock of the charge, wheeled away rather than engage in an unruly melee, and that left the rear momentarily free.

The dwarves fled through the opening, first in ones and twos, then in a kind of mass brawl that saw them fighting each other to escape. The Carinthian spears surged forward to give chase, but Sophia wanted them back. Let Clovis have the duty of running them down before they could cross into the smoking Gehenna that Thaler had created.

"Hold," she called, and the drummers sounded the retreat.

They re-formed, and Sophia ordered that the abandoned wagons be rolled back through her lines and set up across the via, blocking it and any way around it. The two they'd destroyed, they pushed into the marsh.

Inside both was a charnel house, blackened with soot, reddened with blood. They'd done this. She'd done this. If she lived through today, this would be what she'd see when she closed her eyes at night, not fire, but ash.

She sent her wounded back across the river to Rosenheim, and had her dead laid out behind the tower. She resented the loss of each and every one of them. They'd been living and breathing that morning, and now they weren't.

Clovis, fine in his plate and with his moustache bristling, rode up beside her. "My lady. We scent victory."

Sophia stared up at him. "The main host hasn't reached us yet, and there are still far more of them than there are of us. We have a saying about chickens and eggs, and when to count them."

Clovis's horse stamped its feet, because its master could not.

"You Carinthians are so gloomy. In the Franklands we would have pressed home our advantage and routed the enemy."

"This," she spread her hands wide, "this is the first time we've ever seen them run. We've slaughtered thousands of them, and still they come at us. You'll keep your hot-headed impetuosity until after we're done."

Clovis leant forward in his saddle. "And what if I take my men and leave the field, my lady?"

"In order to lead an army of free people, a commander needs the respect of their soldiers, my lord. I'm confident I have the respect of everyone in my army, including your sergeants. How confident are you?"

He sat bolt upright. "You will not call me that name again."

"I'll have no need to call you that name again if you follow my orders. Pretend that they're yours, if you prefer, but an army has to act with a single mind."

"Yours."

There was no time for an argument, so she simply said "Yes", and turned to shout up at the tower. "Aelinn? What can you see?"

"Master Thaler is running out of things to shoot at. The horde are massing at the southern end of the field. The wagons next to Master Büber's position are staying still."

"We absolutely have to get them out into the open." She regarded Clovis. "Take your men around the back of Büber's position. Be ready."

The Frank snorted. "We are always ready."

"Good. A general can't ask for any more." It would sour him further, and she needed to be careful. But her blood was up, and she wasn't about to take lessons from this nudnik.

Clovis wheeled his horse around and rode back to his men. She had to trust that he'd do what she said, because anything else was unthinkable.

"Horst? To me." Then, to the tower: "Aelinn? I need a message taken." Finally, to her centurions: "Form up. We're marching."

Aelinn was at her side, presenting her with her distance-pipe. "My lady."

"Tell Master Thaler he's to stop firing his . . . his things. Wait for a double-horn, then fire at the southern end of the field, into the forest."

She was gone, running for the bridge, and Horst came trotting over on his horse, carrying one of the Frankish pennants on his spear.

"Have you switched sides, sir?" she asked.

He dragged his eyes back from Aelinn's flying skirts. "I might carry this pigeon, my lady, but I've a leopard over my heart. What do you need?"

"A message. Find Master Büber and tell him to pull back to the very eastern edge of the woods and take cover. Then you need to find Master Reinhardt, and tell him he's to join Rabbi Cohen behind the dwarvish host. Tell him to go back up the valley, deep into the trees. Once Master Thaler's finished, they're to move up and kill any dwarves who come their way." She frowned. "Did I need to say that?"

"No, my lady. From what I've heard, your priest won't need telling."

"You're a good man, Horst. Do me a favour and stay alive."

Horst touched his hand to his forehead. "As my lady commands."

He rode off, going wide of the road and across country, chasing the rest of the Frankish horse. Across the river, Thaler's Gunnhildes fell silent, and the breeze cleared the smoke from their emplacements. She could see the people stationed there start to work at turning their weapons to the south. If she squinted, she could also see the observation tower they'd built, and, below it, a table, where a figure sat crouched over. Her father.

How had it come to this, that her father was here, that Thaler was here, that Cohen was here, that she was here, and that Felix was not?

Aelinn was on her way back. Sophia pursed her lips and stepped out onto the via, among the blood and scorch-marks and debris of war. Her spear centuries faced her, solid and battle-proven as

714

she was now. She lifted her spatha into the air and jerked it in the direction of travel.

"Follow me."

99

The ground was shaking. He'd felt that happen before – avalanches, mainly, where he'd have a heartbeat to decide the direction he needed to run. And once it had been a dragon. He'd actually pissed himself then, but that hadn't been so much fear itself as the aura of fear the dragon had magicked up, trying to flush him out from his hiding place.

He'd held firm then, and he held firm now, despite the urge to bury his hands in the soft soil to try to cling to the earth. He wasn't the only one terrified. With every crack and boom, some of his men crouched lower than ought to be possible, cowering like dogs.

And every so often, something would go astray, and the leaves above his head would shiver as a fast-moving sliver of metal punctured the canopy and buried itself in the bark of a tree.

They could do nothing about that. They had to wait. To move forward would be to killed along with the dwarves. It was like being at Obernberg all over again, watching Nikoleta spit fire from her fingers at anything and everything that moved, with him no more than a passive spectator at a unique and ghastly event.

When the first shots had been fired, and that sharp, broken-quartz smell started to drift through the trees, they'd whispered to each other, keeping a watch for attack while trying to see what was happening further up the via.

Their voices had been bludgeoned into silence. Büber wasn't sure he could even speak any more. Nikoleta's flames had been part of her, extending from her body. Thaler's were different: impersonal, chemical, mechanical. Nikoleta had targeted her fury, while Thaler merely pointed his roughly in the direction he wanted it to go, and had little choice who it struck.

Clovis's Franks were another five stadia back from the wooded ridge. He wished he was there with them, or with Cohen's Jews, deep in the forests with their steep valleys and thick walls of rock. Instead, he had this thin place that lied about the amount of cover it could provide and the depth of defence it offered.

Worse than the noise was the anticipation. The certain knowledge that when the ground stopped moving and the air fell still, whoever had survived would surge up the via. He half-wished it would come soon, while the other half of him hoped it never would.

There was one moment when a stray ball had hurtled through the wood at them. It cleared the crest of the ridge and struck a tree-trunk at mid-height. Where it hit, the tree vanished in a cloud of whirling white splinters that flew in all directions. Those underneath had barely started to recover when the crown of the severed tree descended like a giant's fist.

Büber lost someone to that, someone who couldn't get out of the way in time, who couldn't quite believe that they were going to be crushed by half a tree that had appeared out of nowhere.

They even managed to die quietly, so as not to give away their position.

After that, the initial sharp crashes and subsequent rushing of wind grew closer. The earth shivered and shook, and debris repeatedly lifted up on the far side of the ridge to patter down on their heads.

Büber pressed his cheek to the prickly leaf mould and begged for it to stop, but it didn't: instead, the cry went up as dwarves started to clamber over the ridge, stunned, shocked, seeking shelter, and finding only Carinthians with spears and bows and swords.

Up, up, he thought as he hugged the ground. Around him, the figures huddled behind trees and in hollows started to stir, and he knew he had to be among the first to rise, if not *the* first. Certainly the first to the ridge line, sword drawn, to fall on whoever dared cross it.

He struggled up and shook his head free of confusion and of that gods' awful sound. Starting forward, he steadied himself against another man who'd reeled into him. It was as though they were drunk – dizzy and incompetent – from the barrage.

Some deep breaths of the tainted air. Hints of slate and copper and pine made him spit. Up through the trees, towards the top, he unsheathed his sword.

The dwarves came in a trickle, all across the long low line. They hadn't expect anyone to be there and oppose them, but fleeing from Thaler's bellowing had simply pushed them against Büber's force.

While all around him, his men picked off dwarves in their ones and twos, Büber faced off against a weary, pale-faced thing with barely the strength to swing its axe any more. It toppled forward as the huntmaster stepped back, its momentum overbalancing it, and it lay there face-down in the ground as he drove his sword through its unprotected back.

His blade was red. And instead of the bloodlust rising within him, he felt only pity.

More blundered over the top to escape the bombardment, and the lee side of the ridge degenerated into a series of brief, brutal encounters in which Carinthia invariably held the upper hand.

Another shell went astray and filled the translucent air with stinging shards of metal. The dwarves, with their backs to the blast, seemed to fold to the ground, as if it were a blessed relief. The men who faced it staggered back, some bleeding from wounds that just opened in their flesh.

The horn on the Roman tower called. And again. Thaler's barrage ceased and left a numb silence hanging over the smoke-streamed woodland. Büber shouted for an advance, and hoped enough had good ears to hear him. He loped up the shallow rise to the top of the ridge, and looked down the other side.

Gods. The trees looked like they'd been chewed, fresh white wood exposed everywhere from blasted branches and torn trunks, and in among the debris were dwarves, scattered over every patch of ground, and not just in the first few feet of the trees, but all the way across the road to the marshes on the far side.

Thousands of them, wading through their own dead, tripping on and over them, grimly levering themselves over fallen logs and fighting their way through severed boughs.

His soldiers took the ridge, and, like him, stared down at the shifting, groaning mass, moving like oil and covering the land as thoroughly.

Why wouldn't they give in? What spirit possessed and animated them? Any human army would have fled the field long ago, and yet they were still trying to head north, to take the tower, take the bridge and take the road to Juvavum.

He stared at them, trying to make sense of it, when he thought

717

he saw a face he already knew. It couldn't be Heavyhammer; he was dead already by Büber's own hand.

Which meant this was a face he'd seen during his audience with King Ironmaker. Now he could see it: the finer armour, the better weapons, the remnants of coloured cloaks. Ironmaker's thanes. And Ironmaker himself, behind those stout bodies and thick shields.

He was the cause of this madness. His death would be the end of it.

Büber looked down his own line. They were waiting for him. Very well, then.

"Ironmaker! Ironmaker!" His voice was unmistakable, his sword pointed at the knot of dwarves where the king was hidden. "Do you yield?"

The shields shifted, and now Büber could see him clearly, his crown welded to the circumference of his helmet, sharp points undulled.

"Yield," screamed Büber.

His answer came quickly enough. Ironmaker roared his defiance and the pole bearing Felix's head was raised up behind the dwarvish thanes, turned to face the ridge, shaken at the men gathered there.

Büber charged as the dwarves surged up towards them. He started to cut his way towards where the dwarven king stood, and he wasn't alone. Every Carinthian wanted to do only two things now; kill the king, and get their prince back. They converged on that point, a wedge of spears with Büber's sword forming its point.

The left roared, and Cohen's Jewish centuries pressed in. The right ululated, and Sophia's men came down the road in a spear wall, pushing and stabbing.

But it was in the centre that the fighting was fiercest. The Franks had followed Büber to the ridge, and Clovis realised it would be disastrous to lead his horses into such a chaotic crush.

Proud and vain, he nevertheless ordered his sergeants to dismount, and they joined Büber's thrust, his men with longswords and oval shields, and himself with a singularly unsophisticated and ungentlemanly mace.

The dwarves' defence began to falter. They were so close to each other that they were finding it difficult to swing, and so exhausted that they had little strength to elbow themselves some space. Every time one of their fellows was cut down, the net around them closed tighter. Büber, lost completely now in the frenzy of slaying and slaughter, stepped on the eviscerated, punctured bodies of the dead to get to his next target, slashing and striking, forehand, backhand, while spears darted out to his flanks, killing all who came in range.

He raised his sword, brought it down, cut deep into a shoulder, raised it again but the dwarf was already falling. He pushed it instead into another bearded face and felt it grind against bone and metal. Pulling it back, he cut up into an exposed armpit, near enough filleting the joint. Bright blood spurted out; the dwarf crumpled, taking Büber's sword-point with it. He would have been left open to a counter, but the dwarves were now running from his onslaught.

As they turned, they ran into their rear ranks still trying to advance. And they fought each other.

The dwarvish army collapsed in a ripple spreading out from Büber; a ripple that turned into a wave, washing backwards through the dwarves' constricted, cramped mass. They broke, and headed towards the only place that offered any respite: the river.

Büber found himself running to keep up with them, at the head of a surge of Carinthian spears and Frankish swords. The way ahead suddenly cleared, and there was the dwarvish elite, exposed like a rock amid melting snow. He trampled the bodies and launched himself into the air, leaping and screaming, his sword a bright stripe over his head. His feet landed square on an angled shield, breaking the wielder behind it, and his sword howled down until it ground against compacted gristle and bone.

Similar impacts collapsed the shield wall: men throwing themselves and their weapons against it, running and jumping and crashing through with their full weight behind their sharp blades. The bearer of the pole carrying Felix's head looked to his left and right and found no way out. The edge of the wood was at his back. The ditch, via and marshland stood between him and the water, but the way was already being barred as the flanks closed in to meet.

He abandoned his trophy and tried to run.

Büber, dragging his sword free, was aware that the pole was starting to topple, that it was significant, that there were only two thanes left, that they were on the verge of victory.

None of that mattered while Ironmaker still lived.

He hit the shield of one thane so hard that he shattered the rim and split the wood all the way down to the boss. That he also severed the dwarf's arm was incidental: his sword was stuck fast.

He lifted it all – sword, shield, arm – and threw it at Ironmaker. It hit him square in the side of his head, knocking his hammer from his grip, his crowned helmet off his head, and forcing him to one knee. Büber was right behind it, his few fingers tightening around the king's neck and his thumbs across his throat.

The remaining thane that might have stopped him was dragged down by Clovis before he could drive his axe between Büber's shoulders, and was swiftly run through by an ordinary Carinthian spearman.

Ironmaker beat at Büber's hands, then started to claw at his face. Büber ignored him, concentrating on crushing the hard lump of windpipe. There'd be more scars, more damage, more ruin. His blood dripped down into the king's beard, his mouth, his nose. The scratching and gouging grew weaker. It was now like the batting of bird's wings against his skin.

Büber pushed, and, at last, something gave. Ironmaker's hands fell back. His chest heaved, once, twice. Then he shuddered and was still.

The dwarf stared out of his white, lined face with eyes of deepest brown, and Büber let go only with difficulty.

He felt himself undo, an unravelling of such profound completeness that it was all he could do to roll off Ironmaker's body into the torn woodland undergrowth. He pulled his knees up and wrapped his arms around them, resting his savaged cheek against his bloody breeks.

A hand rested on his shoulder for a moment, mailed and heavy. Clovis's moustache had lost all of its former grandeur and now resembled a pair of rats' tails hanging down the sides of his mouth. His own face, from the brow of his helmet to his chin, was speckled with drying scabs.

"It's done," said the prince.

Büber nodded mutely. If he never had to do it again, it would be too soon. Men drifted past him, touching his back, his shoulders, as they carried on to the via and the marshes beyond to watch the remnants of the dwarvish army fall and splash their way through the open pools and mires of mud, then topple into the river.

Someone – several someones – found Felix, and pulled the sharpened poll from under his chin. A Frankish sergeant took off his surcoat and wrapped the head in it before resting it on the ground at Büber's feet.

Büber looked up sharply, and stopped gnawing at one of his finger stumps.

"It would be better coming from you, Master," said the man, and Clovis, still standing beside Büber, agreed.

"This is a Carinthian grief. We can only watch."

Everything ached. He hurt. His face, his hands were cut and bleeding from wounds he didn't even remember receiving. Nevertheless, he got to his knees and slowly picked up the blue-wrapped bundle.

It was surprisingly heavy, and he had to hold it close to him while he steadied himself to stand. Willing hands came down and pulled him up, and he acknowledged their assistance with a grunt of pain.

There was barely anywhere he could tread that wasn't on one of the dead, and it took him time to pick his way into the open. The ditch was full – he had no option but to step on the bodies there – then it was up to the via, its stone surface ripped up and thrown aside. Sophia's spears were strung out along the road, leaning on their weapons or sitting. Sophia herself was viewing the dwarves' progress into the river with concern.

"Get Clovis's cavalry across the bridge to Master Thaler's position," she shouted, and Aelinn took off towards the woods, past Büber.

When she saw what he was carrying, she faltered, then ran on. Perhaps she was glad she'd not be present when he handed Sophia the head of her dead prince.

Sophia grew deathly still as Büber approached her. She knew what he held, he could see that. At least he wouldn't have to explain to her. Her spatha, notched and bent, slipped from her fingers to rattle on the stones.

She was cut, too. Nicks on her forearm, a gash on the side of her head that ran from eyebrow to ear. The side of her face was as bloody as his.

There was no protocol for this. He simply didn't know what to do, and it was clear that neither did she. He had Felix's head clutched to his chest as though it were a newborn baby, his arms cradling it, his hands wrapped around it to protect it from further harm.

They met like that, in the middle of the via. She put her arms around Büber and held him, put her face against his neck, pressed the head between them and wept for the child they had both lost.

100

Agathos was shouting something from his rickety tower, but Thaler was too deaf to hear him.

"Curse the boy, can't he be clearer?" He waggled his little finger in his ear, and Tuomanen frowned at him.

"He's perfectly clear. He's saying 'nanoi', and pointing at the river."

"Nanoi? Little . . . dwarves. Coming this way?"

"Yes, Master Thaler, and we're almost completely unprotected."

"Who knew they could swim?" he muttered and set off at a lumbering run toward the tower and Morgenstern's table. He put one hand on his hat, the other waved his unicorn-horn stick. "Agathos, Aaron. Come away from there at once."

Morgenstern was calmly closing his books and stacking them in the crate at his feet, while the boy waved manically at Thaler and jabbed his finger at the near bank.

"Despotis! Nanoi!"

Thaler, red-faced and sweaty, strode up and struck the table with his walking-stick's brass ferrule.

"Yes, yes. I can see that. Down off there now." He pointed firmly at the ground. "Aaron, leave that."

Morgenstern ignored him and carefully laid another book in the crate. "I have spent literally weeks of my life tabulating these figures, and I will not leave them behind."

"Gods, man. They'll kill us if they reach us, and neither of us is likely to outrun one of them."

"I don't have to outrun them, Frederik," said Morgenstern, picking up his calculating circle, "I just have to outrun you."

"Oh nonsense, man." Thaler banged on the table even harder. "I insist you come with me at once. What would Sophia say if she were to lose you as well?"

Agathos swung himself down the tower, making it sway

alarmingly as he climbed, and Morgenstern managed to stop thinking about his books for a moment. Thaler took the distance-pipe from the boy and trained it on the marshy ground inside the bend of the river. Those dwarves who had made it across the open water flapped and flopped like stranded fish. Those that hadn't gained the bank had simply sunk under the weight of their armour, plunging into the sluggish brown Enn as if they didn't know that it would drag them down to their deaths.

"How many?" asked Morgenstern.

"A few hundred. More than enough if they're determined to take their revenge." Thaler snapped the tube shut and brooded. "Our forces are too far away to make a difference to us. Our fates are in our own hands."

"But my books . . ."

"Bugger your books, Aaron Morgenstern. You are more important – we are all more important – and we should simply leave, now, at once." Thaler took hold of Agathos's collar and pulled him in the direction of the emplacements. "You too, Aaron. Bring the disk if you must, but we must go."

The first of the dwarves had made dry land, about a stadia away. He was a filthy, dirty thing caked in gelatinous mud from the waist down, and he levered himself upright only with the greatest of effort.

Thaler thought he didn't look much of a threat, but, on the other hand, he didn't have much of an army. They had no ball or shell left and they'd used their experimental case-shot very early on. The bottles filled with powder and tacks they'd given to Sophia. They had half a dozen charges of powder remaining, the tools they used to rake and tamp the barrels, and some crowbars.

His firing crews assembled around the closest pot.

"I think we should retreat," Thaler said to them. "There are too many of them and too few of us."

Bastian, already grasping one of the spike-ended scraping rods, disagreed. "No," he said without elaboration.

"No? We've won, apparently. What good would it do to let them kill us?"

"None," said Tuomanen, "but the smith's right. The field's ours, and there's no reason why we should fear them."

"I've already lost six people to the exploding Gunnhilde: that was unfortunate, but at least it was in battle, and the Valkyries

723

will take them as surely as they would any warrior. This? This is idiocy, and I won't lose any more of you."

"No part of our army has run today." Bastian spun the rod with its heavy iron head as though it were a drumstick. "You think we should be the first?"

"Your army?" Thaler turned on the giant of a man. "Your army?"

"It's as much mine as it yours, Carinthian."

"And mine," said Tuomanen, unhelpfully. "And his." She pointed at Agathos.

"Gods, you're all as contrary as each other."

"We want to hold our heads up when we get home," said Morgenstern. "No matter what we did here, all they'll remember is a few drowned rats chasing us off."

"But—"

"They're beaten, Frederik. Beaten by us." Morgenstern waved his hands to cover all those still standing. "Beaten by you. They're nothing any more. We don't have to run from them."

Thaler turned around. The dwarves were massing on the dry ground, and yes, there seemed to be a couple of centuries' worth of them, compared with his barely forty.

"Right then," he said. "Since you all seem determined to get yourselves killed and me with you into the bargain, I suppose we'd better get on with it. Pick something heavy up, and follow me. And for gods' sake, Aaron, stay behind Bastian and shout encouragement or something."

He took a deep breath and started to stride the way he'd come, back towards the tower, swishing at the grass with his walking-stick. Across the river, the cavalry were beginning to form up at the north end of the ridge, but there were only half a dozen of them so far. It would take a while to reach them, even on horse-back: up the via, across the bridge, then down the western bank.

Thaler was by Morgenstern's table, and he stopped briefly to lay his hat down. No point in that getting damaged. Then he faced the dwarves again, purpose in every step.

As he walked, he stopped using his stick to bruise leaves and played with the catches in the handle. It twisted and clicked, then he unscrewed the ash-wood pole from the horn. The two separated to reveal a thin triangular blade.

He made a couple of practice swipes with it, then a lunge that was not so much threatening as comical. All the same, the point was sharp and the blade long: in the hands of someone who knew how to use it, it would be lethal.

The dwarves would have no idea whether Thaler was that someone or otherwise.

Tuomanen, crowbar in hand, unwound the still-smouldering long fuse from around her shoulders and shrugged it off. "You came prepared," she said.

"I thought it prudent. Who could tell what madness might descend and cause us to close with an enemy, armed with little more than a few sticks?" He sucked his teeth. "You realise this is almost the very definition of hubris?"

"The gods won't destroy us, Master Thaler. If there are any gods left who depend on magic rather than prayer, that is." She brushed her hair behind her oddly pointed ears. "We carved out our own destiny here. We spent our blood and our treasure, and look: most of us get to go home. Isn't that the real victory?"

"Except you, Mistress. You don't get to go home, do you?"

She looked down at the ground, at the bright green grass and the water meadow flowers turning to seed beneath her feet, then at her arms black with patterned ink beneath her skin. "Home is where you decide it is, Master Thaler. And I've been away a very long time."

They were where they needed to be. The dwarves were no more than a well-thrown stone away, and Thaler slowed and stopped. His crew drew up behind him, and he took an extra step forward.

The dwarves looked at them. Those sitting or lying down slowly stood, until all were staring. Thaler's people were soot-marked, flint-reeked, tired but unbowed. The dwarves were simply pitiable: half drowned, mud-coated, defeated.

Thaler chewed the side of his tongue. He wondered what to say, if anything at all. He had no guarantee that anything he said would be the least bit comprehensible to the dwarves. He could try his Latin and his Greek, but he'd have to send back to the library for anyone able to speak even a few words of Dwarvish.

No matter: he had to do something, so he raised his sword and levelled it at the dwarf closest to him. He had no reason to assume this was a leader of any sort. These bedraggled things were merely the remnants, the random sweepings from the horde that had been brushed together one last time. So one was as good as another.

"Can you understand me?"

The dwarf looked blankly at him, blinking.

"Does anyone on your side speak German? Latin? Ellenikos?"

Nothing. Why were they suddenly so passive?

"What else can we try? Aaron?"

"Ebrit?" he offered. "Parsi? Aramaic?"

"Donsk tunga," said Tuomanen, and there was an immediate reaction. Heads turned and re-centred on her.

"Mistress? The old language of the north it is, then. Can you tell these gentlemen . . ." Thaler tailed off. He still didn't know what to say. Morgenstern squeezed through to tug on his sleeve.

"Frederik, the cavalry's on its way."

Thaler nodded. "Thank you, Aaron. Mistress, can you tell them that if they surrender to me, I'll save them from the Frankish horse."

"Before I do that," she said, "do you think you can do that?"

"I'm the master librarian and a prince's man. That has to carry some weight, even on a battlefield. So yes, go ahead. Make them understand." He turned to face his own people. "Does anyone here have any problem with asking them to surrender, or do you think we should have some more slaughter to end the day with?"

There were few sceptical faces, but if any had concerns, they kept them quiet.

Tuomanen cleared her throat. "Gefast upp, eða hestamenn vilja drepa þig."

The dwarves seemed to experience a collective shudder, and whispered to themselves. The ground began to sound with the beating of hooves, and Thaler looked over his shoulder to see horsemen, their blue and white pennants fluttering, gallop over the bridge and towards the emplacements.

"What are they saying?" he asked Tuomanen.

"Discussing your offer. There's more shame in defeat than there is in death."

"They can stick their shame up their arses. I'm willing to let them live, not as slaves, but as free men."

"I'll tell them." She composed the phrase in her mind, then spoke it. "Þér mun ekki vera þrælar. Þér vilja hafa frelsi. I'm sure I'm getting all this wrong: it's been a long time, Master Thaler."

"You're doing your best. But please tell them to hurry."

"Veldu nú," she said to them. Her voice was dispassionate, but the horses were almost on them.

Thaler was as desperate as she was calm. It made no sense, since he'd spent all his time previously trying to kill the dwarves, but suddenly it mattered a very great deal to him whether these poor benighted creatures lived or died.

One by one, they made their choices. Those who were willing to be taken captive, to trust Thaler's word, knelt among the tall grasses and flowerheads. There were some, even then, who would not yield. Half a dozen broke out of the main mass and started to run south, towards the notch of the valley and the forest between the mountainsides.

The first of the Franks thundered by, and those six never made it anywhere near the tree line. The other riders circled the remaining dwarves, spears down, ready.

"They've surrendered," called Thaler. "They've surrendered to me and they're my prisoners."

Clovis wheeled about in front of Thaler and Tuomanen. "Master Thaler, isn't it? For a bookish sort, you seem surprisingly martial."

"I had expert teachers, my lord. Homer, Pliny and Caesar himself." Thaler slipped his sword into its ash sheath. "How did it go across the river?"

"How did it go? Grimly well. There was no artistry to it: your low-born commanders live, while King Ironmaker and his lords are dead, his army destroyed and his ambitions as cold as his grave will be." He sniffed. "Your engines of war, Master Thaler. I would like to discuss them with you later. Over a cup of wine, perhaps."

"If you'll call your sergeants off, I'll happily agree."

Clovis turned his attention to the surrounded dwarves. "They raised their arms against you with no warning or reason. Why you suffer some of them still to live is beyond me. Say the word, Master Thaler, and my men will use them for spear practice."

"I don't think that'll be necessary." He screwed his walking-stick back together, and released the catch to turn the hilt back into an innocuous grip. "I have other plans for them."

"Ah, the mines," said Clovis. "Be sure to chain them well, and sweat the labour out of them."

"Something like that," said Thaler, who had no intention of going back on his word. The water courses and drains beneath Juvavum could still do with some expert attention, and yes, the mines, too, which were always in danger of flooding. But only if they wanted to work there. That was what Felix had wanted all along: a few dwarves to pass on their knowledge. It would be a legacy, of sorts.

"I'll leave some of my men to escort your prisoners to their pen." Clovis kicked his heels and his horse trotted away, tail up. "Hah. Beaten by a woman and caught by a librarian. These are dread dwarves indeed."

Thaler watched him go. "I suppose he didn't have to stay and fight with us."

"I don't think the Lady Sophia gave him much choice. I understand she was really very rude to him." Tuomanen smiled. "So what do we do now, Master Thaler?"

"We pack up and we . . . well, carry on as we were before." Thaler shrugged. "Perhaps we can get back to some proper work instead of blowing holes in things. There really is an awful lot to be getting on with."

"And who will lead Carinthia?" she asked.

"I don't know." He looked across the river, more pensive than he had been before. "I'm sure we'll muddle through somehow."

"Why not you?"

He baulked. "Good gods, no. Give it to someone else: I'm far too busy for that sort of thing. I have a library to run."

She smiled again.

IOI

Seeing the mountains covered with snow was a relief that was fresh every morning. Winter was here, at last. The passes to the south were closed by deep, dense drifts, and there was no way through for either the Doge or his old sparring partner, the Duke of Milano.

Wien had collapsed under a mountain of its own: debt. The Protector had fled, and Carinthia had subtly suggested that he keep away from their palatinate. The people of Wien continued their flight from the city. Some would move into Carinthia and learn how they ran things there. After they'd overwintered with their kin, they might take their new ideas back home. That would be interesting.

And Bavaria? Standing before Kossler, Lord of München, had

been more than a little embarrassing, given that he'd so nearly met his end at the point of a dagger wielded by one of Ullmann's agents. Her apology had been heartfelt, and she'd assuaged the man's anger – and turned away the possibility of a war that neither of them wanted – by telling him that she'd killed Ullmann herself. It had become quite beery after that, and Kossler had drunkenly agreed to Carinthia keeping both Rosenheim and Simbach.

When he'd sobered up, she'd reminded him of his promise. She would remind him again when she saw him later.

Carinthia was safe for now, until next spring at least. They'd had a harvest, good enough to last them through, even with the extra mouths to feed, and with some to spare for their neighbours.

All of this, everything from affairs of state to the fullness of a pig farmer's stomach, was now officially going to be her concern. It served her right, really, for being so competent.

She could have refused. She'd talked it over with Thaler, her father, and Wess, and they'd all urged her to accept, though she hadn't been able to tell whether Thaler was encouraging her to do so to ensure that no one would ask him.

She hadn't talked to Peter Büber. She didn't have to. She knew what he'd say.

There'd be no coronation. She wasn't nobility, and her father was vague enough as it was about his genealogy without trying to work his way back to King David. Knowing her luck, she'd be related to Herod Antipas instead.

So she wouldn't be their queen, nor their princess. Some might have hoped for that, but their prince was gone, and that was the end of it. They'd burnt his head, and what she'd been assured was the rest of his body, on a barge in the middle of the Salzach.

In the end, picking a title had proved more difficult than picking the person to fill it.

Thaler had suggested all sorts of impractical names based on offices from Athenian democracy. She was not, absolutely and definitely, going to be an archon, no matter how much sense it made in an Athenian context. She pointed out, and pointedly stuck to the idea, that this was Carinthia, and Athens had flourished and dwindled some two thousand years before them.

Instead, they were going to install her – which made her sound like a piece of furniture – using the title of provost. She would be someone who'd been placed in charge of the palatinate. She hadn't inherited it, or seized it. She'd been given it by the only people qualified to do so: the Carinthians themselves. And she wouldn't be ruling on her own. There'd be an assembly in the spring, after the snows melted, and two in summer, and, oh, everything would be fine: she'd hardly ever have to make a decision on her own, though she'd kept the title strategos. Just in case.

Her spatha, old and battered when she'd worn it, had been retired to over the fireplace in the solar. She turned around to see it held against the stonework by two wire brackets, thin enough so it looked as if it was floating there. If she ever needed it, she knew where it was. Today, they'd present her with the Sword of Carinthia: Felix's sword, and Gerhard's before him, along with all the others who'd wielded it since it had been forged and enchanted, and disenchanted again.

She turned back to the windows, and the snow was still there.

They'd survived. The Germans thanked their gods with more equivocation than she thanked hers. Then again, HaShem had never promised them magic.

There was a knock at the door. She was used to that: the knock, the creak, the unnecessary bow or curtsy, the fumbling conversation and almost always the entirely obvious answer. The door stayed closed this time, and she was distracted more by that than by an announcement that Clovis, King of the Franks, had arrived, or some other dignitary.

"You can come in," she said, loud enough to be heard on the other side of the door.

The latch clicked, the door creaked, Büber stepped in.

"I . . . hello. Is this a good time?"

"Peter. It's always a good time."

"I can come back later," he said, halfway out of the doorway.

"Peter. Come in. Close the door."

He did so, albeit reluctantly. He looked as if this room was the last place on earth he wanted to be, and she the last person he wanted to be with. She sympathised with that, and wondered if he knew just how much she shared those sentiments.

He'd scrubbed up. If it hadn't been for the scars, the part-missing ear, the shaved head and the stubbled cheeks, he'd almost be handsome. Not that she cared any more, but she cared on his behalf, because he was always so painfully aware of how he looked.

Of course, she had her own scar now, a reminder of a time that could have ended so very differently. His clothes were clean, if tired, and she wondered if he'd ever owned anything new.

"You look—"

"Like a pile of shit," he said. "Sorry, I didn't mean to say that."

"I was going to say respectable. They – whoever they are – seem to believe I have to wear something suitable for the occasion. I should, perhaps, have let them fight to the death as to what suitable means." She raised her arms to show that her sleeves were slashed to show the material underneath, and her intricately embroidered cuffs were shot with gold thread. "Black and yellow really isn't my colour."

She let her arms fall back, and he shuffled his feet. She seemed to blind him, and he looked away.

"I won't be there when they, you know . . ."

"Make me provost?" She nodded, and almost choked on the dryness in her mouth. "I'd guessed you might not be. You can change your mind, whenever you want. Up to the moment they do it, of course. After that, it's too late."

"I . . ." he said, and he appeared to be having as much difficulty with his words as she was. "I'm not a ceremony sort of man."

"Neither am I," she said, and she managed to get a wry smile from him, even though he was staring at the toes of his worn boots. "But we do what we have to, Peter."

"I wanted to wish you luck. Do you believe in luck?" He scratched the back of his down-turned head. "I don't know."

"We don't. Not really. Mazel doesn't mean . . ." She stopped, and walked across the room towards him. When she was close enough, she cupped his chin and got him to actually look at her. "You can wish me luck if you want. I won't be offended."

He stepped away from her, just out of reach. He put the back of his hand to his jaw as if she'd burnt him with her touch.

"Good luck, then. Not that you'll need it."

"HaShem orders everything except our choices," she said. "Peter, what are you going to do?"

"I had thought about running away. When I took Felix's message to Farduzes, I intended to keep going. Reach the ocean. I've never seen the sea before." Büber took the opportunity to move further from her, towards the window where he'd be able to see the snow covering the mountains. "This is all I've ever known. I should really go and have a look for myself at what else is out there. Vulfar the Frank wants to try his latest river barge out before the rivers ice up. I might even get all the way down the Donau."

"There's a sea there," said Sophia. "And another beyond it."

"Then perhaps that's what I'll do. Go and explore for a while."

"For a while? How long?"

Büber's breath condensed white on the cold glass of the window. "I don't know. How long were you thinking of being provost?"

"Five years? They should be bored with me by then."

"Five years. It's a long time to be away from home. Long enough to lay some ghosts to rest, for certain."

"We both have things we need to forget. Things we need to be forgiven." She hadn't told him what she knew about Ullmann. She wasn't going to, either: that was one of the choices she'd made. She didn't need any other explanation than Ullmann's cowardice on the battlefield for what she'd done, and, unsurprisingly, no one thought to dig any further. "Will you need anything? Money? Letters? Weapons?"

"I've got a good sword. And I want to see the world, not find new things to kill. I've got money." He shrugged. He was now staring at the window, rather than through it. "Letters are a bit of a waste of time for me. I'll manage without."

"So there's nothing I can give you?"

He was quiet for a while. She watched him reach his hand to his mouth and chew at one of his knuckles.

"Peter?"

"Will you . . ." he said, ". . . will you wait?"

"Yes," she said.

He nodded, and left the room, leaving nothing but his breath on the window pane.

She shivered, even though the room was more than warm enough.

The door was still open, and a hand reached out to tap on it.

"My lady?"

She steeled herself. "Master Thaler."

He stepped in uneasily, and she realised that she wasn't the only one uncomfortable with her costume.

"Is that what they're making you wear?" she asked.

"Yes. Yes it is. Apparently, it's traditional for the master librarian to look like a pig trussed up for the Yule roast."

"We should really find out who they are and banish them from the palatinate for crimes against comfort and utility."

"I'd vote for that." Thaler glanced behind him at the open door. "Was Peter all right? He seemed" – and he frowned – "almost happy."

"I told him I wasn't going to insist on him coming to the investiture." She realised that she had that lost inflection to her voice. She glanced to the window, to the diamond-shaped pane that was now perfectly clear.

"Ah, that would do it." Thaler seemed content with the explanation. "They were going to send someone to get you. I said I would come myself."

"Is everything ready then?"

"People are making their way down to the field. By the time we get there, yes. If you're still going to insist on walking, that is."

"I can't ride in this, so I'll walk. It's not far."

"I meant a carriage," said Thaler, looking disappointed.

"A cup of wine before we go?" she said.

"Gods, yes."

The wine was kosher, and the cups had been tovelled in the new mikveh. She poured them both out a decent measure, enough to stave off the cold and make all the standing that lay ahead of them bearable.

Thaler raised his cup to her. "A toast, my lady provost. Carinthia. Long may we be at peace."

"I'll drink to that," she said, knowing that she had every incentive to work hard for that peace: not just in the palatinate, or between her neighbours, but further afield – Italy, Byzantium, the wild northlands. Because that was where Peter Büber would be for the next five years.

She drained her wine in a most unladylike fashion. "Shall we go?"

"I suppose we should." He finished his own drink, and carefully placed the cup on the table. "I've a present for you. I want to give it to you now, rather than later, because this is for Sophia, not for the provost."

"I'm intrigued, Frederik."

He patted himself down in order to find it, and eventually discovered it in a pocket of his ceremonial robe. It was a padded bag, velvet with a drawstring. He handed it to her, and she was surprised by the weight of it.

She frowned, and, on his urging, started to pull the bag open.

"It'll break if you drop it," he warned, "but it's meant to be used. I thought – we thought – that you might not spend so long in so many interminable meetings."

It was like a flattened brass egg, circular in circumference and as thick as a thumb-width. The surface was plain, and gave no hint as to what it might be.

"We were going to have it engraved, but we ran out of time. Making it proved just a little bit more difficult than we thought."

She turned it in her hands. There were two catches on the rim, and she pressed one of them.

The whole of one side popped up, with a hidden hinge allowing it to be pulled upright. Inside were fine brass cogs, a coiled ribbon of metal like a snail's shell, and some tiny rods and shafts.

"Sorry, that's the wrong side," said Thaler. He reached forward and pushed the lid down until it clicked, and turned it over. "Now try it."

Sophia pressed the other catch, and this time when the brass case popped up, it revealed a white horn disk with numbers written in a circle around its edge, and a tiny metal finger which pointed to them.

"It's very fine," she said. "What is it?"

"There's a key that goes in that little hole in the face of the dial." Thaler shook the bag, and a little brass key tied with a scrap of velvet fell into his palm. He supported her hand underneath while he inserted the key and gave it a few turns. Then he took the key out. "Listen to it," he said.

She brushed the hair away from her ear and held the device next to her head. She could hear a distinct clicking sound coming from it.

"The finger moves to mark out the hours, as long as the spring is wound. Good for cutting insufferable windbags, like myself, off in their prime."

"And you made this?"

"No one can claim sole credit. A dwarf called Thorvald Icehewer did a lot of the internal work, but the principles go all the way back to a water clock we found in a drawing." Thaler put the key back in the bag. "It's very much a working model. The next one we make will be more accurate."

Sophia was captivated by its regular, mechanical heartbeat. "It's perfect, Frederik. Thank you. Thank everyone."

He beamed. "Well, that's good. We do have to go now, though, or they'll be sending someone else to find the pair of us."

She closed the lid, and slid the disk back into its bag. "Yet again, I find myself without pockets."

"You won't need it today," said Thaler, "and it'll still be here in the morning."

She placed the bag on the table next to the two empty cups before slipping her arm through his.

"We can't put this off any longer. No matter how scared I am." She took a deep breath, and was glad of the extra space she'd insisted they allow for her bodice. Still she hesitated.

"Sophia? What's wrong?"

"I'm unworthy of this," she said.

"Oh, we all are. If that's the only thing that's bothering you . . ."

It wasn't. Peter could be on Vulfar's barge already, slipping down the Salzach and away from her. She chewed her lip.

"I'm ready now. Why don't we go and make the world a better place?"

extras

about the author

Dr Simon Morden is a bona fide rocket scientist, having degrees in geology and planetary geophysics, and is one of the few people who can truthfully claim to have held a chunk of Mars in his hands. Simon Morden lives in Gateshead with a fierce lawyer, two unruly children and a couple of miniature panthers.

Find out more about Simon Morden and other Orbit authors by registering for the free monthly newsletter at www.orbitbooks.net.

if you enjoyed
ARCANUM

look out for

SHAMAN

by
Kim Stanley Robinson

We had a bad shaman.

This is what Thorn would say whenever he was doing something bad himself. Object to whatever it was and he would pull up his long gray braids to show the mangled red nubbins surrounding his earholes. His shaman had stuck bone needles through the flesh of his boys' ears and then ripped them out sideways, to help them remember things. Thorn when he wanted the same result would flick Loon hard on the ear and then point at the side of his own head, with a tilted look that said, You think you have it bad?

Now he had Loon gripped by the arm and was hauling him along the ridge trail to Pika's Rock on the overlook between Upper and Lower Valleys. Late afternoon, low clouds rolling overhead, brushing the higher ridges and the moor, making a gray roof to the world. Under it a little line of men on a ridge trail, following Thorn on shaman's business. It was time for Loon's wander.

—Why tonight? Loon protested. —A storm is coming, you can see it.

—We had a bad shaman.

And so here they were. The men all gave Loon a hug, grinning ruefully at him and shaking their heads. He was going to have a miserable night, their looks said. Thorn waited for them to finish, then croaked the start of the good-bye song:

> This is how we always start
> It's time to be reborn a man
> Give yourself to Mother Earth
> She will help you if you ask

—If you ask nicely enough, he added, slapping Loon on the shoulder. Then a lot of laughing, the men's eyes sardonic or encouraging as they divested him of his clothes and his belt and his shoes, everything passed over to Thorn, who glared at him as if on the verge of striking him. Indeed when Loon was entirely naked and without possessions Thorn did strike him, but it was just a quick backhand to the chest. —Go. Be off. See you at full moon.

If the sky were clear, there would have been the first sliver of a new moon hanging in the west. Thirteen days to wander, therefore, starting with nothing, just as a shaman's first wander always started. This time with a storm coming. And in the fourth month, with snow still on the ground.

Loon kept his face blank and stared at the western horizon. To beg for a month's delay would be undignified, and anyway useless. So Loon looked past Thorn with a stony gaze and began to consider his route down to the Lower Valley creekbed, where knots of trees lined the creek. Being barefoot made a difference, because the usual descent from Pika's Rock was very rocky, possibly so rocky he needed to take another way. First decision of many he had to get right. —Friend Raven there behind the sky, he chanted aloud,— lead me now without any tricks!

—Good luck getting Raven to help, Thorn said. But Loon was from the raven clan and Thorn wasn't, so Loon ignored that and stared down the slope, trying to see a way. Thorn slapped him again and led the other men back down the ridge. Loon stood alone, the wind cutting into him. Time to start his wander.

But it wasn't clear which way to get down. For a time it seemed like he might freeze there, might never start his life's journey.

So I came up in him and gave him a little lift from within.

I am the third wind.

He took off down the rocks. He looked back once to show his teeth to Thorn, but they were out of sight down the ridge. Off he plunged, flinging the thought of Thorn from him. Under his feet the broken gritstone was flecked with pock snow, which collected in dimples and against nobbles in a pattern that helped him see where to step. Go as agile as a cat, down rock to rock, hands ready to grab and help down little jumps. His toes chilled and he abandoned them to their cold fate, focused on keeping his hands warm. He would need his hands down in the trees. It began to snow, just a first little pricksnow. The slope had big snow patches that were easier on his feet than the rocks.

He tightened his ribs and pushed his heat out into his limbs and skin, grunting until he blazed a little, and the pricksnow melted when it touched him. Sometimes the only heat to be had is in hurry.

He clambered down and across the boulder-choked ravine seaming the floor of Lower Valley, across the little stream. On the other side he was able to run up the thin forest floor, which was all too squishy, as the ground was wet with rain and snowmelt. Here he avoided the patches of snow. First day of the fourth month: it was going to be trouble to make a fire. The night would be ever so much more comfortable if he could make a fire.

The upper end of Lower Valley was a steep womb canyon. A small cluster of spruce and alder surrounded the spring there, which started the valley's creek. There he would find shelter from the wind, and branches for clothing, and under the trees there wouldn't be much snow left. He hurried up to this grove, careful not to stub his senseless toes.

In the little copse around the spring he tore at live spruce branches and broke several off, cursing their wetness, but even damp their needles would hold some of his heat against him. He wove two spruce branches together and stuck his head through a middle gap in the weave, making it into a rough cloak.

Then he broke off a dead bit of brush pine root to serve as the base of his firestarter. Near the spring he found a good rock to use as a chopper, and with it cut a straight dead alder branch for his firestick. His fingers were just pliable enough to hold the rock. Otherwise he didn't feel particularly cold, except in his feet, which were pretending not to be there. The black mats of spruce needles under the trees were mostly free of snow. He crouched under one of the biggest trees and forced his toes into the mat of needles and wiggled them as hard as he could. When they began to burn a little he pulled them out and went looking for duff. Even the best fire kit needs some duff to burn. He reached into the center of dead spruce logs, feeling for duff or punk. He found some punk that was only a little damp, then broke off handfuls of dead twigs tucked under the protection of larger branches. The twigs were damp on their outsides, but dry inside; they would burn. There were some larger dead branches he could break off too. The grove had enough dead wood to supply a fire once it got going. It was a question of duff or punk. Neither spruce nor alder rotted to a good punk, so he would have to be lucky, or maybe find some ant-eaten wood. He got on his knees and started grubbing around under the biggest downed trees, avoiding the snow, turning over bigger branches and shoving around in the dirt trying to find something. He got dirty to the elbows, but then again that would help keep him warm.

Which might matter, as he could not find any dry punk, or any duff at all. He squeezed water out of one very rotten mass of wood, but the brown goo that remained in his hand resembled dead moss or mullein, and was still damp. The firestick's rough tip would never light such shit.

—Please, he said to the grove. He begged its forgiveness for cursing as he had approached it. —Give me some punk, please goddess.

Nothing. It became too cold for him to keep kneeling on the wet ground digging in downed logs. To make some heat in him he got up and danced. With this effort he could warm his hands, and it was important they not go numb like his feet had. Oh, a fire would make the night so much more comfortable! Surely something could be found here that would burn under the heat of his firestick's tip! Nothing. His belt contained in its fold many little gooseskin bags in which there were spark flints, dry moss, firestick, and base. Dressed and carrying all his things, he could have survived this night and the fortnight to follow in style. Which was why he had been sent out naked: the point of the wander was to prove you could start with nothing but yourself, and not just survive but prosper. He needed to come back into camp on the night of the full moon in good style.

But first he had to get through this night. He began to work hard in his dance, throwing his arms around, spinning his hands in big circles. He sang a hot song and wiggled all over. After doing this for a while, everything but his feet began to burn. But he was also getting tired. He tried to find a balance between the cold and his efforts, walking in a tight circle while also inspecting the forest floor for likely punk and duff shelters. Nothing!

In every grove some wood will burn.

This was one of the sayings that Heather often repeated, though seldom when talking about fire. Loon said it aloud, emphatically, beseechingly: —In every grove some wood will burn! But on this night he wasn't convinced. It only made him mad.

Dig!

He went at the underside of a log which had broken over another one in its fall, a long time ago. They were two crossing mounds of dirt, almost; not an impossible source. But at this moment, wet through and through. And cold.

When he saw how it was, he beat his fist on the soft wet logs. Then he had to start walking in circles again.

Later, more digging into another log gained him only a knot that was still hard, with two spurs extending away from it at an angle much like the angle needed to make a spear thrower. He replaced his first firestarter base with this flat knot, which was better. His alder firestick still looked good. All was ready, if only he had something dry enough to catch fire.

And if only it would stop raining so hard. For a while it pelted down, cold enough to be a little sleety, and all on a gusty wind. In the hard gusts it was like getting hit with cold sand. He simply had to take shelter, and so he crawled under a spruce with big branches right against the ground, where he could snuggle in tight around the trunk and feel only a few drips on him, a few tickles of wind. The spruce needles were scratchy and the ground was cold, but he flexed his shoulder up and down, and sang a hot song and swore vengeance against Thorn. Talk about bad shamans!

But all boys have to become men one way or another. Their wanders had to be trials of skill and endurance. Hunters' wanders were just as bad. And other packs' shamans insisted on even harder trials, it was said.

Loon banished Thorn again. He tested all the branches at the bottom of the spruce. If a dead one could be broken, a dead one well dried but still a little resiny, possibly he could pulverize a spot in it with a rock point and make a mash of splinters fine enough to catch fire under the spin of the firestick. Worth a try, and the effort itself would help keep him warm.

But it turned out there didn't seem to be a branch around the bottom of this tree that he could break.

When the rain let off, he squirmed back out and crawled around under the other spruces looking for such a branch. His hands were so cold he could scarcely grasp the branches to test them.

After a while he had broken off a few likely-looking branches. If he could get a fire started in one of them, the others would be good wood to feed to it.

He found an adequate hearth rock, and a better smasher rock. He took the best one of his dead dry spruce branches and placed it on the hearth, then hit it with the smasher. It resisted, and it was clear it would take a while to get it right, but it seemed promising. Smash smash smash. He had to be more careful than usual not to catch a finger, his hands were so clumsy. Once two years before he had smashed a fingertip, and it was still fat and a little numb at the end, its flat claw lined with grooves. He called that finger Fatty. So he hit his smasher on the side of the broken branch very carefully, once or twice hitting the hearth instead. A spark or two from those accidents made him long for his flint firestrikers. A few scattered sparks were not going to be enough to do it on a night like this. The wet wind whooshed its laughter at him, loud in the trees.

Eventually a spot on the side of his target branch was squashed into a splay of splinters, perfectly dry. He sat cross-legged with his body arched over the branch, and it seemed like the mash of splinters might burn. Breathing hard, warm except for his feet, he crawled under the best of the spruces in his grove and arranged his new kit around him. Smashed branch on the hearth rock, held there between his feet; firestick placed almost upright in the mash of splinters on the branch, held at its tilt between his palms. All set: spin the firestick back and forth.

Back and forth, back and forth between his hands, gently pushing the point of the stick down into the branch. Back and forth, back and forth. His palms ran down the stick with the force of his pushing down, and when they reached the lower end of the stick he had to grasp it with one hand, put the other against the top, and move up and catch it and begin over again, with as little a pause as he could manage. Meanwhile it kept raining outside the shelter of the spruce, and under it, even right against the trunk, drips were dripping. Really it began to look impossible, given the conditions. But he didn't want to admit that. It would get an awful lot colder the moment he admitted that.

After a long time, maybe a fist or more, he had to give up, at least on this branch. The mash of splinters was a bit too massy, and after a while, a little damp. He could get the spot just under the firestick so hot that it slightly burned his fingertip to touch it, and the splinters around that spot had even blackened a little, but they would not burst into flame.

Loon sat there. This was going to be a hard thing to tell Thorn about, assuming he survived to tell the tale. The old sorcerer would flick him on the ears for sure. You had to be able to start a fire, anytime, anywhere; the worse conditions were, the more important it got. Thorn, like most of the shamans at the corroboree, was exceptionally good with fire, and had spent a lot of time with Loon and the other kids, teaching them the tricks. He had put a firestick to their forearms and spun it, to teach them how hot the spinning got. Eventually Loon had learned how to make fire no matter how the old man complicated the task. But there had always been some dry duff, one way or another.

Now he crawled out from under the spruce and stood up, sobbing with frustration, and danced until the cold was held off him by a thin envelope of sweat. When the rain let up a little, he steamed. Already he was hungry, but there was nothing for it. Time to chew on a pebble and think about other things. Chew a pebble and dance in the rain. Cold or not, this was his wander. When daylight came at last he would find better shelter, find some dry duff, find an abri or some smaller overhang. Begin outfitting himself for his return at full moon. He would walk into camp fully clothed, belly full, spear in hand! Clothed in lion skins! Beartooth necklace draped around his neck! He saw it all inside his eyes. He shouted the story of it at the night.

After a while he sat again under the best spruce, his head on his knees, arms wrapped around his legs. Then he got back out and shuffled around in the grove, looking for a better tuck, finding one after another and testing them. If they were good, he added them to a growing little round of camps, each with its own strengths and weaknesses. He chanted for long stretches, cursed Thorn from time to time. May your pizzle fall off, may a lion eat you . . . Then also from time to time he would shout things out loud. —It's cold! Thorn would sometimes howl his thoughts that way, using old words from the shamans' language, words that sounded like the things themselves: Esh var kalt! Esh var k-k-k-kaaaal-TEE!

He stubbed a big toe and only felt it in the bone; the flesh was numb. More curses. May the ravens shit on you, may your babies die . . . Lie on the ground under one big spruce, only his kneecaps and toes and the palms of hands and his forehead touching the earth. Push himself up and down with his arms, staying rigid. If only he could fuck the earth to get warm, but it was too cold, he couldn't get his poor pizzle to antler, it was as numb as his toes, and would hurt like crazy when it next warmed up, prickle and burn till he cried. Maybe if he thought of that girl from the Lion pack, a raven like him, therefore forbidden to him, supposedly, but they had made eyes anyway, and it would warm him to think of plunging her. Or Sage, from his own pack.

That line of thought trapped some time: seeing it all inside his eyelids, seeing her spread her legs to him. Be there inside her kolby, forget this cold rain. Her kolby, her baginaren, her vixen. Start a little fire behind his belly button, get his prong to spurt. But it was too cold. He could only mash the poor flesh around and make it burn a little, warm it in the hope it would not get frostbit. That would be so bad.

After a time the rain relented. The sky's cloudy dark gray seemed a bit lighter. No moon, no stars to tell him how close dawn was. But it felt close. It had to be close. It had been a long, long night.

He stood and swayed. It was surely a lighter gray overhead. He sang a hot song, he sang a song to the sun. He called for the sun, the great god of warmth and good cheer. He was tired and cold. But he wasn't so cold he would die. He would make it to dawn, he could feel it. This was his wander, this was how a shaman was born. He howled till his throat was raw.

Finally dawn came, wet, gray, dull, cold. Under the storm the colors of things did not quite return, but he could see. Low clouds scudded in from the west, cutting off the ridgetops. The undersides of the clouds hung in fat dark tits. A sheet of rain fell on Lower Valley downstream from him, a black broom standing in the air between cloud and forest. With the big snow patches everywhere, the ground was lighter than the sky.

Then in just a few blinks everything got much lighter, and a white spot glowed in the clouds over the east ridge. The sun, wonderful god of warmth, over the ridge at last. Cloudy or not, the air would almost certainly get warmer. Only the worst storms had days colder than the previous night. And now the sky didn't look too bad to windward; the clouds tumbling over the gray hills had little breaks between them that were bright white. It was still windy, however, and the rain began to come down in little freshets.

Whether this day proved to be warmer than the night or not, he was going to have to keep moving to stay warm. There would be no relief from that until he got a fire lit. So he gathered his unsuccessful fire kit and held the two pieces of it in his left hand, and clasped a good throwing rock in his right hand, and took off downstream. He wanted a bigger copse of trees, with a good mix of spruce and pine and cedar and alder. The ridges and hillsides and valley slopes, and the upland behind and above them, were mostly bare rock dotted with grasses, and now covered by old snow; but in the valleys against the creeks, trees usually grew, making ragged dark green lines in the palm of any valley. Downstream a short walk, where Lower Valley's creek was met by a little trickle down its eastern flank, a flat spot held a bigger clump of trees, surrounding a little oval meadow and climbing the slopes to each side.

He made his way around the wet part of the little meadow and went to the thickest part of this grove. He slipped between the trees, grateful for their shelter. It was windier now, and there was more rain falling than he had thought when he left his night copse. In this larger grove things were very much better. He was well protected, and now that it was day he could see what he was doing. A broken cedar at the center of the grove had exposed a big curve of its inner bark, which he could pull free and use to make some rough clothes. A couple of snow-rimmed anthills spilling out of the end of a decomposed cedar log gave him sign of potential punk. There was a small hole at the end of the log; he bashed it in with his rock and tore the hole deeper, then reached in and up: on the underside of the still solid wall of the log was a section of punky duff, quite dry— Ah mother! he cried. —Thank you!

He pulled out a big handful and carried it quickly to the lee of a gnarled old pine. —In every grove OF SUFFICIENT SIZE some wood will burn, he said aloud, shouting his correction. He was going to tell that to Heather in no uncertain terms. She would laugh at him, he knew, but he was going to do it anyway. It was important to get things right, especially if you were going to make sayings out of them.

He left the dry duff well protected in a cleft at the base of a broken old pine tree, and quickly gathered a bunch of branches and broke off several more. He stashed these with the duff and then broke off ten or twenty smallish live branches and arranged them around and behind and over the broken pine tree he had chosen, making its wind protection even better. Bush pines like this old one had multiple trunks, and were thickly needled; this one was a great tuck to begin with, and with his branch walls added, hardly any wind or rain was making it through to his fire area.

After that he gathered the pile of firewood next to him, then sat down with his back against the trunk, curled in a crouch to make his body the last part of the windbreak. He crossed his legs and placed his unfeeling feet against the sides of his base.

He chopped at his firestick's tip until it was a little cleaner and sharper, then placed it in the dent on the knot base, very near his new duff. When all seemed right, he began to spin for dear life, back and forth, back and forth, feeling his hands sliding slowly down the stick, feeling also the pressure of the stick against the base as it spun, trying to hold the combination of speed and pressure that would make the most heat. There was a feel to that, and a dance with each return of the hands from the bottom of the stick to the top, a quick little move. When he had it going as well as he could, and had made several swift hand shifts from bottom to top, he toed some of the duff closer to the blackening cup spot, a little depression in the knot which was what had caused him to pick this base in the first place; it was just what you would have cut with a blade in a flat base.

He watched the duff blacken, holding his breath; then some of the newly black spots glowed yellow and white at their edges. He gently blew on these white points, contorting so his face was closer to them, breathing on them in just the way that would push the white away from the cup into the bigger mass of duff. He bent his backbone like Loop Meadow and blew as gently as seemed right, coaxing the white heat to grow, feeding it a little wind that would not blow it out, giving it just what it needed, emptying himself out to it, puff puff puff, puffffff, this he could do, this he knew how to do, puff puff puff, puff puff puff, pufffff and the duff burst into flame. FIRE! Even this tiny flame lofted a little waft of heat into his face, and he sucked in a breath and blew even more ardently than before, still very gently but with a particular growing urgency, like blowing in a hole on the flute when you want to make a wolf 's cry jump. As he did this he also shifted to his knees and elbows, using his face as the closest windbreak for this gorgeous little flame, and breathing on it in just the way that made it bigger, making love to it, oh how he wanted it to feel good, to be happy and grow! He gave it his breath, his spirit, his love, he wanted it to spurt, to leap up like the spurtmilk out of a prong, to burn in his face: and it did!

When he saw that the little spurt of flame was holding, he began placing the littlest and driest twigs over it, in a way that would catch as much of them alight as possible without harming the blaze below. It was a delicate balance, but one very well known to him; something he was good at, Thorn having forced him to practice it twentytwentytwentytwenty times. Oh yes, fire, fire, FIRE! Almost everyone was pretty good at fire, but Loon thought of himself as exceptionally good at it, which was part of what made the previous night's failure so galling. He was going to be embarrassed to tell the story of that first night. He would have to emphasize the terrible power of the storm, but then again, as his pack had spent the night just one valley over, they weren't going to believe much of an exaggeration. He would just have to admit he had had a bad night.

But now it was morning, and he had a fire started, and the first twigs were catching and adding their burn, so he could add more, including some bigger ones. Soon there were ten or twenty twigs alight in a fiery stack over the first burn, and their flames were a tangible yellow. Very soon the moment came when it was safe to put a pretty large handful of dry twigs gently atop the little blaze, and they would all catch almost immediately. He did that and said—Ha! Ha! and put on some larger branches. Finger sticks, then wrist branches. Happily he watched as the growing flames blackened the rounded sides of so many twigs and branches. A fire makes all right with the world.

Smoke now flew up, and the hiss and crackle from the wood showed how hot the fire was getting. The heat smacked his naked chest and belly and pizzle, which burned horribly as it warmed, in the usual agonizing tingle. He squeezed it in one hand to hold the pain in, and felt that it was a good pain, so good it was easy to feel it as a harsh form of pleasure; ah, the too-familiar burn of numbed flesh coming back to life, the itch deep under the skin, the painful tingle of being alive! Now he was going to be able to warm up even his feet! They would burn like mad as they came back to him. Ah fire, glorious fire, so friendly and warm, so beautiful!

—Such a blessing, such a friend! Such a blessing, such a friend! One of Heather's little fire songs.

Now things were really looking good. The previous night was put in its place as a mere problem, a dark prelude. With a fire lit, the storm still blowing overhead did not matter anything like as much. He could keep this fire going for the whole fortnight, if that seemed best, or he could take it with him a certain distance, if he wanted to move, and reestablish it elsewhere. He could focus his efforts on food, shelter, and clothing, and no matter how those went, he would always have the most important thing. And it was only the first day of his wander!

He sat on the windward side of the fire and stretched out his legs around it, held up his arms over it. Hands catching the heat from right in the smoke. Oh the tingle of life coming back: —OW! It was a very different howl than the ones of the night before. Like the wolves, like his namesake the loons, he had a whole vocabulary of howls. This was the happy one, the triumphant one: —OWWW!